NEW TOEIC

新制

閱讀超高分

最新多益改版黃金試題1000題

作者 • **Ki Taek Lee**

審訂 • **Maddie Smith/**
Richard Luhrs

U0033655

READ

目錄 Contents

多益測驗改制介紹
&
高分戰略

多益測驗的出現

TOEIC 多益測驗（Test of English for International Communication）是針對非英語人士所設計的英語能力測驗。多益測驗的內容主要與職場環境的英語使用有關，能測驗一個人在工作場合上使用英語與人溝通的能力，故有「商業托福」之稱。多益測驗在許多國家施行多年，如今已經成為「職場英語能力檢定」的國際標準。

多益英語測驗是由「美國教育測驗服務社」（Educational Testing Service, ETS）所研發出來。ETS 於 1947 年成立，總部位於美國紐澤西州，是全球最大的私立教育考試機構。ETS 提供標準化的考試和測評服務，除了多益測驗，還包括托福（TOEFL）、GRE 和 GMAT 等等。ETS 在 1979 年時，應日本企業領袖的要求，制定出一套可以用來評估員工英語能力的測驗，以了解員工在貿易、工業和商業領域上所具備的英語程度，以利人力規劃與發展。

如今，多益測驗是全球最通行的職場英語能力測驗，共有超過 165 個國家在施行多益測驗，每年的測試人口超過五百萬。此外，許多校園也要求畢業生須接受多益測驗，而且成績須達一定的分數，以幫助學生在畢業後能更加順利地進入職場。

多益測驗考哪些內容？

多益測驗的研發者強調「國際英語」，而不以「美式英語」和「英式英語」來區分，並著重於測驗非英語人士對母語人士的英語溝通能力。多益的測驗內容不會考專業知識或詞彙，而是測試在日常生活中使用英文的能力。2006 年改版的新多益測驗，還特別加入了四種不同的英語口音，包括：

1 美式英語
2 英式英語
3 澳洲英語
4 加拿大英語

多益題目的設計，以「職場需求」為主，測驗題目的內容則是從全球各地職場的英文資料中蒐集而來，題材多元（但考生毋需具備專業的商業與技術辭彙），包含各種地點與狀況：一般商務、製造業、金融／預算、人事、企業發展、辦公室、採購、技術層面、房屋／公司地產、旅遊、外食、娛樂、保健等主題大類。

多益測驗的方式

①	考試方式	「紙筆測驗」
②	出題方式	所有試題皆為「選擇題」
③	題目類型	聽力測驗（又細分成 4 大題） 閱讀測驗（又細分成 3 大題）
④	考試題數	總共有 200 題（聽力 100 題，閱讀 100 題）
⑤	作答	考生選好答案後，要在與題目卷分開的「答案卷」上劃卡
⑥	考試時間	總計 2 小時（聽力考 45 分鐘，閱讀考 75 分鐘，兩者分開計時）

＊但在考試時，考生尚須在答案卷上填寫個人資料，並簡短的回答求學與工作經歷的問卷，
　因此真正待在考場內的時間會比較長。

多益計分方式

多益測驗沒有「通過」與「不通過」之區別──考生用鉛筆在電腦答案卷上作答，考試分數由答對題數決定，將聽力測驗與閱讀測驗答對之題數換算成分數，聽力與閱讀得分相加即為總分；答錯並不倒扣。聽力得分介於 5-495 分、閱讀得分介於 5-495 分，兩者加起來即為總分，範圍在 10 到 990 分之間。

答對題數	聽力分數	閱讀分數	答對題數	聽力分數	閱讀分數	答對題數	聽力分數	閱讀分數	答對題數	聽力分數	閱讀分數
100	495	495	85	465	420	70	365	320	55	295	230
99	495	495	84	455	415	69	360	315	54	290	225
98	495	495	83	450	410	68	355	310	53	280	220
97	495	490	82	445	400	67	350	300	52	275	215
96	495	485	81	440	395	66	350	295	51	265	210
95	495	480	80	435	385	65	345	290	50	260	205
94	495	475	79	430	380	64	340	285	49	255	200
93	490	470	78	425	375	63	335	280	48	250	195
92	490	465	77	420	370	62	330	270	47	245	190
91	490	460	76	410	365	61	325	265	46	240	185
90	485	455	75	400	360	60	320	260	45	230	180
89	485	450	74	390	350	59	315	255	44	225	175
88	480	440	73	385	345	58	310	250	43	220	170
87	475	430	72	380	335	57	305	245	42	210	165
86	470	425	71	375	330	56	300	240	41	205	160

＊此表格僅供參考，實際計分以官方分數為準 。
＊分數計算方式，例如：聽力答對 70 題，閱讀答對 78 題，總分為 365+375=740 分。

2018年新制多益變革表

多益英語測驗有什麼改變？為什麼？

為確保測驗符合考生及成績使用單位之需求，ETS 會定期重新檢驗所有測驗試題。本次多益英語測驗題型更新，反映了全球現有日常生活中社交及職場之英語使用情況。測驗本身將維持其在評量日常生活或職場情境英語的公平性及可信度。其中一些測驗形式會改變，然而，**測驗的難易度、測驗時間或測驗分數所代表的意義不會有所更動**。

新舊制多益測驗結構比較

聽力測驗 Listening Comprehension　45 分鐘　100 題　495 分
測驗總題數、整體難易程度及測驗時間不變

Part	題型	舊制題數	新制題數	題型題數變更說明
1	**Photographs** 照片描述	10 題	6 題	題型不變，題數減少 4 題。
	說明：從四個選項當中，選出一個和照片最相近的描述，問題與選項均不會印在試卷上。			
2	**Question-Response** 應答問題	30 題	25 題	題型不變，題數減少 5 題。
	說明：從三個選項當中，選出與問題最為符合的回答，問題與選項均不會印在試卷上。			
3	**Conversations** 簡短對話	30 題 3 題×10 組	39 題 3 題×13 組	加入三人對話、加入圖表，題數增加 9 題。
	說明：從四個選項中，選出與問題最為符合的回答，對話內容不會印在試卷上。 對話中將會有較少轉折，但來回交談較為頻繁。 部分對話題型將出現兩名以上的對談者。			
4	**Talks** 獨白	30 題 3 題×10 組	30 題 3 題×10 組	新增圖表作答題型，題數不變。
	說明：從四個選項中，選出與問題最為符合的回答，獨白內容不會印在試卷上。			

◆ 聽力測驗將包含母音省略（elision，如：going to → gonna）和不完整的句子
（fragment，如：Yes, in a minute. / Down the hall. / Could you? 等省去主詞或動詞的句子）。
◆ 配合圖表，測驗考生是否聽懂對話，並測驗考生能否理解談話背景與對話中隱含的意思。

閱讀測驗 Reading Comprehension　75 分鐘　100 題　495 分

測驗總題數、整體難易程度及測驗時間不變

Part	題型	舊制題數	新制題數	題型題數變更說明
5	**Incomplete Sentences** 句子填空	40 題	30 題	題型不變，題數減少 10 題。
	說明：從四個選項中，選出最為恰當的答案，以完成不完整的句子。			
6	**Text Completion** 段落填空	12 題 4 題 X 3 篇	16 題 4 題 X 4 組	加入將適當的句子填入空格的題型，題數增加 4 題。
	說明：從四個選項中，選出最為恰當的答案，以完成文章中不完整的句子。選項類別除原有之片語、單字、子句之外，另新增完整句子的選項。			
7	**Reading Comprehension–Single Passage** 單篇文章理解	28 題 共 9 篇 每篇 2 到 5 題	29 題 共 10 篇 每篇 2 到 4 題	題型不變，題數增加 1 題。
	Reading Comprehension– Multiple Passage 多篇文章理解	20 題 雙篇閱讀共 4 篇 每篇 5 題	25 題 雙篇閱讀 2 篇 三篇閱讀 3 篇 每篇 5 題	少 2 篇雙篇閱讀文章，加入 3 篇三篇閱讀文章。
	說明：閱讀單篇或兩或三篇內容相關的文章，從四個選項中，選出最為恰當的答案以回答問題。加入篇章結構題型，測驗考生能否理解整體文章結構，並將一個句子歸置於正確的段落。			

◆ 閱讀測驗將包含文字簡訊、即時通訊，或多人互動的線上聊天訊息內容。
◆ 新增引述文章部分內容，測驗考生是否理解作者希望表達之意思。

◆ 為新制題型說明

資料來源：ETS 官方網站
http://www.toeic.com.tw/2018update/info.html

各大題答題技巧戰略

聽力部分答題技巧

第一大題	照片描述 （6題）	這個部分是要考你看圖片、選答案的能力。你可以用以下的方法來練習：自己找一些照片來看，並思索根據照片的內容，有哪些問題可以提問。
第二大題	應答問題 （25題）	這個部分是提出各種問題，問題的開頭—— What、How、Why、When、Where、Who 六大問句——可以提示我們需要什麼樣的答案。
第三大題	簡短對話 （39題）	這個部分會先播放簡短的對話，再考你對對話的理解程度。回答技巧是你可以**先看問題、答案選項和圖表**，然後再聽對話內容，這樣你在聽的時候會比較知道要專注答案的線索。
第四大題	獨白 （30題）	這個大題可以說是聽力測驗中最難的部分，平時就需要多聽英文對話和廣播等來加強聽力能力。

聽力題目前的英文指示 & 高分戰略

In the Listening test, you will be asked to demonstrate how well you understand spoken English. The entire Listening test will last approximately 45 minutes. There are four parts, and directions are given for each part. You must mark your answers on the separate answer sheet. Do not write your answers in your test book.

聽力測驗在測驗考生聽懂英語的能力。整個聽力測驗的進行時間約 45 分鐘，共分四大題，每一大題皆有做答指示。請把答案寫在另一張答案卡上，而不要把答案寫在測驗本上。

I. Photographs 第一大題：照片描述

Part 1

Directions: For each question in this part, you will hear four statements about a picture in your test book. When you hear the statements, you must select the one statement that best describes what you see in the picture. Then find the number of the question on your answer sheet and mark your answer. The statements will not be printed in your test book and will be spoken only one time.

Look at the example item below. Now listen to the four statements.

(A) They're pointing at the monitor.
(B) They're looking at the document.
(C) They're talking on the phone.
(D) They're sitting by the table.

Statement (B), "They're looking at the document," is the best description of the picture, so you should select answer (B) and mark it on your answer sheet.

第一大題

指示：本大題的每一小題，在測驗本上都會印有一張圖片，考生會聽到針對照片所做的四段描述，然後選出最符合照片內容的適當描述，接著在答案卡上找到題目編號，將對應的答案選項圓圈塗黑。描述的內容部會印在測驗本上，而且只會播放一次。

（A）他們正指著螢幕。
（B）他們正在看文件。
（C）他們正在講電話。
（D）他們正坐在桌子旁。

描述 (B)「他們正在看文件」是最符合本圖的描述，因此你應該選擇選項 (B)，並在答案卡上劃記。

〔 **高分戰略** 〕

❶ 以人物為主的照片，要注意該人物的動作特徵。

照片題中有 70 ～ 80％的題目是以人物為照片主角，這些照片時常會考人的動作特徵，因此要先整理好相關的動作用語。舉例來說，一看到人在走路的照片，就立刻想到 walking、strolling 這些和走路有關的動詞，聽題目的時候會更有幫助。

❷ 以事物為中心的照片，要注意事物的狀態或位置。

以事物為中心的照片，其事物的狀態或位置是出題的要點。所以，表示「位置」時經常會用到的介系詞，還有表現「狀態」的片語，要先整理好。舉例來說，在表示位置「在……旁邊」時，要整理出 next to、by、beside、near 等用語，最好整個背下來。另外，多益時常出現的事物名稱，也要事先準備好。

❸ 要小心出人意料之外的問題。

不同於過往題型，題目的正確答案可能會出現描寫事物，這已成為一種出題趨勢。舉例來說，照片是一個男人用手指著掛在牆上的畫，按照常理，會想到是要考這個人的動作，要回答 pointing 這樣的動詞。但意外地，本題以掛在牆上的畫當作正確答案（The picture has been hung on the wall.）。所以出現人的照片時，不僅要注意人的動作，連周邊事物也必須要注意一下。只有提到照片中出現的內容，才會是正確答案；想像的內容絕對不會是正確答案。

Part 2

Directions: You will hear a question or statement and three responses spoken in English. They will be spoken only one time and will not be printed in your test book. Select the best response to the question or statement and mark the letter (A), (B), or (C) on your answer sheet.

第二大題

指示： 考生會聽到一個問題句或敘述句，以及三句回應的英語。題目只會撥放一次，而且不會印在測驗本上。請選出最符合擺放內容的答案，在答案卡上將 (A)、(B)、(C) 或 (D) 的答案選項塗黑。

高分戰略

❶ 新制有言外之意的考題增加

PART 2 少了五題，但命題方式變得更巧妙、難度也隨之提升。有言外之意的考題增加，考生必須要聽出背後的含意才能找出答案。碰到此類題型時，在聽完題目後，需要思考一番，才能挑出正確的答案。只要稍不留神，很容易就錯失下一題的解題機會。請務必勤加練習，熟悉此類題型的模式。

❷ 沒聽清楚題目最前面的疑問詞，很可惜。

大部分 Part 2 出現的疑問句都會在最前面提示核心要點，尤其是以疑問詞（Who、What、Where、When、Why、How）開頭的疑問句題目，會出約 9 ～ 10 題。這些題目只要聽到句首的疑問詞，幾乎就能找到正確答案，所以平常要常做區分疑問詞的聽力練習。

❸ 利用錯誤答案消去法。

Part 2 是最多陷阱的部分，所以事先把常見的陷阱題整理起來，是很重要的。舉例來說，以疑問詞開頭的疑問句題目，用 yes 或 no 回答的選項，幾乎都是錯誤答案，可以先將其刪除。另外，重複出現題目中的單字，或出現與題目中字彙發音類似的單字，如 copy 與 coffee，也是常出的錯誤答案模式。平常一邊做題目，一邊將具代表性的陷阱題整理好是必要的。

❹ 常考的片語要整個背起來。

多益中常出現的用語或片語，最好當作一個單字一樣地整個背起來。舉例來說，疑問句「Why don't you . . . ?」的用法並非要詢問原因，而是「做……好嗎？」的代表句型。像這樣的用語，時常會快速唸過，所以事先整個背起來，考聽力時會很有幫助。

因此平常花功夫多做聽力訓練，並跟著一起唸，把重要的用語整段背下來，征服 Part 2 之路就不遠了。

III. Conversations 第三大題：簡短對話

Part 3

Directions: You will hear some conversations between two or more people. You will be asked to answer three questions about what the speakers say in each conversation. Select the best response to each question and mark the letter (A), (B), (C), or (D) on your answer sheet. The conversations will not be printed in your test book and will be spoken only one time.

第三大題

指示：考生會聽到一些兩個人或多人的對話，並根據對話所聽到的內容，回答三個問題。請選出最符合播放內容的答案，在答案卡上將 (A)、(B)、(C) 或 (D) 的答案選項塗黑。這些對話只會播放一次，而且不會印在測驗本上。

高分戰略

❶ 一定要先瞄題目，以找出要聆聽的重點。

Part 3 是兩到三人的對話，每組對話要回答三道題，所以**事先把題目快速掃描過**，找出重點，是很重要的。若不事先看題目，就不知道要把注意力集中在哪裡，而必須理解並記下整個對話，十分吃力。所以事先看一下題目問什麼，會對接下來的對話有概念，並知道要注意聽哪些地方。

有關圖表的試題，要**先看一下圖表訊息**，再綜合試題和選項後，仔細聽對話的內容。有策略地去聽是很重要的。

❷ 一面聽一面找答案！

即使先掃描過了題目，卻沒有練習邊聽邊找答案，容易會出現漏掉正確答案的情況。因為即使之前非常注意聽的對話，但有些細微的訊息，之後可能會記不起來，尤其是新制多益中，出現三個人的對話，所以談話者的性別，及彼此間的關係會更加複雜。所以一聽到答案出現，立刻作答，是最有利的。這麼做剛開始可能有點困難，但只要勤奮地練習，以後瞄過題目就大概就能猜出答案

❸ 千萬不要錯失對話開頭！

在 Part 3 中，時常出現問**職業、場所或主題**的問題，這些問題的答案時常會出現在對話開頭。要快速掌握對話一開始揭示的主題，才能判斷出接下來會出現什麼內容，對解其他的題目很有幫助。所以要勤加練習，把對話開頭確實聽清楚。

IV. Talks 第四大題：簡短獨白

Part 4

Directions: You will hear some talks given by a single speaker. You will be asked to answer three questions about what the speaker says in each talk. Select the best response to each question and mark the letter (A), (B), (C), or (D) on your answer sheet. The talks will not be printed in your test book and will be spoken only one time.

第四大題

指示： 考生會聽到好幾段單人獨白，並根據每一段話的內容，回答三個問題。請選出最符合播放內容的答案，在答案卡上將 (A)、(B)、(C) 或 (D) 的答案選項塗黑。每一段話只會播放一次，而且不會印在測驗本上。

高分戰略

❶ 要事先整理好常考的詢問內容！

和 Part 3 不同，Part 4 的談話種類是有一定類型的。也就是說，會重複聽到有關**交通廣播、天氣預報、旅行導覽、電話留言**等的談話，內容大同小異。所以只需要按這些談話種類，整理出常考的問題類型即可。舉例來說，跟電話溝通相關的主題，時常都在談話一開始出現「I'm calling to . . .」，聽到這個敘述後，要找出正確答案就容易多了。

❷ 具備背景知識的話，答題會更加容易上手。

Part 4 的談話種類是有固定框架的，會感覺好像談話的內容及題目都很類似。所以即使不聽談話，光看題目，就能推測出答案是什麼。舉例來說，若是機場的情境談話，也許會出有關飛機誤點或取消的問題。這時誤點或取消的原因，最常出現的可能是天候不佳。這就是多益的背景知識，即使沒聽清楚，光看題目，也能選出最接近正確答案的選項。所以平常要努力累積多益常考題型的背景知識，不能懶惰。

❸ 要花功夫訓練自己找出問題的要點。

和 Part 3 一樣，Part 4 也是每段談話出三道題，所以要養成先掃描過題目和表格並整理出重點的習慣。由於 Part 4 的談話內容更長，不太可能把全部內容聽完後再答題。因此可以先找出題目的要點，利用背景知識，在試題本上推敲正確答案。不像 Part 3，Part 4 的答案通常會按照題目的順序，一一出現在對話中，答案逐題出現的機率很高。

閱讀部分答題技巧

第五大題	句子填空 （30 題）	在第五大題中，字彙和文法能力最重要。其所考的字彙大都跟職場或商業有關，平時就要多背誦單字。
第六大題	段落填空 （16 題）	除了單字，也需要將比較長的片語或子句，甚至是一整個句子填入空格中，要掌握整篇文章來龍去脈才能找出最合適的答案。
第七大題	單篇文章理解 （29 題） 多篇文章理解 （25 題）	第七大題比較困難，你需要知道有哪幾類的商業文章，像是公告或備忘錄等。平時就要訓練自己能夠快速閱讀文章和圖表，並且能夠找出主要的內容。當然，在這個部分字彙能力也是很重要的。

閱讀題目前的英文指示 & 高分戰略

In the Reading test, you will read a variety of texts and answer several different types of reading comprehension questions. The entire Reading test will last 75 minutes. There are three parts, and directions are given for each part. You are encouraged to answer as many questions as possible within the time allowed.

You must mark your answers on the separate answer sheet. Do not write your answers in your test book.

在閱讀測驗中，考生會讀到各種文章，並回答各種型式的閱讀測驗題目。整個閱讀測驗的進行時間為 75 分鐘 。本測驗共分三大題，每一大題皆有做答指示。請在規定的時間內，盡可能地作答。

請把答案寫在另一張答案卡上，而不要把答案寫在測驗本上。

Part 5

Directions: A word or phrase is missing in each of the sentences below. Four answer choices are given below each sentence. Select the best answer to complete the sentence. Then mark the letter (A), (B), (C), or (D) on your answer sheet.

第五大題

指示：本測驗中的每一個句子皆缺少一個單字或詞組，在句子下方會列出四個答案選項，請選出最適合的答案來完成句子，並在做答卡上將 (A)、(B)、(C) 或 (D) 的答案選項塗黑。

高分戰略

❶ 要先看選項。

試題大致可分為**句型、字彙、文法**以及**慣用語**四種試題。要先看選項，掌握是上述四種題型中的哪一種，便能更快速解題。所以，要練習判斷題型，並正確掌握各題型的解題技巧。

❷ 找出意思最接近的單字。

Part 5 是填空選擇題，若能找出和空格關係最密切的關鍵字彙，便能快速又正確地解題。所以，要練習**分析**句子的**結構**，並找出和空格關係最密切的字彙作為答題線索。一般來說，**空格前後的單字，就是線索**。舉例來說，如果空格後有名詞，此名詞就是空格的線索單字，以此名詞可以猜想出空格可能是個形容詞。

❸ 要盡力廣泛地蒐羅字彙。

多益會拿來出題的字彙，通常以**片語**形式出現。最具代表的是：動詞和受詞、形容詞和名詞、介系詞和名詞、動詞和副詞等。有些詞組中每個單字都懂，但合起來就很難猜出它的中文意思，所以不要直接用中文而要用英文去理解。因此，平日要養成將這些片語詞組視為整體一起背下來的習慣。

舉例來說，中文說「打電話」，但英文是「make a phone call」；而付錢打電話不能用「pay a phone call」，要用「pay for the phone call」。但是多益中 Part 5 考「pay for the phone call」的可能性很低，因為多益大多出常見用語，而這句不是。所以，要用英文去理解常見用語，要整個背起來，不要直接用中文理解，因為這是得高分最大的障礙。

Text Completion 第六大題：短文填空

Part 6

Directions: Read the texts that follow. A word, phrase, or sentence is missing in parts of each text. Four answer choices for each question are given below the text. Select the best answer to complete the text. Then mark the letter (A), (B), (C), or (D) on your answer sheet.

第六大題

指示：閱讀本大題的文章，文章中的某些句子缺少單字、片語或句子，這些句子都會有四個答案選項，請選出最適合的答案來完成文章中的空格，並在做答卡上將 (A)、(B)、(C) 或 (D) 的答案選項塗黑。

高分戰略

❶ 要研究空格前後句子連結關係，掌握上下文。

Part 5 和 Part 6 不同的地方是，Part 5 只探究一個句子的結構，而 Part 6 要探究句子和句子間的關係，因此要練習觀察空格前後句子彼此的連結關係。如果有空格的句子是第一句，要看後一句來解題；如果有空格的句子是第二句，就要看前一句來解題。偶爾，也有要看整篇文章才能作答的題目。

PART 6 最難處在於要從選項的四個句子中，選出適當的句子填入空格中。此為新制增加的題型，不僅要多費時解題，平時也得多花功夫如何掌握上下文意上。

❷ Part 6 的動詞時態問題

Part 5 的動詞時態問題，只要看該句子內的動詞是否符合時態即可，但 Part 6 的動詞時態，要看其他句子才能決定該句空格中的時態。大部分的時態題目都區分為：已發生的事或尚未發生的事。從上下文來看，已發生的事，要用現在完成式或過去式；尚未發生的事，就選包含 will 等與未來式相關的助動詞（will、shall、may 等）選項，或用「be going to . . .」。針對 Part 6 的時態問題，多練習區分已發生的事和尚未發生的事便能順利答題。

❸ Part 6 的連接副詞

所謂的連接副詞，是指翻譯時要和前面的內容一起翻譯的副詞。一般來說，這不會出現在只考一句話的 Part 5，而會出現在考句間的關係的 Part 6。舉例來說，副詞 therefore 是「因此」的意思，所以若前後句的內容有因果關係，用它就對了。若是轉折語氣的話，用有「然而」含意的 however 準沒錯。此外，連接副詞還有 otherwise（否則）、consequently（因而導致）、additionally（此外）、instead（反而）等。另外，連接詞用於連接句子，而介系詞是連接名詞，連接副詞是單獨使用的，這是區分它們最便捷的方法。

Part 7

Directions: In this part you will read a selection of texts, such as magazine and newspaper articles, emails, and instant messages. Each text or set of texts is followed by several questions. Select the best answer for each question and mark the letter (A), (B), (C), or (D) on your answer sheet.

第七大題

指示：這大題中會閱讀到不同題材的文章，如雜誌和新聞文章、電子郵件或通訊軟體的訊息等。每篇或每組文章之後會有數個題目，請選出最適合的答案，並在做答卡上將 (A)、(B)、(C) 或 (D) 的答案選項塗黑。

高分戰略

❶ 要熟記類似的字彙及用語。

做 Part 7 的題目，字彙能力最為重要，它能幫助你正確且快速地找出與題目或文章用語最接近的選項。一邊研究 Part 7 的題目，一邊整理並熟記意思相似的字彙或用語，能快速增加字彙。

❷ Part 7 的問題也是有類型的。

Part 7 的題目乍看好像很多元，事實上可以分作幾種類型，如：
① **具體訊息類型**：詢問文章的一些訊息。
② **主題類型**：要找出文章主題。
③ **NOT 類型**：提供的選項中有三項是對的，而要找出錯誤項目。
④ **邏輯推演類型**：從一些線索中推知內容。
⑤ **文意填空類型**：閱讀段落，將題目中的句子填入文中適當的地方。
解題時先將題目分類，再來研究該如何解題，速度會快很多。

❸ 要注意複合式文章題目。

從 176 題開始，是由兩篇到三文章組成的複合式文章類型，有許多問題出自多篇文章內容的相關性。所以在這部分，相關或相同的地方要連貫起來作答。出這種相關連帶問題時，要注意文章的共通點是以何種方式連接。

❹ 培養耐力。

Part 7 是最後一個單元，解題實力雖然重要，但長時間解題能否集中注意力也是勝負的關鍵。平常要訓練自己，至少要持續一個小時不休息地解題，時常以這種方式來訓練閱讀十分重要。多做解題耐力練習，是考高分的必要條件。

ACTUAL TEST

READING TEST

In the Reading test, you will read a variety of texts and answer several different types of reading comprehension questions. The entire Reading test will last 75 minutes. There are three parts, and directions are given for each part. You are encouraged to answer as many questions as possible within the time allowed.

You must mark your answers on the separate answer sheet. Do not write your answers in your test book.

PART 5

Directions: A word or phrase is missing in each of the sentences below. Four answer choices are given below each sentence. Select the best answer to complete the sentence. Then mark the letter (A), (B), (C), or (D) on your answer sheet.

101. When filling out the order form, please ------- your address clearly to prevent delays.

(A) fix
(B) write
(C) send
(D) direct

102. Ms. Morgan recruited the individuals whom the company ------- for the next three months.

(A) will employ
(B) to employ
(C) has been employed
(D) employ

103. The contractor had a fifteen percent ------- in his business after advertising in the local newspaper.

(A) experience
(B) growth
(C) formula
(D) incentive

104. The free clinic was founded by a group of doctors to give ------- for various medical conditions.

(A) treatment
(B) treat
(C) treated
(D) treating

105. Participants in the walking tour should gather ------- 533 Bates Road on Saturday morning.

(A) with
(B) at
(C) like
(D) among

106. The artist sent ------- best pieces to the gallery to be reviewed by the owner.

(A) him
(B) himself
(C) his
(D) he

107. The figures that accompany the financial statement should be ------- to the spending category.

(A) relevance
(B) relevantly
(C) more relevantly
(D) relevant

108. The building owner purchased the property ------- three months ago, but she has already spent a great deal of money on renovations.

(A) yet
(B) just
(C) few
(D) still

109. We would like to discuss this problem honestly and ------- at the next staff meeting.

(A) rarely
(B) tiredly
(C) openly
(D) highly

110. The store's manager plans to put the new merchandise on display ------- to promote the line of fall fashions.

(A) soon
(B) very
(C) that
(D) still

111. During the peak season, it is ------- to hire additional workers for the weekend shifts.

(A) necessitate
(B) necessarily
(C) necessary
(D) necessity

112. ------- that the insulation has been replaced, the building is much more energy-efficient.

(A) Now
(B) For
(C) As
(D) Though

113. Mr. Sims needs a more ------- vehicle for commuting from his suburban home to his office downtown.

(A) expressive
(B) reliable
(C) partial
(D) extreme

114. The company ------- lowered its prices to outsell its competitors and attract more customers.

(A) strategy
(B) strategically
(C) strategies
(D) strategic

115. ------- Mr. Williams addressed the audience, he showed a brief video about the engine he had designed.

(A) Then
(B) So that
(C) Before
(D) Whereas

116. For optimal safety on the road, avoid ------- the view of the rear window and side-view mirrors.

(A) obstructs
(B) obstructed
(C) obstruction
(D) obstructing

GO ON TO THE NEXT PAGE

117. Having proper ventilation throughout the building is ------- for protecting the health and well-being of the workers.

(A) cooperative
(B) visible
(C) essential
(D) alternative

118. ------- sales of junk food have been steadily declining indicates that consumers are becoming more health-conscious.

(A) In addition to
(B) The fact that
(C) As long as
(D) In keeping with

119. The sprinklers for the lawn's irrigation system are ------- controlled.

(A) mechanically
(B) mechanic
(C) mechanism
(D) mechanical

120. The library staff posted signs to ------- patrons of the upcoming closure for renovations.

(A) notify
(B) agree
(C) generate
(D) perform

121. Mr. Ross, ------- is repainting the interior of the lobby, was recommended by a friend of the building manager.

(A) himself
(B) he
(C) who
(D) which

122. The guidelines for the monthly publication are ------- revised to adapt to the changing readers.

(A) curiously
(B) initially
(C) periodically
(D) physically

123. ------- an ankle injury, the baseball player participated in the last game of the season.

(A) In spite of
(B) Even if
(C) Whether
(D) Given that

124. The governmental department used to provide financial aid, but now it offers ------- services only.

(A) legal
(B) legalize
(C) legally
(D) legalizes

125. At the guest's -------, an extra set of towels and complimentary soaps were brought to the room.

(A) quote
(B) graduation
(C) request
(D) dispute

126. The upscale boutique Jane's Closet is known for selling the most stylish ------- for young professionals.

(A) accessorized
(B) accessorize
(C) accessorizes
(D) accessories

127. The company started to recognize the increasing ------- of using resources responsibly.

(A) more important
(B) importantly
(C) importance
(D) important

128. ------- restructuring several departments within the company, the majority of the problems with miscommunication have disappeared.

(A) After
(B) Until
(C) Below
(D) Like

129. The riskiest ------- of the development of new medications are the trials with human subjects.

(A) proceeds
(B) perspectives
(C) installments
(D) stages

130. ------- seeking a position at Tulare Designs must submit a portfolio of previous work.

(A) Anyone
(B) Whenever
(C) Other
(D) Fewer

GO ON TO THE NEXT PAGE

PART 6

Directions: Read the texts that follow. A word, phrase, or sentence is missing in parts of each text. Four answer choices for each question are given below the text. Select the best answer to complete the text. Then mark the letter (A), (B), (C), or (D) on your answer sheet.

Questions 131-134 refer to the following email.

To: samsmith@digitalIT.com
From: sharronb@bmail.com
Date: September 24
Subject: Business Contract

Dear Mr. Smith,

I am Sharron Biggs, CEO and founder of BiggsGraphics. I recently came across your

advertisement ------- the partnership of a graphic design company for a number of your
          131.

projects. BiggsGraphics has ------- experience working with various small businesses and
          132.

companies in designing advertising campaigns, logos, and websites. ------- Our website,
          133.

www.biggs-graphics.com, also has more information about our company.

I'm interested in working with your company on your projects and hope we can build a

beneficial partnership. I look forward ------- your reply.
          134.

Sincerely,

Sharron Biggs

CEO, Biggs Graphics

131. (A) seek
    (B) to seek
    (C) seeking
    (D) are seeking

132. (A) extensive
    (B) restricted
    (C) generous
    (D) limitless

133. (A) I would really appreciate the opportunity to work with you.
    (B) I heard that DigitalIT is a great company.
    (C) In fact, our designs are often copied by other companies.
    (D) I have attached a number of our past designs to illustrate what we specialize in.

134. (A) at
    (B) to
    (C) with
    (D) from

Questions 135-138 refer to the following announcement.

Thank you for shopping at Larson's China. Our products are known for their modern and unique patterns and color combinations, as well as ------- and strength. ------- Please note,
135.   136.
however, that repeated drops and rough handling will ------- eventual breakage. We suggest
137.
that you store them carefully and that you don't use harsh chemicals, steel sponges, or

------- scrubbing when cleaning them. Please visit our website at www.larsonchina.com for
138.
information about handling and care, or call us at 555-1234 if you have any questions or

concerns.

135. (A) durable
(B) durability
(C) durableness
(D) duration

(NEW)
136. (A) Larson's utensils and silverware go great with the dinnerware.
(B) Our most popular line, the Spring Flower China, is sold out at most locations.
(C) Visit our store to check out our other beautiful products.
(D) They are dishwasher and microwave safe, and we're confident that you'll be using them for years to come.

137. (A) result in
(B) occur to
(C) ending at
(D) stop with

138. (A) ambitious
(B) combative
(C) aggressive
(D) complacent

GO ON TO THE NEXT PAGE

Entry Position: Gold & Slide Accounting Firm

We are looking for enthusiastic candidates with an educational background in finance or

-------. All candidates should have some computer experience. Job experience is not
139.

-------, but preferred. Candidates with bilingual language ability ------- favored. Positions
140.   **141.**

include jobs in accounting, statistics, and general office assistant. If you are interested,

please visit our website at www.G&Saccountingfirm.com/employment for more information.

You can send your cover letters and résumés to Karen Hill at khill@G&S.com. We will begin

interviewing candidates on Monday, November 5th. -------
                                                142.

139. (A) account
(B) accountant
(C) accounting
(D) accounted

140. (A) basic
(B) decisive
(C) additional
(D) necessary

141. (A) is being
(B) will be
(C) has been
(D) were being

142. (A) We sincerely thank you for your kindness.
(B) The position will begin work the following month.
(C) Please call us for more information.
(D) We apologize for any inconvenience.

Questions 143-146 refer to the following email.

To: Kitchen Staff, Office Employees

From: Manager, Larry Park

Date: March 23

Subject: Renovations

To all kitchen staff and Harmon employees,

From Sunday, March 23rd to Thursday, March 27th, the employee cafeteria kitchens will

undergo renovations as new appliances and equipment ------- in to replace the old ones.
                                                              143.

------- Instead, the convenience shops will carry more sandwiches, prepared lunch boxes,
144.

and snacks for the employees during this time.

The renovations will increase the number of sinks, ovens, and stove tops, so that a larger

volume of meals can be provided ------- the lunch and dinner rushes. We apologize for the
                                     145.

inconvenience, but we hope that the changes will ------- the services in the cafeteria.
                                                     146.

---

143. (A) are bringing
    (B) have brought
    (C) bring
    (D) are brought

(NEW)
144. (A) This will take a lot of work.
    (B) As a result, the convenience shops will
        be closed.
    (C) Because of this, hot meals will not be
        available for the patrons.
    (D) There will be noise and chaos as a
        result.

145. (A) before
    (B) after
    (C) during
    (D) outside

146. (A) develop
    (B) improve
    (C) rectify
    (D) recover

GO ON TO THE NEXT PAGE

PART 7

Directions: In this part you will read a selection of texts, such as magazine and newspaper articles, emails, and instant messages. Each text or set of texts is followed by several questions. Select the best answer for each question and mark the letter (A), (B), (C), or (D) on your answer sheet.

Questions 147-148 refer to the following email.

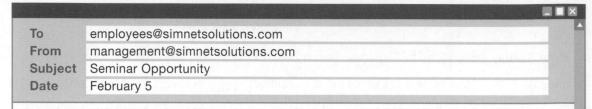

To	employees@simnetsolutions.com
From	management@simnetsolutions.com
Subject	Seminar Opportunity
Date	February 5

Dear female employees,

Only one week remains until registration will be closed for the Women's Leadership Seminar. This seminar is offered free of charge to all of our female employees at Simnet Solutions. To accommodate our female employees' busy schedules, identical seminars will be held on two different dates—February 21 and February 23.

In order to register for this specially designed seminar, you must email James Taylor in human resources by 5:00 P.M. on February 12. This seminar will teach our female employees how to communicate with confidence and credibility in the workplace.

The Simnet Solutions Management Team

---

147. What is indicated about the seminar?

(A) It will feature speaker James Taylor.
(B) It is held annually.
(C) Its fee is more expensive than the last one.
(D) It is designed for women.

148. When will the free registration offer end?

(A) On February 5
(B) On February 12
(C) On February 21
(D) On February 23

Questions 149-150 refer to the following text message chain.

Kyle   **2:42**
Nancy, it's Kyle. I'm in Conference Room B setting up for the meeting at 5. The projector doesn't work. Can you search for another in the supply room?

Nancy   **2:45**
Hey. No problem, I'm heading there now.

Kyle   **2:46**
Thanks, I really appreciate it.

Nancy   **2:57**
Kyle, there are no projectors here. I've called the IT Department and asked if they have any spare ones. I'll get back to you when I get a reply.

Kyle   **3:00**
Thanks again. Oh, and can you check for extra microphones?

Nancy   **3:08**
There are two here. I'll take them both. Meanwhile, the IT department says they don't have extra projectors, but they'll send a guy down now to check what's wrong. They say it worked fine at yesterday's presentation.

Kyle   **3:09**
Great! I'll see you soon then.

149. Where is Nancy most likely located?

(A) In a conference room
(B) At the IT Department
(C) In the supply room
(D) In her office

150. What did Nancy mean when she said, "I'm heading there now"?

(A) She was going to the location.
(B) She would lead the presentation.
(C) She knew where the room was.
(D) She was going straight to meet him.

GO ON TO THE NEXT PAGE

Purchased By: Tim Bailey

Tate Theater

The Kelly Cooper Concert

Time: 7:00 P.M.
Date: Friday, May 20
Section: General Admission
Row: F
Seat: 26

- Guests seated in general admission should arrive at least 30 minutes before the concert begins.
- For those coming by car, the location of the theater can be found on our website at www.tatetheater.com.
- All ticket sales are non-refundable.

151. What is Mr. Bailey advised to do?

(A) Contact the theater for a refund
(B) Select his preferred seat on a website
(C) Arrive at the venue in advance
(D) Post a review later

152. According to the ticket, what can be viewed on the theater's website?

(A) A list of past performances
(B) Driving directions
(C) Concert reviews
(D) Pictures of the theater

Gilmore Good Buy

Order Confirmation

Name: Jenny Collins
Customer ID: F833J
Address: 808 Columbus Avenue, New York, NY 10025
Order date: August 22

Item(s)	Price
Springform pans (5 @ $5.00 each)	$25.00
4 oz. cocoa butter	$10.99
Confectioner's glaze (3 @ $5.90 each)*	$17.70
Cupcake pans (2 @ $4.00 each)	$8.00
Merchandise Total	$61.69
Delivery	$8.99
Total	$70.68
Payment: Credit Card XXXX XXXX XXXX 4026	

* Notes: Will be delivered at a quicker speed to prevent melting or damage

153. What kind of business are the items most likely intended for?

(A) A shopping mall
(B) A bakery
(C) An appliance store
(D) A convenience store

154. What is indicated about the order?

(A) It will be paid in installments.
(B) It will be sent separately.
(C) It has been discounted.
(D) It will be delivered at no charge.

GO ON TO THE NEXT PAGE

Community Victory

After a months-long battle to stop the development of a new shopping mall on the location of the former Rivervalley Courthouse, residents, local businesses, and civic groups are cheering the decision to keep the 150-year-old building intact. – [1] – "We're disappointed," added Branford Construction's CEO. "We felt that the community would benefit and grow, but obviously, residents want to preserve their history, and I respect that."

Instead, efforts are being made to restore the old, deserted courthouse to its former glory. – [2] – "The community is getting together for this, and we are collecting donations to have the building renovated," said local resident Enid Tran. "We hope to make a public library or school out of the building."

– [3] – "It's been here for as long as I can remember. In fact, my grandfather worked as a clerk there," added a local business owner, Kevin Lamb. "It's an iconic symbol of our community, and we don't want it destroyed." The community has already raised over $100,000 through an online petition, and donations keep pouring in. – [4] – The community hopes that restoration of the building will begin within the next couple of months.

155. What is indicated about the old courthouse?

(A) Branford Construction wants to renovate the building.
(B) The residents want to turn the building into a shopping mall.
(C) It may become a public library or school.
(D) It may be destroyed.

156. In which of the positions marked [1], [2], [3], and [4] does the following sentence best belong?

"Branford Construction, the development company that originally planned to build the shopping mall, is looking to build the mall outside of the Rivervalley Community."

(A) [1]
(B) [2]
(C) [3]
(D) [4]

157. What is suggested about the fundraising efforts?

(A) The community made a lot of money from the land.
(B) It has been occurring online.
(C) The city government has been helping.
(D) They haven't raised enough money.

Questions 158-160 refer to the following email.

To: Stacey Johnson <sjohnson@toplineelec.com>
From: Josh Fleck <jfleck@toplineelec.com>
Date: October 22
Subject: Strategic Planning

Dear Ms. Johnson,

District management at Topline Electronics would like to inform you about a new development that will be affecting your store. Another competing consumer electronics store will be opening in the Crayville area on November 12.

In order to ensure that Topline Electronics does not lose business to this new store, district management is advising you to run a special sale on our new line of curved UHD televisions. These televisions provide state-of-the-art features at moderate prices. By showing your customers that Topline Electronics offers the best deals in the area, you will be able to maintain customer loyalty. We will be shipping the new televisions to your store within the next week. We suggest you prepare a prominent display space in your store to feature them. You should also update your website to advertise the sale.

Smooth communication between you and us is vital to effective operational practices. If you have any questions concerning the new televisions or the marketing campaign in general, please don't hesitate to contact district management.

Sincerely,

Josh Fleck, District Manager
Topline Electronics

---

158. Who most likely is Ms. Johnson?

(A) A store manager
(B) A customer
(C) A product developer
(D) A marketing specialist

159. What is indicated about Topline Electronics?

(A) It recently opened a new store location.
(B) It will be relocated to the Crayville area.
(C) It is concerned about market competition.
(D) It was nominated for an annual award.

160. What is Ms. Johnson NOT instructed to do?

(A) Add new information to a website
(B) Hire additional staff
(C) Contact management if necessary
(D) Arrange a sale display area

GO ON TO THE NEXT PAGE

Nickson, Harry   **10:10**
Any word yet from the distributers about the desks and office chairs we were supposed to get on Tuesday?

Jordan, Johnny   **10:11**
Monica is waiting to hear from them. Last I heard, there has been a bit of a delay due to problems at the manufacturing site. Apparently, one of the conveyor belts is down.

Nickson, Harry   **10:12**
Have you told this to our clients at P&R Industries?

Jordan, Johnny   **10:13**
No, because I want to get a definitive answer from our manufacturers first before I relay any sort of a message about a delay. Hey Monica, have you gotten a response yet?

Stein, Monica   **10:14**
Yes, I just spoke with them. Great news; it looks like we can get the job done on Friday as originally scheduled. The desks and chairs will arrive directly at P&R Industries from the assembly lines on Thursday.

Nickson, Harry   **10:15**
That's great to hear. Please inform Mr. Kline about this. We can get started on the 5th floor offices and work our way down once the furniture arrives.

Stein, Monica   **10:15**
I'm on it.

Jordan, Johnny   **10:16**
Alright, and I'll get a large crew there, so that the work can be finished by Friday as planned.

Nickson, Harry   **10:17**
Yes, please make sure that the job is done not only efficiently but also well. They have a couple of other buildings that they may want our services for.

Jordan, Johnny   **10:18**
I'll keep that in mind.

161. What kind of business do the online speakers work at?

(A) A law firm
(B) An office supply company
(C) A furniture shop
(D) A moving company

162. When will the crew begin work?

(A) Tuesday
(B) Wednesday
(C) Thursday
(D) Friday

163. What will Johnny Jordan probably do next?

(A) Contact the distributors
(B) Organize a meeting
(C) Gather a large crew
(D) Call the client

164. What does Monica Stein mean by "I'm on it"?

(A) She'll organize the movers.
(B) She'll wait until she gets more information.
(C) She'll visit the manufacturers.
(D) She'll contact the client.

GO ON TO THE NEXT PAGE

Fulton Stainless Steel Products

Fulton Stainless Steel Products is a large-scale manufacturer making stainless steel industrial kitchen appliances in factories in Germany and France. The company's products are trusted by chefs and bakers around the world to be durable, long-lasting, and of superb quality. The company produces kitchen stoves, ovens, microwaves, refrigerators, food processors, electric kettles, coffee makers, and other products.

After acquiring the Visor Home Products Company in a deal last month, the company expects its overall profits to increase 20% compared to the last fiscal year. As a result, to meet increased demand, the company will employ more than 300 full-time workers in its six factories and offer good pay with an excellent benefits package. The company considers all of its employees valuable members of the Fulton family. Additionally, the company continues to research and develop new products to satisfy its customers and compete with other companies.

165. Who is most likely to be a customer of Fulton Stainless Steel Products?

(A) A car manufacturer
(B) A restaurant
(C) A real estate agency
(D) A clothing store

166. What did Fulton Stainless Steel Products do last month?

(A) It held a press conference.
(B) It opened a new factory.
(C) It obtained a company.
(D) It laid off some workers.

167. What is mentioned about Fulton Stainless Steel Products?

(A) It recently provided extra funding for research and development.
(B) It has released a budget proposal for next year.
(C) It offers a benefits package to its part-time employees.
(D) It plans to hire additional employees to work in factories.

Questions 168-171 refer to the following article from a company newsletter.

Employee Winner of National Contest

One of our employees here at Arrow Design Laboratory, Jennifer Holt, has won first place in a Web design contest hosted by the Association of Web Designers (AWD). Entrants were judged according to clarity of idea, quality of execution, and aesthetics. Ms. Holt was selected among over 300 different applicants. We applaud her achievement and are so happy to have her as an employee at Arrow Design Laboratory.

The Association of Web Designers is an organization founded in 2002 with the goal of emphasizing the importance of Web design and protecting the rights of Web designers. The AWD has members all over the world and is constantly gaining new members. The AWD hosts a variety of contests in order to promote Web design as a professional field. The AWD believes that good design can enhance people's lives and build better communities.

As a recipient of the first place for the Web design contest, Ms. Holt will receive a cash prize as well as free membership in the Association of Web Designers. In addition, she has been invited to give a speech at the Annual Web Designers' Conference to be held next month in Los Angeles, California. The AWD will be holding more contests in the future, and those interested should visit the website at www.awd.com/contests to find out more information.

---

168. Why most likely was the article written?

(A) To introduce a new employee
(B) To report on an award winner
(C) To announce an annual competition
(D) To describe a change in company policy

169. The word "founded" in paragraph 2, line 1, is closest in meaning to

(A) discovered
(B) learned
(C) established
(D) equipped

170. What is suggested about the Association of Web Designers?

(A) It holds a conference every year.
(B) It is based in Los Angeles.
(C) It currently offers free membership.
(D) It donates to community projects.

171. According to the article, what can be found on the website?

(A) A transcript of a speech
(B) An application for an open position
(C) Details about upcoming contests
(D) A list of Ms. Holt's accomplishments

GO ON TO THE NEXT PAGE

16 July, Newtown—Health Shack is downtown Newtown's hottest new hangout for fitness buffs and corporate employees alike. – [1] – Owners Jill and Barry Baker opened the shop last month to rave reviews and long lines. Getting a seat or table at Health Shack can take as long as 30 minutes on a good day, and the place is always crowded no matter the time of day. Health Shack offers only six items on its menu—all protein shakes including the best sellers, Apple Pie, Peanut Butter Cup, and Tuity Fruity. – [2] –

"We were overwhelmed by the response," says Jill Baker. "In fact, everything spread by word of mouth so we didn't even need to advertise." Fitness Instructor Julian Miles said, "I love coming here for a quick lunch that won't wreck my fitness goals. I even recommend this place to all my patrons." – [3] – "I come here to get a healthy but satisfying meal during my short break with my co-workers," added business man Tim Hammer. "Without Health Shack, we'd be eating junk food." – [4] – Health Shack is open from 7 A.M. to 8 P.M. on Monday through Friday, and from 9 A.M. to 7 P.M. on Saturday. It closes on Sunday. The owners hope to add new flavors to the menu in the coming months.

172. What is suggested about the shop?

(A) It is very successful.
(B) It only offers takeout.
(C) It has been open for a long time.
(D) Only fitness experts patron the shop.

173. What is suggested about Health Shack products?

(A) They are very delicious.
(B) They are healthy.
(C) They are cheap.
(D) They are easy to get.

174. Why don't the owners advertise?

(A) They don't have enough money.
(B) They are too busy.
(C) Their customers recommend the place to others.
(D) They don't want to.

175. In which of the positions marked [1], [2], [3], and [4] does the following sentence best belong?

"Despite the limited number of items on the menu, customers can't get enough of the tasty but healthy shakes that are on offer."

(A) [1]
(B) [2]
(C) [3]
(D) [4]

Summer Lecture Series

Sponsored by the Department of City Planning at Wurnster University

The Department of City Planning is excited to announce a summer lecture series that will be focusing on budgeting issues that concern local residents and municipalities. Financial management is one of the most important duties of local government's operations. We hope to improve the status of budgeting at the local government level across the nation through community involvement and participation. All lectures will be held in the Hayston Building on the Wurnster campus.

> Monday, February 1, 6:00 P.M., Room 401
Speaker: Tim Powell, Professor of Policy Analysis at Wurnster University
Strategic Planning—Learn how to develop budgets in order to monitor progress toward community goals and successful outcomes.

> Wednesday, February 3, 7:00 P.M., Room 305
Speaker: Melissa Simmons, Kennedy Institute for Policy Making
Focusing on Our Children—Studies show that building playgrounds and sports facilities for children helps make better communities.

> Monday, February 8, 6:00 P.M., Room 202
Speaker: Hank Ross, Michigan Municipal League
Managing Our County's Parks—Learn how to preserve our local parks as a valuable community resource.

> Wednesday, February 10, 5:30 P.M., Room 404
Speaker: Scott Watson, Executive Director, Local Government Academy
Economic Opportunities and Local Ecology—Economic opportunity is often accompanied by potential risks to the surrounding ecosystem, and balancing the two can be difficult.

Please contact Patricia Flores at pflores@wurnster.edu for additional information

---

To: Patricia Flores <pflores@wurnster.edu>
From: Jake Patterson <jpatterson@wurnster.edu>
Subject: Lecture Series
Date: January 24

Dear Ms. Flores,

I work for facilities management here at Wurnster University. It was recently brought to my attention that there is a scheduling conflict concerning one of your lecture dates. Room 305 has been reserved for every Wednesday this semester by the Wurnster Debate Club. Therefore, I'm sorry to inform you that you will need to move the location or the time of this talk. You can visit the facilities management website in order to check the availability of other room locations and reschedule the talk.

Jake Patterson

GO ON TO THE NEXT PAGE ➡

176. For whom is the lecture series most likely intended?

(A) Community members
(B) Building superintendents
(C) University professors
(D) College students

177. In the brochure, the word "through" in paragraph 1, line 5, is closest in meaning to

(A) over
(B) via
(C) across
(D) until

178. What will most likely be discussed at the lecture on February 10?

(A) How to balance yearly budgets
(B) How to meet infrastructure needs
(C) How to avoid environmental damage
(D) How to stimulate economic development

179. According to Mr. Patterson, whose lecture must be rescheduled?

(A) Mr. Watson's
(B) Mr. Ross's
(C) Ms. Simmons's
(D) Mr. Powell's

180. What is Ms. Flores instructed to do on a website?

(A) Download a document
(B) Check room availability
(C) Update personal information
(D) Facilitate a forum

Questions 181-185 refer to the following email and list.

To:	Sally Russell <srussell@ptmail.com>
From:	Kelly Bennett <kbennett@msplanning.com>
Date:	December 7
Subject:	Wedding Services
Attachment:	Packages

Dear Ms. Russell,

We received your email on Tuesday, December 4, inquiring about our wedding planning and event services. We specialize in all kinds of weddings (small- or large-scale, indoor or outdoor, and various kinds of decor tailored to your dream wedding). We are sure to have a solution just right for you.

You wrote that you want a wedding package that is less than $5,000 and will be held at a large venue close to a major highway because you expect many guests from all over the country. As I understand it, your other preferences are as follows:

• an outdoor venue
• a photographer and videographer available at all times for documentation
• decorations including colorful flowers and elegant tablecloths

I've attached a list of all our possible wedding packages that you might be interested in. They are all located within 15 minutes' drive of Highway 519. Please look through the provided information to decide which location fits your needs best. Once you have made a decision, please inform me via email when you would like the wedding to be held. This will help me secure a reservation for you.

Thanks,

Kelly Bennett
MS Planning

Package	Total Fee	Location	Notes
Diamond	$5,500	Hardy Theater	Everything from the Emerald package, plus a live string quartet
Emerald	$4,300	Zenith Park	Everything from the Ruby package, plus photo and video shoots
Ruby	$3,000	Country Springs Hotel	Everything from the Sapphire package, plus decorated tables and beautiful flowers
Sapphire	$1,750	Jubilee Garden	Buffet lunch and a variety of beverages

GO ON TO THE NEXT PAGE

181. What can be inferred about Ms. Russell?

(A) She is Ms. Bennett's co-worker.
(B) She is planning a honeymoon.
(C) She is currently engaged.
(D) She works for a catering company.

182. Which occupation does Ms. Bennett most likely have?

(A) A professional musician
(B) A wedding photographer
(C) An interior designer
(D) An event planner

183. What is suggested about all the locations on the list?

(A) They are close to a main road.
(B) They are indoor venues.
(C) They are located in the same city.
(D) They require a down payment.

184. What information is Ms. Russell asked to provide?

(A) A potential date
(B) A meal selection
(C) A list of guests
(D) A honeymoon location

185. What package would probably best suit Ms. Russell's needs?

(A) Diamond
(B) Emerald
(C) Ruby
(D) Sapphire

Questions 186-190 refer to the following emails.

To:	<info@bountifulharvest.com>
From:	Emily Hall <emilyhall@zipline.com>
Date:	June 3
Subject:	Food Delivery

To whom it may concern,

My name is Emily Hall, and I am the owner of a vegetarian restaurant located in downtown Huntsville. I am contacting you because I am interested in receiving regular shipments of fresh, organic vegetables to my restaurant weekly. My restaurant is just starting, so I do not need a large quantity of goods. After looking into different farms in the area, I chose to contact Bountiful Harvest because of your promise to deliver certified organic food. Therefore, I would like to receive a price estimate for the cost of having fresh vegetables delivered directly to our restaurant on a weekly basis.

Emily Hall

To:	Emily Hall <emilyhall@zipline.com>
From:	Bountiful Harvest <info@bountifulharvest.com>
Date:	June 4
Subject:	RE: Food Delivery

Dear Ms. Hall,

Thanks for contacting our farm. At Bountiful Harvest, we offer fresh organic produce that can be delivered directly to a customer's location on a regular basis. Our vegetables are harvested from the field and delivered immediately, which means that you are getting wholesome, nutritious, organic produce to serve at your restaurant. We also offer additional items such as fresh meat, cheese, and milk. Below is a table detailing the various pricing options we offer.

Package Option	Features	Weight	Delivery Frequency	Price Per Delivery
Personal	This package feeds approximately two to three people and contains fresh, seasonal vegetables.	5 lb.	Once a week	$15
Small	This package is ideal for small businesses and includes fresh, seasonal vegetables.	50 lb.	Once a week	$140
Medium	This package is for medium-sized businesses needing a constant supply of fresh vegetables and meats.	130 lb.	Twice a week	$500
Large	This package is our largest package and includes vegetables, meats, and dairy products.	250 lb.	Twice a week	$800

The prices listed above do not include the delivery price. Customers who do not pick up their packages in person will have to pay an extra $6 per package to be delivered. However, for customers who sign up for an entire year's worth of deliveries, we will deliver your package for free. The purchase of additional items will also affect the final price of your package. Additional options are available on our website. Payments can be made via cash, credit card, check, or money order on the day of delivery.

We know that our customers especially care about the quality of the food. Therefore, we offer a mini-package free of charge so you can assess our food. Please call Greg Lemons at 555-8141 to take advantage of this opportunity.

Indira Singh

GO ON TO THE NEXT PAGE

To: Bountiful Harvest <info@bountifulharvest.com>
From: Emily Hall <emilyhall@zipline.com>
Date: June 5
Subject: Harvest Schedule

Dear Ms. Singh,

Thank you for responding so promptly to my email. I appreciate the offer of the complimentary delivery, but I think I would like to just go ahead and set up regular deliveries. I may be interested in setting up a year's worth of deliveries, but I would first like to get a list of the range of produce that you will be offering through the different seasons. As I own a vegetarian restaurant, I will need to have an idea of the types of produce that will be delivered, so I can prepare my menus accordingly. Thank you so much for your consideration, and I look forward to working with Bountiful Harvest!

Kind regards,
Emily Hall

---

186. What is the purpose of the first email?

    (A) To request cost information
    (B) To inquire about a policy change
    (C) To postpone an order
    (D) To report an incorrect invoice

187. What package option most likely fits Ms. Hall's needs best?

    (A) Personal
    (B) Small
    (C) Medium
    (D) Large

188. What information is NOT needed for a final price?

    (A) Length of contract
    (B) Method of delivery
    (C) Additional items
    (D) Distance of shipping

189. What is indicated in Emily Hall's email?

    (A) She wants to try it for a month.
    (B) She wants the free gift.
    (C) She is interested in a long term contract.
    (D) She doesn't want winter produce.

190. Why does Emily Hall want to know about the vegetables that will be available throughout the year?

    (A) She loves vegetables.
    (B) She is thinking about adding meat.
    (C) She might hire another employee.
    (D) She wants to plan her future menus.

Important Notice

Dear Castelli customers,

Our quality assurance team has revealed that five hundred jars of Castelli's Classic Spaghetti Sauce do not meet our high standards of product quality.

The defect has been caused by an improper seal on the lid of the jar, and may have resulted in the contents spoiling due to contact with air. We are currently warning customers not to eat this product.

What you should do: If you have already purchased a jar of Castelli's Classic Spaghetti Sauce, please send an email to our Customer Service Department at cs@castellifood. com. One of our employees will provide you with a product replacement voucher. Please include your name, full address, phone number, and the product's serial number in the email. Customers will receive a $12 voucher for each jar purchased. Please do not try to get a refund for this product at a retailer.

Please remember that no other Castelli food products are affected. We encourage you to continue purchasing our products.

To:	<cs@castellifood.com>
From:	Tony Hester <tonyhester21@webzit.com>
Date:	March 29
Subject:	Replacement Voucher

To whom it may concern,

My name is Tony Hester, and I appreciate the precautionary step. Around two weeks ago I purchased two jars of Castelli's Classic Spaghetti Sauce from an Ace grocery store in Hermantown, Minnesota. A week later, I purchased one more jar of it at the same place.

I have attached the image file of both receipts to this email. I would like to receive a product replacement voucher for these defective products. My address is:

Tony Hester
27 Bloom Street
Hermantown, MN 55811

I look forward to receiving a reply soon.

Tony Hester

GO ON TO THE NEXT PAGE

To: Tony Hester <tonyhester21@webzit.com>
From: <cs@castellifood.com>
Date: March 30
Subject: Voucher

Dear Mr. Hester,

Thank you very much for contacting Castelli Foods. We are committed to ensuring that our customers can continue to rely on the Castelli line of quality foods for all their dining needs. As such, we are happy to provide you with three vouchers for the cans of Classic Spaghetti Sauce you recently purchased. Please find the vouchers enclosed.

In addition to the vouchers for the Classic Spaghetti Sauce, we would like to offer you vouchers for our new line of linguini and spaghetti pasta, Pasta Prima. Please accept these as another way for us to say that we are sorry, and we hope that you continue to turn to us for delicious Italian flavors.

Sincerely,
Jan Olson, Customer Care Specialist

191. Where would the notice most likely be found?

(A) In a restaurant
(B) In a staff break room
(C) In a shipping agency
(D) In a grocery store

192. What is indicated about the jars?

(A) They were not closed tightly.
(B) They are currently out of stock.
(C) They were priced incorrectly.
(D) They were delivered to the wrong address.

193. According to the notice, what is NOT mentioned as advice for customers?

(A) Avoiding consuming the product
(B) Reporting on the product
(C) Returning the product to a store
(D) Purchasing other Castelli products

194. In the letter to Mr. Hester, what additional gift does Castelli offer?

(A) Pasta sauce
(B) A recipe book
(C) Vouchers for produce
(D) Vouchers for new products

195. Castelli is sending the vouchers for several reasons; which of the following is NOT one of them?

(A) To keep customers loyal
(B) To say that they were sorry
(C) To be fair to their customers
(D) To gain new customers

Questions 196-200 refer to the following form, email, and notice.

Auburn City Restaurant Inspection

Restaurant Name: Polito's Pizza **Location:** 43 Clark Street **Inspection Date:** January 22

A: Comply completely with safety and health requirements with no violations
B: Conform to most safety and health requirements with a few minor violations
C: Not meet some safety and health requirements with some violations
D: Not satisfy many safety and health requirements with serious violations that could result in harm or illness for a customer
(Fines will be imposed for any C or D level violations related to food preparation and storage.)

Item	Score
1. Personnel regularly wash hands and follow hygienic practices.	B
2. Raw meats and vegetables are refrigerated at proper temperatures.	A
3. All ingredients are properly stored and labeled.	C
4. Dishes and utensils are cleaned and sterilized.	A
5. Fire extinguishers are easily accessible.	B
6. Fire exits are clearly marked.	C
7. Floors are clean and dry.	B

To avoid additional penalties, restaurants are warned to correct violations before their next inspection.

Restaurant Owner: Greg Kluck
Inspector: Melissa Tenner

To: All Employees <employees@politospizza.com>
From: Greg Kluck <gregkluck@politospizza.com>
Subject: Inspection results
Date: January 25

Dear employees,

The results from our recent inspection on January 22 indicate that there are a few problems that we need to address.

First, it was brought to my attention that fire exit signs need to be installed again.

The most serious violation concerned the improper storage and labeling of food. All ingredients stored for later use must be labeled with an exact date and detailed contents. If we do not label containers properly, spoiled food could accidentally be served to customers.

We received relatively low grades for employee hygiene and the cleanliness of our facilities. All employees are required to wear their uniform and hairnet at all times and to wash their hands after every bathroom visit. We also need to mop floors more often and keep them dry.

In order to correct these poor situations, I will be posting a checklist that all employees will be required to complete every morning. It will include necessary preparations to ensure that we are not breaking any regulations. This measure will go into effect on January 29.

If you have any questions about these changes, please bring them up at the staff meeting tomorrow.

GO ON TO THE NEXT PAGE ➡

NOTICE TO ALL EMPLOYEES

The checklist below must be signed by every employee every day that they have a shift at Polito's Pizza. Only sign the task once it has been completed or checked. Failure to fill out the checklist with the date, time, and signature will be treated as a violation of Polito's new health standards.

POLITO'S CHECKLIST

Polito's	Sun	Mon	Tue	Wed	Thu	Fri	Sat
Rotate Food	K.P.	K.P.	K.P.	K.P.			K.P.
Mop Floors	K.P.	K.P.	K.P.	K.P.			K.P.
Uniforms	K.P.	K.P.	K.P.	K.P.			K.P.
Wash hands	K.P.	K.P.	K.P.	K.P.			K.P.

196. Why was the inspection conducted?

(A) To monitor compliance with food industry regulations
(B) To rate the taste and quality of the cuisine
(C) To inspect the structural safety of the building
(D) To evaluate the effectiveness of new policies

197. Why has Polito's Pizza been charged a fine?

(A) Because fire extinguishers were not in place
(B) Because containers of food were not marked appropriately
(C) Because raw meats and vegetables were handled incorrectly
(D) Because the facilities were not cleaned according to standards

198. What does Mr. Kluck ask his employees to do?

(A) Apologize to customers
(B) Wear a name tag at all times
(C) File a complaint with Ms. Tenner
(D) Fill out a required form

199. What will happen if an employee fails to sign the work checklist?

(A) They will have a violation on their record.
(B) They will have to pay a fine.
(C) They will have to come in on the weekends.
(D) They will be fired.

200. Based on Polito's Checklist, what can we infer about K.P.?

(A) He works at night.
(B) He did not work on Thursday and Friday.
(C) He will be fired for violations.
(D) He is slow at work.

NO TEST MATERIAL ON THIS PAGE

Stop! This is the end of the test. If you finish before time is called, you may go back to Parts 5, 6, and 7 and check your work.

READING TEST

In the Reading test, you will read a variety of texts and answer several different types of reading comprehension questions. The entire Reading test will last 75 minutes. There are three parts, and directions are given for each part. You are encouraged to answer as many questions as possible within the time allowed.

You must mark your answers on the separate answer sheet. Do not write your answers in your test book.

PART 5

Directions: A word or phrase is missing in each of the sentences below. Four answer choices are given below each sentence. Select the best answer to complete the sentence. Then mark the letter (A), (B), (C), or (D) on your answer sheet.

101. With the help of one of the IT technicians, the missing accounting files have been -------.

(A) recover
(B) recovers
(C) recovering
(D) recovered

102. A private reception for gallery donors will be ------- on March 5, prior to the grand opening of the exhibit.

(A) held
(B) faced
(C) claimed
(D) made

103. Aurora Furnishings is finding it difficult to make a profit in its ------- competitive market.

(A) increases
(B) increased
(C) increasingly
(D) increase

104. A minor electrical malfunction was discovered by the pilot ------- before the plane took off.

(A) barely
(B) shortly
(C) absolutely
(D) exclusively

105. We will make a final decision about changing the landscaping of the property after reviewing the ------- costs.

(A) estimation
(B) estimate
(C) estimated
(D) estimating

106. MyHealth Co. has produced a wide range of vitamin supplements for ------- two decades.

(A) along
(B) during
(C) over
(D) when

107. The April edition of *Fishing and More* magazine looks ------- different from previous issues because of the new art editor.

(A) completed
(B) complete
(C) completely
(D) completing

108. The customer's order ------- will be sent by email within twenty-four hours.

(A) confirmation
(B) confirms
(C) confirmed
(D) confirm

109. The maintenance team's repair requests should be ------- in groups according to the urgency.

(A) organizing
(B) organize
(C) organized
(D) organizes

110. Following Ms. Rivera's ------- statement, the official awards ceremony for Plex Industries will commence.

(A) brief
(B) straight
(C) former
(D) steep

111. Due to the high volume of foot traffic, the shop must polish its floors more ------- than usual during the peak season.

(A) frequent
(B) frequented
(C) frequency
(D) frequently

112. The Master Gardeners Club had to ------- its monthly meeting because the community center's conference room was double-booked.

(A) prepare
(B) oppose
(C) postpone
(D) extend

113. Financial advisors report that older investors tend to be ------- than their younger counterparts.

(A) cautious
(B) cautioned
(C) more cautious
(D) caution

114. Mr. Albrecht's ------- in replying to the HR director's email demonstrated that he was highly interested in the position.

(A) promptness
(B) prompted
(C) prompt
(D) promptly

115. The soccer players usually practice on the main field at Waterbury Park, but they sometimes practice -------.

(A) everybody
(B) twice
(C) yet
(D) elsewhere

116. The accountants were unable to produce a full report by the deadline, but promised that ------- would give a summary of the important points.

(A) their
(B) themselves
(C) they
(D) theirs

GO ON TO THE NEXT PAGE

117. Despite having some problems with the sound system during the performance, the concert was an ------- experience for everyone.

(A) enjoyable
(B) enjoyment
(C) enjoys
(D) enjoyably

118. ------- the building has an excellent location and a modern interior, it is popular among visitors.

(A) In view of
(B) Provided that
(C) Other than
(D) Seeing that

119. The Parks and Recreation Department offers ------- opportunities for volunteers to improve the community.

(A) reward
(B) rewards
(C) rewarded
(D) rewarding

120. The vacant rooms on the inn's second floor have ------- been cleaned.

(A) most
(B) every
(C) some
(D) all

121. The short story cannot be reprinted ------- explicit permission from the writer.

(A) without
(B) regarding
(C) among
(D) unlike

122. The restaurant has a ------- decorated room that is perfect for hosting children's parties.

(A) cheerful
(B) cheerfully
(C) cheerfulness
(D) cheer

123. A wildlife expert is scheduled to give a talk on the ------- that the factory has had on the surrounding forest.

(A) components
(B) degree
(C) requirements
(D) impact

124. The landlord raised the monthly rent for the first time in several years, and ------- so.

(A) reasonable
(B) reasonably
(C) reason
(D) reasons

125. As long as there are no further delays, the factory will be fully ------- by June 18.

(A) operational
(B) operate
(C) operates
(D) operation

126. Thanks to his experience, Mr. Warren is ------- capable of completing the job on his own.

(A) certainly
(B) certain
(C) certainty
(D) certify

127. Because of ------- fuel costs, some people are choosing to stay home for the summer vacation rather than drive to tourist sites.

(A) rising
(B) above
(C) dependable
(D) lengthy

128. The green light on the side of the water purifier lights up ------- the filter needs to be replaced.

(A) likewise
(B) whenever
(C) therefore
(D) whereas

129. Two items in Ms. Burke's order were out of stock, so her invoice was adjusted -------.

(A) continuously
(B) accordingly
(C) immeasurably
(D) recognizably

130. The notice indicated that a first aid training course will be provided free of charge to ------- next month.

(A) residents
(B) residence
(C) residential
(D) resides

GO ON TO THE NEXT PAGE

PART 6

Directions: Read the texts that follow. A word, phrase, or sentence is missing in parts of each text. Four answer choices for each question are given below the text. Select the best answer to complete the text. Then mark the letter (A), (B), (C), or (D) on your answer sheet.

Questions 131-134 refer to the following notice.

Employee Spring Training

Lawrence Paper is dedicated to helping all of its employees fulfill their potential. That is why we have once again organized two days of spring training. Human Resources has put together a wide range of topics for this year's workshops, ------- sales techniques, computer
131.
skills, communication strategies, and goal setting. We still have two workshop time slots available, so if there is something you've been dying to learn about, please let us know. It's quite possible we ------- it into this year's spring training. ------- Feel free to ------- any ideas
132.   **133.**   **134.**
you might have to Nancy Kensington in the Human Resources department.

131. (A) distributing
    (B) locating
    (C) including
    (D) advancing

132. (A) were incorporating
    (B) have incorporated
    (C) are incorporating
    (D) could incorporate

133. (A) If we get many suggestions, we could also hold a workshop on the following weekend, December 4th.
    (B) We'll be finalizing our choices by the end of the week.
    (C) A large amount of time and energy has gone into organizing this conference.
    (D) Inviting friends and family to these events is always encouraged.

134. (A) create
    (B) request
    (C) submit
    (D) transfer

Questions 135-138 refer to the following advertisement.

Vander Properties

Vander Properties has been serving Houston for over 29 years. It is through our commitment to providing the highest degree of expertise market knowledge and ------- service that we
135.
are recognized as an industry leader.

We specialize in ------- and corporate real estate here in the Denver area. ------- you are
136. **137.**
looking to buy a new home or start a new business, we are the people you should be talking

with. With our office centrally located in downtown, we have our eyes on the whole city.

Browse our site for available listings, or give us a call today. -------
138.
www.vanderproperties.com

Phone: (313) 782-9919

Address: 834 Walton St.

---

135. (A) personalize
(B) personalizes
(C) personalizing
(D) personalized

136. (A) productive
(B) promoted
(C) relevant
(D) residential

137. (A) Whether
(B) Even if
(C) Even though
(D) However

138. (A) Take a drive out of town and come see
us today.
(B) We appreciate your assistance.
(C) Of course, drop-ins are always
welcome.
(D) Our kitchen is open from eight to five
daily.

GO ON TO THE NEXT PAGE

Pizza Chef Wanted

Papa Gino's is hiring, and all ------- applicants will be considered. ------- Even If you have no
          139.   **140.**

experience, training will be provided if you meet our requirements. To meet our requirements

you must have a ------- health card, have reliable transportation, and be able to work
          141.

evenings and weekends. Please apply in person at Papa Gino's on State and Pine. -------
                                           142.

look forward to meeting you.

---

139. (A) qualify
    (B) qualifying
    (C) qualified
    (D) to qualify

(NEW)
140. (A) We are looking for candidates that have
        some experience in Italian food.
    (B) We are looking for candidates that can
        speak Italian.
    (C) We are looking for people who like to
        eat pizza.
    (D) We are looking for people who want to
        practice.

141. (A) valid
    (B) working
    (C) effective
    (D) strong

142. (A) She
    (B) They
    (C) We
    (D) He

Questions 143-146 refer to the following letter.

November 11th

John Adams

Tri-State, Apt. 408

New York, NY 10873

Dear Mr. Adams,

I am pleased to inform you that you ------- as one of the finalists for the position of sales
143.
director at Goldie Saks. Over 100 applicants applied for the ------- but we have narrowed
144.
down our list to eight candidates. You will be called in for an interview on November 15th

from 1 P.M. to 6 P.M. ------- The location of the interview will be the company headquarters.
145.
Our assistant, Miss Lane, will meet you in the main lobby and take you to the interview room.

For the candidates that do well in these interviews, there will be a second interview. We will

let you know as soon as possible whether you -------.
146.

Please call us at 555-1234 if you have any further questions.

We hope to see you soon.

Sincerely,

Jennifer Law

Executive Manager

143. (A) were choosing
(B) had chosen
(C) have been chosen
(D) chose

144. (A) position
(B) location
(C) career
(D) appointment

145. (A) The building is easy to locate.
(B) We would like you to come in at 1 P.M.
(C) Our interviewers will ask you several
questions.
(D) You will be given a specific schedule.

146. (A) enable
(B) approve
(C) refuse
(D) qualify

GO ON TO THE NEXT PAGE

Directions: In this part you will read a selection of texts, such as magazine and newspaper articles, emails, and instant messages. Each text or set of texts is followed by several questions. Select the best answer for each question and mark the letter (A), (B), (C), or (D) on your answer sheet.

Questions 147-148 refer to the following advertisement.

This Amazing World Photography Competition

The monthly travel magazine *This Amazing World* is offering a discounted subscription rate for those who sign up during the month of November. *This Amazing World* has been in print for over 30 years and offers readers insider tips and expert know-how to help you plan the vacation of your dreams. The magazine includes vacation package advertisements, reviews from travelers, and insightful essays to introduce you to various cultures, cuisines, and travel destinations.

Submit your travel photos to our This Amazing World Photography Competition for a chance to win a fantastic vacation to Scotland! The winner of the top prize will receive round-trip tickets and a $2,000 travel voucher for a hotel stay for you and one other person.

147. What is mentioned about the magazine?

(A) It is a literary journal.
(B) It includes a recipe book as a supplement.
(C) It provides travel advice.
(D) It has an online version.

148. What is suggested about the competition?

(A) It is sponsored by professional photographers.
(B) It awards a complimentary vacation to the winner.
(C) It accepts digital photos only.
(D) It features photos of Scotland.

Questions 149-151 refer to the following text message chain.

Liz Bradley		**8:14**

Sir, the arrangements have been made for your meeting with Mr. Johnson tomorrow afternoon. I've reserved a table for two at Sheraton Restaurant at 1 P.M.

Bernie Gibbs   **8:17**

Thank you. And have you compiled the reports that I'll need at the meeting?

Liz Bradley   **8:18**

Most of them, yes. I'm still waiting for Michael Steel's reports. He told me that he would have them ready for me sometime this morning.

Bernie Gibbs   **8:20**

Well, they should have been completed last night. Can you contact him and see what's going on?

(Michael Steel was added to the conversation at 8:26)

Liz Bradley   **8:27**

Michael, Mr. Gibbs wants to know where the reports are. Are you finished with them?

Michael Steele   **8:28**

I apologize for the delay. Our intern accidentally deleted some files. I had to scour the database to locate the back-up material. It was a bit of a headache sorting through the files that I needed, but I think I have everything organized, and I'm printing them out now.

Liz Bradley   **8:29**

Can you bring them to me as soon as you're done?

Michael Steel   **8:30**

Of course. I'll be there in 10 minutes.

GO ON TO THE NEXT PAGE

149. Who most likely is Liz Bradley?

(A) An intern
(B) An assistant
(C) A business partner
(D) An executive

150. Why was Michael Steel added to the conversation?

(A) To have him give an update about the missing reports
(B) To inform him about the upcoming meeting
(C) To let him know about the deadline
(D) To scold him for his lack of punctuality

151. What does Michael imply when he says, "I had to scour the database to locate the back-up material"?

(A) He took his time writing the report.
(B) He had to back up all the information first.
(C) He needed time to find the missing data.
(D) The computer was out of order.

www.turnerandco.com

Turner & Co.

158 Baskin Road, Redwood Bay, UK
Phone: 243-555-1541

| HOME | ABOUT US | PRODUCTS | REPLACEMENT | CONTACT US |

Turner & Co. has produced beautiful, energy-efficient windows that meet the taste and expectations of our customers since its founding in 1949. When you choose Turner & Co., you are buying more than just a window. You will be receiving the excellent services of our professionals who have been performing superb work for decades. We are passionate about helping you choose a quality window that exactly fits the specifications of your home. Additionally, we are fully committed to environmental protection and have recently been recognized for our sustainable business practices by the Environmental Protection Agency (EPA).

152. What is being advertised?

(A) An insurance company
(B) A window manufacturer
(C) A landscaping company
(D) A window cleaning service provider

153. What is indicated about Turner & Co.?

(A) It is a family-run business.
(B) Its branches are located nationwide.
(C) It is an eco-friendly company.
(D) It has recently hired experienced employees.

GO ON TO THE NEXT PAGE

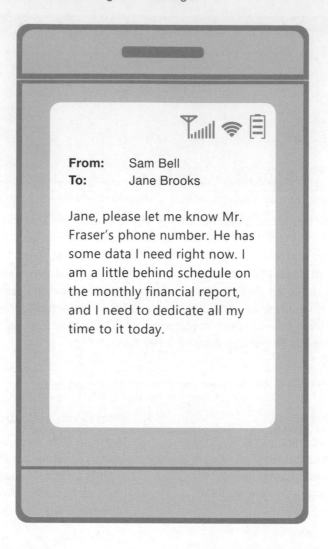

From: Sam Bell
To: Jane Brooks

Jane, please let me know Mr. Fraser's phone number. He has some data I need right now. I am a little behind schedule on the monthly financial report, and I need to dedicate all my time to it today.

154. Why was the message sent?

(A) To ask for a favor
(B) To postpone a deadline
(C) To cancel a meeting
(D) To request a document

155. What is indicated about Mr. Bell?

(A) He is unable to attend a meeting.
(B) He expects profits to increase.
(C) He is trying to meet a deadline.
(D) He was recently hired.

Questions 156-158 refer to the following article.

SEOUL (July 19) – Breamin's Group opened the doors to its first B&G clothing shop on the famed Abgujeong Rodeo street in South Korea to long lines and frantic shoppers. – [1] – The frenzy was over the limited edition line designed by Marichio Bucci in partnership with B&G. Within just a couple of hours of opening the doors, most of the Bucci design items were sold out. Similar reports of chaos and empty shelves which once held items from the Bucci line were echoed in major cities around the world including New York, London, Tokyo, and Milan. – [2] – Although B&G has released limited edition collaborations with other famous designers, this is the first time that B&G shops have reported a complete depletion of items within hours of its release. The Bucci and B&G collaboration is the most successful to date, and talks are already in progress over future collaborations for more clothing lines. – [3] – Meanwhile in Seoul, shoppers who were unable to purchase from the Bucci line were disappointed but excited to have the popular retailer open in Korea. – [4] –

156. What is indicated about B&G?

(A) They have stores around the world.
(B) They only sell items designed by Bucci.
(C) The company has a few branches in Korea.
(D) Their products usually sell out within hours.

157. What is reported about the Bucci and B&G collaboration?

(A) It took years to put together.
(B) It was only sold in select stores.
(C) It's one of the most profitable collaborations for the company.
(D) It will only be a one-time event.

158. In which of the positions marked [1], [2], [3], and [4] does the following sentence best belong?

"This is a first for the company since all previous limited designer edition lines were simply a one-time partnership."

(A) [1]
(B) [2]
(C) [3]
(D) [4]

GO ON TO THE NEXT PAGE

MEMO

To: All staff
From: Elizabeth Paine
Date: January 24
Subject: Sick leave

Attention employees,

We are going to make adjustments to our policies concerning sick leave here at Zimnet Corporation. We are considering reducing the number of paid vacation days and instead increasing the number of paid sick days available to employees. Before we make any changes, we would like to gather the opinions of employees on this matter. Please email Tony Nugent at tonynugent@zimnet.com. He will be collecting and analyzing your responses. Afterward, management will produce a corresponding policy proposal by February 24. Once the proposal has been made, a meeting will be called to discuss its implementation among all of our employees. I hope this process can be helpful to all of our employees. Please be active in your participation.

Sincerely,

Elizabeth Paine

159. What is the purpose of the memo?

(A) To suggest a budget proposal
(B) To solicit feedback
(C) To revise incorrect information
(D) To announce survey results

160. Which job is Mr. Nugent most likely to have?

(A) A sales representative
(B) A product developer
(C) An investment analyst
(D) A personnel employee

161. According to the memo, what will Ms. Paine probably do soon after February 24?

(A) Announce a merger
(B) Hire a medical specialist
(C) Participate in a tour
(D) Schedule a meeting

Questions 162-165 refer to the following text message chain.

Penny Jones   3:27

I just got a call from Martin. His client, Mr. Patrick, would like to have his order two weeks earlier than originally planned. Essentially, by next week Monday. Do you think this is possible? I'd like your input.

Karen Norman   3:28

There's no problem on our end. Most of the leather has already been cut. We've already sent many of the pieces to be sewn. The rest of the work should take a couple of hours.

Neil Park   3:29

The handles are complete, and about half the bags are near completion. I'll get them to Lauren soon. I think we should be able to finish sewing the bags by tomorrow evening.

Penny Jones   3:30

I'm glad to hear that most of the handbags are almost finished. Lauren, how long will it take to get the hardware attached or sewn in?

Lauren Nichols   3:31

We're currently working on the Jenk and Cenk twins orders.

Penny Jones   3:32

We have more than enough time to complete the twin's orders, so I can authorize your workers to put aside that project for now. How long will Mr. Patrick's order take?

Lauren Nichols   3:33

The zippers need to be sewn in, but the studs will be glued, which makes the work easier. I think we need about a day.

Kevin Harding   3:34

It'll only take us a couple of hours to have the order packaged safely to be shipped.

Penny Jones   3:35

Thank you so much. I'll let our client know.

GO ON TO THE NEXT PAGE

162. What kind of business does the client most likely own?

    (A) A clothing shop
    (B) A furniture company
    (C) A shoe store
    (D) A handbag business

163. According to the conversation, whose department must complete the work first?

    (A) Karen Norman's
    (B) Neil Park's
    (C) Lauren Nichols's
    (D) Kevin Harding's

164. At 3:31, why does Lauren Nichols say, "We're currently working on the Jenk and Cenk twins orders"?

    (A) To inform everyone that they have their own clients
    (B) To explain why they refuse to help
    (C) To imply that they are busy with another project
    (D) To make everyone speed up their work

165. What will Penny Jones most likely tell Mr. Patrick?

    (A) That his order will be finished two weeks later
    (B) That his request can be fulfilled
    (C) That his order will cost him extra money
    (D) That there may be a delay to his order

Questions 166-168 refer to the following notice.

Business Hours in Early March

Monday	Tuesday	Wednesday	Thursday	Friday	Saturday	Sunday
2:00 p.m.	2:00 p.m.	3:00 p.m.	4:00 p.m.	2:00 p.m.	2:00 p.m.	9:00 a.m.
|	|	|	|	|	|	|
9:00 p.m.	8:00 p.m.	9:00 p.m.	9:00 p.m.	9:00 p.m.	10:00 p.m.	6:00 p.m.

Due to the current construction on Shilling Street, we have been forced to revise our business hours for the first week in March (see the chart above). During the morning hours, the construction makes it difficult for customers to reach our location by car. We will be extending our evening hours to accommodate this change. Additionally, due to the construction, our parking lot is also currently inaccessible. Therefore, during this period, customers are asked to utilize public parking spaces available on Patch Street. We apologize for this inconvenience and strive to be back to normal soon.

166. What is being announced?

(A) A renovation project
(B) A store expansion
(C) A change in operating hours
(D) A work schedule

167. When is the construction most likely NOT being performed?

(A) On Monday
(B) On Wednesday
(C) On Saturday
(D) On Sunday

168. Why are customers asked to go to Patch Street?

(A) To find a place to park
(B) To visit a new store location
(C) To take part in a promotional event
(D) To receive a sample

GO ON TO THE NEXT PAGE

For Sale by Owner

Palmer Standard Cabin Yacht

Asking price: $45,000 or best offer

Basic Specifications:
This boat was built four years ago. It is 12 feet wide by 36 feet long. The hull is made of fiberglass, making it light yet strong. The boat includes two double bedrooms as well as a sleeper sofa, kitchen, and bathroom.

Features:
This boat is very stable and offers a spacious deck. It is perfect for large families and social gatherings. It includes an eight-speaker sound system with USB connectivity. It also has a lockable storage compartment where personal belongings can be kept.

Additional Information:
I have owned and operated this boat for three and a half years. The boat comes with a five-year warranty that still has one and a half years remaining. The warranty is transferable to the buyer upon purchase.

If you would like to see or test-ride the boat, contact Gary Thompson at (654) 555-8715.

169. What is indicated about the Palmer Standard Cabin Yacht?

(A) It is a fishing boat.
(B) Its original paint color has been changed.
(C) It can accommodate a group of people.
(D) It is currently being repaired.

170. What is NOT mentioned as a feature of the Palmer Standard Cabin Yacht?

(A) Capability to play music
(B) A lightweight construction material
(C) Ample sleeping accommodations
(D) A fuel-efficient engine

171. What is most likely true about Mr. Thompson?

(A) He will give a boat tour to a potential buyer.
(B) He has young children.
(C) He works at a shipyard.
(D) He wants to sell the warranty separately.

Travel & Recreation
123 Gilmore Street
Orange County, CA 48857

November 15
Mr. Peter Kang
3820 Rivervalley Heights
Seattle, WA 19387

Dear Mr. Kang,

We at Travel & Recreation thank you for your subscription to our magazine. As you have been a long time subscriber, I am excited to inform you about our new subscription plan for our VIP members. – [1] – As a member, you will continue to receive monthly editions of our magazine and access to our new online e-magazine services. You can simply download a digital version of the print magazine to any mobile device at no extra cost. – [2] – Furthermore, you can access background information about our authors, journalists, and guest writers, as well as detailed information about the locations and places that are covered in the magazine. In addition, you can access the recipes to the most popular restaurants around the world, and most exciting of all, we will hold an exclusive competition for our VIP members with a chance to win a trip for two to Hawaii. – [3] – Our regular subscribers, as well as VIP members, will have a chance to win a dining experience at 5-star restaurant Bellisimo.

Again, we thank you for your continued support, and we hope you enjoy the many changes we have made to our services as we strive to entertain and educate our loyal subscribers. – [4] – Please fill out the application form that is attached to this letter. Please check which subscription plan you wish to join. If you send in a $100 fee, you will receive the regular subscription plan. If you send in a $200 fee, you will become a VIP member.

We appreciate your support and hope to hear from you soon.

Sincerely,

Victoria Adams

GO ON TO THE NEXT PAGE →

172. Why was a letter sent to Mr. Kang?

(A) To remind him to send in his travel journals
(B) To explain about a new subscription plan
(C) To inquire about his travel plans
(D) To determine his qualifications for a position

173. What did Ms. Adams send with the letter?

(A) A travel itinerary
(B) A new contract
(C) An application form
(D) A revised schedule

174. In the middle of the first paragraph of the letter, the term "at no extra cost" is closest in meaning to

(A) for a small fee
(B) with a donation
(C) quite easily
(D) for free

175. In which of the positions [1], [2], [3], and [4] does the following sentence best belong? "Your subscription expires next month, but we invite you to consider joining our VIP membership."

(A) [1]
(B) [2]
(C) [3]
(D) [4]

Questions 176-180 refer to the following invoice and email.

Taylor Fabrics
Invoice

Ordered by: Tammy Fleck
Order date: August 11
Delivery address: 628 Green Circle Drive, Austin, TX 78701
Email: tfleck@capnet.com

Order taken by: Craig Dell
Estimated delivery date: August 14–16
Mobile phone: (512) 555-9782

Quantity	Item	Description	Price
4 yards	Fabric 10	Solid white	$28.00
5 yards	Fabric 38	Floral pattern	$50.00
6 yards	Fabric 41	Checkered pattern	$48.00
2 yards	Fabric 48	Leopard pattern	$30.00
		Tax	$15.60
		Shipping	$12.00
		Total	$183.60

Payment method: Billed to credit card account ending in 4680
If you have questions about your order, please email us at customerservice@taylorfabrics.com.
All of our packages sent within the United States are guaranteed to arrive within 10 days of
order confirmation. If they don't arrive on time, we promise to reimburse you for 30% of your
total purchase.

To: customerservice@taylorfabrics.com
From: Tammy Fleck <tfleck@capnet.com>
Date: August 25
Subject: Delivery Delay

Dear Customer Service,

I received my order from Taylor Fabrics yesterday that I placed two weeks ago. Not only was
the package delivered later than promised, but one of my orders was incorrectly shipped.
The invoice correctly reflects my wish to receive 5 yards of the floral pattern fabric, but only
2 yards of it were delivered. Because of this error, I won't be able to complete the dress I
was making for my friend's birthday. I am very disappointed.

Once this issue has been resolved and the additional fabric has been sent, please send a text
message to my mobile phone.

Thank you,

Tammy Fleck

GO ON TO THE NEXT PAGE

176. What job is Mr. Dell most likely to have?

    (A) A designer
    (B) A salesperson
    (C) A customer
    (D) A manufacturer

177. What is implied about Ms. Fleck?

    (A) She is a long-term customer of Taylor Fabrics.
    (B) She is a professional fashion designer.
    (C) She is a former employee of Taylor Fabrics.
    (D) She will be partially paid back for her purchase.

178. Why did Ms. Fleck send the email?

    (A) Her credit card was incorrectly charged.
    (B) She wants to return an item.
    (C) She received the incorrect quantity of an item.
    (D) One of her orders had the wrong pattern.

179. Which fabric will Ms. Fleck need more of to make a dress?

    (A) Fabric 10
    (B) Fabric 38
    (C) Fabric 41
    (D) Fabric 48

180. How should Taylor Fabrics customer service contact Ms. Fleck?

    (A) By text message
    (B) By voice mail
    (C) By email
    (D) By letter

Next Month at the Belmont Historical Society

Documentary Film Night: *Exploring the Arctic*
May 5, Spruce Theater

Photo Exhibition: "America in the 20th Century"
Opening Night, May 9, Linda Cameron Art Gallery

Author Talk: Glen Campbell, "The Culture of Early America"
May 14, Chris Charlton Auditorium

Musical Performance: "American Folk Masters"
May 22, Spruce Theater

Children and seniors are allowed free entry to all events. Additionally, if you pay the registration fee and become a member of the Belmont Historical Society on our website, you can attend any event free of charge.

For questions about booking group visits, contact David Smith at dsmith@belmonthistoricalsociety.com. For more details regarding upcoming events and venue locations, or to rent one of our venues, visit us at www.belmonthistoricalsociety.com.

ACTUAL TEST 02

To:	David Smith <dsmith@belmonthistoricalsociety.com>
From:	Jared Tate <jtate@clarkuniversity.com>
Date:	April 22
Subject:	Group Visit

Dear Mr. Smith,

Hello, my name is Jared Tate, and I am a professor in the History Department at Clark University in downtown Maryville.

I am teaching an introductory history course for freshmen this semester, and I thought it would be helpful to attend the event featuring Mr. Campbell. His talk is very pertinent to the subjects we are currently covering in class.

I was also wondering if it would be possible to arrange a question-and-answer session between Mr. Campbell and my group of about 50 students. Please tell him that we are looking forward to seeing him.

I appreciate your reading my email, and I hope to hear back from you soon.

Jared Tate

History Department, Clark University

GO ON TO THE NEXT PAGE

181. What is indicated about the Belmont Historical Society?

(A) It does not allow children into some events.
(B) It is run by the city of Belmont.
(C) It was founded by Linda Cameron.
(D) It will hold its events at several places.

182. What is Mr. Tate most likely currently teaching?

(A) Environmental conditions of the Arctic
(B) Early American history
(C) American folk music
(D) Modern photography

183. What is NOT mentioned as being available on the Belmont Historical Society website?

(A) Information about scheduled events
(B) Member registration
(C) Rental details
(D) Descriptions of previous events

184. In the email, the word "introductory" in paragraph 2, line 1, is closest in meaning to

(A) basic
(B) required
(C) profound
(D) optional

185. What does Mr. Tate request?

(A) A signed copy of a book
(B) A detailed survey
(C) A chance to meet a speaker
(D) A group discount

Questions 186-190 refer to the following schedule and emails.

Newton Library

April Program and Events Schedule

Date and Time	Event	Location	Additional Notes
April 2 7 P.M.	A Trip to the Past: Silent Film Series	Decker Hall	Join us for a viewing of several films showcasing early American film history.
April 5 3 P.M.	Youth Creative Writing Workshop	Youth Wing, Room 304	Open to all students in high school who want to improve their writing skills.
April 10 11 A.M.	Beginner English Conversation Club	Education Center, Room 102	Join other adults who are learning to speak English. This class is free.
April 16 5 P.M.	Never Too Late to Learn	Media Lab, Room 202	Learning to use a computer is not just for young people. Join us as we explore the sea of information, using computers. (For senior citizens)
April 29 10 A.M.	Story Play	Youth Wing, Room 301	Play with toys and hear a story. (For ages 0-5)

We would like to thank all of you who made financial donations that allowed for the purchase of new laptops and the construction of the Media Lab.

To: Richard White <rwhite@newtonlibrary.edu>
From: Linda Carter <lcarter121@seprus.com>
Date: April 1
Subject: Beginner English Conversation Club

Hi Mr. White,

My name is Linda Carter, and I am the instructor for the Beginner English Conversation Club to be held on April 10. I noticed that the library recently built the Media Lab with funds raised by library patrons. I was hoping to change classrooms in order to use my new educational resources to integrate computers into my English conversation class. Could you please reschedule my class to be held in the same classroom as Never Too Late to Learn instead of the Education Center? I think my students will appreciate the practical English skills they can learn on computers. Also, could you please send an email to all of the students who have signed up for the class? They will need to be informed about the room change.

Thank you in advance for your assistance,

Linda Carter

GO ON TO THE NEXT PAGE

To: Linda Carter <lcarter121@seprus.com>
From: Richard White <rwhite@newtonlibrary.edu>
Date: April 2
Subject: Room Change

Dear Ms. Carter,

I would be happy to move your Beginners English Conversation course to the classroom with the updated media lab; for your reference, this is room 3A. Unfortunately, I do not have the emails for all of the students who signed up for your course. Many students only provided their names. I could post a sign at the entrance to the library advertising your course and noting the room change if that would be acceptable for you. Please let me know if you would like me to do this.

Thank you and all the best,

Richard White, Library Projects Coordinator

---

186. What is suggested about Newton Library?

(A) It recently renovated its facilities.
(B) It will hold a fundraising event soon.
(C) It offers educational activities for various ages.
(D) It is closed on Mondays.

187. What event is most suited for film students?

(A) Story Play
(B) Youth Creative Writing Workshop
(C) A Trip to the Past
(D) Never Too Late to Learn

188. In the first email, the word "held" in paragraph 1, line 2, is closest in meaning to

(A) carried
(B) attended
(C) delayed
(D) conducted

189. Why can't Richard White send Linda's students an email?

(A) He doesn't have their emails.
(B) It is not his job.
(C) He does not have the time.
(D) The library is not equipped with that kind of technology.

190. What is Richard White's solution to the problem of informing Linda's students about the room change?

(A) He can email them.
(B) He can direct them to the right room when they enter.
(C) He will post a sign.
(D) He will draw them a map with directions.

To:	Tony Walker <twalker@icmcorp.com>
From:	Suzie Mason <smason@icmcorp.com>
Date:	May 4
Subject:	Summer Calendar
Attachment:	budget.doc

Dear Mr. Walker,

I am finalizing the calendar of summer events for our company. Because we went over budget last year on employee appreciation events, I think it would be wise to find more affordable recreational activities. Attached is a breakdown of projected expenses for the summer events that I have planned.

July 6: Anchorage Flower Festival

July 22: Art in the Park at Lawrence Park

August 6: Bicycle Tours of the Anchorage Countryside

August 19: Horseback Riding at Sweet Meadow Ranch

I have scheduled fewer outdoor activities this year compared to last year. This year I would like to take advantage of a new outdoor recreational opportunity that I read about on the Anchorage Reporter website. You can read the article by clicking on this link: www.anchoragereporter.com/new_trails.

Please let me know your opinion.

Suzie Mason
Human Resources Manager

Anchorage Reporter
Bike Tours of the Anchorage Countryside to Start August 6

May 2—The Anchorage Bike Club will be hosting an annual bike riding event this summer, beginning on August 6 and running through August 7. The event will start at 10 A.M. on both days at the Anchorage Community Center. If you are driving a vehicle to the starting point, it would be better to use the parking lot behind the community center.

Anchorage Bike Club President Jean Frost stated, "The rides will range from 5 to 20 miles and will take bikers through scenic areas in Anchorage. Overall, the bike tours will go ahead at a leisurely pace so that bikers of all skill levels can participate. However, local bikers with ample experience might lead a faster-paced group."

Bikers participating in the tours will learn about riding techniques, bicycle maintenance, and proper nutrition half an hour before the event starts. All participants must have biking helmets on. They are also encouraged to bring their own water to prevent dehydration while biking.

GO ON TO THE NEXT PAGE

BICYCLE TOUR SIGN UP SHEET

If you intend to participate in the August 6 bicycle tour, please write down your name, department, and level of experience or fitness. If we have enough people sign up as advanced, we can coordinate two separate tours. If there are not enough for two tours, we would like to encourage all riders to stay together so that everyone can join in the team building exercises we have planned. Thank you for your participation, and we look forward to seeing everyone at the event!

Name	Department	Fitness/experience
Tom Cruz	Sales	Beginner
Vin Jones	Inventory	Beginner
Sally Jenkins	Inventory	Beginner
Barbara Blaster	Reception	Advanced
Hope Kinski	Sales	Beginner

191. What does Ms. Mason suggest doing?

(A) Keeping within a budget for recreational activities
(B) Appointing a new manager of human resources
(C) Increasing the number of temporary employees
(D) Scheduling more outdoor activities compared to last year

192. What date does Ms. Mason suggest for this year's new activity?

(A) July 6
(B) July 22
(C) August 6
(D) August 19

193. In what section of the website would the article most likely appear?

(A) Economy
(B) Leisure
(C) Entertainment
(D) Politics

194. Based upon the Bicycle Tour Sign Up Sheet, what can we infer about the upcoming bicycle tour?

(A) It will be canceled.
(B) There will be two groups, one for beginners, one for advanced.
(C) There will be only one group.
(D) They will stop along the way for a group meal and photo.

195. What will Barbara Blaster most likely do on the bicycle tour?

(A) She will become bored and quit the tour.
(B) She will complain that more people should sign up as advanced.
(C) She will join a faster paced group of more experienced bikers.
(D) She will stay with the group to participate in group activities.

GO ON TO THE NEXT PAGE

Four Seasons Apparel Outlet

All returns must be sent back to Four Seasons Apparel Outlet within seven days of delivery. They can be exchanged for a different item or returned for a refund. If you choose a refund, we will credit the card used for purchase.

Individuals with official memberships can utilize our delivery tracking service and receive frequent shopper discounts.

Return shipment(s) to:
Four Seasons Apparel Outlet, 144 Fenton Rd., Denver, CO 80725 (303-555-4387)

Check the box that best describes your problem:
___ Product contained a defect or damage   ___ Product did not match expectations
✔ Wrong item was delivered   ___ Other: _____

Personal Information:
Name: _Sally Nelson_   Order Number: _2245_   Phone: _432-555-6729_
Address: _2154 Oak St., Denver, CO 80725_   Email: _snelson@clandon.net_

✔ Exchange   ___ Refund

I ordered a medium-sized Snowy Christmas Sweater from your online store on April 22, but I mistakenly received a small-sized one. I would like to exchange it for the correct one.

From: Debra Clarke <debraclarke@fourseasons.com>
To: Sally Nelson <snelson@clandon.net>
Date: April 30
Subject: Exchange

Dear Ms. Nelson,

We have received your request to exchange the sweater you purchased. We sincerely apologize for this mistake. We shipped the correct item immediately as per your request. Your shipment can be tracked on our website using the following tracking number: 447H57J.

Because this was our mistake, we have returned $7 to your credit card in order to reimburse you for the return shipping costs. Please check your balance to confirm this.

If you experience any future problems with this order, you may call me at 303-555-4387. I will help you solve any problem that may arise.

Debra Clarke

To: Debra Clarke <debraclarke@fourseasons.com>
From: Sally Nelson <snelson@clandon.net>
Date: May 4
Subject: Return Error

Dear Ms. Clarke,

I was glad to receive your email regarding my return and am thankful that Four Seasons was thoughtful enough to refund my shipping cost.

That being said, I checked my account and have received the promised refund. Additionally, the new sweater that was sent to me was the right size, but I had ordered the Snowy Christmas design. What I received was Winter Festival. They are both nice sweaters, but my husband really liked Snowy Christmas better. Could you please send the design that I originally ordered? I will send the Winter Festival sweater back after I receive the correct order and my shipping refund.

Thank you!

Sally Nelson

---

196. What problem with the original shipment does Ms. Nelson report?

(A) It was damaged.
(B) It does not fit.
(C) It arrived late.
(D) It has not reached its destination.

197. In the email from Debra Clarke, the phrase "as per" in paragraph 1, line 2, is closest in meaning to

(A) regardless of
(B) except for
(C) rather than
(D) according to

198. What is indicated about Ms. Nelson?

(A) She recently moved to Denver.
(B) She ordered a gift for a friend.
(C) She has a Four Seasons Apparel Outlet membership.
(D) She waited too long to request a refund.

199. What problem with the replacement shipment does Ms. Nelson report?

(A) The size was incorrect.
(B) The design was incorrect.
(C) The size and design were incorrect.
(D) Too much money was refunded to her from her original purchase.

200. When will Ms. Nelson return her Winter Festival sweater?

(A) When she receives her correct order and the shipping refund.
(B) When she has time.
(C) When her husband is happy with his sweater.
(D) When Four Seasons apologizes for her inconvenience.

Stop! This is the end of the test. If you finish before time is called, you may go back to Parts 5, 6, and 7 and check your work.

READING TEST

In the Reading test, you will read a variety of texts and answer several different types of reading comprehension questions. The entire Reading test will last 75 minutes. There are three parts, and directions are given for each part. You are encouraged to answer as many questions as possible within the time allowed.

You must mark your answers on the separate answer sheet. Do not write your answers in your test book.

PART 5

Directions: A word or phrase is missing in each of the sentences below. Four answer choices are given below each sentence. Select the best answer to complete the sentence. Then mark the letter (A), (B), (C), or (D) on your answer sheet.

101. Not far ------- the train station lies Starlight Park, which is a popular destination for tourists and locals alike.

(A) from
(B) with
(C) next
(D) until

102. The sales director will give a brief talk ------- the keynote speaker is introduced.

(A) before
(B) opposite
(C) about
(D) between

103. The charity's new reading program is ------- to increase literacy rates in developing countries over the next ten years.

(A) project
(B) projecting
(C) projected
(D) projects

104. Engaging in social -------, Ms. Mason quickly expanded her network after moving to a new city.

(A) active
(B) activities
(C) activates
(D) activated

105. Artists wanting to participate in the contest should submit their work by the ------- of June 30.

(A) admission
(B) possibility
(C) deadline
(D) output

106. Drake Pharmaceuticals is ------- to have world-renowned chemist Jonas Lund as its senior lab technician.

(A) absent
(B) fortunate
(C) approximate
(D) respective

107. The Zans Corporation ------- manufacturing all of its luxury wallets and footwear domestically next year.

(A) was starting
(B) started
(C) will start
(D) has started

108. Some voters have a clear ------- for candidates who have practiced law.

(A) selection
(B) reflection
(C) component
(D) preference

109. The clerk said that ------- fifteen customers had been waiting outside the store for it to open.

(A) rougher
(B) roughly
(C) rough
(D) roughness

110. The leaky faucet has been repaired, so visitors may ------- use the first-floor restroom.

(A) however
(B) once
(C) now
(D) quite

111. The ------- of the disease can be significantly slowed by taking the medicine developed by Dr. Toft's team.

(A) progressed
(B) progression
(C) progressive
(D) progressively

112. Unfortunately, when the hurricane hit the area, residents as well as public officials were ------- unprepared.

(A) subsequently
(B) totally
(C) beneficially
(D) currently

113. The company plans on ------- the salespeople for the expenses they incurred while attending the conference.

(A) reimbursement
(B) reimbursed
(C) reimburse
(D) reimbursing

114. Ms. Carlton felt comfortable crossing the road because there were no vehicles coming in her -------.

(A) directly
(B) direction
(C) direct
(D) directs

115. ------- the television coverage of the general election, a number of high-profile candidates were interviewed live on air.

(A) During
(B) About
(C) While
(D) Since

116. Mr. Hicks ------- seating near the stage in the concert hall for important clients.

(A) cooperated
(B) entertained
(C) loosened
(D) reserved

GO ON TO THE NEXT PAGE

117. Fritz Center, the venue ------- hosts the film industry's awards banquet, is undergoing an ambitious expansion project.

(A) that
(B) where
(C) what
(D) even

118. The monthly staff dinners give employees from different departments the chance to interact with ------- on a personal level.

(A) other
(B) neither
(C) every
(D) each other

119. Landlords are required to ------- with the regulations set by the Regional Department of Safe Housing.

(A) reinforce
(B) comply
(C) fulfill
(D) interfere

120. A sturdy support beam was added to the first story of the building for ------- reasons.

(A) structures
(B) structurally
(C) structure
(D) structural

121. Eco Unite is a non-profit organization ------- to educating the public about environmental issues.

(A) proposed
(B) deferred
(C) dedicated
(D) observed

122. It is essential that the logo for Prime Vitamins be integrated ------- all of its catalogs and mailings.

(A) into
(B) of
(C) as
(D) than

123. Despite receiving rejections from several major publishers, Ian Wright ------- to become a world-famous novelist.

(A) gave up
(B) figured out
(C) brought down
(D) went on

124. Mr. Burrows was praised for creating ------- user manuals which can be easily understood.

(A) inform
(B) informant
(C) informs
(D) informative

125. Even though Ms. Garcia had a small account at the financial institution, the employee treated her ------- she were a major investor.

(A) rather than
(B) in spite of
(C) as if
(D) provided that

126. When you return an item by mail, be sure the receipt is ------- to the request form to expedite processing.

(A) attachment
(B) attached
(C) attaching
(D) attach

127. The witness saw only a ------- figure
standing near the lamppost shortly before
the crime was committed.

(A) solitary
(B) spare
(C) previous
(D) random

128. Ben Sanders ------- designed the suitcase
to fold up easily for compact storage.

(A) innovatively
(B) innovate
(C) innovative
(D) innovation

129. Because the weather was warmer than
usual this summer, the crops ------- a few
weeks early.

(A) have been harvesting
(B) will have harvested
(C) are harvesting
(D) will be harvested

130. ------- auditing the financial records of
Rockford Consulting, the accountant will
submit an official report.

(A) In addition
(B) Given
(C) For example
(D) Upon

GO ON TO THE NEXT PAGE

PART 6

Directions: Read the texts that follow. A word, phrase, or sentence is missing in parts of each text. Four answer choices for each question are given below the text. Select the best answer to complete the text. Then mark the letter (A), (B), (C), or (D) on your answer sheet.

Questions 131-134 refer to the following notice.

Urgent! Journeyman Plumber Needed

Ace Plumbing is looking for an experienced plumber to join our ------- business here in
                                                                131.
Columbia. ------- We have always been a family owned and run business, but with the
              132.
------- increase in Columbia's population over the last three years, we have an opportunity to
133.
welcome in a new journeyman plumber. The candidate should have experience with all -------
                                                                                    134.
of plumbing, both commercial and residential. Please send your résumé to aceplumbing@

gmail.com, and we will schedule an interview.

---

131. (A) expanding
    (B) expecting
    (C) contracting
    (D) controlling

(NEW)
132. (A) Ace Plumbing has been servicing the
       Columbia area since 1954.
    (B) We have little connection to the
       community.
    (C) We have been struggling to pay our
       bills.
    (D) Ace Plumbing is in financial trouble.

133. (A) monstrous
    (B) dramatic
    (C) impossible
    (D) insane

134. (A) pieces
    (B) flows
    (C) constructions
    (D) types

Learn Social Media Marketing Tactics
Only at Genius Marketing's Power Conference

Are you ready to take your social media marketing to the next level? Then ------- Genius
135.
Marketing's Power Conference and learn cutting edge social media marketing tactics. -------
136.
This could be the most educational two days of your year.

Genius Marketing will give you real-world tactics to boost your paid and organic social media
marketing efforts. ------- you buy social media advertising or focus on organic social media
137.
engagement, Genius Marketing's Power Conference is the conference you need to attend
this year. You'll be inspired by experts, meet others with your challenges, and get actionable
tactics to drive traffic, increase sales, and ------- customer satisfaction.
138.
To apply, just click the link below.

APPLICATION

---

135. (A) attend
(B) attends
(C) attended
(D) attending

136. (A) Guide people in the industry to
greatness by joining today.
(B) The conference will be held in Houston
on May 3rd and 4th.
(C) Registration for this two-week course
will be on November 20.
(D) Classes will be held throughout the
month of March.

137. (A) Either
(B) Whether
(C) Rather
(D) Not only

138. (A) divide
(B) gain
(C) devalue
(D) endure

GO ON TO THE NEXT PAGE

Questions 139-142 refer to the following email.

To: Nancy Craft

From: Omar Patel

Date: January 16

Subject: Pre-shipping Procedures

At the manufacturing team meeting, ------- was raised that inventory wasn't always being
                                       139.
properly stored before being shipped. ------- to that concern, the team decided to review
                                        140.
the written procedure to determine if additional steps should be added. ------- Please try to
                                                                          141.
arrange the schedules of the team in the packaging and storage wing so a majority of the

managers can attend this meeting.

I am confident that the packaging and storage team management ------- that the written
                                                                142.
procedure leaves no room for any inventory to accidently be improperly stored. Any

suggestions made by the packaging and storage team will only lead to a superior checklist.

139. (A) understanding
     (B) concern
     (C) challenges
     (D) patience

140. (A) However
     (B) Due
     (C) Regardless of
     (D) Provided

141. (A) A meeting of the packaging and storage
         team has been set for Tuesday, January
         23.
     (B) All employees should be asked to
         review the procedure before starting
         work on Tuesday.
     (C) The meeting will investigate the
         possibility of redundancies in the
         packaging process.
     (D) Additional training sessions are planned
         to be added sometime at the end of
         December.

142. (A) is discovering
     (B) have been discovered
     (C) will discover
     (D) has discovered

June 3
Yui Minakuchi
143 Dean St. Apt. 3
Brooklyn, NY 10787

Dear Ms. Minakuchi,

It is my pleasure to inform you that Hannover Design would like ------- you to interview for
143.
our summer intern program. We are only interviewing fifteen candidates this year for the six

positions we have available. You will be pleased to know that you were selected out of a

group of over 200 people ------- applied for an interview.
144.

We will be holding interviews on March 6th and 7th from 1 to 6 P.M. We would like for you

to come on the 6th at 1:30 P.M. if you are able to. If not, we can ------- for you to come on
145.

the 7th. ------- If you have any questions, feel free to call our office (212-347-9919), and the
146.
human resources department will be able to assist you. We look forward to hearing from you

soon.

Sincerely,

Max Wright
Office Manager
Hannover Design
212-326-1268
M.Wright@hannoverdesign.com

143. (A) to invite
(B) will invite
(C) has invited
(D) will be inviting

144. (A) whom
(B) that
(C) whose
(D) which

145. (A) order
(B) arrange
(C) oblige
(D) attend

146. (A) You will need to bring a completed
application and some type of
identification card.
(B) Please let us know as soon as possible
if you will be able to attend.
(C) We wish we were able to accept your
offer, but we must decline it.
(D) Please RSVP and indicate if you plan
on bringing a guest.

GO ON TO THE NEXT PAGE

Directions: In this part you will read a selection of texts, such as magazine and newspaper articles, emails, and instant messages. Each text or set of texts is followed by several questions. Select the best answer for each question and mark the letter (A), (B), (C), or (D) on your answer sheet.

Questions 147-148 refer to the following memo.

MEMO

To: All Employees
From: David Koch
Subject: Important information
Date: May 22

We will be holding our annual meeting for shareholders on June 3. I will be giving a short presentation during the opening ceremony, and I hope everyone can attend. Below is a basic schedule of the meeting.

Opening ceremony	1:00 P.M.
Annual report	2:00 P.M.
Discussion	4:00 P.M.
Dinner	6:00 P.M.

147. What is the purpose of the memo?

(A) To remind employees of a project deadline
(B) To suggest revisions to an annual report
(C) To provide a schedule for an event
(D) To report to shareholders on annual profits

148. At what time will David Koch speak?

(A) 1:00 P.M.
(B) 2:00 P.M.
(C) 4:00 P.M.
(D) 6:00 P.M.

Questions 149-150 refer to the following text message chain.

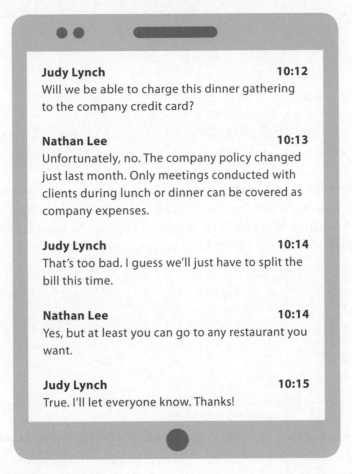

Judy Lynch   **10:12**
Will we be able to charge this dinner gathering to the company credit card?

Nathan Lee   **10:13**
Unfortunately, no. The company policy changed just last month. Only meetings conducted with clients during lunch or dinner can be covered as company expenses.

Judy Lynch   **10:14**
That's too bad. I guess we'll just have to split the bill this time.

Nathan Lee   **10:14**
Yes, but at least you can go to any restaurant you want.

Judy Lynch   **10:15**
True. I'll let everyone know. Thanks!

149. Why does Judy contact Nathan?

   (A) To get him to pay for the dinner
   (B) To get information about company expenses
   (C) To ask if he wanted to join the dinner
   (D) To get recommendations for a good restaurant

150. At 10:14, what does Judy mean when she writes "we'll have to split the bill this time"?

   (A) They will charge the company.
   (B) They will ask the accounting department.
   (C) They will have to choose who will pay.
   (D) They will each have to pay a portion of the cost.

GO ON TO THE NEXT PAGE

January 19

Dear Mr. Peterson,

The results have come back from the blood test you had done. Please call us at your earliest convenience to reserve a time to meet with Dr. Herman.

We would like to remind you that, due to changes in laws pertaining to health insurance, all patients are encouraged to make sure that their contact and insurance information is current and accurate. This can be done either by calling our customer service line at 555-6842 or stopping by the front desk on your next visit.

Sincerely,

Laura Pinkerton
Superior Health Clinic

151. What will Mr. Peterson most likely do in the near future?

(A) Renew an insurance policy
(B) Schedule a doctor's appointment
(C) Apply for a clerical position
(D) Run a blood test

152. What is Mr. Peterson asked to do?

(A) Submit an insurance form
(B) Reply to the letter
(C) Verify personal information
(D) Fill out a survey

Shopping Local

Seattle Business District Association

Did you know?

- **Shopping local puts twice as much revenue into the economy than using chain retailers.**
- **Shopping local supports the city of Seattle through local taxes.**
- **Shopping local helps the environment. It saves gas and causes less air pollution.**
- **Shopping local creates more jobs in Seattle and improves living standards in the community.**

We would like to encourage all residents of Seattle to support their local communities by shopping at traditional local stores and markets.

To find out more and learn about all the great shops and services available to local residents, visit the website of the Seattle Business District Association at www.sbda.org.

153. What is the purpose of the flyer?

(A) To promote sustainable living
(B) To notify shoppers about a sale
(C) To announce a new business opening
(D) To influence shopping patterns

154. What is NOT mentioned as a benefit of shopping local?

(A) It facilitates a job market.
(B) It is environmentally friendly.
(C) It supports the local economy.
(D) It encourages foreign investments.

GO ON TO THE NEXT PAGE →

Grandview Business News

The Burnelles launched their meal delivery service for busy families just six months ago, and the business is flourishing, exceeding expectations. – [1] – Their small shop, Farm-to-Table, located in Central Grandview Heights, has been forced to increase staff by 120% to keep up with demand.

The whole premise of the idea came up after Rachel and Robert Burnelle had their first child. Both working parents had constantly turned to fastfood for their meals and realized that many of their friends did as well. They wanted healthier options, which most fast-food franchises don't provide. – [2] –

The business is so popular that they have been getting orders from outside the city. "The response has been overwhelming," says Rachel. "Our customers especially appreciate the freshness and quality of our meals." Janet, a customer from the start, added, "Not only is the food healthy, it's not that much more expensive than fast-food meals, but it's much better for you." – [3] –

The Burnelles say they are planning to expand their delivery routes and open three Farm-to-Table grocery shops with ready-made meals around the city of Grandview within the next year. – [4] –

---

155. What is the article about?

(A) The changing role of fast-food companies

(B) The importance of healthy eating

(C) The expansion of farmland at Grandview

(D) The success and growth of a small business

156. What is the main selling point of Farm-to-Table meals according to the article?

(A) It is delivered very quickly.

(B) It is very inexpensive.

(C) It is healthy.

(D) It is delicious.

 157. In which of the positions marked [1], [2], [3], and [4] does the following sentence belong?

"That is when the Burnelles decided to quit their office jobs and start their own healthy food delivery service for working people."

(A) [1]

(B) [2]

(C) [3]

(D) [4]

Attention Shoppers

We regret to inform you that there has been a general recall on all Kent brand ladders manufactured between March 30 and July 30 this year.

- The ladders do not comply with mandatory safety standards and could be unstable.
- The ladders could move while standing on them and could contribute to dangerous falls.
- Do not use the ladders for any reason. Contact the Kent Company to receive a refund or a replacement product. Customers will receive a full refund even without proof of purchase as long as they return the ladders.

The Kent Company can be reached by calling 1-800-555-2493. Press 8 in order to be transferred to a representative who deals exclusively with product recalls. We sincerely apologize for this inconvenience.

158. Where could this notice most likely be found?

(A) At a real estate office
(B) At a hardware store
(C) At a recycling center
(D) At a grocery store

159. What are customers warned about?

(A) Using a defective product
(B) Renewing a warranty
(C) Submitting an order form
(D) Filing a complaint

160. According to the notice, how can more information be obtained?

(A) By filling out a form
(B) By consulting an instruction manual
(C) By contacting a company
(D) By watching a video tutorial

GO ON TO THE NEXT PAGE

Questions 161-164 refer to the following online chat discussion.

J&R International Group Discussion		
9:15	**Patricia Noble (moderator)**	Good morning, everyone. I've posted some ideas for the upcoming Leadership Workshop in June.
9:16	**Patricia Noble (moderator)**	Please share some of your ideas. We would like some input.
9:20	**Jared Davis**	It looks very standard. Can we add some activities such as camping expeditions or something?
9:21	**Lawrence O'Donnell**	I don't know if I'll be able to attend this time. My group is finishing up a major project. Camping sounds great, though.
9:22	**Patricia Noble (moderator)**	Camping is a good idea, but it'll take more time to plan. We'll definitely keep this in mind for the next workshop.
9:24	**Jimmy Rhee**	I don't think videos are very effective. How about getting more speakers to present? I'd rather interact with someone.
9:27	**Monica Choi**	I'm looking forward to the camping idea. But for this workshop, I agree with Jimmy. Videos can be quite boring.
9:30	**Jared Davis**	I noticed that John Olive is not presenting this time. What happened? He was very popular. I'd like to attend his workshop.
9:41	**Patricia Noble (moderator)**	John hasn't confirmed with us yet because he may have conflicting schedules. He's trying to work around his schedule.
9:52	**Isabella Price**	I'd like to attend John's workshop as well. I noticed that there are still a couple of empty slots. Would anyone be interested in hearing Ge Xi? I'd love to get a different, cultural aspect.
9:58	**Jared Davis**	Great idea! Ge Xi has had a lot of experience as a supervisor in China, and she always has some interesting stories.
10:01	**Jimmy Rhee**	I second that. I would certainly like to hear what Ge Xi presents. And speaking of cultural perspectives, Adam has had experience managing employees in a number of countries. He'd be interesting, I think.
10:09	**Isabella Price**	Yes, let's get Adam to present in the workshop.
10:15	**Adam Cruz**	Wow, I'm flattered by your vote of confidence. I certainly wouldn't mind participating in the workshop. I'm free in the afternoons.
10:19	**Patricia Noble (moderator)**	Thank you, Adam. I'll put you down for the 3 to 4 P.M. slot if that's OK with you.
10:30	**Adam Cruz**	That sounds great. And could you send me a guideline if you have one?

161. Who is most likely participating in this group discussion?

(A) The general public
(B) All employees of the company
(C) Employees from different countries
(D) Managers and other group leaders of the company

162. What's being discussed?

(A) The best presentations from the meeting
(B) The best speakers at the company
(C) The schedule for the workshop
(D) International co-workers

163. At 10:15, what does Adam Cruz mean when he writes, "I'm flattered by your vote of confidence"?

(A) He's thankful that people want him to be manager.
(B) He's grateful that people see him as a good leader.
(C) He's happy that his favorite speaker has been invited.
(D) He's honored to have won the election.

164. What will Patricia Noble probably do next?

(A) Email some information to a co-worker
(B) Set up a meeting for employees
(C) Meet with international workers
(D) Call co-workers about the changes

GO ON TO THE NEXT PAGE

To	Samantha Russell <srussell@speednet.com>
From	Sam Berger <sberger@highlandshotel.com>
Subject	Reservation
Date	July 1
Attachment	receipt

Dear Ms. Russell,

Thank you for choosing Highlands Hotel as the location for your upcoming celebration. We are contacting you to confirm the details of your reservation for rooms on the nights of July 12 and 13. You have reserved all 12 rooms on the fourth floor of our hotel. Additionally, you will have unrestricted access to the main conference room for exclusive use on both of those days. You mentioned that family members from all around the country will be gathering for this event. We will provide you with any assistance you need during your stay.

Our hotel supplies free Wi-Fi as well as access to our Internet café, where guests can use our computers for free when they want to surf the Internet or send email. This café will be available from 5:00 A.M. to 12:00 P.M. Also, guests are encouraged to eat at our awarding-winning restaurant, which is open from 7:00 A.M. to 10:00 P.M. This email also contains a receipt for your $100 deposit paid by credit card on June 30. If you would like to view the layout and seating for our conference room, you can visit our website at www.highlandshotel.com.

Sincerely,

Sam Berger
Highlands Hotel

165. What kind of event is being held on July 12 and 13?

(A) A family reunion
(B) A business conference
(C) A shareholders' meeting
(D) A job fair

166. What is NOT mentioned as a benefit of the reservation?

(A) Exclusive use of an entire floor
(B) Complimentary meals
(C) Access to a conference room
(D) Free Internet access

167. According to the email, what can Ms. Russell find on the Highlands Hotel website?

(A) A reservation number
(B) A hotel restaurant menu
(C) A seating plan
(D) A discount coupon

Questions 168-171 refer to the following notice.

Attention Members of Super Fit Gym

One workout plan doesn't work for everyone. That is why here at Super Fit Gym we offer the largest variety of fitness programs in the area. You are sure to find something fun and exciting that helps you meet your fitness goals. Now we are excited to bring you a new dance fitness program. The class will run this summer from June 12 to August 23. Dance is an interesting and interactive way to exercise. It is also appropriate for those individuals who are not able to engage in strenuous physical activity.

Those who wish to sign up for this dance class are encouraged to sign up in pairs. If you don't have someone to sign up with, you will team up with another individual on the first day of class. Registration will be available from May 10 to June 1. You can register on our website by filling out a registration form. A class fee must be paid at the time of registration by credit card.

In accordance with our rules and regulations, those who wish to receive a class fee refund must withdraw from class a week or more before the scheduled start date. No refund will be given to those who withdraw from class after that deadline.

For more details concerning class content, schedules, and fees, contact our manager, Scott Peterson, at (231) 555-2523.

Sincerely,

Super Fit Gym Staff

168. What is the purpose of the notice?

(A) To postpone an opening ceremony
(B) To hire new instructors
(C) To explain payment options
(D) To announce a new class

169. What will most likely happen on June 12?

(A) Some instructors will be absent.
(B) Some members will be assigned partners.
(C) Some refunds will be given.
(D) Some certificates of completion will be issued.

170. According to the notice, what is the latest date that participants can receive a refund for the class?

(A) May 10
(B) June 5
(C) June 12
(D) August 23

171. What is mentioned as a reason to contact Mr. Peterson?

(A) To schedule an appointment
(B) To inquire about a class
(C) To update personal contact details
(D) To find a partner to dance with

GO ON TO THE NEXT PAGE

Questions 172-175 refer to the following memo.

MEMO

To: All employees
From: Veronica Jackman, Executive Manager
Date: October 10
Subject: staffing

– [1] – Sheila Roberts, our marketing director will be away on a business trip to Singapore from October 21st to November 5th. In her absence, Michael Lee will temporarily take over some of her responsibilities at Goldman's Department Store. However, for those of you who have projects near completion with Ms. Roberts, we ask that you make final arrangements with her before October 15th. – [2] – Some of the urgent projects have already been discussed with Michael. If your project can wait for Sheila's return, we ask that you inform both Sheila and Michael so that other projects can go forward.

– [3] – I realize this may seem like an inconvenience, especially so close to the holiday season, but I have great confidence that Michael will be able to handle the responsibilities in Sheila's absence. Michael has worked closely with Sheila and will deal with the newer projects handed to him. – [4] –

If you have further questions or concerns about this, please contact Sheila before October 20th or me at any time.

172. Where do the recipients of the memo work?

(A) At a marketing firm
(B) At a law office
(C) At a department store
(D) At a travel agency

173. What is indicated about Sheila Roberts?

(A) She is getting a new job.
(B) She has been promoted.
(C) She is going on vacation.
(D) She is going on a business trip.

174. When should employees with nearly completed projects contact Sheila by?

(A) October 15th
(B) October 20th
(C) October 21st
(D) November 5th

175. In which of the positions marked [1], [2], [3], and [4] does the following sentence belong?

"Michael will arrange separate meetings with different departments during Sheila's absence to ensure a smooth transition and communication during his temporary tenure."

(A) [1]
(B) [2]
(C) [3]
(D) [4]

http://www.instituteforruralservice.com

Rural Community Outreach Program

As part of its ongoing commitment to enhance the standard of living in rural communities across the state, the Institute for Rural Service provides annual grants for rural communities. The goal of this program is to support local efforts to sustain a convenient and satisfying life in the countryside. The grants available this year are as follows:

Business Development Grant: $250,000
Community Development Grant: $150,000
Communications Development Grant: $200,000
Educational Development Grant: $100,000

The institute will give priority to proposals that reflect a comprehensive approach to community development, promote community engagement, and make rural communities a better place to live and work. The grants will allow rural communities to take the first step toward a project or plan that can help improve the lives of rural community members. For the past decades, the grants have been used for a variety of purposes such as state-of-the-art farming equipment, road maintenance, communications infrastructure, educational facilities, and investments for young rural entrepreneurs.

Download this application to apply for a grant. The deadline for submission is February 28.

ACTUAL TEST

03

Village of Cranton Wins Funding

CRANTON, March 22—The Institute of Rural Service announced today that the village of Cranton is this year's recipient of the Educational Development Grant. The grant will be used to fund the construction of a large playground that will provide recreational activities for children under 12. Since the opening of the new electronics factory last year, the number of families in the area has risen dramatically. As a result, children have been left with less and less space to play in. The new playground will allow children to play and enjoy themselves when they are not at school.

Cranton is proud to be the recipient of this grant and plans to apply for more grants in the future to improve the living conditions of the town and attract more residents.

GO ON TO THE NEXT PAGE

176. What is the purpose of the Web page?

 (A) To report that a project has been completed
 (B) To encourage applications for a grant
 (C) To announce a recipient of a grant
 (D) To introduce local entrepreneurs

177. According to the Web page, what is NOT mentioned as a purpose of an Institute of Rural Service grant?

 (A) Providing funds for local business people
 (B) Building the basic systems for communications
 (C) Organizing community health checkups
 (D) Purchasing farming equipment

178. How much funding did Cranton receive?

 (A) $100,000
 (B) $150,000
 (C) $200,000
 (D) $250,000

179. According to the article, what will the grant enable Cranton to do?

 (A) Improve local farming conditions
 (B) Renovate an elementary school
 (C) Hire more qualified teachers
 (D) Provide a play area for children

180. What is indicated about Cranton?

 (A) It has received grants in the past.
 (B) It plans to open a new factory.
 (C) Its population has increased.
 (D) It will hold a community festival.

Questions 181-185 refer to the following email and form.

To: Charles Bell <charlesbell434@globalnet.com>
From: Carrie Cook <carriecook@freshfarmsgrocery.com>
Subject: Membership Card
Date: May 4

Dear Mr. Bell,

Your Silver Star Membership Card at Fresh Farms Grocery will expire on the 28th of this month. Your membership card entitles you to special sale prices as well as special points on most Fresh Farms Grocery purchases. Once you accumulate enough points, they can be redeemed for a discount on your next purchase. Without a valid Silver Star Membership Card, you will lose the ability to accumulate these frequent shopper points.

Please do not attempt to renew your membership over the phone. In order to do that, please stop by the customer service desk at one of our store locations. If you have any other questions, please call us at 204-555-2648.

Carrie Cook
Customer Service Representative
Fresh Farms Grocery

Fresh Farms Grocery

Membership Card Form

First Name: CHARLES
Last name: BELL
Membership Number: 14245FDA

- ☐ Create my membership card
- ☑ Renew my membership card
- ☐ Cancel my membership card

Membership card categories and fees:
Gold Star: Premium membership, $90 a year
Silver Star: Business membership, $70 a year
Bronze Star: Household membership, $50 a year
Shooting Star: Short-term membership, $10 a month

Please note:

Premium membership is reserved for those who hold shares in the Fresh Farms Grocery company.

Food vendors and restaurant owners are eligible to apply for the Silver Star Membership Card.

GO ON TO THE NEXT PAGE ➡

181. What is the purpose of the email?

(A) To announce seasonal discounts
(B) To notify Mr. Bell of an outstanding fee
(C) To remind Mr. Bell to renew a membership
(D) To offer a free upgrade to Mr. Bell

182. What does the membership card allow Mr. Bell to do?

(A) Benefit from frequent shopping
(B) Park in designated spaces
(C) Receive expedited shipping
(D) Purchase new products in advance

183. What is Mr. Bell asked to do?

(A) Call the customer service desk
(B) Visit the store in person
(C) Write a customer review
(D) Attend a regular event

184. How much does Mr. Bell currently pay a year?

(A) $50
(B) $70
(C) $90
(D) $120

185. What is indicated about Mr. Bell?

(A) He is a celebrated chef.
(B) He runs a food-selling business.
(C) He is a shareholder of Fresh Farms Grocery.
(D) He applied for his membership this year.

May 12

Dear Mr. Gray,

You are a long-time member of the Georgian Society of Architects (GSA). We would like to inform you that we are adding some changes to the services provided to members this year. Specifically, we will be adding a new Gold Class level membership that will give privileged members access to more resources than ever before. We are excited to tell you that you meet all of the qualifications for this special membership offer and may sign up immediately. You should be receiving a brochure in the mail soon that will provide more information. We hope that you decide to join this amazing Gold Class membership.

As you know, the GSA's annual members' conference will be held on June 14 at the Stargate Conference Center in Atlanta, Georgia. We noticed you have already registered your attendance. We can't wait to see you there. If you need any further assistance making arrangements, don't hesitate to call our offices at (124) 555-5251.

Yours truly,

Joan Ross
Georgian Society of Architects

Georgian Society of Architects
GOLD CLASS MEMBERSHIP

In order to qualify for this special membership, applicants must have at least 20 years of experience in the field, in addition to holding a degree in architecture from an accredited university.

Benefits include: instantly expanding your contacts through access to our database of over 50,000 practicing colleagues, paying half the regular price when registering for conferences hosted by GSA, and receiving our monthly newsletter, which contains the latest market research and economic analysis to help your business.

Gold Class members will also be eligible to apply for professional liability insurance coverage offered exclusively to our Gold Class members.

To apply, simply fill out the form attached to this brochure and mail it to our headquarters. The $40.00 application fee can either be paid by check or credit card by calling our accountant at (124) 555-5253.

GO ON TO THE NEXT PAGE

STARGATE CONVENTION CENTER SCHEDULE OF EVENTS

JUNE 14th
GEORGIAN SOCIETY OF ARCHITECHTS

9:00 A.M.—9:45 A.M.	Sign in at the desk in the lobby
10 A.M.—11:45 A.M.	Guest Speaker Jerry Jenkins Jr. in Conference Room A
12:00 P.M.—1:30 P.M.	Lunch in the Diamond Room
2:00 P.M.—4:00 P.M.	Regional Presentations in Conference Room A
6:00 P.M.—9:00 P.M.	Dinner and cocktails in the Sapphire Lounge

Please remember to bring your Society ID to ensure a smooth registration for the day's events!

186. What is the purpose of the letter?

(A) To publicize a conference
(B) To advertise a new membership
(C) To confirm an appointment
(D) To attract a new member

187. What is Mr. Gray encouraged to do?

(A) Register for a conference
(B) Reschedule an appointment
(C) Upgrade his service
(D) Pay by credit card

188. What is indicated about Mr. Gray?

(A) He has worked as an architect for over two decades.
(B) He spoke at last year's GSA members' conference.
(C) He contributes to an architecture journal.
(D) He forgot to pay his membership fee in April.

189. What time should Mr. Gray sign in on the day of the conference?

(A) 8:45 A.M. to 10:00 A.M.
(B) 9:00 A.M. exactly
(C) Anytime
(D) 9:00 A.M. to 9:45 A.M.

190. How many meals are included in the event?

(A) Breakfast, lunch, and dinner
(B) Brunch and dinner
(C) Dinner and cocktails
(D) Lunch and dinner

Colonial Heights Nursing Home

Colonial Heights is proud to have served the elderly population of Houston, Texas for over 30 years. Our nursing home is equipped with state-of-the-art facilities. Our five-story building allows each floor to offer individualized levels of care for our residents. Our building houses a rehabilitation gym, and we also provide psychological counseling services for residents.

We currently have openings for several positions. We are looking to hire a nursing home administrator who has at least three years of experience and a valid license. There is also an opening for an admissions coordinator. Those applying for the admissions coordinator job must have a bachelor's degree and at least two years of related experience. We are also looking for hospice workers who can provide personal care to residents in a compassionate and caring manner. Previous experience is not necessary, so everyone interested is welcome to apply for this position.

You can see this job listing and submit an application online by visiting our website at www.chnh.com.

To:	Tommy Jenkins <tommyjenkins7@zeusnet.com>
From:	Greg Parker <g_parker@chnh.com>
Subject:	Hiring procedure
Date:	September 14

Dear Mr. Jenkins,

Congratulations! You have made it through the first round of the application process for the position of admissions coordinator. We require that all applicants visit Colonial Heights Nursing Home in order to attend an in-person interview. I would appreciate it if you let me know a convenient time for your interview on September 17.

I look forward to meeting you.

Sincerely,

Greg Parker
Human Resources Manager
Colonial Heights Nursing Home

GO ON TO THE NEXT PAGE ➡

Dear Mr. Parker,

Thank you so much for giving me the opportunity to interview for the position of admissions coordinator. You requested that I inform you about my availability for September 17. I have another interview at 10 A.M., but I will be able to be at Colonial Heights Nursing Home by 1 P.M. I hope this is convenient for you. Shady Pines Nursing Home, as you know, is a competing facility located on the other side of town, and the hours they offer are very attractive. I would prefer to work in a modern facility such as Colonial Heights. I look forward to interviewing with you and touring your facilities.

Sincerely,

Tommy Jenkins

191. What is mentioned about Colonial Heights Nursing Home?

(A) It has five locations in Texas.
(B) It has operated for over half a century.
(C) It provides art classes.
(D) It offers mental health services.

192. According to the notice, which position does not require experience?

(A) Nursing home administrator
(B) Hospice worker
(C) Admissions coordinator
(D) Front desk receptionist

193. What is indicated about Colonial Heights Nursing Home?

(A) It plans to expand its facilities.
(B) It accepts applications through its website.
(C) It offers the highest wages in the state.
(D) It recently renewed its operating certificate.

194. Why might Tommy Jenkins decide NOT to work for Colonial Heights Nursing Home?

(A) They do not have physical fitness centers.
(B) Their facilities are not modern.
(C) The job is too far away.
(D) Shady Pines Nursing Home can give him a better schedule.

195. When can Tommy Jenkins be at the interview at Colonial Heights?

(A) 10 A.M.
(B) before 1 P.M.
(C) after 1 P.M.
(D) after 4 P.M.

To: Jake Baldwin <baldwinj@technet.com>
From: Dream Oasis Hotel <booking@dreamoasishotel.com>
Date: September 22
Subject: Your Reservation
Attachment: invoice.html

Dear Mr. Baldwin,

Thank you for reserving a room at the Dream Oasis Hotel. You have booked a room with a double bed for the nights of October 13 and 14. Your reservation number is 5259.

I am writing to inform you that you must pay your balance by September 29 in order to confirm your reservation. Your total room fee is $165.25 for both nights. Payment can be made via credit card by visiting our website at www.dreamoasishotel.com and entering your reservation number. You may also call us and complete your payment over the phone. If payment is not received by September 29, your reservation will be canceled automatically. Please see the attached invoice for related details.

When you arrive at the airport, the easiest way to travel to our hotel is by subway. We are located next to exit 3 at City Hall Station. If you have trouble finding us, please don't hesitate to call us at 555-2134. A staff member is available 24 hours a day to assist you.

Thank you again for choosing our hotel.

Amy Lee
Customer Services Manager
Dream Oasis Hotel

To: Dream Oasis Hotel <booking@dreamoasishotel.com>
From: Jake Baldwin <baldwinj@technet.com>
Date: September 23
Subject: RE: Your Reservation

Dear Ms. Lee,

I am writing in regard to my reservation at the Dream Oasis Hotel for October 13 and 14. I received your email about the payment for my upcoming stay at the hotel. However, I would like to inquire about extending my stay for an extra night. I recently heard that there will be a local food festival held on October 16 and I would like to attend it. Therefore, I would like to stay at your hotel through October 15. Please let me know a revised room fee so that I can make the correct payment as soon as possible.

Jake Baldwin

GO ON TO THE NEXT PAGE

To: Jake Baldwin <baldwinj@technet.com>
From: Amy Lee <alee@dreamoasishotel.com>
Date: September 24
Subject: The 15th

Dear Mr. Baldwin,

You are right to be excited about the food festival that will be held on the October 16th. Unfortunately, this event has become so popular that the city fills up for that weekend. I regret to inform you that there is no vacancy at the Dream Oasis Hotel for the night of the 15th. I went ahead and looked into some of our partner hotels in the area, but those properties are also at full occupancy. I do hope you are able to find someplace to stay in the city so you can enjoy the festival while you are in town; I just wish it could have been with us. You could try the Executive Inn, in Fairview. It is a large hotel, and they do have vacancies.

Sincere apologies,

Amy Lee
Customer Service Manager
Dream Oasis Hotel

196. What is the purpose of the first email?

(A) To explain a cancellation policy
(B) To request a payment
(C) To schedule a reservation
(D) To offer a special service

197. What is Mr. Baldwin asked to provide when making a payment online?

(A) His telephone number
(B) His email address
(C) His room number
(D) His reservation number

198. What information is NOT included in Ms. Lee's email?

(A) The cost of the stay
(B) The travel insurance
(C) The location of the hotel
(D) Staff contact information

199. Why can't Mr. Baldwin stay at the Dream Oasis Hotel on the night of the 15th?

(A) The hotel is full because of the food festival.
(B) The hotel is full because it is very popular.
(C) The hotel is full because there is a convention in town.
(D) The hotel is full because the food at the hotel is very good.

200. What does Amy Lee recommend?

(A) That Mr. Baldwin try another hotel in town
(B) That Mr. Baldwin try a hotel in Fairview
(C) That Mr. Baldwin try to attend the food festival next year
(D) That Mr. Baldwin ask again on the 14th, in case there is a cancellation

NO TEST MATERIAL ON THIS PAGE

Stop! This is the end of the test. If you finish before time is called, you may go back to Parts 5, 6, and 7 and check your work.

READING TEST

In the Reading test, you will read a variety of texts and answer several different types of reading comprehension questions. The entire Reading test will last 75 minutes. There are three parts, and directions are given for each part. You are encouraged to answer as many questions as possible within the time allowed.

You must mark your answers on the separate answer sheet. Do not write your answers in your test book.

PART 5

Directions: A word or phrase is missing in each of the sentences below. Four answer choices are given below each sentence. Select the best answer to complete the sentence. Then mark the letter (A), (B), (C), or (D) on your answer sheet.

101. All of the trees on the property were damaged by the storm ------- the one near the rear entrance.

(A) except
(B) considering
(C) still
(D) along

102. Mr. Hotei had to undergo several medical tests before receiving ------- diagnosis from the physician.

(A) he
(B) him
(C) himself
(D) his

103. Entrepreneur James Mosby is featured in the most ------- issue of the magazine.

(A) final
(B) former
(C) recent
(D) later

104. The judge's decision must be based ------- on the evidence presented.

(A) cooperatively
(B) strictly
(C) tensely
(D) remarkably

105. Due to his decades of experience, Mr. Finley was responsible for training the ------- for the new gym.

(A) instructors
(B) instructive
(C) instructively
(D) instructed

106. Customers at Blaze Restaurant may use the valet parking service or park their vehicles -------.

(A) their
(B) themselves
(C) they
(D) theirs

107. Last year, the young chemists contributed ------- to the development of a new adhesive.

(A) construction
(B) constructively
(C) constructive
(D) constructed

108. The experts at Prime Carpentry can restore any piece of wooden furniture ------- its original condition.

(A) to
(B) by
(C) at
(D) with

109. The library has requested funding for ------- doors for the convenience of patrons.

(A) underway
(B) automatic
(C) frequent
(D) energetic

110. After noticing the wardrobe's ------- condition, the owner of the antique shop lowered its price.

(A) deteriorates
(B) deteriorating
(C) deterioration
(D) deteriorate

111. For the past decade, Henley Vivian ------- to be a talented and motivated journalist.

(A) is proving
(B) proving
(C) prove
(D) has proven

112. ------- who suffers from sleep problems could benefit from drinking this herbal tea.

(A) Ourselves
(B) Whichever
(C) Anyone
(D) Others

113. An additional route was added to the rail line to reduce travel times in the southern -------.

(A) accent
(B) function
(C) distance
(D) region

114. During the holiday season, Schwartz Department Store will ------- special make-up gift sets.

(A) solve
(B) carry
(C) impress
(D) occupy

115. Buying a home for the first time can be complicated and even ------- without help from a licensed real estate agent.

(A) nervous
(B) risky
(C) decreased
(D) initial

116. The Brownsville Homeless Shelter has helped thousands of people since its ------- last year.

(A) creative
(B) created
(C) create
(D) creation

GO ON TO THE NEXT PAGE

117. The semifinalists of the community art contest will be ------- by a panel of judges tomorrow.

(A) selected
(B) ignored
(C) prevented
(D) complemented

118. The penalties for canceling the cell phone contract early are ------- stated in the agreement.

(A) express
(B) expression
(C) expressly
(D) expressed

119. ------- the researchers' report, eating fresh fruits and vegetables more often is a better health goal than avoiding fast food.

(A) Even though
(B) Rather than
(C) According to
(D) Because of

120. To make the tour accessible to Spanish speakers, the ------- plans to provide translation services.

(A) interpreted
(B) interpretation
(C) interpreting
(D) interpreter

121. Joggers are asked to keep to the right side of the path, as ------- cyclists need space to pass on the left.

(A) many
(B) each
(C) much
(D) either

122. Before potential buyers view a home, the real estate agent makes sure it is -------.

(A) presentation
(B) presenting
(C) presentable
(D) present

123. For the payment ------- last week, the necessary state and federal taxes must be paid by the recipient.

(A) was remitted
(B) remitted
(C) remitting
(D) to remit

124. Everyone is in favor of shortening working hours, but ------- the president approves the change, nothing will happen.

(A) after
(B) until
(C) yet
(D) because

125. The manufacturing company's recent ------- to reduce on-site accidents was appreciated by the staff.

(A) attempt
(B) industry
(C) value
(D) faculty

126. The dining room furniture was ------- left in the house because the new owner had bought it.

(A) intended
(B) intention
(C) intentional
(D) intentionally

127. The Garrison Theater will ------- allow student groups to view rehearsals during the day.

(A) vaguely
(B) substantially
(C) occasionally
(D) previously

128. *Pro Sports* magazine made a name for itself ------- the publication of a series of exclusive interviews with top athletes.

(A) like
(B) both
(C) so
(D) with

129. Only ------- delegates wearing their ID badges will be allowed into the conference venue.

(A) those
(B) who
(C) each
(D) that

130. ------- his announcement that he would run for office, the candidate met privately with his advisors.

(A) In advance of
(B) As long as
(C) On behalf of
(D) So as to

GO ON TO THE NEXT PAGE

PART 6

Directions: Read the texts that follow. A word, phrase, or sentence is missing in parts of each text. Four answer choices for each question are given below the text. Select the best answer to complete the text. Then mark the letter (A), (B), (C), or (D) on your answer sheet.

Questions 131-134 refer to the following notice.

Employee Workshop

T&R Group strives to help employees reach their potential by offering leadership retreats, employee training, and various workshops. This month, we ------- workshops for those
131.
interested in ------- their computer skills with several classes on how to use Professional
132.
Office, create a personal website, and run the messagecorp app. We have a couple of other slots that are currently ------- and will accept suggestions from employees. ------- Please
133.   **134.**
email Jonas at jsmith@TRgroup.com if you are interested in attending any of the workshops.

We hope you will all take advantage of the programs offered.

131. (A) offers
    (B) were offering
    (C) are offering
    (D) have offered

132. (A) correcting
    (B) diminishing
    (C) elaborating
    (D) improving

133. (A) dependent
    (B) independent
    (C) free
    (D) obtainable

134. (A) Questions related to gaming and entertainment will not be answered.
    (B) The most popular requests will be considered for the workshops.
    (C) We ask all managers to make a suggestion.
    (D) We hope the workshop is a success and wish you the very best.

Citrusine Total Flu for Nighttime

Get ready for cold and flu season with Citrusine. Citrusine is a ------- medicated nighttime
                                                                    135.

tea that can treat symptoms of the flu including fever, aches and pains, nasal congestion,

cough, and sore throat. Wake up feeling ------- and ready to conquer another day. Citrusine
                                         136.

should not be taken if you're planning to operate machinery or drive a vehicle. Keep out of

reach of children. -------
                    137.

Citrusine is the number-one-selling medication ------- the flu and is guaranteed to provide
                                                138.

relief if taken as directed. Visit our website for more information.

www.citrusine.com

---

135. (A) reassuring
     (B) stimulating
     (C) soothing
     (D) consoling

136. (A) refreshing
     (B) refreshed
     (C) refreshes
     (D) refresh

(NEW)
137. (A) This medication may cause serious side
         effects if not taken properly.
     (B) Children should take Citrusine for Kids
         instead.
     (C) The packets look like candy and may
         pose problems.
     (D) And if symptoms persist for more than
         10 days, consult a physician.

138. (A) for
     (B) during
     (C) with
     (D) after

ACTUAL TEST

04

GO ON TO THE NEXT PAGE

Questions 139-142 refer to the following email.

To: Janet Don
From: Greenscape
Date: June 28
Subject: Inquiry

Dear Ms. Don,

We thank you for your inquiry. Greenscape has been the leading landscaper for businesses in the greater downtown area for over 10 years. ------- we specialize in gardens and Japanese-
139.
style landscape art, we also maintain lawns and fields. But to answer your question, yes, we even clear away thick shrubbery and trees. We can send a representative to ------- the
140.
amount of time it will take and the approximate costs. Furthermore, if you ------- to replace
141.
the dense shrubs with a lawn or garden, you can work with one of our designers to come up with a landscape you can be happy with.

------- We are more than happy to serve you.
142.

139. (A) Although
     (B) Because
     (C) Therefore
     (D) However

140. (A) conclude
     (B) count
     (C) estimate
     (D) guess

141. (A) wishing
     (B) wish
     (C) wished
     (D) wishes

142. (A) We welcome any opportunity to do
         business with you.
     (B) Please don't cancel the order.
     (C) Please call us at 555-1245 if you are
         interested in a consultation.
     (D) Go to the park to see the city's
         landscape.

Questions 143-146 refer to the following advertisement.

Black Hill Beans

Black Hill Beans is a Louisianan coffee company and the pioneer of the Louisiana coffee fruit. We oversee a vertically ------- supply chain that starts with the highest quality coffee
143.
and coffee fruit from Black Hill, Louisiana. We ------- three award-winning beans: summer
144.
harvest, dark southern, and black earth. All can be shipped to you ------- 24 hours anywhere
145.
in the continental U.S. Black Hill Beans' coffee is also sold at every Launders Superstore in the U.S.

Whether you're looking for excellent coffee or a bit of southern comfort, Black Hill Beans is the right choice for your coffee. ------- It's nice to feel patriotic while you drink. Visit us
146.
online today to hear more of our story. www.blackhillbeans.com

---

143. (A) integrates
(B) to integrate
(C) integrated
(D) integration

144. (A) locate
(B) select
(C) evaluate
(D) maintain

145. (A) within
(B) by
(C) until
(D) at

146. (A) Try the best-selling frozen beverage around.
(B) It's American-made and organic.
(C) Let us help you find the right supplier.
(D) This discount is only available through October 1st.

GO ON TO THE NEXT PAGE

Directions: In this part you will read a selection of texts, such as magazine and newspaper articles, emails, and instant messages. Each text or set of texts is followed by several questions. Select the best answer for each question and mark the letter (A), (B), (C), or (D) on your answer sheet.

Questions 147-148 refer to the following notice.

Notice

Crawford Apparel has refurbished dressing rooms where you can try on clothes before you make a purchase.

– Please take only an item or two at a time into a dressing room.

– You may leave your personal belongings, such as wallets and purses, with one of our clerks for safekeeping.

– Any personal items left behind in a dressing room will be kept in the lost and found room near the entrance.

147. For whom is this notice most likely intended?

(A) Storekeepers
(B) Customers
(C) Designers
(D) Clerks

148. According to the notice, where can missing items be found?

(A) At a police station
(B) At an information center
(C) In a storage area
(D) Behind a counter

Questions 149-150 refer to the following text message chain.

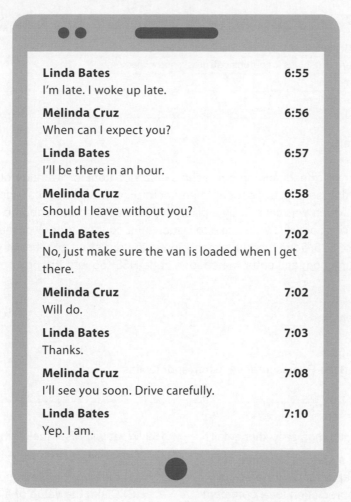

Linda Bates	6:55
I'm late. I woke up late.	
Melinda Cruz	**6:56**
When can I expect you?	
Linda Bates	**6:57**
I'll be there in an hour.	
Melinda Cruz	**6:58**
Should I leave without you?	
Linda Bates	**7:02**
No, just make sure the van is loaded when I get there.	
Melinda Cruz	**7:02**
Will do.	
Linda Bates	**7:03**
Thanks.	
Melinda Cruz	**7:08**
I'll see you soon. Drive carefully.	
Linda Bates	**7:10**
Yep. I am.	

149. What is suggested about Ms. Bates?

(A) She works for Ms. Cruz.
(B) She is being held up in traffic.
(C) She is currently operating an automobile.
(D) She is frequently late.

150. At 7:02, what does Ms. Cruz mean when she writes, "Will do"?

(A) She will be waiting for Ms. Bates.
(B) She plans to load the vehicle.
(C) She is frustrated by Ms. Bates' tardiness.
(D) She has finished packing the van.

GO ON TO THE NEXT PAGE

Questions 151-152 refer to the following email.

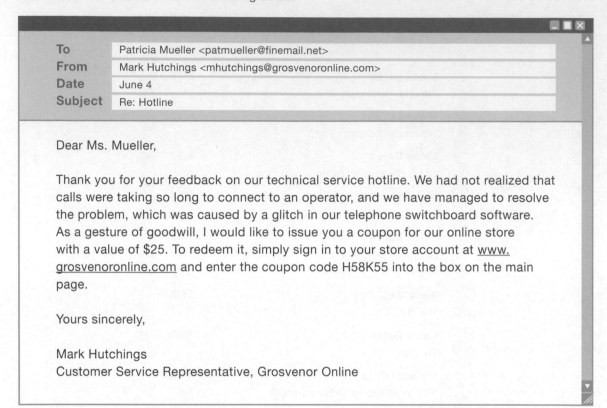

To   Patricia Mueller <patmueller@finemail.net>
From   Mark Hutchings <mhutchings@grosvenoronline.com>
Date   June 4
Subject   Re: Hotline

Dear Ms. Mueller,

Thank you for your feedback on our technical service hotline. We had not realized that calls were taking so long to connect to an operator, and we have managed to resolve the problem, which was caused by a glitch in our telephone switchboard software. As a gesture of goodwill, I would like to issue you a coupon for our online store with a value of $25. To redeem it, simply sign in to your store account at www.grosvenoronline.com and enter the coupon code H58K55 into the box on the main page.

Yours sincerely,

Mark Hutchings
Customer Service Representative, Grosvenor Online

151. Why did Mr. Hutchings send this email?

(A) To promote a special seasonal offer
(B) To confirm an address for an order
(C) To show appreciation for a comment
(D) To request further information about a problem

152. What will Ms. Mueller most likely do on her next visit to Grosvenor Online?

(A) Sign up for a membership program
(B) Claim the value of a coupon
(C) Use the customer feedback form
(D) Update her billing information

Questions 153-154 refer to the following web page.

http://www.jannisar.com

| Home | Products | Contact | About Us | Account |

Congratulations! Because of your high level of regular activity on our site, you have been selected to become a Premium Gold member. Please fill out the following form to complete the process:

First name	
Surname	
Shipping address	
Authorization code	
Email address	
Comments:	

Check the boxes for the merchandise categories that are of interest to you.
(You may check more than one.)

Electronics [ ]   Music [ ]   Books [ ]   Furniture [ ]   Computer Games [ ]

Please note that as a Premium Gold member you will receive email notifications four times a year on special offers for the categories selected. Your account details will be verified by email within 24 hours. An email confirmation will be sent to you. Follow the instructions in that email to confirm your membership.

153. Whom is this web page most likely aimed at?

(A) A new customer on an auction website
(B) An online marketing agency representative
(C) A supplier for a retail outlet
(D) A long-term customer of an online retailer

154. What is the reader asked to do?

(A) Indicate product preferences
(B) Supply payment details
(C) Print and sign the form
(D) Report shipping delays

GO ON TO THE NEXT PAGE

It's Raining Cats and Dogs

Brentwood City (May 2) — – [1] – Brentwood finally has its very own cat café called Catastrophe and dog café called Hotdogs, both opened by owners Kevin and Ginger Blake. Both cafés opened last month to fanfare and a great deal of press coverage. – [2] – "Business has been booming," says Kevin Blake. "We knew we'd be successful; we just didn't think we'd be this successful." Not only are customers enthusiastically flocking to both cafés to hang out with the animals while drinking coffee and tea; many of them are adopting the animals and giving them forever homes. – [3] – "We thought it would be a good idea to take in some of the animals because of the overcrowding in many of the shelters," explained Ginger Blake. "And customers have a chance to interact with the animals, which is the best form of advertisement for the shelters."

Since the cafés' opening, more than 10 dogs and 15 cats have been adopted. "I don't yet own a dog, but I've always wanted one," says Laurie Jordan, a regular customer. "I come here to play with them. Maybe one day I'll find a dog that I really want." – [4] –

Because of their success, the Blakes are considering expanding by purchasing the adjacent shops. "We need more space to fit all our customers and the animals," explained Kevin. "It can get very crowded at times." The Blakes are looking to renovate the dog café next month and the cat café during the fall.

155. What is indicated about the cafés?

(A) They serve an assortment of snacks.
(B) They sell puppies and kittens.
(C) They serve coffees and teas.
(D) They offer pet products.

156. What is reported about the cats and dogs?

(A) Several have been adopted.
(B) They are permanent residents of the cafés.
(C) They are friendly towards the customers.
(D) They are trained to entertain.

157. In which of the positions marked [1], [2], [3], and [4] does the following sentence belong?

"But the hype hasn't slowed down."

(A) [1]
(B) [2]
(C) [3]
(D) [4]

Relax and Unwind at New Wave Spa!

Take a break from your hectic day with professional spa treatments from New Wave Spa, located at 458 Worley Avenue. Whether you stay for an hour or a full day, you'll leave feeling refreshed and energized. Check out our regular packages below.

Classic Getaway ($120)—Try this basic package that's perfect for those on the go.
   30-minute back and neck massage / cucumber facial treatment /
   lilac body wrap

Rose Garden ($155)—Let the scent of roses revive your senses.
   45-minute full-body massage / rosewater skin treatment / manicure

Ocean Experience ($180)—Take advantage of the ocean's healing powers in our most popular package.
   60-minute full-body massage / head-to-toe sea salt scrub /
   hot stone treatment / seaweed facial treatment

Complete Rejuvenation ($210)—Indulge yourself in the luxury of a full day of treatments.
   90-minute full-body massage / relaxation scalp massage /
   mud mask facial treatment / rosemary purifying scrub / manicure / pedicure

Book in advance to secure your spot by calling 555-2940. Groups of four or more people will receive a free lunch of sandwiches, steamed vegetables, and freshly squeezed juices. All patrons will be given a free New Wave lounging robe on their third visit to our facility.

158. What is the advertisement mainly about?

(A) The expansion of a health facility
(B) A discount on luxury services
(C) The relocation of a spa
(D) A business's standard options

159. Which package includes a heat treatment?

(A) Classic Getaway
(B) Rose Garden
(C) Ocean Experience
(D) Complete Rejuvenation

160. What will groups of four or more people be given?

(A) A free robe
(B) A reduced rate
(C) A complimentary meal
(D) A private room

GO ON TO THE NEXT PAGE

Bill Flake (9:41)

Hello. I'd like to get an update on the progress of the drapes that the Manillo family ordered.

Lucy Mitt (9:41)

We're still waiting for the lace silks from Hand-Made Lace but we received most of the other fabrics yesterday. Our seamstresses will get to work on those today.

Bill Flake (9:42)

Then do you think the project will be completed by this Friday as the Manillos wanted?

Lucy Mitt (9:43)

I'm not sure. It'll depend on when the lace arrives. Our group can start sewing some of the pieces together, but we need the lace to complete the intricate designs.

Bill Flake (9:44)

Can you contact Hand-Made Lace and find out when the shipment will arrive?

Lucy Mitt (9:45)

Actually, Richard is taking care of that. Any word from them, Richard?

Richard Choi (9:45)

Yes, I just got off the phone with them. There was a bit of a delay because the lace artisans used the wrong silks. They had to rework the lace. We'll receive them this afternoon. They sent a rush delivery to us.

Bill Flake (9:46)

Excellent. Then can the drapes be finished by the end of this week?

Lucy Mitt (9:47)

No problem. We'll work around the clock to get them finished on time.

Bill Flake (9:48)

I'm glad to hear that. They are long-time customers and they need the drapes for their new condo this weekend.

161. What kind of business do the participants in this online chat probably work for?

(A) A clothing company
(B) A bridal shop
(C) A custom drapery shop
(D) A fabric warehouse

162. When will the shipment of lace arrive?

(A) In the morning
(B) In the afternoon
(C) The next day
(D) At the end of the week

163. At 9:47, what does Lucy Mitt mean when she says, "We'll work around the clock?"

(A) Her team will watch the time carefully.
(B) Her team will work as quickly as possible.
(C) Her team will take as much time as they need.
(D) Her team will work all day and night if they have to.

164. What will Bill Flake probably do next?

(A) Call the client
(B) Cancel the order
(C) Request a shipment of lace
(D) Organize a meeting

GO ON TO THE NEXT PAGE

Duluth City
5th Annual Summer Fun Festival
Sunday, July 23

10:00 A.M. to 6:00 P.M. *Local Nature Art Competition*
Duluth artists will be displaying their paintings of local nature and wildlife in the Duluth Community Center. Visitors are asked to cast their vote for their favorite painting. The winner will be announced at the start of the singing competition.

11:00 A.M. to 12:00 P.M. *Magic Show*
Please join us for an astonishing magic show. Magician Mick Turner is famous for his creative and entertaining magic tricks.

12:00 P.M. to 2:00 P.M. *Live Jazz Concert*
Enjoy live jazz in the park performed by New York-based jazz band The Holloway Band. They will be playing a variety of jazz standards. They will also have their most recent record for sale.

10:00 A.M. to 7:00 P.M. *Renewable Energy Expo*
Local company Sunshine Energy will be displaying some of its newest renewable energy projects, including solar panels and portable cell phone chargers.

7:00 P.M. to 9:00 P.M. *Singing Competition*
Local residents are encouraged to take part in this year's singing competition. Those who would like to participate can register by visiting our website at www.duluthcitysff.com and filling out the necessary form.

For more information, please call us at 555-0157.

---

165. When will the winner of the art competition be announced?

(A) 2:00 P.M.
(B) 6:00 P.M.
(C) 7:00 P.M.
(D) 9:00 P.M.

166. According to the schedule, what will be available for purchase?

(A) A work of art
(B) A musical album
(C) A cell phone accessory
(D) A solar panel

167. How can participants sign up for the singing competition?

(A) By visiting an information booth
(B) By contacting the community center
(C) By visiting a website
(D) By sending an email

Movies in the Park

This fall, Glenwood Springs Park will host a weekly Movies in the Park night for residents of Glenwood Springs in cooperation with various local business sponsors including Paxton, Inc. and GS Mall. Family-friendly movies will be shown every Friday night at the center of the park. Tickets are not necessary for these events because they are free to the public.

Running from September through November, Movies in the Park promises a wonderful lineup of fun and touching movies for the whole family. You are encouraged to bring blankets and chairs as well as picnic snacks. Movie starting times depend on sunset times, so it is advised to come early to secure your spot beforehand. Please visit our website at www.glenwoodsprings.org/movies to see a schedule of upcoming films and a list of our local sponsors.

In the event of heavy rain, low temperatures, or strong winds, film screenings may be canceled. If this occurs, the announcement of the film cancellation will be made both on our website and on local radio. You can also ask about event cancellations by calling the Glenwood Springs Department of Parks and Recreation at 715-555-5358.

168. What is the purpose of the flyer?

(A) To announce park renovation plans
(B) To publicize a community event
(C) To solicit donations
(D) To promote a new film

169. Who will provide funding for Movies in the Park?

(A) A local radio station
(B) The residents of Glenwood Springs
(C) The Department of Parks and Recreation
(D) The businesses of Glenwood Springs

170. What is NOT mentioned as a recommendation for participants?

(A) Bringing food
(B) Purchasing tickets in advance
(C) Consulting a schedule
(D) Arriving early

171. According to the flyer, why would the phone number be used?

(A) To make a reservation
(B) To inquire about a schedule change
(C) To ask for driving directions
(D) To cancel an appointment

ACTUAL TEST

04

GO ON TO THE NEXT PAGE

Wrightman Towers

1234 Broadway Street
New York, NY 49858

– [1] – Located in the financial district of the city, Wrightman Towers offers spectacular views of the skyline and office spaces that are ideal for any company that wishes to operate within the heart of New York. Just one block from the subway station and within walking distance of public buses and taxis, Wrightman Towers is conveniently located. – [2] – The first-floor lobby offers security as employees must scan their way through the gates to the elevators behind. At the same time, the spacious lobby is welcoming with its luxurious interior designs and friendly staff of attendants. – [3] –

The third and fourth floors are available for rent to businesses and corporations. High ceilings and tall glass windows offer open space and beautiful natural lighting. Hurry and send in your requests today. – [4] – Only serious inquiries will be taken and interviews must be conducted in person. Please visit our website at www. wrightmantowers.com/rent for more information. You can take a virtual tour of the premises, or you can call our offices at 555-1234.

172. What is indicated about the rental space?

(A) It is only for private residents.
(B) It is only for businesses.
(C) It is available to the public.
(D) It is very expensive.

173. What is indicated about the location of Wrightman Towers?

(A) It is near public transportation.
(B) There is heavy traffic around the building.
(C) There are no parking spaces.
(D) It is just outside the city.

174. What is featured on the website?

(A) A listing of all occupied spaces
(B) An exclusive discount promo code
(C) A virtual tour of the rental space
(D) A history of the building

175. In which of the positions marked [1], [2], [3], and [4] does the following sentence belong?

"These spaces are in high demand."

(A) [1]
(B) [2]
(C) [3]
(D) [4]

Kenneth Global Journalism Internship

The Kenneth Global Journalism Internship will provide you with the chance to train with the world's most renowned international multimedia news agency, work with professional reporters and editors, and gain valuable experience in fast-paced newsrooms in big cities such as London, Berlin, and Paris. It will offer talented college graduates an opportunity to learn and develop strong journalistic skills while acquiring first-hand knowledge.

This is a paid internship that offers free lodging as well as lunch and dinner. Interns will receive several weeks of formal training focused on writing skills, journalistic ethics, and basic workplace knowledge. They are also able to take advantage of other regularly scheduled training opportunities during the internship, free of charge. The internship will last four months, beginning on August 1.

Applications for the internship can be found on our website at www.kennethglobal.com and must be submitted by June 20. Applicants who advance past this stage will be asked to interview at our headquarters on June 27. Any questions can be directed to Ruby Hart at rubyhart@kennethglobal.com or asked in person at our headquarters in Austin.

From: Kyle Lane <kylelane12@mpnet.com>
To: Ruby Hart <rubyhart@kennethglobal.com>
Subject: Internship
Date: June 23

Dear Ms. Hart,

I am extremely grateful to have advanced past the first round of the Kenneth Global Journalism Internship's selection process. Applicants are supposed to interview in person on the specified date, but unfortunately I am scheduled to attend an important conference in Dallas with my professor. However, since I live just a few minutes from your headquarters, it would not be difficult to arrange an alternative time for an interview.

Thanks again for considering me for this position. I look forward to hearing back from you concerning a possible interview date. In the meantime, I will do my best to prepare myself.

Regards,

Kyle Lane

GO ON TO THE NEXT PAGE

176. What is indicated about internship applicants?

(A) They must have prior work experience.
(B) They must attend an upcoming conference.
(C) They must submit a letter of recommendation.
(D) They must hold a bachelor's degree.

177. What is true about the internship?

(A) It includes meals and accommodations.
(B) It is for professional journalists only.
(C) It will end in August.
(D) It is an unpaid position.

178. What other benefit is offered to interns?

(A) Health insurance
(B) Additional training
(C) Employee discounts
(D) Paid vacation

179. When is Mr. Lane supposed to attend an interview?

(A) On June 20
(B) On June 27
(C) On June 23
(D) On August 1

180. Where does Mr. Lane live?

(A) In Dallas
(B) In Austin
(C) In Berlin
(D) In London

Questions 181-185 refer to the following email and announcement.

To:	Sam Berry <sberry@princetheater.com>
From:	Bessie Wagner <bessiewagner@linsuniversity.edu>
Date:	July 4
Subject:	Openings

Dear Mr. Berry,

My name is Bessie Wagner and I am currently a student in the theater department at Lins University. I have almost finished my degree, and I am starting to look into possible career opportunities for the future. A professor of mine recommended that I contact you at the Prince Theater to ask about possible positions with your company.

At Lins University, I have specialized in the production elements of theater. Through both academic and practical experience, I have learned the skills necessary for stage management. As of September, I will be available to work either part-time or full-time and apply myself fully to whatever task is assigned to me.

I would really appreciate it if you would let me know if there are any available positions at the Prince Theater starting this fall. Thank you.

Bessie Wagner

Prince Theater

Job Openings

• Artistic Intern
Unpaid internship in the artistic department dealing with all aspects of administration and production. This person will perform assistant duties for the artistic director.

• Assistant Technical Director
Part-time position responsible for production management and stage machinery. Applicants should have related experience in stage management.

• Director of Ticket Operations
Full-time position responsible for overall management of ticket operations for all events taking place at the theater. Responsibilities include box office operations as well as planning and implementing all ticket sales processes, and supervision of the ticketing staff.

• Marketing Director
Full-time position responsible for marketing concerning all of the productions put on by the theater. Oversee the preparation of high-quality promotional materials to attract theatergoers to our plays, musicals, and concerts.

– All full-time employees of Prince Theater are eligible for complimentary access to all productions.
– All of the positions will be open starting this October.
– For more information or to apply, contact Sam Berry by email at sberry@princetheater.com.

GO ON TO THE NEXT PAGE

181. What is indicated about Ms. Wagner?

   (A) She is a stage actress.
   (B) She teaches classes in stage design.
   (C) She will graduate soon.
   (D) She is Mr. Berry's coworker.

182. Why did Ms. Wagner write to Mr. Berry?

   (A) To seek a job opportunity
   (B) To schedule an interview
   (C) To express her gratitude
   (D) To register for a training course

183. What is NOT suggested about the director of ticket operations?

   (A) He or she has to manage various types of events.
   (B) He or she must direct the work of other employees.
   (C) He or she can watch any show free of charge.
   (D) He or she must plan promotional events.

184. What do all of the advertised jobs have in common?

   (A) They require musical talent.
   (B) They will be available in the fourth quarter.
   (C) They are part-time positions.
   (D) They require a degree in theater arts.

185. Which job is most suitable for Ms. Wagner?

   (A) Artistic intern
   (B) Assistant technical director
   (C) Director of ticket operations
   (D) Marketing director

April 5—Clearwater Hospital in downtown Scranton has launched a new pen pal letter-writing program between terminally ill hospital patients and adult volunteers. Hospital director Zack Chambers, who was recently presented with an Outstanding Leader Award from the National Health Care Alliance, started the program to create stronger connections between the hospital and the community. Mr. Chambers encourages adults of all types and occupations to apply even if they don't feel completely qualified. Simply visit the Clearwater Hospital website and become a member of the hospital free of charge.

"I hope through this program, volunteers can form close relationships with patients to help them get through these difficult times in their lives," said Mr. Chambers. He also hopes that the program will lead to more people visiting terminally ill patients in person.

Clearwater Hospital

May 4

Monica Greene
4100 Washington Road
Scranton, Wisconsin 54481

Dear Ms. Greene,

I was delighted to receive your letter. I am very excited to have been paired with you as a pen pal. I hope we can learn a lot from each other and build a lasting friendship.

As you know, I live in California, which is a long way from Wisconsin. I hope that in the coming months I can take some time off work and visit you. Please let me know when the most convenient time would be for me to meet you.

I look forward to hearing from you,

Jessica Wright

GO ON TO THE NEXT PAGE

Dear Jessica,

You don't know how much I appreciate your kind words. Although the staff at Clearwater is very kind, I feel the need to connect with people who are not part of the staff. My surviving family also lives a great distance away, in Florida, and so most of the time I am just communicating with the paid staff or the other patients. I would welcome a visit if you truly wanted to come, and the best time would be for our Thanksgiving party here at the center, I suppose. My own family might be here as well. If it is too much for you, or if you can't get the time off from work, don't worry about it too much. I do hope that we can continue to communicate through our letters.

All the best,

Monica Greene

186. What is the article about?

(A) A volunteer program
(B) A doctor's retirement
(C) A new hospital
(D) A writing competition

187. What is mentioned about Mr. Chambers?

(A) He is a patient at Clearwater Hospital.
(B) He teaches writing skills to adults.
(C) He is the head of a government organization.
(D) He was honored for his leadership.

188. What does Mr. Chambers invite people to do?

(A) Sign up for a newsletter
(B) Schedule regular health checkups
(C) Visit patients in critical condition
(D) Write a letter of recommendation

189. Who does Monica Greene spend most of her time with?

(A) Clearwater's staff
(B) Her family
(C) Jessica Wright
(D) Her friends

190. When does Monica want Jessica to visit?

(A) On Monica's birthday
(B) This Saturday
(C) The 7th of June
(D) Thanksgiving

Mr. John Morris
1423 Bernard Avenue
Millville, CA 90117

Dear Mr. Morris,

24/7 Fitness is the most successful workout facility in the United States. With over 3 million members nationwide, our franchise has become known as a reputable and trustworthy brand. Our success is a result of great relationships between us and our franchisees.

You are receiving this mailing because you expressed interest in partnering with 24/7 Fitness in order to open a new location in your town. According to our preliminary research, your town has a large population of young, single people working in professional fields. This is our target demographic, and means the business outlook for your 24/7 Fitness location positive. If you would like more information about the specific terms and regulations when partnering with 24/7 Fitness, please don't hesitate to call me at 347-555-3363. Additionally, if you would like to talk to another franchise owner, that information can be supplied by one of our associates.

Sincerely,

Lori Swanson
Chief Operating Officer

To: Zack Carter <zcarter@zenmail.com>
From: John Morris <jmorris@cbnet.com>
Subject: 24/7 Fitness
Date: March 6

Dear Mr. Carter,

My name is John Morris and I am a small business owner living in the Millville area. I am currently in negotiations with 24/7 Fitness to open my own location here in Millville. As someone who works with 24/7 Fitness, you would help me a lot by sharing your opinions.

I am interested in how you assess 24/7 Fitness as a franchiser. I have operated several franchises in the past, and I have always found that trust and honesty are the most important factors in a successful relationship. More importantly, I was also wondering what kind of support is provided by the parent company. Before opening your location, did you receive adequate training to allow you to smoothly begin operating your business? Any advice you can give me would be much appreciated.

Sincerely,

John Morris

GO ON TO THE NEXT PAGE

To: John Morris <jmorris@cbnet.com>
From: Zack Carter <zcarter@zenmail.com>
Subject: 24/7 Fitness
Date: March 7

Dear Mr. Morris,

I am happy to provide some insight into the operation of a 24/7 Fitness franchise. I have been working with 24/7 Fitness as a franchise owner for 10 years now. I actually run three different branches. I completely agree with you that trust and honesty are the two most important aspects of any business relationship. On that count, I believe the fact that I own three franchises is testament to my faith in the franchiser.

Let me put your mind at ease. First off, 24/7 Fitness has a very specific way that it wants its brand to develop, no matter who owns the branch. The parent company will not only provide training; it insists on controlling the actual layout of the facilities from the locker rooms to the free weights. The owners want any of their 3 million members to be able to walk into any one of their gyms and feel at home. Until you have been operating for one full year, you must make monthly reports to corporate headquarters detailing all aspects of sales, membership, and a flow chart describing the usage of the facilities. It really is hands-on until they have confidence that you can represent the brand. I hope all this helps you decide to join the 24/7 Fitness team!

All the Best,

Zack Carter

---

191. According to the letter, what is the key to 24/7 Fitness's success?

(A) Effective communication with regional owners
(B) Rapid nationwide expansion
(C) A team of experienced researchers
(D) Comprehensive training of employees

192. Where did Mr. Morris most likely get Mr. Carter's contact information?

(A) From a 24/7 Fitness representative
(B) From 24/7 Fitness's website
(C) From Mr. Carter's blog
(D) From Mr. Carter's employee

193. What concerns Mr. Morris most about 24/7 Fitness?

(A) Its reputation
(B) Its financial status
(C) The types of assistance it offers
(D) The regulations for its franchisees

194. What is the purpose of Zack Carter's email?

(A) To ask for information about a franchise
(B) To tell John Morris about 24/7 Fitness and the training it provides
(C) To persuade John Morris not to become the owner of a 24/7 Fitness franchise
(D) To remind 24/7 of its responsibility to its franchisees

195. In Zack Carter's email, what is indicated about 24/7 Fitness?

(A) It wants all of its fitness centers to be nearly identical.
(B) It would like its franchisees to personalize their locations.
(C) It would like to sell more supplements and memberships next year.
(D) It requires its franchisees to send quarterly reports about usage.

To:	Kevin Scott <kevinscott@starrealty.com>
From:	Steven Mason <smason@turnerelectronics.com>
Date:	February 2
Subject:	A warehouse

Dear Mr. Scott,

My name is Steven Mason and I work for the consumer electronics company Turner Electronics. I am currently scouting for a warehouse in the Pittsburgh area. As you know, having an effective distribution strategy is critical for every company in today's fast-paced business world.

Therefore, I am looking for a warehouse located on the outskirts of Pittsburgh. The warehouse needs to be located close to the highway. We are shipping a high volume of products, so we would prefer a dedicated warehouse to be used exclusively for Turner Electronics' operations. A warehouse with a spacious loading bay for large trucks is necessary. Additionally, a warehouse that also has office space would be ideal. Because of the valuable nature of our products, we would like a warehouse that provides security against theft and damage.

I look forward to hearing your response as soon as possible.

Steven Mason
Turner Electronics

To:	Steven Mason <smason@turnerelectronics.com>
From:	Kevin Scott <kevinscott@starrealty.com>
Date:	February 3
Subject:	Re: A warehouse

Dear Mr. Mason,

It seems that as your company expands, you would like to improve the operations of your distribution network and deliver products to sellers more quickly. We have a variety of warehouse options, and I trust one of them will fit your company's needs. All locations have a state-of-the-art security system as well as experienced staff.

Location 1—$3,499 per month for a 10,000-square-foot warehouse space shared by multiple businesses. Because this location is a shared operations site, we offer it at a discounted price.
Location 2—$5,500 per month for an older warehouse located in downtown Pittsburgh. This warehouse is currently empty, and therefore can be used by your company exclusively. It also features a walk-in freezer.
Location 3—$6,500 per month for a very spacious warehouse located a few miles outside of Pittsburgh. Although currently used by two other businesses as a storage space, it can be converted into a warehouse only for your company.
Location 4—$2,600 per month for a medium-size warehouse. This warehouse is provided at a discounted price because it has no area for trucks to unload cargo conveniently. It is best for smaller-sized operations.

These are the locations currently available for use. If you have any questions or would like to visit a location in person, please contact me.

Kevin Scott

GO ON TO THE NEXT PAGE

To: Kevin Scott <kevinscott@starrealty.com>
From: Steven Mason <smason@turnerelectronics.com>
Date: February 3
Subject: Location 3

Dear Mr. Scott,

Thank you so much for responding to my inquiry so quickly. Although none of the warehouses is exactly what I was looking for, I think the best option for our business will be warehouse Location 3. This, of course, is contingent on the other two businesses moving their storage to another warehouse. Our operations, as I noted in my first email, are expanding, and I want to make sure that we have ample room to grow. I am delighted that there is security at your warehouses as well.

I have some time early next week if it would be possible to take a walk through Location 3. I think once I get a feel for the space I will be able to make a firm decision. Please contact me by phone at your convenience so we can set up a time.
You can reach me at (351) 546-9899.

All the best,

Steve Mason
Turner Electronics

---

196. What is the purpose of the first email?

(A) To look for a rental space
(B) To finalize a business proposal
(C) To ensure the arrival of a shipment
(D) To advertise a property for sale

197. Who most likely is Mr. Mason?

(A) A warehouse manager
(B) A truck driver
(C) A security guard
(D) A distribution manager

198. According to Mr. Scott, what does Turner Electronics intend to do?

(A) Hire more experienced truck drivers
(B) Enhance supply chain efficiency
(C) Improve overall product quality
(D) Expand into the Asian market

199. According to the third email, what has to happen for Turner Electronics to move into Location 3?

(A) The rent must be reduced.
(B) Two businesses must find other places to store their belongings.
(C) The space must be converted to include an office.
(D) A security system must be added to the building.

200. According to the third email, what is the most likely day that Mr. Mason will be available for a walk-through of Location 3?

(A) Monday
(B) Thursday
(C) Friday
(D) Saturday

NO TEST MATERIAL ON THIS PAGE

Stop! This is the end of the test. If you finish before time is called, you may go back to Parts 5, 6, and 7 and check your work.

READING TEST

In the Reading test, you will read a variety of texts and answer several different types of reading comprehension questions. The entire Reading test will last 75 minutes. There are three parts, and directions are given for each part. You are encouraged to answer as many questions as possible within the time allowed.

You must mark your answers on the separate answer sheet. Do not write your answers in your test book.

PART 5

Directions: A word or phrase is missing in each of the sentences below. Four answer choices are given below each sentence. Select the best answer to complete the sentence. Then mark the letter (A), (B), (C), or (D) on your answer sheet.

101. Should the customer feel that the proposed color scheme is not -------, the interior designer can make adjustments.

(A) attract
(B) attractive
(C) attracted
(D) attractively

102. For Friday's dinner reservation, please ------- the number of seats from eight to ten.

(A) increase
(B) reflect
(C) merge
(D) invite

103. Mr. Brandt asked for the banner to be hung ------- the exterior wall of the building.

(A) up
(B) next
(C) on
(D) with

104. In case you have problems with the device in the future, you should retain your newly ------- receipt.

(A) expressed
(B) predicted
(C) issued
(D) approached

105. If the patient's nasal problem does not show signs of improvement ------- two days, he should visit the clinic again.

(A) because of
(B) regarding
(C) apart from
(D) within

106. The people giving demonstrations at the department store ------- explained the product's features and benefits.

(A) enthusiasm
(B) enthusiast
(C) enthusiastically
(D) enthusiastic

107. Because its latest exhibit is highly valuable, the Gabe Gallery has taken more precautions than it ------- has in the past.

(A) ever
(B) yet
(C) such
(D) much

108. ------- making structural changes to a house must first apply for a building permit.

(A) Our
(B) Who
(C) Them
(D) Anyone

109. Employees who attend the workshop on improving communication skills will be given a certificate of ------- by the instructor.

(A) achieved
(B) achieving
(C) achieve
(D) achievement

110. ------- its distinguished science department faculty, the university has state-of-the-art laboratory facilities.

(A) In addition to
(B) Otherwise
(C) As well
(D) Hardly ever

111. The donations received at the fundraiser ------- among the charity's three locations equally.

(A) have divided
(B) is being divided
(C) are dividing
(D) will be divided

112. ------- the building's age, the ventilation system must be up-to-date with all safety codes.

(A) Instead of
(B) Toward
(C) Regardless of
(D) Since

113. The delays on the Trenton train line were caused by a ------- error at one of the stations.

(A) proceed
(B) proceeded
(C) procedural
(D) procedurally

114. As we expect to receive hundreds of applications for the position, please ------- your résumé to two pages.

(A) limit
(B) follow
(C) refrain
(D) unfold

115. The lecturer ------- on the country's struggle for independence when he gives his talk.

(A) has focused
(B) is focused
(C) will focus
(D) focusing

116. The welcome activity is an opportunity to improve communication ------- volunteers before the project begins.

(A) among
(B) like
(C) above
(D) under

GO ON TO THE NEXT PAGE

117. The balconies in the rooms at the Orwell Hotel provide a ------- view of the hotel's private beach.

(A) stunningly
(B) stuns
(C) stunning
(D) stunned

118. The travel agent's ------- of the ticket purchase was sent to the customer by email as soon as the payment had been made.

(A) extent
(B) confirmation
(C) awareness
(D) proposal

119. After examining the vehicle, the mechanic ------- identified the reason why the engine had lost power.

(A) corrections
(B) correctly
(C) correct
(D) corrects

120. Because of her hearing disability, Ms. Frasier will be ------- by a sign language expert so she can participate in the meeting.

(A) convinced
(B) anticipated
(C) accompanied
(D) cautioned

121. The project development team is partially responsible for the selection and ------- of potential building sites.

(A) appraisal
(B) appraises
(C) appraise
(D) appraised

122. The easy-to-prepare meal packets come with all the ingredients necessary for an individual dinner ------- boiling water.

(A) except
(B) despite
(C) elsewhere
(D) past

123. The education center provides training in key skills ------- that the unemployed can find jobs more easily.

(A) so
(B) ever
(C) only
(D) as

124. The terms of the licensing agreement are quite ------- and do not require a legal background to be understood.

(A) energetic
(B) frequent
(C) straightforward
(D) accomplished

125. The information sent to conference attendees ------- the presentation schedule and social events.

(A) expands
(B) solicits
(C) allows
(D) outlines

126. You may have the merchandise sent directly to your home or pick it up in person at the store, ------- you prefer.

(A) both
(B) whichever
(C) everybody
(D) another

127. ------- occurring substances are used in the vitamin supplement instead of chemicals.

(A) Naturally
(B) Natural
(C) Naturalize
(D) Nature

128. The bus driver used a side street rather than the main highway, ------- avoiding rush-hour traffic.

(A) such as
(B) than
(C) unless
(D) thereby

129. The crew members ------- the main section of the building by the time the waste removal trucks arrive at 3:30.

(A) demolish
(B) will have demolished
(C) demolished
(D) had demolished

130. Should you find any manufacturing ------- in your ultra-high-definition television, contact the place of purchase as soon as possible.

(A) premises
(B) defects
(C) impacts
(D) distractions

GO ON TO THE NEXT PAGE

PART 6

Directions: Read the texts that follow. A word, phrase, or sentence is missing in parts of each text. Four answer choices for each question are given below the text. Select the best answer to complete the text. Then mark the letter (A), (B), (C), or (D) on your answer sheet.

Questions 131-134 refer to the following advertisement.

Come visit Wild Water Parks, the summer destination for families and friends of all ages.

We have kiddie pools, we have outdoor pools, we have indoor pools, we have waves, and

we have ------- water slides—including our Death Fall, the largest slide in the state. We
        131.

have everything for everyone in ------- group. Don't forget our delicious snack stands and
                              132.

restaurants. We also have gift shops and playgrounds. ------- You can get tickets by calling
                                                    133.

123-5555, or get a season pass for a ------- of the price. Call now and experience the fun!
                                 134.

131. (A) excite
 (B) excited
 (C) exciting
 (D) excitement

132. (A) their
 (B) his
 (C) our
 (D) your

133. (A) The pools are the best place to stay.
 (B) We even have a dog park for that furry companion of yours.
 (C) The chefs are top notch and the food is second to none.
 (D) Hurry before the season is over and the promotion is finished.

134. (A) fraction
 (B) section
 (C) division
 (D) total

From: Rhonda Cross

To: Mike Harris

Date: June 21

Subject: Re: Landscaping and Maintenance

Thank you for your ------- about our services. Arbor Care is a green lawn care and
                      135.
landscaping business. We only use environmentally friendly techniques and products when

caring for the grounds of any business. We've been working in the Portland area for -------
                                                                                     136.
20 years. Currently, we are serving more than 150 businesses in the downtown area.

As for your specific request, yes, we can easily remove dead trees and replace them with

something that fits the ------- landscaping. To give you an exact quote, we would need to
                        137.
stop by and assess the situation in person. To have one of our garden technicians stop by,

please call us at (713) 678-9916. -------
                                  138.

135. (A) submission
     (B) placement
     (C) review
     (D) inquiry

136. (A) over
     (B) less
     (C) until
     (D) through

137. (A) exist
     (B) existed
     (C) existing
     (D) exists

138. (A) It is a pleasure doing business with you.
     (B) We hope to hear from you soon.
     (C) Please send us an email.
     (D) Best wishes for your continued
         success.

GO ON TO THE NEXT PAGE

ACTUAL TEST

05

Outbound Sales Lead Specialist/Telemarketer

Location: Atlanta, GA

Job Code: 3766

# of openings: 4

The sales lead specialist will place outbound calls to ------- customers seeking to purchase
                                                           139.
various services such as insurance, tax help, financial help, telecommunications, or

transportation. They will also call on leads from our existing customer base. Cold calls are

required.

You will work directly with customers via the telephone and email to describe products and

services in order to persuade potential and current customers to purchase new products

and services. The job will also require you to educate customers on product and service

offerings. ------- There is also a minimum requirement for monthly sales that is set at $7,500
          140.
in net revenue. -------, all employees must regularly attend our product education course in
                141.
order to better serve our customers.

To be eligible for the position you must have one or more years in telesales, strong customer

service skills, and superior closing skills.

If you feel you ------- these requirements and are looking for an exciting, lucrative
              142.
experience, please click below.

---

139. (A) substantial
(B) potential
(C) optimal
(D) logical

(NEW)

140. (A) The more you sell, the more opportunity
you'll have for advancement.
(B) This managerial position will require
an organized and highly motivated
individual.
(C) If you could help find your replacement,
it would be much appreciated.
(D) It will be crucial for you to place a
minimum of 150 outbound calls each
day.

141. (A) Actually
(B) However
(C) Additionally
(D) Therefore

142. (A) meet
(B) to meet
(C) meeting
(D) met

Questions 143-146 refer to the following notice.

From: James Jones, Executive Manager

To: Sales Agents

Date: July 15

Subject: policy change

Dear Sales Agents,

There has been a recent change to our reimbursement policy. In the past, you simply had to pay out of pocket first and then provide your receipts after renting vehicles, taking business trips, or ------- other business expenses. -------, from now on you will be required to fill out
         143.   **144.**
an application form which must be approved by the accounting department first. ------- If
                                                                              145.
you spend anything beyond the amount on the card, you will have to pay out of your own pocket and will not be reimbursed for that.

Please read the attachment for further details on what expenses can and cannot be -------
                                                                                   146.
by the company.

---

143. (A) incur
    (B) incurred
    (C) incurring
    (D) to incur

144. (A) However
    (B) Therefore
    (C) Furthermore
    (D) Since

145. (A) They will not approve any card not authorized by a bank.
    (B) You will have to spend with your own credit card.
    (C) Then you will be provided with a company card which holds limited funds.
    (D) They must decide whether our budget allows for our expenses.

146. (A) certain
    (B) acknowledged
    (C) established
    (D) approved

GO ON TO THE NEXT PAGE

PART 7

Directions: In this part you will read a selection of texts, such as magazine and newspaper articles, emails, and instant messages. Each text or set of texts is followed by several questions. Select the best answer for each question and mark the letter (A), (B), (C), or (D) on your answer sheet.

Questions 147-148 refer to the following calendar.

Time	Monday	Tuesday	Wednesday	Thursday	Friday
9:00 A.M.–11:00 A.M.	Yoga Level 1: **Room 4**		Fitness Training: **Room 1**	Kickboxing Level 1: **Room 3**	
11:00 A.M.–2:00 P.M.		Weight Training: **Room 2**			Yoga Level 2: **Room 4**
2:00 P.M.–4:00 P.M.	Cycling: **Room 1**	Kickboxing Level 2: **Room 3**		Nutrition Advice: **Room 5** (book a personal appointment at reception)	
4:00 P.M.–6:00 P.M.	Yoga Level 3: **Room 4**		Fitness Training: **Room 1**		Marathon Training: **Room 2**

147. Where would this calendar most likely be seen?

(A) In the sports section of a newspaper
(B) In a travel itinerary
(C) On the wall in a gym facility
(D) In a program for a sports tournament

148. Which activities take place in the same room?

(A) Yoga and kickboxing
(B) Marathon training and cycling
(C) Yoga and nutrition advice
(D) Cycling and fitness training

Questions 149-150 refer to the following text message chain.

WANDA KNIGHT   9:04
I just sent you the itinerary for your trip to Chicago on Friday.

TED GALEZNIC   9:05
Perfect. Thanks!

WANDA KNIGHT   9:05
Mike Ross wants you to add a meeting with Diamond Publishing while you're up there.

TED GALEZNIC   9:10
No problem.

WANDA KNIGHT   9:11
OK. I can reach out to them. If you're too busy, that is.

TED GALEZNIC   9:13
It won't be a problem. I'm supposed to have a drink with Javier Sanchez from Diamond on Sat. night.

WANDA KNIGHT   9:13
Nice.

TED GALEZNIC   9:20
When the guy is married to your sister, you're bound to see him.

WANDA KNIGHT   9:21
Ah, that's right.

149. What is suggested about Mr. Sanchez?

(A) He works for an accounting company.
(B) He is related to Wanda Knight.
(C) He was recently married.
(D) He will visit Chicago on Friday.

150. At 9:11, what does Ms. Knight mean when she writes, "I can reach out to them"?

(A) She can thank them.
(B) She can contact them.
(C) She can visit them.
(D) She can assist them.

GO ON TO THE NEXT PAGE ➡

Questions 151-152 refer to the following email.

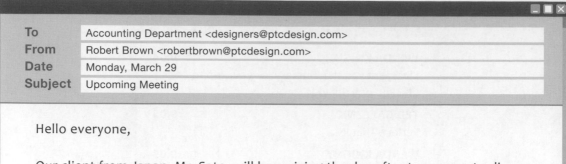

To	Accounting Department <designers@ptcdesign.com>
From	Robert Brown <robertbrown@ptcdesign.com>
Date	Monday, March 29
Subject	Upcoming Meeting

Hello everyone,

Our client from Japan, Mr. Sato, will be arriving the day after tomorrow to discuss an upcoming merger of our two companies. I ask that our accounting department work as a group to produce a financial statement for the first quarter in preparation for this meeting. Anyone who needs further data in order to complete this document should email me without hesitation. Please finish this task by Tuesday afternoon. This document needs to detail all of our company's financial activities, including all of our assets and investments.

Thanks,

Robert Brown, CEO
PTC Design

151. When is Mr. Sato scheduled to arrive at Mr. Brown's company?

(A) On March 28
(B) On March 29
(C) On March 30
(D) On March 31

152. Who will most likely contact Mr. Brown?

(A) Employees who want to transfer to the accounting department
(B) Employees who need additional information
(C) Employees who need a deadline extension
(D) Employees who disagree about a merger

Questions 153-154 refer to the following invitation.

American Architects Society Annual Awards

You are cordially invited to attend this year's event, to be held at the Merriton Hotel in Houston, Texas on Friday, July 24. As a member, you may bring up to two guests.

7:00 P.M.	**Reception**
7:30 P.M.	**Welcome speech and introduction**
	by Barry Humphreys, President of the American Architects Society
7:45 P.M.	**Dinner (Vegetarian options available; please specify when confirming attendance.)**
9:00 P.M.	**Awards ceremony—Best Design, Best Newcomer, Best Residential Building, Best Public Building—presented by comedian Alex Dashwood**
10:30 P.M.	**A special live performance by award-winning band The Pop Tones**

RSVP to event coordinator Janice Harton at <u>janice.harton@amarchsoc.net</u> no later than April 21.

153. Who most likely are the invitation recipients?

(A) Directors of building companies
(B) Members of an association
(C) Architects for the local government
(D) Award ceremony nominees

154. How can attendance be confirmed?

(A) By calling the Merriton Hotel
(B) By emailing Barry Humphreys
(C) By visiting Alex Dashwood
(D) By contacting a coordinator

GO ON TO THE NEXT PAGE ➝

Northshore Financial News

June 29— A local mainstay of Northshore City may soon go national. – [1] – The Northshore Creamery first opened its doors in 1951 under owner Bill Bradley and has become an iconic landmark of the city with its huge rotating ice cream cone on the roof of the shop. Over the years it has remained a favorite local hangout for the residents of the city and captured the eyes of tourists driving through. – [2] – Bill Jr. took over the business 25 years ago and expanded the shop to keep up with the demand of locals and tourists. Northshore Creamery was even selected as a top ten shop to visit by *Travel & Tour Magazine*.

In 1988, Northshore Creamery was featured in the hit Hollywood movie *Future Then and Now*, which made it the top ice cream shop to visit by out-of-towners and tourists.

– [3] – Efforts have been made by various corporations to buy the business from the Bradley family, but Bill Jr. and his son William have insisted on keeping the business within the family, which pleases the residents of Northshore. – [4] – "We're keeping things small in scale and we're slowly expanding," explains William. "In order to maintain the quality and freshness of our ice cream and keep our recipes just the way my grandfather created them, we can't take any shortcuts. That's why we need time."

155. What is the article's purpose?

(A) To advertise the products of a shop
(B) To explain the details of a new business venture
(C) To discuss the history of a family business
(D) To explain the prices of some products

156. What is indicated about Northshore Creamery?

(A) It was purchased by a large corporation.
(B) It became famous in town because of a movie.
(C) It is the pride and joy of the locals.
(D) It doesn't have enough money to expand.

157. In which of the positions marked [1], [2], [3], and [4] does the following sentence belong?

"Now the family is ready to open two new franchises in neighboring cities, and within five years plans to open six new shops around the country."

(A) [1]
(B) [2]
(C) [3]
(D) [4]

Announcement from Acreton City Council

April 3

The Acreton City Council will be creating a new task force charged with reducing unnecessary spending over the next fiscal year. The team of 12 people will be comprised of local business leaders, union representatives, civil servants, and financial consultants. Group members are due to be selected by the 30th of this month and will begin working almost immediately, planning ways to reduce annual local government costs by 10 percent over the next year by eliminating waste.

Applications for positions on the task force are being accepted at this time. Please contact the city council at admin@acretoncc.gov for information on how to get yourself or your organization involved in this project.

158. What is the announcement mainly about?

(A) The formation of a new employees' union.
(B) The creation of a financial oversight committee
(C) The launch of a recruitment effort
(D) The start of a change in local legislation

159. When is the group due to begin work?

(A) At the beginning of May
(B) At the end of the year
(C) At the beginning of the summer
(D) At the end of April

160. What should interested parties do to get involved?

(A) Sign a petition
(B) Attend a meeting
(C) Send an email
(D) Fill out a form

Janet Logan	**[2:15]**	I just got off the phone and Mr. King informed me that he wanted his order a couple of weeks earlier than originally planned. Do you think this may be possible?
Margaret Lee	**[2:16]**	There's no problem on our end. We have all the fabrics ready and cut into their appropriate shapes and sizes. They are ready for the sewing machines.
Jason Brown	**[2:17]**	My team is currently working on the orders from Mr. Bartelli. We have over 1,000 units to sew and another order from Carla Bean after that.
Janet Logan	**[2:18]**	Mr. Bartelli doesn't need his order until the end of the month, and Ms. Bean's orders can wait until next week. I can authorize your team to begin this order first.
Jason Brown	**[2:19]**	What is being made and how many units are needed?
Janet Logan	**[2:20]**	Long-sleeved men's dress shirts. We need 100 units in small, 300 in medium, 300 in large, and 100 in extra large.
Jason Brown	**[2:21]**	OK, then. I think we can finish those in two days.
Peter Williams	**[2:22]**	We can get buttons on all 800 units within two to four hours.
Janet Logan	**[2:23]**	Thank you so much. I appreciate your help. I'm glad that we can accommodate one of our best clients this way.

161. At 2:16, what does Margaret Lee mean when she writes, "There's no problem on our end"?

(A) Her team can achieve the goal.
(B) Her team can help the other teams.
(C) Their project will take some time.
(D) The problems will be minimal.

162. For what type of company does Janet Logan work?

(A) A shoe shop
(B) A clothing manufacturer
(C) A fashion magazine
(D) A menswear boutique

163. According to the discussion, which department needs the most time?

(A) Ms. Lee's department
(B) Mr. Brown's department
(C) Mr. Williams' department
(D) Ms. Logan's department

164. What will Janet Logan most likely tell Mr. King?

(A) That his order will be delayed for a month
(B) That his order can be completed within two weeks
(C) That his request will be difficult to achieve
(D) That his order can be completed early

Unsworthy Manufacturing

Date: Wednesday, October 17
Subject: Recycling

In response to pressure from local environmental groups, as of November 1 we will be separating all of our industrial waste for recycling. Collections will be made twice weekly on Tuesdays and Fridays from the regional recycling center, which will be supplying colored receptacles for different kinds of waste. All oils should be placed in the green container. All metals and glass belong in the red one. All paper waste should go into the blue one. Plastics will be collected for recycling as normal.

As this new policy also carries a financial benefit for the company, managers in all manufacturing bays are responsible for ensuring that the new protocols for waste disposal are followed, and failure to comply with the policy could result in disciplinary action.

Further information about our updated environmental practices will shortly be available on the website. Training sessions for managers will be held on Monday, October 22, but please contact me if you have any further questions in the meantime.

Regards,

Davis Jeeland
Operations Director, Unsworthy Manufacturing

---

165. What is the reason for the change?

(A) The company owners want to save money on labor.
(B) A new recycling center has opened near the business.
(C) The local government has changed its regulations.
(D) Environmentalists in the area have requested it.

166. What can be inferred about Unsworthy Manufacturing?

(A) It has good relations with local authorities.
(B) It already recycles its plastic industrial waste.
(C) It recently increased its workforce.
(D) It updates its environmental policy regularly.

167. What should supervisors do next week?

(A) Attend a workshop on the new procedures
(B) Update the company's website pages
(C) Make room for new waste receptacles
(D) Inform their teams of the changes

GO ON TO THE NEXT PAGE

Normanville Farmers' Market

April 9

Dear Normanville Resident,

This year's first Normanville Farmers' Market will take place on Saturday, April 14 on Clark Street between Main Street and Park Street. The farmers' market will be open from 9 A.M. to 5 P.M. The mayor of Normanville, Tom Daley, will be present to deliver an address at the opening ceremony. A lot of local farmers, food vendors, and street performers will be at the venue.

"This vibrant market will give our local farmers a nice place to sell their fresh produce. Additionally, because we cut out some middle processes, our prices are lower than those of average grocery stores," said Suzy Hammer, executive director of the Normanville Farmers' Association.

Ms. Hammer also mentioned that currently there is not enough parking space to accommodate shoppers. The Normanville Farmers' Association plans to expand parking space over the coming months. In the meantime, she advises Normanville residents who will visit the market to use public transportation in order to avoid parking difficulties.

The Normanville Farmers' Market is different from grocery stores that supply mass-produced food products. The market will provide organic produce that is full of essential vitamins and minerals. As you know, the market will also help the local economy.

Please come this Saturday and see what the Normanville Farmers' Market has to offer!

Sincerely,

Normanville Farmers' Association

168. Why was the letter written?

(A) To describe a policy change
(B) To introduce a new grocery store
(C) To advertise a market opening
(D) To announce election results

169. What is indicated about Ms. Hammer?

(A) She is a vendor at the farmers' market.
(B) She represents other farmers.
(C) She owns a family-run farm.
(D) She is the mayor of Normanville.

170. What problem is mentioned?

(A) Inadequate parking spots
(B) Unfair product pricing
(C) Lack of quality control
(D) Inclement weather

171. What is NOT mentioned as a benefit of shopping at the venue?

(A) A boost for the local economy
(B) Competitive prices
(C) Healthy produce
(D) Longer opening hours

Lost and Found

Parkway City is bracing for another holiday season and urging its citizens and tourists to keep track of their belongings. – [1] – Every year more than 2,000 items show up at the city lost and found located at Parkway City Hall. "But we get even more lost items during the holiday season," explains Jean King, the managing director of the lost and found. "From around November 25th to January 2nd we get a 25-percent increase in the number of items that are brought to us."

– [2] – Everything from keys, sunglasses, umbrellas, and jewelry to electronic devices, luggage, and shopping bags full of newly purchased items has been brought to the center over the years. "The strangest item we ever got was a suitcase full of period piece costumes," says Jean. "The intern working on a film at the time was happy to get it back."

– [3] – If the items are not claimed within 90 days, they are auctioned off at a public event to raise money for the community center. – [4] –

172. What is the purpose of the notice?

(A) To advertise an event for the holidays
(B) To warn citizens of increasing crime
(C) To inform people about lost and found items
(D) To give information about an auction

173. What is suggested about Jean King?

(A) She searches for lost items.
(B) She works for the city.
(C) She is an intern.
(D) She manages the community center.

174. What is suggested about the lost items?

(A) They are not kept at the center indefinitely.
(B) They are usually claimed by their owners.
(C) They are destroyed when unclaimed.
(D) They are generally new items.

175. In which of the positions marked [1], [2], [3], and [4] does the following sentence belong?

"Many people do come to claim their missing items, but the vast majority is still left unclaimed."

(A) [1]
(B) [2]
(C) [3]
(D) [4]

GO ON TO THE NEXT PAGE

Tech Life Hires New CEO

New York, April 12—Amid a crisis of low sales and disappointing performance, the technology company Tech Life has hired Steve Cross as its new chief executive officer. Previously, he was the chief financial officer at the technology investment firm Esta Resources in San Francisco, California. He assumed the position of CEO at the company—based in Dallas, Texas—just this Monday. Stockholders voted unanimously for the appointment, hoping the new CEO would bring renewed vitality and strength to the company.

"Mr. Cross has an impressive record as a business leader who makes smart decisions," commented Lynn Dyer, the director of human resources at Tech Life. "We have faith that he will lead us in a new direction that will help develop new markets and optimize our company operations in general."

Steve Cross graduated from Chester University in Harrisburg, Pennsylvania with a master's degree in business administration. He once served as head of the American League of Business Leaders and is a dedicated family man.

To: Steve Cross <scross@techlife.com>
From: Lynn Dyer <ldyer@techlife.com>
Subject: Welcome!
Date: April 15

Dear Mr. Cross,

It has been almost two years since we met. I am so glad to be collaborating with you again after we worked in the same department at Esta Resources. I felt we cooperated very well at that time, and I had been hoping to work with you again. You will find that we have very dedicated and hard-working teams here. If there is anything I can do to help you make the transition, please don't hesitate to ask.

Additionally, Tech Life has recently added five new managers to our company. If you have time, please visit them at 3:00 P.M. this afternoon, when they will all be attending a mandatory training session in Room 403.

Sincerely,

Lynn Dyer
Director of Human Resources

176. What problem is Tech Life facing?

(A) A shortage of employees
(B) An urgent audit
(C) A decline in profitability
(D) A potential competitor

177. What is mentioned about the shareholders?

(A) They are allowed to share financial information.
(B) They will hold a meeting next week.
(C) They are demanding more dividends.
(D) They agreed on the appointment of a new leader.

178. In the article, the word "optimize" in paragraph 2, line 6 is closest in meaning to

(A) merge
(B) improve
(C) analyze
(D) maintain

179. Where did Ms. Dyer work previously?

(A) In Harrisburg
(B) In Dallas
(C) In New York
(D) In San Francisco

180. What is Mr. Cross asked to do?

(A) Teach a training course
(B) Meet new employees
(C) Attend a stockholders' meeting
(D) Hire new managers

GO ON TO THE NEXT PAGE

The Association of Future and Culture (AFC)

Quarterly Conference
Homer Conference Center, January 10

2:00 P.M.   Kelly O'Neill, President, AFC; Principal, Mulligan Elementary School
Welcoming speech

2:30 P.M.   Mark Kreskas, CEO, SEM Development Group
Enhancing global awareness: leadership and diversity

3:30 P.M.   Lucy Hoover, Co-owner, Piedmont Adult Education Center
Gender and fairness in leadership

4:30 P.M.   Jon Kimura, Store Manager, Kent Grocery Store
The foundations of leadership in the workplace

5:30 P.M.   Kenneth Schneider, Professor, Brookstone University
Ethics and morality in leadership

6:30 P.M.   Question-and-answer session

To: AFC Members <members@futureculture.org>
From: Kelly O'Neill <kellyoneill@futureculture.org>
Date: January 11
Attachment: free_talk.jpg
Subject: Quarterly Conference

Dear AFC Members,

This quarterly conference has been another monumental success. I thank all of you for participating and sharing your expertise with others. I hope you can take the skills learned during the conference and apply them in your local offices and workplaces. Additionally, I encourage all of you to consider giving a presentation at the next conference. If you are interested in doing so, contact Amy Garcia at amygarcia@ futureculture.org.

I would also like to inform you of the invitation made by Kenneth Schneider, who will be giving a talk entitled "Gaining confidence through leadership" at his workplace next month. The talk will be free and open to the public. For more information, please see the attached file.

Finally, it has come to my attention that some members were not able to attend the conference due to scheduling conflicts. Therefore, all future conferences will be streamed simultaneously on our website so that distant members can watch and listen.

Sincerely,

Kelly O'Neill, President

181. What was the topic of the conference on January 10?

(A) How to start a small business
(B) How to manage finances
(C) How to lead other people
(D) How to expand business globally

182. When most likely will inquiries start being made?

(A) At 3:30 P.M.
(B) At 4:30 P.M.
(C) At 5:30 P.M.
(D) At 6:30 P.M.

183. Where will a talk be given at no charge?

(A) At Mulligan Elementary School
(B) At Brookstone University
(C) At Piedmont Adult Education Center
(D) At SEM Development Group

184. What does Ms. O'Neill invite AFC members to do?

(A) Attach a receipt
(B) Fill out a survey
(C) Prepare a presentation
(D) Evaluate speakers

185. What is mentioned about the next conference?

(A) It will be held at a new location.
(B) Its presentations will start later in the day.
(C) Its attendance fees will be increased.
(D) It will be broadcast online.

GO ON TO THE NEXT PAGE

Stark Bank

Announcements	My Accounts	Transfer	Loans

Overdraft Fee

On the date of June 3, you withdrew $100.00 from an ATM in Jacksonville, Florida, exceeding the limit of your debit card account. Therefore, you will be charged an overdraft fee of $30.00. This may have resulted from an accumulation of account withdrawals that were in process at the time you withdrew money from the ATM. We regret having to charge this amount whenever a member's debit card transactions exceed his or her funds.

In the future, this mistake can be avoided by signing up for our Stark Bank mobile banking service. This service only costs two dollars a month. Using your smartphone, you can access your accounts no matter where you are. You can check the amount of money in your accounts, your history of deposits and withdrawals, and most importantly, pending transactions. To sign up, please email us at customerservice@starkbank.com or call us at 904-555-4514.

To: customerservice@starkbank.com
From: ssummers@zippynet.com
Subject: Overdraft Fee
Date: June 5

I am concerned that someone may have illegally accessed my account and made a withdrawal. I lost my debit card on June 2, and upon noticing the next day, I immediately froze all of my accounts. Considering these unfortunate circumstances, I politely ask that the bank refrain from charging a fee for this unforeseen overdraft.

I would like to sign up for the banking service you recommended. It sounds like a useful service that can help me manage my finances in a more efficient manner.

Thank you for your assistance.

Suzie Summers

To: Suzie Summers<ssummers@zippynet.com>
From: Customer Service<customerservice@starkbank.com>
Subject: Overdraft Review
Date: June 6

Dear Ms. Summers,

I am sorry to hear of your misfortunes. According to our account data, you did contact us and freeze your accounts, though it looks like it was too late to prevent the withdrawal and subsequent overdraft from your account. It is a little bit unusual that the transaction that caused the overdraft was at an ATM machine a day after you say that you lost your card. Have you given your access pin to anybody recently? I would be happy to pass your request for overdraft relief on to our fraud department, but you will need to file a police report and then send us the case number that the investigating officer gives you. Once we receive this number we can proceed with our review of your case.

Thank you and good day,

Laura Massey
Customer Service Specialist, Stark Bank

186. What is the purpose of the Web page information?

(A) To announce a new company policy
(B) To explain an upcoming relocation
(C) To inform a user about a charge
(D) To notify a user of phishing attempts

187. What is NOT mentioned as being able to be checked using the mobile banking service?

(A) Account balances
(B) Interest rates
(C) Unresolved transactions
(D) Account history

188. What request does Ms. Summers make?

(A) That her accounts be frozen
(B) That her contact information be updated
(C) That her overdraft fee be waived
(D) That her withdrawal limit be increased

189. In her customer service email to Suzie Summers, what does Laura Massey think is odd about Suzie's story?

(A) Suzie didn't have very much money in her account.
(B) Suzie didn't file a police report.
(C) Suzie lost her card on June 2 but her card was used at an ATM machine on June 3.
(D) Suzie does not live in Florida.

190. What does Laura Massey instruct Suzie Summers to do if she wants to get relief from the overdraft fee?

(A) Write the fraud department of Stark Bank
(B) File a police report and give the case number to Stark Bank
(C) File a claim against the criminal in a court and give the court number to Stark Bank
(D) File a case number with the fraud department of Stark Bank

GO ON TO THE NEXT PAGE

From: customerservice@thomsonapp.com
To: dkerry@coolmail.com
Date: July 6
Subject: Malfunction

Dear Ms. Kerry,

We are very sorry to hear about the malfunction of your deluxe refrigerator model MK1213, purchased from Thomson Appliances. You indicated that the ice dispenser on the door of the fridge has stopped functioning. Actually, several other customers have reported the same problem. It turns out that the manufacturers made an error in the production process. Fortunately, this problem can easily be fixed by one of our technicians. Currently, our technicians are available next Monday, Wednesday, and Thursday. Please specify what day and what time work for you.

Additionally, if your refrigerator is under warranty, this repair will be absolutely free. Please let us know your warranty number so we can verify this before sending a technician to your house.

We apologize for this inconvenience. Thank you again for choosing Thomson Appliances.

Sincerely,

Greg Lewis
Customer Service

From: dkerry@coolmail.com
To: customerservice@thomsonapp.com
Date: July 7
Subject: Re: Malfunction

Dear Mr. Lewis,

Thank you for your prompt response. Actually, next week I will be away on a business trip in Arkansas and won't return until Saturday. However, I have a housekeeper who comes to clean on Monday and Friday. If your technician visits on either of those days, she can let him or her in.

My warranty number is A344F56J and is still valid. I will leave this document with my housekeeper in case you need to see it during your visit.

Dana Kerry

From: customerservice@thomsonapp.com
To: dkerry@coolmail.com
Date: July 7
Subject: repair time

Dear Ms. Kerry,

Our technician will be able to come by your house on Monday. You will need to be sure to leave the warranty documents so the technicians can scan them into our system. This is necessary for us to be reimbursed by the manufacturers. Our technicians will come by in the morning and try to be gone by lunch. Even though you have a housekeeper, they will try not to leave a mess. Safe travels and we appreciate your patience. Thank you for your loyalty to Thomson Appliances.

Sincerely,

Greg Lewis
Customer Service

191. What is one reason the first email was sent?

(A) To specify a warranty number
(B) To ask for a date for a visit
(C) To confirm an order
(D) To apologize for a shipping delay

192. According to the first email, what is true about the refrigerator?

(A) It is a newly released model.
(B) It is no longer covered by the warranty.
(C) It has a manufacturing defect.
(D) It is currently on sale.

193. What information does Mr. Lewis request from Ms. Kerry?

(A) Her current address
(B) Her warranty number
(C) Her refrigerator model
(D) Her contact information

194. Why do the technicians need to scan the warranty?

(A) To make sure it is still valid
(B) To make sure that the model is correct
(C) To make sure that there are enough spare parts to make the repairs
(D) To make sure that the manufacturer covers the repair costs

195. Why do you think the technicians will come on Monday?

(A) Because that is when they are available
(B) Because they are too busy on Friday
(C) Because the housekeeper will be there to let them in
(D) Because Ms. Kerry will be in Arkansas

GO ON TO THE NEXT PAGE ➡

To: Lillian Ross <lillianross@kingstonsportinggoods.com>
From: Eric West <ericwest@jmsolutions.com>
Date: November 4, 10:34 A.M.
Subject: Website Development
Attachment: Details

Dear Ms. Ross,

You contacted us last week to ask some of our computer programmers to help your company develop a website. JM Solutions would be happy to offer you our services.

As I said on the phone, we will help design and program a website that will attract more customers and offer an online sales platform. During this time, we will need to hold meetings with your marketing division in order to best capture your company's goals. Once the website has been completed in mid-February next year, we will hold a training seminar in order to train your employees in the skills necessary to maintain and update your website. The website development and training seminar will cost a total of $32,000. We request that a deposit of 10 percent be paid in advance. Please see the attached file for detailed costs and schedules.

We look forward to working with you in the near future. Our staff members will strive to meet all your needs. Just let me know when your marketing division is available to meet us in person and discuss some of the details of the project. Please contact me at your convenience.

Eric West

To: Lillian Ross <lillianross@kingstonsportinggoods.com>
From: Raymond Wells <raymondwells@kingstonsportinggoods.com>
Date: November 4, 10:37 A.M.
Subject: First Quarter Budget
Attachment: Q1_Budget

Dear Ms. Ross,

I have attached the current draft of the company's budget for the first quarter of next year. As you will notice, all of the profits made from this year's back-to-school sale are planned to be spent on billboard advertisements on major highways. I will call a design team later this afternoon and ask them to create eye-catching images for the advertisements.

At our last meeting, you mentioned that you would like to review the budget before it is finalized. I have already included employee raises in the first quarter's expenses, but if you can think of anything else, please let me know. I would like to have the budget finalized before next week's planning meeting.

Raymond Wells

To:	Raymond Wells <raymondwells@kingstonsportinggoods.com>
From:	Lillian Ross <lillianross@kingstonsportinggoods.com>
Date:	November 4, 10:40 AM
Subject:	Emergency Budget Addition

Dear Mr. Wells,

I am glad you forwarded me your proposed budget when you did. Just prior to receiving your email I received an estimate for our planned website development. It looks like it is going to be more expensive than I had anticipated. Although the final bill of $32,000 is not due immediately, we will have to find an extra $3,200 in next year's first quarter budget if we want to proceed with JM Solutions' proposal.

If you have any questions regarding this matter, please just come to my office and we can go over how to make the tough cuts needed to come up with this funding.

196. Why did Mr. West write the first email?

(A) To inquire about a service
(B) To schedule a meeting
(C) To report on a budget
(D) To apply for a position

197. What service does JM Solutions provide?

(A) Recruitment and employee training
(B) Graphic design
(C) Web programming
(D) Marketing strategy consultation

198. According to the second email, how will the profits from the back-to-school sale be spent?

(A) On repairing some roads
(B) On purchasing advertising space
(C) On paying for JM Solutions' service
(D) On hiring more employees

199. What is indicated by the third email?

(A) The budget for the first quarter of next year looks good.
(B) JM Solutions has a strong reputation.
(C) It will be easy for Kingston Sporting Goods to find money in its budget for web development.
(D) Some items in the budget may lose their funding in order to pay for web development.

200. Why does Kingston Sporting Goods need to allow for $3,200 for web development?

(A) They need the best website money can buy.
(B) They have to expand their business into other territories.
(C) They have to pay JM Solutions 10 percent of the overall cost as a deposit.
(D) They have to negotiate a better price after the deposit.

Stop! This is the end of the test. If you finish before time is called, you may go back to Parts 5, 6, and 7 and check your work.

READING TEST

In the Reading test, you will read a variety of texts and answer several different types of reading comprehension questions. The entire Reading test will last 75 minutes. There are three parts, and directions are given for each part. You are encouraged to answer as many questions as possible within the time allowed.

You must mark your answers on the separate answer sheet. Do not write your answers in your test book.

PART 5

Directions: A word or phrase is missing in each of the sentences below. Four answer choices are given below each sentence. Select the best answer to complete the sentence. Then mark the letter (A), (B), (C), or (D) on your answer sheet.

101. Pet owners are encouraged to register ------- the workshop on pet training and health offered by the community center.

(A) of
(B) from
(C) in
(D) for

102. The CEO held a press conference to ------- for the negative health effects caused by her company's products.

(A) apologized
(B) apologize
(C) apologizes
(D) apologizing

103. There is a ------- difference between the business's revenues during the peak season and during the off-peak season.

(A) prosperous
(B) rural
(C) significant
(D) preparatory

104. The path through Morrison Park was constructed not only for cyclists ------- for joggers.

(A) but also
(B) though
(C) in addition to
(D) neither

105. One of the supervisors questioned Ms. Marshall ------- her role in the misuse of the investment funds.

(A) unless
(B) among
(C) about
(D) into

106. The occupancy rate at Starburst Hotel has ------- by 24 percent due to increased competition.

(A) relied
(B) fallen
(C) expired
(D) coincided

107. A certificate of ------- was given to the participants in the public speaking skills course.

(A) accomplishment
(B) accomplish
(C) accomplished
(D) accomplishing

108. The chef ------- prepares the entrée for a restaurant critic often comes out to greet him or her in person.

(A) whose
(B) what
(C) either
(D) who

109. The negotiators made a few minor changes to the contract to make the terms ------- to both parties.

(A) agreeable
(B) agreement
(C) agree
(D) agreeing

110. The allocation of funds to local schools is ------- on the number of children living in the district.

(A) seen
(B) based
(C) placed
(D) taken

111. This palace was ------- used for public ceremonies and celebrations.

(A) traditionally
(B) traditional
(C) tradition
(D) traditions

112. The successful candidate will be contacted by an HR representative once the hiring committee has made its ------- decision.

(A) disposable
(B) numerous
(C) final
(D) portable

113. The chairperson ------- by an anonymous vote involving all members.

(A) has been selecting
(B) had to select
(C) is selecting
(D) will be selected

114. Providing low-interest loans to small businesses is a key ------- of the recovery plan.

(A) vacancy
(B) status
(C) component
(D) rate

115. The project would not have been a success without Mr. Ratcliffe's complete -------, which was demonstrated on several occasions.

(A) dedicated
(B) dedicate
(C) dedicates
(D) dedication

116. City politicians will debate this ------- issue at the town hall meeting so that voters can have a better understanding of it.

(A) competent
(B) observant
(C) complicated
(D) confused

GO ON TO THE NEXT PAGE

117. ------- the hospital experiences a power outage, power generators will turn on automatically to supply the necessary electricity.

(A) If
(B) Until
(C) What
(D) So

118. After the tellers at Stewart Bank had undergone extensive training, they treated the customers -------.

(A) more courteously
(B) courteous
(C) most courteous
(D) courtesy

119. A gate agent at the airport announced a flight ------- caused by severe weather at the destination.

(A) canceling
(B) cancels
(C) cancellation
(D) cancel

120. ------- the outdated equipment is replaced with state-of-the-art machinery, productivity will be more than double.

(A) Whether
(B) Later
(C) When
(D) Momentarily

121. In order to be eligible for this position, you must have at least five years' experience in the insurance -------.

(A) preservation
(B) figure
(C) industry
(D) description

122. Through his extensive research into the acquisition of language skills, Dr. Harvey Ward has proven ------- to be a leader in the field.

(A) he
(B) his
(C) himself
(D) him

123. The seafood sold by Pacific Plus is ------- and therefore must be transported in a temperature-controlled vehicle.

(A) suitable
(B) widespread
(C) cautious
(D) perishable

124. The novelist said that his writing was ------- influenced by the late writer Edward Truitt.

(A) manually
(B) insecurely
(C) regretfully
(D) profoundly

125. As had been ------- by the researchers, the new environmentally friendly laundry detergent performed as well as its competitors.

(A) observing
(B) observed
(C) observation
(D) observe

126. The Green Society is dedicated to ------- public parks and other natural areas for future generations.

(A) preserving
(B) consulting
(C) escorting
(D) inquiring

127. The manufacturing plant that was damaged in the typhoon should ------- its operations later this month.

(A) resumed
(B) be resuming
(C) had resumed
(D) resuming

128. Because the team was already behind schedule, the manager did not ------- to Ms. Norton's vacation request.

(A) accept
(B) ensure
(C) consent
(D) finalize

129. The nasal spray allowed Bert to keep his seasonal allergies ------- control without having to get a prescription.

(A) against
(B) under
(C) around
(D) unto

130. Our sales ------- are unavailable to take your call at the moment, but will call you back as soon as possible.

(A) representation
(B) represents
(C) representatives
(D) representative

GO ON TO THE NEXT PAGE

PART 6

Directions: Read the texts that follow. A word, phrase, or sentence is missing in parts of each text. Four answer choices for each question are given below the text. Select the best answer to complete the text. Then mark the letter (A), (B), (C), or (D) on your answer sheet.

Questions 131-134 refer to the following email.

To: Olivia Paulson

From: Jonathan Hicks

Date: July 19

Subject: Procedural Review

An issue was brought up at the executives' meeting last Thursday. Complaints about goods damaged after being shipped ------- dramatically in the last month. This may be a result of
131.
more fragile items' being added to the products we now ship. ------- We are reviewing our
132.
packaging procedures and looking to introduce additional steps to ------- that our products
133.
are packaged securely and delivered without damage.

Please inform all manufacturing managers to attend a(n) ------- meeting tonight at 7 P.M. We
134.
hope to address this problem and come up with a sound solution as quickly as possible so that normal business can resume.

---

131. (A) increasing
(B) have increased
(C) were increased
(D) increases

132. (A) We are thinking of dropping such items from our product list.
(B) We may need to increase shipping and handling costs.
(C) An added insurance cost for such items has been suggested.
(D) Because of this, we have temporarily suspended the shipping of accessories and other fragile items.

133. (A) secure
(B) affect
(C) ensure
(D) warrant

134. (A) emergency
(B) necessity
(C) decisive
(D) extensive

172

Questions 135-138 refer to the following advertisement.

Green Clean Services

Call us: 347-281-7834

------- 2005, Green Clean has been providing professional and environmentally friendly
135.

cleaning services of consistently high quality to all types of commercial and industrial

facilities. ------- We understand the contribution a good employee makes toward our -------,
136. **137.**

and we are committed to selecting the best available people to work for you.

Green Clean's mission is to satisfy our customers' needs on a daily basis while providing the

best possible combination of quality, price, and delivery. We accomplish this by continually

improving our systems of -------. Our goal is to make your facility extremely clean in the
138.

greenest way possible. Visit us at www.greeenclean.com today.

---

135. (A) Until
(B) Around
(C) Since
(D) Through

136. (A) Drop in today to schedule a tour of one
of our 20 facilities.
(B) We are the biggest manufacturer of
environmentally friendly cleaning
supplies in the Northwest.
(C) As a service company, we consider our
employees to be our most important
asset.
(D) Allow us to work for you by calling
us today to take care of all of your
accounting needs.

137. (A) success
(B) drive
(C) support
(D) determination

138. (A) to operate
(B) operates
(C) operated
(D) operation

GO ON TO THE NEXT PAGE

Florist Wanted

Do you love making people smile? Does the idea of ------- your day being creative and
 **139.**

working with nature appeal to you? If so, we would like to encourage you to apply to join our

team at Wild Flowers Florists. ------- We are looking for someone who is customer- -------
 **140.** **141.**

first. Creativity is important, but it is secondary to the vision of the client. If you think -------
 **142.**

have what it takes to make people smile, please fill out the application form on our website,

www.WildFlowersFlorists.com.

---

139. (A) spend
(B) to spend
(C) spending
(D) spent

(NEW)
140. (A) You must be good with animals.
(B) Our company is committed to providing
the best floral arrangements for our
clients, no matter what their needs.
(C) We use the best fabrics in our designs.
(D) Everyone loves our commitment to
safety.

141. (A) oriented
(B) prime
(C) located
(D) sourced

142. (A) you
(B) I
(C) they
(D) we

Questions 143-146 refer to the following letter.

October 21

Larry Mills

226 Highland Rivers

Fairbank, WA 20037

Dear Mr. Mills,

I am writing in reply to your complaint about the noise coming from the businesses around your apartment complex. -------, a few people living in the west wing of the building ------- concern over the noise levels. The building committee has held meetings on this issue and we have talked to the businesses involved. ------- Because of this, we are also looking to fortify the complex's windows with noise proof glass in the west wing. Once we have agreed upon these proposals, we will post an announcement on our bulletin board and you may receive a call. Until then, we ask for your ------- patience.

143. (A) As a result
(B) Moreover
(C) On the other hand
(D) Unfortunately

144. (A) is expressing
(B) have expressed
(C) expression
(D) be expressive

145. (A) However, some of the noises are inevitable due to the nature of those businesses.
(B) They will fully cooperate with our committee.
(C) They have responded to our concerns and will work to keep noise levels low.
(D) However, they are losing money over this matter.

146. (A) continue
(B) continues
(C) continued
(D) be continuing

GO ON TO THE NEXT PAGE

Directions: In this part you will read a selection of texts, such as magazine and newspaper articles, emails, and instant messages. Each text or set of texts is followed by several questions. Select the best answer for each question and mark the letter (A), (B), (C), or (D) on your answer sheet.

Questions 147-148 refer to the following invoice.

Henderson, Inc.

1576 Stevens Road, Pleasantville, NY 10571

(231) 555-0786 www.hendersoninc.com

Order Number: 6694
Date: April 2
Customer: Susan Ward
               709 Praise Street
               Pleasantville, NY 10571
               (203) 555-0167

Item	Model	Quantity	Price
Extra-large microwave	MW132	1	$150.00
Four-door refrigerator	RF4D	1	$2,399.99
Smart toaster	TR512	1	$45.50

Subtotal $2,595.49
Tax $230.18
Total due $2,825.67

Local customers are eligible for free shipping on purchases over $1,000.

147. What does Henderson, Inc. sell?

(A) Home appliances
(B) Office furniture
(C) Computer equipment
(D) Construction materials

148. What is indicated about Ms. Ward?

(A) She must pick up her items in person.
(B) She is eligible for a special discount.
(C) She will receive her deliveries at no charge.
(D) She paid with a check.

Questions 149-150 refer to the following text message chain.

DAN COOPER   10:10
Have you finished your meeting?

HEATHER BERRY   10:10
Not yet.

DAN COOPER   10:11
OK. Message me when you're done.

HEATHER BERRY   10:11
I'm free now. We're on a snack and bathroom break.

DAN COOPER   10:13
Great. I was wondering if you'd take the interns to lunch today.

HEATHER BERRY   10:13
Are you bailing on it?

DAN COOPER   10:14
I have to. I need to be in North Point by two.

HEATHER BERRY   10:14
No worries. I'll take them.

DAN COOPER   10:16
Thanks. I'd hate to cancel on them.

149. What is suggested about Ms. Berry?

(A) She is eating a snack.
(B) She will be promoted.
(C) She is in the middle of a meeting.
(D) She plans on cancelling a lunch appointment.

 150. At 10:13, what does Ms. Berry mean when she writes, "Are you bailing on it?"

(A) She's asking if Mr. Cooper has finished his meeting.
(B) She's inquiring whether Mr. Cooper will be missing an appointment.
(C) She wants to know if Mr. Cooper will go to North Point.
(D) She would like Mr. Cooper to notify her when he leaves.

GO ON TO THE NEXT PAGE ➡

Superbox Theaters

Superbox Theaters are now offering reduced prices on matinée tickets for December. Use this early bird special to pay half the regular price for our first matinée show. This offer applies to all movies, seven days a week, including new releases!

Group visits from schools and companies are welcome. If you have a large group, you might want to reserve your tickets in advance. Tickets can be purchased in person from theater staff, or online at www.superboxtheaters.com and www.abcticketworld.com. When buying tickets online, you have the convenience of choosing your seat. Additional information and reviews of current and upcoming films are also available on our website. Come on down to Superbox Theaters and take advantage of this great offer!

151. What is indicated about Superbox Theaters?

(A) They will screen fewer films this December.
(B) They are hiring part-timers.
(C) They will soon be adding a new theater location.
(D) They are offering reduced prices for certain screenings.

152. What are customers able to do on the theaters' website?

(A) Demand a refund
(B) Select a seat location
(C) Sign up for a newsletter
(D) Renew their membership

Questions 153-154 refer to the following email.

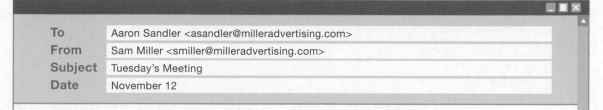

Dear Mr. Sandler,

This month's business review meeting is scheduled for Thursday, November 15. As you know, this meeting is a great opportunity for us to assess our operating plan and make any adjustments that might help us keep up with the constant changes in the marketplace. As an advertising agency, we must stay informed about the newest market trends. So I was very excited when I heard that Tsuyoshi Ito, manager of our Japanese branch, would be visiting this Friday. In order to take full advantage of Mr. Ito's expertise and knowledge, I would like to change the meeting date so that he can attend.

This will be Mr. Ito's first time in the country, so I would like you to pick him up from the airport. A company car will be provided to you for this purpose. I will email again once I have more details concerning Mr. Ito's arrival time.

Sincerely,

Sam Miller
President

153. What is the purpose of the email?

(A) To reschedule a meeting
(B) To request a monthly operating report
(C) To introduce a new employee
(D) To propose a new marketing strategy

154. What does the email indicate about Mr. Ito?

(A) He is changing positions.
(B) He often travels on business.
(C) He works in advertising.
(D) He is a client of Mr. Miller's.

GO ON TO THE NEXT PAGE

Questions 155-157 refer to the following email.

To: Bridget Lee
From: Victor Thomas
Subject: shipment
Date: June 25

Hello Bridget,

– [1] – Our shipment of beverages will arrive tomorrow morning around 10 A.M. Please keep inventory and make sure that all the shipments are accurate as they are unloaded. Also, some of the beverages will need to be refrigerated right away so please make sure that the issue is taken care of in a timely fashion. – [2] – The temperatures are expected to be high tomorrow, so we'll need to get all the shipments into storage as soon as possible. – [3] – We have two refrigerated trucks that we'll send with you and there will be a crew waiting for you at the warehouse. – [4] –

If there are any problems or if you need any help with issues that arise, please contact me by phone. I'll be in the office early tomorrow.

Thanks,

Victor

155. What is the purpose of the email?

(A) To inform suppliers of a mistake
(B) To give an employee instructions
(C) To order a shipment of beverages
(D) To keep inventory of products

156. Why is Victor concerned about the shipment?

(A) The products are fragile.
(B) It may arrive late.
(C) It is temperature-sensitive.
(D) It is for an important client.

157. In which of the places marked [1], [2], [3], and [4] does the following sentence belong?

"I'm worried about the weather."

(A) [1]
(B) [2]
(C) [3]
(D) [4]

Questions 158-160 refer to the following advertisement.

Marigold Bakery
451 Clark Street, Ellis Town
253-555-1298

Marigold Bakery is a family-run business that has been making delicious and irresistible sweet treats for over 30 years. Our store is located in historic downtown Ellis Town, and offers a warm decor and inviting atmosphere.

We offer:
- Made-to-order pastries for parties, weddings, and corporate events
- Gluten- and sugar-free refreshments and vegetarian sandwiches
- Custom cake designs

Hours:
Monday to Saturday, 9:00 A.M. to 5:00 P.M.
We will be closing this September in order to expand our store.

Sunday cooking class:
Marigold Bakery values positive interactions with the community. Therefore, we are currently holding a cooking class for local teenagers. Baking teaches the values of patience and hard work!

158. What is mentioned about Marigold Bakery?

(A) It is internationally known.
(B) It employs local students.
(C) It offers options for those with dietary restrictions.
(D) Its store space can be rented for various events.

159. According to the advertisement, what will happen in September?

(A) The store will shut down for renovations.
(B) A classroom will be constructed.
(C) The menu will be expanded.
(D) The shop will cater a community event.

160. What is indicated about the cooking class?

(A) It will be held at a community center this year.
(B) It has been going on for over 30 years.
(C) It is taught by an experienced baker.
(D) It is designed for young people in the community.

GO ON TO THE NEXT PAGE

Peter Jones Lunch

Peter Jones [12:10] I'm heading to the new pizza parlor across the street for lunch. Does anyone want to join me?

Martin Lee [12:10] Count me in!

Laura Vans [12:11] Theo and I are working on our presentation for tomorrow so we can't.

Theo Gibbs [12:12] Can you bring back some pizza for us?

Peter Jones [12:13] Sure. What kind do you want?

Laura Vans [12:14] I'll take whatever their best-selling pizza is. One large slice will be enough for me.

Theo Gibbs [12:15] Pepperoni for me. One slice.

Peter Jones [12:15] No problem. I'll be back in one hour. Is your presentation about the new product line?

Laura Vans [12:16] Yes, we're almost finished, but we're working on making the visuals more impressive.

Martin Lee [12:17] If you'd like, I can help you with the visuals. I have a bit of a background in computer graphics.

Theo Gibbs [12:17] That would be great. Laura and I are good with basic computer programs, but neither of us is very good at making visuals.

Peter Jones [12:18] When Martin and I come back, we can help you finish your presentation.

Laura Vans [12:18] Thanks so much!

Theo Gibbs [12:19] Awesome!

161. Where most likely are the writers?

(A) At a restaurant
(B) At a pizza shop
(C) At a company
(D) In an electronics shop

162. At 12:10, what does Martin Lee mean when he says, "Count me in"?

(A) He's doing a presentation.
(B) He's in his office.
(C) He would like to go out for lunch.
(D) He's currently in a meeting.

163. What is indicated about the presentation?

(A) It will be presented after lunch.
(B) It is about new products.
(C) It is very long.
(D) It needs more information.

164. What will Martin Lee most likely help the presenters with?

(A) Their graphics
(B) Their information
(C) Their computer use
(D) Their presentation format

Questions 165-167 refer to the following email.

To: All Employees <staff@jointsystems.com>
From: Fred Hanes <fhanes@jointsystems.com>
Subject: Community Park Cleanup
Date: February 12

Joint Systems is a company that tries to take every opportunity to give back to our community. Therefore, I am urging all of our employees to take part in the upcoming community park cleanup sponsored by the city of Harrisburg. Without the dedication of volunteers, our parks and public spaces would not be free of litter. Donate some of your free time to keeping Harrisburg a beautiful and inviting city.

The community park cleanup will be held next Friday, February 18, from 1:00 to 5:00 P.M. Employees who wish to participate will leave work at lunchtime, yet will still be paid as if they had worked a full day. Volunteers are asked to bring supplies such as protective outerwear, tools, insect repellent, trash bags, and snacks.

A shuttle bus will depart from the company parking lot at 1:20 P.M. on Friday to take volunteers to the cleanup location. If you have a specific preference concerning the type of work you would like to do, please contact event organizer Don Lewis at 435-555-6768.

We appreciate everyone's enthusiasm and support.

Fred Hanes
Human Resources

---

165. What is the purpose of the email?

(A) To organize a business trip
(B) To request updated information
(C) To offer additional skills training
(D) To promote a community event

166. What would probably NOT be necessary for participants?

(A) A company uniform
(B) A can of mosquito spray
(C) A rake
(D) A sandwich

167. According to the email, what is Mr. Lewis responsible for?

(A) Raising awareness about food waste
(B) Analyzing customer feedback
(C) Assigning individuals tasks
(D) Cleaning a community center

GO ON TO THE NEXT PAGE

http://www.sanchezcardealership.com/about

Sanchez Motors

| ABOUT | NEWS | MODELS | SERVICES | COMMUNITY |

About Sanchez Motors

Carlos Sanchez dreamed of owning his own car dealership from the time he started working as an assistant at an auto repair shop. After saving his money for 10 years, he finally opened Sanchez Motors, and has been serving the community with integrity and pride ever since. Sanchez Motors carries all kinds of vehicles, from sports cars and vans to SUVs and trucks. Not sure what car fits your needs? Then come on down and try driving a variety of vehicles to see what's right for you.

Until the end of the year, Sanchez Motors is offering an amazing deal on our popular lines of Spitfire pickup trucks and Stark SUVs. If you make a down payment of just $3,000, you will be eligible for an extremely low interest rate on your monthly installments.

Sanchez Motors is located off Highway 5, just outside of the town of Stockton. We are open seven days a week, from 9:00 A.M. to 9:00 P.M. Don't hesitate; come pay us a visit!

168. What is indicated about Mr. Sanchez?

(A) He works at an auto repair shop.
(B) He started his own business.
(C) He is a race car driver.
(D) He designs a variety of vehicles.

169. The word "carries" in paragraph 1, line 4 is closest in meaning to

(A) moves
(B) manufactures
(C) sells
(D) develops

170. What is suggested about Sanchez Motors?

(A) It allows customers to test products.
(B) It operates a store in downtown Stockton.
(C) It offers vehicle customization.
(D) It closes on weekends.

171. What is available to customers until the end of the year?

(A) Discounts on sports cars and vans
(B) An extended warranty at no extra cost
(C) A special payment option
(D) A free oil change with any purchase

Questions 172-175 refer to the following article.

Clean and Green

The town of Korden has much to celebrate as the new hydrogen fuel car company, Newmark, plans to open a massive manufacturing plant here in the next few months. – [1] – Newmark already supplies some of the greenest cities around the world including Vancouver, Singapore, Honolulu, and Amsterdam with hydrogen-fueled public buses and taxis. – [2] –

The company is forecast to grow by 120% in the next five years. Furthermore, the opening of the plant in Korden is expected to bring in 300 new jobs. – [3] – The old Handai facilities will be the site of the new Newmark facilities. The mayor of Korden is also working to provide government subsidies for those who purchase hydrogen-fueled cars in the hope that gas-guzzling conventional cars will eventually become a thing of the past. – [4] –

---

172. What is the main topic of the article?

(A) Alternative energy sources
(B) Environmentally friendly cities
(C) The opening of a new factory
(D) The future of car companies

173. What will happen to the town's old car factories?

(A) They will be destroyed and rebuilt.
(B) They will be the new site of the hydrogen fuel car company.
(C) They will be turned into office buildings.
(D) They will house all the old conventional cars.

174. What is suggested about Korden?

(A) It will become one of the greenest cities.
(B) Its economy will stay stagnant.
(C) It will attract new car companies.
(D) It will grow economically.

175. In which of the places marked [1], [2], [3], and [4] does the following sentence belong?

"This is welcome news for a town that has suffered economically since the closure of its car manufacturing plants in the 1990s and its stagnant growth since then."

(A) [1]
(B) [2]
(C) [3]
(D) [4]

GO ON TO THE NEXT PAGE

To: Sam Brown <sbrown@zippy.com>
From: Kevin Draper <kdraper@fivestarbank.com>
Date: April 22
Subject: Home Loan

Dear Mr. Brown,

Thank you for choosing Five Star Financial Bank as the provider of your home loan. We strive to offer you the most competitive repayment plans as well as superb customer support. Below is a summary of the loan you have taken out with us.

Mortgage Type	Amount	Repayment Period
Home Opportunity Loan	$70,000.00	15 years

During the period of your loan, senior banker Martha King will be in charge of your repayment plan. Understanding the terms of your loan is crucial to successfully paying back the loan and avoiding penalties. We advise you to schedule a time to meet with Ms. King so she can further familiarize you with your home loan.

If you sign up for our online banking services, you will be able to quickly and conveniently check on your repayment progress.

Thanks again for trusting Five Star Financial Bank with your home loan.

Sincerely,

Kevin Draper
Loan Specialist
Five Star Financial Bank

Listed below are the various home loans available to customers of Five Star Financial Bank. Learning about different kinds of loans will help you make an informed decision. Review the loan choices below and decide which loan is right for your situation.

Fixed-Rate Mortgage Loan – This loan ensures that your interest rate and monthly principal repayment remain the same during the entire period of your loan. This loan protects you from rising interest rates and may be a good choice if you plan to live in your home for a long time.

Adjustable-Rate Mortgage Loan – Your interest rate remains fixed for the initial five years, and is then adjusted annually. Typically, this loan has a lower initial interest rate than a fixed-rate mortgage.

Interest-Only Mortgage Loan – During the initial five years of the loan, you are required to make payments on interest only. This option is suitable for those with fluctuating incomes. When your finances are tight you can make interest-only payments, and when your earnings increase you can make payments on the principal.

Home Opportunity Loan – This special loan is designed for first-time home buyers. You do not need a large down payment or a perfect credit rating in order to qualify for this loan.

176. What does Mr. Draper suggest that Mr. Brown do?

(A) Apply for a position
(B) Arrange a meeting
(C) Make a down payment in April
(D) Become a bank customer

177. How is Mr. Brown advised to keep track of his loan?

(A) By meeting with Mr. Draper
(B) By reading regular emails from the bank
(C) By using banking services on the Internet
(D) By calling a bank hotline

178. What information does the Web page provide?

(A) Bank account statements
(B) Quarterly interest rates
(C) Repayment options
(D) A roster of customers

179. Which plan is suitable for those with unstable earnings?

(A) Fixed-Rate Mortgage Loan
(B) Adjustable-Rate Mortgage Loan
(C) Interest-Only Mortgage Loan
(D) Home Opportunity Loan

180. What is indicated about Mr. Brown?

(A) He made a large down payment.
(B) He earns a steady salary.
(C) He recently bought his first home.
(D) He will retire in the near future.

GO ON TO THE NEXT PAGE

Madison Business Update

November 15—Sun Microchips is the country's largest producer of the integrated circuits that go into computers, smartphones, and other digital electronics. The company has recently built a new factory in Madison and will begin operations in January of next year. The chief executive officer of Sun Microchips, Melinda Piers, stated that "As the market for consumer electronics continues to become larger and larger globally, companies like Sun Microchips are expanding to meet its needs."

"We are looking to hire a variety of people such as factory workers, personnel employees, and accountants. We expect the opening of the factory to create over 200 jobs in Madison," said Ms. Piers. She noted that the company will try to hire local applicants first, but that those living outside of Madison are also encouraged to apply.

Applicants must submit their résumés by November 25 by emailing Tina Zimmerman at tzimmerman@sunmicrochips.com. Sun Microchips will be holding two separate sets of interviews next month. Those applying as general laborers for jobs on the assembly line should schedule an interview between December 3 and 8. Those interested in positions in personnel, accounting, and customer service are required to schedule an interview between December 9 and 11.

To:	<tzimmerman@sunmicrochips.com>
From:	<jakehenry@tnamail.com>
Date:	November 21
Subject:	Opening at Sun Microchips
Attachment:	résumé.doc

Dear Ms. Zimmerman,

I recently read an article in the *Madison Business Update* about the openings at your new factory in Madison. As a former employee of Sun Microchips, I am excited by the prospect of joining your company again.

Please see the attached file. I would really appreciate it if you would schedule me for an interview. Anytime on December 10 will work for me. If you would like to learn more about my past work experience with Sun Microchips, you can contact my former supervisor, Todd Smith. He is still working there.

I look forward to meeting you.

Jake Henry

181. According to Ms. Piers, what is true about consumer electronics?

(A) The demand for them is constantly increasing.
(B) They are becoming more and more expensive.
(C) They will soon be produced in only a few countries.
(D) They can affect users' health.

182. What is Sun Microchips planning to do?

(A) Launch its latest model of smartphone
(B) Build a new factory overseas
(C) Give preference to local job candidates
(D) Hire a new chief executive officer

183. Who most likely is Ms. Zimmerman?

(A) A computer technician
(B) A human resources manager
(C) A factory worker
(D) An accountant

184. What is the purpose of the email?

(A) To quit a job
(B) To postpone an appointment
(C) To ask for an interview
(D) To accept a job offer

185. What can be inferred about Mr. Henry?

(A) He is a resident of Madison.
(B) He has a degree in computer science.
(C) He currently works at Sun Microchips.
(D) He wants an office position.

GO ON TO THE NEXT PAGE

From: Henry Choi <henrychoi@neatsolutions.com>
To: Jenny Davis <jennydavis@endlessacresgolfclub.com>
Date: August 8
Subject: Endless Acres Golf Club
Attachment: draft

Dear Ms. Davis,

Attached is the newest draft of the advertisement for Endless Acres Golf Club. I have incorporated the advertising slogan you sent me into my design. I've used a combination of eye-catching graphics to grab the attention of newspaper readers. I've also added some helpful information at the end of the advertisement. Please let me know if the design and new additions meet your expectations. Along with the concurrent television ad, I think this advertisement will help bring a lot of new customers to Endless Acres Golf Club.

Sincerely,

Henry Choi

Endless Acres Golf Club
1232 Hilly Meadows Drive, Mapleview, CO

Take a break from all the stress of life and play a round of relaxing golf at Endless Acres Golf Club. After your game, enjoy a meal at our restaurant in a sophisticated and welcoming environment.

We are currently offering the following promotion:
Reserve a tee time for a party of seven or more golfers and receive a 20-percent discount. Additionally, every member of your group will receive a coupon for $5 off any purchase from our golf shop.

We were recently praised by *The Rolling Meadows Daily* for the superb maintenance of our golf course and grounds. Come in and enjoy the best golf course in the state of Colorado. We are located off Exit 21 on Highway 5. Just look for our billboard. You can't miss it!

Reservations can now be made on our website at www.endlessacresgolf.com or by calling 555-4834.

From:	Logan Mankins <lmankins@crushing.com>
To:	<reservations@endlessacresgolfclub.com>
Date:	July 6
Subject:	Re: Tee time and dinner for 10

Hello,

I saw your ad in the newspaper and I have a couple of quick questions about your deals. First, we have a group of 10 golfers. Now, I know most courses generally limit a group to four players to keep up the pace of play, but I was really hoping you could make an exception for us and allow two groups of five. We will even rent golf carts to ensure that we don't cause a delay. As for the $5 gift cards for the pro shop, I was wondering if they could be pooled together for one large purchase. It is my son's birthday and I would like to buy him a new putter, but they are awfully expensive these days. Fifty bucks would go a long way toward giving him a great gift!

We would like to tee off at around 11:30 a.m. on Saturday, July 20th and then have dinner there at about 6 p.m. Please write back to confirm our tee time and answer my queries. Thank you for your time!

Have a great day,

Logan Mankins

GO ON TO THE NEXT PAGE

186. How does Logan Mankins propose to keep his two groups of five golfers from delaying the other golfers on the course?

(A) He guarantees they will play fast.
(B) He promises that they are very good at golf.
(C) He writes that he will buy a new putter for his son.
(D) He informs the club that the two groups will be driving golf carts.

187. Where would the advertisement most likely appear?

(A) On television
(B) In a magazine
(C) In a newspaper
(D) On a billboard

188. What has been added to the advertisement?

(A) Promotional details
(B) Driving directions
(C) Contact information
(D) Customer reviews

189. What does Logan Mankins want to do with the $5 credits the players get for the golf shop?

(A) He wants to buy his son a putter with his.
(B) He wants to use them to pay his green fees.
(C) He wants to combine them with the 20-percent group discount.
(D) He wants to combine them all and apply the amount to one purchase.

190. What did *The Rolling Meadows Daily* indicate about Endless Acres Golf Club?

(A) Its location is convenient.
(B) Its facilities are well kept.
(C) Its membership fees are affordable.
(D) Its restaurant updates its menu regularly.

To: Library Members <members@claytonlibrary.edu>
From: Holly Allen <hollyallen@claytonlibrary.edu>
Subject: Events This Month
Date: August 1
Attachment: August Events Calendar

Dear Members of the Clayton Library,

Thank you for your continued support of the Clayton Library. Your monthly membership fees help us to obtain new books, computers, journal subscriptions, and other resources that are useful to the entire community. We would like to inform you of some upcoming special events this month that you may be interested in attending.

First, famous children's book author and storyteller Ebert Butler will be visiting our library. He will be reading from his new book, *The Mysterious Cat*, and signing autographs. His book was recently nominated for the Children's Book of the Year Award. Kathy Butler, Mr. Butler's wife, will also be in attendance at this event. She has drawn the pictures for most of Mr. Butler's books, including *The Mysterious Cat*. This event costs $10, but is free for library members.

Later in the month, renowned wildlife photographer Nina Brooks will be holding an exhibition on the main floor of the library. Ms. Brooks recently returned from a trip to Kenya, where she photographed cheetahs, giraffes, elephants, and other animals. Her photographs capture the vividness of wildlife and the majesty of nature.

In addition to these two featured events, there will be a variety of workshops, games nights, and other events this month. Check the attached calendar for details. All events, including Movie Night, are free unless otherwise noted.

Sincerely,

Holly Allen
Library Events Coordinator

Clayton Library Events Calendar

August

Date/Time	Event Title	Notes
Saturday, Aug. 2, 5:00 P.M.	Creative Writers' Workshop	Led by Donna Ward
Friday, Aug. 8, 7:00 P.M.	Movie Night	Family-friendly event
Sunday, Aug. 17, 6:00 P.M.	*The Mysterious Cat* Reading	Entrance cost of $10
Wednesday, Aug. 20, 3:00 P.M.	Knitting Club	Complimentary refreshments
Saturday, Aug. 30, 2:00 P.M.	Photo Exhibition Opening	Entrance cost of $5

GO ON TO THE NEXT PAGE

Clayton Library Community Chat Board

August 1

> User ID: Jjohnson231
Subject: Creative Writers' Workshop, August 2

Hey, is anybody going to go to the writers' workshop tomorrow? I heard that Donna Ward is an outstanding teacher. I could really use some feedback on my latest short story, too. Post if you are going! ~Jim

---

> User ID: Storytimechuck
Subject: re: Creative Writers' Workshop, August 2

Hey Jjohnson231! I am going for sure. You are right; Donna is the best. Her knowledge of narrative and pacing have really helped me with my screenplay. Maybe I could read through your short story after the workshop and give you my feedback, too? The more eyes the better, I always say! I'll let you take a look through my screenplay, too, if you are interested. See you tomorrow! ~Chuck

---

191. What is the purpose of the email?

(A) To introduce new members
(B) To promote upcoming events
(C) To announce some schedule adjustments
(D) To solicit donations

192. What is indicated about Ebert Butler?

(A) His wife is an illustrator.
(B) He has recently published his first book.
(C) He has several cats.
(D) He will receive an award soon.

193. According to the chat board, what does Donna Ward excel at?

(A) Creating vivid photographs
(B) Writing successful screenplays
(C) Understanding the roles of timing and storyline
(D) Working with young poets

194. When can library users meet Kathy Butler?

(A) On Wednesday
(B) On Friday
(C) On Saturday
(D) On Sunday

195. What will likely happen after the creative writers' workshop on August 2?

(A) Everyone will know how to write better poetry.
(B) Chuck and Jim will trade their work to give each other feedback.
(C) Donna Ward will publish her novel.
(D) Chuck and Donna will work on Jim's short story.

(NEW) **Questions 196-200** refer to the following information, form, and letter.

Red Rock Leather Goods

Thank you for purchasing a leather product from Red Rock Leather Goods. We manufacture all of our products to meet the highest quality standards and pride ourselves on excellent customer service. All of our products are individually and meticulously made by skillful craftsmen. We offer a lifetime guarantee that covers all defects in craftsmanship except normal wear and tear. We will repair or replace any faulty piece for as long as you own your Red Rock product.

If your Red Rock product is not under warranty, we offer repairs at the following rates:

	Wallets	Handbags	Jackets
Missing button replacement	$10	$15	$20
Zipper repair or replacement	$20	$30	$45
Seam repair and stitching	$40	$50	$60

The warranty is non-transferable and covers only the original purchaser. Additionally, a sales receipt is required to validate your warranty and receive service. This warranty does not apply to products purchased from second-hand stores or unauthorized dealers.

Red Rock Leather Goods
Repair Request Form

Name: Melisa Perkins
Date: February 28
Address: 458 Center Circle Drive, Chicago, IL
Product: Coco TX Handbag

Description of repairs to be made:
I bought this item last year from a Red Rock Leather Goods store in Chicago, IL. However, after just six months, the zipper became jammed and no longer opens or closes. Because this is a manufacturing defect, I assume it will be covered by the warranty. I have been a regular customer of Red Rock Leather Goods for 12 years, and this is the first time I have had a problem.

I have read and agree to all the terms concerning returns and repairs. I certify that this product was purchased at an official Red Rock Leather Goods store and that I am the original purchaser of this product.
Signature: Melisa Perkins   **Date:** February 28

Note: It may take some time for your product to be returned to you. If you have any questions, please call us at 812-555-8541.

GO ON TO THE NEXT PAGE →

Dear Ms. Perkins,

Thank you for submitting your request for repairs to your Red Rock Leather Goods Coco TX Handbag. We have received and inspected your item and documents, and concluded that it falls within our warranty. It is scheduled to go in for repair this coming week. Once it has been returned to working order, we will express mail it to the address you provided on your repair request form. I would like to thank you on behalf of Red Rock Leather Goods for your 12 years of patronage and apologize for any inconvenience the failure of your Coco TX Handbag has caused you.

Sincerely,

Cheryl Timmins
Customer Service Specialist
Red Rock Leather Goods

196. What is indicated about Red Rock Leather Goods' products?

(A) They are sold nationwide.
(B) They are relatively expensive.
(C) They are made by hand.
(D) They come in a variety of colors.

197. Why did Ms. Perkins fill out a form?

(A) To receive a cash refund for a product
(B) To report a defective item
(C) To file a customer service complaint
(D) To extend a warranty period

198. How much would Ms. Perkins be charged if her item had been purchased at a second-hand store?

(A) $15
(B) $20
(C) $30
(D) $45

199. In the letter to Ms. Perkins, the word "patronage" in line 6 is closest in meaning to which of the following words?

(A) marketing
(B) business
(C) competition
(D) investment

200. What can you infer from the letter to Ms. Perkins approving her request for warranty coverage?

(A) Her handbag suffered normal wear and tear.
(B) Red Rock Leather Goods is a local brand.
(C) She included her receipt from an authorized Red Rock Leather Goods store.
(D) She included $30 for zipper repair to her Coco TX Handbag.

NO TEST MATERIAL ON THIS PAGE

Stop! This is the end of the test. If you finish before time is called, you may go back to Parts 5, 6, and 7 and check your work.

READING TEST

In the Reading test, you will read a variety of texts and answer several different types of reading comprehension questions. The entire Reading test will last 75 minutes. There are three parts, and directions are given for each part. You are encouraged to answer as many questions as possible within the time allowed.

You must mark your answers on the separate answer sheet. Do not write your answers in your test book.

PART 5

Directions: A word or phrase is missing in each of the sentences below. Four answer choices are given below each sentence. Select the best answer to complete the sentence. Then mark the letter (A), (B), (C), or (D) on your answer sheet.

101. Recyclable materials such as glass and plastic are collected ------- weekly on Mondays and Thursdays.

(A) twice
(B) much
(C) yet
(D) far

102. Due to congestion on the roads, an increasing number of manufacturers ------- transport their goods by train.

(A) either
(B) very
(C) now
(D) rather

103. Employees have been instructed ------- the supervisor on duty when a customer has a complaint.

(A) to inform
(B) to have informed
(C) to informing
(D) to be informed

104. Old furniture, vintage jewelry, and other ------- are available for purchase at this market.

(A) quantities
(B) antiques
(C) compartments
(D) statements

105. ------- the necessary safety precautions are not taken, there could be a higher risk of injury.

(A) Just
(B) If
(C) That
(D) From

106. Dissatisfied customers of Maple Housekeeping may terminate their contracts ------- three days of their first cleaning session.

(A) as
(B) by
(C) within
(D) unless

107. The free clinic on Warren Street is ------- by volunteer doctors and nurses.

(A) retained
(B) staffed
(C) founded
(D) produced

108. Ms. Fox extended the operating hours of the store because she agreed ------- Mr. Arbor that they were not long enough.

(A) for
(B) against
(C) to
(D) with

109. Investigators visited the site to ensure that it complied with the ------- industry regulations.

(A) applicability
(B) apply
(C) applies
(D) applicable

110. The majority of people ------- live in Regal Towers are upset about the ongoing problems with their air conditioning systems.

(A) what
(B) where
(C) they
(D) who

111. Mr. Hughes divided the staff into small discussion groups to improve ------- at meetings.

(A) participation
(B) participates
(C) participant
(D) participated

112. The exchange rate has increased by 3.2 percent since the ------- time last year.

(A) only
(B) same
(C) later
(D) true

113. Brenda Tipton is ------- to win the race for the mayor's office because she has the most experience of all the candidates.

(A) predictable
(B) predict
(C) predicts
(D) predicted

114. Those who attend the creative writing workshop will learn a variety of useful skills ------- the next two days.

(A) above
(B) at
(C) toward
(D) over

115. By ------- planning the relocation in advance, we can minimize unexpected expenses and maximize efficiency.

(A) carefully
(B) cares
(C) to care
(D) cared

116. According to company policy, ------- requests for reimbursement of business expenses must be accompanied by receipts.

(A) since
(B) every
(C) all
(D) much

GO ON TO THE NEXT PAGE

117. Safe-Co has ------- home security products since its founding in 2008.

(A) corresponded
(B) functioned
(C) manufactured
(D) enrolled

118. ------- of an error on the order form, some of the construction materials were never shipped.

(A) Because
(B) Even if
(C) In spite
(D) Instead

119. The new policies were implemented in an effort to inspire better ------- among the corporation's departments.

(A) communication
(B) communicative
(C) communicate
(D) communicator

120. Private tours of the old castle will be limited ------- ten people.

(A) to
(B) during
(C) than
(D) of

121. Please do not use metal utensils when cooking with the pan ------- its surface won't get scratched.

(A) since
(B) in order to
(C) while
(D) so that

122. To ------- the monthly mortgage payment, Mr. Tyler would need a substantial salary increase.

(A) admit
(B) suppose
(C) convene
(D) afford

123. Environmentalists were pleased with the community's ------- in increasing recycling in the area.

(A) indifference
(B) cooperation
(C) allocation
(D) separation

124. The National Health Organization reported on the ------- cases of the disease.

(A) confirmation
(B) confirms
(C) confirm
(D) confirmed

125. Due to a ------- in his political beliefs, the senator no longer supported the proposed law on immigration.

(A) shift
(B) compliment
(C) shortage
(D) description

126. ------- buildings in a neighborhood can lead to a net loss of property values for neighboring homeowners.

(A) Fertile
(B) Mandatory
(C) Vacant
(D) Compliant

127. Rather than decorate each conference room -------, the owner of Norris Hall bought furnishings in bulk and gave all the spaces the same appearance.

(A) differing
(B) difference
(C) differently
(D) differs

128. The director attributed the success of the film ------- to the experience and talent of the leading actor in the lead role.

(A) punctually
(B) attentively
(C) primarily
(D) importantly

129. The company's new online banking software is ------- with most smartphone models.

(A) tangible
(B) extensive
(C) mechanical
(D) compatible

130. Employees are allowed to use vacation time whenever they want ------- it does not disrupt their assignments.

(A) except for
(B) as well as
(C) depending on
(D) so long as

GO ON TO THE NEXT PAGE

Directions: Read the texts that follow. A word, phrase, or sentence is missing in parts of each text. Four answer choices for each question are given below the text. Select the best answer to complete the text. Then mark the letter (A), (B), (C), or (D) on your answer sheet.

Questions 131-134 refer to the following email.

From: Vice President Donna Johnson

To: Helio Tech employees

Date: July 5th

Subject: Lobby Renovation

The federal grant money we received last month ------- us to invest in upgrading a few areas
                                              131.
of our building. ------- We will be remodeling the lobby starting July 12th. It should take
                132.
approximately two weeks. ------- that time, if you have a meeting with anyone from outside
                        133.
the company, please arrange to have it at the Rose Street Café on the corner. We have set up
a special account that any employee can use for those two weeks. Please just sign and date
your check and return it to your server. We are ------- that this is a bit of an inconvenience,
                                             134.
and we thank you for your cooperation.

131. (A) did allow
     (B) has allowed
     (C) allows
     (D) are allowing

132. (A) Construction will begin when the
         building permits are received.
     (B) This celebration will last for most of the
         month of July.
     (C) Considering the cost, the renovation
         might be postponed.
     (D) The first area that will benefit from this
         is the lobby.

133. (A) Upon
     (B) During
     (C) Around
     (D) Until

134. (A) aware
     (B) disciplined
     (C) reluctant
     (D) content

Part-Time Cook Needed

Paradise Café is looking ------- a part-time line cook. Applicants must be able to work in a
                        135.
fast-paced environment and be familiar with all standard breakfast fare. ------- This weekend
                                                                          136.
schedule could change in the future. Ideally we are looking for an applicant that has -------
                                                                                      137.
one year of experience working as a short-order cook. Paradise Café is located right next

to the post office in downtown Millstown. Please apply in person with a résumé and be

prepared to cook an egg dish to order. We ------- forward to welcoming you to our team!
                                          138.

---

135. (A) hiring
(B) hire
(C) to hire
(D) to hiring

(NEW)
136. (A) Applicants should know how to make
scrambled eggs.
(B) People applying should know how to
wash dishes.
(C) Anyone applying should be able to
speak Spanish.
(D) Currently we can only offer weekday
shifts, but the applicant must be willing
to work weekends if required.

137. (A) at most
(B) below
(C) at least
(D) the least

138. (A) look
(B) looking
(C) looked
(D) looks

GO ON TO THE NEXT PAGE

Questions 139-142 refer to the following advertisement.

City Realty

City Realty is Washington's number-one real estate company, having served the state for

over 50 years. We ------- recognized as the state's leading experts in the industry, and
     139.

many of our agents have been awarded for their excellence in service by *Forbes Property*

magazine. Our agents are ------- to bringing all of their knowledge and expertise to the table,
     140.

and their knowledge of the housing market's dos and don'ts is second to none. Our agents

specialize in different areas of the industry including corporate real estate, residential real

estate, and rental properties. -------
     141.

Our headquarters, where you can meet with one of our agents ------- a free consultation, is
     142.

located in the central downtown area. You can also visit our website at www.cityrealty.com

for property listings and further information.

---

139. (A) been
    (B) had be
    (C) are being
    (D) have been

140. (A) attached
    (B) faithful
    (C) committed
    (D) loyal

(NEW)

141. (A) You can be confident that they will serve your specific needs.
    (B) You can choose from hundreds of properties in our listings.
    (C) The corporate real estate agents make the most money.
    (D) The residential agents are very busy due to the rising housing market.

142. (A) with
    (B) for
    (C) to
    (D) from

Questions 143-146 refer to the following posting on a website.

Employee Message Board

Holiday Office Party

Success and Appreciation

Posted by Julie Norton

I want to thank everyone who ------- make this party a success. ------- We had some ups
                                    143.   **144.**
and downs when we started preparing for this, but the final result was extraordinary. In fact,

the ------- consensus seems to be that this year's party was the best yet. We had the highest
       145.
turnout ever and many seem to agree that this year's activities contributed to the party's

success. It was a joy to see everyone get along so well and participate in all the events. We

even ------- our children's charity fundraising goals by over $1,000. Once again, I would like
        146.
to thank everyone.

---

143. (A) helps
(B) helped
(C) helping
(D) had help

(NEW)

144. (A) We should order more food and wine.
(B) I worked really hard to plan this event.
(C) Special thanks to Keith, Grant, Vanessa,
and Melissa, who spent many hours
outside of work to help plan everything.
(D) I'm glad to see that everyone dressed
up for the event.

145. (A) regular
(B) familiar
(C) different
(D) general

146. (A) overstepped
(B) surrendered
(C) exceeded
(D) overwhelmed

GO ON TO THE NEXT PAGE

PART 7

Directions: In this part you will read a selection of texts, such as magazine and newspaper articles, emails, and instant messages. Each text or set of texts is followed by several questions. Select the best answer for each question and mark the letter (A), (B), (C), or (D) on your answer sheet.

Questions 147-148 refer to the following letter.

April 3

Larry Martin
Kansas Neat & Tidy
5448 Lakeside Drive
Arlington, Kansas 67514

Dear Mr. Martin,

We are interested in using your company's cleaning services for this year's Halley Valley Rock Festival. The festival will begin on Friday, June 14, and last the entire weekend, ending on the night of Sunday, June 16. However, unlike in previous years, this year we would like your company to clean the festival grounds intermittently throughout the festival. Therefore, we will be providing your company with a temporary office trailer where your workers can take breaks from the heat.

We look forward to working with your company again this year.

Sincerely,

Karen Johnson

Karen Johnson
Festival Coordinator, Halley Valley Foundation

---

147. Who most likely is Mr. Martin?

(A) A musical performer
(B) A truck driver
(C) A cleaning company's representative
(D) A festival coordinator

148. According to the letter, what will be provided?

(A) Food and water
(B) A sheltered area
(C) Musical equipment
(D) Cleaning supplies

Questions 149-150 refer to the following text message chain.

LAURA BURKE	**5:09**
Are you back in the city on Monday?	
ADVIK SHAN	**5:15**
I might be.	
LAURA BURKE	**5:16**
So you're undecided?	
ADVIK SHAN	**5:17**
Yeah. This factory is running into all kinds of problems. Fix one thing and then something else comes up.	
LAURA BURKE	**5:17**
I heard. Well, at least it's nice not to be stuck in the office.	
ADVIK SHAN	**5:18**
That's true.	
ADVIK SHAN	**5:19**
What's happening on Monday?	
LAURA BURKE	**5:20**
Ms. Harris wants to have a meeting with you when you get back. Nothing urgent.	
ADVIK SHAN	**5:22**
OK. I'll let you know when I get my schedule set.	

149. What is suggested about Mr. Shan?

(A) He has missed a meeting.
(B) He is considering a transfer.
(C) He has recently taken over the operations of a manufacturing facility.
(D) He doesn't know when he will be returning to his office.

150. At 5:18, what does Mr. Shan mean when he writes, "That's true"?

(A) He is worried about the conditions in the factory.
(B) He agrees that being out of the office is enjoyable.
(C) He has discovered an error.
(D) He is positive he will be back on Monday.

GO ON TO THE NEXT PAGE

To: Pat Blackburn <pblackburn@fastweb.com>
From: Go Natural Health Products <cs@gonatural.com>
Date: February 4, 3:34 P.M.
Subject: Product Order

We appreciate that you have chosen Go Natural Health Products for your vitamin and mineral supplements. All of our products are carefully inspected for quality and meet all government standards. Additionally, during the month of February, customers making purchases over $100.00 do not have to pay any shipping fees.

Order number: 4330XM21
Order date: February 4, 3:31 P.M.
Shipping address: Pat Blackburn, 2709 Michigan Ave., Clinton, WI
Details: six bottles of Green Source multivitamin pills
Total: $180.00, paid with credit card (XXXX XXXX XXXX 8766)

All our products come with a 100-percent customer satisfaction guarantee. If you are dissatisfied, please call our customer service center at 987-555-3427 for a full refund within a week of your order.

Go Natural Health Products

151. What is indicated about Ms. Blackburn's order?

(A) It has been insured against loss.
(B) It is out of stock.
(C) It was placed by her husband.
(D) It will be delivered free of charge.

152. Why might Ms. Blackburn call the customer service center by February 11?

(A) To revise her order
(B) To change payment options
(C) To get her payment back
(D) To apply for a membership

Questions 153-154 refer to the following article.

Midnight Moon, the new jazz album by guitarist Nick Stanton, will start being sold in stores this Thursday. *Midnight Moon* is Mr. Stanton's first album in five years and has received praise from numerous music critics. Mr. Stanton will be signing copies of his new album at Emerson Department Store, located at 4532 Main Street, this Saturday, March 12. An autograph is free with the purchase of the new album.

153. Who is Nick Stanton?

(A) A record producer
(B) A recording artist
(C) A music critic
(D) A music agent

154. According to the article, what will happen on March 12?

(A) A concert will be held.
(B) A book will be released.
(C) An autograph session will take place.
(D) Some tickets will go on sale.

GO ON TO THE NEXT PAGE

MEMO

To: All employees
From: Betty Franklin, General Manager
Date: August 19
Subject: Receptionist

To all employees:

– [1] – Greta Jones, the receptionist at our studio, will be taking some time off to deal with a personal matter. She will be gone from August 21st to September 5th. – [2] – Ms. Blanche will take care of Ms. Jones' usual responsibilities including taking phone calls, handling appointments, organizing schedules, and dealing with clients. Please welcome Ms. Blanche to the studio and be available for her to ask questions if she has any.

Furthermore, if you have any long-time clients that you give special prices and discounts to, please let Ms. Blanche know ahead of time. – [3] – She will charge the fees that are programmed into the computer system.

If you have any urgent concerns you need to discuss with Ms. Jones, or if you need to purchase any special hair dyes, treatment shampoos, or other such items for customers, please do so today or tomorrow before Ms. Jones leaves. – [4] – You can contact me at any time if you have any further questions.

---

155. Where do the recipients of the memo most likely work?

(A) At a department store
(B) At a hair salon
(C) At a spa
(D) At a makeup studio

156. What is indicated about Greta Jones?

(A) She is retiring.
(B) She is going on vacation.
(C) She will take some time off from work.
(D) She will work only temporarily.

157. When should employees contact Ms. Jones with urgent business?

(A) Before she leaves
(B) After she leaves
(C) Anytime
(D) When she gets back

158. In which of the places marked [1], [2], [3], and [4] does the following sentence belong?

"For this period, we have hired a temporary replacement, Judith Blanche."

(A) [1]
(B) [2]
(C) [3]
(D) [4]

Shoe Shine

Your number one source for sneakers

We see that you are currently registered as a basic member on our website. Click here to upgrade to our premium membership.

Once you become a premium member, you will enjoy the following benefits:
- Expedited shipping for $3 ($5 for a basic member)
- Exchanges on all items within 60 days of purchase at no extra charge (30 days for a basic member)
- Returns on all items within 30 days of purchase at no extra charge (seven days for a basic member)

Upgrading your service from basic to premium takes just one click. To welcome customers to our new online store, this month we are offering the upgrade to annual premium membership at a discounted rate of just $50.

159. What is the purpose of the web page?

(A) To advertise a new line of shoes
(B) To confirm an order
(C) To recommend a service upgrade
(D) To solicit donations

160. What is NOT mentioned as a benefit of premium membership?

(A) Discounts on new items
(B) Faster shipping at a reduced price
(C) A longer period for free returns
(D) A longer period for free exchanges

161. What is indicated about Shoe Shine?

(A) It has been in business for decades.
(B) It was founded by a local entrepreneur.
(C) Its merchandise is available through the Internet.
(D) It has three types of membership.

GO ON TO THE NEXT PAGE

Lisa Hancock 9:39
I'm stopping by a coffee shop on my way to work. What does everyone want? It's on me.

Nick Morton 9:39
Wow! Thanks! I'll just have black coffee.

Lilly Smith 9:40
Thanks. I'd like a latte. Can you also bring some sugar?

Lisa Hancock 9:41
Sure. I'll bring a couple of sugar packets.

Richard Park 9:42
I can never turn down coffee. I'll also have a latte with some sugar.

Emily Jordan 9:42
I'd like an herbal tea if they have any. I don't drink anything caffeinated, so any tea without caffeine would be great. Thanks.

Lisa Hancock 9:43
All right, then. I'll be there in about 20 minutes with your drinks. See you soon. Oh, and before I forget, please make sure that our order from Cindy's Boutique gets set up in our showroom for our clients.

Richard Park 9:44
The boxes arrived this morning and our interns are unpacking them now. However, the order from Chantelle seems to have gone missing.

Lisa Hancock 9:45
What do you mean?

Nick Morton 9:45
We're trying to locate the package. We contacted Chantelle; they sent it to the wrong address.

Lisa Hancock 9:46
That's a disaster. Please try to find out where those dresses went.

Richard Park 9:47
Good news! I just got a message from the shipping company and they found the Chantelle order. They're redirecting the shipment to us.

Lisa Hancock 9:48
I almost had a panic attack. When will it get there?

Richard Park 9:48
This afternoon.

162. What type of business do the speakers probably work at?

(A) A fashion company
(B) A clothing shop
(C) A costume company
(D) A coffee shop

163. At 9:39, what does Lisa Hancock mean when she says, "It's on me"?

(A) She'll bring the coffee.
(B) She'll buy the drinks.
(C) She'll remember everyone's order.
(D) It's her turn to get drinks.

164. What is indicated about one of the speakers' shipments?

(A) It was incorrectly priced.
(B) It was returned to the boutique.
(C) It will arrive later in the day.
(D) It hasn't been located yet.

165. What kind of business is Chantelle?

(A) A fabric company
(B) A magazine company
(C) A shipping company
(D) A boutique

GO ON TO THE NEXT PAGE

Questions 166-168 refer to the following email.

> To   All <csall@cherishedgoods.com>
> From   Eric Nixon <enix@cherishedgoods.com>
> Date   January 5, 10:00 A.M.
> Subject Shipping Error
>
> Hello everyone,
>
> Lilia Kent, the head of the shipping department, has informed me that yesterday our customer database experienced a system error and as a result many orders were sent to the wrong addresses. This morning our department has already received multiple calls from customers complaining that they received the wrong packages. Ms. Kent's department has been working hard to locate the cause of the mistake. Therefore, any customer that calls about a wrong delivery should be asked to return the package. Additionally, please inform the customers that they will be given a 10-percent discount on their next purchase.
>
> Eric Nixon

166. Who most likely received this email?

(A) Employees in the shipping department
(B) Dissatisfied customers
(C) Customer service representatives
(D) Internet technology specialists

167. According to the email, what is Ms. Kent's staff trying to do?

(A) Create a customer database
(B) Fix a system malfunction
(C) Locate a lost package
(D) Take calls from customers

168. What are recipients of the email advised to do?

(A) Update their personal information
(B) Deliver packages in person
(C) Enter data into a customer database
(D) Offer a price reduction to some customers

Questions 169-171 refer to the following email.

To:	carlhurst@nicknet.com
From:	m_winters@tatecc.com
Date:	June 1, 1:34 P.M.
Subject:	Community Events

Dear Mr. Hurst,

As a loyal customer with a family membership at the Tate Community Center, you have sponsored us with your continued donations. We really appreciate your support.

The following table provides information on upcoming family events this month. We welcome your participation.

Crafts Day, June 7	Paul Simpson, June 15	Summer Picnic, June 22
A variety of craft supplies will be available for kids to make their own unique creations.	Come and listen to the beautiful music of local singer and songwriter Paul Simpson.	Everyone needs to bring a tasty dish to share with others. Free beverages will be provided.

For members, no purchase of tickets is necessary for participation in these events. We encourage you to attend these events and spend quality time with your family.

We look forward to seeing you.

Minnie Winters
Program Coordinator
Tate Community Center

---

169. What is suggested about Mr. Hurst?

(A) He is a local musician.
(B) He donates to an orphanage.
(C) He supports a public organization.
(D) He works at a community center.

170. Why was the email sent?

(A) To announce a community board meeting
(B) To apply for a family membership
(C) To publicize upcoming events
(D) To give information about a local election

171. What is indicated about the Tate Community Center?

(A) Its members gain free admission to events.
(B) It offers regular music classes.
(C) It takes reservations by phone.
(D) It serves beverages at all events.

GO ON TO THE NEXT PAGE

J&P Industries

1462 Swinton Street
Cameron, NY 10288

March 29
Mr. Grant Lee
287 Silver Plains Road
Cameron, NY 18729

Dear Mr. Lee,

We thank you for your continued work and your dedication to your job at J&P Industries. We are sending all employees information about recent changes that have been made to your health insurance benefits with our company. You will continue to be covered by the same insurance company, but because of the new state regulations that have been put forth, all employees must now undergo a basic medical checkup at a local clinic or hospital. – [1] – This checkup will be covered by your health insurance, so you do not need to pay any extra fees and this will by no means affect your monthly insurance deductions. – [2] – Included in this envelope is detailed information about the new medical program for employees.

The medical checkup must include a blood test, urine test, eye test, height and weight measurements, hearing test, and chest X-rays. – [3] – Please make an appointment with a local clinic. You should have your results sent to Karen Leigh in human resources by December 30th at the latest. If you fail to get a medical exam, you may be subject to a fine of up to $2000. – [4] – We thank you for your cooperation and hope you will abide by the new changes.

If you have any further questions or concerns, please contact Karen at leighk@jpindustries.com.

Sincerely,

John Black

Executive Manager

J&P Industries

172. What is the purpose of the letter?

(A) To inform an employee about a mandatory exam
(B) To encourage employees to donate blood to a hospital
(C) To discuss the changes made to employees' health insurance coverage
(D) To advertise the services of a new clinic

173. What did Mr. Black send with the letter?

(A) An application form
(B) An insurance document
(C) A contract
(D) Extra information about the changes

174. The term "subject to" at the end of the second paragraph is closest in meaning to:

(A) dependent on
(B) responsible for
(C) withdrawn from
(D) added to

175. In which of places marked [1], [2], [3], and [4] does this sentence belong?

"The appointments should take no longer than 30 minutes."

(A) [1]
(B) [2]
(C) [3]
(D) [4]

GO ON TO THE NEXT PAGE

Blooming Flower Yoga Studio

Summer Yoga Classes

This summer we will be offering a variety of yoga classes for all age groups and skill levels.

Summer Class Schedule and Prices (registration fee):
· Beginner class, twice a week for two months ($150)
· Intermediate and advanced class, twice a week for two months ($200)
· Yoga for senior citizens, once a week for two months ($100)
· Hot power yoga, three times a week for two months ($250)

All necessary supplies will be provided by the Blooming Flower Yoga Studio. Students should wear comfortable clothes that allow for free movement.

45 Clark Street
Indianapolis, IN 46202
715-555-5832
www.bloomingfloweryoga.com

To: Tammy Glenn <tammyglenn@mxmail.com>
From: Dwayne Moore <dwaynemoore@bloomingfloweryoga.com>
Date: May 23
Subject: New Student
Attachment: New member form

Dear Ms. Glenn,

I'm writing to let you know that you have one more student who has signed up for your class. Your new student is Jane Meyers and she will bring the $100 registration fee with her to the first class on Monday.

Also, on Monday, please give Ms. Meyers and any other new members the form they will need to fill out. I have attached the necessary paperwork to this email. All you have to do is print out copies and hand them out.

Your class now has nine students that will attend and is, therefore, almost at full capacity. In fact, all of the classes this summer have proven very popular, and I anticipate that they will all fill up by the end of the month. Thank you so much for your many years of hard work as a teacher here at Blooming Flower Yoga Studio. If you have any questions, let me know.

Dwayne Moore

176. What is stated about the summer classes?

(A) They started last week.
(B) They will be held outdoors.
(C) They are available to both children and adults.
(D) They are being offered at a discounted price.

177. What is suggested about Ms. Meyers?

(A) She has never studied yoga before.
(B) She is an elderly person.
(C) She wants to become a yoga instructor.
(D) She is a long-time student.

178. What is Ms. Glenn asked to do?

(A) Develop a new curriculum
(B) Attend a training seminar
(C) Sign a work contract
(D) Distribute some documents

179. In the email, the word "capacity" in paragraph 3, line 1, is closest in meaning to:

(A) volume
(B) ability
(C) vacancy
(D) role

180. What is indicated about Ms. Glenn?

(A) She works well with children.
(B) She is a long-time employee.
(C) She will be retiring soon.
(D) She will be receiving a pay raise.

GO ON TO THE NEXT PAGE

Mega Hobby Models Community Forum

Issue with the Blackbeard's Pirate Ship Model

August 3, 10:55 A.M.

Post by John Taylor

I recently purchased a model kit from the Mega Hobby online store. I bought the Blackbeard's Pirate Ship model to put together with my son, and I am having a problem. After carefully reading the instruction manual, I noticed that a few essential parts had been left out of the box. Specifically, some parts that make up the mast and sail seem to be absent from the kit. I have bought many Mega Hobby models over the years, and have always been happy with the products I've received.

Has anyone else had the same problem with this kit? My son and I were planning to submit our finished model to a local model-building contest at the end of the month, and we are very disappointed by this setback. If anyone else has experienced this problem and solved it, I would greatly appreciate your advice.

Mega Hobby Models Community Forum

RE: Issue with the Blackbeard's Pirate Ship Model

August 3, 4:24 P.M.

Post by Catherine Maxwell

Hi John,

I also recently purchased the Blackbeard's Pirate Ship model from the Mega Hobby online store for my son and had the same problem that you did. At first I thought I must have been mistaken, but after checking the list of all parts in the instruction manual, I determined that several parts must have been missing from the kit at the time of sale. I took the kit back to my local Mega Hobby store and a staff member confirmed my suspicion. The Mega Hobby employee was nice enough to exchange my model kit for one that had all of the parts. With the new kit, my son and I were able to put the model together exactly like the picture on the box. I suggest that you go to the Mega Hobby store closest to your home and ask to exchange your defective product. Be sure to make a note of the order number when you go there.

181. What is the subject of the first post?

(A) A defect with a purchased product
(B) Mistakes in an instruction manual
(C) A discrepancy with an advertised price
(D) Registration for a competition

182. What is suggested about Mr. Taylor?

(A) He knows Ms. Maxwell personally.
(B) He is a product designer at Mega Hobby.
(C) He owns a sailboat.
(D) He will enter a competition with his son.

183. How did both Mr. Taylor and Ms. Maxwell realize there was a problem?

(A) By talking with a customer service agent
(B) By watching an instructional video
(C) Be consulting a user manual
(D) By looking at a photograph

184. What is indicated about Ms. Maxwell?

(A) She is a regular customer of Mega Hobby.
(B) She works with Mr. Taylor at Mega Hobby.
(C) She successfully assembled the model.
(D) She received a full refund.

185. What does Ms. Maxwell recommend?

(A) Visiting a nearby store
(B) Canceling a membership
(C) Downloading a new instruction manual
(D) Purchasing replacement parts

GO ON TO THE NEXT PAGE

Dreamspace Bed Emporium

Beds, Bedding, and Furniture
3600 Wilshire Road, Springfield, IL 62751
www.dreamspacebeds.com

Don't let yourself suffer tossing and turning, not getting a good night's sleep. Come down to Dreamspace Bed Emporium and treat yourself to a comfortable bed catered to your exact needs. Customers are welcome to lie on any bed in the store.

First Floor: Beds (single, double, queen, king, etc.)
Second Floor: Bedding (sheets, pillows, blankets, cushions, etc.)
Third Floor: Furniture (chairs, sofas, tables, etc.)

In response to customer suggestions, our store now stays open two hours later to accommodate those who may work irregular shifts.

Do you need express delivery of a bed? Simply ask one of our staff members at the checkout counter and it will be easily arranged.

If you have any comments or suggestions for our store, a comment box can be found inside the main entrance.

Comment and Suggestion Form

Dreamspace Bed Emporium

Customer name: Willy M. King
Date: August 9
Contact number: 456-555-6123

Comment: Last week, I came into your store to shop for a new pillow, sheet, and blanket set for my bed. However, when I went to that section, I couldn't find any available staff members to assist me. I waited for about half an hour, but no one came to me. I needed help determining what sheet and blanket set would fit the dimensions of my bed, but ended up just leaving the store frustrated. I hope you can provide better service to customers so something like this doesn't happen again in the future. I have been a loyal customer of yours for years. If you don't explain why no one helped me, I may have to start shopping at one of your competitors' stores.

Hello everybody. I have called this meeting to talk about some of the problems that our new store policy of staying open later has caused. At first, this seemed like a great idea to help customers who work all day. I know it can be hard to find time to do chores and shopping when you work from 9 to 5. Unfortunately, staying open later means that we have had to spread our staff too thin while we wait to hire and train more people.

As a result, we have been neglecting some of our customers lately. The photocopied comment and suggestion form I have passed out to you all from Willy King sums up our shortcomings better than I ever could. Please give it a read and think about ways we can be made to be aware of a customer in need in a store as large as ours. I understand that with our thin staff we have to cover more space than we used to, so this meeting isn't about punishment or blame; it's just about solutions. Please do some brainstorming on this and drop by my office if you think you have an idea. I have to go call Willy King.

186. What is NOT mentioned about the beds at Dreamspace Bed Emporium?

(A) They come in a variety of sizes.
(B) They can be tested by customers.
(C) They are displayed on the first floor.
(D) They come with a lifetime warranty.

187. According to the advertisement, what is true about Dreamspace Bed Emporium?

(A) It is located in a department store.
(B) It sells home appliances.
(C) It is hiring additional staff.
(D) It has extended its operating hours.

188. Where did Mr. King most likely search for the products he wanted?

(A) On the first floor
(B) On the second floor
(C) On the third floor
(D) Near the main entrance

189. Who do you believe is speaking at the meeting?

(A) The Dreamspace Bed Emporium manager
(B) Willy King
(C) A district manager from another city
(D) A checkout clerk

190. What is most likely true based upon the information from the meeting?

(A) Dreamspace Bed Emporium will change its hours back to what they used to be.
(B) Dreamspace Bed Emporium will extend its hours to serve more customers like Willy King.
(C) Dreamspace Bed Emporium will hire more employees so there are enough people to cover the whole store.
(D) Dreamspace Bed Emporium will hold a raffle event and invite Willy King.

GO ON TO THE NEXT PAGE

http://www.acestafftraining.com

| Home | Contact Us | Location | About Ace |

Ace Training is a company that offers developmental courses for the employees of your store or business. You can rely on our team of successful professionals to improve the quality of your staff and help your company achieve its goals. We provide effective and results-oriented programs. Below are the training courses available:

Leadership	Sales
This program helps staff members develop strategic planning and management skills. It also enhances the supervisory skills of employees in leadership positions.	We teach innovative strategies to increase sales and market share. This class is suitable for both in-store salespeople and employees who work over the phone.
Customer Service	Technologies
Never undervalue the importance of your customers' satisfaction. Your employees need the skills to be helpful and efficient when working directly with customers.	In rapidly changing work environments, staff members should keep up with new trends and developments in the technological field. Your staff members will learn how to research and master new technologies quickly and accurately.

To enroll staff members in a program, contact Joshua York at josh@acestafftraining.com.

From: Tiffany Tran <tifftran@zellengifts.com>
To: Joshua York <josh@acestafftraining.com>
Subject: Staff Training for Our Employees
Date: October 9

Dear Mr. York,

I'm contacting you about running a training program for some of our employees here at Zellen Gifts. We are planning on expanding our telemarketing department next month, but we don't have enough properly trained employees to fill the new positions. Therefore, we will be transferring some employees from the customer service department to the telemarketing department to solve this problem. As our products are mainly targeted towards children, we are hoping to increase our profits as much as possible during this Christmas season. Please let me know the maximum number of trainees that you can accommodate at one time.

Thank you,

Tiffany Tran
Zellen Gifts

PROPOSED ACE TRAINING SCHEDULE
FOR ZELLEN GIFTS
November 1–5

Group Code and Trainee Numbers	Monday Sales Strategies	Tuesday Successful Negotiation	Wednesday Customers First!	Thursday Closing the Deal	Friday Start Polite, Stay Polite
Red Team 10 people	9–11	9–11:30	8–10:30	8–11	9–11
Blue Team 10 people	1–3	1–3	1–3	1–3	1–3
Green Team 10 people	3–5	3–5	3–5	3–5	3–5
White Team 10 people	5–7	5–7	5–7	5–7	5–7

Here is our proposed schedule for transitioning your customer service staff into successful telemarketers. You can see that we have an ambitious amount of material to cover, but I am confident that the program will be a success. We have tried to balance your need for a swift transition with your need to continue running Zellen Gifts while the training is in session. Therefore, we have divided your staff into groups and staggered them throughout the day. This will result in better trainee-to-trainer numbers for your staff, and should cause minimal disruption to your business. We look forward to a great week of training!

Joshua York,
Ace Training Coordinator

GO ON TO THE NEXT PAGE

191. Where does Mr. York work?

    (A) At an accounting firm
    (B) At a sports management agency
    (C) At a skills development organization
    (D) At an advertising agency

192. What is stated about the program on technologies?

    (A) It is open to the public.
    (B) It includes current web programming skills.
    (C) It teaches environmental protection.
    (D) It keeps employees up-to-date.

193. What program is Ms. Tran most likely interested?

    (A) Leadership
    (B) Sales
    (C) Customer Service
    (D) Technologies

194. What is indicated by the proposed training schedule and accompanying memo?

    (A) It is an easy course to complete.
    (B) There are five key topics that will be covered.
    (C) Fifty employees will take part.
    (D) Joshua York will be one of the trainers.

195. Based upon the proposed training schedule and accompanying memo, what can be inferred about Zellen Gifts?

    (A) They are trying to become better at customer relations.
    (B) They want to conduct business as usual during their training period.
    (C) They have a small customer service staff.
    (D) They want to finish their training before the end of October.

Midcity Performing Arts Hall

Support the Midcity Performing Arts Hall in downtown Brenton by becoming a member. You can choose from the following membership plans:

General – For only $100 you can get a one-year membership and attend any two performances that have seats available in the D area of the theater.

Silver – For a fee of $200, you can attend any two performances that have seats available in the B area of the theater.

Gold – For a fee of $500, you will receive early alerts about popular programs, tickets to any two performances with seats in the B area, and a guaranteed front row seat at any show of your choice within a one-year period.

Diamond – For a fee of $1,000, you will have exclusive access to performers' autograph signings, invitations to two exclusive pre-showings of popular programs, and a guaranteed VIP seat at any show of your choice within a one-year period.

*Some restrictions do apply.

*Admission to orchestral performances excluded.

To:	bates@midcityarthall.com
From:	Alicia Norton
Date:	January 16
Subject:	membership

Thank you for your email about Midcity Performing Arts Hall memberships. I have paid a fee of $1,000. I was a general member last year, and I enjoyed a couple of the musicals that were performed. I have become a theater enthusiast thanks to that experience, and I look forward to the benefits of the new membership plan.

By the way, the arts hall has done a phenomenal job on its renovations. I'm excited to come back this year.

GO ON TO THE NEXT PAGE ➡

Below is the tentative schedule for shows at the Midcity Performing Arts Hall in the coming months. Please have a look and call anytime if you wish to get seats.

Brenton Philharmonic Orchestra	January 28 to January 30
Dancing Princess	February 3 to February 23
Jazz that Dance	March 1 to March 26
Opera Ghost	April 3 to April 29

196. Which membership did Alicia Norton most likely purchase?

(A) General
(B) Silver
(C) Gold
(D) Diamond

197. What is suggested about the Midcity Performing Arts Hall?

(A) It hosts various sports programs.
(B) Some changes have been made to its building.
(C) It is a place popular among celebrities.
(D) It is an old museum.

198. When is a performance NOT free for members?

(A) January
(B) February
(C) March
(D) April

199. What is implied about the schedule?

(A) The shows have all sold out.
(B) More shows may be added.
(C) It is fixed.
(D) It may change.

200. What is meant by the expression "some restrictions do apply"?

(A) Only certain people will be considered for membership.
(B) The membership plans may change without notice.
(C) Not all performances are available to members.
(D) Non-members will not be admitted.

NO TEST MATERIAL ON THIS PAGE

Stop! This is the end of the test. If you finish before time is called, you may go back to Parts 5, 6, and 7 and check your work.

READING TEST

In the Reading test, you will read a variety of texts and answer several different types of reading comprehension questions. The entire Reading test will last 75 minutes. There are three parts, and directions are given for each part. You are encouraged to answer as many questions as possible within the time allowed.

You must mark your answers on the separate answer sheet. Do not write your answers in your test book.

PART 5

Directions: A word or phrase is missing in each of the sentences below. Four answer choices are given below each sentence. Select the best answer to complete the sentence. Then mark the letter (A), (B), (C), or (D) on your answer sheet.

101. Our spokesperson will explain an ------- opportunity for property investors.

(A) excitedly
(B) excitement
(C) excited
(D) exciting

102. Some of the leather used in this handbag must ------- from Italy.

(A) will import
(B) be imported
(C) to import
(D) have imported

103. Rockwell Bank's automated teller machines are ------- located in various sections of the city.

(A) abruptly
(B) conveniently
(C) fluently
(D) periodically

104. As soon as both sides reach ------- terms, the licensing contract will be signed.

(A) agreeable
(B) agree
(C) agreement
(D) agreed

105. Anyone who cannot ------- one of the safety training workshops before September 1 should inform his or her manager.

(A) impress
(B) employ
(C) attend
(D) reply

106. ------- for using the hotel's spa and dining services will appear on your final invoice.

(A) Charge
(B) Charges
(C) Charging
(D) Charged

107. Members of the security team have been instructed to report ------- unattended bag to the local police department.

(A) any
(B) much
(C) most
(D) all

108. The head chef has the restaurant manager ------- the order for ingredients every evening.

(A) authoritative
(B) authority
(C) authorities
(D) authorize

109. The automotive company ------- pursued technologies that would improve the efficiency of its engines.

(A) aggressive
(B) aggressiveness
(C) aggressively
(D) aggression

110. On the first day of the painting course, students should provide the teacher with proof of -------.

(A) registration
(B) proposal
(C) accumulation
(D) copyright

111. The furniture in this apartment is not -------, but belongs to the landlord and must be returned at the end of the lease.

(A) ours
(B) we
(C) our
(D) us

112. The driver ------- Mr. Dwight is expected to arrive at the conference venue 20 minutes prior to the finishing time.

(A) until
(B) in
(C) for
(D) among

113. Three of the new chemists, who ------- developed the material, will be recognized by the CEO at Saturday's ceremony.

(A) collaborating
(B) collaborate
(C) collaboratively
(D) collaborative

114. The goal of the program is to make health services readily available to those in both rural and urban -------.

(A) purposes
(B) settings
(C) monuments
(D) standards

115. Please send a check in the amount of £550 ------- the document that needs to be checked by our agency.

(A) despite
(B) while
(C) with
(D) through

116. Fingerprint systems are generally ------- as the primary form of security at laboratories in this country.

(A) to accept
(B) accept
(C) accepting
(D) accepted

GO ON TO THE NEXT PAGE

117. Living further from the city center will
------- your rental costs, but will also affect
your commute.

(A) shorten
(B) misplace
(C) lower
(D) collapse

118. FryMate brand cookware can be purchased
directly from the company's website or at a
retailer ------- you.

(A) against
(B) to
(C) along
(D) near

119. Weekly ------- of the facility help to
ensure that minor maintenance issues are
discovered and resolved early.

(A) investigations
(B) investigated
(C) investigative
(D) investigates

120. Patients should call the emergency line
immediately if they experience -------
changes in temperature.

(A) sudden
(B) contemporary
(C) ideal
(D) reasonable

121. Those who are taking part in the half-day
historical tour should be at the meeting
point ------- than 7:45 A.M.

(A) as for
(B) particularly
(C) whenever
(D) no later

122. The supervisor allowed Mr. Martin to take
three additional vacation days because of
his ------- achievement.

(A) unlimited
(B) noteworthy
(C) identical
(D) satisfied

123. Ms. Stevens ------- acknowledged that she
had been unable to complete the task in
the specified time frame.

(A) regretfully
(B) regret
(C) regrets
(D) regretful

124. The customer's steak was -------
undercooked, so he requested that it be
sent back to the kitchen.

(A) rather
(B) such
(C) many
(D) rarely

125. The contact details provided on this survey
are for in-house purposes and will not be
------- to any third party.

(A) suspended
(B) responded
(C) equipped
(D) released

126. Mr. Brannon can assemble the shelves for
the booth ------- as long as he has a set of
tools.

(A) his
(B) himself
(C) him
(D) his own

127. Ms. Stevenson contacted the real estate agent ------- name and phone number appeared in the advertisement.

(A) what
(B) which
(C) whose
(D) who

128. The home's sale becomes ------- when the official document is recorded at the county office.

(A) finally
(B) finalize
(C) finals
(D) final

129. The main activity at the workshop required team members to ------- with each other.

(A) cooperate
(B) oversee
(C) shrink
(D) encounter

130. According to the physician, Ms. Oliver's pain ------- within two hours of her taking the medication.

(A) alleviated
(B) will be alleviated
(C) is alleviating
(D) should be alleviated

GO ON TO THE NEXT PAGE

PART 6

Directions: Read the texts that follow. A word, phrase, or sentence is missing in parts of each text. Four answer choices for each question are given below the text. Select the best answer to complete the text. Then mark the letter (A), (B), (C), or (D) on your answer sheet.

Questions 131-134 refer to the following advertisement.

International Goods Fair

If you want ------- your packaged goods to an international audience, join the eighth annual
131.

International Goods Fair. The fair runs from March 5th to March 7th at the Galaxy Convention

Center in downtown New York City. With over 200 companies from all over the world

-------, you can make business connections while promoting your own products to interested
132.

customers and businesses. The products should be mainly packaged foods ranging -------
133.

desserts and snacks to canned meats and dried jerky. ------- Spots are limited and going
134.

fast.

---

131. (A) promotion
(B) promoting
(C) to promote
(D) have promoted

132. (A) represented
(B) expressed
(C) delivered
(D) revealed

133. (A) to
(B) for
(C) from
(D) with

134. (A) Ice creams will not be allowed on the premises.
(B) You can sample items as you browse.
(C) You'll have a chance to promote your food of choice.
(D) Apply for a booth now before they're all taken.

Questions 135-138 refer to the following notice.

From: Vice President, Jordan Smith

To: K Group Employees

Subject: Company Renovations

Date: February 26

To all employees,

This weekend the renovations to our second-floor offices -------. We ask that you take home
135.

all important documents and file away any loose materials on your desks. All electronic

devices should be turned off and unplugged. -------, all cabinets and drawers should be
136.

locked.

The renovations will take approximately five days. ------- If you have any meetings scheduled
137.

with clients next week, please arrange to meet them outside the company premises due to

the noise. We apologize for the inconvenience but we ask for your -------. Thank you.
138.

135. (A) has began
     (B) will begin
     (C) beginning
     (D) begun

136. (A) Furthermore
     (B) As a consequence
     (C) Because
     (D) Therefore

137. (A) If they need more space, we will notify
         you.
     (B) All business will be suspended until the
         renovations end.
     (C) During this time, your temporary
         workspace will be the first-floor
         conference room.
     (D) Your office space will look new and
         improved after the renovations.

138. (A) service
     (B) association
     (C) connection
     (D) cooperation

GO ON TO THE NEXT PAGE

ACTUAL TEST

08

Attorney Opening

Johnson and Kindness PLC has an immediate opening for a contract attorney. The ideal candidate would have at least three years of experience ------- on complex business
              139.
transactions. ------- The types of contract work that we ------- at Johnson and Kindness
              140.   **141.**
deal exclusively with business relationships between private companies and the government.

If ------- feel that you are qualified to join our team, please email our HR manager at JK@law.
    142.
com.

---

139. (A) working
     (B) work
     (C) to work
     (D) worked

140. (A) Government experience would also be a plus.
     (B) Working with children would help your résumé.
     (C) Experience with animals is essential.
     (D) Working with disabled people is a bonus.

141. (A) perform
     (B) achieve
     (C) allow
     (D) transform

142. (A) you
     (B) I
     (C) we
     (D) they

Questions 143-146 refer to the following email.

To:	bobsaget@BobsJobs.com
From:	HarrisonG@gmail.com
Date:	September 20
Subject:	business proposal

Dear Mr. Saget,

My name is Harrison Goodbody. I am ------- in response to the advertisement you placed
                                       143.
in the *Times* for a new human resource manager. I have five years' ------- working in a fast-
                                                                        144.
paced corporate environment. I understand that your firm employs upwards of 300 people

and many of them speak Spanish. ------- I have attached my résumé and would be happy
                                  145.

------- provide excellent references should you request them. Thank you for your time.
146.

Sincerely,

Harrison Goodbody

GO ON TO THE NEXT PAGE

143. (A) message
(B) to write
(C) writing
(D) looking

144. (A) experience
(B) knowledge
(C) work
(D) internship

145. (A) I am a certified level five speaker of Spanish.
(B) Spanish people can be hard to work with.
(C) I don't know any Spanish, but I could study.
(D) Spanish speakers are good workers.

146. (A) in
(B) to
(C) for
(D) will

PART 7

Directions: In this part you will read a selection of texts, such as magazine and newspaper articles, emails, and instant messages. Each text or set of texts is followed by several questions. Select the best answer for each question and mark the letter (A), (B), (C), or (D) on your answer sheet.

Questions 147-148 refer to the following information.

The new Sensonic curved television is now on sale at the shockingly low price of just $1,999. Enjoy your favorite television shows, movies, and games on a 55-inch screen that offers ultra-high-definition images! Best of all, you don't have to struggle with a complicated instruction manual. Just take the television home and install it, and it begins working with your preferences immediately without the need for annoying adjustments.

147. Where would this information most likely appear?

(A) In an instruction manual
(B) On a product receipt
(C) In a promotional flyer
(D) In a letter

148. What is mentioned as a convenient feature of the product?

(A) Its simple set-up procedure
(B) Its long warranty period
(C) Its compatibility with other devices
(D) Its detailed instructions

Questions 149-150 refer to the following text message chain.

Tom Arnold	**11:55**
Are you coming back to the office today?	
Richard Hewitt	**12:08**
Yeah. I just finished that pitch to Anderson & Wright about the riverside restaurant.	
Tom Arnold	**12:13**
Great. How did it go?	
Richard Hewitt	**12:13**
I think they might bite.	
Tom Arnold	**12:13**
Nice. It'd be great to have them in on this project.	
Richard Hewitt	**12:14**
Exactly!	
Tom Arnold	**12:35**
Can you join Harold and me for lunch at one at the Kettle Room?	
Richard Hewitt	**12:35**
Sure. I'll have the cab change directions and meet you there.	
Tom Arnold	**12:39**
Good. See you soon.	

149. What is suggested about Mr. Hewitt?

    (A) He is late for a lunch appointment.
    (B) He has accepted a new position.
    (C) He is in a taxi.
    (D) He is on his way to a presentation.

150. At 12:14, what does Mr. Hewitt mean when he writes, "Exactly"?

    (A) He would like to know where they're having lunch.
    (B) He is looking forward to meeting Anderson & Wright.
    (C) He is on his way back to the office.
    (D) He would also like Anderson & Wright to join the project.

GO ON TO THE NEXT PAGE

The buzz at New York's premier book fair is all about the upcoming book from poet-turned-novelist Harry S. Tepper. *The Nightingales of Fall* is the eagerly awaited sequel to his best-selling debut novel, *The Swallows of Spring*. The book follows the journey of Sally Harknett through the weird world of Underfell, mixing social commentary with sharp wit and just a dash of magic and mystery. Tepper burst onto the scene over a decade ago with the acclaimed poetry collection *King Harmon's Castle*, and the expectation is that this latest novel will be another chart-topping success. Later this week the first copies will be made available in a prize drawing at the New York Book Fair, with the official launch at major bookstores next month.

151. How would Mr. Tepper's latest book most likely be classified?

(A) Romance
(B) Historical fiction
(C) Fantasy
(D) Poetry

152. Where will copies of the book be available this week?

(A) At all major bookstores
(B) On a website
(C) At a literary event
(D) In selected public libraries

```
                                                              ⬛⬛❌
```

To: All Subscribers
From: Customer Support <customersupport@stylefashionmz.com>
Date: June 5
Subject: New Edition

Dear loyal subscribers,

Style & Fashion Magazine is excited to announce the launch of the new digital edition of our monthly magazine this summer. Although the print and digital edition will be nearly identical, the digital edition will contain some longer articles and images that won't appear in the print edition.

Current subscribers to the print edition of our magazine will automatically receive a code that will allow access to the digital edition. Your code will be included with next month's print magazine when it is delivered to your house.

153. What is the purpose of the email?

(A) To offer a discounted subscription rate
(B) To advertise a new online shopping mall
(C) To introduce a digital publication
(D) To remind some subscribers to renew their subscriptions

154. What can subscribers find in the paper edition in July?

(A) A discount coupon
(B) A special supplement
(C) An exclusive interview
(D) An access code

GO ON TO THE NEXT PAGE

Questions 155-158 refer to the following article.

More Buses During the Holidays

November 28— – [1] – Although the holiday season signals a nice week-long vacation for many, bus drivers will work longer hours and straight through the holidays to accommodate the many tourists that are flooding the city at this time of year and the shoppers that are busy buying those last-minute gifts. – [2] – The city has announced new bus schedules for the next few weeks which include some routes on which buses will run all day and all night. While most buses stop running by 1 A.M., some parts of downtown will see buses running all night. The Bingham shopping district will see buses running until 3 A.M. "This is when we have the most tourists and out-of-town folks coming to visit," explained Mayor Bill Nate. "We felt it was important to provide the necessary services during this time." – [3] –

When the bus drivers' union leader, Nathan Reiner, was asked about the new schedules, he responded, "We worked out a payment plan that is agreeable on both sides and have enough drivers that can work in shifts so that there is no danger of overworking or exhaustion. Many of us will still get some time off during the holidays with our families." – [4] –

---

155. What is the purpose of the article?

(A) To report changes in public transportation
(B) To describe the city during the holidays
(C) To inform the public about traffic delays
(D) To advertise new shopping centers

156. What is suggested about Mr. Reiner?

(A) He is happy with the mayor.
(B) He may stage a protest.
(C) He is satisfied with the working conditions.
(D) He would like some time off for the holidays.

157. What is stated about the city during the holiday season?

(A) It closes down for the holidays.
(B) Many visitors come from out of town.
(C) Many taxi drivers lose business.
(D) The citizens travel to other cities.

158. In which of the places marked [1], [2], [3], and [4] does the following sentence belong?

"Overall, the city seems prepared for the influx of tourists and holiday shoppers as Christmas draws near."

(A) [1]
(B) [2]
(C) [3]
(D) [4]

Channel 19 Program Schedule

March 3

6:00 A.M. – 7:00 A.M.
Life in Alaska
Follow the life of Ken Ruskin, a fisherman living in the remote Alaskan tundra.

7:00 A.M. – 9:00 A.M.
Amazing Sights of Africa
Learn about the diverse animals and plants of the African savanna.

9:00 A.M. – 10:30 A.M.
Anatomy of a Dinosaur
In this episode, paleontologist Dr. Kerry Peterson tells you everything you want to know about the tyrannosaurus.

10:30 A.M. – 11:00 A.M.
Rocky
Host Dan Reed demonstrates how to survive the extreme conditions of the Canadian outdoors in winter.

11:00 A.M. – 1:00 P.M.
Natural Phenomenon
Host Julia Fromm investigates the most mysterious naturally occurring phenomena on Earth.

1:00 P.M. – 2:00 P.M.
Blue Ocean
Travel with us to the ocean waters around Australia, where diver Pat Russell finds dolphins, sharks, seals, and much more.

ACTUAL TEST

08

159. What is the focus of the channel?

(A) Plants
(B) Sports
(C) Nature
(D) Lifestyle

160. According to the schedule, who is a scientist?

(A) Pat Russell
(B) Dan Reed
(C) Kerry Peterson
(D) Ken Ruskin

161. Which program will teach viewers survival skills?

(A) *Anatomy of a Dinosaur*
(B) *Amazing Sights of Africa*
(C) *Blue Ocean*
(D) *Rocky*

GO ON TO THE NEXT PAGE

Questions 162-165 refer to the following online chat discussion.

J&R International Group Discussion

Sunny Rhee [5:37] Is anyone unable to make it to Friday's office party?

Kevin King [5:38] I can be there for the first hour, but I need to leave early for a family get-together.

Patrick Stone [5:39] I have a business trip to Hong Kong the next day so I'm going to take a pass this year.

Sunny Rhee [5:42] Is that everyone, then? I just want to make sure that we have enough snacks. Eva, have you contacted the caterers yet?

Eva Sanderson [5:43] I called a couple of different places, but only Four-Leaf Catering offers vegan options.

Sunny Rhee [5:44] Why don't we give them a try, then? I think a couple of people here are vegans.

Holly Johnson [5:45] I don't normally like to advertise my eating preferences, but I would love to have vegan options this time.

Eva Sanderson [5:46] I agree. I think it would make everything more interesting. I'm thinking of trying to go vegan myself and this would be a good first step for me.

Holly Johnson [5:47] Well, it's not easy, but I'll be there to support you.

Eva Sanderson [5:47] Thanks. I'll order our platters from the caterers, then.

Angelo Smith [5:48] But make sure there are some meat dishes for us meat-lovers.

Eva Sanderson [5:49] Of course. I've emailed everyone our tentative menu and most of you seem to like the choices.

Sunny Rhee [5:50] Don't forget to email the caterers about the security clearance they'll need to enter the building.

Eva Sanderson [5:51] I'll work on that now.

---

162. What is the discussion mainly about?

(A) Those who can't attend a party
(B) The best caterers
(C) Becoming a vegan
(D) Ordering food for a party

163. At 5:39, what does Patrick Stone mean by "I'm going to take a pass this year"?

(A) He'll stop by for a short time.
(B) He'll decline this time.
(C) He'll be late.
(D) He wants to get a free pass.

164. What is mentioned about Four-Leaf Catering?

(A) It offers vegan food.
(B) It has only vegan options.
(C) It has catered previous office parties.
(D) It specializes in special orders.

165. What will Eva Sanderson most likely do next?

(A) Work on the menu
(B) Contact the caterers
(C) Confirm a meeting
(D) Order some lunch

Midas Touch Internet Provider

Contract Summary

Date: March 22

Customer: Ms. Tanya Sullivan
Address: 345 Oak Street, Parsons, WY 54055
Purchase Date: March 13

Services Purchased:

Item	Price
Midas Internet multimedia package	$40.00/month
– Download speed of 100 Mbps	
– 32 free movie channels	
– Video streaming services of the five latest movies every month	
Security Guard virus protection	$5.00/month
Modem and router rental service	$3.00/month

	Subtotal	$48.00/month
	Tax	$3.45/month
	Total	$51.45/month

Just call us at 341-555-6487 and our technician will come to your house to take care of everything that you need to connect to the Internet via the modem and router.

ACTUAL TEST 08

---

166. What did Ms. Sullivan do on March 13?

(A) She purchased a home security system.
(B) She returned a product.
(C) She signed up for Internet service.
(D) She made an appointment.

167. What is suggested about Ms. Sullivan?

(A) She teaches a computer skills class.
(B) She had trouble installing some software.
(C) She will have access to movies.
(D) She has recently moved into her home.

168. What is indicated about Midas Touch Internet Provider?

(A) It dispatches its employees for installation work.
(B) It sells computer accessories.
(C) Its headquarters are located in Parsons.
(D) It offers website developing services.

GO ON TO THE NEXT PAGE →

April 2—Repairs will begin next Friday on the historic Marion Hall in downtown Marion. In its heyday, Marion Hall was a popular downtown destination for residents to dance, enjoy live music, and watch movies. However, it has lost its popularity gradually since the multiplex building was completed on Henson Street four years ago.

After all of the necessary repairs have been made to Marion Hall, city officials will begin to invite various performers including famous theater companies, musicians, comedians, and speakers to the newly renovated theater. "We hope Marion Hall can serve as a new cultural center here in Marion," says Mayor Greg Fields.

The revitalization of Marion Hall is part of a larger project to enhance the public facilities in Marion. On April 29, the Marion Children's Park, which features a baseball field as well as several playgrounds, is scheduled to have its grand reopening.

169. What is suggested about Marion?

(A) It will restore an old building soon.
(B) It has closed a park for repairs.
(C) It is planning a music festival.
(D) Its population is decreasing.

170. What is the purpose of Marion Hall?

(A) To serve as a play center for children
(B) To hold city council meetings
(C) To offer public education classes
(D) To host cultural events

171. What will happen in April?

(A) A famous speaker will give a presentation.
(B) A new mayor will be elected.
(C) Some improved public facilities will open.
(D) A new play will be performed.

Questions 172-175 refer to the following article from a company newsletter.

As I'm sure you're aware, this week we must decide if we want to continue working with CC Wheel Delivery. As we learned at yesterday's meeting, they are being sued for the accident that happened last week. – [1] – We all agreed that the whole company shouldn't be held liable for the mistakes of a few careless workers, but that was a conversation we had before we had really thought about the ramifications of our decision. – [2] – Unfortunately, the situation is escalating and there is about to be a lot of bad press. – [3] – It's true that many of them are our friends, but we must protect our company. We can't handle anything that might affect our sales.

For the last four months we've been operating with a very thin margin for error. If our sales drop even slightly, it could be disastrous. So I'm suggesting that, as a means of protecting ourselves from any negative backlash, we cut our ties with CC Wheel Delivery. Maybe later, if they're able to rehabilitate their name, we'll work with them again. – [4] – I propose we vote one more time on whether or not to work with them.

172. What is true about CC Wheel Delivery?

(A) A contract of theirs has just been canceled.
(B) Legal action is being taking against them.
(C) Their president has just stepped down.
(D) Two of their trucks were in an accident.

173. What is indicated about the company that the writer works for?

(A) It is financially insecure.
(B) It has recently been created.
(C) It will be closing.
(D) It is a delivery company.

174. Why does the writer wish to stop working with CC Wheel Delivery?

(A) To protect his company from financial damage
(B) To cut production costs over the next four months
(C) To lower the price of an individual product
(D) To avoid legal trouble in the future

175. In which of the places marked [1], [2], [3], and [4] does this sentence belong?

"Yes, we've worked with them for a long time."

(A) [1]
(B) [2]
(C) [3]
(D) [4]

GO ON TO THE NEXT PAGE

September 21—What is the secret to delicious home-cooked meals? Kimberly Lee, host of the *My Home Cooking* television show and owner of her own restaurant chain, seems to know all the secrets. Her show has been on the air for over two years, and now she has a devoted group of followers around the country. When she sat down for an interview with us, she said that fresh vegetables and local produce are the key to cooking healthy and tasty food.

Ms. Lee is scheduled to publish her very first cookbook near the end of the month. The book is entitled *Kimberly Lee's My Home Cooking*, and it provides easy-to-follow recipes that can be made in less than 30 minutes. Over 40,000 copies have already been pre-ordered.

Ms. Lee says that the final page of the book will include a detachable fan club membership form. Those who fill the form out and send it in to the provided address will receive a monthly newsletter and exclusive recipes available only to those in the fan club. Fan club members will also receive a password that allows access to the *My Home Cooking* website.

To:	Kimberly Lee <kimberlylee@kimberlylee.com>
From:	Suzie Sanders <suziesanders@kimberlylee.com>
Date:	October 12
Subject:	Update

Dear Ms. Lee,

Great news! I'm happy to report that not only has your book been selling well, but the number of new members joining the fan club has been increasing drastically since it was published. I'm certain that the article in the newspaper helped generate considerable publicity for your book.

Also, we have received a lot of feedback from new members expressing a desire for more recipes for cakes, cookies, and candies to be featured in next month's newsletter. I think it would be a good idea to satisfy their requests this time.

Sincerely,

Suzie Sanders
Publicity Coordinator

176. What is the main purpose of the article?

(A) To publicize an upcoming book
(B) To provide advice for professional chefs
(C) To advertise a new restaurant
(D) To describe a television show

177. According to Ms. Lee, what is the secret to successful cooking?

(A) Following a recipe book
(B) Using quality ingredients
(C) Balancing all the flavors
(D) Choosing the correct spices

178. What is the thing one has to do in order to become a fan club member?

(A) Access a website
(B) Call a hotline
(C) Visit Ms. Lee's restaurant
(D) Purchase a book

179. In the email, what does Suzie Sanders say about the article?

(A) It was written by a famous journalist.
(B) It was featured on a popular cooking website.
(C) It helped increase fan club membership.
(D) It contained excerpts from Ms. Lee's book.

180. What is suggested about next month's newsletter?

(A) It will be mailed behind schedule.
(B) It will feature a column about healthy eating habits.
(C) It will contain an article on desserts.
(D) It will include a copy of Ms. Lee's book.

GO ON TO THE NEXT PAGE

From: Stacey Watkins <staceywatkins@titus.com>
To: Ann Rose <annrose@putkincomp.com>
Subject: Conference of Bank Managers
Date: February 12

Dear Ms. Rose,

You recently contacted us about using our conference center again this year to host your annual conference of bank managers. This year we have updated our conference room with new projectors and more comfortable seating. We will be providing shuttle buses from the airport and a premium buffet in the dining hall as well as an Internet café where guests can use computers or print documents at no cost. For your convenience, we will also be providing useful supplies such as flip charts, 10-foot whiteboards, and projector screens.

Once you decide on a date, we ask that you please make a down payment of $1,000 as soon as we've confirmed that it is available. The remaining balance should be paid upon your arrival. We also ask that, as the organizer of the event, you arrive at the conference center one day before the conference begins. That way, any unforeseen issues can be taken care of beforehand.

We appreciate your doing business with the Titus Conference Center once again. We are looking forward to providing you with the best service possible.

Stacey Watkins, Director

From: Ann Rose <annrose@putkincomp.com>
To: Stacey Watkins <staceywatkins@titus.com>
Subject: RE: Conference of Bank Managers
Date: February 16

Dear Ms. Watkins,

I am also pleased to be working with you again this year. We would like to reserve your conference space for the weekend of August 15 to 16. The down payment will be handled by our financial department. I will have one of the employees contact you soon.

Also, there is one thing that I would like to ask of you. Last year, some of our attendees were disappointed because the dining hall didn't offer enough vegetarian options. I hope this issue can be dealt with in advance this year.

Thank you,

Ann Rose
Organizer, Annual Conference of Bank Managers

181. What is indicated about the Titus Conference Center?

(A) It recently improved its facilities.
(B) It demands full payment at the time of reservation.
(C) It is located next to an international airport.
(D) It currently has no vacancies for the month of August.

182. What is NOT mentioned as a benefit of using the Titus Conference Center?

(A) Convenient transportation
(B) Laptop rental services
(C) A printing service
(D) Presentation supplies

183. When will Ms. Rose most likely arrive at the Titus Conference Center?

(A) On August 7
(B) On August 14
(C) On August 15
(D) On August 16

184. What is the main purpose of the second email?

(A) To reserve tickets for an upcoming conference
(B) To request help in making a payment
(C) To confirm a reservation
(D) To inquire about payment options

185. What does Ms. Rose suggest about the Titus Conference Center?

(A) This will be her first time working with it.
(B) It will relocate in August.
(C) It has several locations across the country.
(D) It failed to satisfy some guests last year.

GO ON TO THE NEXT PAGE

To: John Masterson <jmasterson@masterstrokeindustries.com>
From: Carl Ennens <cennens@gmail.com>
Date: December 30
Subject: Internship

Dear Mr. Masterson,

My name is Carl Ennens and I am entering my final year at Evergreen State College. I am majoring in industrial engineering here, and my liquid dynamics professor, Dr. Alcobar, recommended Master Stroke Industries for a possible internship opportunity. Your company is recognized as a leader in flow research. If you would be willing to accept an intern for the coming spring semester, I could give you up to 15 hours per week of work, provided that you are able to write some performance evaluations that I can turn in to Dr. Alcobar for credit. Thank you for your consideration, and if you would like to see my transcript, I would be happy to forward it to you.

All the best,

Carl Ennens

To: Carl Ennens <cennens@gmail.com>
From: John Masterson <jmasterson@masterstrokeindustries.com>
Date: December 31
Subject: RE: Internship

Dear Carl,

I appreciate your interest in interning with us here at Master Stroke Industries. We have not accepted a lot of interns in the past, but I know Dr. Alcobar personally, and if he recommended that you contact us, he must have faith in your ability. I think we should set up an interview at our headquarters downtown on Holly Street. We can get to know each other a bit over some coffee and I will show you around our facilities. Don't worry about your transcripts; like I said, If Dr. Alcobar thinks you'd be a good fit, I'll trust his judgment. How about this coming Friday at 10 A.M.?

Looking forward to meeting you,

John Masterson

CEO, Master Stroke Industries

Memorandum To Master Stroke Industries Employees

This spring Master Stroke Industries will have an intern assisting us with everything from making coffee to solving complex equations. Carl Ennens is a student at the state college here and the University and has kindly offered his services in exchange for a piece of our operational knowledge. Please treat him with respect and don't be afraid to use him for an extra pair of hands or eyes or an opinion should you need it. And I do hear he makes a good cup of coffee!

186. What is indicated about Carl Ennens?

(A) He is a senior in high school.
(B) He will be a junior in college.
(C) He will graduate in two years.
(D) He will be a senior in college.

187. What is indicated about Dr. Alcobar?

(A) Nobody knows who he is.
(B) People do not appreciate his opinion.
(C) He is respected by John Masterson.
(D) He has done a lot of prominent research.

188. In the second email, the term "headquarters" in the fourth line is closest in meaning to:

(A) basement
(B) main office
(C) warehouse
(D) distribution center

189. According to the memorandum, what will Carl Ennens be expected to do?

(A) Research fluid dynamics
(B) Cook
(C) Help wherever he is needed
(D) Watch and learn

190. What position does John Masterson have in the company?

(A) Chief Executive Officer
(B) Chief Financial Officer
(C) Sales Executive
(D) Owner

GO ON TO THE NEXT PAGE

Brand-X Coming to Town

March 9 – Popular Danish skin care company Brand-X is finally launching its best-selling line in America. The 88-year-old company is Denmark's leading skin-care brand and its top-selling cream, Xtreme 7, has been Europe's most popular facial cream for over 10 years. Though Americans may not have had access to these creams before, the brand is already generating much excitement.

Dermatologist Dr. Francis Keenan explains, "Tests have shown that Xtreme 7 dramatically reduces the fine lines around the eye area and laugh lines after only 30 days of use, but the price of the cream is only a fraction of what department store brands sell for. I'll definitely recommend this cream to my clients."

"People have been asking about Xtreme 7, but the product hasn't even arrived yet!" added Susan Chan, an employee at a beauty counter. "People are already calling in to pre-order."

A spokesperson for the company explained that Brand-X is making moves to expand into the North American and Asian markets. For now, only the company's best-selling line will be available outside of Europe (starting next month), but within a year more products will be available.

Brand-X Positions at American Headquarters in Westminster, California

Don't miss your chance to work in an exciting career in skin care and beauty with Brand-X. Eighty administrative and customer service positions are available with no experience necessary. Applicants must have strong communication and computer skills. Knowledge of both English and Spanish is preferred but not essential. Applicants with experience in cosmetics, dermatology, or marketing may qualify for management positions. Please visit our website at www.brandx.com/jobs for more information. Application forms must be sent in before March 20th. Interviews will take place at the Hillway Building at 143 Garden Road. Be sure to bring your résumé and reference letters.

```
□ ■ ☒

To          Professor David Mills
From        Jacqueline O'Hare
Date        March 28
Subject     job
```

Dear Professor Mills,

Thank you so much for the reference letter you wrote for me. I was recently hired by Brand-X, and my orientation begins next Wednesday at 10 A.M. Unfortunately, we have our statistics test at that time. Is there any way that I can take a make-up test at a different time or hand in another assignment in place of the test? The orientation is mandatory, and I don't want to disappoint my new employers. The job should not have any impact on my school work otherwise. I appreciate your kind consideration in this matter.

Sincerely,

Jacqueline O'Hare

191. What does Dr. Keenan suggest about Xtreme 7?

(A) It is the most effective cream on the market.
(B) It is worth the high price.
(C) It is both effective and cheap.
(D) It is the only cream that a doctor would recommend.

192. What is suggested about Brand-X?

(A) Its products are currently only available in Europe.
(B) It is Europe's most popular brand.
(C) It is a luxury skin-care company.
(D) It was first launched 10 years ago.

193. According to the article, what does Brand-X plan to do?

(A) Sell more products in Europe
(B) Expand outside of Europe
(C) Develop a makeup line
(D) Build a factory in America

194. What is indicated in the advertisement?

(A) None of the positions requires previous work experience.
(B) Applicants must be bilingual.
(C) Experience in certain fields can lead to management positions.
(D) The available positions are only temporary.

195. For what position was Jacqueline most likely hired?

(A) Management
(B) Human Resource
(C) Marketing
(D) Customer Service

GO ON TO THE NEXT PAGE ➡

To: Bill Johnson<bj@action.net>
From: Laurie Wheeler<lwheeler@zipnet.com>
Date: October 11
Subject: Reservation info

Dear Mr. Johnson,

I am writing to you on behalf of the company I work for, Competitive Excellence. We specialize in productivity and efficiency training for corporations and small businesses. Lately our staff has been suffering from low morale, and while searching the Internet for solutions I came across your website www.action.net. I am interested in hearing more about the motivational speaking that you do. Specifically, could you tell me if your speeches are religious in nature? We have a diverse staff, and I am looking for something secular. Please write me back with an overview of what you do and what your presentation rates are.

Laurie Wheeler,

Managing Director, Competitive Excellence

To: Laurie Wheeler<lwheeler@zipnet.com>
From: Bill Johnson<bj@action.net>
Date: October 13
Subject: RE: Reservation info

Dear Ms. Wheeler,

Thank you so much for your interest in Action. I am happy to answer your questions and provide you with a full breakdown of what we can do for you, your team, and your company. To begin with, all of our talks are secular, though not necessarily free from the concept of spirituality. Our professional speakers seek to motivate people to look internally to find their own spirit and help it rise. Morale, after all, is an intangible but essential aspect of an effective team. Please refer to the topic list and pricing guide I have attached to this email. Once you have chosen a theme, speaker, and appropriate class size for your company, please send me a follow-up email to schedule your event.

Bill Johnson,
Action Coordinator

Action Course Topics and Price Guide

Theme	Location	Speaker	Class Size	Duration	Price
Stay in the Moment!	On-Site	Jim Grey	15-20	3 hours	$450
New You Every Day	Off-Site	Darlene Woodward	20-25	3 hours	$400
Stay Positive for the Team!	Off-Site	Jeff Boxer	15-30	3 hours	$400
Blessed Are We All	Off-Site	John Brown	20-30	4 hours	$500

196. How did Laurie Wheeler learn about Action?

(A) From a friend
(B) Through a client
(C) In a newspaper
(D) On the Internet

197. What is indicated about Action?

(A) They do not promote a religion.
(B) They are Christian.
(C) They are just building their brand.
(D) They are moving to a new location.

198. According to the graphic, what is NOT an option for customers?

(A) Off-site courses
(B) Classes for 10
(C) A four-hour course
(D) Courses to build positivity

199. What course will Laurie Wheeler likely sign her staff up for?

(A) Stay in the Moment!
(B) New You Every Day
(C) Stay Positive for the Team!
(D) Blessed are We All

200. What is indicated about Competitive Excellence?

(A) They are struggling financially.
(B) The mood in their office is not good.
(C) They are having a booming year of sales.
(D) They want to change their business focus.

Stop! This is the end of the test. If you finish before time is called, you may go back to Parts 5, 6, and 7 and check your work.

READING TEST

In the Reading test, you will read a variety of texts and answer several different types of reading comprehension questions. The entire Reading test will last 75 minutes. There are three parts, and directions are given for each part. You are encouraged to answer as many questions as possible within the time allowed.

You must mark your answers on the separate answer sheet. Do not write your answers in your test book.

PART 5

Directions: A word or phrase is missing in each of the sentences below. Four answer choices are given below each sentence. Select the best answer to complete the sentence. Then mark the letter (A), (B), (C), or (D) on your answer sheet.

101. The projector borrowed by Ms. Reid is ------- back at the IT department by five o'clock.

(A) due
(B) set
(C) paid
(D) prompt

102. Now that the annual conference is over, the planning committee will hold meetings ------- often.

(A) below
(B) less
(C) decreased
(D) lower

103. Before you distribute the report, ask Ms. Burns to make sure that ------- contains all the necessary information.

(A) them
(B) our
(C) her
(D) it

104. According to consumers, using the new website is no ------- than calling the help center directly.

(A) easily
(B) easy
(C) easiest
(D) easier

105. Anyone who participates ------- the city's annual baking competition will receive a coupon from Fresh Supermarket.

(A) to
(B) beside
(C) in
(D) among

106. City officials are still debating Irving Enterprises' request ------- the outdated building.

(A) demolishes
(B) have demolished
(C) to demolish
(D) demolished

107. Heron Glassworks ------- student groups of all ages for weekday tours of its warehouse and production floor.

(A) conveys
(B) preserves
(C) encloses
(D) welcomes

108. To combat mental illness, the clinic will take a more comprehensive ------- than it has in the past.

(A) approachably
(B) approached
(C) approach
(D) approachable

109. Brandy can withdraw money at any Salis Bank branch, but she usually visits the ------- one.

(A) closing
(B) closely
(C) closure
(D) closest

110. As a ------- for signing contracts with a lot of new clients, Mr. Skinner was given additional vacation days.

(A) reward
(B) progress
(C) solution
(D) routine

111. Please seat yourselves according to the ------- name cards that have been placed on each table.

(A) personalizes
(B) personalizing
(C) personalize
(D) personalized

112. The memo sent out by Mr. Lee addressed a few ------- that were discovered during the quarterly inspection.

(A) issuing
(B) issue
(C) issues
(D) issued

113. Many voters in this city are uninterested in the issues, and only about 15% of them are ------- active.

(A) politically
(B) political
(C) politics
(D) politician

114. This year's award winner, Cheryl Garner, taught basic first aid skills to students and adults ------- the region.

(A) between
(B) throughout
(C) during
(D) toward

115. -------, the cabin will be rented for the entire month, but the owner will agree to four weekly rentals instead.

(A) Reluctantly
(B) Absolutely
(C) Ideally
(D) Mutually

116. The non-profit organization released several documents to the press ------- its largest donors and how much they had contributed.

(A) detailed
(B) detail
(C) details
(D) detailing

GO ON TO THE NEXT PAGE

117. No passengers are allowed to board ------- the aircraft's door has been closed.

(A) that
(B) despite
(C) once
(D) rather

118. A government ------- will visit the site to speak with the protesters directly and seek a resolution.

(A) representative
(B) representation
(C) represent
(D) represented

119. An extensive ------- conducted by Ivanex Communications revealed that Internet speed was one of the most important factors for consumers.

(A) inventory
(B) strategy
(C) coverage
(D) survey

120. Mr. Denson wanted to purchase a special edition gold-plated watch from Utica Watches, but there were ------- left.

(A) none
(B) nothing
(C) something
(D) some

121. Ms. May reminded us that the agreement was only ------- as it had not been approved yet.

(A) perishable
(B) imperative
(C) accustomed
(D) tentative

122. Following the restoration project, the lobby of the historical Kirkwood Hotel looked ------- like it originally had.

(A) remarkably
(B) remarking
(C) remark
(D) remarked

123. ------- the right environmental conditions, this tree will yield fresh fruit for most of the year.

(A) With
(B) About
(C) On
(D) As

124. One of the interns ------- that the logo on the second page of the sales report was upside down.

(A) looked after
(B) accounted for
(C) pointed out
(D) came across

125. ------- the parking lot is closed, both employees and customers will have to park on the street.

(A) As if
(B) Until
(C) So that
(D) While

126. If the new athletic shoes do well in smaller test markets, their nationwide launch could be -------.

(A) convinced
(B) accelerated
(C) directed
(D) circulated

127. The city hosted an ------- fireworks display
to celebrate the 100th anniversary of its
founding.

(A) impressive
(B) impress
(C) impression
(D) impressively

128. After investing heavily in Internet marketing
campaigns, Bailey Coffee increased its
annual profits ------- 15 percent.

(A) by
(B) among
(C) between
(D) on

129. The receptionists ------- change the artwork
in the clinic's waiting room and rearrange
the layout of the furniture.

(A) periodically
(B) relatively
(C) tightly
(D) narrowly

130. The policy requiring businesses to provide
medical insurance applies only to those
------- more than 25 people.

(A) employs
(B) employ
(C) employed
(D) employing

GO ON TO THE NEXT PAGE

PART 6

Directions: Read the texts that follow. A word, phrase, or sentence is missing in parts of each text. Four answer choices for each question are given below the text. Select the best answer to complete the text. Then mark the letter (A), (B), (C), or (D) on your answer sheet.

Questions 131-134 refer to the following notice.

Beverly Boutique: Sales Assistant Position

Our boutique is looking for enthusiastic candidates for a sales assistant position. ------- **131.** Previous experience in a similar position is preferred, but not necessary. Organizational skills are a must, as is some experience with computers. Most of all, we need someone who is personable, can make customers feel -------, and is passionate about fashion. Duties will **132.** include serving customers, taking inventory, and minor jobs around the boutique such as sweeping the floor and locking the doors at closing time. Payment is by sales commission, which gives employees more ------- to provide our customers with the very best service they **133.** can. Hours will be flexible. For more information, please visit our website.

If you ------- in the position, please send your résumé to Rita at rlan@bboutique.com. **134.**

---

131. (A) Our boutique is a leader in trendy fashions.
(B) Hurry before the promotion ends.
(C) Candidates need to be friendly and able to communicate with customers in all kinds of situations.
(D) Come visit our store to see what our business is about.

132. (A) comfortable
(B) appropriate
(C) neglected
(D) convenient

133. (A) influence
(B) incentive
(C) insistence
(D) consideration

134. (A) be interesting
(B) were interesting
(C) interest
(D) are interested

Handy Maids Home Service

Call us at 555-1244

Handy Maids Home Service ------- professional cleaning services for your business or home.
135.

We steam vacuum carpeted areas, polish hardwood flooring, wipe away all traces of dust

and dirt in hard-to-reach areas, and clean out clutter. Our ------- service is second to none in
136.

the Tri-State Area. We provide one-day service after giving an estimate. -------, we provide
137.

weekly and monthly services for customers who request them.

The cleaning products we use are environmentally friendly and pet- and child-safe. -------
138.

Please visit our website at www.handymaids.com or call us for more information.

---

135. (A) provide
(B) provides
(C) provided
(D) providing

136. (A) unusual
(B) peculiar
(C) best
(D) exceptional

137. (A) In addition
(B) Because
(C) On the other hand
(D) As a result

138. (A) We make sure that your pets and children don't go near the chemicals.
(B) In fact, we aim to make your home or business a safe and clean place without the use of harsh chemicals.
(C) Our all-natural cleaning agents may not be as effective as chemicals, but they are safe.
(D) Pets and children will be asked to leave the premises during cleaning.

GO ON TO THE NEXT PAGE

October 09

Bob Prosser

342 Winkler Ave

Fairbanks, AK 99705

Dear Mr. Prosser,

The information that you ------- about changes to the hunting permit scheme is enclosed.
139.
Please note that each permit you require must be applied for separately. When filling out

your application(s), you must print all answers clearly in block letters with a black or blue

pen. Please do not use cursive script, print only. Each application ------- enclosed in its own
140.
envelope and received before the applicable deadline. -------. Because of this, you must
141.
plan your submission(s) in a timely fashion to make sure that you receive your permit(s) while

the applicable season is still open. I hope that the information ------- answers all of your
142.
questions. Take care and happy hunting.

Sincerely,

Shirley Horn, Executive Secretary

Department of Wildlife

Fairbanks, AK 99701

139. (A) provided
    (B) provide
    (C) request
    (D) requested

140. (A) won't be
    (B) can be
    (C) must be
    (D) couldn't be

141. (A) Once received, applications can take
        up to five weeks to process.
    (B) Applications are never approved before
        the season is over.
    (C) Sometimes applications get lost.
    (D) Never make an application in person.

142. (A) enclose
    (B) enclosing
    (C) encloses
    (D) enclosed

Questions 143-146 refer to the following notice.

Date: August 22

To: All Sales Team Members

From: Melinda Lackey, Sales Manager

Subject: Rental Policy

For some ------- now we have allowed sales reps to pay for their car rentals up front with
        143.
their personal cards or cash, and then be reimbursed later. This is no longer our policy, and

has not been our policy for over two months now. As of June 15th, all payments for rentals

were supposed to have ------- with the company card that was assigned to you. Larry in
                    144.
accounting has informed me that he has received six separate reimbursement forms since

then. I have gone ahead and allowed him to process those six forms. ------- I'm sorry for the
                                                                   145.
------- tone of this message, but everyone was asked to do this back in June. If you have
 146.
any questions, please contact me directly.

143. (A) distances
     (B) place
     (C) event
     (D) time

144. (A) making
     (B) to be made
     (C) makes
     (D) been made

145. (A) Only Fonitna Rental should be used to book cars in the future.
     (B) As of tomorrow, however, no one will be reimbursed for car rentals anymore.
     (C) He will redesign the form by the beginning of next week.
     (D) All sales reps are required to turn in their cards as soon as possible.

146. (A) overreaching
     (B) gracious
     (C) benevolent
     (D) harsh

GO ON TO THE NEXT PAGE

Directions: In this part you will read a selection of texts, such as magazine and newspaper articles, emails, and instant messages. Each text or set of texts is followed by several questions. Select the best answer for each question and mark the letter (A), (B), (C), or (D) on your answer sheet.

Questions 147-148 refer to the following flyer.

Jay Furniture

3105 Michigan Avenue, Chicago, IL 60611

Black Friday Weekend Sale
November 29 to December 1

Tables—20% off
Couches—30% off
Mattresses—20% to 50% off
Desks and Chairs—25% to 50% off

- During the sale, any customer who purchases over $500 worth of merchandise will receive a coupon for an extra 5% off any purchase during our Christmas sale. Coupons will be valid from December 9 to December 28.
- Mention the code BLKFRI for an additional $10 off any table or mattress during the sale.

Note: Jay Furniture will be closed the day before the weekend sale to prepare for it. Doors will open at 9:00 a.m. on November 29.

147. What is the purpose of the flyer?

(A) To announce the opening of a store
(B) To advertise a sale on furniture
(C) To introduce new products
(D) To inform customers of a business's relocation

148. When will the store be closed?

(A) On November 28
(B) On November 29
(C) On November 30
(D) On December 9

Questions 149-150 refer to the following text message chain.

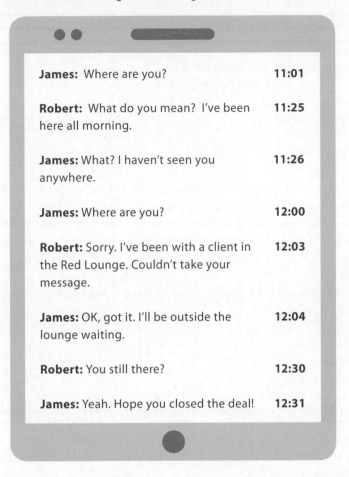

James: Where are you?	**11:01**
Robert: What do you mean? I've been here all morning.	**11:25**
James: What? I haven't seen you anywhere.	**11:26**
James: Where are you?	**12:00**
Robert: Sorry. I've been with a client in the Red Lounge. Couldn't take your message.	**12:03**
James: OK, got it. I'll be outside the lounge waiting.	**12:04**
Robert: You still there?	**12:30**
James: Yeah. Hope you closed the deal!	**12:31**

149. Why does James most likely say, "Hope you closed the deal!"?

(A) He thinks there will be a bonus.
(B) He has been waiting a long time.
(C) He loves the Red Lounge.
(D) There are too many deals open.

150. What can be inferred by the length of time between James's messages and Robert's responses?

(A) Robert isn't interested in James.
(B) Robert wants time to himself.
(C) Robert's phone has died.
(D) Robert cannot check his phone all the time.

GO ON TO THE NEXT PAGE

To: Operations Team <operations@acemfg.com>
From: Thomas Wheeler <t.wheeler@acemfg.com>
Date: Monday, June 16
Subject: New Equipment

To the operations team,

The company will order a new set of heavy equipment tomorrow and it will be delivered to the warehouse the following afternoon. Our employees' work schedules will have to be adjusted in line with this addition of new equipment. Please submit a report stating the new tasks and responsibilities of each worker regarding this equipment by 5:00 P.M. on Thursday.

If I am not in the office, please give it to my secretary, Ms. Hardy.

Thanks,

Thomas Wheeler
Director of Manufacturing

151. When will the new equipment most likely arrive at the warehouse?

(A) On Monday
(B) On Tuesday
(C) On Wednesday
(D) On Thursday

152. What should be included in the report?

(A) Workers' contact information
(B) Workers' assignments
(C) Workers' résumés
(D) Workers' suggestions

To:	R&D Department
From:	Rick Campbell, Director of R&D
Subject:	Change in Staff
Date:	Tuesday, April 4, 3:40 P.M.

I am writing to share news with you regarding recent changes in the research and development office. Starting April 7, Bob Denkle will be our new project manager in the research and development department. He has just completed a month-long training session and will replace Benjamin Palmer by the end of the week.

Mike Garcia, the HR director, will post an announcement of several openings in different departments by next week. For those who wish to transfer into a different department within the company, now would be a good time to apply.

Please congratulate Benjamin Palmer, who will transition into a new position at Ion Industries, and welcome Bob Denkle as he joins our department.

153. What is expected to happen by next week?

(A) A new department will be formed.
(B) Job offers will be announced.
(C) An interview will be conducted.
(D) A training session will take place.

154. Who is leaving the company?

(A) Bob Denkle
(B) Mike Garcia
(C) Rick Campbell
(D) Benjamin Palmer

GO ON TO THE NEXT PAGE

Re-Fit Closing Stores

February 9 – Neway Group has announced that 80 Re-Fit stores will be closing down around the country in the next six months, with 100 more to follow within the year. – [1] – However, the past ten years have seen a steady decline in sales as consumers have turned to other clothing retailers such as Zanas and HRM. – [2] – "I don't know. I just found the clothing to be outdated," says a former customer. "They should have updated the styles and offered non-sporty options."

CEO Derrick Greenwich agrees. "We focused so much on particular styles of sportswear that we lost sight of the changing tastes of consumers. We're working on restructuring the company and offering consumers what they want. We'll come back bigger than ever." – [3] –

An internal review of the losses will continue to be conducted as nervous shareholders consider their next moves. – [4] – Neway is hoping that a good number of the Re-Fit stores will remain in operation as the company struggles to reinvent its brand.

155. What is indicated about the Re-Fit brand?

(A) Its popularity has dropped dramatically.
(B) It specializes in sports gear.
(C) The CEO is renaming the company.
(D) The brand has a 100-year history.

156. The phrase "lost sight of" in the second paragraph is closest in meaning to:

(A) restricted
(B) were not blinded by
(C) ignored
(D) selected

157. In which of the positions marked [1], [2], [3], and [4] does the following sentence belong?

"The clothing store, best known for its affordable but trendy sportswear, was very popular in the 1990s and early 2000s."

(A) [1]
(B) [2]
(C) [3]
(D) [4]

Questions 158-160 refer to the following table of contents from a booklet.

CONTENTS

9 *Easy Snacks*
Donald Cohen offers recipes that are suitable for those who are always on the move.

14 *The Perfect Resort*
Melissa Green discusses the features of the world's top 10 resorts.

19 *Passport Guide*
Henry Carroll shows you how to apply for a passport in five easy steps.

23 *Safety First*
Tricia Oldham discusses basic first aid for first-time travelers.

26 *Wish You Were Here*
Rebecca Barajas shares her pictures from her amazing trip to New Zealand.

30 *Delicious Diners*
Barry Eason shares his tasty experiences on the road.

33 *On a Budget*
Edward Boyd shares tips on how to save money on your next trip.

35 *Light My Way*
Reviews of the most popular guidebooks

158. What is the focus of the booklet?

(A) Food
(B) Transportation
(C) The environment
(D) Travel

159. Where in the booklet would pictures most likely be found?

(A) On page 9
(B) On page 19
(C) On page 26
(D) On page 30

160. According to the table of contents, who writes about spending less money?

(A) Ms. Green
(B) Mr. Carroll
(C) Mr. Eason
(D) Mr. Boyd

GO ON TO THE NEXT PAGE →

Questions 161-164 refer to the following online chat discussion.

Ginger Lin	**[4:59]**	Just a reminder to everyone to please clear your desks and shut down all electronic devices before you leave today. The floors will be polished and cleaned over the weekend.
Dimitri Roberts	**[5:00]**	Should we lock all the cabinets and drawers as well?
Ginger Lin	**[5:01]**	Yes. Please make sure that when the furniture is moved around, nothing falls out.
Dimitri Roberts	**[5:02]**	I'll make sure that everything is secure and locked before I leave.
Janet Leigh	**[5:03]**	Ginger, I've finished our budget reports. I'll have copies emailed to you soon before I send them off.
Ginger Lin	**[5:04]**	Thank you. And Lance, you'll have to reschedule your meeting with your client tomorrow.
Lance Sibley	**[5:04]**	I've already rescheduled our meeting for a week from Monday. And just to be on the safe side in case our offices are not ready by then, we'll be meeting at a café nearby.
Ginger Lin	**[5:05]**	All right. It looks like most things are in order. Let me know if I've missed anything.
Janet Leigh	**[5:06]**	Actually, not everyone has sent me his or her overtime hours yet. I was still able to confirm through the sign-up sheets, but I need everyone to confirm by email before I send the payment forms to the finance department.
Dimitri Roberts	**[5:07]**	Oops! That's me. I'll send you an email right now.
Karen Walker	**[5:07]**	Me, too.
Janet Leigh	**[5:08]**	Great. I can send the forms once I get your emails.

161. What will take place on Saturday and Sunday?

(A) An office party
(B) A meeting with clients
(C) A renovation
(D) A cleaning services

162. Who most likely is Ginger Lin?

(A) A secretary
(B) A manager
(C) A technician
(D) A security guard

163. At 5:04, what does Lance Sibley mean by "just to be on the safe side?"

(A) The offices may not be safe.
(B) The client may need help.
(C) Just as a precaution.
(D) He's been given a warning.

164. What will Janet Leigh most likely do next?

(A) Check her email
(B) Contact the finance department
(C) Call some employees
(D) Print out some reports

Questions 165-167 refer to the following job advertisement.

Helping Hands
8732 Bakersfield Avenue, Santa Clara, California

Regional Manager—Employment Opportunity

Helping Hands is dedicated to providing quality affordable housing for low-income individuals and families. For over 25 years, we have been acquiring multifamily communities and improving these properties to maintain their availability for those earning less than 50 percent of the areas' average incomes. Our properties are currently located in cities throughout the state of Texas including Austin, Dallas and Houston, and our plans are to expand and make more homes available to more people.

We are looking for someone to fill the position of regional manager. The new manager will be stationed in Austin and will supervise and evaluate the performance of on-site management to ensure that all properties are well maintained. The candidate must have a bachelor's degree or higher in a business or management field, a minimum of three years of experience in supervising personnel, and certain certificates (more details are on the application page).

Applications can be submitted in person Monday through Friday from 9:00 A.M. to 5:00 P.M. or by mail or email. They will be accepted only if they are received before 5:00 P.M. on October 14.

165. What is mentioned about Helping Hands?

(A) It offers services for senior citizens.
(B) It is committed to nature conservation.
(C) It is sponsored by the government.
(D) It supplies homes to a disadvantaged group.

166. Where will the successful candidate be required to work?

(A) In Santa Clara
(B) In Austin
(C) In Dallas
(D) In Houston

167. What is NOT suggested about the position?

(A) It includes supervision of our local staff.
(B) It requires an academic degree.
(C) It requires official documents.
(D) It is limited to California residents.

GO ON TO THE NEXT PAGE ➡

Questions 168-171 refer to the following email.

To	cmason@centersports.com
From	sdixon@instaprinting.com
Date	November 3
Subject	Your Inquiry

Dear Mr. Mason,

We are responding to the inquiry you made through our website yesterday. Insta Printing promises to provide faster, cheaper, and more reliable service than any of our competitors in the area. We also guarantee that we will beat any price offered by a competitor.

As per your request, our company would be happy to help design and print jerseys for your soccer team. In addition to casual wear, we have plenty of experience producing athletic wear for sports teams and clubs.

Customers can choose from a variety of materials and printing methods. Our materials include denim, cotton, flannel, nylon, and many more, and we use several printing methods including screen printing, heat press, and direct-to-garment printing.

Please feel free to contact me directly at 712-555-9804 to discuss further details about working with Insta Printing. We look forward to working with you and helping your organization achieve its goals.

Sincerely,

Stephen Dixon
Client Relations Representative, Insta Printing

168. Why did Mr. Dixon send the email?

(A) To give a quote for a project
(B) To explain a new policy
(C) To persuade a client to agree to a deal
(D) To confirm a reservation

169. What does Mr. Mason want to do?

(A) Purchase a set of shirts
(B) Apply for a position
(C) Devise a new printing technique
(D) Expand his business internationally

170. What is mentioned about Insta Printing?

(A) It opened a second branch yesterday.
(B) It offers various production options.
(C) It only produces athletic wear.
(D) It sponsors a local soccer team.

171. The word "further" in paragraph 4, line 1, is closest in meaning to:

(A) urgent
(B) official
(C) additional
(D) careful

Questions 172-175 refer to the following information.

(Man) – [1] – I remember when Sergio Hernandez first came to work here at Trout & Lee. He was a young man of 30 with a heart and mind filled with ambition and drive. – [2] – It is that ambition and drive, along with a lot of integrity and intelligence, that have made him one of the most valuable players in the garment business, and us one of its most successful companies.

– [3] – I can't help but remember how emotional I was when I left the company to pursue a life of leisure last year. – [4] – The speech Sergio gave then helped me during the difficult transition into living without an office to go to or colleagues to be continually inspired by, and I hope the few humble words I've strung together will remind him of how well respected he is and what an astounding life he has lived as he goes through the same process. Please put your hands together for Mr. Sergio Hernandez.

172. What is implied about Mr. Hernandez?

(A) He is the CEO of Trout & Lee.
(B) He is receiving a promotion.
(C) He is transferring to a new department.
(D) He is retiring from the company.

173. What is indicated about Trout & Lee?

(A) It is an international company.
(B) It is a real estate company.
(C) It has manufacturing plants in the U.S.
(D) It has existed for many decades.

174. What is NOT mentioned about Mr. Hernandez?

(A) When he started working for the company
(B) The type of employee he is
(C) The type of industry he works in
(D) His position in the company

175. In which of the places marked [1], [2], [3], and [4] does this sentence belong?

"I feel it a great honor to be asked to speak about him here today."

(A) [1]
(B) [2]
(C) [3]
(D) [4]

GO ON TO THE NEXT PAGE

Maple Outdoor
387 Maple Street, York, WA

Order # 23710

Date: May 6

ITEM	BRAND	1 Unit	PRICE
Hiking Boots	Nordic Heights	$149.95	$149.59
Camping Stove	Avalanche	$58.79	$58.79
Fuel Canister	Avalanche	$9.98	$19.96
Socks	Northern Wool	$12.85	$00.00 (Comp.)*

Total: $228.34

* We've included a free pair of socks to keep you warm on your next camping trip.

Thank you for being a loyal patron of Maple Outdoor for more than a year!

As always, if there is anything we can assist you with, don't hesitate to ask. If you are contacting us about a specific order, remember to give us the order number and your name.

Call us: (601) 478-2129

Email us: MapleOutdoor@zmail.com

To: Customer Service, Maple Outdoor
From: Shana Sandberg
Date: May 9
Subject: Delivery Issues

I received my order yesterday, and it wasn't what I had expected. I ordered an Avalanche camping stove, but I received an MT Elite stove instead. I'd like to receive my Avalanche stove as soon as possible, as I'm going on a camping trip next weekend. Do you think you can get it to me in time, or should I just come in and exchange the MT stove at your store? Please get back to me soon. I'll be waiting.

Thank you,

Shana Sandberg

176. What does Maple Outdoor mention about Ms. Sandberg's order?

(A) It will be delayed for up to a month.
(B) They have expedited it for free.
(C) It may not be returned if it is damaged through misuse.
(D) They have included a complimentary item with it.

177. How much does an Avalanche fuel canister cost?

(A) $58.79
(B) $9.98
(C) $19.96
(D) $12.85

178. Why did Ms. Sandberg write the email?

(A) To praise the service she received
(B) To request a monthly newsletter
(C) To ask if she could return an item
(D) To complain about an incorrect item

179. What requested information did Ms. Sandberg forget to include?

(A) Her name
(B) Her mailing address
(C) Her order number
(D) Her credit card number

180. What is true about Ms. Sandberg?

(A) She has shopped at Maple Outdoor before.
(B) She frequently goes camping.
(C) She didn't receive her hiking boots.
(D) She will be visiting the Maple Outdoor store soon.

GO ON TO THE NEXT PAGE ⟶

Attention Passengers

Clinton Bus Lines

In response to customer feedback, Clinton Bus Lines will be expanding its bus routes connecting Texas to other metropolitan centers in the Southwest. Starting on May 1, the new routes listed below will take effect. In order to promote these new bus lines, we will be offering tickets at half price during the first week of operation. Improving your satisfaction is our main priority. To get more detailed information such as departure and arrival times, please visit our website at www.clintonbuses.com.

• **From Dallas Bus Terminal to Phoenix, Arizona Bus Terminal**
• **From Austin Bus Terminal to Santa Fe, New Mexico Bus Terminal**
• **From Fort Worth Bus Terminal to Denver, Colorado Bus Terminal**

To: erichanson@prplanning.com
From: dangregory@trentonlogistics.com
Date: April 27
Subject: Upcoming Visit

Dear Mr. Hanson,

I am currently finalizing all the details of my visit to your company's headquarters in Santa Fe. Thank you for inviting me down to take part in these negotiations. Please let me know what time I should arrive. Will the meeting begin after lunch like it did last time?

You won't need to pick up me up, as I have arranged for a cab to pick me up at the Santa Fe bus terminal. Fortunately, a new bus line has been established between where I live and your offices. This has made transit in the region considerably more convenient. There are now routes to Denver and Phoenix as well. Best of all, thanks to a bit of good luck, I will be able to buy my ticket to Santa Fe at half the usual price.

I can't wait to see you and your coworkers again.

Dan Gregory

181. In the notice, what are Clinton Bus Lines' passengers encouraged to do on the company's website?

(A) Reserve tickets in advance
(B) Check bus schedules
(C) Apply for membership
(D) Request discount coupons

182. What is indicated about Mr. Gregory's previous meeting with Mr. Hanson?

(A) It took place in Texas.
(B) It lasted an entire week.
(C) It commenced in the afternoon.
(D) It was canceled due to bad weather.

183. In the email, the word "transit" in paragraph 2, line 3 is closest in meaning to:

(A) participation
(B) transportation
(C) investigation
(D) collaboration

184. Where does Mr. Gregory most likely live?

(A) In Santa Fe
(B) In Austin
(C) In Dallas
(D) In Denver

185. When is the meeting scheduled to take place?

(A) Before April 24
(B) Between April 24 and April 30
(C) Between May 1 and May 7
(D) After May 7

GO ON TO THE NEXT PAGE

To: Brian Petersen <bpetersen@atasteofclass.com>
From: Jason Hostrum <jhostrum@jhfurnishing.com>
Date: November 20th
Subject: Office Christmas Party

Dear Mr. Petersen,

I am looking to engage the services of your catering company, A Taste of Class, for our Christmas party at the end of the year. Ideally, we would like to have our event on Saturday, December 20th. I just have a few questions about your services. First, do you provide decorations? I really want this year's party to be a hit; it is my first time being responsible for it and I really want to impress the boss. Second, do you offer a wide range of vegetarian dishes? We have 12 vegetarians on our staff of 35, so it will be important to provide them with a full meal, not just appetizers. If you could get back to me with the answers to my questions and your availability on the 20th, I would greatly appreciate it.

Sincerely,

Jason Hostrum
Junior Secretary, Johnson Home Furnishing

To:	Jason Hostrum <jhostrum@jhfurnishing.com>
From:	Brian Petersen <bpetersen@atasteofclass.com>
Date:	November 21st
Subject:	RE: Office Christmas Party

Dear Mr. Hostrum,

I am delighted that you have contacted A Taste of Class to help make your Christmas party one to remember. Let me answer all of your questions and put your mind at ease. To begin with, we have one team left that can cater you on the 20th of December, so you are in luck! As far as the decorations are concerned, we have several different themes to choose from, so please visit our website at www.atasteofclass.com to see pictures of some of our successful events from the past. They are labeled with themes, so you can just choose one that appeals to you.

Your final inquiry regarding vegetarian options will also require some decision-making on your part. We offer gourmet dining, and are happy to specially prepare 12 vegetarian meals, but that could be a little expensive. I don't know what your budget is, but might I suggest making the entire menu vegetarian? We have an outstanding vegetarian chef, Julia Monroe, who can prepare a full vegetarian buffet so delicious a lion would eat it! This option is also a lot more cost-effective than preparing two separate menus. After reviewing your options, please let me know what choices are best for you.

Sincerely,

Brian Petersen
Booking and Sales Manager
A Taste of Class

To:	Brian Petersen <bpetersen@atasteofclass.com>
From:	Jason Hostrum <jhostrum@jhfurnishing.com>
Date:	November 22nd
Subject:	RE: Office Christmas Party

Dear Mr. Petersen,

Thanks for your reply. I want to go ahead and book the event for Saturday the 20th of December. I want the decoration theme Winter Wonderland, and I have decided to take your advice and go with whatever menu your chef Julia Monroe can put together for us. I really appreciate all of your recommendations and I just know this will be a great event!

All the best,

Jason Hostrum
Junior Secretary, Johnson Home Furnishing

GO ON TO THE NEXT PAGE

186. Why is Jason Hostrum anxious about the party?

(A) His family will be there.
(B) It is the first time the boss will join in.
(C) This is the first party he has had to plan for the company.
(D) There is too much food for him to prepare.

187. In the third email, what is indicated about Jason Hostrum?

(A) He has visited atasteofclass.com.
(B) He has created his own theme.
(C) He wants to cancel the party.
(D) He wants to add more food and guests.

188. According to the emails, what kind of food will be served?

(A) Only meat
(B) A mixture of meat and vegetarian
(C) Only vegetarian
(D) Only appetizers

189. In the first email, what is a big concern about the food?

(A) The flavor
(B) The types of side dishes
(C) The dietary restrictions of some employees
(D) Where the buffet will be located

190. What is indicated about A Taste of Class?

(A) They are busy this holiday season.
(B) They have lots of free teams on the 20th.
(C) They would prefer to cater on another date.
(D) They are too busy to work Johnson Home Furnishing's party.

To: <cservice@starproducts.com>
From: Jose Ramos <jramos@zipnet.com>
Date: October 14
Subject: Defective Hose

Dear Ms. Jenkins,

Recently I purchased 5,000 yards of XP100 industrial hosing from your company, Star Products. The hosing was listed as being capable of handling up to 1,000 pounds of pressure per square inch (psi). My company, Advanced Dynamic Cleaning, refitted all of our pressure washers with your hosing, at a considerable cost of both money and time. Every single one of our pressure washers has since failed at some point along the hosing from the joint of the gun to the compressor. Our compressors only generate 500 psi, so I have to conclude that there is some defect in the design of your hose. I would like to get a refund for my purchase, or a replacement of my order with hosing that meets industry standards. I have included my purchase order and a copy of the invoice.

Sincerely,

Jose Ramos

To: Jose Ramos <jramos@zipnet.com>
From: Raquel Jenkins <cservice@starproducts.com>
Date: October 16
Subject: RE: Defective Hose

Dear Mr. Ramos,

We have received your report of defective hosing and reviewed the attached documents. We truly value your business, and are sorry that you went through such a waste of time and energy with our hosing. However, I am sorry to say that the mistake appears to be on your end. Your purchase order clearly shows that you ordered XP100 hosing x 5,000 yards. If you look at the specs for that hosing, you will see that it is only rated as appropriate for 100 psi. This could explain why all of your hosing failed. What I can offer you is an exchange of the remaining XP100 hosing in your inventory for a hosing more appropriate for your needs. We will do this at no charge, and pay for the shipping as a show of our appreciation for your business. Please fill out the purchase order that I have attached and include it with the XP100 hosing when you ship it back to us for exchange.

Thank you,

Raquel Jenkins

GO ON TO THE NEXT PAGE

Star Products Purchase Order Form

Product Name	PSI	Length required	Price per yard	Applicable discount
XP1000	1,000	2,500 yards	$.50	Total discount as per agreed-upon exchange with product XP100

191. Why did Jose Ramos write to Star Products?

(A) To inquire about a price
(B) To order new hosing
(C) To report a hosing malfunction
(D) To compliment them on their hosing

192. What is indicated about the hosing that Jose Ramos ordered?

(A) It did not have the right psi rating for his use.
(B) It was defective.
(C) It was installed incorrectly.
(D) It was delivered to the wrong address.

193. According to the purchase order form, how much XP100 hosing is Jose Ramos returning?

(A) 1,000 yards
(B) 2,000 yards
(C) 2,500 yards
(D) 5,000 yards

194. What is indicated in the letter from Star Products?

(A) Star Products does not value Jose Ramos's business.
(B) Star Products appreciates Jose Ramos's patronage.
(C) Star Products doesn't need any more business.
(D) Star Products wants to expand its business.

195. What job does Raquel Jenkins likely have?

(A) CEO
(B) CFO
(C) Customer service representative
(D) Sales representative

To: Jason Roberts <jroberts@robertsparties.com>
From: Leroy Jenkins<ljenkins@smope.com>
Date: Sept. 24
Subject: Fall Party

Dear Mr. Roberts,

My name is Leroy Jenkins and I am planning a family reunion for the first weekend of October. I have heard from some friends that your parties are absolutely the best. I really want to make a good impression on my sister's new in-laws, as it will be the first time that they join our family for our annual reunion. I just have a few questions for you.

First, I need to know how much you would charge for a party for 25 people. I can afford $25 per person, not including alcohol. My family is also a little bit picky about food, so if it is possible for you to send a list of the foods that you offer and the cost per person, I would like to go through it and create my own menu.

The last question I have for you is about staffing. I really don't want to be cleaning up and doing dishes during the party. Do you provide staff, and if so how much do you charge for their service? Please write me back as soon as possible so we can get this party planned!

All the best,

Leroy Jenkins

ACTUAL TEST

09

GO ON TO THE NEXT PAGE

Dear Mr. Jenkins,

So glad to hear that our parties have been such a success. We do have a catering menu for you to choose items from; and feel free to mix and match based on your own budget and tastes. I have included a menu as well as a staffing guide. I recommend hiring a banquet captain if you're nervous about the event. Our banquet captains are trained to engage and charm the guests at the parties we host; hence our strong reputation.

I look forward to making your party a success!

Jason Roberts

ROBERTS PARTIES CATERING LIST

Appetizer	Entrée	Salad	Dessert
Chips and dip 1.00	Steak 2.50*	Caesar 1.00	Cake .50*
Pastry bites 1.00	Chicken 1.50*	Cobb 2.00*	Pie .50*
Onion rings 1.00*	Pork 1.50	Wild Greens 2.00*	Ice Cream .50

ROBERTS PARTIES STAFFING PRICES

Chef	$5.00 per hour
Wait Staff	$2.50 per hour
Banquet Captain	$3.50 per hour

*recommended items

196. Who most likely is Jason Roberts?

   (A) A chef
   (B) A business owner
   (C) A banquet captain
   (D) A receptionist

197. Who is Leroy Jenkins worried about impressing?

   (A) His boss
   (B) His brother
   (C) His sister's husband's family
   (D) His parents

198. What does Jason Roberts recommend that Leroy Jenkins include for his event?

   (A) An extra chef
   (B) A banquet captain
   (C) A vegetarian option
   (D) Extra waiters

199. What is indicated about Leroy Jenkins' budget?

   (A) He cannot afford Roberts Parties.
   (B) He needs to choose a very small menu.
   (C) He can afford everything that Roberts Parties recommends.
   (D) He will have to cut out appetizers.

200. Who will be at Leroy Jenkins' reunion?

   (A) His sister's in-laws
   (B) 25 Jenkins family members
   (C) Family members that live in town
   (D) Every member of his family

Stop! This is the end of the test. If you finish before time is called, you may go back to Parts 5, 6, and 7 and check your work.

READING TEST

In the Reading test, you will read a variety of texts and answer several different types of reading comprehension questions. The entire Reading test will last 75 minutes. There are three parts, and directions are given for each part. You are encouraged to answer as many questions as possible within the time allowed.

You must mark your answers on the separate answer sheet. Do not write your answers in your test book.

PART 5

Directions: A word or phrase is missing in each of the sentences below. Four answer choices are given below each sentence. Select the best answer to complete the sentence. Then mark the letter (A), (B), (C), or (D) on your answer sheet.

101. ------- the difference between the two brands is minimal, most consumers purchase the cheaper one.

(A) Until
(B) Because
(C) Before
(D) So

102. Audience members were impressed that the questions asked of the candidate were answered -------.

(A) clearly
(B) clear
(C) cleared
(D) clearing

103. In an attempt ------- sustainable energy, city officials have had solar panels affixed to some public buildings.

(A) generates
(B) generated
(C) generating
(D) to generate

104. The slow ------- of the fire department resulted in severe damage to the building.

(A) duration
(B) response
(C) treatment
(D) maintenance

105. After hours of searching, the plumber ------- identified the source of the leak.

(A) routinely
(B) finally
(C) rarely
(D) strongly

106. Please tell ------- that the workshop has been moved to Conference Room 402.

(A) whatever
(B) themselves
(C) everyone
(D) something

107. Highway 16 was widened over the summer to ------- the increasing number of vehicles using it.

(A) duplicate
(B) extend
(C) accommodate
(D) propose

108. Meal vouchers were given to Beta Airways passengers ------- were not able to depart on time because of booking errors.

(A) when
(B) because
(C) recently
(D) who

109. The gallery's catalog contains an accurate ------- of each piece of artwork that is being offered for sale.

(A) described
(B) description
(C) descriptive
(D) describes

110. To ensure that old appliances are disposed of properly, the city will offer free removal of them ------- April 2 and April 5.

(A) into
(B) from
(C) until
(D) between

111. A buffet dinner is available for the guests, so they may eat ------- looks appetizing to them without having to place an order.

(A) anyway
(B) whatever
(C) wherever
(D) anything

112. During the music festival, goods will be sold only by ------- vendors who have registered with the organizers.

(A) controversial
(B) increased
(C) confident
(D) approved

113. The grocery store chain Refresh Foods has ------- in organic products since it opened in 2001.

(A) participated
(B) certified
(C) specialized
(D) admired

114. The malfunctioning of the printer was ------- a component that had been inserted incorrectly during the assembly process.

(A) due to
(B) whereas
(C) as though
(D) instead of

115. The proposed holiday schedule is ------- to most workers because they know it is fair.

(A) acceptably
(B) accept
(C) acceptable
(D) accepting

116. The test will ------- confirm whether or not the patient has the disease.

(A) like
(B) liking
(C) likable
(D) likely

GO ON TO THE NEXT PAGE →

117. With over 200 unique stores, the Plainview Mall ------- millions of shoppers annually.

(A) attracts
(B) implements
(C) postpones
(D) contributes

118. The participants will be judged on ------- performance, and the winners will be announced later during the awards ceremony.

(A) athletically
(B) athletic
(C) athletes
(D) athlete

119. The York Foundation is an organization that has been supporting ------- in medical technology for the past decade.

(A) to advance
(B) advanced
(C) advances
(D) advancing

120. ------- the volleyball tournament is held indoors or outdoors depends primarily on the weather forecast for that day.

(A) Because
(B) Although
(C) Whether
(D) Whereas

121. The company came under investigation after several former employees made allegations of unfair -------.

(A) compositions
(B) assurances
(C) momentums
(D) practices

122. ------- joined Vince's Gym, Mr. Pinter could attend group classes and health counseling sessions for free.

(A) Being
(B) Having
(C) To have
(D) To be

123. The best way to improve the ------- of your home inexpensively is to give the exterior a fresh coat of paint.

(A) privacy
(B) appearance
(C) control
(D) location

124. Marketers believed that if the packaging were more ------- colored, consumers might pay more attention to the product.

(A) variously
(B) vary
(C) various
(D) variety

125. The police officer directed traffic ------- the detour ramp so that drivers could find the route easily.

(A) toward
(B) like
(C) of
(D) during

126. Every employee is asked to pair up with a ------- and find him or her at the predetermined meeting place during fire drills.

(A) reliance
(B) supervision
(C) colleague
(D) calculator

127. The car's owner submitted ------- evidence of the damage along with a mechanic's report to his insurance company.

(A) photographer
(B) photographically
(C) photographic
(D) photogenic

128. The restrooms on the second floor are ------- unavailable because one of the sinks is being replaced.

(A) temporarily
(B) previously
(C) respectively
(D) vitally

129. Because our sales representatives meet with high-level clients in the industry, ------- those with a professional manner will be considered for the position.

(A) only
(B) moreover
(C) except
(D) however

130. On next week's program, our host will interview Kristen Dabney about her time working as an ------- for a UN official.

(A) interpretation
(B) interpret
(C) interpreting
(D) interpreter

GO ON TO THE NEXT PAGE

PART 6

Directions: Read the texts that follow. A word, phrase, or sentence is missing in parts of each text. Four answer choices for each question are given below the text. Select the best answer to complete the text. Then mark the letter (A), (B), (C), or (D) on your answer sheet.

Questions 131-134 refer to the following notice.

To: All Staff

From: Michael Davis, Head Technician

Subject: Network Upgrade

We regret to inform everyone that from Monday the 13th of November until sometime midweek, the employee key card system will not be active. In order to get into and out of the building, you will need to buzz security. In order to lock or unlock any door, you will -------
131.
assistance from the security team.

The old system was reviewed and many vulnerabilities were discovered. -------, the company
132.
has decided to replace the old system. This process should take three to four days.

As part of the process, new key cards will be issued to all staff members. These key cards will be available for you to pick up starting Wednesday, the 15th of November, in the security office. Please feel free to stop by anytime ------- the day to collect yours. -------
133.   **134.**
We apologize for any inconvenience this may cause.

131. (A) is requesting
(B) has requested
(C) have to request
(D) had to request

132. (A) Unfortunately
(B) Therefore
(C) Regardless
(D) Finally

133. (A) upon
(B) during
(C) before
(D) at

134. (A) The switch from keys to keyless entry should make the facility more secure.
(B) We look forward to seeing you sometime next week.
(C) The security office is open 24 hours a day.
(D) This is for product security.

Music Teacher Needed

Mike's Music School is ------- seeking a new piano instructor for weekend and evening
       135.

classes. Mike's Music School has been operating in the Central district since 1992. -------
             136.

Because of this, we hope to hire a long-time resident of Central to join our team. Applicants

should be well versed in ------- teaching techniques. If you are interested in ------- for the
        137.   **138.**

position, we will be holding interviews and auditions this Saturday at 12 noon at our main

studio on Elm Street and Du Pont Avenue.

---

135. (A) active
(B) activation
(C) actively
(D) activated

(NEW)

136. (A) Our company tries to work with outside communities.
(B) Our commitment to the community is as important as our commitment to our students.
(C) Our company is unique and uses strange instruments.
(D) Our company is in a special location, next to an auto service center.

137. (A) contemporary
(B) unknown
(C) strange
(D) boring

138. (A) apply
(B) applied
(C) applying
(D) to apply

Saldesta

Rest Your Mind and Body

It's what you've been dreaming of. Peaceful sleep without a struggle is what you need. That's what Saldesta -------. Saldesta helps people fall asleep quickly, and stay asleep the entire
139.
night. It's the only nonnarcotic sleeping aid, and it's ------- for long-term use. ------- Talk to
140. **141.**
your doctor before using sleeping aids for extended periods. Tonight, just close your eyes and leave everything else to Saldesta.

Find out how to improve your sleep at www.saldesta.com, or call 1-800-SALDESTA.

Important Safety Information: Saldesta works quickly, and should be taken right -------
142.
bed. Be sure you have at least eight hours to devote to sleep before becoming active. Do not drink alcohol while taking Saldesta. Most sleep medications carry some risk of dependency.

---

139. (A) offers
(B) sustains
(C) mitigates
(D) maintains

140. (A) to approve
(B) approves
(C) approving
(D) approved

141. (A) So you can feel comfortable taking it night after night.
(B) Talk to your doctor today to see if it's right for you.
(C) This is the only stimulant approved for prolonged use by the FDA.
(D) Enter this code for a free sample and discounts.

142. (A) during
(B) around
(C) before
(D) after

Questions 143-146 refer to the following posting on a website.

Employee Message Board

Request for Feedback

Posted by James Frohm, Human Resources Director

Hello colleagues,

The holiday season is fast approaching and we need to ------- our office party! There have
                                                    143.

been several ------- for locations and themes made to me directly, but I wanted to invite
            144.

everyone in the office to give me his or her feedback. All ideas are welcome, but I must

remind everyone that our office -------. Our party can include all forms of secular celebration,
                              145.

but out of respect for everyone there can be no religious themes. Please respond to me

directly by email at <u>jamesfrohm@ccn.net</u>, so I can get started making plans. -------
                                                                            146.

Sincerely,

James

---

143. (A) make
    (B) plan
    (C) conceive
    (D) deliver

144. (A) comments
    (B) suggestions
    (C) spots
    (D) suggested

145. (A) is a safe space for all customs and
       cultures
    (B) stays open late on Tuesday
    (C) needs a new janitor
    (D) will move next week

146. (A) I look forward to hearing your ideas!
    (B) I don't want you to be late!
    (C) I look forward to your undivided
       attention.
    (D) I hope you reply before it's too late.

GO ON TO THE NEXT PAGE

Directions: In this part you will read a selection of texts, such as magazine and newspaper articles, emails, and instant messages. Each text or set of texts is followed by several questions. Select the best answer for each question and mark the letter (A), (B), (C), or (D) on your answer sheet.

Questions 147-148 refer to the following flyer.

TriStar Sports Gear

5477 Fairmont Avenue
Bemidji, MN 56634
218-555-3412
www.tristarsportsgear.com

Summer Sale from July 1 to July 14

The school year has ended and summer has arrived. Stop by TriStar Sports Gear and take advantage of our huge annual summer sale beginning this Friday. Now is the time to get ready for summer fun. We will be selling jerseys featuring your favorite sports teams for 20 percent off our regular price. Also, if you buy two pairs of athletic shoes, you can get a third pair at half price. There is much more on sale, so please see our sale list on the back page.

* Bring this flyer to our store and you can get a 10-percent discount on all kinds of balls.

147. What is indicated about TriStar Sports Gear?

(A) It is a family business.
(B) It is located next to a school.
(C) It holds a sale every year.
(D) It mainly sells weight training equipment.

148. How can customers receive a discount on athletic shoes?

(A) By buying more than two pairs
(B) By visiting the store on July 1
(C) By placing an order online
(D) By presenting a flyer

Questions 149-150 refer to the following text message chain.

Sylvia: What movie are we going to?   **19:01**

Jason: The one we agreed on last night!   **19:08**

Phyllis: Yeah. It looks sooooo good! I love   **19:08**
horror movies!

Bern: !!! What do you mean?? I thought   **19:20**
we decided on a comedy, that new one!

Sylvia: That's right! The comedy with   **19:21**
Ruffle Yellowbeard, the famous mime!

Jason: Comedy? I was thinking horror too,   **19:25**
but I do love Ruffle Yellowbeard. I'm in!

Phyllis: OK, comedy it is. Meet you   **19:35**
outside the theater at 10 P.M. SHARP!

---

149. What kind of movie did Phyllis think the group was going to see?

(A) Horror
(B) Science fiction
(C) Comedy
(D) Romance

150. What does Jason mean when he texts, "I'm in"?

(A) He wants to see the horror movie they agreed on.
(B) He wants to be in a comedy movie.
(C) He wants to be included in the group.
(D) He wants to stay at home tonight.

GO ON TO THE NEXT PAGE

Brixton Science Journal

On March 3, famed archeologist Douglas Price will be presenting on the results of his year-long excavation of ancient burial sites in Egypt. The presentation will be held at the Brixton Public Library beginning at 6:00 P.M.

Attendees are encouraged to come early in order to view some ancient Egyptian tools and instruments that will be on display. These precious items were retrieved by Mr. Price during his expedition to Egypt, and they are truly one of a kind. They are believed to have been used for farming by ancient Egyptian people.

Those who want to attend can reserve seats by visiting www.brixtonlibrary. com. You can also find more information concerning Mr. Price's most recent research on the website.

151. What is mentioned about the event?

(A) It is sponsored by the Egyptian government.
(B) It will feature an artifact exhibition.
(C) It will be held in Egypt.
(D) It is already sold out.

152. What can be found on the library's website?

(A) An events calendar
(B) A detailed map of the area
(C) Facts about ancient Egypt
(D) A guide to Egyptian food

Questions 153-154 refer to the following invitation.

Spring Valley Center

Grand Opening on Birch Street

Monday, February 23

Spring Valley Center of Spring Valley, California
is happy to invite you to
tour our new office spaces available for rent!

All day Monday we will host an open house
and all are welcome to tour the premises.

Spring Valley Center is conveniently located off Highway 10.

153. What most likely is Spring Valley Center?

(A) A department store
(B) A conference center
(C) A logistics company
(D) A business park

154. Why is the event being held?

(A) To attract new employees to a company
(B) To schedule a sales conference
(C) To advertise commercial rental space
(D) To announce the opening of a shopping center

Lockland Business News

September 8 — – [1] – This should come as a relief for residents on both sides of the Canadian-American border, as many shoppers from Lockland often make the one-and-a-half-hour drive into Canada to shop at the Cashco warehouse in Brentwood. – [2] – This usually results in long waits at the border and a very crowded Canadian Cashco with more than half its shoppers coming from across the border. Many Brentwood residents are resentful of the large crowds in their tiny town and Lockland residents have complained that the closest American Cashco is located almost five hours away. – [3] –

"I'm very excited," says Lockland resident Janice Burrows. "I heard it'll be huge. Maybe Canadians might start coming here to shop. But all kidding aside, we've been petitioning for a branch here for a long time." – [4] – The new Lockland Cashco is rumored to be one of the largest warehouses in America, with its own gas station, a pet center, a restaurant, cafeterias, a garden center, and a medical clinic.

155. What is the article about?

(A) Tension at the border
(B) Competition between neighboring residents
(C) Cross-border shopping expeditions
(D) The opening of a new Cashco branch in the near future

156. What is implied about Canadian residents?

(A) They want a Cashco branch.
(B) They dislike Americans' coming to shop.
(C) They don't like going to America.
(D) They have to travel far to get to a Cashco.

157. In which of the places marked [1], [2], [3], and [4] does the following sentence belong?

"A spokesperson for wholesale giant Cashco confirmed on Monday that a branch will finally open in Lockland next month."

(A) [1]
(B) [2]
(C) [3]
(D) [4]

Centerville County Shelter to Hold Marathon to Raise Money for the Homeless

A walking marathon will be held in Centerville County next Saturday. All proceeds from the event will be donated to the Centerville County Shelter. The shelter is a public institution that provides food, lodging, and support services for the homeless, the elderly, and anyone else in need.

This will be the second time the event has been held, and organizers expect more participants than they had last year. This event is open to children and adults of all ages. However, children must be accompanied by an adult family member at all times.

Centerville County Shelter was founded in 1981 with the mission of alleviating the hardships of homelessness, poverty, and hunger.

158. Why most likely would someone register for the event?

(A) To learn about staying fit
(B) To win a cash prize
(C) To apply for a job
(D) To contribute to the community

159. According to the article, who is NOT allowed to participate in the event?

(A) Senior citizens
(B) Students without student ID cards
(C) Unaccompanied children
(D) Foreign tourists

160. What is the main goal of the Centerville County Shelter?

(A) To build affordable housing
(B) To provide basic necessities
(C) To train professional athletes
(D) To educate community members

GO ON TO THE NEXT PAGE

ACTUAL TEST

10

Questions 161-164 refer to the following online chat discussion.

Molly	Who wants to go to the victory parade with me tomorrow?
Susan	I do! I've been following the team all season! Their games have been great, and their quarterback may be the best the school has ever had! It will also be a great opportunity to network and promote our new brand of beer, Winner's Ale!
Jeff	That might be fun. But I worry about our competition and their contracts with the university and the stadium's sponsors.
Molly	Ahhhhhhh. True; I didn't think of that . . . Well, we could do it "off the record." hahaha
Susan	Yeah, right. If corporate finds out, we will be fired for sure, or worse.
Jeff	True, true, but I still want to see the game and at least analyze our competitors' marketing strategies.
Susan	Good point, Jeff. We will go, but you'd better keep your mouth shut.
Jeff	Thanks, Susan. I will. So we'll all go and take notes, right?

161. What is indicated about Winner's Ale?

(A) It is an old variety of beer.
(B) People don't know about it yet.
(C) It is delicious.
(D) It is cheap.

162. What will the group most likely do next?

(A) Report to corporate about Jeff
(B) Go to the victory parade
(C) See a movie
(D) Go dancing and drink Winner's Ale

163. What does Molly mean when she says, "off the record"?

(A) An unreleased song
(B) A record of their activities is being kept.
(C) They won't go on official business
(D) Everything is being recorded and they want it to stop.

164. What is suggested about Jeff?

(A) He takes good notes.
(B) He likes to drink.
(C) He likes to talk.
(D) He loves parades.

Lichtenberg Air

September 24

To our passengers:

Beginning October 1, Lichtenberg Air will ask passengers to pay an extra 20 percent in baggage fees. As you know, the reason for this increase is rising fuel costs. We regret that our baggage fees have to be increased.

However, passengers are still allowed to bring one carry-on bag free of charge. We would also like to emphasize that this is the first increase in baggage fees for Lichtenberg Air in 10 years.

As always, our goal is to provide safe and reliable transportation at a reasonable price. If the price of fuel lowers, we expect to reverse this fee increase.

We thank you for choosing Lichtenberg Air.

165. What is indicated about Lichtenberg Air?

(A) It is asking passengers to stay within a baggage limit.
(B) It is responding to customer complaints.
(C) It has not increased its baggage fees for a decade.
(D) It has added new destinations.

166. What is suggested about passengers?

(A) They are allowed to bring electronics on board.
(B) They can take one bag onto a plane at no charge.
(C) They must pay an increased ticket price from October 1.
(D) They can get a 20-percent discount next month.

167. According to the notice, what will happen when the price of fuel drops?

(A) The stock price for Lichtenberg Air will increase.
(B) Passengers will be offered gift certificates.
(C) More flight attendants will be employed.
(D) The extra charge will be eliminated.

GO ON TO THE NEXT PAGE →

ACTUAL TEST

10

April 4

Paula Lynch
344 Culler Boulevard
Ellie, MN 42195

Dear Ms. Lynch,

We are pleased that you have accepted our request to give a presentation at this year's Conference on Second Language Education. As you know, this conference will gather teachers of German, French, Chinese, and many other foreign languages in one place to share classroom techniques and approaches. Aside from attending workshops and seminars, attendees will have ample opportunity to converse and network at a variety of events. This is an opportunity not to be missed.

This year's conference will be held at the Wilson Convention Center in Salem, Oregon. It will begin on Thursday, July 12, and last through Sunday, July 15. If requested, laptops and other equipment can be loaned to speakers for use during the conference. Any borrowed supplies must be returned on the final day of the conference. In addition to your fee for speaking, all speakers are also allowed to attend any other workshops and seminars free of charge.

Please provide us with your detailed travel itinerary. One of our staff members will be at the airport to meet you and give you a ride to the venue. Please call our office at (456) 555-1345 to provide the requested information before April 10.

We are looking forward to seeing you at the conference.

Sincerely,

Dirk Klein
Conference Organizer

168. What can be inferred about Ms. Lynch?

(A) She lives in Salem, Oregon.
(B) She can speak a second language.
(C) She is a motivational speaker.
(D) She is a conference organizer.

169. What is the purpose of the conference?

(A) To attract foreign investment
(B) To share teaching methods
(C) To set curriculum standards
(D) To establish a charitable foundation

170. When must speakers return borrowed supplies?

(A) April 4
(B) April 10
(C) July 12
(D) July 15

171. What is Ms. Lynch asked to inform Mr. Klein about?

(A) When she will arrive
(B) What supplies she will need
(C) What room she will use
(D) Who will accompany her

Bandit Pharmaceuticals
255 Highway Road
Boston, MA 48573

April 23
Mr. Timothy Jean
6844 Sylvia Place
Fresno, CA 97658

Dear Mr. Jean,

We at Bandit Pharmaceuticals are delighted you have accepted the position of research assistant. You will begin work on May 5th. The first day will be an orientation for all new hires with a workplace safety workshop, a seminar explaining your responsibilities on the job, and a tour of the facilities. – [1] –

Because you are coming in from out of town, we would like to make your move as smooth as possible. We understand that you will be arriving on April 29th and staying at the Boston Family Inn for a few days. The Inn is about a 10-minute taxi ride from the Bandit Pharmaceutical Headquarters. – [2] – You can go to the front desk in the main lobby and ask for Ms. Jenna Rhimes in human resources. She helps new out-of-town employees settle into the city and will answer any questions you may have. I have also attached the telephone numbers of some places and organizations that may be relevant to your move here. – [3] –

If you have any further questions or concerns, please feel free to call me at 555-1234 during my office hours, Monday to Friday from 9 A.M. to 7 P.M. – [4] – All the best with your move here and I will see you on May 5th.

Sincerely,

Joan Noonan
Human Resources

GO ON TO THE NEXT PAGE

172. Why did Ms. Noonan send a letter to Mr. Jean?

(A) To give him details about the time and place of a job interview

(B) To give him information about his first day of work

(C) To provide information about places for rent

(D) To confirm whether he would accept a job

173. What did Ms. Noonan send with the letter?

(A) Telephone numbers

(B) A copy of a contract

(C) Contact information of company employees

(D) A schedule

174. The phrase "settle into" in the second paragraph is closest in meaning to:

(A) look for

(B) explore

(C) become comfortable in

(D) navigate within

175. In which of the places marked [1], [2], [3], and [4] does the following sentence belong?

"Your laboratory manager will give you further details at the end of the first day."

(A) [1]

(B) [2]

(C) [3]

(D) [4]

Blackrock Education Foundation

| HOME | ABOUT US | NEWS | RESOURCES | CONTACT |

February 10

Language Scholarship

The Blackrock Education Foundation would like to announce that we will begin taking applications for the 24th German Language Scholarship starting March 10 and ending on March 31. Applicants from diverse backgrounds are encouraged to apply. To qualify for the scholarship, applicants must:
– be currently enrolled in a master's program
– prove advanced proficiency in the German language
– submit a complete health check
– submit a recommendation from a previous language instructor

The German Language Scholarship is intended for students who already speak German at an advanced level. Therefore, this scholarship is for students who plan to use the German language to study in Germany in the near future.

Recipients of the scholarship must complete monthly progress reports, submit all monthly expenses to the foundation, and maintain a B+ grade average.

Applications can be downloaded under the RESOURCES tab on our website. Please submit all necessary materials to Mr. Hans Richter, Blackrock Education Foundation's director. The address is 459 Pearson Road, Chicago, IL 60616. The review and selection process will take approximately two weeks. Any application with incomplete or missing documents will be rejected without exception. Results will be announced on April 15.

To: Clint Porter <cporter@umc.com>
From: Hans Richter <richter@blackrockedu.com>
Date: April 15
Subject: Blackrock Scholarship
Attachment: scholarship_information

Dear Mr. Porter,

I would like to congratulate you on being chosen as a recipient of the 24th German Language Scholarship. As a recipient of the scholarship, you will be supplied with travel expenses to Germany, tuition fees, and living expenses for one year. Attached is a booklet containing information on scholarship regulations and requirements. Please make sure you read it carefully. If you have any questions or concerns, feel free to contact me. I will be emailing you within the next week with specific details on how to prepare for your upcoming studies.

Thanks,

Hans Richter

Director, Blackrock Education Foundation

ACTUAL TEST

10

GO ON TO THE NEXT PAGE

176. According to the web page, what must scholarship recipients do?

(A) Keep track of monthly expenses
(B) Write a research paper
(C) Submit an annual report
(D) Take an entrance examination

177. What is indicated about scholarship applications?

(A) They must be received by mid-April.
(B) They will be accepted only if requirements are met.
(C) They will be reviewed and selected by German professors.
(D) They must be submitted online.

178. On the web page, the word "proficiency" in paragraph 1, line 6 is closest in meaning to:

(A) system
(B) practice
(C) experience
(D) mastery

179. What is the purpose of the email?

(A) To confirm a departure date
(B) To schedule an interview
(C) To give some information to a scholarship winner
(D) To enroll in required courses at a university in Germany

180. What is suggested about Mr. Porter?

(A) He worked at the Blackrock Foundation.
(B) He is an entrepreneur working in Germany.
(C) He has a good command of German.
(D) He wants to be a language instructor.

Sunny Day Cleaning
The only choice for your professional cleaning

Bill to: Randall Auto Body   **Invoice #:** 2348   **Date:** March 3
957 Pacific Trail Rd.
Troutdale, Oregon 97055

Date	Description of Service	Amount
February 5	Full office cleaning (Including: three rooms, two bathrooms, windows, carpet deep clean, furniture)	$95
February 19	Full office cleaning (Including: three rooms, two bathrooms, windows, carpet deep clean, furniture)	$95

Total: $190

*Payments received after April 1st will be subject to a $20 late charge.

Sunny Day Cleaning
283 Main St.
Troutdale, Oregon 97055

Questions or Additional Services: Please call 1-345-737-2209

GO ON TO THE NEXT PAGE

March 8

Dear Sunny Day Cleaning,

I have received your invoice for the services we received in February, which I have to say were excellent. I see we were charged 95 dollars for each time you cleaned our offices. This is what we had initially agreed upon and have been paying for your services since last year at this time. However, Rod Sanford told me we'd be receiving a five-dollar discount each time you visited us because we have arranged for you to clean our other location just off of Highway 26. He said that this new price would go into effect starting in February. I have included a copy of the email he sent me. Could you please adjust the price to reflect our new agreement and send us a new bill? I'd appreciate it. We look forward to seeing you again.

Thank you for your assistance,

Patricia Collins

Patricia Collins

Manager
Randall Auto Body

---

181. According to the invoice, what amount is due by April 1?

(A) $20
(B) $90
(C) $95
(D) $190

182. What service was NOT provided to Randall Auto Body?

(A) Window cleaning
(B) Floor cleaning
(C) Furniture cleaning
(D) Carpet cleaning

183. Why did Ms. Collins write a letter?

(A) The cleaning service missed an appointment.
(B) She was overcharged for a service.
(C) The cleaning service added an extra fee to her bill.
(D) She would like to renew her contract.

184. What is implied about Sunny Day Cleaning?

(A) They provide decent service.
(B) They are often late for appointments.
(C) They frequently overcharge their clients.
(D) They offer late payment options.

185. What did Ms. Collins send besides her letter?

(A) A coupon for auto repairs
(B) A copy of an email
(C) A signed contract
(D) A check for the amount due

Respite for Commuters

A new ride-sharing app is gaining in popularity as bus and taxi fees continue to rise and commuters continue to look for more efficient routes. Jordan Mills, a small business owner who commutes into the city from his home in Brentwood, had to change buses twice and then take the subway to get to his workplace. Not only did he find the commute quite costly and uncomfortable with the rush-hour crowds; he also found it time-consuming. But with the availability of the new Freewheel app, he found that he could save time and money with a quick ride available within five minutes from any location he was at. "This is definitely the future of transportation," says Jordan. "I wouldn't go to work and back any other way now."

Jordan Mills isn't the only commuter who feels this way. An estimated 2,000 commuters in the city of Sherwood alone are expected to use the ride-sharing app within the next year and almost 500 drivers have signed up for the program.

Freewheel is available for download on the Freewheel website and on Miniapp.com and Amacom.com.

---

www.freewheel.com/history

The idea for Freewheel began when Michael Owens and his coworkers started a carpooling program at the company they worked at. Owens had to change subways three times and buses twice to get to work and although he could drive, parking was limited. He managed the carpooling group by assigning drivers and mapping out a route to each coworker's home. He then created an app that everyone could connect and communicate through so that the designated drivers and passengers could easily find each other. Five years later, Freewheel is a major company with tens of thousands of users, both drivers and commuters, around the country.

Freewheel is dedicated to keeping the cost of commuting down and the efficiency up. In time, it hopes to offer its services to people around the world.

GO ON TO THE NEXT PAGE

ACTUAL TEST

10

Technology Initiatives
is proud to present the
New Innovation Award to:
Michael Owens, CEO of Freewheel

This award recognizes the innovation and creativity of new talent in the technology industry. It also acknowledges efforts to help consumers through the use of technology with novel ideas that have transformed the nature of transportation.

Susan Vaneer

Executive Manager, Technology Initiatives

186. How are Jordan Mills and Michael Owens similar?

(A) Both started technology companies.
(B) Both wanted an efficient way to commute.
(C) Both were employed in public transportation.
(D) Both won awards for their achievements.

187. What is indicated about Freewheel?

(A) It started out small.
(B) It is an international company.
(C) It employs bus drivers.
(D) It is good for the environment.

188. What is most likely true about Michael Owens?

(A) He dislikes driving.
(B) He owns a taxi company.
(C) He wants to expand his business.
(D) He has met Jordan Mills.

189. The word "Respite" in the title of the article is closest in meaning to:

(A) employment
(B) immunity
(C) a refund
(D) a break

190. What is the certificate rewarding?

(A) The best driver
(B) Environmental efforts
(C) A good idea
(D) The highest-earning company

To: Ken Alberts <kalberts@emergentsolutions.com>
From: Clarissa Pierce <cpierce@actionservices.com>
Date: June 13
Subject: shipping contracts

Hello Mr. Alberts,

I am writing on behalf of my company, Action Services. Our company specializes in creating personalized flower arrangements, gift baskets, and novelty gifts. Recently we have been going over our books and have realized we have been paying too much to our current shipping company. We would be interested in offering you the opportunity to take over our account if you could offer us more competitive rates. I have included a recent invoice of shipping cost from our current carrier, Express Corp. If you feel that you could beat their prices, we would like to try working with you. Please let me know what you think.

Sincerely,

Clarissa Pierce
Account Manager, Action Services

To: Clarissa Pierce <cpierce@actionservices.com>
From: Ken Alberts <kalberts@emergentsolutions.com>
Date: June 14
Subject: shipping contracts

Dear Ms. Pierce,

Thank you for contacting us at Emergent Solutions. I have taken a look at your invoice from your last bill from Express Corp. and I believe that we can beat their prices. I would be happy to send over my account director to try to tailor a delivery package that is perfect for your needs. Since most of the shipping that you do is within the state, and composed of relatively small items, I believe our express courier service would be perfect. We use fuel-efficient hybrid vehicles to run our small deliveries and are able to pass the savings on to our customers. As account director, I look forward to working with Action Services in the future.

Sincerely,

Ken Alberts

GO ON TO THE NEXT PAGE

To: Ken Alberts <kalberts@emergentsolutions.com>
From: Clarissa Pierce <cpierce@actionservices.com>
Date: June 16
Subject: shipping contracts

Dear Mr. Alberts,

This sounds amazing! You have no idea how much it means to our company that you are using environmentally responsible transportation. Action Services was originally formed by a group of environmental studies majors at City College here. Everything we sell is ethically sourced and recyclable. We can't wait to meet with your team.

Best,

Clarissa Pierce
Account Manager, Action Services

191. What job does Mr. Alberts have?

(A) President
(B) HR manager
(C) CEO
(D) Account director

192. What is indicated about Action Services?

(A) They care about art.
(B) They are concerned about the environment.
(C) They need to sell more packages.
(D) Their old delivery service delivered packages to the wrong addresses.

193. From the emails, what can you infer?

(A) Emergent Solutions offers lower shipping costs than Express Corp.
(B) Emergent Solutions will not be efficient.
(C) Emergent Solutions' business ethics are at odds with those of Action Services.
(D) Action Services is in debt.

194. Why did Action Services contact Emergent Solutions?

(A) They needed new customers.
(B) They were spending too much on shipping.
(C) They wanted to expand their operation.
(D) They wanted to ship internationally.

195. What kind of business is Action Services?

(A) Technology consultants
(B) Leadership experts
(C) Hotel and resort specialists
(D) Florists and novelty suppliers

To:	Aaron Donald <adonald@acemail.com>
From:	James Holt <holtrain@zipnet.net>
Date:	Jan. 12
Subject:	First Quarter Performance Review

Dear Aaron,

I just wanted to give you a heads-up that the performance evaluations will be going forward as discussed. I know this was an area of stress for you in the fourth quarter of last year, so I wanted to give you plenty of advance warning. You will need to bring your numbers up significantly if you want to pass the review. As you know, we have been struggling to meet our sales goals over the past several years, and I am afraid Mr. Jones is determined to trim the staff if things don't change. I have far exceeded my target numbers, so I have included an attachment with some possible leads for sales; give them a shot.

Good Luck,

James

To:	James Holt <holtrain@zipnet.net>
From:	Aaron Donald <adonald@acemail.com>
Date:	Jan. 12
Subject:	RE: First Quarter Performance Review

James,

Thank you so much for the leads. I will get on them right away. I don't know why my sales in the technology division are slumping so much lately. It seems like every sales technique I learned in school isn't working anymore. I am thinking about changing industries if I don't pass our review when it comes out in March. My sister is opening a beauty parlor and she's been asking me to become a barber. Imagine that! Anyway, thank you again for the notice about the possible layoffs coming up. I will try to get my numbers up to standard, but I think that Mr. Jones may have already decided to let me go.

All the best,

Aaron

GO ON TO THE NEXT PAGE

Possible Sales Leads for January

Name	Division	Account Potential	Rating
Sally Jones	technologies	$35,000-$50,000	Silver
Bob Knuddle	technologies	$100,000 and up	Gold
Marquise Lee	technologies	$12,000-$20,000	Bronze/Silver

196. What is most likely true about James and Aaron?

(A) They are competitors.
(B) They are related.
(C) They are married.
(D) They are friends.

197. What is indicated about Aaron?

(A) He is not very good at his job these days.
(B) The owner loves him.
(C) He has problems with all of his coworkers.
(D) He will keep his job after the evaluations are reviewed.

198. According to the information provided, what is true about James?

(A) He has done very well at work.
(B) He needs more sales.
(C) He wants to work with Aaron.
(D) He will become a barber.

199. What is the problem with the sales leads James gave to Aaron?

(A) They are rated too highly.
(B) They aren't worth very much money.
(C) Aaron doesn't know the contacts.
(D) They are in a field Aaron is struggling in.

200. What job does Mr. Jones most likely have?

(A) Human resources agent
(B) Sales executive
(C) Owner
(D) Associate secretary

Stop! This is the end of the test. If you finish before time is called, you may go back to Parts 5, 6, and 7 and check your work.

TRANSLATION

ACTUAL TEST ①

PART 5　P.18-21

◎ Part 5 解答請見 P.457

101. 填寫訂購單時，請清楚**寫上**您的地址以避免延誤。

102. 摩根女士招募了公司接下來三個月**將聘用**的人員。

103. 在本地報紙刊登廣告後，承包商的生意**成長**了百分之十五。

104. 這間免費診所是由一群醫生設立的，為各種疾病提供**治療**。

105. 參加徒步行程的人應該在星期六上午**於**貝茲街 533 號集合。

106. 藝術家將**他**最棒的作品送到藝廊讓老闆品評。

107. 財務報表所附的數據應該與支出項目**有關**。

108. 業主三個月前**才**買下這棟大樓，但她已經花了一大筆錢裝潢了。

109. 我們打算在下次的員工會議上開誠**布公**地討論這個問題。

110. 店經理打算**趕快**展示新產品以宣傳秋季系列時裝。

111. 在旺季時，僱用更多員工來輪週末的班是**必要的**。

112. **既然**已經換成了隔熱材料，這棟大樓就更節能了。

113. 西蒙斯先生需要一部更**可靠**的車以往返郊區的住家和市中心的辦公室。

114. 為了比其他競爭對手銷售更多產品並吸引更多顧客，這家公司**策略性地**降低售價。

115. **在**威廉斯先生對聽眾演講**前**，他播放了一部短片，是關於他所設計的引擎。

116. 為了在道路駕駛時的安全起見，避免**阻擋**後車窗與左右後視鏡的視線。

117. 整棟大樓有良好的通風，對保護員工健康和福祉來說是**必要**的。

118. 垃圾食物銷售量持續下滑的**事實**顯示出消費者已經更有健康概念了。

119. 草地灑水系統的灑水器是由**機械**控制的。

120. 圖書館員張貼公告，**通知**讀者因裝修即將閉館的消息。

121. 幫大廳內部重新粉刷**的**羅斯先生，是由大樓經理的朋友推薦的。

122. 月刊的撰寫體例會**定期地**修改，以因應不斷變化的讀者。

123. **儘管**腳踝受傷，那位棒球員還是參加了該季的最後一場比賽。

124. 政府部門以前會提供財務協助，但現在只提供**法律**服務。

125. 應房客**要求**，多送了一組毛巾與免費香皂到客房。

126. 高檔精品店珍的衣櫥以銷售最時髦的**飾品**給年輕專業人士著名。

127. 公司開始體認到有責任地運用資源這件事日益增加的**重要性**。

128. **在**重組公司內部幾個部門**後**，大多數溝通不良的問題都消失了。

129. 新藥物研發中最危險的**階段**就是人體實驗。

130. 應徵圖萊里設計公司**的人都**必須繳交作品集。

PART 6　P.22–25

131–134 電子郵件

收件者：samsmith@digitalIT.com
寄件者：sharronb@bmail.com
日期：9 月 24 日
主旨：商業合約

親愛的史密斯先生：

我是雪倫・畢格斯，我是畢格斯平面設計公司的創辦人兼執行長。最近看到您的廣告，是為貴公司的一些專案尋求配合的平面設計公司。畢格斯設計有豐富的經驗，與各種小型企業與公司合作過設計廣告活動、商標與網站。我已附上本公司之前的設計案，以說明我們的專項。本公司的網站 www.biggs-graphics.com 上也有相關資訊。

我對與貴公司合作進行您的專案相當感興趣，希望彼此能夠建立有利的合作關係。期待收到您的回覆。

畢格斯平面設計執行長

雪倫・畢格斯 敬上

131. Ⓐ 尋求
　　　 Ⓑ 以尋求
　　　 Ⓒ 尋求
　　　 Ⓓ 正在尋求

132. **Ⓐ 大量的**
　　　 Ⓑ 受限制的
　　　 Ⓒ 慷慨的
　　　 Ⓓ 無限的

133. Ⓐ 我會很感激有機會與您合作。
　　　 Ⓑ 我聽聞數位 IT 是一間很棒的公司。
　　　 Ⓒ 事實上，我們的設計常被其他公司抄襲。
　　　 Ⓓ 我已附上本公司之前的設計案，以說明我們的專項。

134. Ⓐ 在
　　　 Ⓑ 對
　　　 Ⓒ 和
　　　 Ⓓ 來自

135–138 公告

感謝您惠顧勞森瓷器店。我們的產品以時尚又獨特的花紋、色彩搭配以及耐用與堅固著名。可使用於洗碗機與微波爐，而且我們有信心您絕對可以用上好幾年。但是，請注意，反覆摔落或粗魯使用將終造成毀損。我們建議您小心存放，在清潔時避免使用刺激性化學藥劑、鋼製海綿或激烈擦洗。有關使用與照料上的資訊，請上本店網站 www.larsonchina.com。若有任何疑慮，也可來電 555-1234。

135. Ⓐ 耐用的
　　　 Ⓑ 耐用性
　　　 Ⓒ 耐用
　　　 Ⓓ 持續時間

136. Ⓐ 勞森的器皿與銀器很適合搭配餐具。
　　　 Ⓑ 我們最受歡迎的春花瓷器系列，在大多數的門市都銷售一空。
　　　 Ⓒ 到我們店裡看看其他美麗的產品。
　　　 Ⓓ 可使用於洗碗機與微波爐，而且我們有信心您絕對可以用上好幾年。

137. Ⓐ 造成
　　　 Ⓑ 想到
　　　 Ⓒ 終止於
　　　 Ⓓ 停止

138. Ⓐ 有野心的
　　　 Ⓑ 好戰的
　　　 Ⓒ 激烈的
　　　 Ⓓ 滿足的

139–142 告示

初級職位：高登暨史賴會計事務所

我們正在徵求充滿熱忱、具財務或會計教育背景的應徵者。所有應徵者需有一定的電腦操作經驗。無工作經驗可，但具工作經驗者尤佳。具雙語能力者將優先考慮。職務包括：會計、統計與總務處助理。意者請上本公司網站 www.

G&Saccountingfirm.com/employment 了解更多資訊。可將求職信與履歷寄給凱倫·希爾，電子郵件是 khill@G&S.com。我們將於 11 月 5 日星期一開始進行面試，該職位從次月到職上班。

139. Ⓐ 帳戶
Ⓑ 會計師
Ⓒ 會計
Ⓓ 説明

140. Ⓐ 基本的
Ⓑ 決定的
Ⓒ 額外的
Ⓓ 必要的

141. Ⓐ 正在
Ⓑ 將會
Ⓒ 已經
Ⓓ 之前在

142. Ⓐ 我們衷心地感謝您的好意。
Ⓑ 該職位從次月到職上班。
Ⓒ 請來電洽詢更多資訊。
Ⓓ 我們為所造成的不便致歉。

143–146 電子郵件

收件者：廚房人員、辦公室員工
寄件者：賴瑞·派克經理
日期：3 月 23 日
主旨：整修

給廚房人員及漢默全體員工：

自 3 月 23 日星期日起至 3 月 27 日星期四止，員工自助餐廳因廚房汰換老舊器具，進駐新廚具設備而進行整修工程。為此，將無法提供熱食給顧客。但這段時間便利商店將為員工們準備更多的三明治、便當及點心。

這個整修工程將增加水槽、烤箱和爐子的數量，這樣在午餐與晚餐的巔峰時段就能提供大量餐點。我們為所造成的不便致歉，但我們也希望這些變革可以改善餐廳的服務。

143. Ⓐ 正帶來
Ⓑ 已經帶來
Ⓒ 帶來
Ⓓ 被帶來

144. Ⓐ 這要花上很多功夫。
Ⓑ 因此，便利商店要關門了。
Ⓒ 為此，將無法提供熱食給顧客。
Ⓓ 因此會出現噪音與混亂。

145. Ⓐ 在……之前
Ⓑ 在……之後
Ⓒ 在……期間
Ⓓ 在……之外

146. Ⓐ 發展
Ⓑ 改善
Ⓒ 矯正
Ⓓ 恢復

PART 7 P.26–47

147–148 電子郵件

收件者：employees@simnetsolutions.com
寄件者：management@simnetsolutions.com
主旨：研討會機會
日期：2 月 5 日

親愛的女性同仁：

距離女性領導力研討會報名截止日期還有一週的時間，這個研討會將免費提供給我們新網顧問公司的所有女性同仁。為了配合女性同仁們忙碌的工作時間表，將分別於 2 月 21 日和 2 月 23 日兩天，舉辦一樣的研討會。

欲報名這場特別安排的研討會，請於 2 月 12 日下午五點前以電子郵件方式告知人力資源部的詹姆斯·泰勒。這場研討會將教導女性同仁如何在職場上以自信與值得信賴的方式表達想法。

新網顧問公司管理團隊 敬上

147. 下列何者和研討會有關？

    Ⓐ 它的特色是主講人詹姆斯‧泰勒
    Ⓑ 它每年都會舉行
    Ⓒ 它的費用比前一場還貴
    Ⓓ 為女性而設計

148. 免費報名何時截止？

    Ⓐ 2 月 5 日
    Ⓑ 2 月 12 日
    Ⓒ 2 月 21 日
    Ⓓ 2 月 23 日

149–150 訊息串

凱爾	2:42

南西，是我，凱爾。我在 B 會議室為五點的會議做準備。投影機不能用，你可以到用品儲藏室拿另一台來嗎？

南西	2:45

嘿，沒問題。我現在就過去。

凱爾	2:46

謝啦。真的很感激。

南西	2:57

凱爾，這裡沒有投影機。我已經打給資訊科技部，問他們有沒有備用機。等我收到回覆再跟你說。

凱爾	3:00

再次感謝你。喔，你可以找一下有沒有多的麥克風嗎？

南西	3:08

這裡有兩個，我會把兩個都帶上。同時，資訊科技部說，他們沒有多的投影機。不過他們現在就派人過去看看出了什麼問題。他們說，昨天簡報時還是好的。

凱爾	3:09

太好了！待會見。

149. 南西最有可能在哪裡？

    Ⓐ 會議室
    Ⓑ 資訊科技部門
    Ⓒ 用品儲藏室
    Ⓓ 她的辦公室

150. 南西說：「我現在就過去」是什麼意思？

    Ⓐ 她要過去那個地方
    Ⓑ 她會帶領簡報
    Ⓒ 她知道那個房間在哪裡
    Ⓓ 她要直接過去找他

151–152 票券

購票者：提姆‧貝利

泰特劇院
凱莉‧庫柏演唱會

    時間：晚上七點
    日期：5 月 20 日，星期五
    區域：搖滾區
    排：F
    座位：26

■ 搖滾區來賓請於演唱會開始前至少 30 分鐘入場

■ 自行開車者，可上網站 www.tatetheater. com 查詢劇院位置

■ 票券售出，概不退款

151. 貝利先生被建議做什麼事？

    Ⓐ 聯絡劇院要求退款
    Ⓑ 在網站上挑選喜歡的座位
    Ⓒ 提早入場
    Ⓓ 稍後發表評論

152. 根據票券，劇院的網站上可以看到什麼？

    Ⓐ 以前的表演清單
    Ⓑ 行車路線
    Ⓒ 演唱會評論
    Ⓓ 劇院照片

153–154 資訊

基墨尚好買
訂單確認

姓名：珍妮‧柯林斯
顧客編號：F833J
地址：10025 紐約州紐約市哥倫布大道
      808 號
訂購日期：8 月 22 日

品項	價格
彈簧圓模烤盤（單價 5 元 5 入）	25 元
可可油四盎司	10.99 元
糖衣（單價 5.9 元 3 入）*	17.70 元
杯子蛋糕烤盤（單價 4 元 2 入）	8.00 元
商品金額	**61.69 元**
運費	**8.99 元**
合計	**70.68 元**

付款方式：
信用卡 xxxx xxxx xxxx 4026

* 備註：為防融化或毀損，將加速送達

153. 這些物品最有可能給哪種行業使用？

- A 購物中心
- **B 麵包店**
- C 電器行
- D 便利商店

154. 下列何者與訂單有關？

- A 將使用分期付款
- **B 商品將分開遞送**
- C 已經打折了
- D 將免費運送

155–157 文章

社區大獲全勝

在歷經長達數月的抗爭，力阻在河谷法院大樓的前院址興建開發新購物商場後，當地居民與民間團體皆歡欣鼓舞，因為最後裁決將完整無缺地保住這棟 150 年的建築。原本計劃興建購物中心的開發公司布蘭福德建設，現在正打算在河谷社區之外另蓋商場。「我們很失望。」布蘭福德建設執行長補充說道，「我們認為這地區可因此受益成長。但顯然地，居民們想保存他們的歷史，而我尊重他們的決定。」

他們正在努力修復廢棄的舊法院大樓，讓它恢復昔日榮景。「整個社區為此凝聚在一起，我們正在募款整修這棟大樓。」當地居民陳依尼表示：「我們希望把這棟大樓改建成公立圖書館或學校。」

「從我有記憶以來，它就在這裡了。事實上，我的祖父就在這裡當過職員。」當地商家老闆凱文・蘭伯說：「它是我們社區的一個象徵標誌，我們不希望它被破壞。」透過線上連署，該社區已經募集了十萬多元，而捐款仍然持續注入。該社區希望大樓的修復工程能在未來的幾個月內展開。

155. 文中提到舊法院大樓的什麼？

- A 布蘭福德建設想修復這棟大樓
- B 居民想把這棟大樓改成購物中心
- **C 它可能會變成公立圖書館或學校**
- D 它可能被破壞

156. 下列句子最適合出現在 [1]、[2]、[3]、[4] 的哪個位置？「原本計劃興建購物中心的開發公司布蘭福德建設，現在正打算在河谷社區之外另蓋商場。」

- **A [1]**
- B [2]
- C [3]
- D [4]

157. 下列何者與募款一事有關？

- A 社區從土地上賺了很多錢
- **B 在網路上進行**
- C 市政府提供協助
- D 他們還沒募到足夠的錢

158–160 電子郵件

收件者：史黛西・強生
<sjohnson@toplineelec.com>
寄件者：喬許・佛列克
<jfleck@toplineelec.com>
日期：10 月 22 日
主旨：戰略規劃

親愛的強生女士：

泰菱電子區域管理部要通知您一個可能會影響您店面的新發展，另一家同您競爭消費者的電器行將於 11 月 12 日在克雷維爾區開幕。

為了確保泰菱電子的生意不會因為這家新店而失去生意，區域管理部建議您針對新型超高畫質曲面液晶電視推出特別優惠活動。這些電視有最先進的功能，卻有平實的價格。只要讓顧客知道泰菱電子會提供本地區中最實惠的價格，您就能維持顧客的忠誠度。我們將於下週內將新電視機配送到您的店裡。建議您在店內安排一塊顯眼的區域做展示，特別介紹它們。您也應更新網頁來宣傳這個促銷活動。

保持您與我們之間的溝通管道暢通對有效經營非常重要。如果您對新電視機或一般的行銷活動有任何問題，請不要猶豫，隨時歡迎與區域管理部聯絡。

泰菱電子 區域經理
喬許·佛列克 敬上

158. 強生女士最有可能是誰？

Ⓐ **店經理**
Ⓑ 顧客
Ⓒ 產品開發人員
Ⓓ 行銷專家

159. 下列何者與泰菱電子有關？

Ⓐ 它最近新開了一家門市
Ⓑ 它將搬到克雷維爾區
Ⓒ **它對市場競爭感到憂心**
Ⓓ 它在一項年度大獎中被提名

160. 強生女士未被指示做哪件事？

Ⓐ 在網站上增加新資訊
Ⓑ **多僱用員工**
Ⓒ 如有需要聯絡管理部
Ⓓ 安排一個銷售展示區

161–164 網路討論區

哈利·尼克森	10:10

批發商那裡有任何關於書桌和辦公椅的消息嗎？我們週二就應該要就收到了。

強尼·喬登	10:11

莫妮卡正在等他們的消息。上回我聽到的是，因為生產線的問題而造成了一些延誤。看樣子，是有條傳輸帶故障了。

哈利·尼克森	10:12

你有把這件事告訴我們在 P&R 企業的客戶嗎？

強尼·喬登	10:13

沒有。我想在轉達任何延誤相關訊息前，先得到製造商的明確說法。嗨，莫妮卡，你收到回覆了嗎？

莫妮卡·史丹	10:14

是的，我剛跟他們談過。好消息，看來我們可以照原先計劃在週五完工。桌椅會在星期四時直接從生產線送達 P&R 企業。

哈利·尼克森	10:15

這消息真是太棒了，請通知克萊先生這件事。一旦家具送達，我們就可以開始進行五樓辦公室的工程，從那裡繼續往下做。

莫妮卡·史丹	10:15

我馬上處理。

強尼·喬登	10:16

好，我會召集一大群工作人員去那裡，這樣就能照計劃在週五時完工。

哈利·尼克森	10:17

好的，請確認不但是要有效率地完工，還要做得完善。他們還有幾間別的大樓，可能也會需要我們的服務。

強尼·喬登	10:18

我會牢記在心的。

161. 這幾位線上交談者從事何種行業？

Ⓐ 法律事務所
Ⓑ **辦公家具公司**
Ⓒ 家具店
Ⓓ 搬家公司

162. 工作人員何時開工？

    A 週二

    B 週三

    C 週四

    D 週五

163. 強尼‧喬登接下來可能會做什麼？

    A 聯絡批發商

    B 籌備會議

    C 召集工作人員

    D 打電話給客戶

164. 莫妮卡‧史丹說的「我馬上處理」是什麼意思？

    A 她會安排搬遷事宜

    B 她會等到有更多資訊

    C 她會拜訪製造商

    D 她會聯絡客戶

165–167 企業介紹

富頓不鏽鋼製品

富頓不鏽鋼製品是一家大規模的製造商，在德國與法國的工廠生產不鏽鋼工業廚房用具。世界各地的廚師與烘焙師都相信本公司的產品耐用、持久，而且品質極佳。本公司生產廚房爐具、烤箱、微波爐、冰箱、食物調理機、電水壺、咖啡機以及其他產品。

本公司在上個月的交易中收購「微舍家庭用品公司」後，與去年財政年度相比，整體利潤可望提高 20%。因此，為了滿足增加的需求量，本公司將在六個廠區中增聘 300 多位全職員工，並提供優渥薪資以及絕佳的福利津貼。本公司視全體員工為富頓家族的寶貴成員。除此之外，本公司也將繼續研發新產品以滿足顧客需求，並與其他公司展開競爭。

165. 誰最有可能是富頓不鏽鋼製品的客戶？

    A 汽車製造商

    B 餐廳

    C 房地產經紀公司

    D 服飾店

166. 富頓不鏽鋼製品上個月做了什麼？

    A 舉辦記者會

    B 開設一家新工廠

    C 取得一家公司

    D 解聘一些工人

167. 文中提到有關富頓不鏽鋼製品的什麼？

    A 它最近提供額外經費用於研發

    B 它已公布明年的預算計劃

    C 它為兼職員工提供了福利津貼

    D 它打算僱用更多員工在工廠工作

168–171 公司通訊

員工榮獲全國比賽優勝

我們艾羅設計研究室的同仁珍妮佛‧霍爾特，在網頁設計師協會（AWD）所舉辦的網頁設計比賽中榮獲第一名。參賽作品的評比準則是依據概念表達清晰度、製作品質以及美學。爾特女士從 300 多位參賽者獲選。我們為她的成就鼓掌，也很榮幸她是艾羅設計研究室的一員。

網頁設計師協會成立於 2002 年，旨在強調網頁設計的重要性及保護網頁設計師的權益。AWD 的會員來自世界各地，並持續增加新會員。為了推廣網頁設計至專業領域，AWD 舉辦各種比賽。AWD 相信好的設計可以改善人們生活，建立更好的社群。

身為網頁設計大賽的第一名得主，霍爾特女士將獲頒獎金，以及免費加入網頁設計師協會的會員資格。除此之外，她也受邀在下個月於加州洛杉磯舉辦的網頁設計師年度大會上發表演說。AWD 未來將舉辦更多比賽，意者可至官網 www.awd.com/contests 了解更多資訊。

168. 撰寫這篇文章最有可能的原因為何？

    A 介紹新員工

    B 報導一名獲獎者

    C 宣布年度競賽

    D 說明公司規定的改變

169. 第二段第一行的「founded」與下列哪個
字意思最接近？

Ⓐ 發現
Ⓑ 學習
Ⓒ 建立
Ⓓ 裝備

170. 文中指出何者與網頁設計師協會有關？

Ⓐ 每年舉辦一場會議
Ⓑ 總部在洛杉磯
Ⓒ 目前提供免費加入會員
Ⓓ 捐錢給社區計劃

171. 根據這篇文章，網站上可以看到什麼？

Ⓐ 演講全文
Ⓑ 職缺的應徵函
Ⓒ 即將舉辦的比賽細節
Ⓓ 霍爾特女士的成就列表

172–175 文章

7 月 16 日新城——健康小屋位於新城市中心，是健身愛好者和公司員工們最熱門的新去處。老闆吉兒和貝瑞・貝克夫婦上個月開了這家店，受到熱烈的好評與大排長龍的人潮。生意好的時候，想在健康小屋等到位子得花上半小時之久，不管是什麼時段，那裡永遠擠滿人潮。健康小屋的菜單上只提供六種餐點：各式乳清蛋白暢銷飲品，有蘋果派、花生醬巧克力杯和什錦水果。儘管菜單的餐點種類有限，顧客們對於其美味又健康的乳清蛋白飲品讚不絕口。

「我們被大家的反應嚇到了，」吉兒・貝克說：「事實上，這一切都靠口耳相傳，所以我們甚至連廣告都不需要。」健身教練朱利安・邁爾斯說：「我喜歡來這裡吃頓不會破壞健身目標的簡單午餐，我甚至把這裡推薦給我所有的客戶。」「我和同事在短暫的午休時間來這裡吃頓健康但令人滿足的餐點」，商業人士提姆・漢默補充說道：「沒有健康小屋，我們就要吃垃圾食物了。」健康小屋的營業時間是每週一至週五的早上七點到晚上八點，週六上午九點至晚上七點，週日休息。老闆希望接下來幾個月內，在菜單上增加新餐點。

172. 文中暗示關於這家店的哪件事情？

Ⓐ 它很成功
Ⓑ 它只提供外帶服務
Ⓒ 它已經營業很久了
Ⓓ 只有健身達人光顧這家店

173. 下列何者與健康小屋的產品有關？

Ⓐ 它們很美味
Ⓑ 它們很健康
Ⓒ 它們很便宜
Ⓓ 它們很容易取得

174. 為什麼老闆不需要廣告宣傳？

Ⓐ 他們沒有足夠的錢
Ⓑ 他們太忙了
Ⓒ 他們的顧客向別人推薦了這家店
Ⓓ 他們不想

175. 下列句子最適合出現在 [1]、[2]、[3]、[4] 的哪個位置？「儘管菜單餐點種類有限，顧客們對於美味又健康的乳清蛋白飲品讚不絕口。」

Ⓐ [1]
Ⓑ [2]
Ⓒ [3]
Ⓓ [4]

176–180 簡章和電子郵件

夏季講座系列

由溫斯特大學城市規劃系主辦

城市規劃系很開心宣布一系列夏季講座，重點關注與本地居民和市政當局有關的預算議題。財務管理是地方政府營運最重要的職責之一。我們希望透過社區參與，來改善全國地方政府層級的預算編列的情況。所有的演講都將於溫斯特大學校區內的海頓斯大樓舉行。

2 月 1 日，星期一，下午 6 點，401 教室
演講者：提姆・鮑爾，溫斯特大學政策分析教授
策略規劃——學習如何編列預算以監督社區目標與成效的達成進度。

2 月 3 日，星期三，晚上 7 點，305 教室

演講者：瑪麗莎・西蒙斯，康乃迪政策制
　　　　定中心

將重點放在孩童──研究顯示為孩童建造
遊樂場與運動設施，有助於營造更好的社
區環境。

2 月 8 日，星期一，下午 6 點，202 教室

演講者：漢克・羅斯，密西根市聯會縣立
公園地管理──學習如何以寶貴的社區資
源來維護地方公園區域。

**2 月 10 日，星期三，下午 5 點 30 分，
404 教室**

演講者：史考特・華生，地方政府研究院
　　　　常務董事

經濟機會與地方生態──經濟機會經常伴
隨著潛在危險，對週遭生態系統造成威
脅，在兩者間取得平衡並非易事。

欲知更多資訊，請洽派翠西亞・弗洛勒斯
pflores@wurnster.edu。

收件者：派翠西亞・弗洛勒斯
　　　　<pflores@wurnster.edu>
寄件者：傑克・彼得森
　　　　<jpatterson@wurnster.edu>
主旨：講座系列
日期：1 月 24 日

親愛的弗洛勒斯女士：

本人任職於溫斯頓大學的設備管理處，我
最近發現您的講座日期出現了排程上的衝
突。溫斯頓辯論社本學期每週三已經預約
了 305 教室，因此，很遺憾地通知您，您
需要更動這場演講的地點或時間。您可以
上設備管理處的網站確認其他教室可使用
的時間，並重新安排演講。

傑克・派得森

176. 這場講座系列最有可能是為誰安排的？

　　Ⓐ 社區成員
　　Ⓑ 大樓管理員
　　Ⓒ 大學教授
　　Ⓓ 大學生

177. 在簡章中，第一段第五行的「through」
與下列哪個字意思最接近？

　　Ⓐ 在……上面
　　Ⓑ 透過
　　Ⓒ 越過
　　Ⓓ 直到

178. 2 月 10 日最有可能在講座中討論什麼？

　　Ⓐ 如何平衡年度預算
　　Ⓑ 如何符合公共建設的需求
　　Ⓒ 如何避免環境傷害
　　Ⓓ 如何刺激經濟發展

179. 根據派得森先生所言，誰的演講必須改
期？

　　Ⓐ 華生先生的
　　Ⓑ 羅斯先生的
　　Ⓒ 西蒙斯女士的
　　Ⓓ 鮑爾先生的

180. 弗洛勒斯女士被指示要在網站上做什麼？

　　Ⓐ 下載檔案
　　Ⓑ 查看空教室
　　Ⓒ 更新個人資料
　　Ⓓ 推行論壇

181–185 電子郵件和清單

收件者：莎莉・羅素
　　　　<srussell@ptmail.com>
寄件者：凱莉・班尼特
　　　　<kbennett@msplanning.com>
日期：12 月 7 日
主旨：婚禮服務
附件：套裝專案

親愛的羅素小姐：

我們在 12 月 4 日星期二收到了您的電子
郵件，詢問我們的婚禮策劃與活動服務。
本公司專長各式婚禮（大小型，室內外，
以及為您夢幻婚禮量身打造的各類場地布
置），我們絕對有適合您的最佳方案。

您寫道，您想要一場低於五千元的婚禮套裝方案，並且要在一個接近主要公路的大型場地舉辦婚禮，因為您預計將有許多來自全國各地的賓客。據我了解，您其他的要求如下：

- 戶外場地
- 拍照攝影師與錄影師全程記錄
- 場地布置，包括各色花卉與高雅桌巾

我已隨信附上本公司所有您可能感興趣的套裝婚禮專案表，它們全位於距 519 號公路 15 分鐘的車程內。請您瀏覽所提供的資訊，決定哪個地點最符合您的需求。請您決定後，透過電子郵件告知您預計舉行婚禮的時間。這能幫助我為您確保預約。

感謝。

MS 婚禮策畫
凱莉‧班尼特 敬上

套裝專案	全額費用	地點	備註
鑽石專案	5,500 元	哈帝劇院	綠寶石專案內容，加上現場弦樂四重奏
綠寶石專案	4,300 元	真立時公園	紅寶石專案內容，加上拍照及錄影服務
紅寶石專案	3,000 元	鄉間溫泉旅館	藍寶石專案內容，加上餐桌布置及美麗花卉
藍寶石專案	1,750 元	銀禧花園	自助式午餐及各式飲料

181. 文中可判斷出羅素小姐的什麼事情？

- A 她是班尼特女士的同事
- B 她正在規劃蜜月旅行
- **C 她現在已經訂婚了**
- D 她在外燴公司上班

182. 班尼特女士最有可能從事哪一行？

- A 職業樂手
- B 婚禮攝影師
- C 室內設計師
- **D 活動策劃員**

183. 下列何者與表單中的所有地點有關？

- **A 它們都接近主要道路**
- B 它們都是室內場地
- C 它們都位在同一城市
- D 它們都要求預付訂金

184. 羅素小姐被要求提供什麼資訊？

- **A 可能的日期**
- B 餐點選擇
- C 賓客名單
- D 蜜月地點

185. 哪一個套裝專案可能最符合羅素小姐的需求？

- A 鑽石專案
- **B 綠寶石專案**
- C 紅寶石專案
- D 藍寶石專案

186–190 電子郵件

收件者：<info@bountifulharvest.com>
寄件者：艾蜜莉‧霍爾
　　　　<emilyhall@zipline.com>
日期：6 月 3 日
主旨：食物配送

敬啟者：

我叫艾蜜莉‧霍爾，是亨茨維爾市中心一家素食餐廳的老闆。會與您連絡，是因為我對每週定期配送新鮮有機蔬菜到本餐廳的服務感興趣。我的餐廳才剛開幕，所以不需要大量貨品。在研究過本地不同的農場後，我選擇聯絡大豐收農場，就是因為你們保證配送有機認證的食物。因此，我想索取一份每週直送新鮮蔬菜到本餐廳的費用估價單。

艾蜜莉‧霍爾

收件者：艾蜜莉・霍爾
　　　　<emilyhall@zipline.com>
寄件者：大豐收農場
　　　　<info@bountifulharvest.com>
日期：6月4日
主旨：回覆：食物配送

親愛的霍爾女士：

感謝您與本農場聯絡。在大豐收農場，我們提供新鮮有機農產品，可定期直送給客戶。我們的蔬菜從田地採收後會立刻配送，這表示您可以收到有益健康、營養、有機的農產品，以供貴餐廳使用。我們也提供其他的商品，像是新鮮的肉類、起士和牛奶。以下是詳列我們各式商品的價目表。

方案選擇	特點	重量	配送頻率	單次配送價格
個人	這個套裝供大約二到三人食用，內含新鮮當季蔬菜。	5磅	一週一次	15元
小型	這個套裝適合小型商家，內含新鮮當季蔬菜。	50磅	一週一次	140元
中型	這個套裝適合需要長期供應新鮮蔬菜與肉類的中型商家。	130磅	一週兩次	500元
大型	這是我們最大的套裝，內含蔬菜、肉類和乳製品。	250磅	一週兩次	800元

以上所列的價格未含運費。無法自取的顧客，則需要多付六元的運費。但是對於簽訂整年度配送合約的顧客，則免運費。若購買其他商品，也會影響該方案的最終價格。其他可選購的商品請參考本農場網站。款項可於出貨日以現金、信用卡、支票或匯票方式給付。

我們知道顧客特別在意食物的品質。因此我們提供了免費的迷你包，方便您先行評估我們的食物。請來電555-8141與格雷格・雷蒙斯聯絡並索取。

英迪拉・辛格

收件者：大豐收農場
　　　　<info@bountifulharvest.com>
寄件者：艾蜜莉・霍爾
　　　　<emilyhall@zipline.com>
日期：6月5日
主旨：收成時間表

親愛的辛格女士：

感謝您如此迅速地回覆我的電子郵件。我很感謝你們提供免費試用品，但我想我乾脆就直接安排定期配送。我對安排整年度的配送很感興趣，但我想先取得不同季節時你們會提供的農產品項目清單。由於我經營的是素食餐廳，我需要對所配送的農產品種類有個概念，這樣我才能依此準備菜單。非常感謝您的體諒，很期待與大豐收農場合作！

祝好

艾蜜莉・霍爾

---

186. 第一封電子郵件的目的是什麼？

　A 要求費用資料
　B 詢問規定更動
　C 延後訂單
　D 通報錯誤的發票

187. 哪一個選擇方案可能最符合霍爾女士的需求？

　A 個人
　B 小型
　C 中型
　D 大型

188. 最終價格裡不需要哪一項資訊？

　A 合約期限
　B 配送方式
　C 加購物品
　D 運送距離

189. 艾蜜莉・霍爾的電子郵件中提到了什麼？

　A 她想要試一個月看看
　B 她想要免費贈品
　C 她對長期合約有興趣
　D 她不想要冬季農產品

190. 艾蜜莉‧霍爾為什麼想知道整年度會收到的蔬菜種類？

[A] 她喜愛蔬菜

[B] 她正在考慮增加肉類

[C] 她可能會多僱用一位員工

[D] 她想規劃未來的菜單

191–195 告示和電子郵件

重要公告

親愛的卡斯泰利顧客：

本公司品保團隊表示，有五百罐卡斯泰利經典義大利麵醬未符合本公司產品品質的高標準。

這個瑕疵是由罐蓋的密封不當所造成的，且因為接觸到空氣，可能已經造成內容物的腐壞。目前我們正警告顧客不得食用該產品。

您該怎麼做：如果您已經購買了卡斯泰利經典義大利麵醬，請寄電子郵件至本公司客服部 cs@castellifood.com，本公司同仁將提供您商品兌換券。請在電子郵件中註明您的姓名、完整地址、電話號碼以及產品序號，顧客所購買的每一罐商品都會收到一張 12 元的折價券。請勿於零售店辦理退貨。

請記得卡斯泰利食品的其他產品都未受影響。我們鼓勵您繼續購買本公司的產品。

收件者：<cs@castellifood.com>

寄件者：湯尼‧赫斯特
　　　　<tonyhester21@webzit.com>

日期：3 月 29 日

主旨：兌換券

敬啟者：

我叫湯尼‧赫斯特，很感謝這個防範措施。大約在兩週前，我在明尼蘇達州赫曼鎮的艾斯雜貨店，買了兩罐卡斯泰利經典義大利麵醬。一週後，我又在同一家店買了另一罐。

我已隨電子郵件附上兩張收據的圖片檔，希望能收到這些不良品的商品兌換券。我的地址是：

湯尼‧赫斯特

55811 明尼蘇達州赫曼鎮布魯街 27 號

期待儘快收到回覆。

湯尼‧赫斯特

收件者：湯尼‧赫斯特
　　　　<tonyhester21@webzit.com>

寄件者：<cs@castellifood.com>

日期：3 月 30 日

主旨：折價券

親愛的赫斯特先生：

非常感謝您與卡斯泰利食品聯繫。我們承諾確保顧客可以繼續信賴卡斯泰利的高品質食品，以滿足其所有用餐需求。為此，我們很樂意為您最近所購買的卡斯泰利經典義大利麵醬，提供您三張兌換券。請查看所附上的兌換券。

除了經典義大利麵醬的兌換券外，我們也提供您本公司新系列細扁麵、義大利麵與通心粉的折價券，請接受這些做為我們表達歉意的另一種方式。我們希望您繼續惠顧本公司美味的義大利食品。

客服專員

珍‧奧森 敬上

---

191. 這張公告最有可能在哪裡看到？

[A] 餐廳

[B] 員工休息室

[C] 航運公司

[D] 雜貨店

192. 下列何者與罐子有關？

[A] 沒有關緊

[B] 目前缺貨

[C] 標價錯誤

[D] 送到錯的地址

193. 根據這張公告，何者不是給顧客的建議？

[A] 不要食用該產品

[B] 通報該產品

[C] 將產品退回商店

[D] 購買卡斯泰利其他產品

194. 在給赫斯特先生的電子郵件中，卡斯泰利公司額外提供了什麼贈品？

Ⓐ 通心粉醬

Ⓑ 食譜

Ⓒ 農產品折價券

Ⓓ 新產品折價券

195. 下列何者不是卡斯泰利公司送出折價券的理由？

Ⓐ 保住客戶忠誠度

Ⓑ 表達歉意

Ⓒ 對顧客公平

Ⓓ 獲得新顧客

196–200 表格、電子郵件和告示

奧本市餐廳查驗

餐廳名稱：波利多比薩
地址：克拉克街 43 號
抽查日期：1 月 22 日

A：無違規，完全符合安全與健康法規。

B：輕微違規，符合大多數安全與健康法規。

C：部分違規，未符合部分安全與健康法規。

D：未符合安全與健康法規，出現可能對顧客造成傷害或致病的嚴重違規。

（食物準備與存放方面出現 C、D 等級違規行為，將處以罰款）

項目	分數
1. 人員定期洗手並遵守衛生規定	B
2. 生肉與蔬菜以適當溫度冷藏	A
3. 所有的食材都適當存放與標示	C
4. 碗盤與用具經清潔與消毒	A
5. 滅火器可方便取用	B
6. 火災逃生口標示清楚	C
7. 地面乾淨並保持乾燥	B

為避免更多罰款，餐廳應於下次查驗前改善違規情況。

餐廳所有人：葛瑞格·克魯克
檢驗員：瑪莉莎·坦蓽

收件者：全體員工
　　　　<employees@politospizza.com>
寄件者：葛瑞格·克魯克
　　　　<gregkluck@politospizza.com>
主旨：檢驗結果
日期：1 月 25 日

親愛的同仁：

最近在 1 月 22 日的檢驗報告指出了一些我們需要注意的問題。

首先，我注意到的就是必須重新裝設火災逃生出口標示。最嚴重的違規是有關食物的不當存放與標示。所有之後會用到的食材都必須標示確切日期與詳細內容，如果沒有將容器標示清楚，可能會不小心把腐壞的食物提供給顧客。我們在員工衛生與設備的清潔度上拿到了相對低的分數，全體員工隨時都要穿著制服，戴上髮網，並在每次使用洗手間之後洗手。我們也需要更常拖地，並保持乾燥。

為了改正這些不良狀況，我會貼一張確認表，全體同仁每天早上都必須完成，裡面包括了必要的準備工作，以確保我們沒有違反任何規定。這個措施將於 1 月 29 日實施。如果您對

這些變革有任何疑問，請在明天的員工會議上提出。

全體同仁注意

每位波利多比薩的同仁在每天輪值時,都必須簽寫以下確認表。只有在工作完成或檢查後才能簽名。未在確認表上填寫日期、時間與簽名者,將視同違反波利多比薩新的健康標準規定。

波利多確認表

波利多	星期日	星期一	星期二	星期三	星期四	星期五	星期六
輪換食物	K.P.	K.P.	K.P.	K.P.			K.P.
拖地	K.P.	K.P.	K.P.	K.P.			K.P.
制服	K.P.	K.P.	K.P.	K.P.			K.P.
洗手	K.P.	K.P.	K.P.	K.P.			K.P.

196. 為什麼要進行檢驗?

　Ⓐ 監督食品業法規的符合狀況
　Ⓑ 評價美食的口味與品質
　Ⓒ 檢查大樓的結構安全
　Ⓓ 評估新政策的效率

197. 波利多比薩為什麼被罰款?

　Ⓐ 因為滅火器沒有在場
　Ⓑ 因為食物容器沒有適當標示
　Ⓒ 因為不當處置生肉與蔬菜
　Ⓓ 因為設備沒有依標準清理

198. 克魯克先生要求員工做什麼?

　Ⓐ 向顧客道歉
　Ⓑ 隨時配戴名牌
　Ⓒ 投訴坦蕁女士
　Ⓓ 填寫必要的表格

199. 如果員工沒有簽寫工作確認表,會發生什麼事?

　Ⓐ 他們的紀錄上會有違規紀錄
　Ⓑ 他們必須付罰款
　Ⓒ 他們必須在週末上班
　Ⓓ 他們會被開除

200. 根據波利多確認表,我們可以推論出有關 K.P. 的什麼事?

　Ⓐ 他上晚班
　Ⓑ 他週四週五休假
　Ⓒ 他因違規被開除
　Ⓓ 他做事動作很慢

TEST 1

PART 7

ACTUAL TEST ②

PART 5　P.48–51

◎ Part 5 解答請見 P.457

101. 有了資訊科技人員的協助，遺失的會計文件已經被**救回來**了。

102. 一場專為藝廊贊助者舉辦的私人招待會將於 3 月 5 日**舉行**，就在展覽盛大開幕會之前。

103. 歐若拉家具發現，要在**日益**競爭的市場中獲利很困難。

104. 機師在飛機起飛前**不久**，發現電機出了一點小問題。

105. 在檢視**估算**成本後，我們將對這棟房子的造景變動做出最終決定。

106. 我的健康公司已經生產**超過** 20 年的各種維他命保養品。

107. 由於新進的美編，四月號的《不僅是釣魚》雜誌看起來與之前的期數**完全**不同。

108. 客戶的訂單**確認函**將於 24 小時內以電子郵件寄出。

109. 維修團隊的修繕申請必須根據緊急程度分組**安排**。

110. 在李維拉女士的**簡短**聲明後，普列士企業的正式頒獎典禮隨即展開。

111. 由於大量人潮往來，商店在旺季時必須比平時更**常**擦地板。

112. 由於社區活動中心的會議室被重複預訂了，大師園藝社的月會必須**延後**。

113. 財務顧問報告説，較年長的投資者往往比年輕人**更謹慎**。

114. 阿爾布雷希特先生**迅速**回了人資主管的電子郵件，這證明他對這個職務有高度興趣。

115. 足球員們通常在沃特伯里公園的主運動場練習，但他們偶爾也會在**其他地方**練習。

116. 會計師們無法在截止日期前提出完整報告，但**他們**保證會給一份重點摘要。

117. 儘管表演中音響系統出了問題，但對每個人來説，這場音樂會仍然是個**愉快的**經驗。

118. **由於**這棟建築有極佳的位置和現代化的內部裝潢，很受遊客的歡迎。

119. 公園與遊憩部門為志工們提供了改善社區的**寶貴**機會。

120. 旅社二樓的空房已經**全部**打掃過了。

121. 這個短篇故事在**沒有**得到作者明確同意的狀況下無法再行印製。

122. 餐廳裡有一間裝潢**活潑**的包廂，非常適合舉辦兒童派對。

123. 一位野生動物專家預定發表一場演講，有關工廠對週遭森林所產生的**影響**。

124. 房東第一次調漲幾年來沒變的每月房租，這樣做是**合理**的。

125. 只要別再出現延誤，工廠就可以在 6 月 18 日前全面**運作**。

126. 多虧他的個人經驗，華倫先生**一定**可以獨力完成這份工作。

127. 由於燃料成本**上漲**，有些人選擇暑假時待在家裡，而非開車到觀光勝地。

128. **每當**需要更換濾心**時**，濾水器側邊的綠燈就會亮起。

129. 伯克女士的訂單中有兩項物品缺貨，所以她的發票也**跟著**修改。

130. 公告指出，有一場急救訓練課程將於下個月免費提供給**居民**參加。

PART 6 | P.52–55

131–134 告示

春季員工培訓

勞倫斯報致力協助全體員工發揮他們的潛能，這就是為什麼我們再度安排了兩天的春季培訓課程。人資部已經為今年的培訓準備了廣泛的主題，包括銷售技巧、電腦技能、溝通策略以及目標設定。培訓還有兩個空的時段，所以如果大家有任何非常渴望學習的事物，請告訴我們，我們或許可以將它納入今年的春季培訓當中。我們將於本週末前確定最終的選擇。如果您有任何想法，歡迎向人力資源部的南西·肯辛頓提出。

131. Ⓐ 分發
Ⓑ 設置
Ⓒ 包括
Ⓓ 促進

132. Ⓐ 當時正納入
Ⓑ 已經納入
Ⓒ 現在納入
Ⓓ 可納入

133. Ⓐ 如果我們收到很多建議，我們也可以在下週週末 12 月 4 日舉辦培訓。
Ⓑ 我們將於本週末前確定最終的選擇。
Ⓒ 我們投入大量的時間和精力籌備這場會議。
Ⓓ 我們一向鼓勵大家邀請親友來參加這些活動。

134. Ⓐ 創造
Ⓑ 要求
Ⓒ 提出
Ⓓ 轉調

135–138 廣告

萬達房地產

萬達房地產已經在休士頓地區服務超過 29 年。我們保證提供最高等級的市場專業知識及客製化服務，因此被公認是業界的領導者。

本公司專營丹佛地區自用與企業房地產。不管您想買新家，還是開展新事業，您都應該與我們洽談。由於本公司就位於市中心，我們關注整個城市的動向。請參考本公司網站上的物件清單，或今天就來電。當然，我們永遠歡迎您隨時大駕光臨。

www.vanderproperties.com
電話：(313) 782-9919
地址：沃頓街 834 號

135. Ⓐ 客製
Ⓑ 客製
Ⓒ 客製中
Ⓓ 客製化的

136. Ⓐ 有成效的
Ⓑ 獲得升遷
Ⓒ 有關聯的
Ⓓ 住宅的

137. **Ⓐ 不論**
Ⓑ 即使
Ⓒ 儘管
Ⓓ 不管怎樣

138. Ⓐ 今天就開車出城來看看我們吧。
Ⓑ 我們感謝您的協助。
Ⓒ 當然，我們永遠歡迎您隨時大駕光臨。
Ⓓ 我們的餐廳每天從八點營業到五點。

誠徵比薩廚師

吉諾老爹正在徵才，所有符合資格的應徵者都將列入考量中。我們正在找具有料理義式餐點經驗的人。即使您沒有經驗，只要符合資格條件，我們將提供訓練。為了符合條件，您必須具備有效的保健卡、可靠的交通工具，還要能夠在晚上與週末時上班。請親自至州街與松街的吉諾老爹應徵。期待見到您。

139. Ⓐ 使合格
　　　Ⓑ 合格的
　　　Ⓒ 合格的
　　　Ⓓ 使合格

140. **Ⓐ 我們正在找具有料理義式餐點經驗的人。**
　　　Ⓑ 我們正在找會說義大利文的人。
　　　Ⓒ 我們正在找喜歡吃比薩的人。
　　　Ⓓ 我們正在找想練習的人。

141. **Ⓐ 有效的**
　　　Ⓑ 工作的
　　　Ⓒ 生效的
　　　Ⓓ 強壯的

142. Ⓐ 她
　　　Ⓑ 他們
　　　Ⓒ 我們
　　　Ⓓ 他

143–146 信件

11 月 11 日
約翰・亞當斯
10873 紐約州紐約市三州區 408 公寓

親愛的亞當斯先生：

很高興通知您，您已經獲選為高第薩克斯公司銷售經理一職的最終人選。在該職位的一百多位應徵者中，我們已經將名單減縮至八位。我們邀請您來參加 11 月 15 日下午一點到六點的面試，我們希望您能在

下午一點時抵達，地點就在公司總部。助理藍恩小姐將於大廳與您碰面，帶您到面試室。

對於面談表現良好的應徵者，我們將進行第二次面試。我們將儘快通知您合格與否。

若有任何疑問，請打 555-1234 與我們聯絡。

希望很快就可以見到您。

行政經理
珍妮佛・羅 敬上

143. Ⓐ 正在選擇
　　　Ⓑ 已經選擇
　　　Ⓒ 已經被選擇
　　　Ⓓ 選擇

144. **Ⓐ 職位**
　　　Ⓑ 地點
　　　Ⓒ 職業
　　　Ⓓ 預約

145. Ⓐ 那棟大樓很容易找。
　　　Ⓑ 我們希望您能在下午一點時抵達。
　　　Ⓒ 我們的面試官將問您一些問題。
　　　Ⓓ 您將拿到一份明確的時程表。

146. Ⓐ 使能夠
　　　Ⓑ 批准
　　　Ⓒ 拒絕
　　　Ⓓ 合格

PART 7　P.56–79

147–148 廣告

驚奇世界攝影比賽

旅遊月刊《驚奇世界》現正為 11 月註冊的人士提供訂閱優惠。《驚奇世界》已經發行 30 餘年，提供讀者行家情報及專業知識，幫助您規劃夢想之旅。本雜誌包含了度假套裝行程廣告、遊客評論以及具有深度見解的短文，介紹您認識各種不同的文化、美食和旅遊勝地。

將您的旅遊照片寄來參加驚奇世界攝影比賽，就有機會贏得一趟蘇格蘭美妙之旅。首獎優勝者將獲贈兩人來回機票，以及價值 2,000 元的旅遊住宿券。

147. 文中提到有關雜誌的什麼？
- Ⓐ 這是一本文學雜誌
- Ⓑ 內含一本食譜副刊
- **Ⓒ 提供旅遊建議**
- Ⓓ 有線上版

148. 下列何者與比賽有關？
- Ⓐ 由專業攝影師所贊助
- **Ⓑ 獲勝者將獲得一趟免費旅程**
- Ⓒ 只接受數位照片
- Ⓓ 以英格蘭的照片為主軸

149–151 訊息串

麗滋・布雷德利	8:14

長官，您與強生先生明天下午的會議都已安排妥當，我已在喜來登餐廳訂了下午一點兩人的座位。

伯尼・吉布斯	8:17

謝謝你，會議所需的報告都彙整好了嗎？

麗滋・布雷德利	8:18

大部分都好了。我還在等麥可・斯蒂爾的報告。他告訴我，他今天早上會準備好給我。

伯尼・吉布斯	8:20

好。這應該要在昨天晚上就弄好，你可以聯絡他看看到底是怎麼一回事？

（麥可・斯蒂爾於 8:26 加入對話）

麗滋・布雷德利	8:27

麥可，吉布斯先生想知道報告在哪裡。你做完了沒？

麥可・斯蒂爾	8:28

很抱歉耽誤了。我們的實習生不小心刪除了一些檔案，我必須搜尋整個資料庫才能找到備份資料。要查看所有我需要的文件並加以分類有點棘手，但我想我已經處理好了，現在要列印出來了。

麗滋・布雷德利	8:29

你可以一印好就拿來給我嗎？

麥可・斯蒂爾	8:30

當然，十分鐘後到。

149. 麗滋・布雷德利最有可能是誰？
- Ⓐ 實習生
- **Ⓑ 助理**
- Ⓒ 生意夥伴
- Ⓓ 行政主管

150. 麥可・斯蒂爾為什麼加入對話？
- **Ⓐ 要他提供缺失報告的最新狀況**
- Ⓑ 通知他即將到來的會議
- Ⓒ 讓他知道截止日期
- Ⓓ 責備他不守時

151. 麥可說：「我必須搜尋整個資料庫才能找到備份資料」是什麼意思？
- Ⓐ 他從容不迫地寫報告
- Ⓑ 他必須先將所有資料備份
- **Ⓒ 他需要時間找遺失的資料**
- Ⓓ 電腦故障了

152–153 網頁

透納公司

英國紅木灣巴金絲路 158 號
電話：243-555-1541

首頁	關於我們	產品	配件	聯絡我們

透納公司自 1949 年成立以來，一直製造美麗且節能的窗戶，以滿足顧客的品味與期望。當您選擇透納公司，您所購買的不只是一扇窗戶，您將獲得我們專業人員數十年來一向表現卓越的絕佳服務。我們熱情地協助您挑選完全符合您住家規格的高品質窗戶，除此之外，我們全心致力於環保，而且我們的永續企業經營最近還通過了環境保護局（EPA）的認可。

152. 這篇文章在廣告什麼？

- A 保險公司
- **B 窗戶製造商**
- C 庭園造景公司
- D 窗戶清潔服務公司

153. 下列何者與透納公司有關？

- A 它是家族企業
- B 它的分公司遍及全國
- **C 它是間注重環保的公司**
- D 它最近聘用了經驗豐富的員工

154–155 簡訊

傳送者：山姆・貝爾
接收者：珍・布魯斯

珍，請告訴我佛雷澤先生的電話號碼。他那裡有一些我現在就要的資料。我的財務月報表進度已經有點落後，我今天需要把所有時間都花在這上面。

154. 為什麼要傳這則訊息？

- **A 請求協助**
- B 延後期限
- C 取消會議
- D 索取文件資料

155. 下列何者與貝爾先生有關？

- A 他無法出席會議
- B 他希望利潤提高
- **C 他試著趕上截止日期**
- D 他最近得到新工作

156–158 文章

首爾（7月19日）——布里明集團在南韓著名的狎鷗亭洞羅德奧街上開設了第一家 B&G 服飾店，開幕便大排長龍，吸引許多狂熱買家。造成瘋狂的是馬利奇歐・布奇和 B&G 合作設計的限量版商品。就在營業後的幾個小時內，大部分由布奇所設計的商品已銷售一空。類似的騷動及被掃蕩一空的布奇商品架的報導，在世界各大城市像是紐約、倫敦、東京和米蘭也曾發生過。雖然 B&G 也曾和其他著名

設計師合作發行限量商品，但這是第一次 B&G 門市回報有商品在推出幾小時後就銷售一空的現象。布奇和 B&G 的合作是目前為止最成功的案例，並已開始著手洽談日後更多服飾系列的合作案。這是該公司的創舉，因為之前的限量設計商品都只是一次性的合作關係。同時，在首爾買不到布奇系列的顧客雖然感到失望，但對於高人氣店家能在進駐韓國也感到興奮。

156. 下列何者與 B&G 有關？

- **A 全世界都有分店**
- B 他們只賣由布奇設計的商品
- C 在韓國有幾家分店
- D 商品通常在幾小時內銷售一空

157. 文中報導什麼關於布奇和 B&G 的合作案？

- A 花好幾年才談妥
- B 只在特定商店才有販售
- **C 對該公司而言是最賺錢的合作案之一**
- D 這將只是一次性的活動

158. 下列句子最適合出現在 [1]、[2]、[3]、[4] 的哪個位置？「這是該公司的創舉，因為之前的限量設計商品都只是一次性的合作關係。」

- A [1]
- B [2]
- **C [3]**
- D [4]

159–161 備忘錄

備忘錄

收文者：全體職員
發文者：伊莉莎白・潘恩
日期：1月24日
主旨：病假

全體同仁，請注意：

本公司星網企業將針對病假規定做出調整。我們正在考慮減少帶薪休假的天數，增加員工們可申請的帶薪病假的天數。在我們做出任何異動前，我們想收集同仁們

對這件事的意見。請寄電子郵件給湯尼·納金特 *tonynugent@zimnet.com*，他會彙集並分析各位的回覆。之後，管理部將於 2 月 24 日前做出相對應的政策提案。一旦完成提案，將召開會議以討論全體員工的實行事宜。希望這個做法對全體同仁有所助益，請大家踴躍參與。

伊莉莎白·潘恩 敬上

159. 這份備忘錄的目的是什麼？

    Ⓐ 建議預算企劃
    Ⓑ 徵求回饋意見
    Ⓒ 修正錯誤資訊
    Ⓓ 宣布調查結果

160. 納金特先生最有可能擔任什麼職務？

    Ⓐ 業務
    Ⓑ 產品開發人員
    Ⓒ 投資分析師
    Ⓓ 人事部職員

161. 根據這份備忘錄，潘恩女士可能會在 2 月 24 日後就做什麼？

    Ⓐ 宣布合併
    Ⓑ 聘用專科醫師
    Ⓒ 參加旅遊
    Ⓓ 安排會議

162–165 訊息串

潘妮·瓊斯　　　　　　　　3:27
我剛接到馬丁的電話，他的客戶派翠克先生希望他的訂單能比原定計劃提早兩週完成。基本上，就是下週一前。你們認為有可能嗎？我想知道大家的看法。

凱倫·諾曼　　　　　　　　3:28
我們這邊沒問題。大多數的皮革都已經裁切好了，我們已經把很多皮革送去縫接了。剩下的工作應該只要幾個小時。

尼爾·帕克　　　　　　　　3:29
把手已經做好了，大約一半的包包都接近完工，我可以儘快送到羅倫那裡。我想我們應該可以在明天傍晚前縫好那些包包。

潘妮·瓊斯　　　　　　　　3:30
很高興聽到大部分的手提包都快完工了。羅倫，把那些金屬貼上去或縫上去要多久時間？

勞倫·尼可斯　　　　　　　3:31
我們現在正在做詹克和堅克雙胞胎的訂單。

潘妮·瓊斯　　　　　　　　3:32
我們有非常充裕的時間來完成那對雙胞胎的訂單，所以我批准你的工作人員先把那邊的工作擱置一旁。那派翠克先生的訂單要花多久時間？

勞倫·尼可斯　　　　　　　3:33
拉鍊需要用縫的，但飾釘可以用黏的，這樣會簡單一點。我想我們需要大約一天的時間。

凱文·哈汀　　　　　　　　3:34
妥善包裝以安全出貨只需要幾小時。

潘妮·瓊斯　　　　　　　　3:35
太感謝各位了。我會告訴客戶的。

162. 這個客戶最有可能經營哪種生意？

    Ⓐ 服飾店
    Ⓑ 家具公司
    Ⓒ 鞋店
    Ⓓ 手提包業

163. 根據對話內容，誰的部門必須先完工？

    Ⓐ 凱倫·諾曼的
    Ⓑ 尼爾·帕克的
    Ⓒ 勞倫·尼可斯的
    Ⓓ 凱文·哈汀的

164. 在 3:31 時，勞倫·尼可斯為什麼會說：「我們現在正在做詹克和堅克雙胞胎的訂單。」

    Ⓐ 為了告訴大家他們現在有自己的客戶了
    Ⓑ 為了解釋他們為什麼拒絕幫忙
    Ⓒ 為了暗示他們正忙著其他的工作
    Ⓓ 為了讓大家加快速度完成工作

165. 潘妮‧瓊斯最有可能跟派翠克先生說什麼？

A 他的訂單兩週後才會完成

B 他的要求可以達成

C 他的訂單要額外加錢

D 他的訂單可能會延誤

166–168 告示

三月初的營業時間

星期一	星期二	星期三
下午 2:00—晚上 9:00	下午 2:00—晚上 8:00	下午 3:00—晚上 9:00
星期四	星期五	星期六
下午 4:00—晚上 9:00	下午 2:00—晚上 9:00	下午 2:00—晚上 10:00
星期日		
早上 9:00—下午 6:00		

由於仙令街目前正在進行工程，我們必須不更動三月第一週的營業時間（請參考上列表格）。早上時間，工程的進行讓顧客很難開車到我們門市，為了順應這個變化，我們將延長夜間營業時間。另外，由於工程的關係，目前我們的停車場也無法使用。因此，在這段期間，請顧客利用沛奇街上的公共停車場。我們為此不便深感抱歉，也會努力儘快恢復正常。

166. 這篇文章公告了什麼？

A 整修計劃

B 展店

C 營業時間異動

D 工作時程表

167. 何時最不可能施工？

A 星期一

B 星期三

C 星期六

D 星期日

168. 顧客為什麼被要求到沛奇街？

A 找地方停車

B 造訪一家新門市

C 參加促銷活動

D 拿樣品

169–171 廣告

船主求售
帕默爾標準艙遊艇

要價：45,000 元或最佳出價

基本規格：

這艘船建於四年前，寬 12 呎，長 36 呎。船身由纖維玻璃打造而成，使得整艘船輕盈但堅固。這艘船內有兩間雙人房、一張沙發床、廚房和浴室。

特點：

這艘船非常平穩並有寬敞的甲板，適合大家族與社交聚會。船上有套八揚聲器的音響系統，可連接 USB，還有一個可存放私人物品的上鎖式儲藏隔間。

其他資訊：

我已經擁有並使用這艘船三年半。這艘船有五年的保固期，所以現在還剩一年半的時間。一經購買後，保固可移轉給買家。

如果您想看看這艘船或試乘，請來電 (654) 555-8715 找格瑞‧湯普森。

169. 下列何者和帕默爾標準艙遊艇有關？

A 它是一艘漁船

B 它原始的油漆顏色已經換了

C 它可容納一群人

D 它目前正在維修中

170. 下列何者不是帕默爾標準艙遊艇的特點？

A 播放音樂的功能

B 輕量建材

C 寬敞的睡眠空間

D 省油引擎

171. 關於湯普森先生，下列何者最有可能為真？

A 他會為潛在買家提供一趟遊艇之旅
B 他有年幼的小孩
C 他在造船廠工作
D 他想要另外賣保證書

172–175 信件

旅遊與休閒
48857 加州橘郡吉爾摩街 123 號

11 月 15 日
彼得‧康先生
19387 華盛頓州西雅圖市河谷高地 3820 號

親愛的康先生：

《旅遊與休閒》雜誌感謝您的訂閱。由於您是我們的長期訂戶，我很高興通知您一個針對我們 VIP 會員的新訂閱方案。您的訂閱方案將於下個月到期，但我們邀請您考慮加入 VIP 會員。以會員來說，您可以繼續收到本雜誌的月刊號，也可以使用我們新的線上電子雜誌服務。您不需額外付費，就可以將紙本雜誌的數位版本下載至任何行動裝置中。而且，您還可以取得本雜誌的作者、記者與特約撰稿人的背景資料，以及雜誌提及之場所與地點的詳細資訊。此外，您還可以得到全世界最受歡迎餐廳的食譜。最棒的是，我們為 VIP 會員舉辦了一場可贏得夏威夷雙人遊的獨家比賽。一般訂戶和 VIP 會員，將有機會贏得在貝利西默五星級餐廳用餐的體驗。

再次感謝您持續的支持，希望您喜歡我們在服務上做的異動，我們努力娛樂並教育忠實訂戶。請填寫本函所附上的申請表，確認您欲參加的訂閱方案。如果您付 100 元的費用，將得到一般訂戶的訂閱方案。如果您付 200 元的費用，即可成為 VIP 會員。

感謝您的支持，希望很快收到您的回音。

維多莉雅‧亞當斯 敬上

172. 為什麼要寄信給康先生？

A 提醒他提交旅遊日誌
B 說明新的訂閱方案
C 詢問他的旅遊計劃
D 確定他合乎某個職位的資格

173. 亞當斯女士隨信附上了什麼？

A 旅遊行程表
B 新合約
C 申請表
D 修改過的時程表

174. 在信件中，第一段中間的「at no extra cost」意思最接近？

A 很少的費用
B 捐款
C 相當簡單
D 免費

175. 下列句子最適合出現在 [1]、[2]、[3]、[4] 的哪個位置？「您的訂閱方案將於下個月到期，但我們邀請您考慮加入 VIP 會員。」

A [1]
B [2]
C [3]
D [4]

176–180 發票和電子郵件

泰勒織品
發票

訂購者：譚米‧弗列克
經手人：克雷格‧戴爾
訂購日期：8 月 11 日
預計送達日：8 月 14 日到 16 日
運送地址：78701 德州奧斯汀綠圓道 628 號
電子信箱：tfleck@capnet.com
行動電話：(512) 555-9782

數量	品項	說明	價格
4 碼	10 號布料	純白色	28.00 元
5 碼	38 號布料	印花	50.00 元
6 碼	41 號布料	方格	48.00 元
2 碼	48 號布料	豹紋	30.00 元

<table>
<tr><td></td><td>稅 15.60 元</td></tr>
<tr><td></td><td>運費 12.00 元</td></tr>
<tr><td></td><td>總計 183.60 元</td></tr>
</table>

付款方式：

以末四碼為 4680 的信用卡支付帳單

如果您對訂單有任何疑問，請寄電子郵件至 customerservice@taylorfabrics.com。所有美國境內的包裹保證於訂單確認後十天內送達。若未於時間內送達，我們保證退還 30% 的全額購物金。

收件者：
customerservice@taylorfabrics.com
寄件者：譚米・弗列克
　　　　　 <tfleck@capnet.com>
日期：8 月 25 日
主旨：運送延誤

客服部您好：

我昨天才收到兩週前在泰勒織品所訂購的東西。包裹不僅比原先承諾的時間要晚到，其中一項物品還寄錯了。發票上正確地載明了我要的是五碼的印花布，但是送來的只有兩碼。因為這個失誤，我無法完成原本要為朋友生日所做的洋裝。我深感失望。

等這個問題一處理好，補寄的織布也寄出後，請傳簡訊到我的行動電話。

謝謝

譚米・弗列克

176. 戴爾先生的工作最有可能是什麼？
　[A] 設計師
　[B] 銷售員
　[C] 顧客
　[D] 製造商

177. 下列何者與弗列克女士有關？
　[A] 她是泰勒織品的長期客戶
　[B] 她是專業的時尚設計師
　[C] 她是泰勒織品的前員工
　[D] 她將拿回部分的購物金

178. 弗列克女士為什麼寄這封電子郵件？
　[A] 她的信用卡被錯誤扣款
　[B] 她想退還一項物品
　[C] 她收到某項數量錯誤的商品
　[D] 她訂的某項商品的樣式是錯的

179. 弗列克女士還需要哪一款布來做洋裝？
　[A] 10 號布料
　[B] 38 號布料
　[C] 41 號布料
　[D] 48 號布料

180. 泰勒織品的客服要如何聯絡弗列克女士？
　[A] 透過簡訊
　[B] 透過語音信箱
　[C] 透過電子郵件
　[D] 透過郵件

181–185 廣告和電子郵件

下個月在貝爾蒙特市歷史協會舉行

紀錄片之夜：《探索北極》
5 月 5 日，雲杉劇院

攝影展：「二十世紀的美國」
5 月 9 日開幕夜，琳達・卡麥隆藝廊

作家演講：葛倫・坎貝爾「早期美國文化」
5 月 14 日，克里斯・查爾頓禮堂

音樂表演：「美國民謠大師」
5 月 22 日，雲杉劇院

兒童與年長者可免費參加所有活動。此外，如果您在網站上支付了報名費，並成為貝爾蒙特市歷史協會的會員，也可免費參加任何活動。

有關團體參觀登記問題，聯絡大衛・史密斯 dsmith@belmonthistoricalsociety.com。有關接下來的活動與場地地點或租借場地的細節，請上本協會網站 www.belmonthistoricalsociety.com。

收件者：大衛・史密斯
<dsmith@belmonthistoricalsociety.com>
寄件者：傑瑞德・泰特
<jtate@clarkuniversity.com>
日期：4 月 22 日
主旨：團體參觀

親愛的史密斯先生：

您好，我叫傑瑞德・泰特，是馬里維爾市中心克拉克大學歷史系的教授。

我這學期教授大一的歷史導論，我認為參加坎貝爾先生主講的活動會對我的課程有益，他的演講與我們現在課堂上正在討論的主題相關。

我也在想，有沒有可能安排一場坎貝爾先生與我班上約 50 名學生之間的問答座談。請告訴他，我們很期待見到他。

感謝您撥冗讀我的電子郵件，希望儘快收到您的回覆。

克拉克大學歷史系
傑瑞德・泰特

181. 下列何者與貝爾蒙特市歷史協會有關？

Ⓐ 它不允許兒童參加某些活動
Ⓑ 它由貝爾蒙特市所經營
Ⓒ 它是由琳達・卡麥隆所創辦的
Ⓓ 它將在幾個不同的地方舉辦活動

182. 泰特先生目前的授課內容最有可能是什麼？

Ⓐ 北極的環境狀況
Ⓑ 美國早期歷史
Ⓒ 美國民俗音樂
Ⓓ 現代攝影

183. 下列何者無法在貝爾蒙特市歷史協會的網站上找到？

Ⓐ 已排定活動的資訊
Ⓑ 會員註冊
Ⓒ 租借細節
Ⓓ 之前活動的記敘

184. 在電子郵件中，第二段第一行的「introductory」意思最接近？

Ⓐ 基本的
Ⓑ 必要的
Ⓒ 深度的
Ⓓ 非必要的

185. 泰特先生要求什麼？

Ⓐ 一本簽了名的書
Ⓑ 一份詳細的調查
Ⓒ 和主講者見面的機會
Ⓓ 團體優惠

186–190 行程表和電子郵件

紐頓圖書館
四月節目與活動時間表

日期與時間	活動	地點	其他備註
4 月 2 日晚上 7 點	昔日之旅：默片系列	德克廳	和我們一起觀賞幾部呈現美國早期電影史的影片。
4 月 5 日下午 3 點	青年創意寫作坊	青年部 304 室	開放給所有想增進寫作技巧的高中生。
4 月 10 日上午 11 點	初級英語會話社	教育中心 102 室	加入其他想學英語會話的成人。此課程免費。
4 月 16 日下午五點	活到老學到老	媒體教室 202 室	學會使用電腦不只是年輕人獨享的權利。加入我們，一起利用電腦探索資訊汪洋。（適合年長者）
4 月 29 日上午 10 點	故事劇	青年部 301 室	邊玩玩具邊聽故事。（給 0 到 5 歲的孩童）

感謝所有捐款讓我們得以購買新筆記型電腦與設立媒體教室的人士。

收件者：李察・懷特
<rwhite@newtonlibrary.com>
寄件者：琳達・卡特
<lcarter121@seprus.com>
日期：4 月 1 日
主旨：初級英語會話社

懷特先生您好：

我叫琳達・卡特，我是即將於 4 月 10 日舉辦的初級英語會話社的指導老師。我注意到圖書館最近用向讀者募集的捐款設立了媒體教室，我希望能更換教室，以便我使用新的教學資源，將電腦融入我的英語會話課程中。您可以將我的班改到和「活到老學到老」同一間教室，而非教育中心嗎？我想我的學生會很喜歡他們從電腦上學到的實用英語技巧。同時，可以請您寄電子郵件給所有已經報名本課程的學生嗎？他們需要被告知教室異動一事。

先感謝您的協助。

琳達・卡特

收件者：琳達・卡特
<lcarter121@seprus.com>
寄件者：李察・懷特
<rwhite@newtonlibrary.com>
日期：4 月 2 日
主旨：教室異動

親愛的卡特女士：

我很樂意將您的初級英語會話課挪至擁有最新媒體設備的教室，請知悉，那是 3A 教室。很遺憾的是，我沒有報名該課程所有學生的電子郵件信箱。很多學生只提供了他們的姓名。如果您可以接受的話，我可以在圖書館入口處貼上告示，公告您的課程，並註明教室異動。請告訴我，您是否要我這樣做。

感謝您，並祝安好

圖書館活動籌劃員
李察・懷特

---

186. 下列何者與紐頓圖書館有關？
　　A 它最近裝修了設施
　　B 它不久後將舉辦募款活動
　　C 它提供各種年齡層的教育活動
　　D 它週一休館

187. 哪一項活動最適合電影系學生？
　　A 故事劇
　　B 青年創意寫作坊
　　C 昔日之旅
　　D 活到老學到老

188. 在第一封電子郵件中，第一段第二行的「held」意思最接近？
　　A 搬運
　　B 參加
　　C 延誤
　　D 進行

189. 李察・懷特為什麼無法發電子郵件給琳達・卡特的學生？
　　A 他沒有他們的電子郵件信箱
　　B 那不是他的工作
　　C 他沒有時間
　　D 圖書館內沒有那種科技

190. 對於無法通知琳達的學生教室異動的問題，李察・懷特提出了什麼解決方法？
　　A 他可以寄電子郵件給他們
　　B 他可以在他們進來時引導他們至正確的教室
　　C 他會張貼告示
　　D 他會畫一張上頭有路線指引的地圖給他們

191–195 電子郵件、文章和報名表

收件者：湯尼・沃克
　　　　<twalker@icmcorp.com >
寄件者：蘇西・梅森
　　　　<smason@icmcorp.com>
日期：5 月 4 日
主旨：夏季行事曆
附件：預算 .doc

親愛的沃克先生：

我正要確定公司的夏季活動行事曆。由於我們去年在員工的感恩活動上超出預算，所以我想比較明智的做法應該是找更實惠的休閒活動。附件是我為已規劃的夏季活動所做的費用預估分析明細。

7 月 6 日：安克拉治花卉節

7 月 22 日：勞倫斯公園的公園藝術

8 月 6 日：安克拉治鄉間自行車之旅

8 月 19 日：甜心牧場騎馬

相較於去年，今年我安排了較少的戶外活動。今年我想利用一個新的戶外休閒活動機會，是我在安克拉治記者網上看到的。您可以點擊這個連結，閱讀這篇文章：www.anchoragereporter.com/new_trails

請告訴我您的看法。

人力資源部經理
蘇西・梅森

安克拉治記者
自 8 月 6 日起安克拉治鄉間自行車之旅

5 月 2 日——安克拉治自行車社今年夏天將舉辦年度騎自行車活動，自 8 月 6 日起至 8 月 7 日止。這個活動將於那兩天的上午 10 點，在安克拉治社區活動中心揭開序幕。如果您欲開車前往起點，最好利用社區活動中心後面的停車場。

安克拉治自行車社社長琴・佛洛斯特表示：「騎車的路程從 5 英里到 20 英里不等，將帶領自行車騎士們穿過安克拉治風景秀麗的地區。整體來說，這些自行車之旅將以一種悠閒的步調進行，所以各種程度的自行車騎士皆可參加。不過，本地經驗豐富的騎士將帶領一組步調較快的隊伍。」

於活動開始前半個小時，參加自行車之旅的騎士們將學到騎車技巧、自行車保養，以及適當的營養補給方式。所有參加者都必須戴上安全帽，也鼓勵他們自行攜帶飲水，以防騎車時脫水。

自行車之旅報名表

如果您有意參加 8 月 6 日的自行車之旅，請寫下您的姓名、所屬部門，以及經驗或體能程度。如果進階組報名人數夠多，我們就可以協調成兩組獨立的行程。如果人數不夠分成兩組，那我們鼓勵所有騎士待在一起，這樣每個人都可以參與到我們所規劃的團體運動。感謝您的參與，希望能在活動上見到各位！

姓名	部門	體能／經驗
湯姆・克魯茲	業務	初級
維恩・瓊斯	倉管	初級
莎莉・杰金斯	倉管	初級
芭芭拉・布雷斯特	接待	進階
哈潑・金斯基	業務	初級

191. 梅森女士提議做什麼？

Ⓐ **休閒活動的支出要限制在預算內**
Ⓑ 派任新的人力資源部經理
Ⓒ 增加臨時僱員的數量
Ⓓ 比去年安排更多戶外活動

192. 梅森女士建議今年的新活動要安排在哪一天？

Ⓐ 7 月 6 日
Ⓑ 7 月 22 日
Ⓒ **8 月 6 日**
Ⓓ 8 月 19 日

193. 這篇文章最有可能出現在網站的哪一個版面？

Ⓐ 經濟
Ⓑ **休閒**
Ⓒ 娛樂
Ⓓ 政治

194. 根據自行車之旅報名表，我們可推知下列何者與即將舉辦的自行車之旅有關？

　Ⓐ 活動將被取消

　Ⓑ 將會有兩個隊伍，初級組與進階組

　Ⓒ 將只有一個隊伍

　Ⓓ 他們將會半路停下來用餐並合照

195. 芭芭拉・布雷斯特最有可能在自行車之旅中做什麼？

　Ⓐ 她會很無聊，然後放棄行程

　Ⓑ 她會抱怨進階組應該要有更多人報名

　Ⓒ 她會加入經驗豐富騎士的快步調隊伍

　Ⓓ 她會留在隊伍參加團體活動

196–200 表格和電子郵件

四季服飾暢貨中心

所有退換貨必須在送達七天內寄回四季服飾暢貨中心，退還的商品可以更換成其他商品或要求退款。如果您選擇退款，我們會將款項退還至購買時所使用的信用卡帳戶中。

具正式會員資格者可利用我們的宅配查詢服務並收到常客優惠。

退換貨請寄至：

80725 科羅拉多州丹佛市芬頓街 144 號（303-555-4387），四季服飾暢貨中心

請勾選最符合您的問題的描述：

＿＿ 商品有瑕疵或毀損

＿＿ 商品不符預期

＿✓＿ 送錯商品

＿＿ 其他：＿＿＿＿＿＿＿＿＿＿

個人資料：

姓名：莎莉・尼爾森

訂單號碼：2245

電話：432-555-6729

地址：80725 科羅拉多州丹佛市橡樹街 2154 號

電子郵件：snelson@clandon.net

＿✓＿ 更換　　＿＿ 退款

我於 4 月 22 日在貴公司的網路商店訂購了一件中號的白雪聖誕毛衣，但我卻收到小號的。我想要更換成正確尺寸的毛衣。

寄件者：黛博拉・克拉克
<debraclarke@fourseasons.com>
收件者：莎莉・尼爾森
<snelson@clandon.net>
日期：4 月 30 日
主旨：更換

親愛的尼爾森女士：

我們已經收到您想更換所購買的毛衣的要求，我們誠心地為此錯誤道歉。我們會立即依照您的要求將正確的商品宅配給您。貨物配送狀況可利用以下貨物追蹤查詢號碼，於本公司網站查詢：447H57J。

由於這是本公司的失誤，我們已經將七元退回您的信用卡帳戶內，以補償您退換貨的運費。請核對餘額進行確認。

如果您對本訂單還有任何問題，歡迎來電 303-555-4387，我將協助您處理所有問題。

黛博拉・克拉克

收件者：黛博拉・克拉克
<debraclarke@fourseasons.com>
寄件者：莎莉・尼爾森
< snelson@clandon.net >
日期：5 月 4 日
主旨：退換錯誤

親愛的克拉克女士：

很高興收到您的電子郵件，內容事關於我退換貨一事，也很感謝四季如此貼心地退還我的運費。

話雖如此，我確認過帳戶，也收到了所說的款項。此外，寄來的新毛衣也是正確的尺寸。但是我訂的是白雪聖誕款，收到的卻是冬季慶典款。這兩款都是很棒的毛衣，但是我先生就是比較喜歡白雪聖誕款。您可以將我原本訂的款式寄給我嗎？待我收到正確貨品與運費退款後，我會將冬季慶典毛衣寄回。

謝謝您！

莎莉・尼爾森

196. 尼爾森女士呈報説原本宅配的商品有什麼問題？

Ⓐ 有受損

Ⓑ 尺寸不合

Ⓒ 延遲收到

Ⓓ 未抵達目的地

197. 在黛博拉‧克拉克寄出的電子郵件中，第一段第二行的「as per」哪個意思最接近？

Ⓐ 不論

Ⓑ 除了……之外

Ⓒ 而不是

Ⓓ 根據

198. 下列何者與尼爾森女士有關？

Ⓐ 她最近才搬到丹佛市

Ⓑ 她訂了禮物要給朋友

Ⓒ 她有四季服飾暢貨中心的會員資格

Ⓓ 她太晚要求退款

199. 尼爾森女士呈報説更換的宅配商品有什麼問題？

Ⓐ 尺寸錯誤

Ⓑ 款式錯誤

Ⓒ 尺寸跟款式都錯了

Ⓓ 原本購買商品的退款金額溢給

200. 尼爾森女士將於何時退還冬季慶典毛衣？

Ⓐ 當她收到正確的貨品與運費退款時

Ⓑ 當她有空時

Ⓒ 當她的老公喜歡他的毛衣時

Ⓓ 當四季為她的不便道歉時

ACTUAL TEST ③

PART 5　P.80–83

◎ Part 5 解答請見 P.457

101. **離**火車站不遠**處**就是星光公園，是個遊客或在地人都喜歡的景點。

102. **在**介紹主講人之**之前**，銷售主任會先簡短致詞。

103. 慈善團體的新閱讀計劃**預計**在未來十年內提升發展中國家的識字率。

104. 搬到新的城市後，梅森女士以參與社交**活動**來快速地擴展她的人際網絡。

105. 欲參賽的藝術家應於**截止日期** 6 月 30 日之前繳交作品。

106. 德瑞克藥廠很**幸運的**聘請到世界知名的化學家喬納斯・倫德成為其實驗室資深技術員。

107. 扎恩公司明年**將開始**在國內製造生產所有高檔皮夾與鞋子。

108. 有些投票者明顯**偏好**那些從事法律工作的候選人。

109. 店員說**大約**有 15 位客人已經在店門外等著店家開門。

110. 漏水的水龍頭已經修好，所以訪客**現在**可以使用一樓的洗手間。

111. 藉由服用托夫特醫生團隊所研發出來的藥，可以明顯地延緩病**程**。

112. 不幸地，當颱風襲擊該地時，居民和官員**完全**措手不及。

113. 公司計劃**補助**業務員出席會議時所產生的開銷。

114. 卡爾頓女士很自在地過馬路，因為沒有車輛朝她的**方向**開來。

115. **在**電視新聞報導大選**期間**，很多備受矚目的候選人接受了現場採訪。

116. 希克斯先生在音樂廳替重要的客戶**保留**靠近舞台的位子。

117. 舉辦電影產業頒獎盛會**的**費里茲中心正在進行浩大的擴建工程。

118. 每月一次的員工晚餐，讓來自不同部門的員工有機會以個人層面**彼此**互動。

119. 房東必須**遵守**由住宅安全區域部門所訂定的法規。

120. 由於**結構**因素，在大樓的一樓加上堅固的支撐橫樑。

121. 生態聯盟是個非營利的組織，**致力於**教育大眾環保相關議題。

122. 將所有目錄與郵件加**入**維他命公司的商標是很重要的。

123. 儘管遭到數大出版商拒絕，伊恩・萊特**仍繼續努力**，後來成為世界知名的小說家。

124. 布洛斯先生因撰寫出**資訊豐富**且簡單易懂的使用手冊而受到讚揚。

125. 雖然賈西亞女士在該金融機構中的資金不多，但其員工仍視她**如**重要投資者。

126. 當您郵寄退貨時，請確保收據已**附**在申請表上以便加速作業。

127. 案發不久前，目擊者看到只有**單**人身影站在路燈旁。

128. 班・山德斯**創新地**設計了一款容易收合，可精巧收納的行李箱。

129. 因為今年夏天氣候較往年溫暖，農作物**將**可提早幾週**收成**。

130. **在一**查完羅克福德顧問公司的財務記錄**後**，會計師即呈交一份正式報告。

131–134 公告

緊急！誠徵熟手水管工

王牌配管工程公司位於哥倫比亞，現正擴大徵求熟手的水管工。自 1954 年起，王牌配管工程就開始在哥倫比亞地區服務。我們一直以來都是家族企業，但是隨著過去三年哥倫比亞人口急遽增長，讓我們有機會歡迎熟練的水管工加入我們。應徵者應具安裝商用與住宅的各型水管之經驗。請將履歷表寄至 aceplumbing@gmail.com，我們將安排面試。

131. A 擴展
B 期待
C 承包
D 控制

132. A 自 1954 年起，王牌配管工程就開始在哥倫比亞地區服務。
B 我們與社區的連結較少。
C 我們一直難以支付帳單。
D 王牌配管工程有財務困難。

133. A 怪異的
B 急遽性的
C 不可能的
D 荒唐的

134. A 片段
B 流量
C 工程
D 種類

135–138 網頁

學習到社群媒體行銷策略
就在天才行銷力研討會

準備好要讓您的社群媒體行銷進入下個階段了嗎？那麼就參加天才行銷力研討會，並學習最前衛的社群行銷策略。研討會將於 5 月 3 日及 4 日在休士頓舉辦。這可能是您一年中最富教育意義的兩天。

天才行銷將傳授您現實世界的策略，來提高您的付費與自然社群媒體的行銷成效。不論您是購買社群媒體廣告，或是把重點放在社群媒體的自然曝光上，天才行銷力研討會都是您今年必須參加的一場研討會。您將獲得專家啟發、與他人交流您面臨的挑戰、取得可行的策略來驅動流量，提高銷售量並增加客戶滿意度。

欲申請者，只需點擊以下連結。

<u>**申請**</u>

135. A 參加
B 參加
C 參加了
D 正參加

136. A 今日就加入，並將業界的人帶往偉大之境。
B 研討會將於 5 月 3 日至 4 日於休士頓舉辦。
C 將於 11 月 20 日開放兩週課程的報名登記。
D 整個三月都有提供課程。

137. A 兩者之一
B 不論
C 寧願
D 不只

138. A 劃分
B 增加
C 貶值
D 忍受

139–142 電子郵件

收件者：南西・克拉夫
寄件者：歐瑪・帕托
日期：1 月 16 日
主旨：宅配前流程

在產製團隊會議中，存貨在出貨前並未全部都有妥善的儲放這點令人疑慮。由於這點疑慮，團隊決定要檢視書面流程來確認是否需要多增加步驟。包裝與倉儲團隊的會議已經安排在 1 月 23 日星期二舉行。請安排時間表，讓包裝與倉儲團隊中大多數的主管都能出席這個會議。

我有信心包裝與倉儲團隊的管理部將會發現，書面流程不會讓儲放不良的這種問題有機會發生。包裝與倉儲團隊所提出的任何建議，只會修改出更完善的檢核表。

139. A 理解
     B 疑慮
     C 挑戰
     D 耐心

140. A 然而
     B 由於
     C 不管
     D 假如

141. **A 包裝與倉儲團隊的會議已經安排在 1 月 23 日星期二舉行。**
     B 在星期二上班前，所有員工都被要求要檢視流程。
     C 會議將會調查包裝過程中冗餘步驟的可能性。
     D 計劃在 12 月底時加入額外的訓練課程。

142. A 正發現
     B 已經被發現
     C 將發現
     D 已經發現

143–146 信件

6 月 3 日
水口結衣
10787 紐約州布魯克林狄恩街
143 號 3 號公寓

水口女士您好：

很高興通知您，漢諾威設計公司想要邀請您參加夏季實習專案的面試。在本公司今年的六個職缺中，我們只面試 15 名應徵者。您會很開心知道您在 200 多位應徵者中脫穎而出。

面試將安排在三月六日和七日下午一至六點。若時間允許，我們希望您能於六日下午 1 點 30 分前來。若時間上不允許，也可安排在七日。請盡快告知我們您是否可以出席。若有任何問題，請撥打辦公室電話（212-347-9919），人力資源部將協助您。期待盡快收到您的回覆。

漢諾威設計公司行政主管
麥克斯・萊特 敬上
212-326-1268
M.Wright@hannoverdesign.com

143. **A 邀請**
     B 將邀請
     C 已經邀請
     D 將被邀請

144. A ……的人
     B ……的那個
     C ……人的
     D ……的那個

145. A 訂購
     B 安排
     C 迫使
     D 參加

146. A 您需要帶一份已填好的應徵函與某種身分證件。
     B 請盡快告知我們您是否可以出席。
     C 我們真希望能接受您的提議，但是我們必須回絕您。
     D 請回覆，若攜伴也請一併告知。

PART 7 　P.88–109

147–148 備忘錄

備忘錄

收文者：全體員工
發文者：大衛・科霍
主旨：重要訊息
日期：5 月 22 日

我們將於 6 月 3 日召開股東年會。在開幕式時，我將發表簡短的演說，希望各位都可以出席。以下是會議的初步時程表。

開幕式　　下午一點
年度報告　下午兩點
討論　　　下午四點
晚宴　　　下午六點

147. 這份備忘錄的目的是什麼？
　　Ⓐ 提醒員工專案截止日期
　　Ⓑ 建議修改年度報告
　　Ⓒ 提供活動時程表
　　Ⓓ 向股東報告年度獲利

148. 大衛・科霍將於幾點發表演說？
　　Ⓐ 下午一點
　　Ⓑ 下午二點
　　Ⓒ 下午四點
　　Ⓓ 下午六點

149–150 訊息串

茱蒂・林區	10:12

我們可以用公司信用卡刷這次的晚餐費用嗎？

奈森・李	10:13

很遺憾地，不行。公司政策上個月才修改過。只有在午餐或晚餐時與客戶開會的餐費才能報公帳。

茱蒂・林區	10:14

太可惜了，我猜我們這次要平均分攤了。

奈森・李	10:14

是的，但至少你可以去任何你想去的餐廳用餐。

茱蒂・林區	10:15

沒錯。我會告訴大家的。謝謝！

149. 茱蒂為什麼要聯絡奈森？
　　Ⓐ 要他付晚餐費用
　　Ⓑ 詢問公司開銷的資訊
　　Ⓒ 詢問他是否要一起用晚餐
　　Ⓓ 請他推薦好的餐廳

150. 在 10:14 時，茱蒂寫：「我們這次要平均分攤了」是什麼意思？
　　Ⓐ 他們將請公司付款
　　Ⓑ 他們將詢問會計部
　　Ⓒ 他們將決定誰要付款
　　Ⓓ 他們每個人必須支付部分帳單

151–152 信件

1 月 19 日

親愛的彼德森先生：

您所做的血液檢測結果已經出爐了。請盡快來電預約可以和赫門醫生會面的時間。

我們要提醒您，由於健康保險法規的變更，所有病患都被鼓勵要確認聯絡方式與保險資訊是最新且準確的，您可以撥打客戶服務專線 555-6842，或下次來診所時在櫃台完成確認。

尊榮健康診所
蘿拉・林克頓 敬上

151. 彼得森先生在不久的未來是可能做什麼？
　　Ⓐ 更新保單
　　Ⓑ 安排與醫生的預約
　　Ⓒ 應徵辦事員一職
　　Ⓓ 做血液檢測

152. 彼得森先生被要求做什麼？
　　Ⓐ 繳交保險表格
　　Ⓑ 回信
　　Ⓒ 確認個人資訊
　　Ⓓ 填寫問卷

153–154 傳單

在地購物
西雅圖商業區協會

您知道嗎？

■ 比起向連鎖零售商購買，在本地店家購物能為經濟帶來兩倍的收益。

■ 在本地店家購物，可以透過地方稅收來支持西雅圖市。

- 在本地店家購物有益於環保，節省汽油並減少空氣污染。

- 在本地購物可以在西雅圖創造更多工作機會，改善社區的生活水準。

我們想要鼓勵所有西雅圖的居民，藉由在當地傳統商店和市場購物來支持在地社區。

想要更了解或知悉所有在地居民可利用的優質商店與服務，請上西雅圖商業區協會的網站 www.sbda.org 查詢。

153. 這份宣傳單的目的是什麼？
- A 推廣永續生活
- B 通知特價訊息
- C 宣布新店開幕
- **D 影響消費模式**

154. 下列何者不是文中所提到在當地店家消費的好處？
- A 促進就業市場
- B 對環境友善
- C 支持當地經濟
- **D 鼓勵外商投資**

155–157 文章

格蘭德維尤商業新聞

柏奈爾餐廳在六個月前開始為忙碌的家庭提供外送服務，其業績之卓越，超乎預期。他們的小店「農場上桌」位於格蘭德維尤中央高地，被迫增加 1.2 倍的人力，才能趕上需求。

當瑞秋和羅伯・柏奈爾夫婦有了第一個孩子之後，整間餐廳的概念發想就出現了。兩位職業父母不斷地以速食當餐點，並發現身邊有許多朋友也是如此。他們需要更健康的選擇，而這正是大多數速食店無法提供的健康選擇。於是柏奈爾夫婦決定在那時辭掉辦公室的工作，開始創業，為上班人士提供健康餐點的外送服務。

他們的生意大受歡迎，一直接到來自外縣市的訂單。「顧客的反應令人覺得吃驚。」

瑞秋說，「顧客特別喜愛餐點的新鮮與品質。」一位在外送服務創始時就訂購的顧客珍娜補充說：「不只是食物健康，價格沒比速食餐點更貴，但卻是更好的選擇。」

柏奈爾餐廳說他們計劃在下年度內擴大外送路線，並且在格蘭德維尤市各地開設三間「農場上桌」販賣熟食餐點。

155. 這篇文章是有關什麼？
- A 速食公司的角色變化
- B 健康飲食的重要性
- C 格蘭德維尤農地的擴展
- **D 小型店家的成功與成長**

156. 根據這篇文章，農場上桌餐點的主要賣點是什麼？
- A 運送速度非常快
- B 價格很便宜
- **C 健康**
- D 美味

157. 下列句子最適合出現在 [1]、[2]、[3]、[4] 的哪個位置？「於是柏奈爾夫婦決定在那時辭掉辦公室的工作，開始創業，為上班人士提供健康餐點的外送服務。」
- A [1]
- **B [2]**
- C [3]
- D [4]

158–160 告示

顧客請注意

很遺憾要通知大家，我們要全面回收肯特牌今年 3 月 30 日至 7 月 30 日間所生產的各類型梯子。

- 梯子不符合強制性安全標準，可能不穩。
- 站在上面時梯子會移動，可能導致危險性摔傷。
- 任何情況下都不要使用梯子，請與肯特公司聯絡進行退換貨。只要將梯子退還，即使沒有購買證明，顧客仍可拿到全額退款。

請撥打 1-800-555-2493 與肯特公司聯絡。按 8 即可轉接專門負責處理產品回收的客服人員。造成您的不便，我們深感抱歉。

158. 這個公告最有可能會在哪裡看到？

 Ⓐ 房地產辦公室

 Ⓑ 五金行

 Ⓒ 回收站

 Ⓓ 雜貨店

159. 公告裡告誡顧客不要做什麼事？

 Ⓐ 使用有瑕疵的產品

 Ⓑ 更新保固

 Ⓒ 繳交訂單

 Ⓓ 提出客訴

160. 根據公告，要如何獲得更多資訊？

 Ⓐ 填寫表格

 Ⓑ 查看使用手冊

 Ⓒ 與公司聯絡

 Ⓓ 看教學影片

161–164 網路聊天室

J&R 國際公司的小組討論區

9:15	派翠西亞·諾貝爾（管理人）	大家早。關於即將於六月舉辦的領袖研討會，我已經張貼了一些構想。
9:16	派翠西亞·諾貝爾（管理人）	請分享你的想法，我們需要大家提供意見。
9:20	傑瑞·戴維斯	看起來非常制式化。可以加入一些像是露營遠征之類的活動嗎？
9:21	羅倫斯·歐丹尼爾	我不知道這次是否可以參加，我的團隊正在為一個重要的企劃案收尾。不過露營聽起來很棒。
9:22	派翠西亞·諾貝爾（管理人）	露營是個好主意，但是需要更多時間規劃。下次研討會絕對會將它納入考慮。
9:24	傑米·李	我不認為影片會很有效。若是找更多演講者來發表演說呢？我比較希望能與他人互動。
9:27	莫妮卡·崔	我很期待那個露營的點子，但是這次的研討會，我同意傑米的看法。影片會很無聊。
9:30	傑瑞·戴維斯	我發現約翰·奧利維這次沒有要發表演說。發生了什麼事嗎？他很受歡迎，我想參加他的研討會。
9:41	派翠西亞·諾貝爾（管理人）	約翰還沒有跟我們確認，因為他行程上可能有衝突。他正努力調整行程。
9:52	伊莎貝拉·普瑞斯	我也想要參加約翰的研討會。我注意到還有幾個空的時段。有人有興趣聽耿欣演講嗎？我想要聽聽不同的文化觀點。
9:58	傑瑞·戴維斯	好主意！耿欣在中國擔任主管經驗豐富，她總是有一些有趣的故事。
10:01	傑米·李	我附議，我真的很想聽聽耿欣的演講。而說到文化觀點，亞當也有在多國管理員工的經驗。我想他應該也會很有趣。
10:09	伊莎貝拉·普瑞斯	好，邀請亞當來研討會演講吧。
10:15	亞當·克魯茲	哇，我很高興你們對我的信任。我很樂意參與研討會，我下午都有空。
10:19	派翠西亞·諾貝爾（管理人）	謝謝你，亞當。如果可以的話，我會把你安排在下午三至四點的時段。
10:30	亞當·克魯茲	聽起來很棒。如果有的話，可以寄一份準則給我嗎？

161. 誰最有可能參加這個小組討論？

    Ⓐ 一般大眾

    Ⓑ 公司全體員工

    Ⓒ 來自不同國家的員工

    Ⓓ 公司經理及其他主管

162. 文中討論了什麼？

    Ⓐ 會議中最佳的演說

    Ⓑ 公司裡最佳的講者

    Ⓒ 工作坊的時程表

    Ⓓ 國際同事

163. 在 10:15 時，亞當·克魯斯說：「我很高興你們對我的信任」是什麼意思？

    Ⓐ 他感謝大家要他擔任經理

    Ⓑ 他感謝大家認為他是一位好主管

    Ⓒ 他很高興他最喜歡的演講者受到邀請

    Ⓓ 他為贏得選舉而感到榮幸

164. 派翠西亞·諾貝爾接下來可能會做什麼？

    Ⓐ 以電子郵件寄一些資料給同事

    Ⓑ 敲定員工會議

    Ⓒ 與全球同仁見面

    Ⓓ 打電話給同事說明異動

165–167 電子郵件

收件者：莎曼珊·羅素

                <srussell@speednet.com>

寄件者：山姆·柏格

                <sberer@highlandshotel.com>

主旨：預約

日期：7 月 1 日

附件：收據

親愛的羅素女士：

感謝您選擇高地飯店作為您即將舉行慶祝活動的場地。與您聯絡是為了確認您 7 月 12 日與 13 日兩晚房間的預約細節。您預定了本飯店四樓整層的 12 間房。除此之外，在那兩天，主會議室將專屬於您，供您無限制使用。您提到家族成員將從全國各地前來出席這個活動。在住宿期間，本飯店將提供任何您所需要的協助。

本飯店提供免費無線網路，也提供免費網路咖啡廳，讓顧客想上網或寄送電子郵件時可免費使用我們的電腦。咖啡廳開放時間為上午 5 點至中午 12 點。另外，也歡迎貴賓至我們獲獎的餐廳用餐，服務時間為上午 7 點至晚上 10 點。

這封電子郵件還附上您的收據，是您在 6 月 30 日以信用卡所支付的訂金 100 元。若您想看看會議室的格局與座椅安排，可至 本 飯 店 網 站 www.highlandshotel.com 瀏覽。

高地飯店

山姆·柏格 敬上

165. 7 月 12 日和 13 日將舉辦什麼活動？

    Ⓐ 家族聚會

    Ⓑ 商務會議

    Ⓒ 股東會議

    Ⓓ 就業博覽會

166. 下列何者不是此次訂房的好處？

    Ⓐ 單獨使用一整層樓

    Ⓑ 免費餐點

    Ⓒ 使用會議室

    Ⓓ 免費上網

167. 根據電子郵件，羅素女士可以在高地飯店網站上查詢到什麼？

    Ⓐ 訂房編號

    Ⓑ 飯店餐廳的菜單

    Ⓒ 座位規劃

    Ⓓ 折價券

168–171 公告

超強健身房會員請注意

一種健身計劃無法適用於每個人，這就是為什麼超強健身房提供本地區最多元的健身課程，保證您能找到有趣又刺激的課程，幫助您達到健身目標。現在我們很興奮地要介紹您一個新的舞蹈體適能課程。上課時間是今年夏季的 6 月 12 日至 8 月 23 日。

舞蹈是種既有趣又能互動的運動方式，也適合那些無法進行高強度健身活動的人。

我們鼓勵想要報名這堂舞蹈課的人，以兩人為一組來登記。如果您沒有其他人可以一起報名，那第一堂課時將與其他人一起配對。報名時間為 5 月 10 日至 6 月 1 日。您可以在網站上填寫報名表。課程費用必須於報名時以信用卡支付。

依照我們的規定，學員必須在課程開始至少前一週取消報名才能退費。在截止日期後取消報名者將不予退費。

欲知更多課程內容、課表及費用的相關資訊，請來電 (231) 555-2523 找經理史考特・彼得森。

168. 這個公告的目的是什麼？
　　Ⓐ 延後開幕典禮
　　Ⓑ 聘用新教練
　　Ⓒ 解釋付款方式
　　Ⓓ 宣布新的課程

169. 6 月 12 日最有可能發生什麼事？
　　Ⓐ 有些教練將會缺席
　　Ⓑ 有些會員將會被分配搭檔
　　Ⓒ 會退費
　　Ⓓ 會核發結業證明

170. 根據公告，報名者能得到退費的最後日期是哪一天？
　　Ⓐ 5 月 10 日
　　Ⓑ 6 月 5 日
　　Ⓒ 6 月 12 日
　　Ⓓ 8 月 23 日

171. 文中提到與彼得森先生聯絡的原因是什麼？
　　Ⓐ 安排預約
　　Ⓑ 詢問課程
　　Ⓒ 更新個人聯絡資料
　　Ⓓ 找舞伴

172–175 備忘錄

備忘錄

收文者：全體員工
發文者：維蘿妮卡・傑克曼執行經理
日期：10 月 10 日
主旨：人員配置

我們的行銷主管席拉・羅伯絲將於 10 月 21 日至 11 月 5 日前往新加坡出差。在她出差期間，麥可・李將暫時代理她在高曼百貨公司的部分職務。但是，對於那些和羅伯絲女士一起執行企劃案且接近完成的人，公司要求你們在 10 月 15 日前與她敲定最後的工作安排。部分緊急的企劃案已經和麥可討論過了。如果你的企劃案可以等席拉出差回來，公司要求你們告知席拉和麥可，好讓其他的企劃案可以先進行。

我知道這可能造成工作不便，特別是如此接近過節的時候，但我相信在席拉出差期間，麥可能夠擔負起這些職責。麥可一直與席拉合作密切，他將會處理交到他手上的新企劃案。在席拉出差期間，麥可將安排與不同部門單獨開會，以確保在他暫代期間能順利交接與溝通。

若有其他問題或疑慮，請在 10 月 20 日前與席拉聯絡，或隨時來找我。

172. 備忘錄的收文者在哪裡工作？
　　Ⓐ 在行銷公司
　　Ⓑ 在法律事務所
　　Ⓒ 在百貨公司
　　Ⓓ 在旅行社

173. 下列何者與席拉・羅伯絲有關？
　　Ⓐ 她得到一份新工作
　　Ⓑ 她升官了
　　Ⓒ 她要去度假
　　Ⓓ 她要出差

174. 專案即將完成的員工要在何時前與席拉聯絡？

[A] **10 月 15 日**
[B] 10 月 20 日
[C] 10 月 21 日
[D] 11 月 5 日

175. 下列句子最適合出現在 [1]、[2]、[3]、[4] 的哪個位置？「在席拉出差期間，參可將安排與不同部門單獨開會，以確保在他暫代期間能順利交接與溝通。」

[A] [1]
[B] [2]
[C] [3]
[D] **[4]**

176–180 網站和文章

鄉村地區擴展計畫

為了持續致力於改善本州各地鄉村社區的生活水準，鄉村服務協會提供鄉村社區年度補助金。這個計劃的目的是要資助當地為維持鄉村生活的便利性及滿意度的人，慰勞他們在地所付出的努力。今年提供的補助金如下：

商業發展補助金：250,000 元
社區發展補助金：150,000 元
交流發展補助金：200,000 元
教育發展補助金：100,000 元

協會將優先補助的提案是那些反映整體社區多元發展，提升社區參與，以及讓鄉村社區成為一個更適合安居樂業的地區。補助金可以讓鄉村社區邁出第一步，利用提案或規劃幫助改善社區居民的生活。在過去數十年中，補助款被用在各種不同用途上，如最先進的耕種器具、道路維護、通訊基礎設施、教育設施以及投資鄉村青年企業家。

下載申請表來申請補助金吧。送件截止日期是 2 月 28 日。

克拉頓村贏得資金補助

克拉頓，3 月 22 日——鄉村服務協會今天宣布克拉頓村是今年教育發展補助金的得主。補助金將用於興建大型遊樂場的工程上，為 12 歲以下兒童提供休閒娛樂用。自從去年新的電子工廠開業以來，該地區的家庭數量急遽上升。因此，留給兒童玩耍的空間變得越來越少。新的遊樂場將可讓兒童在放學時玩樂。

克拉頓很榮幸能獲得這筆補助金，計劃未來要申請更多的補助金，以改善該村的生活條件，吸引更多居民。

176. 網頁的目的是什麼？

[A] 報告企劃案已完成
[B] **鼓勵申請補助金**
[C] 宣布補助金的得主
[D] 介紹當地企業家

177. 根據網頁，下列何者不是鄉村服務協會補助金的目的？

[A] 提供資金給當地商業人士
[B] 建設通訊基礎設施
[C] **安排社區健康檢查**
[D] 購買農耕器具

178. 克拉頓村獲得多少補助？

[A] **100,000 元**
[B] 150,000 元
[C] 200,000 元
[D] 250,000 元

179. 根據這篇文章，補助金讓克拉頓村可以做什麼？

[A] 改善當地農耕條件
[B] 整修小學
[C] 聘用更多合格教師
[D] **提供兒童遊樂場所**

180. 下列何者與克拉頓村有關？

[A] 以前也曾獲得補助
[B] 計劃開設新的工廠
[C] **人口數增加**
[D] 將舉辦社區慶祝活動

181–185 電子郵件和表格

收件者：查理斯·貝爾
<charlesbell434@globalnet.com>
寄件者：凱莉·庫克
<carriecook@freshfarmsgrocery.com>
主旨：會員卡
日期：5 月 4 日

親愛的貝爾先生：

您在新鮮農產商場的銀星會員卡將於本月 28 日到期，您的會員卡讓您享有特價以及購買大多數產品的特別積點權益。一旦您累積到足夠的點數，就可以於下次購物時享有折扣。若無有效的銀星會員卡，您將無法累積這些常客點數。

請勿以電話續延您的會員資格。若欲續延會員資格，請至各分店的客戶服務櫃台辦理。若有任何疑問，請來電 204-555-2648。

新鮮農產商場 客戶服務專員
凱莉·庫克

新鮮農產商場
會員卡申請表

名： 查理斯
姓： 貝爾
會員編號： 14245FDA

☐ 建立我的會員卡
☑ 續延我的會員卡
☐ 取消我的會員卡

會員卡種類與費用：

金星：頂級會員，每年 90 元
銀星：商業會員，每年 70 元
銅星：家庭會員，每年 50 元
流星：短期會員，每月 10 元

請注意：

頂級會員僅限新鮮農產商場股東申請。食品賣家和餐廳老闆有資格申請銀星會員。

---

181. 這封電子郵件的目的是什麼？
　Ⓐ 宣布季節性折扣
　Ⓑ 通知貝爾先生未付款項
　Ⓒ 提醒貝爾先生續延會員資格
　Ⓓ 提供貝爾先生免費升等

182. 會員卡讓貝爾先生可以做什麼？
　Ⓐ 受惠於經常性的消費
　Ⓑ 在指定的區域停車
　Ⓒ 獲得快速配送
　Ⓓ 預先購買新產品

183. 貝爾先生被要求做什麼？
　Ⓐ 打電話給客戶服務櫃台
　Ⓑ 親自到店
　Ⓒ 填寫客戶評價
　Ⓓ 參加定期活動

184. 貝爾先生目前一年要付多少會費？
　Ⓐ 50 元
　Ⓑ 70 元
　Ⓒ 90 元
　Ⓓ 120 元

185. 下列何者與貝爾先生有關？
　Ⓐ 他是個著名的廚師
　Ⓑ 他經營食品販賣的商店
　Ⓒ 他是新鮮農產商場的股東
　Ⓓ 他今年才申請加入會員

186–190 信件、小手冊和時間表

5 月 12 日

親愛的葛瑞先生：

您是喬治亞建築師協會（GSA）的長期會員。我們要通知您協會今年為所提供的會員服務增加一些變化。具體而言，我們新增了金級會員，讓有特殊權限的會員能獲得比以往更多的資源。很開心通知您符合這個特殊會員的所有資格條件，現在就可立即註冊。您很快就會收到一份郵寄的手冊，裡面有更多資訊。我們希望您決定加入這個令人驚奇的金級會員。

如您所知，GSA 年度會員大會將於 6 月 14 日在喬治亞洲亞特蘭大市的星門會議中心舉行。我們注意到您已經報名了，我們等不及在那與您相會。如您需要任何安排上的協助，歡迎來電本會，電話是 (124) 555-5251。

喬治亞建築師協會
喬安·蘿絲 敬上

喬治亞建築師協會
金級會員

為符合這特別會員的資格，申請者在該領域須有 20 年以上的工作經驗，並擁有認可大學的建築學位。

福利包含：透過登入擁有超過 50,000 筆執業同業的資料庫，立即擴展您的聯絡網、只需繳交一半的報名費即可報名由 GSA 所舉辦的研討會、收到每月會訊，內容包含最新的市場研究及經濟分析，有助您的事業發展。

金級會員同時也符合申請該級會員專屬的專業責任保險資格。

如欲申請，只需填寫手冊所附的表格，寄至總部。40 元的申請費可以支票給付，或來電 (124) 555-5253 洽會計人員，以信用卡支付。

星門會議中心活動時程表
6 月 14 日
喬治亞建築師協會

上午 9:00 – 上午 9:45	大廳櫃台報到
上午 10:00 – 上午 11:45	演講貴賓傑瑞·詹金斯二世於 A 會議室
中午 12:00 – 下午 1:30	鑽石廳午宴
下午 2:00 – 下午 4:00	地區簡報於 A 會議室
晚上 6:00 – 晚上 9:00	藍寶石宴客廳晚宴與雞尾酒會
為確保當天活動報到順利，請記得攜帶您的協會會員證！	

186. 這封信的目的是什麼？
- Ⓐ 宣傳會議
- **Ⓑ 推銷新的會員身分**
- Ⓒ 確認預約
- Ⓓ 吸引新會員

187. 葛瑞先生被鼓勵做什麼？
- Ⓐ 報名參加會議
- Ⓑ 重新安排預約
- **Ⓒ 升級他的服務**
- Ⓓ 以信用卡付款

188. 下列何者與葛瑞先生有關？
- **Ⓐ 他當建築師已經超過 20 年了**
- Ⓑ 他在去年 GSA 會員大會上發表演說
- Ⓒ 他投稿至建築期刊
- Ⓓ 他在四月時忘記繳交會費

189. 葛瑞先生在會議當天應該要幾點報到？
- Ⓐ 上午 8:45 到上午 10:00
- Ⓑ 上午 9:00 整
- Ⓒ 任何時間
- **Ⓓ 上午 9:00 到上午 9:45**

190. 活動中包含幾餐？
- Ⓐ 早餐、午餐和晚餐
- Ⓑ 早午餐和晚餐
- Ⓒ 晚餐和雞尾酒會
- **Ⓓ 午餐和晚餐**

191–195 告示和電子郵件

科洛尼爾高地安養院

科洛尼爾高地很自豪已經在德州休士頓服務長者超過 30 年了。本安養院擁有最先進的設備，本院的五樓大樓讓每一層樓都可提供住戶個人化的照護。大樓裡設有復健用健身房，另外也提供住戶心理諮詢服務。

本院現正有數個職缺。我們希望聘用一名安養院行政人員，至少具三年的經驗及有效執照。另外，徵求一位住院協調員，應徵者需具備大學學歷及至少兩年的相關工作經歷。我們還招募臨終照護工作人員，需要能以富同情心與關懷的方式來提供住戶個人化照護，無須相關經驗，所以歡迎任何有興趣的人來應徵。

您可到本安養院網站查詢職缺，並上傳求職表，網站是 www.chnh.com。

收件者：湯米・詹金斯
<tommyjenkins7@zeusnet.com>
寄件者：貴格・帕克
<g_parker@chnh.com>
主旨：聘用程序
日期：9 月 14 日

親愛的詹金斯先生：

恭喜您！您已經通過住院協調員的第一輪應徵程序。我們要求所有應徵者親自前來科洛尼爾高地安養院參加面試。請您告知在 9 月 17 日方便前來面試的時間。

期盼與您見面。

科洛尼爾高地安養院 人力資源部主管
貴格・帕克 敬上

收件者：貴格・帕克
<g_parker@chnh.com>
寄件者：湯米・詹金斯
<tommyjenkins7@zeusnet.com>
日期：9 月 15 日
主旨：回覆：聘用程序

親愛的帕克先生：

感謝您給我住院協調員一職的面試機會。您要求我告知 9 月 17 日有空的時間。我在上午 10 點有另一場面試，但下午 1 點就可以到科洛尼爾高地安養院，希望您那個時間方便。如您所知，位於市區另一頭的松蔭安養院是另一家與您競爭的安養機構，而他們所提出的時數非常誘人。但我更想在像科洛尼爾高地安養院這樣有現代化設備的場所工作。期盼這次與您的面談，並參觀貴院設施。

湯米・詹金斯 敬上

---

191. 文中提到與科洛尼爾高地安養院有關的什麼事？
　　Ⓐ 在德州有五個據點
　　Ⓑ 已經營運超過半世紀
　　Ⓒ 提供藝術課程
　　Ⓓ 提供心理健康服務

192. 根據公告，哪個職位不需要經驗？
　　Ⓐ 安養院行政人員
　　Ⓑ 臨終照護人員
　　Ⓒ 住院協調員
　　Ⓓ 櫃台接待員

193. 下列何者與科洛尼爾高地安養院有關？
　　Ⓐ 計劃要擴大設施
　　Ⓑ 接受網站上遞出求職表
　　Ⓒ 提供該州最高的薪水
　　Ⓓ 最近更新了營業執照

194. 下列何者可能是湯米・詹金斯決定不去科洛尼爾高地安養院工作的原因？
　　Ⓐ 他們沒有健身中心
　　Ⓑ 他們的設備不先進
　　Ⓒ 工作地點太遠
　　Ⓓ 松蔭安養院可以提供他更好的時間表

195. 湯米・詹金斯幾點可以到科洛尼爾高地安養院？
　　Ⓐ 上午 10 點
　　Ⓑ 下午 1 點以前
　　Ⓒ 下午 1 點以後
　　Ⓓ 下午 4 點以後

196–200 電子郵件

收件者：傑克・包德溫
<baldwinj@technet.com>
寄件者：夢幻綠洲飯店
<booking@dreamoasishotel.com>
日期：9 月 22 日
主旨：您的訂房紀錄
附件：請款單 .html

親愛的包德溫先生：

感謝您在夢幻綠洲飯店訂房。您預約了 10 月 13 日和 14 日兩晚一間一張雙人床的房間。您的訂房編號是 5259。

僅以此信通知您，您必須於 9 月 29 日前支付尾款以便確認訂房。兩晚的費用總額為 165.25 元。您可以在飯店網站上以信用卡支付帳款，網址為 www.dreamoasishotel.com，支付時需輸入訂房編號。您也可以來電以電話完成支付手續。若未於 9 月 29 日前收到款項，將自動取消您的預約。有關詳細資訊，請參考附件的請款單。

當您抵達機場時，前往本飯店最簡單的方式就是搭乘地鐵。本飯店位於市政廳站三號出口旁。若找不到飯店，請隨時來電 555-2134。我們 24 小時皆有人員提供協助。

再次感謝您選擇本飯店。

夢幻綠洲飯店 客戶服務部經理
艾咪‧李

收件者：夢幻綠洲飯店
<booking@dreamoasishotel.com>
寄件者：傑克‧包德溫
<baldwinj@technet.com>
日期：9 月 23 日
主旨：回覆：您的訂房紀錄

親愛的李小姐：

這封信是有關我在夢幻綠洲飯店 10 月 13 日和 14 日這兩天的訂房。您在電子郵件中提到我即將入住貴飯店的款項問題。但是，我想要詢問住宿時間是否能延長一晚。我最近聽說 10 月 16 日將舉辦在地美食節，我想要參加。因此，我打算在貴飯店住到 10 月 15 日。請告知我修改後的費用，這樣我就能盡快支付正確的款項。

傑克‧包德溫

收件者：傑克‧包德溫
<baldwinj@technet.com>
寄件者：艾咪‧李
<alee@dreamoasishotel.com>
日期：9 月 24 日
主旨：15 號

親愛的包德溫先生：

將於 10 月 16 日舉辦的美食節的確值得讓您感到興奮。遺憾的是，這個活動太熱門了，所以該週末整個市區都已經客滿了。很遺憾要通知您，夢幻綠洲飯店在 10 月 15 日已經沒有空房。我逕自查了附近合作的飯店，但是也都沒有空房。我真的希望您能在市區找到住宿的地方，這樣就能在此享受這個節慶，我多麼希望您能和我們一同歡度。您可以試試位於費爾維尤的高檔旅舍，那是一間大型飯店，他們還有空房。

誠摯地深感抱歉。

夢幻綠洲飯店 客戶服務部經理
艾咪‧李

---

196. 第一封電子郵件的目的是什麼？

  Ⓐ 解釋取消的規定
  Ⓑ 要求付款
  Ⓒ 安排預約
  Ⓓ 提供特殊服務

197. 當包德溫先生線上付款時，會被要求提供什麼？

  Ⓐ 他的電話號碼
  Ⓑ 他的電子郵件信箱
  Ⓒ 他的房間號碼
  Ⓓ 他的訂房編號

198. 李小姐的電子郵件中不包含以下哪一項資訊？

  Ⓐ 住宿的費用
  Ⓑ 旅遊保險
  Ⓒ 飯店位置
  Ⓓ 員工聯絡方式

199. 包德溫先生 15 號那晚為什麼無法住在夢幻綠洲飯店？

Ⓐ **飯店因為美食節而客滿了**
Ⓑ 飯店因為太熱門而客滿了
Ⓒ 因為市區要舉辦會議，所以客滿了
Ⓓ 因為飯店餐點太好吃，所以客滿了

200. 艾咪‧李提供了什麼建議？

Ⓐ 要包德溫先生試試市區另一間飯店
Ⓑ **要包德溫先生試試位於費爾維尤的飯店**
Ⓒ 要包德溫先生明年再來參加美食節
Ⓓ 要包德溫 14 號再來問看看是否有人取消訂房

TEST 3

PART 7

ACTUAL TEST ④

◎ Part 5 解答請見 P.457

101. **除了**靠近後門的那棵樹外,這塊地上所有的樹木都在暴風雨中受損了。

102. 在內科醫生為**他**確診前,賀帝先生必須先進行幾項醫療檢查。

103. 企業家詹姆斯·莫斯比是**最近**一期雜誌的專題人物。

104. 法官的判決必須**嚴格地**依據所提供的證據。

105. 基於他數十年的經驗,芬利先生負責訓練新健身房的**指導員**。

106. 火焰餐廳的顧客可使用代客泊車服務,也可**自行**停車。

107. 去年,那些年輕的化學家**積極地**投入新黏著劑的研發。

108. 第一木業的專家可以將任何木頭家具修復**到**其原始的狀況。

109. 圖書館為了讀者的方便,要求資助裝設**自動**門。

110. 在注意到衣櫃**耗損的**狀況後,骨董店的老闆降低了價格。

111. 過去的十年來,亨利·維維安**證明**是位有才華又有上進心的記者。

112. **任何**患有睡眠問題**的人**在喝了這種花草茶後能獲得改善。

113. 為了減少南部**地區**的交通時間,在原有的鐵路線外又新增了一條。

114. 在節日期間,施瓦茨百貨公司將**推出**特別的化妝品禮盒組。

115. 沒有合格房地產經紀人的協助,首次購屋會是複雜甚至**有風險的**事情。

116. 布朗斯維爾的遊民之家自去年**創立**以來,已經幫助了數千人。

117. 明天評審小組將**評選出**社區美術大賽的準決賽參賽者。

118. 手機提早解約的罰金**明確地**記載在合約書中。

119. **根據**研究者報告,更常食用新鮮蔬果比避免吃速食是更好的健康終極目標。

120. 為了讓西班牙文母語者也能參加導覽,**口譯者**打算提供翻譯服務。

121. 慢跑者被要求靠道路右側跑,因為**很多**自行車騎士需要利用左邊的空間通行。

122. 在潛在買家看屋前,房地產經紀人要確定那房子是**美輪美奐的**。

123. 至於上週的**匯款**,必繳的州稅與聯邦稅須由領款者支付。

124. 每個人都支持縮短工時,但是**直到**總裁批准之前,一切都將依照原樣。

125. 該製造公司最近在減少工地意外事件上的**努力**受到了全體員工的讚賞。

126. 飯廳的家具**故意**留在屋內,因為新屋主已經買下它們。

127. 葛瑞森劇院**偶爾**會讓學生團體在白天時觀看彩排。

128. 《專業運動》雜誌**以**出版一系列頂尖運動員的獨家專訪而出名。

129. 只有**那些**配戴識別證的代表人員,才能進入會議場地。

130. **在**候選人正式宣布參加競選**前**,他私下與顧問群會面。

131–134 告示

員工工作坊

T&R 集團以提供領導能力進修、員工訓練及各種工作坊等方式，盡力幫助員工發揮潛能。這個月，我們為那些有意加強電腦技能的員工提供了工作坊，包括如何操作專業文書套件軟體、架設個人網站和操作通訊應用軟體等數種課程。我們目前還有幾個空檔時段，歡迎同仁提供建議，最受歡迎的提案將會考慮列入工作坊。如果您有意參加任何一個工作坊，請寄電子郵件給瓊納斯 jsmith@TRgroup.com。我們希望大家都能善用所提供的課程。

131. A 提供
　　 B 當時正提供
　　 C 現正提供
　　 D 已提供

132. A 改正
　　 B 減少
　　 C 詳述
　　 D 改善

133. A 依賴的
　　 B 獨立的
　　 C 閒置的
　　 D 能得到的

134. A 有關賭博與娛樂的問題恕不回答。
　　 B 最受歡迎的提案將會考慮列入工作坊。
　　 C 我們要求所有主管提出建議。
　　 D 我們希望這個工作坊成功，並祝您一切順利。

135–138 廣告

西卓辛：夜間型流感全效

以西卓辛做好迎接感冒與流感季節。西卓辛是一種含藥物成分的舒緩夜飲，可治療流感症狀，包括發燒、全身疼痛、鼻塞、咳嗽和喉嚨痛。讓您醒來感到精神充沛，準備好戰勝新的一天。如果您打算操作機械或開車，請勿服用西卓辛。請置於孩童不易接觸之處。如果症狀持續十天以上，請向醫生諮詢。

西卓辛是銷售第一的流感治療藥物，請依指示服用，保證有效。欲知詳情請上網站 www.citrusine.com。

135. A 使人放心的
　　 B 增強活力的
　　 C 舒緩的
　　 D 安慰的

136. A 提神的
　　 B 恢復精神的
　　 C 恢復活力
　　 D 恢復活力

137. A 若不當服用，可能造成嚴重副作用。
　　 B 兒童應該服用兒童用西卓辛。
　　 C 小包裝看起來像糖果，可能會引起問題。
　　 D 如果症狀持續十天以上，請向醫生諮詢。

138. **A 為了**
　　 B 在……期間
　　 C 和……一起
　　 D 在……之後

139–142 電子郵件

收件者：珍娜・唐
寄件者：綠景
日期：6 月 28 日
主旨：詢問

唐女士您好：

感謝您的提問。十多年來，綠景向來是郊區商家愛用的主要庭園設計公司。雖然本公司專長園藝與日式庭園造景，但我們也保養草坪與運動場。至於您的提問，是的，我們也清除茂密的灌木叢和樹木。我們可以派專人前去估算所需的時間與大概的費用。此外，如果您希望將稠密的樹叢改成草地或花園，您可與我們的設計師合作，一起發想您喜歡的造景設計。

若您有意洽詢，請來電 555-1245。我們很樂意為您服務。

139. A 雖然
   B 因為
   C 因此
   D 然而

140. A 斷定
   B 計算
   C **估算**
   D 猜測

141. A 正希望
   B **希望**
   C 過去希望
   D 希望

142. A 我們歡迎任何與您合作的機會。
   B 請勿取消訂單。
   C **如果您有意洽詢，請來電 555-1245。**
   D 去公園看看本市的景色。

143–146 廣告

黑山豆

黑山豆是路易西安納的一間咖啡公司，也是路易西安納咖啡豆的先驅。本公司監管一條垂直整合供應鏈，以來自路易西安納州黑山最高品質的咖啡豆為始。本公司嚴選了三種獲獎咖啡豆：夏收、烏南與黑地。所有產品都可在 24 小時內配送至全美各地。黑山豆的咖啡也在全美所有隆德超商中販售。

不論您要的是優質咖啡，還是想來點南方風情的安逸。黑山豆都會是您正確的咖啡選擇，全部都是美國生產製造且有機。當您飲用的同時，還可以感受到愛國情操。今天就上本公司網站 www.blackhillbeans.com 聽聽我們更多的故事吧！

143. A 結合
   B 結合
   C **整合的**
   D 整合

144. A 位於
   B **挑選**
   C 評估
   D 維持

145. A **在⋯⋯範圍內**
   B 在⋯⋯之前
   C 直到
   D 在

146. A 試試這附近最暢銷的凍飲。
   B **全部都是美國生產製造且有機。**
   C 讓我們幫您找到適合的供應商。
   D 這個優惠只在 10 月 1 日前有效。

147–148 公告

公告

克勞佛服飾已整修試衣間，讓您可以在購買前試穿衣服。

■ 一次請拿一到兩件衣物進試衣間。

■ 您可以將個人物品，像是皮夾或皮包交由店員保管。

■ 任何留在試衣間的個人物品，將存放在入口旁的失物招領處。

147. 這張公告最有可能是給誰看的？

 A 店長
 B 顧客
 C 設計師
 D 店員

148. 根據這張公告，在哪裡可以找到遺失物品？

 A 警察局
 B 服務中心
 C 存放處
 D 櫃台後方

149–150 訊息串

琳達・貝茲	6:55
我遲到了。我睡太晚了。	

梅琳達・克魯茲	6:56
那你幾點會到？	

琳達・貝茲	6:57
我一個小時內可以到。	

梅琳達・克魯茲	6:58
我要先走嗎？	

琳達・貝茲	7:02
不用，只要確定我到時，貨物都裝上車就行了。	

梅琳達・克魯茲	7:02
好的。	

琳達・貝茲	7:03
謝了。	

梅琳達・克魯茲	7:08
等會見，小心開車。	

琳達・貝茲	7:10
好，我會的。	

149. 下列何者與貝茲女士有關？

 A 她為克魯茲女士工作
 B 她被困在車陣中
 C 她目前正在開車
 D 她常遲到

150. 在 7:02 時，克魯茲女士寫：「好的。」是什麼意思？

 A 她會等貝茲女士
 B 她打算把貨裝到貨車上
 C 她對貝茲女士的遲到很不滿
 D 她已經裝滿貨車了

151–152 電子郵件

收件者：派翠西亞・穆勒
<patmueller@finemail.net>
寄件者：馬克・哈欽斯
<mhutchings@grosvenoronline.com>
日期：6 月 4 日
主旨：回覆：熱線

親愛的穆勒女士：

感謝您對我們技術服務熱線的指教，我們並不知道電話轉到總機要花這麼久的時間。我們已經設法解決了這個因電話總機軟體的小故障而引發的問題。作為善意的表示，謹在此提供您一張本公司網路商店價值 25 元的折價券。只要在 www.grosvenoronline.com 登入您的帳戶，在主頁欄位中輸入折價券序號 H58K55，即可兌換。

格羅夫納網路公司 客服專員
馬克・哈欽斯 敬上

151. 馬克・哈欽斯為什麼會寄這封電子郵件？

    Ⓐ 為了促銷當季特別優惠

    Ⓑ 為了確認訂單地址

    Ⓒ 為了對一份意見表達感謝

    Ⓓ 為了對某個問題要求更多資訊

152. 穆勒女士下次登上格羅夫納網路公司時，
最有可能會做什麼？

    Ⓐ 報名加入會員

    Ⓑ 兌換優惠券

    Ⓒ 使用顧客意見表

    Ⓓ 更新帳單資料

153–154 網頁

http://www.jannisar.com

首頁	產品	聯絡我們	關於我們	帳戶

恭喜！因為您經常造訪本站，已經獲選成為白金會員。請填寫下列表格，以完成整個程序：

名	
姓	
郵寄地址	
授權碼	
電子郵件信箱	
意見：	

勾選您有興趣購買的商品類別（可複選）

電子用品〔 〕　音樂〔 〕　書籍〔 〕
家具〔 〕　電腦遊戲〔 〕

請注意，身為白金會員，您將於一年內收到四次電子郵件，通知您所勾選類別之商品優惠。您的帳戶資料將於 24 小時內以電子郵件查核。我們會寄給您一封電子郵件確認函，請遵照郵件中指示，確認您的會員資格。

153. 這個網頁針對的對象是誰？

    Ⓐ 拍賣網站上的新客戶

    Ⓑ 網路行銷公司專員

    Ⓒ 零售商店的供應商

    Ⓓ 網路零售店的長期客戶

154. 該網頁的讀者被要求做什麼？

    Ⓐ 說明喜歡的商品

    Ⓑ 提供付款資料

    Ⓒ 列印表格並簽名

    Ⓓ 報告配送延誤

155–157 文章

貓狗風潮

布蘭特伍德市（5月2日）——布蘭特伍德市終於有了自己的貓咪咖啡廳，叫做喵喵浩劫，還有一家叫做熱狗的小狗咖啡店。這兩家店是凱文和金潔・布萊克夫婦所開設的。這兩家咖啡廳於上月熱烈開幕，並受到大篇幅的媒體報導，但這股熱潮並未消退。「生意很興隆，」凱文・布萊克說，「我們知道我們會很成功，只是沒想到會這麼成功。」客人不僅熱情蜂擁到這兩家咖啡廳，和動物們一同消磨喝茶或咖啡的時光，還有很多人認養了這些動物，給牠們永遠的家。「我們認為能為一些動物提供住處是很棒的，因為許多收容所都已經過度擁擠。」金潔・布萊克解釋，「同時客人也有機會和動物們互動，這對收容所而言是最好的宣傳方式。」

自咖啡廳開幕以來，已經有超過 10 隻狗和 15 隻貓被認養。「我還沒養狗，但我一直想養一隻。」一位常客蘿莉・喬登說，「我來這裡和牠們玩，或許有一天我會找到一隻自己真正想要的小狗。」

由於他們的成功，布萊克夫婦正考慮買下鄰近的店面來拓展商機。「我們需要更多空間以容納所有客人和動物們，」凱文解釋道，「有時候真的很擠。」布萊克夫婦正計劃於下個月整修小狗咖啡店，並於秋天時整修貓咪咖啡廳。

155. 下列何者與咖啡廳有關？

    Ⓐ 它們供應各種點心

    Ⓑ 它們販賣小狗和小貓

    Ⓒ 它們提供咖啡和茶

    Ⓓ 它們提供寵物用品

156. 文中報導了什麼有關貓和狗的敘述？

A 有好幾隻已經被認養

B 牠們會永遠住在咖啡廳裡

C 牠們對客人都很友善

D 牠們被訓練來娛樂大家

157. 下列句子最適合出現在 [1]、[2]、[3]、[4] 的哪個位置？「但這股熱潮並未消退。」

A [1]

B [2]

C [3]

D [4]

158–160 廣告

> ### 來新浪潮水療中心休息放鬆！
>
> 從忙亂的一天中，享受新浪潮水療中心的專業水療服務來好好休息一下吧。我們位於沃利大道 458 號。不管您只待上一小時或是一整天，在您離開時都將感到神清氣爽並充滿活力。請參考我們以下的一般療程：
>
> **經典假期（120 元）**——試試這個最適合忙碌人士的基本療程
> 30 分鐘背部與肩頸按摩／小黃瓜臉部護理／紫丁香全身裹敷
>
> **玫瑰花園（155 元）**——讓玫瑰的香氣喚醒您的所有感官
> 45 分鐘全身按摩／玫瑰水護膚療程／手部美甲
>
> **海洋體驗（180 元）**——來體驗我們最受歡迎的療程，海洋療癒之力
> 60 分鐘全身按摩／全身海鹽去角質／熱石療程／海草臉部護理
>
> **完美活化（210 元）**——讓自己沉浸在一整天的豪華療程中
> 90 分鐘全身按摩／頭皮放鬆按摩／火山泥臉部護理／迷迭香純淨去角質／手部美甲／足部護理
>
> 請事先來電 555-2940 預約，以免向隅。四人以上同行，可享免費三明治、清蒸蔬食與鮮榨果汁午餐組。所有貴賓在第三次光臨時將免費獲贈新浪潮浴袍。

158. 這則廣告主要和什麼有關？

A 保健機構的擴展

B 奢華服務的優惠

C 水療中心的搬遷

D 店家的標準方案

159. 哪一項療程包含了熱氣護理？

A 經典假期

B 玫瑰花園

C 海洋體驗

D 完美活化

160. 四人以上的團體可獲贈什麼？

A 免費浴袍

B 減價優惠

C 免費餐點

D 私人包廂

161–164 網路討論區

比爾·佛萊克	9:41

你好，我想知道米蘭諾家窗簾訂單的最新進度。

露西·米特	9:41

我們還在等手工蕾絲的花邊絲綢，不過我們昨天收到大部分的布料，我們的裁縫師今天就會進行處理。

比爾·佛萊克	9:42

那你認為這些工作可以如米蘭諾家要求的在本週五完成嗎？

露西·米特	9:43

我不確定。這要看那些花邊何時到。我們的小組可以開始接縫其中一部分，但我們需要那些花邊來完成複雜的圖樣。

比爾·佛萊克	9:44

你可以聯絡手工蕾絲，了解一下貨運幾時到嗎？

露西·米特	9:45

事實上，理查正在處理。理查，他們那裡有消息嗎？

理查‧崔　　　　　　　9:45
是，我剛和他們通完電話。出貨有些延誤，因為他們的花邊師傅用錯絲綢，他們必須重做花邊。我們可以在今天下午收到，他們會用急件送來。

比爾‧佛萊克　　　　　9:46
太好了。這週末就可以把這些窗簾做好嗎？

露西‧米特　　　　　　9:47
沒問題。我們會日夜趕工讓它們準時完工。

比爾‧佛萊克　　　　　9:48
很高興聽到你這樣說。他們是長期老客戶了，他們的新公寓這週末需要用到這些窗簾。

---

161. 在線上聊天的這些人可能從事何種行業？
　 A 服飾公司
　 B 婚紗店
　 C 窗簾客製店
　 D 布料批發行

162. 花邊的貨運何時會到？
　 A 早上
　 B 下午
　 C 隔天
　 D 週末

163. 在 9:47 時，露西‧米特說：「我們會日以繼夜地工作」是什麼意思？
　 A 她的團隊將仔細注意時間
　 B 她的團隊會盡快工作
　 C 她的團隊完全不用趕時間
　 D 如果有必要，她的團隊將日夜趕工

164. 比爾‧佛萊克接下來可能會做什麼？
　 A 打電話給客戶
　 B 取消訂單
　 C 要求花邊配送
　 D 安排會議

165–167 時間表

> **杜魯斯市**
> **第五屆夏季歡樂慶**
> **7 月 23 日 星期日**
>
> **早上 10 點到下午 6 點《鄉土自然美術大賽》**
> 杜魯斯的藝術家們將於杜魯斯社區活動中心展出畫作，作品描繪本地大自然與野生動物。來賓可票選自己最喜愛的畫作，優勝者名單將於歌唱比賽開始時宣布。
>
> **早上 11 點到中午 12 點《魔術秀》**
> 請和我們一起來欣賞令人驚奇的魔術表演吧。魔術師米克‧透納以他頗富創意與娛樂效果的魔術花招著名。
>
> **中午 12 點到下午 2 點《現場爵士音樂會》**
> 在公園享受現場爵士樂，由來自紐約的爵士樂團哈洛威樂團所演奏。他們將演奏各種經典爵士樂曲，也將販售他們最新發行的唱片。
>
> **早上 10 點到晚上 7 點《可再生能源博覽會》**
> 本地的陽光能源公司將展示最新的可再生能源專案，包括太陽能面板與手機行動電源。
>
> **晚上 7 點到晚上 9 點《歌唱大賽》**
> 歡迎當地居民參加今年的歌唱大賽。有意參賽者可上網站報名並填寫必要表格 www.duluthcitysff.com。
>
> 欲知更多資訊，請來電 555-0157。

165. 畫畫比賽的優勝者將於何時宣布？
　 A 下午 2 點
　 B 下午 6 點
　 C 晚上 7 點
　 D 晚上 9 點

166. 根據時程表，有什麼可供購買？
　 A 藝術品
　 B 音樂專輯
　 C 手機配件
　 D 太陽能面板

167. 參賽者要如何報名歌唱大賽？

　　Ⓐ 前往詢問處
　　Ⓑ 聯絡社區活動中心
　　Ⓒ 上網站
　　Ⓓ 寄電子郵件

168–171 傳單

公園露天電影

今年秋天，格倫伍德溫泉公園將為格倫伍德溫泉居民每週舉辦名為「公園露天電影夜」的活動，並與帕克斯頓企業、GS 購物商場等的本地商家合作。將於每週五晚上在公園中心播放適合闔家觀賞的電影。這些活動不需門票，因為它們是免費開放給大眾的。

自 9 月到 11 月，公園露天電影夜保證為全家帶來一系列有趣又感人的電影，鼓勵您帶著毛毯、椅子和野餐點心前來。電影開演時間依日落時間而定，因此建議您提早到場以優先選定位置。請上我們的網站 www.glenwoodsprings.org/movies 查看即將播放的電影時刻表及本地贊助商的名單。

如果遇上大雨、低溫或強風，將有可能取消電影播放。如果發生這種狀況，將於網站與本地電台公告電影取消事宜。您也可以來電 715-555-5358 格倫伍德溫泉的公園與休憩部，詢問活動取消的相關訊息。

168. 這個傳單的目的是什麼？

　　Ⓐ 宣布公園整修計劃
　　Ⓑ 宣傳社區活動
　　Ⓒ 請求捐款
　　Ⓓ 宣傳新電影

169. 誰會提供公園露天電影的資金？

　　Ⓐ 當地廣播電台
　　Ⓑ 格倫伍德溫泉的居民
　　Ⓒ 公園與休憩部門
　　Ⓓ 格倫伍德溫泉的商家

170. 下列何者不是給參加者的建議？

　　Ⓐ 帶食物
　　Ⓑ 事先買票
　　Ⓒ 參考時間表
　　Ⓓ 提早到場

171. 根據這張傳單，為什麼會用到這個電話號碼？

　　Ⓐ 做預約
　　Ⓑ 詢問時間表的異動
　　Ⓒ 詢問交通路線
　　Ⓓ 取消預約

172–175 廣告

賴特曼塔
49858 紐約州紐約市百老匯街 1234 號

位於本市金融區，賴特曼塔提供了壯麗的市景，更提供了辦公空間，適合任何有意在紐約市中心營運的企業。離地鐵站僅一個街區，步行即可抵達公車與計程車站，賴特曼塔的位置相當便利。一樓大廳提供保全措施，所有職員都需經過安檢門的掃瞄檢查才能到達後方的電梯。同時，寬敞的大廳以豪華的室內裝潢與親切的服務員迎賓。

三樓與四樓可出租給公司企業使用。高挑的樓板與高聳的玻璃窗提供了開放空間與完美的自然採光。今天就盡快提出申請吧。市場上對這些場地的需求極高。必須親自面談，非誠者勿試。更多資訊請上網站 www.wrightmantowers.com/rent，您可以在網路上參觀或來電 555-1234 洽詢本公司。

172. 下列何者與出租的場所有關？

　　Ⓐ 只提供給私人住戶
　　Ⓑ 只提供給企業
　　Ⓒ 提供給大眾
　　Ⓓ 非常昂貴

173. 下列何者與賴特曼塔的地點有關？

　　Ⓐ 靠近大眾運輸
　　Ⓑ 大樓周遭交通繁忙
　　Ⓒ 沒有停車場
　　Ⓓ 在市郊

174. 網站有什麼特色？

    Ⓐ 列出所有使用中的場所

    Ⓑ 獨家優惠促銷代碼

    Ⓒ 出租場所的虛擬導覽

    Ⓓ 大樓的歷史

175. 下列句子最適合出現在 [1]、[2]、[3]、[4] 的哪個位置？「市場上對這些場所的需求極高。」

    Ⓐ [1]

    Ⓑ [2]

    Ⓒ [3]

    Ⓓ [4]

176–180 公告和電子郵件

肯尼斯環球新聞實習

肯尼斯環球新聞實習職將提供您大好機會，可以在世界最知名的國際多媒體新聞通訊社接受培訓，與專業的記者及編輯一起工作，並且在各大都市（如倫敦、柏林和巴黎）中步調快速的新聞編輯室獲得寶貴經驗。這將為才華橫溢的大學畢業生提供一個機會，學習並培養新聞工作的專業技能並習得第一手知識。

這是一份帶薪的實習職，提供免費住宿與午晚餐。實習生將接受數週的正式培訓，著重於寫作技巧、新聞倫理和職場基本知識等方面的訓練。實習生也可在實習期間免費利用其他固定安排的培訓機會。這個實習將自 8 月 1 日起，歷時四個月。

實習申請表可於網站 www.kennethglobal.com 取得，必須在 6 月 20 前繳交。通過此階段的應徵者必須於 6 月 27 日到總部進行面談。任何問題都可寫信至 rubyhart@kennethglobal.com 向露比·哈特提出，或親至我們位於奧斯汀的總部詢問。

寄件者：凱爾·蘭恩 <kylelane12@mpnet.com>

收件者：露比·哈特 <rubyhart@kennethglobal.com>

主旨：實習

日期：6 月 23 日

親愛的哈特女士：

我相當高興能夠通過肯尼斯環球新聞實習職的第一階段甄選。應徵者應該要在指定日期親自參加面試，但是很遺憾地，我預計要和教授一起參加一場在達拉斯舉辦的重要會議。但因為我就住在離貴公司總部只有幾分鐘路程的地方，安排另一場面談時間應該不是難事。

再次感謝貴公司將我列入該職務的考量人選。期待收到您有關面談日期的回覆。同時，我也會盡全力做好準備。

凱爾·蘭恩 敬上

176. 下列何者與實習應徵者有關？

    Ⓐ 他們必須先有工作經驗

    Ⓑ 他們必須參加即將舉辦的會議

    Ⓒ 他們必須交一封推薦信

    Ⓓ 他們必須有學士學位

177. 關於實習職，下列何者為真？

    Ⓐ 含餐點與住宿

    Ⓑ 只提供給專業新聞工作者

    Ⓒ 將於八月結束

    Ⓓ 是無薪職務

178. 實習生還可享有什麼好處？

    Ⓐ 健康保險

    Ⓑ 額外的培訓

    Ⓒ 員工優惠

    Ⓓ 帶薪假

179. 蘭恩先生應該在何時參加面談？

    Ⓐ 6 月 20 日

    Ⓑ 6 月 27 日

    Ⓒ 6 月 23 日

    Ⓓ 8 月 1 日

180. 蘭恩先生住在哪裡？

- A 達拉斯
- **B 奧斯汀**
- C 柏林
- D 倫敦

181–185 電子郵件和宣布

收件者：山姆·貝瑞
<sberry@princetheater.com>
寄件者：貝思·華格納
<bessiewagner@linsuniveristy.edu>
日期：7 月 4 日
主旨：職缺

親愛的貝瑞先生：

我叫貝思·華格納，目前是林斯大學戲劇系的學生。我即將完成學業，正開始探詢未來可能的就業機會。有位教授推薦我可與在王子劇院服務的您聯絡，詢問貴公司可能開缺的職缺。

在林斯大學就讀時，我專攻戲劇製作。透過學術與實務經驗，我學到舞台管理的必要技能。從九月開始，我就可以從事兼職或全職的工作，並全力投入所有指派給我的工作中。

若王子劇院於今年秋季開始有任何職缺的話，煩請您不吝告知，我將感激不盡。

貝思·華格納

王子劇院
工作職缺

- **美術實習**
在美術部門的無償實習，處理各層面行政與製作職務。此人須執行美術主管的助理職務。

- **技術副總監**
兼職職務，負責演出管理與舞台機械設備。應徵者須具備舞台管理相關經驗。

- **票務管理主管**
全職職務，負責劇院所有活動的整體票務管理工作。職責包括管理售票處，規劃並執行售票流程，以及督導售票員工。

- **行銷主管**
全職職務，負責行銷劇院推出的所有演出活動。監督高品質宣傳資料的準備工作，以吸引戲迷來看我們的戲劇、音樂劇與音樂會。

- 所有王子劇院的全職員工皆能免費觀賞所有演出。

- 所有職務皆自今年十月起出缺。

- 欲知更多資訊或有意應徵，請以電子郵件聯絡山姆·貝瑞 sberry@princetheater.com。

181. 下列何者與華格納女士有關？

- A 她是舞台演員
- B 她教舞台設計
- **C 她即將畢業**
- D 她是貝瑞先生的同事

182. 華格納女士為什麼寫信給貝瑞先生？

- **A 要尋求工作機會**
- B 要安排面試
- C 要表達感謝之意
- D 要報名訓練課程

183. 下列何者與票務管理主管無關？

- A 他／她必須管理各種活動
- B 他／她必須指導其他員工的工作
- C 他／她可以免費看所有表演
- **D 他／她必須規劃宣傳活動**

184. 這些刊登的職務有什麼共同點？

- A 都需要音樂才華
- **B 都將在第四季開缺**
- C 都是兼職工作
- D 都需要戲劇學位

185. 哪一個工作最適合華格納女士？

- A 美術實習生
- **B 技術副總監**
- C 票務管理主管
- D 行銷主管

TEST
4

PART 7

4月5日——斯克蘭頓市中心的清水醫院發起了一項筆友計劃，讓絕症患者和成人志工相互通信。這項計劃由院長查克·錢伯斯發起，他最近才剛獲得全國健康護理聯盟所頒發的傑出領導獎。這計劃將使醫院與社區間有更穩固的關係。錢伯斯先生鼓勵各行各業的成人提出申請，即使他們可能覺得自己不完全合乎資格。只要上清水醫院網站，就可免費成為醫院會員。

錢伯斯先生說：「我希望透過這個計劃，讓志工可以和病人形成緊密的關係，幫助他們度過生命中這些艱難的時刻。」他也希望這個計劃能引起更多人親自探訪這些絕症患者。

清水醫院

5月4日

莫妮卡·格尼
54481 威斯康辛州斯克蘭頓市華盛頓路4100 號

親愛的格尼女士：

很高興收到您的來信。我非常興奮能和您配對成為筆友。希望我們可以從彼此身上學到很多東西，建立起永恆的友誼。

正如您所知，我住在加州，離威斯康辛州很遠。希望接下來的幾個月中我能休假去探望您。請告訴我最適合去探訪您的時間。

期待收到您的回音。

潔西卡·萊特

親愛的潔西卡：

您不知道您那親切的話語讓我有多感激。雖然清水醫院的工作人員非常和善，我仍然有種渴望，想與醫護人員以外的人交流。我其他的家人也住在遙遠的地方，在佛羅里達州，因此大多數的時候，我只能和工作人員或其他病友說話。如果您真的想來的話，我非常歡迎，我想最適合的時間應該就是中心的感恩節派對了。我自己的家人也可能會來這裡。如果您覺得這樣太勉強，或您無法休假，也別太掛心。我真的希望我們可以透過信件繼續交流。

祝安好。

莫妮卡·格尼

---

186. 這篇文章是有關什麼？

A 志工計劃
B 醫生退休
C 新醫院
D 寫作比賽

187. 下列何者和錢伯斯先生有關？

A 他是清水醫院的病人
B 他教授成人寫作技巧
C 他是政府機構的首長
D 他因領導長才受到表揚

188. 錢伯斯先生邀請人們做什麼事？

A 訂閱商務通訊
B 安排定期健康檢查
C 探視病情嚴重的病人
D 寫推薦信

189. 潔西卡·格尼大部分的時間都和誰一起度過？

A 清水醫院員工
B 她的家人
C 莫妮卡·萊特
D 她的朋友

190. 莫妮卡要潔西卡何時去探訪？

A 在莫妮卡的生日
B 這週六
C 6月7日
D 感恩節

191–195 信件和電子郵件

約翰·莫里斯先生
90117 加州米爾維爾伯納爾大道 1423 號

親愛的莫里斯先生：

24/7 健身中心是全美最成功的健身中心。我們全國有超過三百萬名會員，我們加盟企業已被公認為聲譽良好且值得信賴的品牌。我們的成功來自於我們與各分店的良好關係。

您之所以收到此函，是因為您表達了有意加盟 24/7 健身中心，要在您的鎮上開設新據點。根據我們初步的研究，您所居住的城鎮有大量在專業領域服務的年輕單身人口。這是我們的目標客群，表示此 24/7 健身中心據點的生意前景頗被看好。如果您想要有更多加盟 24/7 健身中心的具體條款和規則等相關資料，請來電 347-555-3363 與我聯絡。此外，如果您想與其他分店店長聯絡，我們的同事也能提供相關資訊給您。

營運總長
洛麗斯·旺森 敬上

收件者：查克·卡特
<zcarter@zenmail.com>
寄件者：約翰·莫里斯
<jmorris@cbnet.com>
主旨：24/7 健身中心
日期：3 月 6 日

親愛的卡特先生：

我叫約翰·莫里斯，是住在米爾維爾地區的小型企業主。目前我正和 24/7 健身中心協商在米爾維爾這裡開設我自己的據點。作為 24/7 健身中心的加盟業者，您或許可以藉由分享您的看法來助我一臂之力。

我想了解您作為加盟業者，對 24/7 健身中心的評價如何。我以前曾經營過數家加盟店，一直認為信任與誠實是一段成功關係中最重要的因素。更重要的是，我也在想知道母公司提供了何種的協助。在開設您的據點前，您是否得到了充足的訓練，讓您得以順利地經營業務？非常感謝您所提供的任何建議。

約翰·莫里斯 敬上

收件者：約翰·莫里斯
<jmorris@cbnet.com>
寄件者：查克·卡特
<zcarter@zenmail.com>
主旨：24/7 健身中心
日期：3 月 7 日

親愛的莫里斯先生：

我很樂意提供對 24/7 健身中心加盟管理的一些看法。截至目前為止，我已經和 24/7 健身中心以加盟身分合作十年了。事實上，我目前經營三家分店。我完全同意您所說的話，信任與誠實是商業關係中最重要的兩個部分。在這方面，我相信擁有三家加盟店的事實，就是我對這加盟總部的信心證明。

我來讓您更放心。首先，不管分店店長是誰，24/7 健身中心對於品牌發展有很明確的方向。母公司不但提供了訓練，他們還堅持掌控設施的實際配置，從更衣間到自由重量訓練區皆是。母公司要自己的 300 萬名會員能夠走進任何一間分店，並且感到自在。在您經營滿一年之前，您每個月都必須向總部詳細報告業績、會員績效，和設備使用的流量表。他們將事必躬親，直到他們有信心您能代表這個品牌。我希望這能有助於您決定加入 24/7 健身中心這個團隊！

祝一切安好。

查克·卡特

191. 根據信件內容，24/7 健身中心的成功關鍵是什麼？

Ⓐ 與分店長有效率的溝通
Ⓑ 快速的全國展店
Ⓒ 有經驗的研究團隊
Ⓓ 員工全面性的訓練

192. 莫里斯先生最有可能從哪裡得到卡特先生的聯絡資料？

Ⓐ 從 24/7 健身中心的專員
Ⓑ 從 24/7 健身中心的網站
Ⓒ 從卡特先生的部落格
Ⓓ 從卡特先生的員工

193. 莫里斯先生最在意24/7健身中心的什麼？

[A] 品牌名聲
[B] 財務狀況
[C] 提供協助方式
[D] 加盟店規定

194. 查克‧卡特寫這封電子郵件的目的是什麼？

[A] 要求有關加盟的資訊
[B] 告訴約翰‧莫里斯有關 24/7 健身中心的事宜與提供的訓練
[C] 説服約翰‧莫里斯不要加盟 24/7 健身中心
[D] 提醒 24/7 健身中心他們對加盟店的責任

195. 在查克‧卡特的電子郵件中，下列何者與 24/7 健身中心有關？

[A] 他們要所有的健身中心幾乎都一樣
[B] 他們要加盟商將分店個人化
[C] 他們明年想賣出更多補給品與會籍
[D] 他們要求加盟商繳交使用的季報

196–200 電子郵件

收件者：凱文‧史考特
<kevinscott@starrealty.com>
寄件者：史蒂文‧梅森
<smason@turnerelectronics.com>
日期：2月2日
主旨：倉庫

親愛的史考特先生：

我叫史蒂文‧梅森，在消費性電子產品公司透納電器服務。我現在正在找位於匹茲堡地區的倉庫，正如您所知，在現今步調快速的商業世界中，擁有高效率的配送策略對每家公司來說都很重要。

因此，我正在尋找位於匹茲堡近郊的倉庫。倉庫需要靠近高速公路。本公司配送大量商品，所以我們想要一個專屬透納電器使用的倉庫。倉庫需備有可供大型卡車使用的寬廣裝卸區。此外，若倉庫也具辦

公空間會更理想。由於本公司產品的貴重性質，我們希望倉庫能有預防竊盜與損害的保全設施。

期待儘快收到您的回覆。

透納電器
史蒂文‧梅森

收件者：史蒂文‧梅森
<smason@turnerelectronics.com>
寄件者：凱文‧史考特
<kevinscott@starrealty.com>
日期：2月3日
主旨：回覆：倉庫

親愛的梅森先生：

聽起來貴公司因為拓展業務，所以想要加強配送網絡的營運，以更快速將商品送到賣家手上。我們有各式的倉庫可供選擇，我相信其中一定有符合貴公司需求的倉庫。所有場地都有最先進的保全系統及經驗豐富的職員。

地點一——月租 3,499 元，10,000 平方英尺，倉庫由不同企業共用。由於該場所屬於共用地，因此我們提供優惠價。

地點二——月租 5,500 元，舊型倉庫，位於匹茲堡市中心。這個倉庫目前閒置中，因此可專屬貴公司使用。特點是還有一個人可進入的冷凍間。

地點三——月租 6,500 元，位於匹茲堡市郊數英哩處非常寬敞的倉庫。雖然目前有其他兩家公司做為儲藏室使用，但可改成讓貴公司專用的倉庫。

地點四——月組 2,600 元，中型倉庫。這個倉庫因為沒有方便卡車卸貨的空間，因此以優惠價提供。最適合小型企業。

以上這些是目前可供使用的場地，如果您有任何疑問或想親自參觀，請與我聯絡。

凱文‧史考特

收件者：凱文・史考特
<kevinscott@startrealty.com>
寄件者：史蒂文・梅森
<smason@turnerelectronics.com>
日期：2 月 3 日
主旨：地點三

親愛的史考特先生：

非常感謝您如此快速地回覆我的詢問。雖然所有的倉庫沒有一間完全符合我正在找的，但我想對本公司最好的選擇應該是地點三的倉庫。當然，這前提是另外兩家公司能將他們所存放的貨物搬到其他倉庫。正如我在第一封電子郵件中提到的，本公司的營運正在擴展中，我要確定我們有大量空間可供成長。我也很樂見倉庫有保全措施。

下週初我有時間，如果有可能的話可以去地點三走走。我想如果我能親自造訪那個地方，才能做出果斷的決定。您方便時，請來電與我聯絡，這樣我們就可以安排時間。您可以打 (351) 546-9899 找我。

祝好。

透納電器
史蒂文・梅森

196. 第一封電子郵件的目的是什麼？

[A] **找出租的場所**
[B] 敲定營運計劃
[C] 確定宅配送達
[D] 宣傳要出售的房地產

197. 梅森先生最有可能是誰？

[A] 倉庫管理人
[B] 卡車司機
[C] 保全警衛
[D] **配送部主管**

198. 根據史考特先生所説，透納電器想做什麼？

[A] 僱用更多有經驗的卡車司機
[B] **提升供應鏈效率**
[C] 改善產品整體品質
[D] 拓展到亞洲市場

199. 根據第三封電子郵件，要怎麼樣透納電器才會搬進地點三？

[A] 租金要減少
[B] **兩家公司必須找到其他地點儲藏它們的東西**
[C] 場地必須改建以容納辦公室
[D] 大樓必須再增加一名警衛

200. 在第三封郵件中，梅森先生最有可能在哪一天去地點三參觀？

[A] **星期一**
[B] 星期四
[C] 星期五
[D] 星期六

TEST
4

PART 7

ACTUAL TEST ⑤

PART 5　P.140–143

◎ Part 5 解答請見 P.457

101. 如果客戶認為所提出的色系不夠**吸引人**，室內設計師是可以調整的。

102. 星期五晚餐的訂位，請將賓客人數由八名**增加**為十名。

103. 白朗特先生要求將橫幅懸掛在大樓的外牆**上**。

104. 為了以免日後設備有問題，你應該保留最近**開立**的收據。

105. 如果病患鼻子的症狀**在**兩天**內**沒有改善的跡象，那他就應該再去診所。

106. 百貨公司裡的展示員**熱情地**解說產品的功能與優點。

107. 因為最近的展品相當珍貴，加貝藝廊比以往**任何時候**採取了更多的防護措施。

108. **任何**要改變房屋結構的**人**必須先申請建物准可。

109. 出席改善溝通技巧工作坊的員工將得到一張由講師頒發的**結業**證書。

110. **除了**科學系優秀的教職員外，該大學也擁有最先進的實驗設備。

111. 募款者募得的捐款**將**平均**分配**給該慈善機構的三個據點。

112. **不論**建築物的年份，通風系統必須符合最新的安全法規。

113. 造成特頓線火車延誤的原因是其中一個車站發生了**程序上的**錯誤。

114. 由於我們預期會收到數百封求職申請書，所以您的履歷表以兩頁**為限**。

115. 講者在演講時，**將把焦點放在**國家爭取獨立的奮鬥上。

116. 在專案開始之前，歡迎活動是個增進志工**之間**交流的好機會。

117. 歐威飯店房間的陽台提供了該飯店**令人驚艷的**私人海灘景色。

118. 一付款後，旅行社人員就以電子郵件將購票**確認函**寄給顧客。

119. 在檢查車子之後，技師已經**正確地**找出引擎失去動力的原因。

120. 由於費雪女士的聽障問題，她將有一位手語專家**陪同**，好讓她可以參加會議。

121. 專案開發小組對挑選**鑑定**可能的大樓位址負有部分責任。

122. 方便烹調的料理包**除了**熱水外，附有一人份晚餐所需要的所有食材。

123. 教育中心提供關鍵技能的訓練，**好讓**失業者更容易找到工作。

124. 授權同意書的條款非常**簡單易懂**，不需要有法律背景即可了解。

125. 寄給研討會與會者的說明資料**羅列**了演講時間表和聯誼活動。

126. 你可以**依**你喜好，讓商品直接送到家或親自前往店家取貨。

127. 維他命補充劑上使用的是**天然**物質，而非化學物質。

128. 巴士司機利用小路而非主要快速道路，**從而**避開尖峰時刻的交通。

129. 當搬運廢棄物的卡車在 3:30 抵達時，組員**將已拆除**大樓的主體部分。

130. 如果您發現超高畫質電視有任何製造**瑕疵**，請盡快與原購買經銷商聯絡。

131-134 廣告

來參觀狂野親水公園，它是個夏季好去處，適合和各年齡層的家人及朋友一起前往。我們有兒童泳池、戶外泳池、室內泳池、海浪以及刺激的滑水道，包括我們的「死亡墜落」，是本州最大型的滑水道。園內能滿足所有人的所有需求。別忘了我們美味的零食攤和餐廳，我們也有禮品店與遊樂園。我們甚至為您的毛小孩提供小狗公園。您可以撥打電話 123-5555 購買門票，或用優惠價格買季票。現在就來電，體驗樂趣吧！

131. Ⓐ 使興奮
　　Ⓑ 興奮的
　　Ⓒ 刺激的
　　Ⓓ 刺激

132. Ⓐ 他們的
　　Ⓑ 他的
　　Ⓒ 我們的
　　Ⓓ 您的

133. Ⓐ 泳池是最棒的遊玩所在。
　　Ⓑ 我們甚至為您的毛小孩提供小狗公園。
　　Ⓒ 廚師是最頂級的，而餐點也是首屈一指的。
　　Ⓓ 在本季與促銷結束前快來玩吧。

134. **Ⓐ 部分**
　　Ⓑ 部分
　　Ⓒ 部分
　　Ⓓ 全部

135-138 電子郵件

寄件者：朗達‧克羅斯
收件者：麥可‧哈利斯
日期：6 月 21 日
主旨：回覆：庭園造景與維護

感謝您詢問本公司的服務內容。「植樹管理」是一間草皮維護與庭園造景公司。在照料所有客戶的草皮時，我們只使用對環

境無害的技術和產品。我們已經在波特蘭營業超過 20 年了。目前，我們在市中心服務逾 150 家企業。

至於您所提出的特定需求，是的，我們可以毫不費力地移除枯木，改種適合目前造景的植物。為了給您正確的報價，我們需要到場親自查看狀況。若要安排本公司的園藝技工前往，請來電 (713) 678-9916。希望能盡快得到您的回覆。

135. Ⓐ 提交
　　Ⓑ 替換
　　Ⓒ 審閱
　　Ⓓ 詢問

136. **Ⓐ 超過**
　　Ⓑ 少於
　　Ⓒ 直到
　　Ⓓ 在……整個期間

137. Ⓐ 存在
　　Ⓑ 存在的
　　Ⓒ 現存的
　　Ⓓ 存在

138. Ⓐ 很高興能與您交易。
　　Ⓑ 希望能盡快得到您的回覆。
　　Ⓒ 請寄電子郵件給我們。
　　Ⓓ 祝福您持續邁向成功。

139-142 告示

電銷線索專員／電銷人員

地點：喬治亞州亞特蘭大市
工作代碼：3766
職缺人數：4

銷售線索專員要撥打電話給有意購買各種服務的潛在客戶，像是保險、稅務協助、財務協助、電信或運輸等。他們也要從現有客戶群中拜訪潛在客戶。必須進行電話行銷。

為說服潛在與現有客戶購買新產品與服務，你需透過電話與電子郵件直接向客戶

說明產品及服務項目。這份工作也要你教導客戶產品與服務的內容。最重要的是，你每天至少要打 150 通電話。每月銷售額最低的要求是淨利 7,500 元。除此之外，全體員工必須定期參加我們的產品教育課程，以提供顧客更好的服務。

為了符合職務要求，你必須擁有至少一年以上的電話銷售經驗、優秀的客服技巧，以及高超的成交技巧。

若您自認符合這些條件，並正在尋求刺激且高薪的經驗，請點擊以下的連結。

139. Ⓐ 實質的
Ⓑ **潛在的**
Ⓒ 最理想的
Ⓓ 合理的

140. Ⓐ 賣的越多，升遷的機會就越多。
Ⓑ 管理職位需要的是一位有組織能力且幹勁十足的人。
Ⓒ 如果你可以幫忙找到替代你的人選，那就太感謝了。
Ⓓ **最重要的是，你每天至少要打 150 通電話。**

141. Ⓐ 實際上
Ⓑ 然而
Ⓒ **除此之外**
Ⓓ 因此

142. Ⓐ **符合**
Ⓑ 去符合
Ⓒ 符合
Ⓓ 符合了

143–146 告示

寄件者：行政經理詹姆斯・瓊斯
收件者：銷售人員
日期：7 月 15 日
主旨：政策變動

親愛的銷售人員：

公司最近修改了核銷規定。過去，你只要先自費付款，然後再提供租車、出差或其

他的業務花費收據來核銷即可。但是，從現在開始你必須填寫申請表，要先通過會計部門的審核。然後你會領到內含有限金額的公司卡。若是支出超過卡片中的金額，你就必須自費，而且無法核銷。

請詳讀附件，以更了解公司接受與拒絕何種支出項目。

143. Ⓐ 產生
Ⓑ 已產生的
Ⓒ **產生**
Ⓓ 會產生

144. Ⓐ **但是**
Ⓑ 因此
Ⓒ 此外
Ⓓ 自從

145. Ⓐ 他們不會核准任何非經銀行授權的卡。
Ⓑ 你必須以你個人信用卡支付。
Ⓒ **然後你會領到內含有限金額的公司卡。**
Ⓓ 他們必須決定我們的預算是否能支付開銷。

146. Ⓐ 確定的
Ⓑ 公認的
Ⓒ 建立的
Ⓓ **批准的**

PART 7　P.148-167

147–148 行事曆

時間	星期一	星期二	星期三	星期四	星期五
上午9點 | 上午11點	瑜伽 1級： **4 號 教室**		健身 訓練： **1 號 教室**	踢拳擊 1級： **3 號 教室**	
上午11點 | 下午2點		重量 訓練： **2 號 教室**			瑜伽 2級： **4 號 教室**

時間				
下午2點 — 下午4點	飛輪： **1號教室**	踢拳擊 2級： **3號教室**		營養建議： **5號教室** （在櫃檯預約個人諮詢）
下午4點 — 下午6點	瑜伽 3級： **4號教室**	健身訓練： **1號教室**		馬拉松訓練： **2號教室**

147. 最有可能在哪裡看到這份行事曆？

   A 報紙上的運動版

   B 在旅遊行程表上

   C 在健身房的牆上

   D 在運動錦標賽的節目手冊上

148. 哪些活動在同一個教室上課？

   A 瑜伽與踢拳擊

   B 馬拉松訓練和飛輪

   C 瑜伽和營養建議

   D 飛輪和健身訓練

149–150 訊息串

> **汪達・奈特**　　　　　　　　9:04
> 我剛剛把你週五要去芝加哥的行程表寄給你了。
>
> **泰德・格列茲尼克**　　　　　9:05
> 太棒了，謝謝！
>
> **汪達・奈特**　　　　　　　　9:05
> 麥克・羅斯希望趁你在那裡時，能增加一場和鑽石出版社的會議。
>
> **泰德・格列茲尼克**　　　　　9:10
> 沒問題。
>
> **汪達・奈特**　　　　　　　　9:11
> 好。我可以和他們連絡，假如你太忙的話，就這樣。
>
> **泰德・格列茲尼克**　　　　　9:13
> 沒問題的。我星期六晚上應該會和鑽石出版社的傑維爾・山伽茲小酌。
>
> **汪達・奈特**　　　　　　　　9:13
> 真好。

> **泰德・格列茲尼克**　　　　　9:20
> 當那傢伙娶了你妹時，見到他是必然的。
>
> **汪達・奈特**　　　　　　　　9:21
> 啊，那倒是。

149. 下列何者與山伽茲先生有關？

   A 他在會計公司上班

   B 他和汪達・奈特有親戚關係

   C 他最近結婚了

   D 他星期五會到芝加哥

150. 在 9:11 時，奈特女士寫：「我可以和他們連絡」是什麼意思？

   A 她可以向他們致謝

   B 她可以和他們聯繫

   C 她可以去拜訪他們

   D 她可以協助他們

151–152 電子郵件

> 收件者：會計部
> <designers@ptcdesign.com>
> 寄件者：羅伯特・布朗
> <robertbrown@ptcdesign.com>
> 日期：3 月 29 日星期一
> 主旨：即將舉辦的會議
>
> ---
>
> 大家好：
>
> 本公司來自日本的客戶佐藤先生將於後天抵達，討論我們兩家公司即將進行的合併事宜。為了準備這個會議，我要求會計部同心協力做出第一季的財務報告。任何需要更多資料來完成這份文件的人，歡迎寄電子郵件給我。請於週二下午前完成這項任務。這份文件需要詳細說明本公司的所有財務活動，包含本公司全部的資產與投資。
>
> 謝謝。
>
> PTC 設計 執行長
> 羅伯特・布朗

151. 佐藤先生預計何時抵達布朗先生的公司？

    A 在 3 月 28 日
    B 在 3 月 29 日
    C 在 3 月 30 日
    D 在 3 月 31 日

152. 誰最有可能和布朗先生聯絡？

    A 想要調職到會計部門的員工
    B 需要額外資訊的員工
    C 需要延長期限的員工
    D 不同意合併的員工

153–154 邀請函

美國建築師協會年度大獎

誠摯地邀請您出席今年於 7 月 24 日星期五，在德州休士頓梅立頓飯店舉辦的盛事。會員可以攜帶兩位貴賓同行。

晚上 7:00	歡迎會
晚上 7:30	歡迎致詞與介紹（由美國建築師協會會長貝里·韓福瑞主持）
晚上 7:45	晚宴（提供素食，請於確認出席時提出）
晚上 9:00	頒獎典禮（最佳設計、最佳新人、最佳住宅建築、最佳公共建築），頒獎人為喜劇演員艾力克斯·達斯伍
晚上 10:30	由得獎樂團流行調調現場特別演出

請於 4 月 21 日前回覆出席意願給活動承辦人珍妮絲·哈頓 janice.harton@amarchsoc.net。

153. 誰最有可能是收到邀請函的人？

    A 建築公司的主管
    B 協會會員
    C 當地政府的建築師
    D 頒獎典禮的提名者

154. 要如何確認出席？

    A 打電話到梅立頓飯店
    B 寄電子郵件給貝里·韓福瑞
    C 拜訪艾力克斯·達斯伍
    D 與承辦人連絡

155–157 文章

北岸財經新聞

6 月 29 日——北岸市的在地支柱即將向全國發展。北岸乳品廠於 1951 年由老闆比爾·布得利創立，以商店屋頂上的大型旋轉冰淇淋甜筒成為北岸市的地標。多年來，它仍舊是當地居民最喜歡的聚會場所，也吸引了許多開車經過遊客的目光。比爾二世於 25 年前接手事業後，為了滿足當地居民與觀光客的需求擴展了商店。北岸乳品廠甚至被《旅遊雜誌》評選為十大商店之一。

1988 年，北岸乳品廠還出現在當紅好萊塢電影《未來、現在與過去》中，此舉讓它成為外地居民與觀光客造訪的首選冰淇淋店。

雖然有很多企業努力想從布得利家族手中買下這事業，但是比爾二世和兒子威廉堅持以家族方式來經營，這點讓北岸市的市民感到滿意。現在，這個家族準備要在鄰近城市開設兩家新分店，而且預計五年內，在全國開設六間新分店。「我們將維持小規模的經營模式，慢慢擴展。」威廉解釋，「為了維持冰淇淋的新鮮品質，並讓產品與我爺爺所創的食譜一樣，我們不想投機取巧，這也就是為什麼我們需要時間的原因。」

155. 這篇文章的目的是什麼？

    A 宣傳商店產品
    B 解釋新創業型態的細節
    C 討論一間家族企業的歷史
    D 解釋某些商品的價格

156. 下列何者與北岸乳品廠有關？

    Ⓐ 被一家大型企業收購
    Ⓑ 因為一部電影而在全市出名
    Ⓒ 是當地居民的驕傲與快樂
    Ⓓ 沒有足夠的經費可以擴展

157. 下列句子最適合出現在 [1]、[2]、[3]、[4] 的哪個位置？「現在，這個家族準備要在鄰近城市開設兩家新分店，而且預計五年內，在全國開設六間新分店。」

    Ⓐ [1]
    Ⓑ [2]
    Ⓒ [3]
    Ⓓ [4]

158–160 公告

> ### 阿克頓市議會公告
>
> 4 月 3 日
>
> 阿克頓市議會局將成立一個新的特別小組，負責在下個會計年度裡減少不必要的支出。這個 12 人小組將由當地企業負責人、工會代表、公務員及財經顧問所組成，小組成員訂於本月 30 號選出，接著立即開始運作，規劃以消除浪費的方式以減少 10% 明年當地政府的支出。
>
> 即日起接受小組成員的申請。有關以個人或單位名義參與這個計劃的資訊，請洽市議會 admin@acretoncc.gov。

158. 這份公告主要是有關什麼？

    Ⓐ 成立新的職業工會
    Ⓑ 成立財務監督小組
    Ⓒ 開始招募工作
    Ⓓ 當地法令變革開始

159. 小組訂於何時開始運作？

    Ⓐ 五月初
    Ⓑ 年底
    Ⓒ 夏季初
    Ⓓ 四月底

160. 有興趣的各方要如何參與？

    Ⓐ 簽署請願書
    Ⓑ 出席會議
    Ⓒ 寄送電子郵件
    Ⓓ 填寫表格

161–164 網路討論區

珍娜·羅根	[2:15]	我剛講完電話，金先生跟我說，他想要比預定時間提早幾個禮拜拿到訂貨。你們覺得可行嗎？
瑪格麗特·李	[2:16]	我們這邊沒問題。所有的布料都準備就緒，也裁切成適當的形狀與大小，已經準備給裁縫機作業了。
傑森·布朗	[2:17]	我的小組正在處理巴特利先生的訂單。有 1,000 多件要縫，之後還得處理卡拉·賓恩的訂單。
珍娜·羅根	[2:18]	巴特利先生月底才需要取貨，而賓恩女士的訂單可以等到下週再處理。我可以授權你的小組先著手處理這筆訂單。
傑森·布朗	[2:19]	正在處理什麼？需要多少件？
珍娜·羅根	[2:20]	長袖的男子襯衫。需要 S 號 100 件，M 號 300 件，L 號 300 件，XL 號 100 件。
傑森·布朗	[2:21]	好，我覺得兩天可以完工。
彼得·威廉斯	[2:22]	我們可以在兩至四小時內縫好 800 件的鈕釦。
珍娜·羅根	[2:23]	謝謝你們，感謝各位的協助。很開心我們可以這樣配合本公司最好的顧客。

161. 在 2:16 時，瑪格麗特·李寫：「我們這邊沒問題」是什麼意思？

    Ⓐ 她的小組可以達成目標
    Ⓑ 她的小組可以協助其他小組
    Ⓒ 他們的計劃需要一點時間
    Ⓓ 問題會很小

TEST 5

PART 7

162. 珍娜·羅根在何種公司上班？

　　Ⓐ 鞋店
　　Ⓑ 服飾工廠
　　Ⓒ 時尚雜誌
　　Ⓓ 男裝精品店

163. 根據這段討論，哪個部門需要最多的時間？

　　Ⓐ 李女士的部門
　　Ⓑ 布朗先生的部門
　　Ⓒ 威廉先生的部門
　　Ⓓ 羅根女士的部門

164. 珍娜·羅根最有可能告訴金先生什麼？

　　Ⓐ 他的訂單將延遲一個月交貨
　　Ⓑ 可以在兩週內完成他的訂單
　　Ⓒ 他的要求不容易達成
　　Ⓓ 他的訂單可以提早完成

165–167 備忘錄

安斯渥西製造公司

日期：10 月 17 日星期三
主旨：回收

為了因應來自當地環保團體的施壓，自 11 月 1 日起，我們將所有的工業廢棄物分類以便回收。資源回收將一週收兩次，地區的回收中心將於每週二和五進行回收，他們會提供彩色的容器來分裝不同種類的廢棄物。所有的油類必須裝在綠色容器裡，所有的金屬和玻璃要裝進紅色容器中，紙類則放進藍色容器裡，塑膠類就依照一般的方式回收。

由於這個新政策也會為公司帶來財務上的獲益，所有製造區的主管要負責確保遵循新的廢棄物處理程序，若是未遵守規定，將受到懲戒處分。

更多有關最新環保措施的資訊，很快就會公告在網站上。主管的培訓講習將於 10 月 22 日星期一舉行。在此期間，若有任何進一步的問題，請與我聯絡。

安斯渥西製造公司 營運主管
大衛·基蘭 敬上

165. 異動的原因是什麼？

　　Ⓐ 公司老闆想要省下工錢
　　Ⓑ 公司附近開了一間新的回收中心
　　Ⓒ 當地政府更改了法規
　　Ⓓ 當地環保人士提出要求

166. 可推論出何者與安斯渥西製造公司有關？

　　Ⓐ 與當地權威人士關係良好
　　Ⓑ 已進行塑膠工業廢棄物的回收
　　Ⓒ 最近增加了人力
　　Ⓓ 定期更新環保政策

167. 公司主管下週應該要做什麼？

　　Ⓐ 參加新程序的工作坊
　　Ⓑ 更新公司網頁
　　Ⓒ 挪出空間來放新的廢棄物容器
　　Ⓓ 通知他們的團隊同仁有異動

168–171 信件

諾門維爾農夫市集

4 月 9 日

親愛的諾門維爾居民們：

今年第一次的諾門維爾農夫市集將於 4 月 14 日星期六開幕，地點是大街和帕克街之間的克拉克街上。農夫市集的開放時間是上午九點至下午五點。諾門維爾市長湯姆·戴倫將於開幕式上致詞。許多當地農夫、食品攤販與街頭藝人都將出席。

諾門維爾農夫協會的執行理事蘇西·漢默說：「朝氣蓬勃的市集將提供在地農夫一個銷售新鮮農產品的好場所。除此之外，因為我們省去一些中間程序，所以價格也會比一般雜貨店便宜。」

漢默女士也提到目前並沒有足夠的停車空間可以容納購物者。諾門維爾農夫協會計劃在未來幾個月內擴大停車空間。在此期間，她建議會來參觀的諾門維爾居民搭乘大眾運輸以避開停車難題。

諾門維爾農夫市集不同於其他食品量販店，市集將提供富含重要維他命和礦物質的有機產品。如大家所知，市集也將有益在地經濟。

本週六請來看看諾門維爾市集賣了那些東西吧！

諾門維爾農夫協會 敬上

168. 這封信的目的是什麼？

[A] 描述政策改變
[B] 介紹新的雜貨店
[C] 宣傳市集的開幕
[D] 宣布競選結果

169. 下列何者與漢默女士有關？

[A] 她是農夫市集的攤販
[B] 她代表其他農夫
[C] 她擁有一座家族經營的農場
[D] 她是諾門維爾市市長

170. 文中提到了什麼樣的問題？

[A] 停車空間不足
[B] 產品價格不公
[C] 缺少品質管控
[D] 天氣險惡

171. 下列何者不是文中提到在市集採買的優點？

[A] 促進當地經濟
[B] 具有競爭力的價格
[C] 健康的農產品
[D] 較長的營業時間

172–175 告示

失物招領

帕克威市正為了即將到來的節慶季做好準備，並強烈要求市民及遊客看顧好個人物品。每一年都會有超過 2,000 件的遺失物品，被送至位於帕克威市政廳的失物招領處。「但節慶季期間我們會收到更多的遺失物品。」失物招領處的管理主任珍‧金恩表示，「從 11 月 25 日左右至 1 月 2 日，被送過來的遺失物大約增加了 25%。」

這幾年送來中心的遺失物品五花八門，從鑰匙、太陽眼鏡、雨傘、珠寶、到電子產品、行李箱、和裝滿新添購戰利品的購物袋。「我們收過最奇特的物品是裝滿了古

裝戲服的行李箱。」珍説，「當時一位在拍片的實習生很高興能尋回失物。」

許多人會來認領他們的遺失物，但是絕大部分的遺失物都無人認領。如果物品在 90 天內沒有人來認領，那些物品就會在公開活動中被拍賣，為社區活動中心募款。

172. 這篇告示的目的是什麼？

[A] 宣傳一項節慶活動
[B] 警告市民犯罪案的增加
[C] 告知民眾失物招領的物品
[D] 提供關於拍賣的訊息

173. 下列何者與珍‧金恩有關？

[A] 她在尋找遺失物
[B] 她在市政府上班
[C] 她是個實習生
[D] 她管理社區活動中心

174. 下列何者與遺失物品有關？

[A] 不會被永久存放在中心
[B] 通常會被失主領回
[C] 無人領取的時候會被銷毀
[D] 通常都是新的物品

175. 下列句子最適合出現在 [1]、[2]、[3]、[4] 的哪個位置？「許多人會來認領他們的遺失物，但是絕大部分的遺失物都無人認領。」

[A] [1]
[B] [2]
[C] [3]
[D] [4]

176–180 文章和電子郵件

科技生活聘僱新執行長

紐約，4 月 12 日──深陷銷售量低迷和表現令人失望的危機當中，「科技生活」科技公司聘用了史帝夫‧克羅斯擔任新的執行長。在此之前，他曾擔任過在加州舊金山的科技投信公司艾斯塔資源的財務長。就在本週一，他接下了該公司的執行長一

職，此公司位於德州達拉斯。股東們一致投票通過這項任命，期盼新執行長可以重新為公司燃起活力與力量。

「克羅斯先生是一位決策睿智的企業主管，擁有令人驚豔的記錄。」科技生活人力資源部主任琳恩・代爾表示。「我們有信心，他將帶領我們走向新方向，協助開發新市場，使公司整體運作更加完善。」

史帝夫・克羅斯畢業於賓州哈里斯堡的徹斯特大學，擁有企業管理碩士學位。他曾經擔任美國商業聯盟會長，也是位盡責的居家好男人。

收件者：史帝夫・克羅斯
<scross@techlife.com>
寄件者：琳恩・代爾
<ldyer@techlife.com>
主旨：歡迎！
日期：4 月 15 日

克羅斯先生您好：

上次見面已是將近兩年前的事了。很開心在艾斯塔資源跟您在同部門共事後，還能再次與您合作。我覺得我們那時合作無間，很期待能再和您一起共事。您會發現我們有非常盡責且認真工作的團隊。過渡時期若有任何我能幫得上忙的，歡迎隨時提出。

此外，科技生活最近新增了五位公司主管。若果您有空，請於下午三點來見見他們，他們將出席在 403 室舉行的強制培訓課程。

科技生活 人力資源部主任
琳恩・代爾 敬上

176. 科技生活面臨了什麼問題？

- Ⓐ 員工短缺
- Ⓑ 緊急查帳
- **Ⓒ 獲利減少**
- Ⓓ 潛在的競爭對手

177. 下列何者與股東有關？

- Ⓐ 他們可以獲取財務資訊
- Ⓑ 他們下週將開會
- Ⓒ 他們要求更多股息
- **Ⓓ 他們同意新主管的任命**

178. 文章中第二段第六行的「optimize」意思最接近？

- Ⓐ 合併
- **Ⓑ 改善**
- Ⓒ 分析
- Ⓓ 維持

179. 代爾女士先前在哪裡工作？

- Ⓐ 在哈里斯堡
- Ⓑ 在達拉斯
- Ⓒ 在紐約
- **Ⓓ 在舊金山**

180. 克羅斯先生被要求做什麼？

- Ⓐ 教授訓練課程
- **Ⓑ 和新員工見面**
- Ⓒ 出席股東會議
- Ⓓ 聘用新主管

181–185 議程表和電子郵件

未來與文化協會（AFC）
季度研討會
荷馬會議中心，1 月 10 日

下午 2:00	凱莉・歐尼爾（AFC 會長，慕里根小學校長），歡迎致詞
下午 2:30	馬克・貴斯克斯（SEM 開發集團執行長），強化全球意識：領導力與多樣化
下午 3:30	露西・胡佛（皮埃蒙特成人教育中心合夥人），領導階層的性別與公平性
下午 4:30	瓊恩・木村（肯特商場經理），工作場域中領導階層的基礎
下午 5:30	肯尼斯・施耐德（布魯克史東大學教授），領導階層的倫理與道德
下午 6:30	問答時間

收件者：AFC 會員
<menbers@futureculture.org>
寄件者：凱莉・歐尼爾
<kellyoneill@futureculture.org>
日期：1月11日
附件：free_talk.jpg
主旨：季度研討會

親愛的 AFC 會員：

這場季度研討會已經成為另一項值得紀念的成功。感謝大家的參與及專業分享，希望大家可以將在研討會中所學到的技能運用在辦公室和工作場合裡。除此之外，我也要鼓勵大家在下一次的研討會中考慮發表演說。若您有意參加，請與艾咪・賈西亞聯絡，電子郵件為 amygarcia@futureculture.org。

我也要通知各位肯尼斯・施耐德的邀請，他將於下個月於其工作地點發表一場演說，主題是〈從領導得來的自信〉。這是場免費的演講，並開放給一般民眾參加。若需更多資訊，請參考附件。

最後，我注意到有些會員因為行程衝突而無法出席研討會。因此，從現在開始，未來所有的研討會將同步在網站上播出，這樣遠距的會員也可以收看收聽了。

會長
凱莉・歐尼爾 敬上

181. 1月10日的研討會主題是什麼？
    Ⓐ 如何創立小型企業
    Ⓑ 如何管理財務
    Ⓒ 如何領導他人
    Ⓓ 如何將企業擴展至全球

182. 提問最有可能從幾點開始？
    Ⓐ 下午 3:30
    Ⓑ 下午 4:30
    Ⓒ 下午 5:30
    Ⓓ 下午 6:30

183. 免費的演講地點在哪裡？
    Ⓐ 慕里根小學
    Ⓑ 布魯克史東大學
    Ⓒ 皮埃蒙特成人教育中心
    Ⓓ SEM 開發集團

184. 歐尼爾女士邀請 AFC 的會員們做什麼？
    Ⓐ 附上收據
    Ⓑ 填寫問卷
    Ⓒ 準備演說
    Ⓓ 評估演講者

185. 文中提到什麼與之後舉辦的研討會有關？
    Ⓐ 將在新的地點舉辦
    Ⓑ 演說將晚點開始
    Ⓒ 將提高出席費用
    Ⓓ 將在網路上播放

186–190 網站和電子郵件

史塔克銀行

公告	我的帳戶	轉帳	貸款

透支費用

6 月 3 日當天，您於佛羅里達州傑克遜威爾市的提款機提領了 100 元，已超過您簽帳金融卡的額度限制，因此，您將被收取一筆 30 元的透支費。這可能是由於您從提款機提款之時，正在進行提款金額的累積所致。只要客戶金融卡交易金額超過其存款金額時，本行很遺憾必須收取這筆款項。

未來，藉由加入史塔克銀行的網銀服務，就能避免這項失誤。這個服務每個月只需 2 元的費用。利用您的智慧型手機，無論您身在何處都能登入帳號。您可以查看帳戶金額，存取款的歷史記錄，最重要的是還能辦理延後交易。欲加入，請寄電子郵件到 customerservice@starkbank.com 或撥打本行電話 904-555-4514。

收件者：customerservice@starkbank.com
寄件者：ssummers@zippynet.com
主旨：透支費用
日期：6 月 5 日

我擔心可能有人非法從我的帳戶提款。我在 6 月 2 日遺失了簽帳金融卡，隔天一發現後，我就立即凍結了所有帳戶。考慮到這些不幸的情況，懇請貴行能免收因這個意外而產生的透支費用。

我想要加入您所建議的銀行服務。這服務聽起來很不錯，可以幫我用更有效率的方式管理我的財務。

感謝您的協助。

蘇西・桑莫斯

收件者：蘇西・桑莫斯
<ssummers@zippynet.com>
寄件者：客戶服務部
<customerservice@starbank.com>
主旨：檢視透支
日期：6 月 6 日

親愛的桑莫斯女士：

本行對於您不幸的遭遇深感遺憾。根據我們所看到的帳戶資料，雖然看來已來不及防止盜領與隨後發生的帳戶透支，但您確實與我們聯繫要求凍結帳戶。在您報告遺失金融卡的隔天後，才發生以提款機交易而產生透支的情況有點不尋常。您最近是否有告訴他人您的密碼呢？我很樂意將您取消透支費的要求轉交給本行負責處理詐騙的部門，但您必須向警方報案，然後將偵查員給您的報案編號傳給我們。等我們一收到那個編號，就可以開始複審您的案件了。

謝謝您，祝您有美好的一天。

史塔克銀行 客戶服務專員
蘿拉・梅西

186. 網頁資訊的目的是什麼？
- Ⓐ 宣布公司的新規定
- Ⓑ 說明即將進行的搬遷
- **Ⓒ 告知使用者需支付的費用**
- Ⓓ 告知使用者網路釣魚的手法

187. 下列何者不是網銀的查詢項目？
- Ⓐ 帳戶結餘
- **Ⓑ 利率**
- Ⓒ 待處理的交易
- Ⓓ 帳戶歷史記錄

188. 桑莫斯女士要求銀行做什麼事？
- Ⓐ 凍結帳戶
- Ⓑ 更新聯絡資料
- **Ⓒ 免除透支費用**
- Ⓓ 提高提款上限

189. 在客戶服務部寄給桑莫斯女士的電子郵件中，蘿拉・梅西認為蘇西的事件有何奇怪之處？
- Ⓐ 蘇西帳戶裡沒有很多錢
- Ⓑ 蘇西沒有去警局報案
- **Ⓒ 蘇西在 6 月 2 日遺失金融卡，但是金融卡卻在 6 月 3 日被拿去提款機提款**
- Ⓓ 蘇西不住在佛羅里達

190. 如果蘇西・桑莫斯想要免除透支的費用，蘿拉・梅西教她該怎麼做？
- Ⓐ 寫信給史塔克銀行負責處理詐騙的部門
- **Ⓑ 去警察局報案，然後提供報案編號給史塔克銀行**
- Ⓒ 去法院向罪犯提告，將法案編號給史塔克銀行
- Ⓓ 向史塔克銀行負責詐騙的部門立案

191–195 電子郵件

寄件者：customerservice@thomsonapp.com
收件者：dkerry@coolmail.com
日期：7 月 6 日
主旨：故障

親愛的凱莉女士：

您在湯森家電行買的豪華冰箱型號 MK1213 發生故障，本公司對此感到非常抱歉。您說冰箱門上的製冰機停止運作，事實上，有幾位顧客也回報了相同的問題。結果是製造商在產品製造過程中產生失誤。所幸，我們的技師可以輕易地解決這個問題。目前技師下週一、三和四都有空。請明確告知您哪天與幾點方便。

此外，如果您的冰箱仍在保固期中，維修完全免費。請告知您的保固編號，以便在技師到訪前，讓我們先行確認。

我們十分抱歉造成不便。再次感謝您光臨湯森家電行。

客戶服務部
貴格·路易斯 敬上

寄件者：dkerry@coolmail.com
收件者：customerservice@thomsonapp.com
日期：7月7日
主旨：回覆：故障

親愛的路易斯先生：

感謝您迅速的回覆。事實上，下週我將到阿肯色州出差，星期六才會回來。但是，星期一和五會有管家來打掃。若您的技師可以在這其中一天過來，那她就可以讓他或她進來。

我的保固編號是 A344F56J，目前仍在保固有效期間內。我會將這個文件留給管家，以備你們來的時候需要查看。

堂娜·凱瑞

寄件者：customerservice@thomsonapp.com
收件者：dkerry@coolmail.com
日期：7月7日
主旨：維修時間

親愛的凱瑞女士：

技師可以在星期一到府維修。請務必留下保固文件，如此一來技師才能將它掃描至系統內，以利我們向製造商報帳。技師將於上午前往，盡量在中午以前修好。雖然您有管家，但他們會盡量維持整潔。祝您旅途平安，感謝您的耐心等候。感謝您對湯森家電行的忠誠惠顧。

客戶服務部
貴格·路易斯　敬上

---

191. 第一封電子郵件寄出的原因是什麼？
　　Ⓐ 說明保固編號
　　Ⓑ 詢問到訪日期
　　Ⓒ 確認訂單
　　Ⓓ 為運送延遲致歉

192. 根據第一封電子郵件，有關冰箱的敘述，下列何者為真？
　　Ⓐ 是最新推出的款式
　　Ⓑ 已超過保固期限
　　Ⓒ 有製造上的缺陷
　　Ⓓ 最近特價中

193. 路易斯先生要求凱瑞女士提供什麼資料？
　　Ⓐ 目前的地址
　　Ⓑ 保固編號
　　Ⓒ 冰箱型號
　　Ⓓ 聯絡資料

194. 技師為什麼要掃描保固文件？
　　Ⓐ 確定仍在保固期內
　　Ⓑ 確定型號正確
　　Ⓒ 確定有足夠的備用零件可以進行維修
　　Ⓓ 確定製造商會支付維修費用

195. 技師星期一可以到訪的原因是什麼？
　　Ⓐ 因為那時候技師才會有空
　　Ⓑ 因為技師星期五太忙了
　　Ⓒ 因為管家那時候會讓他進門
　　Ⓓ 因為凱莉女士會在阿肯色州

196–200 電子郵件

收件者：莉莉安·羅斯
<lillianross@kingstonsportinggoods.com>
寄件者：艾瑞克·衛斯特
<ericwest@jmsolutions.com>
日期：11月4日上午 10 點 34 分
主旨：網站開發
附件：明細

親愛的羅斯女士：

您上週與本公司聯絡，詢問要本公司的電腦程式工程師協助貴公司開發網站。JM科技很樂意為您提供服務。

正如在電話中所說的，我們將會協助設計並開發一個可以吸引更多顧客的網站，並提供線上銷售平台。在這期間，我們需要和貴公司的行銷部門開會，以完整掌握貴公司的銷售目標。明年二月中網站一完成後，我們將舉辦訓練課程，教導貴公司員工維護與更新網站所需的技巧。網站開發與訓練課程的總金額是 32,000 元。依規定貴公司需先支付 10% 的金額作為訂金。詳細的費用與時間表請參考附檔。

本公司期待在不久的未來能跟貴公司合作。本公司全體職員將努力滿足您的需求。因此，請告知貴公司行銷部門何時可以親自與我們會面，討論此案的一些細節。請在方便時與我聯絡。

艾瑞克‧衛斯特

收件者：莉莉安‧羅斯
<lillianross@kingstonsportinggoods.com>
寄件者：雷蒙‧威爾斯
<raymondwells@kingstonsportinggoods.com>
日期：11 月 4 日上午 10 點 37 分
主旨：第一季預算
附檔：Q1_ 預算

親愛的羅斯女士：

我已隨信附上明年第一季公司的預算草案附上。如您將注意到的，今年開學特賣的所有獲利，將用在主要公路上的廣告看板上。今天下午晚點我會打電話給設計組，請他們為廣告設計吸睛的圖案。

在我們上次的會議中，您提到希望在定案前再檢視一次預算。我已經將員工調薪加入第一季的支出中，但若您想到其他的部分，請告訴我。我打算在下週的籌劃會議前將預算定案。

雷蒙‧威爾斯

收件者：雷蒙‧威爾斯
<raymondwells@kingstonsportinggoods.com>
寄件者：莉莉安‧羅斯
<lillianross@kingstonsportinggoods.com>
日期：11 月 4 日上午 10 點 40 分
主旨：緊急追加預算

親愛的威爾斯：

很開心收到你做好的預算表。就在收到你的電子郵件前，我收到規劃中的網站建置估價單，看起來比我預期的還貴。雖然不需立即支付總額 32,000 元的帳單，但若要與 JM 科技公司合作進行企劃案的話，明年第一季的預算表需要另外撥出 3,200 元來。

如果你對這件事有任何的問題，請到我辦公室來，我們可以看看哪邊還可以再緊縮一些以支付這筆費用。

196. 衛斯特先生為什麼會寫第一封電子郵件？
- Ⓐ 詢問服務
- **Ⓑ 安排會議**
- Ⓒ 報告預算
- Ⓓ 求職

197. JM 科技公司提供什麼服務？
- Ⓐ 徵才與員工訓練
- Ⓑ 平面設計
- **Ⓒ 網路程式設計**
- Ⓓ 行銷策略諮詢

198. 根據第二封電子郵件，開學特賣的獲利將用在哪裡？
- Ⓐ 道路維修
- **Ⓑ 購買廣告空間**
- Ⓒ 支付 JM 科技公司的服務費用
- Ⓓ 聘請更多員工

199. 下列何者與第三封電子郵件有關？

    Ⓐ 明年第一季的預算看起來沒有問題

    Ⓑ JM 科技公司的名聲很好

    Ⓒ 對於金斯頓運動用品公司來說，要從
        預算裡找到經費來支付網站建構是很
        容易的

    **Ⓓ 為了要支付網站建構費用，一些項目
        可能會失去資金**

200. 金斯頓運動用品公司為什麼要花 3,200 元
在網站建構上？

    Ⓐ 他們需要能購買到最好的網站

    Ⓑ 他們須將生意擴展到其他領域

    **Ⓒ 他們須支付 JM 科技公司總金額的
        10% 作為訂金**

    Ⓓ 在付訂金後，他們需要協商一個更好
        的價格

ACTUAL TEST ⑥

◎ Part 5 解答請見 P.457

101. 寵物主人被鼓勵**報名**由社區活動中心所提供的寵物訓練與健康工作坊。

102. 執行長舉行了記者會，為該公司產品造成的不良健康影響**道歉**。

103. 旺季與淡季期間的營業收入有**明顯的**差異。

104. 貫穿莫里森公園的步道不僅是為了自行車騎士，**也是**為了慢跑者而建。

105. 其中一位主管質疑馬歇爾女士**有關**她在濫用投資基金中所扮演的角色。

106. 由於競爭增加，星霸飯店的住房率已經**下滑**了 24%。

107. **結業**證書已經發給公開演說技巧課程的參加者。

108. 為餐廳評論家準備主菜**的**主廚，通常會親自出來打招呼。

109. 協商者對合約做了些微更動，讓雙方都能**接受**那些條款。

110. 給當地學校的資金是**根據**住在該地區的孩童數量來分配。

111. 這座宮殿**傳統上**是作為公開典禮與慶祝活動之用。

112. 一旦招聘委員會做出**最終**決定，人力資源部代表將聯絡獲選的應徵者。

113. 主席**將由**所有會員匿名投票**選出**。

114. 提供低利貸款給小型企業是經濟復甦計劃的關鍵**要件**。

115. 這個計劃若沒有拉特克里夫先生的全力**付出**就不會成功，這從幾個時機點上得到證明。

116. 本市政治人物將於市政廳上辯論這個**複雜的**議題，讓投票者更加了解。

117. **如果**醫院遭逢斷電，發電機將自動運轉以供應所需電力。

118. 在史都華銀行的行員接受大量的訓練後，他們對待客戶**更有禮貌**了。

119. 登機門的地勤人員宣布航班**取消**，是由於目的地的天氣狀況惡劣所導致。

120. **當**老舊的設備被汰換成最先進的機械，產量將超過兩倍。

121. 要符合這個職位的資格，你必須要有至少五年的保險**業界**經驗。

122. 透過他對語言技巧習得上的廣泛研究，哈維・沃德博士已經證明**自己**是這個領域的領導者。

123. 太平洋食品公司所販售的海鮮容易**腐敗**，因此必須以溫控車輛運送。

124. 那位小說家說他的寫作，**深遠地**受到已故作家愛德華・特魯伊特的影響。

125. 正如研究者**所觀察**到的那樣，這新環保洗衣精和它的競爭對手一樣表現出色。

126. 綠化社致力為未來世代**維護**公立公園及其他自然區域。

127. 在颱風中受損的製造工廠將於本月稍後**重新恢復**運作。

128. 由於整個團隊的進度已經落後，經理沒有**同意**諾頓女士的休假申請。

129. 那個鼻塞噴劑讓伯特得以控制**好**他的季節性過敏，不必去索取醫師處方。

130. 我們的業務**代表**目前無法接聽您的電話，但將盡快回電給您。

PART 6 P.172–175

131–134 電子郵件

收件者：奧莉維亞·鮑爾森
寄件者：強納生·希克斯
日期：7月19日
主旨：流程檢視

上週四在主管會議上提出了一項議題，針對上個月商品在出貨後的毀損客訴遽增加，原因可能是因為我們現在配送易碎品的量增加。因此，我們已經暫停配送飾品與其他易碎物品。我們正在檢視產品的包裝流程，並打算增加更多步驟來確保產品有妥善包裝，並在毫無毀損的狀況下送達。

請通知所有產製主管參加今晚七點的緊急會議。我們希望提出這個問題，並盡快想出一個妥善的解決方案以恢復正常營運。

131. Ⓐ 增加中
　　 Ⓑ 已增加
　　 Ⓒ 被增加
　　 Ⓓ 增加

132. Ⓐ 我們正考慮將這類商品從產品清單上除名。
　　 Ⓑ 我們可能需要增加運費與處理費。
　　 Ⓒ 已經建議增加這類商品的保險費。
　　 Ⓓ 因此，我們已經暫停配送飾品與其他易碎物品。

133. Ⓐ 使安全
　　 Ⓑ 影響
　　 Ⓒ 確保
　　 Ⓓ 授權

134. **Ⓐ 緊急情況**
　　 Ⓑ 必需
　　 Ⓒ 決定的
　　 Ⓓ 廣泛的

135–138 廣告

綠潔服務公司
請來電：347-281-7834

自 2005 年起，綠潔一直為各類商業或工業場所提供一貫高品質專業又環保的清潔服務。做為一間服務公司，我們視員工為最重要的資產。我們了解一名好員工對公司成就所做的貢獻，我們也承諾挑選出最佳人員為您服務。

綠潔的使命就是滿足客人的每日需求，同時提供最佳品質、價格與服務，我們藉由不斷改善營運制度以達成此任務。我們的目標就是盡可能以最環保的方式讓您的處所極整潔。今天就上我們的網站看看 www.greenclean.com。

135. Ⓐ 直到
　　 Ⓑ 大約
　　 Ⓒ 自從
　　 Ⓓ 在……期間

136. Ⓐ 今天就來安排參觀我們 20 家分店的其中一家吧。
　　 Ⓑ 我們是西北部最大的環保清潔用品製造商。
　　 Ⓒ 做為一間服務公司，我們視員工為最重要的資產。
　　 Ⓓ 今天就來電讓我們為您處理所有的會計需求。

137. **Ⓐ 成就**
　　 Ⓑ 驅使
　　 Ⓒ 支持
　　 Ⓓ 決心

138. Ⓐ 操作
　　 Ⓑ 操作
　　 Ⓒ 操作
　　 Ⓓ 營運

誠徵花藝師

您喜歡讓人們微笑嗎？過著充滿創造力的一天並和大自然緊密工作的想法吸引您嗎？若是如此，我們想鼓勵您加入我們野花花藝團隊。本公司致力於為客戶提供最棒的花藝設計，無論他們的需求為何。我們尋求以客戶為優先導向的人士。創意很重要，但與客戶的想像力相較之下卻是其次。如果您認為自己有具備讓人們微笑的才能，請填寫本公司網站 www.WildFlowersFlorists.com 的線上求職表。

139. A 度過
B 度過
C 度過
D 已度過

140. A 你必須善於和動物相處。
B 本公司致力於為客戶提供最棒的花藝設計，無論他們的需求為何。
C 我們在設計中使用了最好的布料。
D 所有人都喜愛我們對安全性的承諾。

141. **A** 以……為導向
B 主要的
C 位於
D 獲得

142. **A** 您
B 我
C 他們
D 我們

143–146 信件

10 月 21 日
賴瑞・米爾斯
20037 華盛頓州費爾班克斯高地河區 226 號

親愛的米爾斯先生：

我來信是為了回覆您投訴公寓大樓週遭商家所發出的噪音。很遺憾，一些住在大樓西翼的住戶已經表達過對這些噪音的關切。大樓委員會已經針對這個問題開過會議，我們也跟那些商家說過了。不過，由於那些商業場所的性質，有些噪音是無可避免的。為此，我們也正打算幫住在西翼的住戶加強窗戶的隔音效果。一旦這些提案核准後，就會在公布欄上張貼公告，您也可能會接到電話通知。在那之前，只好請您繼續耐心等待。

143. A 因此
B 此外
C 另一方面
D 遺憾地

144. A 正在表達
B 已經表達
C 表達
D 表情豐富的

145. **A** 不過，由於該那些商業場所的性質，有些噪音是無可避免的。
B 他們將完全配合我們委員會。
C 他們已經回應了我們的關切，將努力減低噪音。
D 但是，他們正因此事而賠錢。

146. A 繼續
B 繼續
C 繼續的
D 連續的

PART 7 　P.176–197

147–148 請款單

韓德森企業

10571 紐約歡樂谷史蒂文斯路 1576 號
(231) 555-0786　www.hendersoninc.com

訂單編號：6694
日期：4 月 2 日
客戶：蘇珊・沃德
　　　10571 紐約歡樂谷讚美街 709 號
　　　(203) 555-0167

品項	型號	數量	價格
加大微波爐	MW132	1	150.00 元
四門冰箱	RF4D	1	2,399.99 元
智慧型烤麵包機	TR512	1	45.50 元

小計：2,595.49 元
稅：230.18 元
總計：2,825.67 元

本地顧客消費滿一千元以上，可獲免運資格。

147. 韓德森企業販售什麼？

Ⓐ **家用電器**
Ⓑ 辦公家具
Ⓒ 電腦設備
Ⓓ 建築材料

148. 下列何者和沃德女士有關？

Ⓐ 她必須親自提貨
Ⓑ 她合乎特別優惠的資格
Ⓒ **她可獲得免費宅配**
Ⓓ 她以支票付款

149–150 對話串

丹·庫柏	10:10
你開完會了嗎？	

海瑟·貝瑞	10:10
還沒。	

丹·庫柏	10:11
好，結束後傳訊給我。	

海瑟·貝瑞	10:11
我現在有空。現在是吃點心和上洗手間的休息時間。	

丹·庫柏	10:13
太好了，我在想你今天可不可以帶實習生去吃午餐？	

海瑟·貝瑞	10:13
你要拋下我嗎？	

丹·庫柏	10:14
沒辦法，我兩點得到北角。	

海瑟·貝瑞	10:14
別擔心。我會帶他們去。	

丹·庫柏	10:16
謝啦。我真的很不想取消跟他們的約會。	

149. 文中提到什麼和貝瑞女士有關？

Ⓐ 她正在吃點心
Ⓑ 她將獲得升遷
Ⓒ **她開會開到一半**
Ⓓ 她打算取消午餐約會

150. 在 10:13 時，貝瑞女士寫道：「你要拋下我嗎？」是什麼意思？

Ⓐ 她在問庫伯先生是否已經開完會了。
Ⓑ **她在問庫伯先生是否無法赴約。**
Ⓒ 她想知道庫伯先生是否會去北角。
Ⓓ 她要庫伯先生在離開時通知她。

151–152 傳單

超級包廂戲院

超級包廂戲院在今年 12 月提供日場票券的減價優惠。利用這個早鳥特別優惠，日場第一場電影只要半價。這個優惠適用於所有電影，每週七天，還包括最新院線片。

歡迎學校及公司團體觀賞。如果您的團體人數較多，可預先訂票，可親自向戲院職員購票或上網 www.superboxtheaters.com 和 www.abcticketworld.com 購買。您在網路購票時還可以順便選位。也可在網站上看到現正上映以及即將上映的影片資訊與評論。來超級包廂戲院，享受這個超棒的優惠吧。

151. 下列何者和超級包廂戲院有關？

Ⓐ 今年 12 月播放的電影較少
Ⓑ 正在招聘兼職人員
Ⓒ 不久將新開一家戲院
Ⓓ **對特定場次提供折價優惠**

152. 顧客可以在戲院的網站上做什麼？

- Ⓐ 要求退款
- **Ⓑ 選座位**
- Ⓒ 訂閱商業通訊
- Ⓓ 續延會員資格

153–154 電子郵件

收件者：亞倫・山德勒
<asandler@milleradvertising.com>
寄件者：山姆・米勒
<smiller@milleradvertising.com>
主旨：週二會議
日期：11 月 12 日

親愛的山德勒先生：

本月的業務審查會議定於 11 月 15 日週四召開。正如您所知，這個會議是個評估營運計劃的好機會，並做出調整讓我們跟上持續不斷的市場變化。做為廣告公司，了解最新市場趨勢是必要的。因此，當我聽到日本分公司的經理伊藤剛將於本週五來訪時，我非常興奮。為了善用他的專長與知識，我想更改會議日期，好讓伊藤先生也可與會。

這是伊藤先生第一次到本國，所以我希望您可以到機場接他。為此，將提供公司車供您使用。一旦我得到更多有關伊藤先生抵達的時間資訊，我會再寄電子郵件給您。

總裁山姆・米勒

153. 這封電子郵件的目的是什麼？

- **Ⓐ 重新安排會議**
- Ⓑ 要求月營運報告
- Ⓒ 介紹新員工
- Ⓓ 提出新的行銷策略

154. 這封電子郵件提到了什麼有關伊藤先生的事？

- Ⓐ 他的職務變動
- Ⓑ 他常出差
- **Ⓒ 他在廣告業工作**
- Ⓓ 他是米勒先生的客戶

155–157 電子郵件

收件者：布麗奇特・李
寄件者：維多・湯瑪斯
主旨：宅配
日期：6 月 25 日

布麗奇特你好：

我們飲料的貨運將於明天早上大約 10 點左右送達。請做好庫存紀錄，並於卸貨時確認所有配送的貨物正確無誤。同時，部分飲料需要即刻冷藏，因此請確保這部分能及時處理。我很擔心天氣的狀況。明天的氣溫預計將會頗高，所以我們需要盡快將所有配送的貨物存放妥當。我們會派兩台冷藏貨車給你，也會有職員在倉庫等你。

如你有任何問題，或你有任何突發狀況需要協助，請打電話給我。我明天一早就會進辦公室。

維多

155. 這封電子郵件的目的是什麼？

- Ⓐ 通知供應商有失誤
- **Ⓑ 給員工指令**
- Ⓒ 訂購一批飲料
- Ⓓ 記錄商品庫存

156. 維多為什麼擔心配送的事？

- Ⓐ 產品易碎
- Ⓑ 可能會晚到
- **Ⓒ 對溫度變化很敏感**
- Ⓓ 要配送給重要客戶

157. 下列句子最適合出現在 [1]、[2]、[3]、[4] 的哪個位置？「我很擔心天氣的狀況。」

- Ⓐ [1]
- **Ⓑ [2]**
- Ⓒ [3]
- Ⓓ [4]

158–160 廣告

金盞花麵包店
艾利斯鎮克拉克街 451 號
253-555-1298

金盞花麵包店是個家族企業，製作美味又誘人的甜點已有三十年多的時間。我們的門市就位在歷史悠久的艾利斯鎮市中心，提供溫馨的裝潢與迷人的氛圍。

我們提供：
- 派對、婚禮與公司活動所需的訂製點心
- 無麩質且無糖的茶點與蔬食三明治
- 客製蛋糕

營業時間：
週一至週六，早上九點至下午五點。
今年九月將因擴展店面而暫停營業。

週日烹飪課程：
金盞花麵包店重視與社區的正面互動關係。因此，我們現正為社區青少年舉辦烹飪課程，烘焙可教我們領悟耐心與努力的價值觀。

158. 文中提到下列何者與金盞花麵包店有關？
- Ⓐ 是國際知名的店
- Ⓑ 僱用當地學生
- **Ⓒ 為有飲食限制的人提供各種選擇**
- Ⓓ 店面空間可出租給各種活動使用

159. 根據這則廣告，九月會發生什麼事？
- **Ⓐ 這家店因整修而歇業**
- Ⓑ 將興建教室
- Ⓒ 將增加菜單內容
- Ⓓ 店家將為社區活動提供外燴服務

160. 下列何者與烹飪課程有關？
- Ⓐ 今年將於社區活動中心舉辦
- Ⓑ 已經進行三十多年了
- Ⓒ 由經驗豐富的烘焙師教授
- **Ⓓ 為社區裡的青少年所設計**

161–164 網路討論區

彼得·瓊斯	[12:10]	我要去對街新開的比薩店吃午餐。有人要一起來嗎？
馬丁·李	[12:10]	算我一份！
蘿拉·文斯	[12:11]	西奧和我要做明天的簡報，所以我們不能去。
西奧·吉伯斯	[12:12]	你可以幫我們外帶些比薩嗎？
彼得·瓊斯	[12:13]	當然可以。你們要哪一種？
蘿拉·文斯	[12:14]	我要他們賣得最好的那種，我吃一片大的就夠了。
西奧·吉伯斯	[12:15]	我要義大利臘腸口味，一片。
彼得·瓊斯	[12:15]	沒問題。我一個小時後回來。你們的報告和新產品系列有關嗎？
蘿拉·文斯	[12:16]	是啊，我們快做好了，但是我們正努力讓視覺圖像更吸睛。
馬丁·李	[12:17]	如果你們願意的話，我可以幫你們做視覺圖像。我在電腦繪圖上有點底子。
西奧·吉伯斯	[12:17]	那太好了。蘿拉和我對基本電腦程式還可以，但我們兩個都不擅長視覺圖像的製作。
彼得·瓊斯	[12:18]	等馬丁和我回來後，我們可以幫你們完成簡報。
蘿拉·文斯	[12:18]	太感謝了！
西奧·吉伯斯	[12:19]	太好了！

161. 對話者有可能在哪裡？
- Ⓐ 餐廳
- Ⓑ 比薩店
- **Ⓒ 公司**
- Ⓓ 電器行

162. 在 12:10 時，馬丁寫下：「算我一份」是什麼意思？

- A 他正在做簡報
- B 他在他的辦公室
- **C 他想外出吃午餐**
- D 他正在開會

163. 下列何者和簡報有關？

- A 將在午餐後報告
- **B 與新產品有關**
- C 很長
- D 需要更多資料

164. 馬丁・李最有可能幫報告者做什麼？

- **A 他們的圖表**
- B 他們的資料
- C 他們使用電腦的方式
- D 他們的簡報格式

165–167 電子郵件

收件者：全體職員
<staff@jointsystems.com>
寄件者：佛瑞德・哈奈斯
<fhanes@jointsystems.com>
主旨：清掃社區公園
日期：2 月 12 日

聯合系統是一家努力把握每個機會回饋社區的公司。因此，我鼓勵所有同仁參加由哈里斯堡市所贊助的社區公園清掃活動。沒有志工們的努力，我們的公園和公共空間將充滿垃圾。貢獻一點休閒時間讓哈里斯堡成為一個美麗又迷人的城市吧。

社區公園的清掃活動將於下週五 2 月 18 日下午一點至五點舉行。有意參加的同仁可以在午餐時間下班，但將仍以全薪計薪。志工須攜帶用具，像是防護性外衣、打掃用具、驅蚊劑、垃圾袋和點心。

接駁車將於週五下午 1:20 從公司停車場出發，載志工到清潔地點。如果您對想做的工作有特定的偏好，請來電 435-555-6768 與活動籌辦人唐・路易斯聯絡。

我們感謝所有人的熱心支持。

佛瑞德・哈奈斯
人力資源部

165. 這封電子郵件的目的是什麼？

- A 安排出差
- B 索取最新資料
- C 提供額外的技能訓練
- **D 宣傳社區活動**

166. 何者對參加者來說不是必要的？

- **A 公司制服**
- B 一罐防蚊劑
- C 耙子
- D 三明治

167. 根據電子郵件，路易斯先生負責什麼？

- A 引起對浪費食物的關注
- B 分析顧客意見
- **C 分派個人任務**
- D 打掃社區活動中心

168–171 網頁

http://www.sanchezcardealership.com/about

桑切斯汽車

認識我們	最新消息	車款	服務	相關社群

有關桑切斯汽車

卡洛斯・桑切斯從開始在汽車修理廠當助理以來，就一直有開設個人汽車代理商行的夢想。在儲蓄十年之後，他終於開設了桑切斯汽車公司，而且從那時起，就一直誠信且自豪為鄉里服務。桑切斯汽車提供各式車輛，從跑車、廂型車、休旅車到卡車皆有。不確定什麼車可以滿足您的需求嗎？那麼就來試駕各種車輛，看看哪款最適合您吧。

到年底為止，桑切斯汽車將提供優惠價給最受歡迎的噴火皮卡車及史塔克休旅車兩款。只要支付 3,000 元的頭期款，您就享有每月超低利率的分期車貸。

桑切斯汽車位於五號公路下，就在史塔克頓鎮外。我們一週營業七天，上午九點至晚上九點。別遲疑，現在就來找我們！

168. 下列何者與桑切斯先生有關？

Ⓐ 他在汽車修理廠工作
Ⓑ 他開創了自己的事業
Ⓒ 他是跑車駕駛
Ⓓ 他設計各種車輛

169. 第一段第四行的「carries」意思最接近？

Ⓐ 移動
Ⓑ 製造
Ⓒ 販售
Ⓓ 開發

170. 文中提到何者與桑切斯汽車有關？

Ⓐ 可讓顧客測試產品
Ⓑ 在史塔克頓市中心開店
Ⓒ 提供客製化汽車
Ⓓ 週末不營業

171. 到年底為止，顧客可以得到什麼？

Ⓐ 跑車與廂型車的優惠
Ⓑ 不加價的延長保固
Ⓒ 特別的付款方式
Ⓓ 購買商品後免費更換一次機油

172–175 文章

> ### 乾淨又環保
>
> 科登鎮有連連好事要慶祝，因為新的氫動力汽車公司紐馬克企業，打算在接下來的幾個月內設立一家大型製造廠。紐馬克企業已經為全球最環保的幾個都市提供氫動力公共汽車與計程車，包括溫哥華、新加坡、檀香山和阿姆斯特丹。
>
> 該公司預測未來五年內的業績將成長百分之 120%。同時，柯登廠的啟用也預計帶來 300 個新的工作機會。該鎮自當地汽車製造廠在 1990 年代關閉後，經濟就一蹶不振，故這對他們而言是個可喜的消息。松山舊廠區將是紐馬克企業的新廠址。科登鎮市長也努力提供政府津貼給那些購買氫動力汽車的人，期盼那些耗油的傳統汽車最終能走入歷史。

172. 這篇文章的主題是甚麼？

Ⓐ 替代能源
Ⓑ 環保城市
Ⓒ 新工廠的啟用
Ⓓ 汽車公司的未來

173. 舊汽車工廠會發生什麼事？

Ⓐ 它們會被摧毀再重建
Ⓑ 它們會成為氫動力汽車公司的新廠址
Ⓒ 它們會變成辦公大樓
Ⓓ 它們將收藏所有傳統舊車

174. 下列何者與科登有關？

Ⓐ 將成為最環保的城市之一
Ⓑ 它的經濟將持續蕭條不振
Ⓒ 它將吸引新的汽車公司
Ⓓ 它在經濟上會有所成長

175. 下列句子最適合出現在 [1]、[2]、[3]、[4] 的哪個位置？「該鎮自當地汽車製造廠在 1990 年代關閉後，經濟就一蹶不振，故這對他們而言是個可喜的消息」？

Ⓐ [1]
Ⓑ [2]
Ⓒ [3]
Ⓓ [4]

176–180 電子郵件和網頁

收件者：山姆·布朗
<sbrown@zippy.com>
寄件者：凱文·德雷伯
<kdraper@fivestarbank.com>
日期：4 月 22 日
主旨：房屋貸款

親愛的布朗先生：

感謝您選擇五星金融銀行為您提供房屋貸款。我們竭力提供您最具競爭力的還款計劃及超優的客戶支助。以下是您向本行申請的貸款摘要：

抵押貸款種類	金額	償還期間
購屋佳機貸款	70,000.00 元	15 年

在您貸款期間，資深行員瑪莎·金將負責您的還款計劃。了解您的貸款條款至關重要，能讓您成功償還貸款並避免罰款。我們建議您安排個時間和金女士會面，這樣她才能協助您進一步了解您的房屋貸款內容。

如果您註冊本行網路銀行服務，您就能快速便利地查詢您的還款進度。

再次感謝您將房屋貸款託付給五星金融銀行。

凱文·德雷伯 敬上
貸款專員

五星金融銀行

以下是提供給五星金融銀行會員的各種房屋貸款。了解不同種類的貸款可幫助您做出明智的決定。檢閱以下的貸款選擇，決定哪一種貸款最適合您的狀況。

固定利率抵押貸款——這項貸款保證在整個貸款期間您的利率與每個月還款的本金維持不變。這項貸款保護您免受利息調升的影響。如果您打算長期居住，這會是一個不錯的選擇。

浮動利率抵押貸款——您的利率在前五年維持固定不變。接下來每年調整。通常，這項貸款一開始的利率都會低於固定利率抵押貸款。

無本金抵押貸款——在貸款最初的五年期間，您只需支付利息。這個選擇適合那些收入不穩定者。當您的財務吃緊時，可以只支付利息。當您的收入增加，就可以支付本金。

購屋佳機貸款——這個特別的貸款是專為首次購屋者所設計的。您不需要一大筆頭期款和良好的信用評等就有資格申請這項貸款。

176. 德雷伯先生建議布朗先生做什麼？
- A 應徵職位
- **B 安排會面**
- C 在四月付頭期款
- D 成為銀行會員

177. 布朗先生被建議如何追蹤貸款？
- A 和德雷伯先生會面
- B 閱讀銀行發的定期電子郵件
- **C 利用網路上的銀行服務**
- D 撥打銀行熱線

178. 網頁提供了什麼資訊？
- A 銀行帳戶明細
- B 季利率
- **C 還款選擇**
- D 會員名冊

179. 哪一項計畫適合那些沒有穩定收入的人？
- A 固定利率抵押貸款
- B 浮動利率抵押貸款
- **C 無本金抵押貸款**
- D 購屋佳機貸款

180. 下列何者與布朗先生有關？
- A 他付了一大筆頭期款
- B 他有穩定收入
- **C 他最近買了第一間房子**
- D 他不久將退休

181–185 文章和電子郵件

《麥迪森商業快報》

11 月 15 日——太陽微晶片是國內積體電路規模最大的製造商，其產品用於電腦、智慧型手機和其他數位電子用品內。這家公司最近在麥迪森設立了新廠房，即將於明年一月開始運作。太陽微晶片的執行長梅琳達·皮爾斯解釋：「隨著消費性電子產品的市場在全球持續成長，像太陽微晶片這樣的公司也要擴大營運來滿足需求。」

「我們正在尋聘各類人員，像是工廠員工、人事部僱員和會計。我們預估開設這個工廠將能為麥迪森地區創造 200 多個工作機會。」皮爾斯女士說。她提到公司將優先僱傭當地居民，但非麥迪森的居民也歡迎應徵。

應徵者必須在 11 月 25 日前將履歷以電子郵件方式寄給蒂娜·齊默爾曼 tzimmerman@sunmicrochips.com。太陽微晶片將於下個月分別舉辦兩場面試。應徵裝配線的一般員工應於 12 月 3 日至 8 日間舉辦面試，至於那些對人事、會計與客服等職務有興趣者，將於 12 月 9 日至 11 日間安排面試。

收件者：
<tzimmerman@sunmicrochips.com>
寄件者：<jakehenry@tnamail.com>
日期：11 月 21 日
主旨：太陽微晶片公司的職缺
附件：履歷表

親愛的齊默爾曼女士：

我最近在《麥迪森商業快報》上看到貴公司新工廠的職缺。身為太陽微晶片的前職員，我對於再次加入貴公司的前景感到很興奮。

請參看附件檔案。如果您能給我面試機會，我將感激不盡。12 月 10 日的任何時段我都可以。如果您想多了解我之前在太陽微晶片的工作經歷，您可以和我的前主管塔德·史密斯聯絡。他仍在公司服務。

期待與您見面。

傑克·亨利

---

181. 根據皮爾斯女士所言，關於消費性電子產品，下列何者為真？

Ⓐ **它們的需求持續增加**
Ⓑ 它們變得愈來愈昂貴
Ⓒ 它們很快地只會在一些國家製造
Ⓓ 它們會影響使用者的健康

182. 太陽微晶片公司打算做什麼？

Ⓐ 推出最新款的智慧型手機
Ⓑ 在海外建新廠房
Ⓒ **優先聘僱當地應徵者**
Ⓓ 聘僱新的執行長

183. 齊默爾曼女士最有可能是誰？

Ⓐ 電腦技師
Ⓑ **人力資源部經理**
Ⓒ 工廠員工
Ⓓ 會計師

184. 這封電子郵件的目的是什麼？

Ⓐ 辭職
Ⓑ 延後約定會面
Ⓒ **要求面試**
Ⓓ 接受工作邀約

185. 下列何者與亨利先生有關？

Ⓐ 他是麥迪森的居民
Ⓑ 他有電腦科學的學位
Ⓒ 他目前在太陽微晶片公司工作
Ⓓ **他想要辦公職務**

186–190 電子郵件和廣告

寄件者：亨利·崔
<henrychoi@neatsolutions.com>
收件者：珍妮·戴維斯
<jennydavis@endlessacresgolfclub.com>
日期：8 月 8 日
主旨：無盡大地高爾夫球俱樂部
附件：草稿

親愛的戴維斯女士：

附件是「無盡大地高爾夫球俱樂部」廣告的最新草稿。我已經將您寄給我的廣告標語加入設計中。我結合了各種吸睛圖像來吸引報紙讀者的注意，我也在廣告結尾加上了實用的資訊，請告訴我這個設計與新添加的部分是否符合您的期望。配合目前的電視廣告，我想這個廣告將為無盡大地高爾夫球俱樂部帶來許多新顧客。

亨利·崔 敬上

無盡大地高爾夫球俱樂部
科羅拉多州美寶市山丘草原大道 1232 號

暫離生活中的所有壓力，來無盡大地高爾夫球俱樂部打一輪輕鬆的高爾夫球吧。在打完球後，來俱樂部餐廳精緻舒適的用餐環境中享用餐點。

我們目前提供了以下的優惠活動：

預約七人以上組團比賽可享八折優惠。除此之外，每位成員都將得到五元折價券，可於本俱樂部的專賣店消費時折抵。

我們最近才受到《滾動草原日報》讚揚我們優質的場地維護，請來享受科羅拉多州最棒的高爾夫球場吧。我們位於五號公路 21 號出口附近，只要找一下我們的看板，您絕對不會錯過！

現在可於本俱樂部的網站 www.endless sacresgolf.com 線上預約，或來電 555-4834。

寄件者：羅根‧曼金斯
<lmankins@crushing.com>
收件者：
<reservations@endlessacresgolfclub.com >
日期：7 月 6 日
主旨：回覆：十人開球與晚餐

您好：

我在報上看到你們的廣告，對於你們的優惠有幾個簡短的問題。第一，我們有十位球員。我知道大多的場地一般都會限制最多四人下場比賽，是為了加速賽程，但我們真的很希望您能為我們破例，一次讓兩隊各五人下場。我們甚至願意租用高爾夫球車來確保不會造成延遲。至於高爾夫球專賣店的五元禮券。我不知道是否可以合起來購買價位較高的物品。這是我兒子的生日。我想送他一支新球桿，但球桿現在真的很貴，50 塊錢應該可以買給他一份很棒的禮物！

我們想在 7 月 20 日星期六早上 11:30 時開打，然後大約在傍晚 6 點時用餐。煩請回信確認開球時間，並回覆我的提問。感謝您撥冗讀信！

祝您有個美好的一天
羅根‧曼金斯

---

186. 羅根‧曼金斯建議要如何讓兩組五人的隊伍不會耽誤到場上其他球員？

[A] 他保證他們會打得很快

[B] 他保證他們都很擅長打高爾夫球

[C] 他寫說他會買新的球桿給他兒子

[D] 他告訴俱樂部那兩隊都會開高爾夫球車

---

187. 這則廣告最有可能在哪裡出現？

[A] 電視上

[B] 雜誌裡

[C] 報紙上

[D] 看板上

---

188. 廣告上加了什麼？

[A] 促銷細節

[B] 交通資訊

[C] 聯絡資料

[D] 顧客評論

---

189. 羅根‧曼金斯想怎麼利用會員在專賣品店可用的五元折價券？

[A] 他想用他的折價券買一支球桿給兒子

[B] 他想用它們來支付果嶺費

[C] 他想和八折的團體優惠合用

[D] 他想集合所有折價券來買一樣商品

---

190. 《滾動草原日報》提到了無盡大地高爾夫球俱樂部的什麼？

[A] 地點便利

[B] 場地維護良好

[C] 會費合理

[D] 餐廳定期更新菜單

191–195 電子郵件、行事曆和網路討論區

寄件者：圖書館會員
<members@claytonlibrary.edu>
收件者：荷莉‧艾倫
<hollyallen@claytonlibrary.edu>
主旨：本月活動
日期：8 月 1 日
附件：8 月活動行事曆

親愛的克萊頓圖書館會員：

感謝您對克萊頓圖書館持續的支持。您所繳的月費幫助我們購買新書、電腦、訂閱期刊還有添購其他對整個社區有益的資源。我們想知會您一些本月即將舉辦的特別活動，您或許會有興趣參加。

首先，著名的童書作家與説書人艾伯特‧巴特勒將來訪本圖書館。他將選讀他的新書《神秘貓》，並親筆簽名。他的書最近被提名入選年度最佳童書獎。他的妻子凱西·巴特勒也將出席這場活動，她為巴特勒先生大部分的書籍繪製插圖，也包括《神秘貓》。這場活動費為 10 元，但圖書館會員免費。

本月底，著名的野生動物攝影師妮娜·布魯克斯將於圖書館一樓舉辦展覽。布魯克斯女士最近剛從肯亞旅行回來，在那裡她拍攝了獵豹、長頸鹿、大象和其他動物。她的照片捕捉了野生動物的生動樣貌與大自然的雄偉。

除了這兩項主打活動，本月還有各種工作坊、遊戲之夜與其他活動。細節請參考附上的行事曆。除非另有註記，所有的活動，包括電影之夜會都可免費入場。

圖書館活動籌辦者
荷莉·艾倫 敬上

克萊頓圖書館活動行事曆
八月

日期／時間	活動名稱	附註
8 月 2 日 星期六 下午五點	創意作家 工作坊	由多娜·沃德 主持
8 月 8 日 星期五 晚上七點	電影之夜	闔家活動
8 月 17 日 星期日 下午六點	《神秘貓》 讀書會	入場費 10 元
8 月 20 日 星期三 下午三點	針織社	免費茶點
8 月 30 日 星期六 下午兩點	攝影展開幕	入場費 5 元

克萊頓圖書館社群聊天室
8 月 1 日
■ 使用者身分：**Jjohnson231**

主旨：8 月 2 日創意作家工作坊
嘿，有人要參加明天的作家工作坊嗎？我聽說多娜·沃德是位優秀的老師。我最新的短篇故事很需要一些意見。如果要去的人請喊個聲吧！～吉姆

■ 使用者身分：**Storytimechuck**

主旨：回覆：8 月 2 日創意作家工作坊

嗨，Jjohnson231！我一定會去。你說的沒錯，多娜超棒的。她對敘事與節奏的知識真的對我的電影劇本助益很大。或許我也可以在工作坊結束後讀你的短篇故事，提供我的意見。就像我一直在說的，愈多人看愈好！如果你有興趣的話，我也可以讓你看一下我的劇本。明天見！～恰克

191. 這封電子郵件的目的是什麼？
Ⓐ 介紹新成員
Ⓑ 宣傳即將舉辦的活動
Ⓒ 公告時間表的調整
Ⓓ 請求捐款

192. 下列何者與艾伯特·巴特勒有關？
Ⓐ 他的妻子是插畫家
Ⓑ 他最近出版了第一本書
Ⓒ 他有好幾隻貓
Ⓓ 他即將得獎

193. 根據聊天室，多娜·沃德擅長什麼？
Ⓐ 拍攝生動的照片
Ⓑ 編寫成功的電影劇本
Ⓒ 了解步調與故事情節的作用
Ⓓ 和年輕詩人合作

194. 圖書館讀者何時可以見到凱西·巴特勒？
Ⓐ 星期三
Ⓑ 星期五
Ⓒ 星期六
Ⓓ 星期日

195. 8 月 2 日創意作家工作坊結束後可能會發生什麼事？
Ⓐ 每個人都知道如何把詩寫得更好
Ⓑ 恰克和吉姆將交換作品提供彼此的意見
Ⓒ 多娜·沃德將出版她的小說
Ⓓ 恰克與多娜將一起寫吉姆的短篇故事

紅岩皮件

感謝您購買紅岩皮件的商品。我們製造的商品都符合最高品質標準，並以優質的客服為豪。我們所有的商品都是由技術純熟的工匠一絲不苟地逐一製作，我們提供終生保固，除了正常磨損以外，所有做工上的瑕疵皆適用。只要在您使用紅岩產品期間，我們將維修或更換任何瑕疵部分。

如果您的紅岩商品不在保固期間，則維修費如下：

	皮夾	手提包	外套
更換遺失鈕扣	10 元	15 元	20 元
拉鍊維修或更換	20 元	30 元	45 元
縫線修補及縫合	40 元	50 元	50 元

保固不可轉讓，且僅限原始購買人使用。此外，必須要有銷售收據以確認保固並使用服務。這個保固不適用於購自二手商店或未獲授權代理商之商品。

紅岩皮件
維修申請表

姓名：梅莉莎・波金斯
日期：2 月 28 日
地址：伊利諾伊州芝加哥中圓大道 458 號
商品：可可 TX 手提包

維修說明：

我去年在伊利諾伊州芝加哥的紅岩皮件店買了這件商品，但才不到在六個月，拉鍊就卡住了，無法開合。由於這是製作上的瑕疵，我想這應該在保固範圍內。12 年來我一直是紅岩皮件的忠實常客，這是我第一次碰到問題。

本人已經閱讀並同意所有退貨與維修的相關條款。本人保證這個商品是在紅岩皮件的官方商店購得，而且本人是這項商品的原始購買人。

簽名：梅莉莎・波金斯
日期：2 月 28 日

備註：您的商品可能需要一段時間才能取回。若您有任何問題，請來電 812-555-8541。

親愛的梅莉莎・波金斯：

感謝您提出了紅岩皮件可可 TX 手提包的維修申請。我們已經收到並檢查了您的商品與文件，確定這的確是在我們的保固範圍內，並安排於下週進行維修。一旦恢復正常，我們將以快遞寄到您在維修申請表中所提供的地址。僅代表紅岩皮件感謝您 12 年來的惠顧，也為這個可可 TX 手提包的瑕疵對您造成的不便感到抱歉。

紅岩皮件客戶服務專員
雪若・蒂明斯 敬上

196. 下列何者與紅岩皮件的商品有關？

    Ⓐ 它們在全國都有販售
    Ⓑ 它們相當昂貴
    Ⓒ 它們是手工製
    Ⓓ 它們有各種顏色

197. 波金斯女士為什麼填寫申請表？

    Ⓐ 要得到商品的退款
    Ⓑ 要告知商品有瑕疵
    Ⓒ 向客服投訴
    Ⓓ 延長保固期限

198. 如果波金斯女士的商品是從二手商店買來的，她會被收多少錢？

    Ⓐ 15 元
    Ⓑ 20 元
    Ⓒ 30 元
    Ⓓ 45 元

199. 在給波金斯女士的信中，第六行的「patronage」意思最接近？

    Ⓐ 行銷
    Ⓑ 惠顧
    Ⓒ 競爭
    Ⓓ 投資

200. 從核准波金斯女士所提出的保固一信中，可推論出什麼？

[A] 她的手提包有正常的磨損

[B] 紅岩皮件是當地的品牌

[C] 她附上了紅岩皮件專賣店的銷售收據

[D] 她為她的可可 TX 手提包附上 30 元的拉鍊維修費

ACTUAL TEST ⑦

PART 5　　P.198-201

◎ Part 5 解答請見 P.457

101. 每週於星期一與星期四收**兩次**可回收物品，如玻璃及塑膠。

102. 因為道路交通壅塞，愈來愈多的製造商**現在**會利用火車來運送商品。

103. 員工被指示當顧客抱怨時，要**通知**值班的主管。

104. 老舊傢俱、復古珠寶和其他的**古董**都可在這個市集裡買到。

105. 如果沒有做好必要的安全預防措施，受傷的風險可能會更高。

106. 不滿意楓葉家庭清潔服務的顧客，可以在首期清潔作業的三天**內**終止契約。

107. 華倫街上免費診所裡的**員工都是**由志工醫師和護士**組成**。

108. 福克斯女士延長店家營業時間，因為她認同亞柏先生**所說的**營業時間不夠長。

109. 偵查員查看了這個地方，確保該地符合**適用的**業界規範。

110. 大部分住在利嘉塔**的**居民，對於冷氣系統不斷出現的問題感到苦惱。

111. 休斯先生將員工分成小型討論小組以加強會議的**參與度**。

112. 自去年**同期**以來，匯率已經上漲了 3.2 個百分比。

113. 布蘭達‧提頓被**預測**將贏得市長競選，因為她是所有候選人中資歷最豐富的。

114. 那些參加創意寫作工作坊的人，在未來兩天**中**將學到各種有用的技巧。

115. 藉由事先**仔細**規劃搬遷事宜，我們可以將意外的支出降至最低，並盡量提高效率。

116. 根據公司規定，**所有**出差費用的申請必須附上收據才能核銷。

117. 安全公司自 2008 年創立以來就一直**生產**居家安全產品。

118. 因為訂單上的一個錯誤，部分建築材料從沒寄送出去。

119. 實施新政策是為了加強公司各部門之間的**溝通**。

120. 古堡的私人旅行團人數將限制**在**十人內。

121. 使用平底鍋烹煮時，請勿使用金屬用具，**這樣**表面才不會被刮花。

122. 為了**負擔**每個月的房貸，泰勒先生需要大幅度的加薪。

123. 環保人士對於社區**配合**提升當地的資源回收再利用感到滿意。

124. 國家健康組織報告了該疾病的**確診**案例。

125. 由於政治傾向的**改變**，參議員不再支持提出的移民法案。

126. 對附近的屋主來說，鄰里裡的**空屋**會造成房產淨值的損失。

127. 諾里斯大樓的屋主大量購進家具，讓每個會議室看起來都一模一樣，而非讓每間有**不同的**裝潢。

128. 導演將影片的成功**主要**歸功於男主角的經驗與才華。

129. 公司新的網路銀行軟體與大多數型號的智慧型手機**相容**。

130. 只要不中斷工作，員工可隨時休假。

PART 6　P.202–205

131–134 電子郵件

寄件者：副總裁堂娜‧強森
收件者：赫力奧科技公司員工
日期：7月5日
主旨：大廳翻新

上個月收到的聯邦政府補助款已可讓我們改善大樓的幾個區域，第一個從中獲益的地方就是大廳，我們將自7月12日起開始改建大廳。大概需要兩個禮拜的時間。在那段期間內，如需與公司以外的人開會，請安排到轉角的羅斯街咖啡店。我們已經設定了一個特別帳目，這兩個禮拜內公司的人都可以使用。請在帳單上簽名並寫上日期，然後將帳單交還給服務生。我們知道這樣會有點不方便，感謝大家的配合。

131. Ⓐ 之前允許
　　　 Ⓑ 已允許
　　　 Ⓒ 允許
　　　 Ⓓ 正允許

132. Ⓐ 當收到建物准許通知後就會開始動工。
　　　 Ⓑ 這個慶祝活動將持續大半個七月。
　　　 Ⓒ 考量到花費，改建將延後進行。
　　　 Ⓓ 第一個從中獲益的地方就是大廳。

133. Ⓐ 一……就
　　　 Ⓑ 在……期間
　　　 Ⓒ 大約
　　　 Ⓓ 直到

134. **Ⓐ 知道**
　　　 Ⓑ 受過訓練的
　　　 Ⓒ 不情願的
　　　 Ⓓ 滿意的

135–138 告示

誠徵兼職廚師

天堂咖啡廳正在找一位兼職廚師。應徵者必須能在步調快速的環境裡工作，且熟悉所有的制式早餐餐點。我們目前只提供平日班，但若有必要，應徵者必須願意在週末上班。週末的時間表日後將有異動。理想上，我們希望應徵者最好有至少一年以上快餐廚師的工作經驗。天堂咖啡廳位於磨坊鎮市區的郵局旁。請親自繳交履歷表，並準備烹煮一份可供點餐的蛋類餐點。我們期盼並歡迎您加入本團隊！

135. Ⓐ 聘用
　　　 Ⓑ 聘用
　　　 Ⓒ 聘用
　　　 Ⓓ 聘用

136. Ⓐ 應徵者必須知道如何炒蛋。
　　　 Ⓑ 來應徵的人必須知道怎麼洗碗。
　　　 Ⓒ 應徵者需要能說西班牙文。
　　　 Ⓓ 我們目前只提供平日班，但若有必要，應徵者必須願意在週末上班。

137. Ⓐ 最多
　　　 Ⓑ 低於
　　　 Ⓒ 至少
　　　 Ⓓ 最少

138. **Ⓐ 期盼**
　　　 Ⓑ 期盼
　　　 Ⓒ 期盼
　　　 Ⓓ 期盼

139–142 廣告

城市不動產

城市不動產是華盛頓州首屈一指的不動產公司，在本州服務超過50年。我們被公認為是本州業界的權威專家，我們的許多仲介人員也因他們傑出的服務而獲得《富比士地產》雜誌頒發的獎項。本公司仲介人員竭盡心力將他們最棒的知識與專業端上檯面，而且他們對於房地產市場的準則也是數一數二的。本公司仲介人員專精房地產業的各個區塊，包含企業不動產、住家不動產及租賃不動產。您可以確信的是他們絕對能滿足您的特定需求。

本公司總部位於市中心，您可以與我們的仲介人員在此會面並做免費諮詢。您也可以上本公司網站 www.cityrealty.com 查看不動產物件列表及更多資訊。

139. Ⓐ 是
　　Ⓑ 曾是
　　Ⓒ 正是
　　Ⓓ 已經是

140. Ⓐ 附屬的
　　Ⓑ 忠誠的
　　Ⓒ 盡心盡責的
　　Ⓓ 忠心的

141. **Ⓐ 您可以確信的是他們絕對能滿足您的特定需求。**
　　Ⓑ 本公司有上百筆的房產清單供您選擇。
　　Ⓒ 企業不動產的房仲賺最多錢。
　　Ⓓ 由於住房市場日漸上漲，住家不動產的房仲很忙。

142. Ⓐ 和
　　Ⓑ 為了
　　Ⓒ 到
　　Ⓓ 來自

143–146 網站貼文

員工留言板

辦公室節慶派對
成就與感恩

發表人：朱利‧諾頓

我要感謝每一位曾經提供協助而讓這場派對成功的人。特別要感謝凱斯、格蘭特、凡妮莎和瑪莉莎，他們在工作之餘還花了

許多時間協助規劃這一切。在開始準備的時候，我們經歷了一些起落，但是最終結果卻是非凡的。事實上，全體一致認為今年的派對是有史以來最棒的。這次參加的人數破了紀錄，而且很多人都覺得今年的活動是派對成功的主因。很開心看到大家都相處融洽，還參與了所有活動。兒童慈善募款甚至超越目標 1,000 多元。再一次地，我要感謝大家。

143. Ⓐ 協助
　　Ⓑ 曾協助
　　Ⓒ 正協助
　　Ⓓ 已協助

144. Ⓐ 我應該再多點些食物和酒。
　　Ⓑ 我很認真地規劃了這次的活動。
　　Ⓒ 特別要感謝凱斯、格蘭特、凡妮莎和瑪莉莎，他們在工作之餘還花了許多時間協助規劃這一切
　　Ⓓ 今天很開心看到各位為此活動盛裝出席。

145. Ⓐ 一般的
　　Ⓑ 熟悉的
　　Ⓒ 不同的
　　Ⓓ 全體的

146. Ⓐ 踰越
　　Ⓑ 投降
　　Ⓒ 超過
　　Ⓓ 征服

PART 7　P.206–229

147–148 信件

4 月 3 日

賴瑞‧馬汀
堪薩斯整齊清潔公司
67514 堪薩斯州阿靈頓湖邊路 5448 號

親愛的馬汀先生：

今年我們哈雷谷搖滾嘉年華有意僱用貴公司的清潔服務。嘉年華將於 6 月 14 日星期五開始，持續一整個週末，到 6 月 16 日星期天晚上結束。但是，和前幾年不同，今年我們希望貴公司能在嘉年華期間不定時地清潔環境。因此，我們將提供貴公司一輛拖車作為臨時辦公室，讓員工可以避暑休息。

期盼今年再次與貴公司合作。

哈雷谷基金會嘉年華籌劃人
凱倫・強森 敬上

147. 馬汀先生最有可能是誰？

　　A 音樂表演者
　　B 卡車司機
　　C 清潔公司的專員
　　D 嘉年華籌劃人

148. 根據這封信，將提供什麼？

　　A 食物與水
　　B 休息區
　　C 音樂器材
　　D 清潔用品

149–150 訊息串

蘿拉・伯克	5:09
你星期一會回市區嗎？	

阿德溫・尚恩	5:15
可能會。	

蘿拉・伯克	5:16
所以，你還沒決定嗎？	

阿德溫・尚恩	5:17
是啊，工廠正面臨各種問題。處理好一件，另一件又出現。	

蘿拉・伯克	5:17
我聽說了。嗯，至少不用被綁在辦公室裡。	

阿德溫・尚恩	5:18
這倒是真的。	

阿德溫・尚恩	5:19
星期一有什麼事嗎？	

蘿拉・伯克	5:20
你回來之後，哈里斯女士想要和你開個會。沒什麼要緊的事。	

阿德溫・尚恩	5:22
好，等我確定好行程之後再告訴你。	

149. 下列何者與尚恩先生有關？

　　A 他錯過了一場會議
　　B 他考慮轉調
　　C 他最近接管了工廠的經營
　　D 他不知道他什麼時候會回辦公室

150. 在 5:18 時，尚恩先生寫下：「這倒是真的。」是什麼意思？

　　A 他擔心工廠的狀況
　　B 他同意不在辦公室還蠻愉快的
　　C 他發現一個錯誤
　　D 他確信星期一會回來

151–152 電子郵件

收件者：派特・布萊克本
<pblackburn@fastweb.com>
寄件者：自然而然健康產品
<cs@gonatural.com>
日期：2 月 4 日，下午 3 點 34 分
主旨：產品訂購

感謝您選擇自然而然健康產品做為您維他命及礦物質的補充品。本公司所有的產品品質都經過仔細的品質檢驗，符合政府所有法規。此外，在二月期間，顧客消費滿 100 元將不需支付任何運費。

訂單編號：4330XM21
訂購日期：2 月 4 日，下午 3 點 31 分
寄件地址：威斯康辛州克林頓密西根大道 2709 號，派特・布萊克本收
明細：六瓶綠源綜合維他命
總價：180 元，以信用卡支付
　　　　（XXXX XXXX XXXX 8766）

本公司所有產品都有顧客百分百的滿意保證。若您有任何不滿，請撥打客戶服務中心電話 987-555-3427，訂單成立一週內皆可全額退費。

自然而然健康產品

151. 下列何者與布萊克本女士的訂單有關？

　　Ⓐ 已保遺失險
　　Ⓑ 缺貨中
　　Ⓒ 她先生下的訂單
　　Ⓓ 將不用支付運費

152. 布萊克本女士為什麼有可能在 2 月 11 日前打電話給客戶服務中心？

　　Ⓐ 為了修改訂單
　　Ⓑ 為了更改付款方式
　　Ⓒ 為了退款
　　Ⓓ 為了申請會員資格

153-154 文章

本週四，吉他手尼克‧史丹頓的新爵士專輯《午夜之月》將開始在店面販售。《午夜之月》是史丹頓先生這五年來的第一張專輯，已經獲得許多音樂評論家的讚賞。史丹頓先生將於 3 月 12 日本週六，在位於主街 4532 號的艾默生百貨公司舉辦簽名會。購買新專輯就能免費獲得親筆簽名。

153. 尼克‧史丹頓是誰？

　　Ⓐ 唱片製作人
　　Ⓑ 唱片藝人
　　Ⓒ 音樂評論家
　　Ⓓ 音樂經紀人

154. 根據文章內容，3 月 12 日會發生什麼事？

　　Ⓐ 將舉辦演唱會
　　Ⓑ 新書發表
　　Ⓒ 將舉辦簽名會
　　Ⓓ 將販售部分門票

155-158 備忘錄

備忘錄

收件者：全體員工
寄件者：總經理貝蒂‧富蘭克林
日期：8 月 19 日

主旨：接待員

致全體員工：

我們工作室的接待員葛瑞塔‧瓊斯將請假一段時間去處理私事，請假時間是從 8 月 21 日至 9 月 5 日。在這段期間，我們聘請了一位臨時代理人，朱蒂絲‧布蘭琪。布蘭琪女士將處理瓊斯女士的平常業務，包括接聽電話、處理預約、安排時間及接待顧客。請歡迎布蘭琪女士的加入工作室，當她有任何問題時，也請協助她。

此外，若各位有提供優惠及折扣給長期客戶，也請提早告訴布蘭琪女士，否則她將依照電腦系統裡設定的價格收費。

若有需要和瓊斯女士討論的緊急狀況，或需要購買特殊染髮劑、調理洗髮精及客戶要的其他品項，請在今天與明天瓊斯女士離開前處理完畢。如果還有其他問題，隨時都可以和我聯絡。

155. 備忘錄裡的接待員最有可能在哪裡工作？

　　Ⓐ 百貨公司
　　Ⓑ 美髮沙龍
　　Ⓒ 水療按摩沙龍
　　Ⓓ 造型工作室

156. 下列何者與葛瑞塔‧瓊斯有關？

　　Ⓐ 她要退休了
　　Ⓑ 她要去度假
　　Ⓒ 她要請假一段時間
　　Ⓓ 她是臨時工

157. 員工應該在什麼時候和瓊斯女士聯絡緊急業務？

　　Ⓐ 在她離開前
　　Ⓑ 在她離開後
　　Ⓒ 隨時
　　Ⓓ 等她回來後

158. 下列句子最適合出現在 [1]、[2]、[3]、[4] 的哪個位置？「在這段期間，我們聘請了一位臨時代理人，朱蒂絲·布蘭琪。」

Ⓐ [1]
Ⓑ [2]
Ⓒ [3]
Ⓓ [4]

159–161 網頁

閃亮鞋店
您運動鞋的最佳首選

我們看到您目前在本公司網站登記為基本會員。

<u>請點選這裡升級為優質會員。</u>

一旦成為優質會員，您將享有以下福利：

■ 快遞只要 3 元（基本會員為 5 元）
■ 購買 60 天以內可免費更換所有商品（基本會員為 30 天）
■ 購買 30 天內可免費退還所有商品（基本會員為 7 天）

只需要點擊一下就能享有從基本會員升級至優質會員的服務。為了歡迎顧客到我們新的網路商店，本月提供優惠價，只要 50 元就能升級成一年期的優質會員。

159. 這個網頁的目的是什麼？

Ⓐ 宣傳新系列鞋款
Ⓑ 確認訂單
Ⓒ 推薦服務升級
Ⓓ 募集捐款

160. 下列何者不是優質會員的福利？

Ⓐ 新產品折扣
Ⓑ 減價快遞費
Ⓒ 免費退貨期限較長
Ⓓ 免費換貨期限較長

161. 下列何者與閃亮鞋店有關？

Ⓐ 已經在業界好幾十年了
Ⓑ 由當地的企業家所創立
Ⓒ 可在網路上購買商品
Ⓓ 有三種會員模式

162–165 網路聊天室

麗莎·漢考克	9:39

我在上班途中會去咖啡店一下。大家想喝什麼？我請客。

尼克·莫頓 9:39

哇，謝謝妳！我只要黑咖啡就好。

莉莉·史密斯 9:40

謝謝。我要拿鐵。你可以順便拿一些糖嗎？

麗莎·漢考克 9:41

好。我會拿幾個糖包。

理查·帕克 9:42

我永遠沒辦法向咖啡說不。我也要拿鐵加糖。

愛蜜莉·喬丹 9:42

如果有的話，我想要花草茶。我不喝含咖啡因的飲料，所以任何沒有咖啡因的茶類都可以。謝謝。

麗莎·漢考克 9:43

好，20 分鐘後我會帶著你們的飲料到。等會見。喔，在我忘記之前，請確認我們從欣蒂精品店訂購的物品，已經在展示間準備給客戶看了。

理查·帕克 9:44

箱子早上送到了，實習生正在把東西從箱子裡拿出來。但是從仙黛爾訂的東西似乎不見了。

麗莎·漢考克 9:45

什麼意思？

尼克·莫頓 9:45

我們正努力確定包裹的下落。我們聯絡過仙黛爾，他們把東西送錯地址了。

麗莎·漢考克 9:46

真是太糟糕了，請盡量查出那些洋裝到哪去了。

理查‧帕克　　　　　　　　　9:47
好消息。我剛從貨運公司接到消息,他們找到仙黛爾的貨了,正重新送過來。

麗莎‧漢考克　　　　　　　　9:48
我差點恐慌症發作。什麼時候會送到?

理查‧帕克　　　　　　　　　9:48
今天下午。

162. 說話者們可能在哪種公司上班?

   A 時裝公司

   B 服飾店

   C 戲服公司

   D 咖啡廳

163. 在9:39分,麗莎‧漢考克寫下:「我請客」是什麼意思?

   A 她會帶咖啡來

   B 她會買飲料

   C 她會記得每個人訂的東西

   D 輪到她去買飲料了

164. 下列何者與他們其中一件配送的貨物有關?

   A 定價錯誤

   B 被送回精品店

   C 當天晚點會到

   D 還沒找到貨物

165. 仙黛爾是何種公司?

   A 布料公司

   B 雜誌公司

   C 宅配公司

   D 精品店

166–168 電子郵件

收件者:全體人員
<csall@cherishedgoods.com>
寄件者:艾瑞克‧尼克森
<enix@cherishedgoods.com>
日期:1月5日,上午10點
主旨:寄送錯誤

大家好:

配送部門主管莉莉亞‧肯特告訴我,昨天公司的客戶資料庫發生了系統錯誤,導致許多訂單送錯地址。今天早上我們部門已經接到了許多顧客的抱怨電話,說他們收到錯的包裹。肯特女士的部門已經很努力地在確認錯誤源頭,因此,任何來電說運送錯誤的顧客,都要請他們退回包裹。除此之外,請告知顧客,他們下次購物時可享有九折的優惠。

艾瑞克‧尼克森

166. 誰最有可能收到這封電子郵件?

   A 配送部門員工

   B 不滿的顧客

   C 客戶服務代表人員

   D 網路技術專員

167. 根據這封電子郵件,肯特女士的員工正在努力做什麼?

   A 建立客戶資料庫

   B 修理系統故障

   C 尋找一個遺失的包裹

   D 接聽客戶電話

168. 電子郵件的收件者被告知要做什麼?

   A 更新個人資料

   B 親自運送包裹

   C 將資料輸入客戶資料庫中

   D 提供減價優惠給某些客戶

169–171 電子郵件

收件者：carlhurst@nicknet.com
寄件者：m_winters@tatecc.com
日期：6 月 1 日，下午 1 點 34 分
主旨：社區活動

親愛的赫斯特先生：

作為泰特社區活動中心家庭會員的忠實顧客，您以持續性捐款的方式資助我們。我們真的很感謝您的支持。

下列表格提供了本月即將舉辦的家庭活動資訊，我們歡迎您的參與。

手工日 6 月 7 日	保羅·辛普森 6 月 15 日	夏季野餐 6 月 22 日
提供孩子各種手工材料，讓他們可以創作個人獨特的作品。	來聆聽本地歌手暨詞曲創作者保羅·辛普森美妙的音樂。	每個人都要帶一道美味的餐點來與大家分享。將免費提供飲料。

對於會員而言，參加這些活動不需買票。我們鼓勵大家來參與這些活動，與家人共享優質時光。

期待見到您。

泰特社區活動中心活動籌劃者
米妮·華特斯

169. 下列何者與赫斯特先生有關？
- Ⓐ 他是當地音樂家
- Ⓑ 他捐款給孤兒院
- **Ⓒ 他支持公共組織**
- Ⓓ 他在社區活動中心工作

170. 寄這封電子郵件的目的是什麼？
- Ⓐ 宣布社區理事會會議
- Ⓑ 申請家庭會員資格
- **Ⓒ 宣傳將舉辦的活動**
- Ⓓ 提供當地選舉資訊

171. 下列何者與泰特社區活動中心有關？
- **Ⓐ 會員可以免費參加活動**
- Ⓑ 提供定期的音樂課程
- Ⓒ 接受電話預約
- Ⓓ 所有活動都將提供飲料

172–175 信件

J&P 企業
10288 紐約州卡麥隆史雲頓街 1462 號

3 月 29 日
格蘭特·李先生
18729 紐約州卡麥隆銀原路 287 號

親愛的李先生：

感謝您在 J&P 企業多年來的服務與工作上的貢獻。我們正將公司健康保險福利近來的異動資訊寄給全體員工。您的保險將由同一間保險公司承保，但是由於新實施的州立規定，現在全體員工都必須在當地的診所或醫院接受基本健康檢查。檢查費用將由健康保險支付，所以您不需支付任何額外費用，而且絕不影響每個月的保費扣減。信封內含供員工參考的新醫療計劃詳細資訊。

健康檢查必須包括血液檢查、尿液檢查、眼睛檢查、身高與體重測量、聽力檢查、以及胸部 X 光檢查，不需 30 分鐘即可檢查完畢，請至當地診所預約。請最晚在 12 月 30 日以前將檢查結果交給人力資源部的凱倫·李，如果沒有做健康檢查，將被處以高達 2,000 元的罰鍰。感謝您的配合且希望您能遵守這個新的異動。

若有任何問題或疑慮，請洽凱倫 leighk@jpindustries.com。

J&P 企業 執行經理
約翰·布雷克 敬上

172. 這封信的目的是什麼？
- **Ⓐ 通知員工一項強制性的檢查**
- Ⓑ 鼓勵員工去醫院捐血
- Ⓒ 討論員工健康保險給付範圍的異動
- Ⓓ 宣傳新診所的服務項目

173. 布雷克先生隨信寄了什麼？

    Ⓐ 申請表

    Ⓑ 保險資料

    Ⓒ 合約

    Ⓓ 有關異動的更多資料

174. 在第二段結尾的「subject to」與下列哪個字意思最接近？

    Ⓐ 取決於

    Ⓑ 對……負責

    Ⓒ 退出

    Ⓓ 增加

175. 下列句子最適合出現在 [1]、[2]、[3]、[4] 的哪個位置？「不需 30 分鐘即可檢查完畢。」

    Ⓐ [1]

    Ⓑ [2]

    Ⓒ [3]

    Ⓓ [4]

176–180 廣告和電子郵件

花兒朵朵開瑜伽工作室

夏季瑜伽課程

今年夏天，我們將為各年齡層與程度的人開設各式瑜伽課程。

夏季課程時間表及價格（註冊費）：

· 初級班，每週兩次，共兩個月（150 元）

· 中級班及進階班，每週兩次，共兩個月（200 元）

· 銀髮族瑜伽，每週一次，共兩個月（100 元）

· 熱力瑜伽，每週三次，共兩個月（250 元）

花兒朵朵開瑜伽工作室將提供所有必需器材。

會員須穿著可活動自如的舒適服裝。

46202 印地安納州印地安納波里克拉克街 45 號

715-555-5832

www.bloomingfloweryoga.com

收件者：潭美‧格倫 <tammyglenn@mxmail.com>

寄件者：德威恩‧摩爾 <dwaynemoore@bloomingfloweryoga.com>

日期：5 月 23 日

主旨：新學員

附件：新會員表

親愛的格倫女士：

我寫信是為了通知您，您班上多了一位報名課程的學員。新學員是珍‧梅爾斯，她星期一上第一堂課時會帶 100 元的註冊費來。

另外，星期一時請給梅爾斯小姐和其他新學員需要填寫的表格。我已在這封電子郵件中附上所需文件，您只要印出紙本交給她們即可。

目前您的課程有九位學員報名，所以幾乎額滿。實際上，今年夏季的所有課程都證明相當受歡迎，我預估在月底時將全部額滿。感謝您多年來在花兒朵朵開瑜伽工作室辛勤的教學。若您有任何問題，請告訴我。

德威恩‧摩爾

176. 下列何者與夏季課程有關？

    Ⓐ 上禮拜開始上課

    Ⓑ 將在戶外上課

    Ⓒ 小孩大人都可以上

    Ⓓ 課程費用有折扣

177. 下列何者與梅爾斯女士有關？

    Ⓐ 她從沒學過瑜伽

    Ⓑ 她是位銀髮族

    Ⓒ 她想要成為瑜伽老師

    Ⓓ 她是位長期會員

178. 格倫女士被要求做什麼？

    Ⓐ 開發新課程

    Ⓑ 參加訓練

    Ⓒ 簽署工作合約

    Ⓓ 發送一些文件

179. 在電子郵件中，第三段第一行的「capacity」意思最接近？

Ⓐ 量

Ⓑ 能力

Ⓒ 空間

Ⓓ 角色

180. 下列何者與格倫女士有關？

Ⓐ 她和小孩相處得很好

Ⓑ **她是位長期員工**

Ⓒ 她即將退休

Ⓓ 她將被加薪

181–185 網站貼文

超級模型愛好社群論壇

黑鬍子海盜模型船有問題

　　　　　　8 月 3 日，上午 10 點 55 分

由約翰·泰勒發布

我最近從超級愛好網路商店買了一組模型。我買了黑鬍子海盜模型船和兒子一起組裝，但是碰到了一個問題。在仔細閱讀使用說明書後，我注意到一些必要的零件不在盒子裡。具體來說，組成桅桿和風帆的零件不在套組裡。幾年來，我已經在超級模型愛好買了許多組模型，也一直對收到的產品感到滿意。

還有其他人在這個套組上碰到一樣的問題嗎？我兒子和我打算在月底將完成的模型送去參加本地的模型組裝比賽，我們對這個狀況都感到很失望。如果有碰過這個問題並且已經解決的人提供建議，我會十分感激。

超級模型愛好社群論壇

回覆：黑鬍子海盜模型船有問題

　　　　　　8 月 3 日，下午 4 點 24 分

由凱瑟琳·麥斯威爾發布

嗨，約翰：

我最近也從超級愛好網路商店買了黑鬍子海盜模型船給我兒子，而且也碰上和你一樣的問題。起初我以為一定是我搞錯了，但在確認使用說明書上所有零件清單後，我確定套組裡幾個零件一定是在販售時就已經不見了。我把套組帶回去本地的超級愛好門市，店員證實了我的懷疑，超級愛好的員工很好心地換給我一組零件完整的套組。有了新套組，我兒子和我就能將模型組裝成和盒子上的圖片一模一樣。我建議你到離家最近的超級愛好門市，要求他們更換瑕疵品。記得去的時候，要寫下訂單號碼。

181. 第一則貼文的主旨是什麼？

Ⓐ **購買的產品有瑕疵**

Ⓑ 使用說明書的錯誤

Ⓒ 售價與廣告不符

Ⓓ 報名一項比賽

182. 下列何者與泰勒先生有關？

Ⓐ 他認識麥斯威爾女士這個人

Ⓑ 他是超級愛好的產品設計師

Ⓒ 他有一艘帆船

Ⓓ **他將和兒子一起參加比賽**

183. 泰勒先生和麥斯威爾女士如何得知套組有問題？

Ⓐ 透過和客服人員談話

Ⓑ 透過觀賞教學影片

Ⓒ **透過參考使用手冊**

Ⓓ 透過查看照片

184. 下列何者與麥斯威爾女士有關？

Ⓐ 她是超級愛好的常客

Ⓑ 她和泰勒先生都在超級愛好上班

Ⓒ **她成功地組裝模型套組**

Ⓓ 她收到全額退費

185. 麥斯威爾女士提供了什麼建議？

A 到附近的門市去
B 取消會員資格
C 下載新的使用手冊
D 購買替代零件

186–190 廣告、表格和會議公告

夢想空間床鋪商場

床鋪、寢具和家具

62751 伊利諾州春田市威爾夏路 3600 號

www.dreamspacebeds.com

別讓自己飽受翻來覆去之苦，不得一夜安眠。來一趟夢想空間床鋪商場，找一張完全符合需求的舒適床鋪來款待自己。歡迎顧客來試躺店裡的任何一張床。

一樓：床鋪（單人床、雙人床、加大床、超級加大床等）
二樓：寢具（床單、枕頭、毯子、靠墊等）
三樓：家具（椅子、沙發、桌子等）

因應顧客的建議，為了那些上班時間不固定的顧客，本商場現在延長營業兩小時。

需要快遞床鋪嗎？只要在結帳時詢問店員就能輕鬆安排妥當。

如果您對本商場有任何意見或建議，請利用大門內側的意見箱。

意見與建議表
夢想空間床鋪商場

顧客姓名：威利・M・金
日期：8 月 9 日
聯絡電話：456-555-6123

意見：上禮拜，我到你們的商場去買我床要用的新枕頭、床單和毛毯組。但是，當我走到那一區時，卻找不到任何員工可以幫我。我等了大概半個小時，也沒有人來。我需要幫忙確認哪種床單和毛毯組能符合我床的尺寸，但最後卻只能洩氣地離開。希望你們可以為顧客提供更好的服務，不讓類似的狀況再度發生。身為貴店多年的忠實顧客，若你們無法說明為什麼沒人可以協助我，我也許得開始光顧貴店競爭對手的商場。

大家好，本人召開這個會議，是想討論延長營業時間這個新政策所帶來的一些問題。首先，這似乎是個好構想，可以幫助全天候上班的顧客。我知道要朝九晚五地上班，很難找空檔處理家務及購物。但遺憾的是，延長營業時間也表示我們人手過於分身乏術，而我們只能等待日後聘用並訓練更多人力。

結果，我們最近忽略了一些顧客。剛傳給大家看的是威利・金所寫的意見與建議表影本，他比我更清楚地歸納出缺失。請看一下，然後想想有什麼方法讓我們在這樣大型的商場裡注意到有需求的顧客。我了解以我們微薄的人力卻得負責比以往更大的空間，所以這個會議並不是要處罰或責怪，而是要想出解決方法。請腦力激盪一下，如果有任何構想，請送到我辦公室來。我必須打電話給威利・金。

186. 下列何者與夢想空間床鋪商場的床無關？

A 有各種不同的尺寸
B 顧客可以試躺
C 陳列在一樓
D 提供終身保固

187. 根據廣告的內容，關於夢想空間床鋪商場，下列何者為真？

A 它位於百貨公司內
B 它銷售居家用品
C 它正在在聘用更多員工
D 它已延長營業時間

188. 金先生最有可能在哪裡找到想買的產品？

A 一樓
B 二樓
C 三樓
D 大門入口附近

189. 您認為會議中講話的人是誰？

A 夢想空間床鋪商場的主管
B 威利・金
C 其他城市的地區經理
D 結帳櫃台職員

190. 根據會議中的資訊，下列何者為真？

Ⓐ 夢想空間床鋪商場將把營業時間改回來。

Ⓑ 夢想空間床鋪商場將延長營業時間來服務更多像威利·金這類的顧客。

Ⓒ 夢想空間床鋪商場將聘用更多員工，才有足夠人力來負責整個商場。

Ⓓ 夢想空間床鋪商場將舉辦抽獎活動並邀請威利·金參加。

191–195 網頁、電子郵件和時間表

www.acestafftraining.com

首頁	與我們聯絡	門市據點	關於我們

王牌教育訓練是一間為商店或企業員工提供開發課程的公司。您可以倚賴我們成功專業人士所組成的團隊來改善員工素質，並幫助公司達成目標。我們提供有效並以結果為導向的課程。以下是現有的訓練課程：

領導力	**銷售**
這個課程幫助員工培養策略規劃與管理技能，同時也改善領導階層的員工管理技巧。	我們傳授創新策略來提高銷售量與市場佔有率。這個課程適合門市銷售員和電話行銷人員。
顧客服務	**科技**
絕對不要低估顧客滿意度的重要性。當直接面對顧客時，您的員工需要有幫助有效果的技能。	在變化快速的工作環境中，員工需要跟上科技領域的新潮流與發展。您的員工將學到如何快速且精準地搜尋並掌控新科技。

為員工報名課程，請洽約書亞·約克
josh@acestafftraining.com

寄件者：蒂芬妮·陳
<tifftran@zellengifts.com>
收件者：約書亞·約克
<josh@acestafftraining.com>
主旨：本公司員工訓練課程
日期：10 月 9 日

親愛的約克先生：

會與您聯絡是因本公司澤聯禮品想為一些員工開設訓練課程。我們打算下個月擴大電話行銷部門，但是我們訓練有素的員工人數不足以填補這些新職缺。因此，我們將從客服部門轉調部分員工到電話行銷部門，以解決這個問題。由於本公司的產品主要針對兒童，我們希望盡可能地能在今年的聖誕季增加獲利。請告訴我一次課程能容納的最多人數是多少。

感謝您。

澤聯禮品
蒂芬妮·陳

澤聯禮品的王牌教育訓練課程企劃
11 月 1 日至 5 日

小組代號與學員人數	星期一 行銷策略	星期二 成功談判	星期三 顧客第一！	星期四 完成交易	星期五 以禮開始，以禮相待
紅色小組 10 人	9–11	9–11:30	8–10:30	8–11	9–11
藍色小組 10 人	1–3	1–3	1–3	1–3	1–3
綠色小組 10 人	3–5	3–5	3–5	3–5	3–5
白色小組 10 人	5–7	5–7	5–7	5–7	5–7

這是我們的課程表企劃，能幫忙貴公司將客服員工轉換為成功的電話行銷人員。您可以看到，這課程雄心壯志地涵蓋大量的資料，但我有信心這是一場勝戰。我們試著在課程進行時，取得順利轉換與保持澤聯禮品公司持續營運這兩個需求之間的平衡。因此，

我們將貴公司員工分成小組，交錯安排在一整天的課程中。這對您的員工來說會有比較好的師生人數比，而且對貴公司業務造成的影響最小。我們很期待這優質教育訓練的一週！

王牌教育訓練籌劃員
約書亞‧約克

191. 約克先生在哪裡上班？
    A 會計事務所
    B 運動管理經紀公司
    C 技能發展機構
    D 廣告公司

192. 下列何者與課程中的科技內容有關？
    A 開放給社會大眾
    B 包括當前的網頁程式設計技巧
    C 教導環境保護
    D 讓員工跟上潮流

193. 陳女士最有可能對哪一個課程感興趣？
    A 領導力
    B 銷售
    C 客戶服務
    D 科技

194. 下列何者與訓練課程的提案及其後的備註有關？
    A 是個能完成的簡單課程
    B 將涵蓋五個重要的主題
    C 將有 50 名員工參與
    D 約書亞‧約克將是其中一名訓練師

195. 根據訓練課程的提案及其後的備註，我們可以推論出澤聯禮品公司的什麼？
    A 他們試著改善客戶關係
    B 他們希望在訓練期間能正常營運
    C 客服員工人數不多
    D 他們想要在十月底前完成訓練

196–200 網頁、電子郵件和時間表

中城藝術表演廳

藉著加入會員來支持位於布倫頓市區的中城藝術表演廳，您可以從以下的會員方案裡選擇：

普級 – 只要 100 元，即可獲得整年度的會員資格，可以觀賞任兩場座位在 D 區的藝術表演。

銀級 – 200 元的費用，您可以觀賞任兩場座位在 B 區的藝術表演。

金級 – 500 元的費用，您可以收到熱門表演的預先通知、任兩場座位在 B 區的藝術表演票，並保證在一年內選到任何表演的前排座位。

鑽石級 – 1,000 元的費用，可以獨家取得表演者的親筆簽名，受邀參加兩場熱門演出的獨家試映會，並保證在一年內選到任何表演的貴賓 VIP 座位。

■ 適用部分限制規定

■ 不含管弦樂表演門票

收件者：bates@midcityarthall.com
寄件者：愛利希亞‧諾頓
日期：1 月 16 日
主旨：會員

感謝您寄給我關於中城藝術表演廳的會員資訊，我已經繳交上 1,000 元的費用。去年我是普級會員，很喜歡幾場音樂劇。自從體驗過後，我就變成劇場狂熱者了，期待新的會員方案所帶來的福利。

順便一提，整修工程為表演廳增色不少。很期待今年回去看表演。

以下是未來幾個月中城藝術表演廳暫訂的節目表。請閱讀，如欲訂位，歡迎隨時來電洽詢。

《布倫頓愛樂管弦樂團》
1月28日至1月30日
《舞動的公主》
2月3日至2月23日
《舞吧爵士》
3月1日至3月26日
《歌劇之魂》
4月3日至4月29日

196. 愛利希雅‧諾頓最可能購買的是何種會員？
　Ⓐ 普級
　Ⓑ 銀級
　Ⓒ 金級
　Ⓓ 鑽石級

197. 下列何者與中城表演藝術廳有關？
　Ⓐ 它舉辦過各種運動競賽
　Ⓑ 建築物有些改變
　Ⓒ 它是個受到名人喜愛的地方
　Ⓓ 它是個老舊的博物館

198. 對會員來說，何時的表演不是免費的？
　Ⓐ 一月
　Ⓑ 二月
　Ⓒ 三月
　Ⓓ 四月

199. 下列何者與時間表有關？
　Ⓐ 表演門票都已銷售一空
　Ⓑ 會增加更多的演出
　Ⓒ 時間表是固定
　Ⓓ 有可能會更改

200. 文中「適用部分限制規定」是什麼意思？
　Ⓐ 只有特定人士才能成為會員
　Ⓑ 會員方案可能在未告知狀況下異動
　Ⓒ 不是所有的演出都開放給會員
　Ⓓ 非會員者不可入場

ACTUAL TEST ⑧

◎ Part 5 解答請見 P.457

101. 我們的講者將為房地產投資人說明一個**令人振奮的**良機。

102. 這個手提包所使用的部分皮革必須是自義大利**進口**的。

103. 洛克威爾銀行的自動櫃員機**便利地**設置於這個城市的不同區域。

104. 待雙方達成**一致的**協議，就立即簽訂這個授權合約。

105. 任何無法在 9 月 1 日之前**參加**安全訓練研習的人必須告知主管。

106. 使用飯店水療中心與用餐服務的**費用**，將列在最終發票上。

107. 保全小組的成員已被囑咐要將**任何**無人看管的包包呈報當地警局。

108. 主廚每天晚上都請餐廳經理**批准**食材的訂單。

109. 這家汽車公司**積極地**追求能夠改善引擎效能的科技。

110. 在繪畫課程的第一天，學生們應該把**報名**證明給老師看。

111. 這間公寓的家具並不是**我們的**而是房東的，必須在租約到期時歸還。

112. 德懷特先生**的**司機預計在結束前 20 分鐘抵達會議地點。

113. **合作**研發新材料的三位新進的化學家，將於週六的典禮上接受執行長的表揚。

114. 這個計劃的目的是要讓住在鄉間與都市**地區**的人，都馬上能得到醫療服務。

115. 請將金額 550 英鎊的支票**及**需要本公司檢核的文件**一併**寄上。

116. 在這國家的實驗室，指紋辨認系統普遍**被接受**當作保全措施的主要方法。

117. 住在遠離市中心的地方將**減少**租屋開銷，但卻會影響你通勤。

118. 煎友的廚具可以直接從該公司的網站購得，也可以在您**附近的**零售點購買。

119. 每週的設備**檢查**有助於確保及早發現及處理細微的維修問題。

120. 病人如果察覺到**突然的**體溫變化，應立即撥打緊急專線。

121. 參加歷史導覽半日遊的人，必須**最晚在**早上 7:45 **前**必須到集合地點。

122. 由於他的**重大**成就，主管允許馬丁先生多休三天假。

123. 史蒂文斯女士**懊悔地**承認她無法在特定的期間內完成這個任務。

124. 這個客人的牛排煎的火侯**有些**不足，所以要求將餐點送回廚房。

125. 這個問卷調查所提供的聯絡資料僅供公司內部使用，不會**透露**給第三方。

126. 只要有一套工具，布蘭諾先生就可以**自己**組裝攤位的隔板。

127. 史蒂文森女士聯絡了**那個**名字和電話出現在廣告上的房地產仲介。

128. 當正式文件被登錄在郡辦公室時，房屋的出售就已**定案**。

129. 工作坊中進行的主要活動需要團隊成員相互**合作**。

130. 根據內科醫師表示，奧利佛女士的疼痛**將**在吃完藥的兩個小時內**緩解**。

131–134 廣告

國際商品展

如果您想把自己的包裝商品推廣到國際，就來參加第八屆年度國際商品展吧。這個商展將從 3 月 5 日到 3 月 7 日，在紐約市中心的銀河會議中心舉行。來自世界各地兩百多家公司代表參展，在您推銷自家產品給有興趣的顧客和商家之時，您也可以建立商業網絡。產品以包裝商品為主，範圍從甜點、零食到罐頭肉品與肉乾。快趁所有攤位被登記一空前申請，攤位有限，而且很快就沒了。

131. Ⓐ 推銷
Ⓑ 正在推銷
Ⓒ 欲推銷
Ⓓ 已推銷

132. **Ⓐ 代理**
Ⓑ 表達
Ⓒ 遞送
Ⓓ 顯露

133. Ⓐ 到
Ⓑ 為了
Ⓒ 從
Ⓓ 和……一起

134. Ⓐ 會場禁止冰淇淋。
Ⓑ 您可以在參觀時試吃商品。
Ⓒ 您有機會推廣食品。
Ⓓ 快趁所有攤位被登記一空前申請。

135–138 告示

寄件者：副總裁喬登・史密斯
收件者：K 集團員工
主旨：公司整修
日期：2 月 26 日

致全體同仁：

本週末我們二樓辦公室的整修工程即將開工，我們要求各位將所有重要文件帶回家，並且把桌上零散的資料歸檔。所有的電子產品都要關閉，並將插頭拔掉。此外，所有的櫃子與抽屜也要上鎖。

這個整修工程大約需要五天的時間。在這段期間，各位的臨時辦公處就在一樓的會議室。由於噪音干擾，如果您預定下週與客戶會面，請安排至公司以外的其他地點。我們為所有的不便深感抱歉，但也懇請各位配合。感謝大家。

135. Ⓐ 已經開始
Ⓑ 即將開始
Ⓒ 開始
Ⓓ 開始

136. **Ⓐ 此外**
Ⓑ 因此
Ⓒ 因為
Ⓓ 因此

137. Ⓐ 如果需要更多空間，我們會通知大家。
Ⓑ 所有的業務都將暫停，直到整修完成。
Ⓒ 在這段期間，各位的臨時辦公處就在一樓的會議室。
Ⓓ 整修後，各位的辦公場所會看起來嶄新且變得更好。

138. Ⓐ 服務
Ⓑ 聯合
Ⓒ 連結
Ⓓ 合作

律師職缺

強生暨慈愛公共有限公司目前有一個合同律師的職缺。理想的應徵者需具備至少三年處理複雜商業交易的經驗,有公家單位服務經驗者尤佳。我們在強生暨慈愛公司處理的合約型態,僅限於私人企業與政府之間的業務關係。如果您認為自己合乎加入本團隊的資格,請寄電子郵件給本公司人資部經理 JK@law.com。

139. **A** 工作
  B 工作
  C 工作
  D 工作

140. **A** 有公家單位服務經驗者尤佳。
  B 和孩子互動可以替你的履歷增色。
  C 必須具備應付動物的經驗。
  D 有與身障人士共事過的經驗會加分。

141. **A** 執行
  B 達成
  C 允許
  D 改變

142. **A** 您
  B 我
  C 我們
  D 他們

收件者:bobsaget@BobsJobs.com
寄件者:HarrisonG@gmail.com
日期:9 月 20 日
主旨:業務企劃

親愛的薩格先生:

我叫哈里遜・谷巴蒂。我寫這封信是要回應您刊登在《泰晤士報》上新人事經理一職的廣告。我有五年在步調快速企業環境中工作的經驗。我知道貴公司僱用了 300 多名員工,其中有許多是講西班牙文的,我有取得西班牙文口語的五級證照,已隨信附上履歷表,如果您有需求,我也很樂意提供推薦函。感謝您撥冗閱讀。

哈里遜・谷巴蒂 敬上

143. A 發訊息
  B 寫
  C 寫
  D 看

144. **A** 經驗
  B 知識
  C 工作
  D 實習

145. **A** 我有取得西班牙文口語的五級證照。
  B 西班牙人有時很難合作。
  C 我不懂任何西班牙文,但我可以學。
  D 講西班牙文的人都是好員工。

146. A 在……之內
  B 為了給
  C 為了
  D 將會

147–148 資訊

新款的聖桑尼克曲面電視現正以驚人的超低價 1,999 元出售。用 55 吋超高畫質的螢幕享受您最喜歡的電視節目、電影和比賽吧！最棒的是，您不必費力搞懂複雜的操作手冊。只要把電視機帶回家並安裝好，不需任何惱人的調整就可以立即依照您的喜好播放節目。

147. 這則資訊最可能在哪裡出現？

- A 操作手冊
- B 商品收據
- **C 宣傳單**
- D 信件

148. 文中提到產品有什麼便利之處？

- **A 簡單的設置程序**
- B 長期保固
- C 與其他器材的相容性
- D 詳細的操作說明

149–150 訊息串

湯姆·阿諾	11:55
你今天會回辦公室嗎？	

理查·休伊特	12:08
會。我剛向安德森和萊特做完有關河濱餐廳的提案報告。	

湯姆·阿諾	12:13
很好。進行得如何？	

理查·休伊特	12:13
我想他們可能有意願。	

湯姆·阿諾	12:13
好。有他們加入這個計劃就太棒了。	

理查·休伊特	12:14
沒錯！	

湯姆·阿諾	12:35
你可以和哈羅德跟我在一點時去釜室吃午餐嗎？	

理查·休伊特	12:35
沒問題。我請計程車掉頭，跟你們在那裡碰面。	

湯姆·阿諾	12:39
好。待會見。	

149. 下列何者與休伊特先生有關？

- A 他的午餐約遲到了
- B 他接受了一個新職位
- **C 他在計程車上**
- D 他正在去做簡報的路上

150. 在 12:14 時，休伊特先生寫下：「沒錯」是什麼意思？

- A 他想知道他們在哪裡吃午餐
- B 他期待和安德森與萊特會面
- C 他正在回辦公室的路上
- **D 他也希望安德森與萊特能加入計劃**

151–152 文章

紐約書展開幕會的熱門話題，全圍繞在詩人轉小說家哈利·S·泰伯的新書上。書迷殷切期盼的《秋之夜鶯》，是他最暢銷的小說處女作《春之燕》的續集。這本書跟著莎莉·哈奈特一起展開奇幻的「地伏世界」之旅，並結合了尖銳機智的社論，及些許魔幻與神秘。十年多前，泰伯以備受好評的詩集《哈蒙王的城堡》嶄露頭角，而這本最新的小說也被預期將登上週暢銷排行榜。本週稍晚，本書首刷將成為紐約書展抽獎的獎品，下個月即將於各大書店正式發行。

151. 泰伯先生最新的作品將如何被歸類？

- A 浪漫愛情
- B 歷史小說
- **C 奇幻小說**
- D 詩集

152. 本週在哪裡可看到書？

- A 各大書店
- B 網站
- **C 文學活動**
- D 選定的公立圖書館

收件者：所有訂戶
寄件者：客服部
<customersupport@stylefashionmz.com>
日期：6 月 5 日
主旨：新版

親愛的忠實訂戶：

《風格與時尚雜誌》很開心地宣布，本月刊的新數位版本即將於今年夏季發行。雖然紙本與數位版幾近相同，但數位版將包含了一些紙本未刊登的長篇文章及圖片。

本雜誌目前的紙本訂戶將自動收到一組代碼，可直接獲得數位版本。您的代碼將附於下個月寄達的雜誌中。

153. 這封電子郵件的目的是什麼？

🄰 提供訂閱優惠價
🄱 宣傳新開的網路購物商場
🄲 介紹數位出版品
🄳 提醒訂戶續訂

154. 訂戶可以在七月號的紙本雜誌中找到什麼？

🄰 優惠折價券
🄱 特刊
🄲 獨家專訪
🄳 代碼

155–158 文章

節日公車增班

11 月 28 日——雖然對很多人而言，節慶季代表了一整週的美好長假，但公車司機將在整個假期裡延長工作時間，以因應每年這個時節湧入市區的大批遊客，以及忙著在最後一刻採買禮物的購物者。市府已經宣布接下來幾週的新公車時刻表，其中包括將全天候營運的部分公車路線。雖然大部分的公車將行駛至凌晨一點收班，市中心的部分地區將有公車運行，整夜不收

班，賓漢購物區的公車將延駛至凌晨三點收班。「這是我們有最多遊客與外地人到訪的時節，」市長比爾·奈特說，「我們認為在這段時間中提供必要的服務是很重要的。」

當公車司機工會會長納森·雷納被問到對新時刻表的看法時，他回道，「我們已經制定出雙方都同意的薪資，也有足夠的司機可以排班，所以不會有過度工作或過勞的危險。我們很多人還是有例假，可以和家人共度佳節。」整體而言，隨著聖誕節的接近，這個城市似乎已經準備好迎接遊客與節慶購物入潮了。

155. 這篇文章的目的是什麼？

🄰 報導公共交通運輸的異動
🄱 描述節日中的城市狀況
🄲 告知大眾交通延遲
🄳 為新的購物中心打廣告

156. 下列何者與雷納先生有關？

🄰 他對市長很滿意
🄱 他可能會發動抗議
🄲 他對工作條件感到滿意
🄳 他想要在節日中休假

157. 文中提到這個城市在節慶季中是怎樣的？

🄰 在節日期間關閉
🄱 很多遊客自外地來
🄲 更多計程車司機業績下滑
🄳 市民要到其他城市去旅行

158. 下列句子最適合出現在 [1]、[2]、[3]、[4] 的哪個位置？「整體而言，隨著聖誕節的接近，這個城市似乎已經準備好迎接遊客與節慶購物的人潮了。」

🄰 [1]
🄱 [2]
🄲 [3]
🄳 [4]

159–161 時間表

19 台節目時間表

三月三日

上午 6:00 – 上午 7:00
《阿拉斯加的生活》

關注住在阿拉斯加偏遠凍原的漁夫肯·拉斯金的生活。

上午 7:00 – 上午 9:00
《非洲奇景》

了解非洲大草原上的各類動植物。

上午 9:00 – 上午 10:30
《恐龍解剖學》

在這一集中，古生物學家凱瑞·彼得森博士將告訴您有關暴龍的一切。

上午 10:30 – 上午 11:00
《洛基》

主持人丹·里德將說明如何在加拿大戶外寒冬的極端條件下生存。

上午 11:00 – 下午 1:00
《自然現象》

主持人茱莉亞·富朗研究了發生在地球上最神秘的自然現象。

下午 1:00– 下午 2:00
《湛藍海洋》

與我們一起遨遊澳洲海域吧，與潛水員派特·羅素一起探索海豚、鯊魚、海豹，還有許多生物。

---

159. 這個頻道的重點是什麼？

- A 植物
- B 運動
- **C 大自然**
- D 生活

160. 根據這個時間表，哪一位是科學家？

- A 派特·羅素
- B 丹·里德
- **C 凱瑞·彼得森**
- D 肯·拉斯金

161. 哪個節目將教導觀眾求生技巧？

- A 《恐龍解剖學》
- B 《非洲奇景》
- C 《湛藍海洋》
- **D 《洛基》**

162–165 網路討論區

J&R 國際小組討論區

桑妮·李	[5:37]	有人不能參加週五的辦公室派對嗎？
凱文·金	[5:38]	我第一個小時可以參加，但我得提早離席去參加家庭聚會。
派翠克·史東	[5:39]	我隔天要到香港出差，所以我今年就免了。
桑妮·李	[5:42]	那還有其他人嗎？我只是要確定我們有足夠的點心。伊娃，你聯絡外燴公司了嗎？
伊娃·山德森	[5:43]	我打電話給好幾家，但只有四葉外燴提供素食。
桑妮·李	[5:44]	那我們就試試那家吧，我想我們有些人是吃素的。
荷莉·強生	[5:45]	我通常不太表明自己對食物的偏好，不過這次我希望有素食的選擇。
伊娃·山德森	[5:46]	我同意，我想這應該會讓這一切變得更有意思。我自己也想嘗試吃素，這對我來說會是個很好的開始。
荷莉·強生	[5:47]	嗯，這並不容易，不過我會到場支持你。
伊娃·山德森	[5:47]	謝啦，那我就跟外燴業者訂餐了。
安傑羅·史密斯	[5:48]	但要確保有肉食給我們這些無肉不歡的人喔。

伊娃・山德森	[5:49]	沒問題。我已經把暫定的菜單以電子郵件寄給大家了，大多數的人好像還蠻喜歡的。
桑妮・李	[5:50]	別忘了寄電子郵件通知外燴業者，他們進入大樓時需要通過安全檢查。
伊娃・山德森	[5:51]	我現在就去處理。

162. 這段討論主要是關於什麼？

- [A] 那些無法參加派對的人
- [B] 最佳外燴業者
- [C] 成為素食者
- **[D] 為派對訂餐**

163. 在 5:39 分時，派翠克・史東寫下：「我今年就免了」是什麼意思？

- [A] 他會到場一下
- **[B] 他這次婉拒參加**
- [C] 他會遲到
- [D] 他想要免費通行證

164. 文中提到什麼和四葉外燴有關？

- **[A] 它提供素食**
- [B] 它只有素食
- [C] 它曾為辦公室派對提供過外燴
- [D] 它擅長處理特殊訂單

165. 伊娃・山德森接下來最有可能會做什麼？

- [A] 處理菜單
- **[B] 聯絡外燴業者**
- [C] 確認會議
- [D] 訂午餐

166–168 合約

點石成金網路服務供應商
契約摘要

日期：3 月 22 日
顧客：譚雅・蘇利文小姐
地址：54055 懷俄明州帕森市橡樹街 345 號
購買日期：3 月 13 日

購買服務：

項目	價格
點石成金網路多媒體套組	40.00 元／月

- 下載速度 100MB
- 32 個免費電影頻道
- 每月五部最新電影的串流服務

防毒軟體	5.00 元／月
數據機與路由器租借服務	3.00 元／月
小計	48.00 元／月
稅	3.45 元／月
總計	51.45 元／月

只要撥打 341-555-6487，我們的技術人員就會到府處理任何經由數據機與路由器連接上網的問題。

166. 蘇利文女士在 3 月 13 日做了什麼？

- [A] 她購買居家保全系統
- [B] 她退還商品
- **[C] 她簽訂網路服務合約**
- [D] 她預約服務

167. 下列何者與蘇利文女士有關？

- [A] 她教授電腦技能課程
- [B] 她在安裝部分軟體上碰到麻煩
- **[C] 她將可以看電影**
- [D] 她最近剛搬家

168. 下列何者與點石成金網路服務供應商有關？

- **[A] 它會派人員進行安裝工作**
- [B] 它販售電腦配件
- [C] 它的總部就在帕森市
- [D] 它提供了網站架設服務

169–171 文章

4月2日——馬里安市中心頗具歷史意義的馬里安會堂即將於下週五展開修復工程。在它的全盛時期，馬里安會堂是市中心頗受居民歡迎的場所，他們在那裡跳舞、欣賞現場音樂跟看電影。但是，自從四年前亨森街上的複合式大樓完工後，它就逐漸失去人氣了。

在馬里安會堂完成所有必要的整修工程後，市府官員將開始邀請不同的表演者（包括知名劇團、音樂家、喜劇演員和演講者）前來新整修的劇院。「我們希望馬里安會堂能夠成為馬里安市的新文化中心。」馬里安市長格雷葛・菲爾斯說。

重振馬里安會堂是改善馬里安市公共設施大型計劃中的一部分。4月29日那天，以棒球場和數個遊樂場為特色的馬里安兒童樂園，預定將重新盛大開放。

169. 何者與馬里安市有關？

　A 即將修復一棟舊建築
　B 已關閉一座公園好進行修復
　C 正在規劃音樂節
　D 人口正在下降

170. 馬里安會堂的用途是什麼？

　A 作為兒童遊樂中心
　B 舉辦市議會會議
　C 提供公共教育課程
　D 舉辦文化活動

171. 四月將發生什麼事？

　A 知名的演說家將發表演說
　B 要選新市長
　C 一些改善後的公共設施將開放使用
　D 將上演一齣新戲

172–175 企業會報中的文章

我相信你已經知道，我們必須在本週決定是否繼續和 CC 貨運公司合作。正如我們在昨天的會議上所了解的，他們將為上週所發生的事故被起訴。我們都同意整個公司不應該為幾個粗心的員工所犯的過錯負責，但是這個想法是出現在我們討論過這個決定的後果之前。不幸地是，現在情況惡化了，而且也出現許多負面報導。沒錯，我們已經跟他們合作很久了，他們之中有許多人確實也是我們的朋友。但是，我們必須保護自己的公司。我們無法承受任何可能影響銷售量的事情。

這四個月來，我們幾乎沒有犯錯的餘地，即便銷售量只掉了一點點，後果可能不堪設想。所以我建議，作為保護本公司不受任何負面反應傷害的方法，我們應該與 CC 貨運公司劃清界限。也許日後如果他們能夠恢復名聲，我們再和他們合作。我提議針對要不要和他們合作一事再投一次票。

172. 關於 CC 貨運公司，下列何者為真？

　A 他們其中一個合約剛被取消
　B 有人對他們提起法律行動
　C 他們的總裁退位了
　D 他們有兩部卡車發生意外

173. 下列何者與撰文者服務的公司有關？

　A 有財務危機
　B 最近才被創立
　C 將停止營業
　D 是一家貨運公司

174. 撰文者為什麼希望停止和 CC 貨運公司合作？

　A 保護他的公司免於財務損害
　B 減少接下來四個月的生產成本
　C 降低個別產品的價格
　D 避免未來法律糾紛

175. 下列句子最適合出現在 [1]、[2]、[3]、[4] 的哪個位置？「沒錯，我們已經跟他們合作很久了。」

A [1]

B [2]

C [3]

D [4]

176–180 文章和電子郵件

9 月 21 日——美味自製餐點的秘密到底是什麼？電視節目主持人暨連鎖餐廳老闆金柏莉‧李，似乎知道所有的秘密。她的節目已經開播兩年多，現在擁有一群來自全國各地的死忠追隨者。當她坐下來接受我們的專訪時，她表示新鮮蔬菜和在地農產品就是烹煮健康美味食物的關鍵。

李女士預計於月底出版她的第一本烹飪書。這本書的書名就叫《金柏莉‧李的家常菜》，書中提供了可以在 30 分鐘內完成的簡易食譜。到目前為止，預購數量已經超過 40,000 本。

李女士表示，書的末頁有一張可撕下的粉絲俱樂部會員申請表。填寫申請表並寄到指定地址的人，將收到一份月訊與粉絲俱樂部會員專屬的獨家食譜。粉絲俱樂部的會員也將收到「我的家常菜」網站的登入密碼。

收件者：金柏莉‧李
<kimberlylee@kimberlylee.com>
寄件者：蘇西‧桑德斯
<suziesanders@kimberlylee.com>
日期：10 月 12 日

主旨：最新狀況

親愛的李女士：

好消息！很開心地向您報告，您的書不僅熱賣，自從書出版後加入粉絲俱樂部的新會員人數也急遽增加。我相信報上的文章為您的書增加了相當的曝光率。

同時，我們也收到了許多新會員的回饋意見，表達希望下個月的會訊能刊出更多蛋糕、餅乾和糖果的食譜。我想，滿足他們這次的需求會是個好主意。

公關協調員
蘇西‧桑德斯 敬上

176. 這篇文章的主要目的是什麼？

A 宣傳即將出版的書

B 為專業廚師提供意見

C 為新餐廳打廣告

D 描述電視節目

177. 根據李女士所說，成功烹飪的秘密是什麼？

A 仿效食譜

B 使用優質的食材

C 調衡所有的味道

D 選擇正確的香料

178. 若要成為粉絲俱樂部會員必須怎麼做？

A 登入網站

B 撥打熱線電話

C 造訪李女士的餐廳

D 買書

179. 在電子郵件中，蘇西‧桑德斯說了什麼有關那篇文章的事？

A 那是由知名記者所寫的

B 它被刊登在一個熱門的烹飪網站上

C 它對增加粉絲俱樂部的會員有所助益

D 它節錄了李女士書中內容

180. 文中提到什麼與下個月會訊有關的事？

A 將會比預定時間晚寄

B 將有一個關於健康飲食習慣的專欄

C 將包含一篇有關甜點的文章

D 將附上一本李女士的書

181-185 電子郵件

寄件者：史黛西・沃金斯
<staceywatkins@titus.com>
收件者：安・羅斯
<annrose@putkincomp.com>
主旨：銀行主管會議
日期：2 月 12 日

親愛的羅斯女士：

您最近聯絡我們，提到今年想再次使用我們的會議中心來舉辦銀行主管年會。今年我們已經為會議室換新的投影機和更舒適的座椅。我們還將提供機場的接駁公車服務、高級餐廳自助餐，以及網咖讓來賓可以免費使用電腦或列印文件。為了您的方便，我們還提供實用的設備，像是掛紙白板、10 英尺的白板以及投影屏幕。

一旦您決定好日期，在我們確認能配合後，將請您先付 1,000 元的訂金，您來的時候再支付餘額。同時我們也要求身為活動籌辦人的您，在會議開始前一天到會議中心，以事先處理任何意外狀況。

感謝您再次與鐵達時會議中心合作，我們期盼提供您最好的服務。

史黛西・沃金斯主任

寄件者：安・羅斯
<annrose@putkincomp.com>
收件者：史黛西・沃金斯
<staceywatkins@titus.com>
主旨：回覆：銀行主管會議
日期：2 月 16 日

親愛的沃金斯女士：

我也很高興今年能再度與您合作。我們想預約 8 月 15 和 16 日這個週末的會議中心。訂金是由我們的財務部門負責處理，我會請本公司同仁盡快跟您聯絡。

同時，有件事想請您幫忙。去年因為餐廳沒有提供足夠的素食選擇，讓我們部分的與會者頗為失望。我希望今年可以提前處理這個問題。

感謝您。

銀行主管年會　籌辦人
安・羅斯

181. 下列何者與鐵達時會議中心有關？
- Ⓐ **最近改善了設備**
- Ⓑ 預約時需支付全額款項
- Ⓒ 位於國際機場旁
- Ⓓ 目前八月全滿

182. 下列何者不是使用鐵達時會議中心的優點？
- Ⓐ 便利的交通
- Ⓑ **筆記型電腦租借服務**
- Ⓒ 列印服務
- Ⓓ 簡報設備

183. 羅斯女士最有可能何時抵達鐵達時會議中心？
- Ⓐ 8 月 7 日
- Ⓑ **8 月 14 日**
- Ⓒ 8 月 15 日
- Ⓓ 8 月 16 日

184. 第二封電子郵件的目的是什麼？
- Ⓐ 為即將到來的研討會預約門票
- Ⓑ 請求協助付款
- Ⓒ **確認預約**
- Ⓓ 詢問付款方式

185. 羅斯女士提到什麼有關鐵達時會議中心的事？
- Ⓐ 她第一次在這裡辦活動
- Ⓑ 將於八月遷移
- Ⓒ 在全國有數個據點
- Ⓓ **去年無法讓一些賓客滿意**

收件者：約翰・馬斯特森
<jmasterson@masterstrokeindustries.com>
寄件者：卡爾・艾尼斯
<cennens@gmail.com>
日期：12 月 30 日
主旨：實習

親愛的馬斯特森先生：

我叫卡爾・艾尼斯，即將升上長春州立大學四年級。我在這裡主修工業工程學，而我的流體動力學教授艾可赫巴博士向我推薦神技企業，認為貴公司是個適合實習的單位。貴公司被公認為流體研究的翹楚，如果您願意在接下來的春季學期接受實習生，並能夠寫表現評估報告讓我交給艾可赫巴博士抵學分的話，我可以一週工作多達 15 個小時。感謝您給予考慮。如果您想要看成績單的話，我很樂意轉寄給您。

祝安好。

卡爾・艾尼斯

收件者：卡爾・艾尼斯
<cennens@gmail.com>
寄件者：約翰・馬斯特森
<jmasterson@masterstrokeindustries.com>
日期：12 月 31 日
主旨：回覆：實習

親愛的卡爾：

感謝你對本公司神技企業的實習工作感興趣。我們以往不太收實習生，不過我認識艾可赫巴博士本人，如果他推薦你跟我們聯絡，那他一定對你的能力非常有信心。我想我們應該在本公司位於市中心合利街的總部安排面試，我們可以邊喝咖啡邊認識彼此，我也會帶你看看我們公司。別擔心成績單的事，就像我說的，如果艾可赫巴博士認為你適合的話，我相信他的判斷。這週五早上十點方便嗎？

期待見到你。

神技企業執行長
約翰・馬斯特森

給神技企業全體員工的備忘錄

今年春季神技企業將有一位實習生協助我們處理大小事，包括從煮咖啡到解出複雜的方程式。卡爾・艾尼斯是本地州立大學的學生，他願意提供服務來交換我們的實務知識。請對他以禮相待，如果有需要，別怕請他幫忙提供見解或意見。而且我聽說他泡得一手好咖啡喔！

186. 下列何者與卡爾・艾尼斯有關？

- Ⓐ 他是高三生
- Ⓑ 他將成為大三生
- Ⓒ 他再兩年就畢業了
- **Ⓓ 他將成為大四生**

187. 下列何者與艾可赫巴博士有關？

- Ⓐ 沒人知道他是誰
- Ⓑ 人們不喜歡他的意見
- **Ⓒ 他受到約翰・馬斯特森的尊敬**
- Ⓓ 他已經做了很多重要的研究

188. 在第二封電子郵件中，第四行的「headquarters」意思最接近？

- Ⓐ 地下室
- **Ⓑ 總公司**
- Ⓒ 倉庫
- Ⓓ 物流中心

189. 根據備忘錄的內容，卡爾・艾尼斯被期待要做哪些事？

- Ⓐ 研究流體力學
- Ⓑ 烹飪
- **Ⓒ 有需要他幫忙的地方就幫忙**
- Ⓓ 觀察學習

190. 約翰・馬斯特森在公司擔任什麼職務？

- **Ⓐ 執行長**
- Ⓑ 財務長
- Ⓒ 業務主管
- Ⓓ 老闆

Brand-X 進駐

3月9日——頗具人氣的丹麥護膚公司 Brand-X 終於在美國推出他們最暢銷的系列產品。這家有 88 年歷史的公司是丹麥的護膚領導品牌，十多年來他們最熱賣的乳霜 Xtreme 7 一直是歐洲最受歡迎的面霜。儘管美國人以前可能沒機會接觸這些乳霜，但這個品牌已經引起相當熱潮。

皮膚科醫師法蘭西斯·基南解釋：「測試結果顯示，在只使用 Xtreme 7 30 天後，眼週的細紋和笑紋明顯地減少了，但乳霜的價格卻只是百貨公司品牌的一小部分。我當然推薦這款乳霜給我的客人。」

「產品都還沒到貨，大家就已經在詢問 Xtreme 7 了，」一位美容專櫃的櫃員蘇珊·陳說，「人們已經來電預購了。」

公司發言人解釋，Brand-X 正進軍北美與亞洲市場。目前只有公司最暢銷的系列產品會在歐洲以外的地方上市（自下個月起），但在一年後將可以買到更多商品。

Brand-X 在美國加州西敏市總部的職缺

不要錯過在刺激的護膚美容行業 Brand-X 的工作機會，有 80 個行政與客服職缺等著您，且不限經驗，應徵者需要有良好的溝通技巧，懂電腦操作。具英文與西班牙雙語能力尤佳，但非必要。若有化妝品、皮膚科或行銷經驗的應徵者，可有資格從事主管職。更多資訊，請參考本公司網站 www.brandx.com/jobs。申請表需於 3 月 20 日前送交。面試將於花園路 143 號的希爾威大樓舉行，請記得攜帶履歷與推薦函。

收件者：大衛·米爾斯教授
寄件者：賈桂琳·歐海爾
日期：3 月 28 日
主旨：工作

親愛的米爾斯教授：

非常感謝您幫我寫推薦信。我最近被 Brand-X 錄取，下週三上午 10 點就要開始新進員工訓練。但是很不巧地，那個時間我們剛好有統計學考試。是不是有方法可以讓我在其他時間補考，或是用交作業的方式來代替考試？新進員工訓練是強制參加的，而我不想讓新老闆失望。除此之外，這份工作應該不會對我的學校課業有任何影響。我衷心地感謝您能考慮這件事。

賈桂琳·歐海爾 敬上

191. 基南醫師提到了有關 Xtreme 7 的什麼事？

- (A) 它是市面上最有效的面霜
- (B) 它值得高價
- **(C) 它有效又便宜**
- (D) 它是醫生唯一會推薦的乳霜

192. 文中提到下列何者與 Brand-X 有關？

- **(A) 商品目前只能在歐洲買到**
- (B) 它是歐洲最受歡迎的品牌
- (C) 它是高檔護膚公司
- (D) 它十年前首次上市

193. 根據文章內容，Brand-X 打算做什麼？

- (A) 在歐洲販售更多商品
- **(B) 拓展到歐洲以外**
- (C) 開發彩妝系列商品
- (D) 在美國建廠

194. 下列何者與廣告有關？

- (A) 所有的職務都不需經驗
- (B) 應徵者必須是雙語人士
- **(C) 在特定領域有經驗的人可以得到管理職**
- (D) 可應徵的職務都是暫時性的

TEST 8 PART 7

195. 賈桂琳最有可能被錄取了什麼職務？

    Ⓐ 管理
    Ⓑ 人資
    Ⓒ 行銷
    Ⓓ 客服

196–200 電子郵件和時間表

收件者：比爾・強生 <bj@action.net>
寄件者：羅莉・惠勒
<lwheeler@zipnet.com>
日期：10 月 11 日
主旨：預約資訊

親愛的強生先生：

本人謹代表所服務的公司競爭優勢公司寫信給您。我們專為公司與小型企業進行生產力與效率訓練。最近，我們的員工士氣低落。在網路上搜尋解決辦法時，我看到了貴公司的網站 www.action.net。我很想多了解你們激勵人心的演講。特別是想請您告訴我，你們的演講是否屬於宗教性質？我們有各類員工，我需要的是非宗教性質的演講。請回信告訴我你們的服務內容概要以及演講費用。

競爭優勢常務董事
羅莉・惠勒

收件者：羅莉・惠勒
<lwheeler@zipnet.com>
寄件者：比爾・強生 <bj@action.net>
日期：10 月 13 日
主旨：回覆：預約資訊

親愛的惠勒女士：

非常感謝您對行動公司的興趣。我很樂意回答您的疑問，並為您、您的團隊以及貴公司提供一份完整的服務內容分析。首先，我們所有的演講雖然無法撇開心靈的概念，但卻是屬於非宗教性的內容。我們的專業講師試圖激勵人們觀看內在，找到自己的心性，並協助其提升。畢竟士氣實

屬無形，卻也是有效率的團隊不可或缺的部分。請參考我隨電子郵件附上的課程主題表以及價目表。一旦您選好主題、講者和適合貴公司的課程規模，請發後續電郵給我以便安排您的活動。

行動公司專員
比爾・強生

行動公司課程主題及價目表

主題	地點	演講者	人數	演講時間	價格
把握當下！	現場	吉姆・葛雷	15–20	三小時	450 元
每天都是全新的自己	非現場	達琳・伍德沃德	20–25	三小時	400 元
為團隊而積極！	非現場	傑夫・巴舍	15–30	三小時	400 元
我們都幸福	非現場	約翰・布朗	20–30	四小時	500 元

196. 羅莉・惠勒是怎麼知道行動公司的？

    Ⓐ 從朋友那
    Ⓑ 透過客戶
    Ⓒ 在報紙上
    Ⓓ 在網路上

197. 下列何者與行動公司有關？

    Ⓐ 他們不推廣宗教
    Ⓑ 他們是基督徒
    Ⓒ 他們正在建立自己的品牌
    Ⓓ 他們正搬到新址

198. 根據圖表，哪一個不是客戶有的選項？

    Ⓐ 非現場課程
    Ⓑ 十人課程
    Ⓒ 四個小時的課程
    Ⓓ 建立積極性的課程

199. 羅莉・惠勒可能會報名何種課程？

    Ⓐ 把握當下！
    Ⓑ 每天都是全新的自己
    Ⓒ 為團隊而積極！
    Ⓓ 我們都幸福

200. 下列何者與競爭優勢有關？

　　A 他們財務困窘

　　B 辦公室的氣氛不好

　　C 他們今年業績大好

　　D 他們想要改變業務重心

ACTUAL TEST ⑨

PART 5　P.258-261

◎ Part 5 解答請見 P.457

101. 李德女士借的投影機**要在**五點前歸還給資訊科技部門。

102. 既然年會結束了，籌備委員會也就**不會那麼常**開會了。

103. 在你分發報告前，問一下伯恩斯女士以確認**報告**有全部所需的資料。

104. 據消費者表示，使用新網頁並不**比**直接打電話給服務中心**簡單**。

105. 參加**了**本市年度烘焙競賽者，將獲得新鮮超市折價券一張。

106. 市府官員們仍然就厄文企業要求**拆除**老舊大樓一事爭論著。

107. 蒼鷺玻璃廠**歡迎**各年齡層的學生團體，參加倉庫與生產區的平日導覽。

108. 為了對抗精神疾病，這診所將採取比過去更全面性的**策略**。

109. 布蘭蒂可以從沙利斯銀行的任何分行提款，但她通常是去離她**最近的**那間。

110. 做為他與許多新客戶簽約的**獎勵**，史金納先生得到了額外的假期。

111. 請依已放置在桌上的**個人**專屬名牌就坐。

112. 李先生所寄的備忘錄中提出了一些在季檢中發現的**問題**。

113. 這城市有很多對這些議題不感興趣的選民，其中大約只有 15% 的人**在政治上**很活躍。

114. 今年的得獎者雪若‧迦納教導**整個**地區的學生與成人基本急救技巧。

115. **理想的狀況是**，這棟小木屋可以出租一整個月，但屋主只同意分成四週各別出租。

116. 這個非營利組織向新聞界發佈幾份文件，**詳細**說明大筆款項的捐贈者以及他們捐款的金額。

117. **一旦**機艙門已經關閉，乘客都不得再登機。

118. 一名政府**代表**將來到現場與抗議者直接對話並尋求解決方案。

119. 由伊旺尼可斯通訊所進行的大規模**民調**顯示，網路速度對消費者來說是最重要的影響因素。

120. 丹森先生想要從尤蒂卡錶店買一支特別版的鍍金手錶，但是卻**沒**貨了。

121. 梅女士提醒我們那份協議只是**暫定的**，因為它還沒有被核准。

122. 依照整修計劃，頗具歷史的柯克伍德飯店大廳看起來與它原始的模樣**神**似。

123. **在**適當的環境條件下，這棵樹一年當中大多可以結出新鮮的果實。

124. 有位實習生**指出**銷售報告第二頁上的商標顛倒了。

125. **當**停車場關閉時，員工和顧客將必須利用路邊停車。

126. 如果新款運動鞋在小型試售市場上表現良好，就可以**加速**在全國上市。

127. 這城市舉辦了**令人驚豔的**煙火表演來慶祝建城一百週年。

128. 在大量投資網路行銷活動後，貝利咖啡的年獲利成長**了** 15%。

129. 接待員**定期地**更換診所候診室的藝術品，並重新布置家具的擺放位置。

130. 要求企業提供醫療保險的規定，只適用於那些**聘僱** 25 人以上的公司。

131–134 告示

貝芙莉精品服飾：誠徵銷售助理

本精品服飾店現正徵求充滿熱忱的銷售助理人員。應徵者必須親切，能夠在各種情況下與顧客交流。有相似工作經驗佳，無經驗可，須具組織能力及電腦使用經驗。最重要的是，我們需要品貌兼優、可讓顧客感到自在，並對時尚充滿熱情的人。工作職責包括服務顧客，記錄庫存以及店內零碎雜務，像是打掃和下班時鎖門。薪資將按銷售佣金計酬，能更激勵員工盡力提供顧客最棒的服務。工作時間彈性，若需要更多資訊，請參考本店網站。如果您對這職位有興趣，請將履歷寄到 rlan@bboutique.com 給瑞塔。

131. Ⓐ 本精品服飾是流行時尚的領導者。
　　 Ⓑ 在促銷結束前，動作要快。
　　 Ⓒ 應徵者必須親切，能夠在各種情況下與顧客交流。
　　 Ⓓ 來參觀門市，看看我們的業務內容。

132. **Ⓐ 自在的**
　　 Ⓑ 適當的
　　 Ⓒ 忽視的
　　 Ⓓ 方便的

133. Ⓐ 影響
　　 Ⓑ 激勵
　　 Ⓒ 堅持
　　 Ⓓ 考量

134. Ⓐ 有趣的
　　 Ⓑ 以前有趣的
　　 Ⓒ 興趣
　　 Ⓓ 感興趣

135–138 廣告

巧傭居家服務

請來電 555-1244

巧傭居家服務為您的公司或住家提供專業的清潔服務。我們以蒸汽吸塵器清理地毯區域、擦亮硬木地板、擦拭所有死角的灰塵與髒汙，並處理雜物。我們的優質服務在三州地區是首屈一指的。在估價後，我們會提供單日服務。此外，我們也為提出要求的顧客提供包週及包月的服務。

我們所使用的清潔用品都是環保的，對寵物和兒童都無害。事實上，我們致力讓住家或公司在不使用刺激性化學藥劑的情況下，成為安全又乾淨的地方。欲知更多資訊，請來電或上本公司網站 www.handymaids.com。

135. Ⓐ 提供
　　 Ⓑ 提供
　　 Ⓒ 提供過
　　 Ⓓ 正提供

136. Ⓐ 不尋常
　　 Ⓑ 特別的
　　 Ⓒ 應最好的
　　 Ⓓ 優秀的

137. **Ⓐ 此外**
　　 Ⓑ 因為
　　 Ⓒ 另一方面
　　 Ⓓ 因此

138. Ⓐ 我們確保您的寵物與小孩不會接近化學藥劑。
　　 Ⓑ 事實上，我們致力讓住家或公司在不使用刺激性化學的情況下，成為安全又乾淨的地方。
　　 Ⓒ 我們的全天然清潔劑也許不如化學藥劑有效，但它們是安全的。
　　 Ⓓ 在清潔時，孩童與寵物將被要求離開該地。

139–142 信件

10 月 9 日
鮑伯·普羅瑟

99705 阿拉斯加州費爾班克斯溫克勒大道 342 號

親愛的普羅瑟先生：

您要求變更狩獵許可計劃的相關資料已經隨函附上。請注意，每一張許可證都必須分開申請。填寫申請書時，請用黑筆或藍筆以大寫清楚地填寫，請勿使用書寫字體，只能以正楷字體書寫。每張申請書需放入個別的信封中，於申請截止日前收件。受理申請後，可能需要長達五週的時間處理。因此，您必須規劃適當的繳交時間，以確保您在收到許可證之時，仍然開放狩獵。希望附上的這些資料能答覆您所有的疑問。祝安好並狩獵愉快。

99701 阿拉斯加費爾班克斯野生動物部
執行秘書 雪莉·宏恩 敬上

139. A 提供
B 供應
C 要求
D 要求

140. A 將不會
B 可以是
C 一定是
D 不可能是

141. **A 受理申請後，可能需要長達五週的時間處理。**
B 在狩獵季結束前，決不會核准申請。
C 申請書有時候會遺失。
D 請勿親自申請。

142. A 附上
B 正附上
C 附上
D 被附上

143–146 告示

日期：8 月 22 日
收件者：業務團隊全體成員

寄件者：業務經理梅琳達·雷基

主旨：租賃規定

好一段時間裡，公司讓業務代表先用個人信用卡或現金支付他們租車的費用，之後再報帳核銷。這已非本公司的規定了，早在兩個月前就沒有此規定，至今已經取消兩個多月。自 6 月 15 日起，所有租車的費用要由分配給各位的公司信用卡支付。會計部的賴瑞通知我，自那之後，他還是收到了六筆核銷申請表。我已經先核准，讓賴瑞處理那六份申請表。但是從明天起，大家都不能再將租車的費用報帳了。很遺憾這封通知要用如此嚴厲的語氣，但我們在六月時就已經要求大家這麼做了。如果您還有任何問題，請直接和我聯絡。

143. A 距離
B 地方
C 事件
D 時間

144. A 做出
B 被做出
C 做出
D 已被做出

145. A 以後只能跟方提那租車公司預約租車。
B 但是從明天起，大家都不能再將租車的費用報帳了。
C 他在下週初會重新設計表格。
D 所有業務代表都必須盡快繳交自己的名片。

146. A 誇大的
B 親切的
C 仁慈的
D 嚴厲的

147–148 傳單

> ### 潔家具
>
> 60611 伊利諾州芝加哥密西根大道 3105 號
>
> ### 黑色星期五週末特賣
> ### 11 月 29 日至 12 月 1 日
>
> 桌子——八折
> 沙發——七折
> 床墊——五折至八折
> 書桌和椅子——五折至七五折
>
> ■ 特賣期間，消費滿 500 元的顧客，皆可獲得聖誕特賣會的 95 折折價券，其有效期限為 12 月 9 日至 12 月 28 日。
>
> ■ 特賣期間出示代碼 BLKFRI，就可多獲得桌子和床墊的 10 元抵扣優惠。
>
> **備註：**潔家具將在週末特賣會前一天暫停營業以做準備。11 月 29 日上午九點開門營業。

147. 這張傳單的目的是什麼？

A 宣布店家開幕
B 宣傳家具特賣
C 介紹新產品
D 通知顧客店家搬遷

148. 店家何時暫停營業？

A 11 月 28 日
B 11 月 29 日
C 11 月 30 日
D 12 月 9 日

149–150 訊息串

詹姆士	**11:01**
你在哪裡？	
羅伯特	**11:25**
什麼意思？我整個早上都在這裡啊。	
詹姆士	**11:26**
什麼？我到處都找不到你。	
詹姆士	**12:00**
你在哪裡？	
羅伯特	**12:03**
抱歉，我一直都和客戶在紅室。無法收到你的訊息。	
詹姆士	**12:04**
好，了解。我會在外面等。	
羅伯特	**12:30**
你還在那裡嗎？	
詹姆士	**12:31**
是啊，希望你已經成交了。	

TEST 9
PART 7

149. 詹姆士為什麼寫下：「希望你已經成交了」？

A 他覺得會有分紅獎金
B 他已經等很久了
C 他喜歡紅室
D 有太多交易未成交

150. 從詹姆士的訊息和羅伯特的回覆中間相隔的時間可推論出什麼？

A 羅伯特對詹姆士毫無興趣
B 羅伯特想要有自己的時間
C 羅伯特的電話壞了
D 羅伯特無法一直查看電話

151–152 電子郵件

收件者：營運小組
<operations@acemfg.com>
寄件者：湯瑪士·惠勒
<t.wheeler@acemfg.com>
日期：6 月 16 日星期一
主旨：新設備

致營運小組：

公司將於明天訂購一套新的重型設備，並於隔天下午送達倉庫。員工工作時間表將配合我們設備的新增有所調整。請在週四下午五點前送交一份報告，說明每位同仁與這套設備相關的新工作與職責。

如果我不在辦公室，請交給我的秘書哈蒂女士。

製造部 主管
湯瑪士·惠勒

151. 新設備最有可能何時抵達倉庫？
- Ⓐ 星期一
- Ⓑ 星期二
- **Ⓒ 星期三**
- Ⓓ 星期四

152. 報告裡應該包括了什麼？
- Ⓐ 員工的聯絡資料
- **Ⓑ 員工的指派任務**
- Ⓒ 員工的履歷表
- Ⓓ 員工的建議

153–154 備忘錄

收文者：研發部
發文者：研發部主管瑞克·坎貝爾
主旨：員工異動
日期：4 月 4 日星期二，下午 3:40

我寫這篇訊息是為了跟各位分享有關研發部門最近的異動消息。從 4 月 7 日起，鮑伯·丹坷將成為研發部的新專案經理。他剛完成了一個月的訓練講習，將於週末前頂替班傑明·帕瑪。

人力資源部主管麥克·賈西亞將於下週前公布不同部門的人事空缺。對那些有意轉調公司其他部門的人來說，現在正是申請的好時機。

請大家恭喜班傑明·帕瑪將轉任「離子企業」的新職，同時也歡迎鮑伯·丹坷加入本部門。

153 下週前預計會發生什麼事？
- Ⓐ 將成立新部門
- **Ⓑ 將宣布職缺**
- Ⓒ 將進行面試
- Ⓓ 將舉辦訓練講習

154. 誰將離開公司？
- Ⓐ 鮑伯·丹坷
- Ⓑ 麥克·賈西亞
- Ⓒ 瑞克·坎貝爾
- **Ⓓ 班傑明·帕瑪**

155–157 文章

Re-Fit 關閉店面

2 月 9 日——紐韋集團剛宣布接下來六個月內即將關閉全國 80 家 Re-Fit 門市，今年內還有 100 家也會跟著結束營業。這家服飾店以價格合理但款式時髦的運動服飾出名，在 1990 年代和 2000 年代初期非常受歡迎。不過，在過去十年它們的業績下滑，因為顧客轉向其他服飾零售店像是扎納斯和 HRM 消費。「我不知道，我只是覺得那些衣服過時了。」一名以前的顧客說，「他們應該要更新款式，提供非運動風的選擇。」

執行長戴瑞克·格林威治同意說：「我們太過單獨專注在特定的運動風格上，以致於忽略了顧客喜好的改變。我們正努力重組公司，提供顧客想要的商品。我們會再次盛大回歸。」

針對虧損的內部檢討將持續進行，而不安的股東們也在考慮他們的下一步。紐韋希望在公司致力於重新改造品牌之際，大部分的 Re-Fit 門市仍能維持營運。

155. 下列何者與 Re-Fit 這品牌有關？

Ⓐ 它受歡迎的程度已經急遽下滑
Ⓑ 專攻運動器材
Ⓒ 執行長要為公司重新命名
Ⓓ 這品牌有百年歷史

156. 在第二段的「lost sight of」意思最接近？

Ⓐ 限制
Ⓑ 沒被蒙蔽
Ⓒ 忽略
Ⓓ 挑選

157. 下列句子最適合出現在 [1]、[2]、[3]、[4] 的哪個位置？「這家服飾店以價格合理但款式時髦的運動服飾出名，在 1990 年代和 2000 年代初期非常受歡迎。」

Ⓐ [1]
Ⓑ [2]
Ⓒ [3]
Ⓓ [4]

158–160 小手冊目錄

158. 這本手冊的重點是什麼？

Ⓐ 食物
Ⓑ 交通
Ⓒ 環境
Ⓓ 旅遊

159. 可以在手冊中的何處找到照片？

Ⓐ 第 9 頁
Ⓑ 第 19 頁
Ⓒ 第 26 頁
Ⓓ 第 30 頁

160. 根據目錄的內容，誰寫了節省花費的議題？

Ⓐ 格林女士
Ⓑ 卡羅爾先生
Ⓒ 伊森先生
Ⓓ 鮑伊先生

161–164 網路討論區

金潔·林	[4:59]	只是想提醒大家在今天下班前清空桌子並關閉所有電子設備，整個地板要在這個週末清理打磨。
迪米崔·羅伯茲	[5:00]	我們也要將所有櫃子跟抽屜上鎖嗎？
金潔·林	[5:01]	是的，麻煩了。請確定家具搬動時，不會有東西掉出來。
迪米崔·羅伯茲	[5:02]	我會在離開前確定所有東西都已放妥且上鎖。
珍娜·李	[5:03]	金潔，我已經做好預算報告了。在我送出前，我會以電子郵件寄一份給妳。
金潔·林	[5:04]	謝謝。對了藍斯，你必須重新安排你明天和客戶的會議。
藍斯·西伯利	[5:04]	我已經把會議重新安排到下週一了。為了慎重起見，以防辦公室屆時還沒弄好，我們將在附近的咖啡廳會面。
金潔·林	[5:05]	好。看起來大部分的事情都已就緒。如果我遺漏了什麼，請告訴我。

珍娜·李	[5:06]	事實上，還有人沒有給我加班時數。我是可以透過簽到表確認，但是在我將薪資表送到財務部前，我需要大家利用電子郵件確認。
迪米崔·羅伯茲	[5:07]	喔！就是我。我現在就寄電子郵件給你。
凱倫·沃克	[5:07]	我也是。
珍娜·麗	[5:08]	好。我一收到你們的電子郵件，就可以把表單送出去。

161. 星期六和星期日會發生什麼事？

Ⓐ 辦公室派對
Ⓑ 與客戶會面
Ⓒ 整修
Ⓓ 清潔服務

162. 金潔·林最有可能是誰？

Ⓐ 秘書
Ⓑ 經理
Ⓒ 技術人員
Ⓓ 保全警衛

163. 在 5:04 時，藍斯·西伯利寫下：「為了慎重起見」是什麼意思？

Ⓐ 辦公室可能不安全
Ⓑ 客戶可能需要協助
Ⓒ 只是個預防措施
Ⓓ 他被警告

164. 珍娜·李接下來最有可能做什麼？

Ⓐ 查看電子郵件
Ⓑ 聯絡財務部門
Ⓒ 打電話給一些員工
Ⓓ 列印一些報告

165–167 徵才廣告

援助之手

加州聖塔克拉貝克斯斐爾德大道 8732 號

就業機會——區域經理

援助之手一直致力為低收入的個人及家庭提供優質且價格合理的住屋。25 多年來，我們一直購進集合住宅式社區，改善住宅並維持供需量以供給那些所得低於地區平均收入一半的人。我們的住宅目前分布在全德州各都市，包括奧斯汀、達拉斯和休士頓，我們的計劃是擴大服務以提供更多的房子給更多人。

我們正在尋找能擔任區域經理的人才。新經理將派駐奧斯汀，負責監督並評估當地管理部門的績效，並確保房產受到良好的維護。求職者需具商業或管理領域學士以上學位、至少三年的人事監督經驗，並具備特定證照（徵才網頁上有更多詳細資訊）。

申請書可於週一至週五上午九點至下午五點間親送，或以郵寄或以電子郵件寄送。於 10 月 14 日下午五點前收件方可受理，逾時不候。

165. 文中提到什麼和援助之手有關？

Ⓐ 它為年長者提供服務
Ⓑ 它致力於自然保育
Ⓒ 它受到政府贊助
Ⓓ 它為弱勢族群提供住屋

166. 成功的應徵者必須到哪裡工作？

Ⓐ 聖塔克拉拉
Ⓑ 奧斯汀
Ⓒ 達拉斯
Ⓓ 休士頓

167. 下列何者與該職務無關？

Ⓐ 包括監督當地員工
Ⓑ 需要學位
Ⓒ 需要正式文件
Ⓓ 僅限加州居民

168–171 電子郵件

收件者：cmason@centersports.com
寄件者：sdixon@instaprinting.com
日期：11 月 3 日
主旨：您的提問

親愛的梅森先生：

這封信是要回覆您昨天在本公司網站上所提出的疑問。即刻印刷承諾提供比同區競爭對手更快速、更便宜且更可靠的服務。本公司也保證能在價錢方面擊敗競爭對手。

至於您的要求，本公司很樂意協助您的足球隊設計及印製運動服。除了休閒服裝之外，本公司也在製作體育隊服和俱樂部運動服上也經驗豐富。

顧客可以選用各種不同的布料與印製方式，我們的布料包括丹寧、棉布、法蘭絨、尼龍等其他布料，而印製方式則有網版印刷、熱印刷和衣物直印法。

歡迎直接來電 712-555-9804 與本人聯絡，以便洽詢更多細節。本公司期盼與您合作，幫助您的單位達成目標。

即刻印刷 客服代表
史帝芬 · 狄克森

168. 狄克森先生為什麼會寄這封電子郵件？

- A 為專案報價
- B 說明新規定
- **C 說服客戶達成交易**
- D 確認預約

169. 梅森先生想做什麼？

- **A 購買一組上衣**
- B 應徵職務
- C 發明新印刷技術
- D 拓展國際業務

170. 下列何者與即刻印刷有關？

- A 昨天第二家分店開張
- **B 提供各種印製方式**
- C 只生產運動服
- D 贊助在地足球隊

171. 第四段、第一行的「further」意思最接近？

- A 緊急地
- B 正式地
- **C 額外地**
- D 謹慎地

172–175 資訊

（男子）我還記得塞爾吉奧 · 赫南德茲剛到「趙特暨李」公司上班的模樣。他是個30 歲的小伙子，充滿了雄心壯志和幹勁。就是那股雄心壯志和幹勁，加上滿懷正直與智慧，讓他成為服裝業界最有價值的一員，也讓本公司成為最成功的企業之一。

今天受邀在此訴說他的事蹟讓我備感榮幸，讓我不由自主地想起去年當我離開公司去追求清閒生活時，心裡有多傷感。塞爾吉奧的那段話幫助我度過難熬的過渡期，過著沒公司可去，也沒有同事激勵的日子，而我希望我這番不足為道的話語能在他經歷同樣的歷程時，讓他記得自己有多麼受人敬重，還有他過了多麼令人敬佩的生活。請大家以熱烈掌聲來歡迎塞爾吉奧 · 赫南德茲先生。

172. 文中提到了什麼有關赫南德茲先生的事？

- A 他是趙特暨李公司的執行長
- B 他被升職
- C 他要轉調到新部門
- **D 他將從公司退休**

173. 下列何者與趙特暨李公司有關？

- A 它是國際性企業
- B 它是房地產公司
- C 它在美國有製造廠
- **D 它已經成立好幾十年了**

174. 關於赫南德茲先生，下列何者未在文中提到？

- A 他從何時開始在公司工作
- B 他是哪一類型的員工
- C 他所服務的產業類型
- **D 他在公司的職務**

175. 下列句子最適合出現在 [1]、[2]、[3]、[4] 的哪個位置？「今天受邀在此訴說他的事蹟讓我備感榮幸。」

A [1]
B [2]
C **[3]**
D [4]

176–180 請款單和信件

訂單號碼：23710

楓林戶外用品

華盛頓州約克楓林街 387 號
日期：5 月 6 日

品項	品牌	單價	總價
登山靴	北歐高地	149.95 元	149.95 元
野營爐	阿凡藍奇	58.79 元	58.79 元
燃油罐	阿凡藍奇	9.98 元	19.96 元
襪子	北國羊毛	12.85 元	0 元（贈品）*
		總計：228.34 元	

* 我們免費附贈一雙襪子，讓您在下次露營時可以保暖。

感謝您在楓林戶外用品一年多來的惠顧。和往常一樣，若有任何我們可協助之處，歡迎洽詢。如果您詢問的是訂單相關事宜，請記得給我們您的訂單號碼與大名。

電話：(601) 478-2129
電子郵件信箱：MapleOutdoor@zmail.com

收件者：楓林戶外用品客服
寄件者：莎娜‧桑德柏格
日期：5 月 9 日
主旨：宅配問題

我昨天收到了訂購的東西，但那並不是我預期會收到的商品。我訂購的是阿凡藍奇野營爐，但我收到的卻是 MT 菁英爐。我希望能盡快收到阿凡藍奇野營爐，因為下個週末我就要參加露營之旅了。你們來得及寄給我嗎？還是我直接到門市更換即可？請盡快與我聯絡。我會等您的回音。

謝謝。
莎娜‧桑德柏格

176. 楓林戶外用品提到了什麼有關桑德柏格女士的訂單？

A 將延誤長達一個月的時間
B 他們已經免費快遞
C 如果因使用不當而毀損將無法退貨
D **他們隨件附送一份贈品**

177. 阿凡藍奇燃油罐價值多少錢？

A 58.79 元
B **9.98 元**
C 19.96 元
D 12.85 元

178. 桑德柏格女士為什麼要寫這封電子郵件？

A 稱讚她所得到的服務
B 要求一份通訊月刊
C 詢問可否退還商品
D **投訴送錯商品**

179. 桑德柏格女士忘記附上什麼資料？

A 她的姓名
B 她的郵寄地址
C **她的訂單號碼**
D 她的信用卡號碼

180. 下列有關桑德柏格女士，何者為真？

A **她以前在楓林戶外用品買過東西**
B 她常去露營
C 她沒有收到登山靴
D 她即將前往楓林戶外用品門市

181–185 告示和電子郵件

各位乘客，請注意

克林頓客運

為回應乘客的反應，克林頓客運將拓展連接德州與西南部其他大都會中心的巴士路線。以下所列的新路線將自 5 月 1 日起運行。為了推廣這些新巴士路線，我們將於營運的第一週提供票券半價優惠。增進大家的滿意程度是我們的首要之務，更多詳細資訊（像是發車與抵達時間），請參考本公司網站 www.clintonbuses.com。

收件者：erichanson@prplanning.com
寄件者：dangregory@trentonlogistics.com
日期：4 月 27 日
主旨：即將到訪

親愛的漢森先生：

我現在正為前往貴公司於聖塔菲的總部拜訪一事確認細節。感謝您邀請我前去參加業務協商。請告訴我應該抵達的時間，會議是否和上次一樣在午餐後開始呢？

您不需要來接我，我已經安排了計程車在聖塔菲巴士總站接我。很幸運地，我住的地方到您的公司有一條新巴士路線，這讓地區間的交通變得更加便利，現在也有到丹佛和鳳凰城的巴士了。最棒的是，我幸運地可以用半價買到到聖塔菲的車票。

等不及再次見到您與您的同事了。

丹‧格雷戈里

181. 根據公告內容，克林頓客運的乘客被鼓勵在網站上做什麼？
    Ⓐ 預先訂票
    Ⓑ 查詢公車時刻表
    Ⓒ 申請會員資格
    Ⓓ 索取優惠券

182. 下列何者與格雷戈里先生和漢森先生之前的會面有關？
    Ⓐ 在德州舉行
    Ⓑ 持續了一整週
    Ⓒ 在下午開始
    Ⓓ 因天候惡劣取消

183. 在電子郵件中，第二段第三行的「transit」意思最接近？
    Ⓐ 參與
    Ⓑ 交通
    Ⓒ 調查
    Ⓓ 合作

184. 格雷戈里先生最有可能住在哪裡？
    Ⓐ 聖塔菲
    Ⓑ 奧斯汀
    Ⓒ 達拉斯
    Ⓓ 丹佛

185. 會議預計何時舉行？
    Ⓐ 在 4 月 24 日前
    Ⓑ 在 4 月 24 日與 4 月 30 日間
    Ⓒ 在 5 月 1 日與 5 月 7 日間
    Ⓓ 在 5 月 7 日後

186–190 電子郵件

收件者：布萊恩‧彼得森
<bpetersen@atasteofclass.com>
寄件者：傑森‧郝士楚
<jhostrum@jhfurnishing.com>
日期：11 月 20 日
主旨：辦公室聖誕派對

親愛的彼得森先生：

我希望於本公司年底舉辦的聖誕派對上，使用貴公司優味的外燴服務。理想上，我們最希望能在 12 月 20 日星期六舉辦活動。我對貴公司提供的服務項目有些問題想請教。第一，你們提供會場布置服務嗎？我真的很希望今年的派對能大成功，這是我第一次負責這個活動，我真的希望能給上司留下好印象。第二，您們素食餐點的種類多嗎？本公司 35 名職員中有 12 位素食者，所以能為他們供應全素食餐點是很重要的，不要只有開胃菜是素食。如果您能回覆這些問題，並告知 20 號當天是否有空，我會非常感激的。

傑森‧郝士楚 敬上
強森家飾 初級秘書

收件者：傑森·郝士楚
<jhostrum@jhfurnishing.com>
寄件者：布萊恩·彼得森
<bpetersen@atasteofclass.com>
日期：11 月 21 日
主旨：回覆：辦公室聖誕派對

親愛的郝士楚先生：

很高興您與優味公司聯繫，讓我們協助您讓聖誕派對成為難以忘懷的一場盛會。就讓我來回答您所有的問題，使您寬心。

首先，我們還有一組人員可以承辦您在 12 月 20 日舉辦的派對，所以您很幸運！至於會場布置一事，我們有好幾種不同的主題可供選擇，請上我們的網站 www.atasteofclass.com 參考我們過去圓滿舉辦的活動照片。上面都已標示主題，所以您只要選出吸引您的就可以了。

您最後關於素食餐點的問題，這需要由您來決定。本公司提供美味佳餚，也很樂意特別準備 12 份素食餐點，但這價格會偏高。我不知道您的預算如何，但我會建議考慮將整份菜單換成素食。我們有非常優秀的素食主廚，茉莉亞·摩爾能準備全素食的自助餐，而且好吃到連獅子都願意吃！這個方案也會比準備兩種不同的餐點要來的划算。在衡量過您可選擇的方案後，請告訴我什麼樣的方案最適合您。

優味 預約暨業務經理
布萊恩·彼得森 敬上

收件者：布萊恩·彼得森
<bpetersen@atasteofclass.com>
寄件者：傑森·郝士楚
<jhostrum@jhfurnishing.com>
日期：11 月 22 日
主旨：回覆：辦公室聖誕派對

親愛的彼得森先生：

感謝您的回覆。我決定將活動訂在 12 月 20 日星期六。我想要的布置主題是冬季仙境。我也決定接受您的建議，採用主廚

茉莉亞·摩爾為我們搭配的餐點。很感謝您所有的建議。我知道這將是一場很棒的盛會！

強森家飾 初級秘書
傑森·郝士楚 敬上

186. 傑森·郝士楚為什麼擔心那場派對？

Ⓐ 他的家人會到場
Ⓑ 這是老闆第一次一起參加
Ⓒ 這是他為公司規劃的第一場派對
Ⓓ 食物太多，他無法準備

187. 在第三封電子郵件中，何者與傑森·郝士楚有關？

Ⓐ 他已看過 atasteofclass.com 網站
Ⓑ 他已自創主題
Ⓒ 他要取消派對
Ⓓ 他要增加更多食物與賓客

188. 根據電子郵件，哪一種食物會供應？

Ⓐ 只有肉類
Ⓑ 肉類與素食混搭
Ⓒ 只有素食
Ⓓ 只有開胃菜

189. 在第一封電子郵件中，和食物有關的大問題是什麼？

Ⓐ 口味
Ⓑ 副食種類
Ⓒ 部分員工的飲食限制
Ⓓ 自助餐擺設的位置

190. 下列何者與優味有關？

Ⓐ 今年節慶季很忙
Ⓑ 還有很多小組在 20 日有空
Ⓒ 他們寧可在其他日期承辦派對
Ⓓ 他們太忙無法承辦強森家飾的派對

191–195 電子郵件和訂購表格

收件者：<cservice@starproducts.com>
寄件者：荷西・拉莫斯
<jramos@zipnet.com>
日期：10 月 14 日
主旨：瑕疵水管

親愛的潔金斯女士：

我最近向貴公司星辰製業購買了 5,000 碼的 XP100 工業用水管。那水管標示可應付每平方英寸 1,000 磅的壓力。我們「先進動力清潔公司」為了配合你們的水管，花了可觀的成本改裝壓力清洗裝置。但每一個壓力清洗裝置，從噴槍到壓縮機間的水管某處都出現故障。我們的壓縮機只能產生 500 磅的壓力，因此我只能推論貴公司的水管在設計上有瑕疵。我想要退款，或是將訂購的產品換成符合工業標準的水管。我已經附上訂購單及請款單影本。

荷西・拉莫斯 敬上

收件者：荷西・拉莫斯
<jramos@zipnet.com>
寄件者：拉蔻兒・潔金斯
<cservice@starproducts.com>
日期：10 月 16 日
主旨：回覆：瑕疵水管

親愛的拉莫斯先生：

我們已經收到您提出的瑕疵水管報告，也審閱過所附上的資料。我們真的很重視貴公司的惠顧，也很遺憾您花如此多時間和力氣來處理我們的水管。但是，我恐怕要告訴您，這個問題可能出在貴公司。您的訂單明確顯示您訂購了 5,000 碼的 XP100 水管。如果您仔細研究過那組水管的規格，就會發現它被列在適用於約 100 磅壓力的等級，這可以解釋為什麼您的所有管線會故障。我可以提供給您的是讓貴公司目前庫存的 XP100 水管更換成更符合您需求的管線。我們將免費處理，並支付運費，

以感謝您的惠顧。請填寫隨信附上的請購單，並於寄回 XP100 水管時一併附上，以便換貨。

感謝您。

拉蔻兒・潔金斯

星辰製業請購單

品名	磅力	需要長度	每碼單價	適用折扣
XP1000	1,000	2,500 碼	0.5 元	總折扣依更換 XP100 時所商定

191. 荷西・拉莫斯為什麼寫信給星辰製造業？
- Ⓐ 要詢問價格
- Ⓑ 要訂購新水管
- **Ⓒ 要提出水管的瑕疵**
- Ⓓ 要稱讚他們的水管

192. 下列何者與荷西・拉莫斯訂購的水管有關？
- **Ⓐ 不在他適用的磅力範圍中**
- Ⓑ 有瑕疵
- Ⓒ 安裝不當
- Ⓓ 送錯地址

193. 根據請購單，荷西・拉莫斯退還了多少 XP100 的水管？
- Ⓐ 1,000 碼
- Ⓑ 2,000 碼
- **Ⓒ 2,500 碼**
- Ⓓ 5,000 碼

194. 下列何者與星辰製造業所發出的信件有關？
- Ⓐ 星辰製造業並不重視荷西・拉莫斯的生意
- **Ⓑ 星辰製造業很感謝荷西・拉莫斯的惠顧**
- Ⓒ 星辰製造業不需要更多的業務
- Ⓓ 星辰製造業想拓展業務

195. 拉蔻兒‧潔金斯最有可能做什麼工作？

    A 執行長

    B 財務長

    C 客服

    D 銷售

196–200 電子郵件和表格

收件者：傑森‧羅伯茲
<jroberts@robertsparties.com>
寄件者：萊羅伊‧杰金斯
<ljenkins@smope.com>
日期：9 月 24 日
主旨：秋季派對

親愛的羅伯茲先生：

我叫萊羅伊‧杰金斯。我正在規劃十月第一個週末的家庭聚會，我聽幾位朋友說貴公司辦的派對絕對是最棒的。我真的想讓我姊姊的新夫家留下一個好印象，這是他們第一次參加我們的家族年度聚會。我有幾個問題想請教您。

第一，我想知道 25 人的團體收費是多少。不含酒類的話，我可以負擔每人 25 元的預算。我家人對食物有點挑剔，所以是否可以請您將所提供的食物清單與每人費用寄給我，我想先看過後，再設計自己的菜單。

最後要請教的問題就是服務人員。我真的不想在派對時還要打掃、洗碗盤。貴公司可提供人員嗎？如果有，服務的收費又是如何計算？請盡快回覆給我，好讓我們可以著手規劃這場派對！

祝好。

萊羅伊‧杰金斯

收件者：萊羅伊‧杰金斯
<ljenkins@smope.com>
寄件者：傑森‧羅伯茲
<jroberts@robertsparties.com>
日期：9 月 25 日
主旨：回覆：秋季派對

親愛的杰金斯先生：

很高興聽您說本公司的派對一向都很成功。我們的確有外繪菜單供您選擇，歡迎您根據您的預算與口味喜好混合搭配。我已經附上菜單和服務人員配置簡介，如果您很擔心活動的進行，那我建議您雇用宴會總召。本公司的宴會總召皆受過培訓，專門在我們所主辦的派對上負責接待賓客，使他們開心；也因此我們有良好的聲譽。

期待讓您的派對大成功！

傑森‧羅伯茲

羅伯茲派對外燴菜單

開胃菜	主菜	沙拉	甜點
玉米片加沾醬 1 元	牛排 2.50 元 *	凱薩 1 元	蛋糕 0.5 元 *
一口酥 1 元	雞肉 1.50 元 *	柯布 2 元 *	派 0.5 元 *
洋蔥圈 1 元 *	豬肉 1.50 元	蔬菜 2 元 *	冰淇淋 0.5 元

羅伯茲派對服務人員價目表

主廚	時薪 5 元
侍者	時薪 2.5 元
宴會總召	時薪 3.5 元

* 推薦品項

196. 傑森‧羅伯茲最有可能是誰？

    A 主廚

    B 老闆

    C 宴會總召

    D 接待員

197. 萊羅伊·杰金斯在擔心要給誰留下好印
象?

   Ⓐ 他的老闆
   Ⓑ 他的兄弟
   Ⓒ 他姊夫的家人
   Ⓓ 他的父母

198. 傑森·羅伯茲建議萊羅伊·杰金斯將什
麼列入他的活動中?

   Ⓐ 多一名主廚
   Ⓑ 宴會總召
   Ⓒ 素食餐點
   Ⓓ 更多服務生

199. 下列何者與萊羅伊·杰金斯的預算有關?

   Ⓐ 他無法負擔羅伯茲派對的價格
   Ⓑ 他需要選一份便宜的菜單
   Ⓒ 他可以負擔羅伯茲派對所有的建議
   Ⓓ 他必須捨棄開胃菜

200. 誰會出席萊羅伊·杰金斯的聚會?

   Ⓐ 他姊夫家的人
   Ⓑ 25 名杰金斯家族成員
   Ⓒ 住在鎮上的家族成員
   Ⓓ 家族中的每位成員

TEST
9

PART 7

ACTUAL TEST ⑩

PART 5　　P.288-291

◎ Part 5 解答請見 P.457

101. **由於**兩個品牌間的差異性很小，大多數的消費者會購買較便宜的那個。

102. 觀眾們對候選人能**清楚地**回答被問到的問題都感到印象深刻。

103. 為了**生產**永續能源，市府官員已經在部分公共建築上加裝了太陽能板。

104. 消防局遲緩的**應變**造成該大樓的嚴重毀損。

105. 在幾個小時的搜尋後，水管工人**終於**找到漏水的源頭。

106. 請告訴**大家**，研討會已經被移至 402 會議室了。

107. 16 號公路於夏季時進行道路拓寬，以**容納**日益增加的交通流量。

108. 餐券發給了那些因訂位錯誤而無法準時起飛**的**貝塔航空旅客。

109. 藝廊的目錄裡包含了每件待售的藝術作品的精確**說明**。

110. 為了確保老舊家電得到妥善處理，本市將於 4 月 2 日至 4 月 5 日**間**免費清除。

111. 賓客們可享用自助式晚餐，所以他們不須點餐就可以吃到**任何**他們想吃的美食。

112. 音樂季期間，只有向籌辦單位登記且**獲得許可的**攤販可以販售商品。

113. 自 2001 年開業以來，快活食品連鎖量販店**專門**販售有機產品。

114. 列表機故障是**因為**組裝過程中有個零件嵌入不當。

115. 大多數的員工能**接受**被提議的假日時間表，因為他們知道它是公平的。

116. 這個檢測**可望**證實病人是否得到該疾病。

117. 擁有兩百多家的獨特店面，普萊恩維爾商場每年**吸引了**上百萬的購物人潮。

118. 參賽者將以**運動**表現接受評比，之後將於頒獎典禮上宣布優勝者。

119. 約克基金會是一個在過去十年來，一直支持醫療科技**發展**的組織。

120. **是否**在室內或室外舉行排球錦標賽，主要取決於當天的天氣預報。

121. 在幾位前職員指控該公司的不當**交易**後，該公司就被調查。

122. 加入文斯健身房**後**，品特先生可免費參加團體課程及健康諮詢。

123. 要以小資改善房屋**外觀**的最好的方式，就是在外牆塗上新漆。

124. 市場營銷員相信，如果包裝的顏色更**繽紛**，消費者可能更容易注意到商品。

125. 警察指揮交通車輛**前往**繞道匝道，好讓駕駛人可以輕易地找到路線。

126. 所有員工被要求與**同事**兩人一組，並在在消防演習中與對方到預定地點集合。

127. 那個車主繳交了車輛的毀損**照片**證據及技師的報告給保險公司。

128. 二樓的洗手間**暫時**無法使用，因為有個水槽正在被更換中。

129. 因為我們的業務代表需要與業界的高層客戶會面，**只有**具專業態度的人才會被列入這個職位人選的考量。

130 在下週的廣播節目中，我們的主持人將訪問克莉絲汀‧達布尼，談談她擔任聯合國官員**口譯員**的時光。

131–134 告示

收件者：全體員工
寄件者：首席技師麥克・戴維斯
主旨：網路升級

我們很遺憾要通知大家，自 11 月 13 日下週一起至下週中的某天，員工鑰匙卡系統將無法使用。要進出大樓，各位需要按電鈴通知警衛。要開門或鎖門，各位也必須請求保全小組的幫忙。

舊系統經檢視後發現有很多漏洞。因此，公司決定更換舊系統。這個過程應該會花上三至四天的時間。

其中一個流程是發新的鑰匙卡給每位員工。鑰匙卡將於 11 月 15 日星期三起在警衛室供您領取。請在當天任何時間內領取，警衛室一天 24 小時全天候開放。若造成您的不便，我們深感抱歉。

131. Ⓐ 正請求
　　 Ⓑ 已經請求
　　 Ⓒ 必須請求
　　 Ⓓ 過去必須請求

132. Ⓐ 不幸地
　　 Ⓑ 因此
　　 Ⓒ 不管怎樣
　　 Ⓓ 終於

133. Ⓐ 一……就
　　 Ⓑ 在……期間
　　 Ⓒ 在……之前
　　 Ⓓ 在

134. Ⓐ 出入從鑰匙轉成無鑰匙，應該可以讓場所更安全。
　　 Ⓑ 我們期待在下週見到您。
　　 Ⓒ 警衛室一天 24 小時全天候開放。
　　 Ⓓ 這是為了產品安全。

135–138 告示

誠徵音樂老師

麥可音樂學校正積極徵求週末及晚間課程的新鋼琴老師。麥可音樂學校自 1992 年起，就在中央區營運至今。我們對社區的責任感，就和我們對學生的責任感一樣重要。為此，我們希望能聘用中央地區的長期住戶加入本團隊。應徵者必須精通現代教學技巧。如果您有意應徵該職，我們將於本週六中午 12 點在榆樹街與杜邦大道的大錄音室舉行面試及甄選。

135. Ⓐ 積極的
　　 Ⓑ 活化的
　　 Ⓒ 積極地
　　 Ⓓ 活性化的

136. Ⓐ 本公司試著與外面的社區合作。
　　 Ⓑ 我們對社區的責任感就和我們對學生的責任感一樣重要。
　　 Ⓒ 本公司非常獨特，使用奇特的樂器。
　　 Ⓓ 本公司地點特殊，就在汽車修理廠旁邊。

137. **Ⓐ 現代的**
　　 Ⓑ 不知名的
　　 Ⓒ 奇怪的
　　 Ⓓ 無聊的

138. Ⓐ 申請
　　 Ⓑ 申請
　　 Ⓒ 申請
　　 Ⓓ 申請

TEST 10
PART 6

薩爾達斯塔

放鬆您的身心

這就是您一直夢寐以求的。不須翻來覆去即可一夜安眠正是您所需要的，這也是薩爾達斯塔所提供的。薩爾達斯塔幫助人們快速入睡，整夜好眠。這是唯一非麻醉性的安眠藥，經驗證能長期使用，因此您可以安心每夜服用。長期服用安眠藥前請先與醫師討論。今晚，只要閉上您的眼睛，把一切都交給薩爾達斯塔。

請參考網站 www.saldesta.com 或撥打 1-800-SALDESTA 看看如何改善您的睡眠。

重要安全資訊：薩爾達斯塔藥效發揮快速，請在睡前服用。甦醒活動前，請確保您至少有八小時的睡眠時間。服用薩爾達斯塔時，請勿飲酒。大部分的安眠藥都有一定的風險，會產生依賴性。

139. Ⓐ 提供
Ⓑ 支撐
Ⓒ 緩和
Ⓓ 維持

140. Ⓐ 核准
Ⓑ 核准
Ⓒ 贊成的
Ⓓ 經過檢驗的

141. **Ⓐ 因此您可以安心每夜服用。**
Ⓑ 今天就和醫生討論，看是否適合您。
Ⓒ 這是唯一經食品藥物管理局核准可長期使用的興奮劑。
Ⓓ 輸入這個代碼就可獲得免費樣品與折扣優惠。

142. Ⓐ 在……期間
Ⓑ 在……附近
Ⓒ 在……前
Ⓓ 在……後

員工留言板

請求回應

人力資源部主管，詹姆斯·弗羅姆發布

同仁們大家好：

節慶季很快就到來了，我們需要規劃一下我們的辦公室派對！已經有好幾個地點和主題的提案直接送到我這來了，但我想邀請辦公室的各位給我一點回應。所有的構想都很歡迎，但我必須提醒各位本辦公室接納各種習俗與文化。我們的派對可涵蓋各種世俗的慶祝活動，但出於對所有人的尊重，不能有與宗教相關的主題。請直接以電子郵件回覆到 jamesfrohm@ccn.net 給我，這樣我就可以開始規劃了。期待收到各位的點子！

詹姆斯 敬上

143. Ⓐ 製作
Ⓑ 計劃
Ⓒ 設想
Ⓓ 遞送

144. Ⓐ 評論
Ⓑ 建議
Ⓒ 地點
Ⓓ 建議的

145. **Ⓐ 接納各種習俗與文化**
Ⓑ 週二會營業到很晚
Ⓒ 需要新的清潔工
Ⓓ 下週要搬家

146. **Ⓐ 期待收到各位的點子！**
Ⓑ 我可不希望你們遲到！
Ⓒ 期待各位的全神留意。
Ⓓ 希望各位來得及回覆。

147-148 傳單

三星運動器材行

56634 明尼蘇達州伯米吉費爾蒙大道 5477 號

218-555-3412

www.tristarsportsgear.com

7 月 1 日至 7 月 14 日夏季特賣

學年已經結束，夏天也已經到了。來三星運動器材行，好好地利用本週五開始的年度盛大夏季拍賣會吧。現在正是準備好迎接夏季樂活的時候。我們將以原價八折的優惠販售您最喜愛的運動隊伍的球衣。此外，如果您購買兩雙運動鞋，就可以用半價購買第三雙。還有更多特價商品，請參考背頁的特賣清單。

■ 持本傳單到本店，即可以九折的優惠購買各種球類。

147. 下列何者與三星運動器材行有關？

Ⓐ 是家族企業

Ⓑ 位於學校旁邊

Ⓒ **每年舉辦特賣會**

Ⓓ 主要販售重量訓練器材

148. 顧客要如何獲得運動鞋的優惠？

Ⓐ **購買兩雙以上的運動鞋**

Ⓑ 7 月 1 日到店

Ⓒ 網路訂購

Ⓓ 出示傳單

149-150 訊息串

希薇亞　　　　　　　**19:01**

我們要去看什麼電影？

傑森　　　　　　　**19:08**

我們昨晚說好的那部啊！

菲利斯　　　　　　　**19:08**

對啊，看起來超好看！我愛恐怖片！

伯恩　　　　　　　**19:20**

！！！你是什麼意思？我以為我們決定的是喜劇片，新的那部！

希薇亞　　　　　　　**19:21**

沒錯！那部有知名諧星黃亂鬍的喜劇片。

傑森　　　　　　　**19:25**

喜劇片？我也以為是恐怖片，不過我喜歡黃亂鬍。算我一份！

菲利斯　　　　　　　**19:35**

好，那就是喜劇片了。晚上 10 點整在戲院外頭見。

149. 菲利斯以為大夥兒要去看哪一類的電影？

Ⓐ **恐怖片**

Ⓑ 科幻片

Ⓒ 喜劇片

Ⓓ 浪漫愛情片

150. 傑森的簡訊寫：「算我一份！」是什麼意思？

Ⓐ 他想看大家同意的恐怖片

Ⓑ 他想演喜劇片

Ⓒ **他想加入大家**

Ⓓ 他今晚想待在家

151-152 文章

布里克斯頓科學期刊

3 月 3 日，知名考古學家道格拉斯·普瑞斯將介紹他長年挖掘埃及古墓遺址的成果。這場演講將於布里克頓公立圖書館舉行，晚間六點開始。

希望與會者能提早到場，以參觀一些展示的古埃及用具和器械。這些寶貴的展品是普瑞斯先生在他遠征埃及時所取得，真的是獨一無二。它們被認為是古埃及人用來耕作的器具。

有意參加者，可上網 www.brixtonlibrary.com 預約席位。您也可以在網頁上找到更多有關普瑞斯先生最近的研究資料。

151. 文中提到有關這個活動的什麼？

Ⓐ 由埃及政府贊助

Ⓑ **將特別介紹工藝品展**

Ⓒ 將於埃及舉行

Ⓓ 票券已經全數售完

152. 在圖書館的網站上可以找到什麼？

 Ⓐ 活動行事曆
 Ⓑ 該地區的詳細地圖
 Ⓒ 有關古埃及的事
 Ⓓ 埃及食物指南

153–154 邀請函

> ### 春谷中心
> #### 在樺木街盛大開幕
>
> 2 月 23 日，星期一
>
> 加州春谷的春谷中心誠摯地邀請您
>
> 參觀我們可供出租的新辦公場所！
>
> 週一整天我們將舉辦開放參觀日
>
> 歡迎所有人到場參觀
>
> 春谷中心交通便利，就在 10 號公路下。

153. 春谷中心最有可能是什麼場所？

 Ⓐ 百貨公司
 Ⓑ 會議中心
 Ⓒ 物流公司
 Ⓓ 辦公園區

154. 為什麼要舉辦活動？

 Ⓐ 吸引新員工到公司
 Ⓑ 安排銷售會議
 Ⓒ 宣傳商業出租場所
 Ⓓ 宣布購物中心的開幕

155–157 文章

> ### 羅克蘭商業新聞
>
> 9 月 8 日——批發商巨擘卡旭可大賣場的發言人星期一證實，下個月終於要羅克蘭開新分店。這消息讓加拿大和美國邊境雙邊的居民都備感安慰，因為許多從羅克蘭來的購物者通常得花上一個半小時，開車進加拿大到布倫特伍德的卡旭可大賣場買東西。這通常造成邊境大排長龍，而且擠滿加拿大卡旭可大賣場的購物者半數以上都是來自邊境。許多住在布倫特伍德的加拿大居民對於大批民眾擠進他們的小城鎮

感到憤怒，而羅克蘭的居民也抱怨美國境內最近的卡旭可大賣場居然相距將近五小時車程之遙。

「我覺得很興奮，」羅克蘭居民珍妮絲·布洛斯説，「聽説賣場很大。或許加拿大人也會開始來這裡買東西。但正經地説，我們要求在這裡開設分店已經很長一段時間了。」有傳聞説新的羅克蘭卡旭可大賣場將成為美國最大的賣場之一，擁有自己的加油站、寵物中心、餐廳、自助餐廳、園藝中心與醫療診所。

155. 這篇文章是有關什麼？

 Ⓐ 邊境的緊張情勢
 Ⓑ 鄰近居民間的競爭
 Ⓒ 跨境遠征購物
 Ⓓ 近期即將開幕的卡旭可新分店

156. 下列何者與加拿大居民有關？

 Ⓐ 他們想要一間卡旭可分店
 Ⓑ 他們不喜歡美國人過來購物
 Ⓒ 他們不喜歡去美國
 Ⓓ 他們要走很遠才能到一家卡旭可賣場

157. 下列句子最適合出現在 [1]、[2]、[3]、[4] 的哪個位置？「批發商巨擘卡旭可大賣場的發言人星期一證實，下個月終於要在羅克蘭開新分店。」

 Ⓐ [1]
 Ⓑ [2]
 Ⓒ [3]
 Ⓓ [4]

158-160 文章

> ### 森特維爾郡立收容所舉辦馬拉松比賽為街友募款
>
> 下週六將於森特維爾郡舉辦一場馬拉松競走比賽。活動的所有收入都將捐給森特維爾郡立收容所。這個公立機構為街友、年長者或任何有需要的人提供食物、住宿與協助服務。
>
> 這活動將是第二次舉辦，籌辦單位期盼能有比去年更多的參與者。這個活動開放給

各年齡層的孩童與成人參加。但是孩童必須全程由成年家人陪伴。

森特維爾郡立收容所成立於 1981 年，其宗旨為減輕無家可歸、貧困及飢餓者的苦難。

158. 最有可能報名這個活動的原因是什麼？
- Ⓐ 學習保持身材的方法
- Ⓑ 贏得現金獎項
- Ⓒ 應徵工作
- **Ⓓ 對社區做出貢獻**

159. 根據本篇文章，誰不可以參加這個活動？
- Ⓐ 該郡的老年民眾
- Ⓑ 沒有學生證的學生
- **Ⓒ 無人陪伴的孩童**
- Ⓓ 外國遊客

160. 森特維爾郡立收容所的主要目標是什麼？
- Ⓐ 建造價格便宜的房屋
- **Ⓑ 提供基本需求**
- Ⓒ 培訓專業運動員
- Ⓓ 教育社區成員

161–164 網路討論區

茉莉	有誰明天要和我一起去勝利遊行的嗎？
蘇珊	我要！我整個球季都有在關注這個球隊。他們的球賽都很好看，而他們的四分衛可能是該校有史以來最厲害的！這也將是個好機會，可以建立關係同時宣傳我們新款的贏家啤酒！
傑夫	可能會很好玩吧。但是我擔心的是我們的競爭對手，以及他們與大學和球場的贊助合約。
茉莉	啊。沒錯，我沒想到那些……嗯，我們可以「私底下」進行……哈哈。
蘇珊	是啊，如果被公司發現，我們一定會被開除……或者更慘。
傑夫	沒錯，但我還是想去看比賽，至少分析我們競爭對手的行銷策略。

蘇珊	説的好，傑夫。我們去吧，但是你最好閉上你的嘴。
傑夫	謝啦，蘇珊，我會的。所以我們都會去，還要做筆記，對吧？

161. 下列何者與贏家啤酒有關？
- Ⓐ 是老牌子啤酒
- **Ⓑ 人們還不知道這個牌子**
- Ⓒ 很好喝
- Ⓓ 價格便宜

162. 這群人接下來最有可能會做什麼？
- Ⓐ 向公司報告傑夫的事
- **Ⓑ 去參加勝利遊行**
- Ⓒ 看電影
- Ⓓ 去跳舞並喝贏家啤酒

163. 茉莉寫：「私底下」是什麼意思？
- Ⓐ 是一條尚未發表的歌
- Ⓑ 是記載他們活動的紀錄
- **Ⓒ 他們不會進行公務**
- Ⓓ 所有事情都被紀錄，而他們不想再被記錄

164. 下列何者與傑夫有關？
- Ⓐ 他的筆記做得很好
- Ⓑ 他喜歡喝酒
- **Ⓒ 他喜歡講話**
- Ⓓ 他熱愛遊行

利希滕貝格航空

9 月 24 日

致旅客:

自 10 月 1 日開始,利希滕貝格航空將要求旅客額外支付 20% 的行李托運費用。如各位所知,調漲的原因是因為燃油價格上揚。本公司很遺憾地必須調漲行李托運費用。

然而,旅客仍可免費攜帶一件隨身行李。本公司也要強調,這是利希滕貝格航空 10 年來第一次調漲行李托運費用。

一如既往,本公司的目標就是以合理的價格來提供既安全又可靠的交通運輸。當燃油價格調降時,本公司亦期盼能調回原先的價格。

感謝您選擇搭乘利希滕貝格航空。

165. 下列何者與利希滕貝格航空有關?
[A] 要求乘客遵守行李限制
[B] 回應顧客的抱怨
[C] 已經 10 年未曾調漲行李託運費用
[D] 已經新增目的地

166. 下列何者與乘客有關?
[A] 允許攜帶電子產品上飛機
[B] 可免費攜帶一件行李上飛機
[C] 從 10 月 1 日起必須支付調漲的機票錢
[D] 下個月可以獲得 20% 的優惠折扣

167. 根據公告所示,當燃油價格調降時,將發生什麼事?
[A] 利希滕貝格航空的股價會上漲
[B] 將提供乘客禮券
[C] 將聘僱更多空服員
[D] 將取消額外收取的費用

4 月 4 日

寶拉・林區

42195 明尼蘇達州埃利市庫勒大道 344 號

親愛的林區女士:

很高興您接受我們的邀請,於今年的第二語言教育研討會上發表演說。如您所知,研討會將有德語、法語、中文與其他許多外國語言的老師,齊聚一堂分享教學技巧與方法。除了參加工作坊與研討會外,與會者也有許多機會在各種活動裡交談以及建立關係。這是個不容錯過的機會。

今年的研討會將於奧勒岡州撒冷市的威爾森會議中心舉行,時間是 7 月 12 日星期四至 7 月 15 日星期日。如果提出申請的話,演講嘉賓可租借筆電與其他器材於研討會期間使用,所有出借的器材必須於研討會最後一天歸還。除了演講費之外,所有的演講嘉賓亦可免費參加所有其他工作坊與研討會。

煩請告知您的詳細行程。我們會請工作人員開車至機場接機,並將您送至會場。請於 4 月 10 日前撥打辦公室電話 (456) 555-1345 以提供資訊。

期待在研討會上與您見面。

研討會籌辦人
德克・克萊 敬上

168. 下列何者與林區女士有關?
[A] 她住在奧勒岡州撒冷市
[B] 她會說第二種語言
[C] 她是位能激發人的講者
[D] 她是研討會的籌辦人

169. 研討會的目的是什麼?
[A] 吸引國外投資客
[B] 分享教學方法
[C] 設定課程標準
[D] 建立慈善基金會

170. 講者必須在何時歸還借用的器材？

    Ⓐ 4 月 4 日
    Ⓑ 4 月 10 日
    Ⓒ 7 月 12 日
    Ⓓ 7 月 15 日

171. 林區女士被要求告知克萊先生什麼事？

    Ⓐ 她何時抵達
    Ⓑ 她需要何種器材
    Ⓒ 她要用哪種會議室
    Ⓓ 誰會陪她一起來

172–175 信件

> ### 班迪特製藥廠
>
> 48573 麻薩諸塞州波士頓高速道路 255 號
>
> 4 月 23 日
> 提摩西・簡恩先生
> 97658 加州佛雷斯諾希微亞區 6844 號
>
> 親愛的簡恩先生：
>
> 班迪特製藥廠很開心您接受了研究助理一職。您的到職日為 5 月 5 日。第一天是安排給全體新進員工的任職培訓會，內容包括職場安全工作坊、工作職責說明會及設施導覽。您的實驗室主管將在第一天尾聲給您更詳細的說明。
>
> 因為您來自外地，公司想讓您的搬遷過程能順利進行。公司知道您將於 4 月 29 日抵達，並在波士頓家庭旅社住幾天。該旅社距離班迪特製藥廠總公司大約 10 分鐘的計程車車程。您可以到大廳櫃台找人力資源部的珍娜・萊姆絲女士。她會協助非本地新進員工適應本地環境，並回答您可能有的疑慮。我也附上與您搬遷相關的場所和機構的電話號碼。
>
> 若您有其他問題或疑慮，請於星期一至五上午 9 點至晚上 7 點上班時間來電 555-1234 與我聯絡。祝您搬遷順利，5 月 5 日見。
>
> 人力資源部
> 瓊安・諾南 敬上

172. 諾南女士為什麼寄信給簡恩先生？

    Ⓐ 提供工作面試的時間與地點細節
    Ⓑ 提供第一天上班的資訊
    Ⓒ 提供租屋資訊
    Ⓓ 確認他是否接受這份工作

173. 諾南女士隨信寄了什麼？

    Ⓐ 電話號碼
    Ⓑ 一份合約
    Ⓒ 公司員工的聯絡資料
    Ⓓ 時間表

174. 第二段的「settle into」意思最接近？

    Ⓐ 尋找
    Ⓑ 探索
    Ⓒ 變得自在
    Ⓓ 引導

175. 下列句子最適合出現在 [1]、[2]、[3]、[4] 的哪個位置？「您的實驗室主管將在第一天尾聲給您更詳細的說明。」

    Ⓐ [1]
    Ⓑ [2]
    Ⓒ [3]
    Ⓓ [4]

TEST 10

PART 7

176–180 網站和電子郵件

> ### 黑石教育基金會
>
> | 首頁 | 關於我們 | 最新消息 | 資源連結 | 與我們聯絡 |
> |---|---|---|---|---|
>
> 2 月 10 日
>
> **語言獎學金**
>
> 黑石教育基金會宣布，我們即將開始受理第 24 屆德語獎學金的申請，時間自 3 月 10 日起至 3 月 31 日為止，鼓勵不同專業背景的人士前來申請。為符合獎學金的申請資格，申請者必須：
>
> - 現為碩士生
> - 證明具進階德語能力
> - 繳交一份完整的健康檢查報告
> - 繳交一份以前的語言教師的推薦信

德語獎學金的對象為具德語口說進階程度的學生。因此，這份獎學金將提供給打算近期以德語到德國求學的學生。

獎學金得主必須完成每月的進度報告，繳交完整的每月支出明細給基金會，並維持平均 B+ 的成績。

申請者可於網站的「資源連結」下載申請表。請將所有必要文件繳交給黑石教育基金會的主任漢斯・里希特先生，地址是 60616 伊利諾州芝加哥市皮爾森路 459 號。審查與選拔程序大約需兩週的時間，不完整或缺件的申請案件一律退件。結果將於 4 月 15 日公布。

收件者：克林特・波特
<cporter@umc.com>
寄件者：漢斯・里希特
<richter@blackrockedu.com>
日期：4 月 15 日
主旨：黑石獎學金
附件：獎學金 _ 資料

親愛的波特先生：

我要恭喜您獲得第 24 屆德語獎學金。身為獎學金得主，您將獲得基金會提供您到德國的旅費、學費以及一整年的生活費。隨信附上簡章一本，內含獎學金規定與條件等相關資料，請務必仔細閱讀。若有任何問題或疑慮，歡迎與我聯絡。下週之內我會把如何準備未來求學的詳細資料以電子郵件寄給您。

謝謝。

漢斯・里希特
黑石教育基金會主任

---

176. 根據網頁，獎學金得主必須做什麼？

　Ⓐ 記錄每月支出
　Ⓑ 寫研究報告
　Ⓒ 繳交年度報告
　Ⓓ 參加入學考試

177. 下列何者與獎學金申請有關？

　Ⓐ 必須在四月中旬前收到
　Ⓑ 只有符合條件才能申請
　Ⓒ 將由德國教授來審查和選拔
　Ⓓ 必須線上繳交

178. 在網頁上，第一段第六行的「proficiency」意思最接近？

　Ⓐ 系統
　Ⓑ 練習
　Ⓒ 經驗
　Ⓓ 精通

179. 這封電子郵件的目的是什麼？

　Ⓐ 確認出發日期
　Ⓑ 安排面試
　Ⓒ 提供獎學金得主一些資料
　Ⓓ 報名德國大學必修課程

180. 以下何者與波特先生有關？

　Ⓐ 他在黑石基金會上班
　Ⓑ 他是在德國工作的企業家
　Ⓒ 他精通德語
　Ⓓ 他想要成為語言教師

181–185 請款單和信件

晴天清潔公司
專業清潔的唯一選擇

付款人：藍道車體公司（97055 奧勒岡州勞特代爾太平洋道 957 號）
請款編號：2348
日期： 3 月 3 日

日期	服務說明	總額
2 月 5 日	辦公室全套清潔（含：辦公室三間、浴室兩間、窗戶、地毯深層清潔、家具）	95 元
2 月 19 日	辦公室全套清潔（含：辦公室三間，浴室兩間、窗戶、地毯深層清潔、家具）	95 元
		總計：190 元

*4 月 1 日後付款需支付滯延金 20 元晴天

清潔公司

97055 奧勒岡州勞特代爾主街 283 號
若有疑問或需額外服務，請撥 1-345-737-2209

---

3 月 8 日

親愛的晴天清潔公司：

我已收到貴公司二月份清潔服務的請款單，我必須說服務品質很棒。我看到每次清潔辦公室的費用是 95 元。這是我們最初達成協議的價格，並且從去年此時就開始支付這樣的價碼。但是，羅德·山福告訴我，因為我們請貴公司去清掃本公司在 26 號高速道路旁的另一間辦公室，因此接下來貴公司的每次清潔服務都將提供五元的優惠折扣。他說新價碼將自二月份開始生效，我附上了羅德·山福寄給我的電子郵件影本。能否請您依照新的協議調整價格，並再寄一份新帳單過來？感謝您。期待再次見到您們。

感謝您的協助！

藍道車體公司經理
派翠西亞·柯林斯

---

181. 根據請款單，4 月 1 日前須支付的金額是多少？

Ⓐ 20 元
Ⓑ 90 元
Ⓒ 95 元
Ⓓ 190 元

182. 下列何者未在提供給藍道車體公司的服務中？

Ⓐ 窗戶清潔
Ⓑ 地板清潔
Ⓒ 家具清潔
Ⓓ 地毯清潔

183. 柯林斯女士為什麼寫這封信？

Ⓐ 清潔公司少打掃一次
Ⓑ 她被多收錢
Ⓒ 清潔公司在帳單裡增加了額外的費用
Ⓓ 她想要續約

184. 下列何者與晴天清潔公司有關？

Ⓐ 提供不錯的服務
Ⓑ 通常比預定時間晚到
Ⓒ 經常向客戶多收錢
Ⓓ 提供延後付款的選擇

185. 除了信之外，柯林斯女士還寄了什麼？

Ⓐ 汽車維修的折價券
Ⓑ 一封電子郵件的影本
Ⓒ 已簽名的合約
Ⓓ 應付金額的支票

186–190 文章、網頁和獎狀

給通勤者的緩解方法

由於公車及計程車費用不斷上漲，加上通勤者不斷地尋求更有效率的交通路線，一個新的共乘應用程式正大受歡迎。小企業老闆喬丹·密爾斯，從布倫特伍德的家必須轉兩趟公車再搭乘地鐵，才能到市中心的公司上班。他發現不只通動的費用頗高，尖峰時段擁擠的人群令人不適外，他也發現太過耗費時間。但是使用新的應用程式飛輪後，他發現不管身在何處，五分鐘之內就有車可搭，節省了時間和金錢。「這絕對是交通運輸的未來樣貌。」喬丹說，「我無法再以其他的方式通勤上下班了。」

喬丹·密爾斯不是唯一有這種感覺的通勤者。估計光在西華市就約有 2,000 名的通勤者將在明年內使用這個共乘應用程式，且將近 500 位駕駛已登記加入了這個計劃。

飛輪應用程式可於飛輪網站以及 <u>Miniapp.com</u> 和 <u>Amacom.com</u> 下載。

---

www.freewheel.com/history

當麥可·歐文斯和他同事在他們工作的公司首次發起汽車共乘計劃時，飛輪的構想便萌芽了。歐文斯必須轉三次地鐵和兩次公車才能到辦公室，雖然他可以開車，但停車位有限。他管理共乘群組的方式，是透過指派不同的駕駛及劃出每位同事家的路線圖。然後，他設計了一個應用程式，讓大家都可以

TEST
10

PART 7

透過它相互連結交流，如此一來，被指派的駕駛與乘客便能輕鬆的找到對方。五年後，飛輪已經是間大公司，在全國擁有數以萬計的使用者包含駕駛和乘客。

飛輪致力於壓低通勤費用並提高效率。希望有天能將這個服務提供給全世界的人使用。

創新科技

很驕傲地將新創獎頒發給飛輪公司的執行長麥可‧歐文斯！

這個獎項表彰了科技產業中新人才的革新與創造力，同時也表揚他努力透過科技的運用及創新的構想，來改革運輸業的本質。

創新科技總經理
蘇珊‧凡尼爾

186. 喬丹‧密爾斯和麥可‧歐文斯有什麼相似之處？

 Ⓐ 都創立了科技公司
 Ⓑ 都想要一個有效率的通勤方式
 Ⓒ 都在公共運輸業上班
 Ⓓ 都因其成就而獲獎

187. 下列何者與飛輪公司有關？

 Ⓐ 以小型企業起家
 Ⓑ 是間國際化的公司
 Ⓒ 聘用公車司機
 Ⓓ 對環境有益

188. 有關麥可‧歐文斯的敘述，下列何者為真？

 Ⓐ 他不喜歡開車
 Ⓑ 他擁有一間計程車公司
 Ⓒ 他想要擴展事業版圖
 Ⓓ 他見過喬丹‧密爾斯

189. 文章標題「Respite」意思最接近？

 Ⓐ 就業
 Ⓑ 免疫力
 Ⓒ 退款
 Ⓓ 改變

190. 獎狀是在獎勵什麼？

 Ⓐ 最佳駕駛人
 Ⓑ 對環保的努力
 Ⓒ 好的構想
 Ⓓ 獲利最高的公司

191–195 電子郵件

收件者：肯恩‧亞伯斯
<kalberts@emergentsolutions.com>
寄件者：克拉麗莎‧皮爾斯
<cpierce@actionservices.com>
日期：6 月 13 日
主旨：運送合約

親愛的亞伯斯先生：
僅代表本公司行動服務寫信給您。本公司專長創作客製化花卉擺設、禮物籃及新穎禮品。最近我們檢視帳冊後，發現我們支付太多運費給目前合作的貨運公司。若貴公司能提供更具競爭力的價格，我們有意讓貴公司接手這項業務。我已附上目前配合的貨運公司快捷公司最近所開立的運費請款單。若貴公司認為您能提供更優惠的價格，本公司願意嘗試與貴公司合作。請告知貴公司的想法。

行動服務 客戶經理
克拉麗莎‧皮爾斯 敬上

收件者：克拉麗莎‧皮爾斯
<cpierce@actionservices.com>
寄件者：肯恩‧亞伯斯
<kalberts@emergentsolutions.com>
日期：6 月 14 日
主旨：運送合約

親愛的皮爾斯女士：
感謝您與本公司緊急物流聯絡。我已看過快捷公司最新一期的單據，我相信本公司能在價格上取勝。我很樂意派本公司的客戶主管制定出一份最符合貴公司需求的運送方案。既然貴公司大部分的運送地點都在本州內，而且運送的是小型物品，我相信我們的快遞服務會很適合。我們使用省油的油電混合車來運送小型物品，將省下的金額回饋給顧客。身為客戶總監，我期盼未來能與行動服務合作。

肯恩‧亞伯斯 敬上

收件者：肯恩・亞伯斯
<kalberts@emergentsolutions.com>
寄件者：克拉麗莎・皮爾斯
<cpierce@actionservices.com>
日期：6月16日
主旨：運送合約

亞伯斯先生：

這聽起來很棒！您不知道貴公司使用節能交通工具這點對本公司有多重要。行動服務最初就是由一群城市大學環境研究的學生所組成的，我們賣的所有產品都透過道德貿易而來並且是可回收的。我們迫不及待與貴公司團隊會面了。

行動服務 客戶經理
克拉麗莎・皮爾斯 敬上

191. 亞伯斯先生的工作是什麼？

    Ⓐ 總裁
    Ⓑ 人資主管
    Ⓒ 執行長
    Ⓓ 客戶總監

192. 下列何者與行動服務有關？

    Ⓐ 他們關心藝術
    Ⓑ 他們關懷環境
    Ⓒ 他們需要販售更多包裹
    Ⓓ 他們舊的貨運公司將包裹送錯地方

193. 根據電子郵件內容，可推論出什麼？

    Ⓐ 緊急物流提供比快捷公司便宜的收費
    Ⓑ 緊急物流的效率不高
    Ⓒ 緊急物流的企業倫理與行動服務不合
    Ⓓ 行動服務目前負債中

194. 行動服務為什麼要與緊急物流聯絡？

    Ⓐ 他們需要新客戶
    Ⓑ 他們在運費上花太多錢
    Ⓒ 他們想要擴展業務
    Ⓓ 他們想要運貨到國外

195. 行動服務是何種企業？

    Ⓐ 科技顧問
    Ⓑ 領導專家
    Ⓒ 飯店與度假村專家
    Ⓓ 花卉與新奇小物供應商

196–200 電子郵件和表格

收件者：亞倫・唐諾
<adonald@acemail.com>
寄件者：詹姆斯・浩特
<holtrain@zipnet.net>
日期：1月12日
主旨：第一季績效評估

親愛的亞倫：

我想要先提醒您績效評估將如同先前討論的要開始進行了。我知道你在去年第四季承受了些壓力，所以我想要先給你一些預警。如果你想要通過評估，就必須讓數字顯著上升。正如你所知道的，我們過去幾年一直很努力要達到銷售目標，我很擔心要是業績毫無起色，瓊斯先生會決定裁員。我的業績數字已經遠遠超過我的目標值，所以我附上一份文件，裡面有一些可能的銷售對象，試看看吧。

祝好運！

詹姆斯

收件者：詹姆斯・浩特
<holtrain@zipnet.net>
寄件者：亞倫・唐諾
<adonald@acemail.com>
日期：1月12日
主旨：回覆：第一季績效評估

詹姆斯：

非常感謝你的客戶名單，我會立刻聯絡他們的。我不知道為什麼最近自己在科技部門的業績會衰退這麼多，在學校學的銷售技巧好像都不管用了。如果我沒通過三月公布的評估，我打算換個跑道。我妹妹要開一間美容院，她要我去當理髮師。想像那畫面吧！不管怎樣，再次感謝你提醒未來可能裁員一事。我會努力將業績提升到公司標準，但我覺得瓊斯先生可能已經決定要叫我走路了。

祝一切順利。

亞倫

一月份可能的銷售客戶名單			
姓名	類別	可能進帳	等級
沙莉・瓊斯	科技類	35,000 元 – 50,000 元	銀級
鮑伯・納德	科技類	100,000 元以上	金級
馬基斯・李	科技類	12,000 元 – 20,000 元	銅級／銀級

196. 下列關於詹姆斯和亞倫的敘述,何者正確?

    Ⓐ 他們是競爭對手
    Ⓑ 他們有親戚關係
    Ⓒ 他們結婚了
    Ⓓ 他們是朋友

197. 下列何者與亞倫有關?

    Ⓐ 他最近在工作上表現不好
    Ⓑ 老闆喜歡他
    Ⓒ 跟所有同事間有些問題
    Ⓓ 評估結果出爐後他還能保住工作

198. 根據所提供的資訊,下列與詹姆斯有關的敘述,何者為真?

    Ⓐ 他工作上的表現非常好
    Ⓑ 他需要更多業績
    Ⓒ 他想要和亞倫一起工作
    Ⓓ 他將成為一名理髮師

199. 詹姆斯給亞倫的銷售名單有什麼問題?

    Ⓐ 等級太高
    Ⓑ 值不了多少錢
    Ⓒ 亞倫不認識這些人
    Ⓓ 正是他處境艱難的領域

200. 下列何者最有可能是瓊斯先生的工作?

    Ⓐ 人力資源仲介
    Ⓑ 銷售經理
    Ⓒ 老闆
    Ⓓ 助理秘書

ANSWER KEY

Actual Test 01

101 (B)	126 (D)	151 (C)	176 (A)
102 (A)	127 (C)	152 (B)	177 (B)
103 (B)	128 (A)	153 (B)	178 (C)
104 (A)	129 (D)	154 (B)	179 (C)
105 (B)	130 (A)	155 (C)	180 (B)
106 (C)	131 (C)	156 (A)	181 (C)
107 (D)	132 (A)	157 (B)	182 (D)
108 (B)	133 (D)	158 (A)	183 (A)
109 (C)	134 (B)	159 (C)	184 (A)
110 (A)	135 (B)	160 (B)	185 (B)
111 (C)	136 (D)	161 (B)	186 (A)
112 (A)	137 (A)	162 (C)	187 (B)
113 (B)	138 (C)	163 (C)	188 (D)
114 (B)	139 (C)	164 (D)	189 (C)
115 (C)	140 (D)	165 (B)	190 (D)
116 (D)	141 (B)	166 (C)	191 (D)
117 (C)	142 (B)	167 (D)	192 (A)
118 (B)	143 (D)	168 (B)	193 (C)
119 (A)	144 (C)	169 (C)	194 (D)
120 (A)	145 (C)	170 (A)	195 (D)
121 (C)	146 (B)	171 (C)	196 (A)
122 (C)	147 (D)	172 (A)	197 (B)
123 (A)	148 (B)	173 (B)	198 (D)
124 (A)	149 (C)	174 (C)	199 (A)
125 (C)	150 (A)	175 (B)	200 (B)

Actual Test 02

101 (D)	126 (A)	151 (C)	176 (B)
102 (A)	127 (A)	152 (B)	177 (D)
103 (C)	128 (B)	153 (C)	178 (C)
104 (B)	129 (B)	154 (A)	179 (B)
105 (C)	130 (A)	155 (C)	180 (A)
106 (C)	131 (C)	156 (A)	181 (D)
107 (C)	132 (D)	157 (C)	182 (B)
108 (A)	133 (B)	158 (C)	183 (D)
109 (C)	134 (C)	159 (B)	184 (A)
110 (A)	135 (D)	160 (D)	185 (C)
111 (D)	136 (D)	161 (D)	186 (C)
112 (C)	137 (A)	162 (D)	187 (C)
113 (C)	138 (C)	163 (A)	188 (D)
114 (A)	139 (C)	164 (C)	189 (A)
115 (D)	140 (A)	165 (B)	190 (C)
116 (C)	141 (A)	166 (C)	191 (A)
117 (A)	142 (C)	167 (D)	192 (C)
118 (D)	143 (C)	168 (A)	193 (B)
119 (D)	144 (A)	169 (C)	194 (C)
120 (D)	145 (B)	170 (D)	195 (D)
121 (A)	146 (D)	171 (A)	196 (B)
122 (B)	147 (C)	172 (B)	197 (D)
123 (D)	148 (B)	173 (C)	198 (C)
124 (B)	149 (B)	174 (D)	199 (B)
125 (A)	150 (A)	175 (A)	200 (A)

Actual Test 03

101 (A)	126 (B)	151 (B)	176 (B)
102 (A)	127 (A)	152 (C)	177 (C)
103 (C)	128 (A)	153 (D)	178 (A)
104 (B)	129 (D)	154 (D)	179 (D)
105 (C)	130 (D)	155 (D)	180 (C)
106 (B)	131 (A)	156 (C)	181 (C)
107 (C)	132 (A)	157 (B)	182 (A)
108 (D)	133 (B)	158 (B)	183 (B)
109 (B)	134 (D)	159 (A)	184 (B)
110 (C)	135 (A)	160 (C)	185 (B)
111 (B)	136 (B)	161 (D)	186 (B)
112 (B)	137 (B)	162 (C)	187 (C)
113 (D)	138 (B)	163 (B)	188 (A)
114 (B)	139 (B)	164 (A)	189 (D)
115 (A)	140 (B)	165 (A)	190 (D)
116 (D)	141 (A)	166 (B)	191 (D)
117 (A)	142 (C)	167 (C)	192 (B)
118 (D)	143 (A)	168 (D)	193 (B)
119 (B)	144 (B)	169 (B)	194 (D)
120 (D)	145 (B)	170 (B)	195 (B)
121 (C)	146 (B)	171 (B)	196 (B)
122 (A)	147 (C)	172 (C)	197 (D)
123 (D)	148 (A)	173 (D)	198 (B)
124 (D)	149 (B)	174 (A)	199 (A)
125 (C)	150 (D)	175 (D)	200 (B)

Actual Test 04

101 (A)	126 (D)	151 (C)	176 (D)
102 (D)	127 (C)	152 (B)	177 (A)
103 (C)	128 (D)	153 (D)	178 (B)
104 (B)	129 (A)	154 (A)	179 (B)
105 (A)	130 (A)	155 (C)	180 (B)
106 (B)	131 (C)	156 (A)	181 (C)
107 (B)	132 (D)	157 (B)	182 (A)
108 (A)	133 (C)	158 (D)	183 (D)
109 (B)	134 (B)	159 (C)	184 (B)
110 (B)	135 (C)	160 (C)	185 (B)
111 (D)	136 (B)	161 (C)	186 (A)
112 (C)	137 (D)	162 (B)	187 (D)
113 (D)	138 (A)	163 (D)	188 (C)
114 (B)	139 (A)	164 (A)	189 (A)
115 (B)	140 (C)	165 (C)	190 (D)
116 (D)	141 (B)	166 (B)	191 (A)
117 (A)	142 (C)	167 (C)	192 (A)
118 (C)	143 (C)	168 (B)	193 (C)
119 (C)	144 (B)	169 (D)	194 (B)
120 (D)	145 (A)	170 (B)	195 (A)
121 (A)	146 (B)	171 (B)	196 (A)
122 (C)	147 (B)	172 (B)	197 (D)
123 (B)	148 (C)	173 (A)	198 (B)
124 (B)	149 (C)	174 (C)	199 (B)
125 (A)	150 (B)	175 (D)	200 (A)

Actual Test 05

101 (B)	126 (B)	151 (D)	176 (C)
102 (A)	127 (A)	152 (B)	177 (D)
103 (C)	128 (D)	153 (B)	178 (B)
104 (C)	129 (B)	154 (D)	179 (D)
105 (D)	130 (B)	155 (C)	180 (B)
106 (C)	131 (C)	156 (C)	181 (C)
107 (A)	132 (D)	157 (D)	182 (D)
108 (D)	133 (B)	158 (B)	183 (B)
109 (D)	134 (A)	159 (A)	184 (C)
110 (A)	135 (D)	160 (C)	185 (D)
111 (D)	136 (A)	161 (A)	186 (C)
112 (C)	137 (C)	162 (B)	187 (B)
113 (C)	138 (B)	163 (B)	188 (C)
114 (A)	139 (B)	164 (D)	189 (C)
115 (C)	140 (D)	165 (D)	190 (B)
116 (A)	141 (C)	166 (B)	191 (B)
117 (C)	142 (A)	167 (A)	192 (C)
118 (B)	143 (C)	168 (C)	193 (B)
119 (B)	144 (A)	169 (B)	194 (D)
120 (C)	145 (C)	170 (A)	195 (C)
121 (A)	146 (D)	171 (D)	196 (B)
122 (A)	147 (C)	172 (C)	197 (C)
123 (A)	148 (D)	173 (B)	198 (B)
124 (C)	149 (B)	174 (A)	199 (D)
125 (D)	150 (B)	175 (C)	200 (C)

Actual Test 06

101 (D)	126 (A)	151 (D)	176 (B)
102 (B)	127 (B)	152 (B)	177 (C)
103 (C)	128 (C)	153 (A)	178 (C)
104 (A)	129 (B)	154 (C)	179 (C)
105 (C)	130 (C)	155 (B)	180 (C)
106 (B)	131 (B)	156 (C)	181 (A)
107 (A)	132 (D)	157 (B)	182 (C)
108 (D)	133 (C)	158 (C)	183 (B)
109 (A)	134 (A)	159 (A)	184 (C)
110 (B)	135 (C)	160 (D)	185 (D)
111 (A)	136 (C)	161 (C)	186 (D)
112 (C)	137 (A)	162 (C)	187 (C)
113 (D)	138 (D)	163 (B)	188 (C)
114 (C)	139 (C)	164 (A)	189 (D)
115 (D)	140 (B)	165 (D)	190 (B)
116 (C)	141 (A)	166 (A)	191 (B)
117 (A)	142 (A)	167 (C)	192 (A)
118 (A)	143 (D)	168 (B)	193 (C)
119 (C)	144 (C)	169 (C)	194 (D)
120 (C)	145 (A)	170 (A)	195 (B)
121 (C)	146 (C)	171 (C)	196 (C)
122 (C)	147 (A)	172 (C)	197 (B)
123 (D)	148 (C)	173 (B)	198 (C)
124 (D)	149 (C)	174 (D)	199 (B)
125 (B)	150 (B)	175 (C)	200 (C)

Actual Test 07

101 (A)	126 (C)	151 (D)	176 (C)
102 (C)	127 (C)	152 (C)	177 (B)
103 (A)	128 (C)	153 (B)	178 (D)
104 (B)	129 (D)	154 (C)	179 (A)
105 (B)	130 (D)	155 (B)	180 (B)
106 (C)	131 (B)	156 (C)	181 (A)
107 (B)	132 (D)	157 (A)	182 (D)
108 (D)	133 (B)	158 (B)	183 (C)
109 (D)	134 (A)	159 (C)	184 (C)
110 (D)	135 (C)	160 (A)	185 (A)
111 (A)	136 (D)	161 (C)	186 (D)
112 (B)	137 (C)	162 (A)	187 (D)
113 (D)	138 (A)	163 (B)	188 (B)
114 (D)	139 (D)	164 (C)	189 (A)
115 (A)	140 (C)	165 (D)	190 (C)
116 (C)	141 (A)	166 (C)	191 (C)
117 (C)	142 (B)	167 (B)	192 (D)
118 (A)	143 (B)	168 (D)	193 (B)
119 (A)	144 (C)	169 (C)	194 (B)
120 (A)	145 (D)	170 (C)	195 (B)
121 (D)	146 (C)	171 (A)	196 (D)
122 (D)	147 (C)	172 (A)	197 (B)
123 (B)	148 (B)	173 (D)	198 (A)
124 (D)	149 (D)	174 (B)	199 (D)
125 (A)	150 (B)	175 (C)	200 (C)

Actual Test 08

101 (D)	126 (B)	151 (C)	176 (A)
102 (B)	127 (C)	152 (C)	177 (B)
103 (B)	128 (D)	153 (C)	178 (D)
104 (A)	129 (A)	154 (D)	179 (C)
105 (C)	130 (B)	155 (A)	180 (C)
106 (B)	131 (C)	156 (C)	181 (A)
107 (A)	132 (A)	157 (B)	182 (B)
108 (D)	133 (C)	158 (D)	183 (B)
109 (C)	134 (D)	159 (C)	184 (C)
110 (A)	135 (B)	160 (C)	185 (D)
111 (A)	136 (A)	161 (D)	186 (D)
112 (C)	137 (C)	162 (D)	187 (C)
113 (C)	138 (D)	163 (B)	188 (B)
114 (B)	139 (A)	164 (A)	189 (C)
115 (C)	140 (A)	165 (B)	190 (A)
116 (D)	141 (A)	166 (C)	191 (C)
117 (C)	142 (A)	167 (C)	192 (A)
118 (D)	143 (C)	168 (A)	193 (B)
119 (A)	144 (A)	169 (A)	194 (C)
120 (A)	145 (A)	170 (D)	195 (D)
121 (D)	146 (B)	171 (C)	196 (D)
122 (B)	147 (C)	172 (B)	197 (A)
123 (A)	148 (A)	173 (A)	198 (B)
124 (A)	149 (C)	174 (A)	199 (C)
125 (D)	150 (D)	175 (C)	200 (B)

Actual Test 09

101 (A)	126 (B)	151 (C)	176 (D)
102 (B)	127 (A)	152 (B)	177 (B)
103 (D)	128 (A)	153 (B)	178 (D)
104 (D)	129 (A)	154 (D)	179 (C)
105 (C)	130 (D)	155 (A)	180 (A)
106 (C)	131 (C)	156 (C)	181 (B)
107 (D)	132 (A)	157 (A)	182 (C)
108 (C)	133 (B)	158 (D)	183 (B)
109 (D)	134 (D)	159 (C)	184 (B)
110 (A)	135 (B)	160 (D)	185 (C)
111 (D)	136 (D)	161 (D)	186 (C)
112 (C)	137 (A)	162 (B)	187 (A)
113 (A)	138 (B)	163 (C)	188 (C)
114 (B)	139 (D)	164 (A)	189 (C)
115 (C)	140 (C)	165 (D)	190 (A)
116 (D)	141 (A)	166 (B)	191 (C)
117 (C)	142 (D)	167 (D)	192 (A)
118 (A)	143 (D)	168 (C)	193 (C)
119 (D)	144 (D)	169 (A)	194 (B)
120 (A)	145 (B)	170 (B)	195 (C)
121 (D)	146 (D)	171 (C)	196 (B)
122 (A)	147 (B)	172 (D)	197 (C)
123 (A)	148 (A)	173 (D)	198 (B)
124 (C)	149 (B)	174 (D)	199 (C)
125 (D)	150 (D)	175 (C)	200 (A)

Actual Test 10

101 (B)	126 (C)	151 (B)	176 (A)
102 (A)	127 (C)	152 (C)	177 (B)
103 (D)	128 (A)	153 (D)	178 (D)
104 (B)	129 (A)	154 (C)	179 (C)
105 (B)	130 (D)	155 (D)	180 (C)
106 (C)	131 (C)	156 (B)	181 (D)
107 (C)	132 (B)	157 (A)	182 (B)
108 (D)	133 (B)	158 (D)	183 (B)
109 (B)	134 (C)	159 (C)	184 (A)
110 (D)	135 (C)	160 (B)	185 (B)
111 (B)	136 (B)	161 (B)	186 (B)
112 (D)	137 (A)	162 (B)	187 (A)
113 (C)	138 (C)	163 (C)	188 (C)
114 (A)	139 (A)	164 (C)	189 (D)
115 (C)	140 (D)	165 (C)	190 (C)
116 (D)	141 (A)	166 (B)	191 (D)
117 (A)	142 (C)	167 (D)	192 (B)
118 (B)	143 (B)	168 (B)	193 (A)
119 (C)	144 (B)	169 (B)	194 (B)
120 (C)	145 (A)	170 (D)	195 (D)
121 (D)	146 (A)	171 (A)	196 (D)
122 (B)	147 (C)	172 (B)	197 (A)
123 (B)	148 (A)	173 (A)	198 (A)
124 (A)	149 (A)	174 (C)	199 (D)
125 (A)	150 (C)	175 (A)	200 (C)

答案紙

ACTUAL TEST 01

READING SECTION

101	Ⓐ Ⓑ Ⓒ Ⓓ	111	Ⓐ Ⓑ Ⓒ Ⓓ	121	Ⓐ Ⓑ Ⓒ Ⓓ	131	Ⓐ Ⓑ Ⓒ Ⓓ	141	Ⓐ Ⓑ Ⓒ Ⓓ	151	Ⓐ Ⓑ Ⓒ Ⓓ	161	Ⓐ Ⓑ Ⓒ Ⓓ	171	Ⓐ Ⓑ Ⓒ Ⓓ	181	Ⓐ Ⓑ Ⓒ Ⓓ	191	Ⓐ Ⓑ Ⓒ Ⓓ
102	Ⓐ Ⓑ Ⓒ Ⓓ	112	Ⓐ Ⓑ Ⓒ Ⓓ	122	Ⓐ Ⓑ Ⓒ Ⓓ	132	Ⓐ Ⓑ Ⓒ Ⓓ	142	Ⓐ Ⓑ Ⓒ Ⓓ	152	Ⓐ Ⓑ Ⓒ Ⓓ	162	Ⓐ Ⓑ Ⓒ Ⓓ	172	Ⓐ Ⓑ Ⓒ Ⓓ	182	Ⓐ Ⓑ Ⓒ Ⓓ	192	Ⓐ Ⓑ Ⓒ Ⓓ
103	Ⓐ Ⓑ Ⓒ Ⓓ	113	Ⓐ Ⓑ Ⓒ Ⓓ	123	Ⓐ Ⓑ Ⓒ Ⓓ	133	Ⓐ Ⓑ Ⓒ Ⓓ	143	Ⓐ Ⓑ Ⓒ Ⓓ	153	Ⓐ Ⓑ Ⓒ Ⓓ	163	Ⓐ Ⓑ Ⓒ Ⓓ	173	Ⓐ Ⓑ Ⓒ Ⓓ	183	Ⓐ Ⓑ Ⓒ Ⓓ	193	Ⓐ Ⓑ Ⓒ Ⓓ
104	Ⓐ Ⓑ Ⓒ Ⓓ	114	Ⓐ Ⓑ Ⓒ Ⓓ	124	Ⓐ Ⓑ Ⓒ Ⓓ	134	Ⓐ Ⓑ Ⓒ Ⓓ	144	Ⓐ Ⓑ Ⓒ Ⓓ	154	Ⓐ Ⓑ Ⓒ Ⓓ	164	Ⓐ Ⓑ Ⓒ Ⓓ	174	Ⓐ Ⓑ Ⓒ Ⓓ	184	Ⓐ Ⓑ Ⓒ Ⓓ	194	Ⓐ Ⓑ Ⓒ Ⓓ
105	Ⓐ Ⓑ Ⓒ Ⓓ	115	Ⓐ Ⓑ Ⓒ Ⓓ	125	Ⓐ Ⓑ Ⓒ Ⓓ	135	Ⓐ Ⓑ Ⓒ Ⓓ	145	Ⓐ Ⓑ Ⓒ Ⓓ	155	Ⓐ Ⓑ Ⓒ Ⓓ	165	Ⓐ Ⓑ Ⓒ Ⓓ	175	Ⓐ Ⓑ Ⓒ Ⓓ	185	Ⓐ Ⓑ Ⓒ Ⓓ	195	Ⓐ Ⓑ Ⓒ Ⓓ
106	Ⓐ Ⓑ Ⓒ Ⓓ	116	Ⓐ Ⓑ Ⓒ Ⓓ	126	Ⓐ Ⓑ Ⓒ Ⓓ	136	Ⓐ Ⓑ Ⓒ Ⓓ	146	Ⓐ Ⓑ Ⓒ Ⓓ	156	Ⓐ Ⓑ Ⓒ Ⓓ	166	Ⓐ Ⓑ Ⓒ Ⓓ	176	Ⓐ Ⓑ Ⓒ Ⓓ	186	Ⓐ Ⓑ Ⓒ Ⓓ	196	Ⓐ Ⓑ Ⓒ Ⓓ
107	Ⓐ Ⓑ Ⓒ Ⓓ	117	Ⓐ Ⓑ Ⓒ Ⓓ	127	Ⓐ Ⓑ Ⓒ Ⓓ	137	Ⓐ Ⓑ Ⓒ Ⓓ	147	Ⓐ Ⓑ Ⓒ Ⓓ	157	Ⓐ Ⓑ Ⓒ Ⓓ	167	Ⓐ Ⓑ Ⓒ Ⓓ	177	Ⓐ Ⓑ Ⓒ Ⓓ	187	Ⓐ Ⓑ Ⓒ Ⓓ	197	Ⓐ Ⓑ Ⓒ Ⓓ
108	Ⓐ Ⓑ Ⓒ Ⓓ	118	Ⓐ Ⓑ Ⓒ Ⓓ	128	Ⓐ Ⓑ Ⓒ Ⓓ	138	Ⓐ Ⓑ Ⓒ Ⓓ	148	Ⓐ Ⓑ Ⓒ Ⓓ	158	Ⓐ Ⓑ Ⓒ Ⓓ	168	Ⓐ Ⓑ Ⓒ Ⓓ	178	Ⓐ Ⓑ Ⓒ Ⓓ	188	Ⓐ Ⓑ Ⓒ Ⓓ	198	Ⓐ Ⓑ Ⓒ Ⓓ
109	Ⓐ Ⓑ Ⓒ Ⓓ	119	Ⓐ Ⓑ Ⓒ Ⓓ	129	Ⓐ Ⓑ Ⓒ Ⓓ	139	Ⓐ Ⓑ Ⓒ Ⓓ	149	Ⓐ Ⓑ Ⓒ Ⓓ	159	Ⓐ Ⓑ Ⓒ Ⓓ	169	Ⓐ Ⓑ Ⓒ Ⓓ	179	Ⓐ Ⓑ Ⓒ Ⓓ	189	Ⓐ Ⓑ Ⓒ Ⓓ	199	Ⓐ Ⓑ Ⓒ Ⓓ
110	Ⓐ Ⓑ Ⓒ Ⓓ	120	Ⓐ Ⓑ Ⓒ Ⓓ	130	Ⓐ Ⓑ Ⓒ Ⓓ	140	Ⓐ Ⓑ Ⓒ Ⓓ	150	Ⓐ Ⓑ Ⓒ Ⓓ	160	Ⓐ Ⓑ Ⓒ Ⓓ	170	Ⓐ Ⓑ Ⓒ Ⓓ	180	Ⓐ Ⓑ Ⓒ Ⓓ	190	Ⓐ Ⓑ Ⓒ Ⓓ	200	Ⓐ Ⓑ Ⓒ Ⓓ

ACTUAL TEST 02

READING SECTION

101	Ⓐ Ⓑ Ⓒ Ⓓ	111	Ⓐ Ⓑ Ⓒ Ⓓ	121	Ⓐ Ⓑ Ⓒ Ⓓ	131	Ⓐ Ⓑ Ⓒ Ⓓ	141	Ⓐ Ⓑ Ⓒ Ⓓ	151	Ⓐ Ⓑ Ⓒ Ⓓ	161	Ⓐ Ⓑ Ⓒ Ⓓ	171	Ⓐ Ⓑ Ⓒ Ⓓ	181	Ⓐ Ⓑ Ⓒ Ⓓ	191	Ⓐ Ⓑ Ⓒ Ⓓ
102	Ⓐ Ⓑ Ⓒ Ⓓ	112	Ⓐ Ⓑ Ⓒ Ⓓ	122	Ⓐ Ⓑ Ⓒ Ⓓ	132	Ⓐ Ⓑ Ⓒ Ⓓ	142	Ⓐ Ⓑ Ⓒ Ⓓ	152	Ⓐ Ⓑ Ⓒ Ⓓ	162	Ⓐ Ⓑ Ⓒ Ⓓ	172	Ⓐ Ⓑ Ⓒ Ⓓ	182	Ⓐ Ⓑ Ⓒ Ⓓ	192	Ⓐ Ⓑ Ⓒ Ⓓ
103	Ⓐ Ⓑ Ⓒ Ⓓ	113	Ⓐ Ⓑ Ⓒ Ⓓ	123	Ⓐ Ⓑ Ⓒ Ⓓ	133	Ⓐ Ⓑ Ⓒ Ⓓ	143	Ⓐ Ⓑ Ⓒ Ⓓ	153	Ⓐ Ⓑ Ⓒ Ⓓ	163	Ⓐ Ⓑ Ⓒ Ⓓ	173	Ⓐ Ⓑ Ⓒ Ⓓ	183	Ⓐ Ⓑ Ⓒ Ⓓ	193	Ⓐ Ⓑ Ⓒ Ⓓ
104	Ⓐ Ⓑ Ⓒ Ⓓ	114	Ⓐ Ⓑ Ⓒ Ⓓ	124	Ⓐ Ⓑ Ⓒ Ⓓ	134	Ⓐ Ⓑ Ⓒ Ⓓ	144	Ⓐ Ⓑ Ⓒ Ⓓ	154	Ⓐ Ⓑ Ⓒ Ⓓ	164	Ⓐ Ⓑ Ⓒ Ⓓ	174	Ⓐ Ⓑ Ⓒ Ⓓ	184	Ⓐ Ⓑ Ⓒ Ⓓ	194	Ⓐ Ⓑ Ⓒ Ⓓ
105	Ⓐ Ⓑ Ⓒ Ⓓ	115	Ⓐ Ⓑ Ⓒ Ⓓ	125	Ⓐ Ⓑ Ⓒ Ⓓ	135	Ⓐ Ⓑ Ⓒ Ⓓ	145	Ⓐ Ⓑ Ⓒ Ⓓ	155	Ⓐ Ⓑ Ⓒ Ⓓ	165	Ⓐ Ⓑ Ⓒ Ⓓ	175	Ⓐ Ⓑ Ⓒ Ⓓ	185	Ⓐ Ⓑ Ⓒ Ⓓ	195	Ⓐ Ⓑ Ⓒ Ⓓ
106	Ⓐ Ⓑ Ⓒ Ⓓ	116	Ⓐ Ⓑ Ⓒ Ⓓ	126	Ⓐ Ⓑ Ⓒ Ⓓ	136	Ⓐ Ⓑ Ⓒ Ⓓ	146	Ⓐ Ⓑ Ⓒ Ⓓ	156	Ⓐ Ⓑ Ⓒ Ⓓ	166	Ⓐ Ⓑ Ⓒ Ⓓ	176	Ⓐ Ⓑ Ⓒ Ⓓ	186	Ⓐ Ⓑ Ⓒ Ⓓ	196	Ⓐ Ⓑ Ⓒ Ⓓ
107	Ⓐ Ⓑ Ⓒ Ⓓ	117	Ⓐ Ⓑ Ⓒ Ⓓ	127	Ⓐ Ⓑ Ⓒ Ⓓ	137	Ⓐ Ⓑ Ⓒ Ⓓ	147	Ⓐ Ⓑ Ⓒ Ⓓ	157	Ⓐ Ⓑ Ⓒ Ⓓ	167	Ⓐ Ⓑ Ⓒ Ⓓ	177	Ⓐ Ⓑ Ⓒ Ⓓ	187	Ⓐ Ⓑ Ⓒ Ⓓ	197	Ⓐ Ⓑ Ⓒ Ⓓ
108	Ⓐ Ⓑ Ⓒ Ⓓ	118	Ⓐ Ⓑ Ⓒ Ⓓ	128	Ⓐ Ⓑ Ⓒ Ⓓ	138	Ⓐ Ⓑ Ⓒ Ⓓ	148	Ⓐ Ⓑ Ⓒ Ⓓ	158	Ⓐ Ⓑ Ⓒ Ⓓ	168	Ⓐ Ⓑ Ⓒ Ⓓ	178	Ⓐ Ⓑ Ⓒ Ⓓ	188	Ⓐ Ⓑ Ⓒ Ⓓ	198	Ⓐ Ⓑ Ⓒ Ⓓ
109	Ⓐ Ⓑ Ⓒ Ⓓ	119	Ⓐ Ⓑ Ⓒ Ⓓ	129	Ⓐ Ⓑ Ⓒ Ⓓ	139	Ⓐ Ⓑ Ⓒ Ⓓ	149	Ⓐ Ⓑ Ⓒ Ⓓ	159	Ⓐ Ⓑ Ⓒ Ⓓ	169	Ⓐ Ⓑ Ⓒ Ⓓ	179	Ⓐ Ⓑ Ⓒ Ⓓ	189	Ⓐ Ⓑ Ⓒ Ⓓ	199	Ⓐ Ⓑ Ⓒ Ⓓ
110	Ⓐ Ⓑ Ⓒ Ⓓ	120	Ⓐ Ⓑ Ⓒ Ⓓ	130	Ⓐ Ⓑ Ⓒ Ⓓ	140	Ⓐ Ⓑ Ⓒ Ⓓ	150	Ⓐ Ⓑ Ⓒ Ⓓ	160	Ⓐ Ⓑ Ⓒ Ⓓ	170	Ⓐ Ⓑ Ⓒ Ⓓ	180	Ⓐ Ⓑ Ⓒ Ⓓ	190	Ⓐ Ⓑ Ⓒ Ⓓ	200	Ⓐ Ⓑ Ⓒ Ⓓ

答案紙

ACTUAL TEST 03

READING SECTION

101	Ⓐ Ⓑ Ⓒ Ⓓ
102	Ⓐ Ⓑ Ⓒ Ⓓ
103	Ⓐ Ⓑ Ⓒ Ⓓ
104	Ⓐ Ⓑ Ⓒ Ⓓ
105	Ⓐ Ⓑ Ⓒ Ⓓ
106	Ⓐ Ⓑ Ⓒ Ⓓ
107	Ⓐ Ⓑ Ⓒ Ⓓ
108	Ⓐ Ⓑ Ⓒ Ⓓ
109	Ⓐ Ⓑ Ⓒ Ⓓ
110	Ⓐ Ⓑ Ⓒ Ⓓ

(Answer grid continues 111–200, each with options Ⓐ Ⓑ Ⓒ Ⓓ)

ACTUAL TEST 04

READING SECTION

101	Ⓐ Ⓑ Ⓒ Ⓓ
102	Ⓐ Ⓑ Ⓒ Ⓓ
103	Ⓐ Ⓑ Ⓒ Ⓓ
104	Ⓐ Ⓑ Ⓒ Ⓓ
105	Ⓐ Ⓑ Ⓒ Ⓓ
106	Ⓐ Ⓑ Ⓒ Ⓓ
107	Ⓐ Ⓑ Ⓒ Ⓓ
108	Ⓐ Ⓑ Ⓒ Ⓓ
109	Ⓐ Ⓑ Ⓒ Ⓓ
110	Ⓐ Ⓑ Ⓒ Ⓓ

(Answer grid continues 111–200, each with options Ⓐ Ⓑ Ⓒ Ⓓ)

答案紙

READING SECTION

101 ⒜ⒷⒸⒹ · 102 ⒜ⒷⒸⒹ · 103 ⒜ⒷⒸⒹ · 104 ⒜ⒷⒸⒹ · 105 ⒜ⒷⒸⒹ · 106 ⒜ⒷⒸⒹ · 107 ⒜ⒷⒸⒹ · 108 ⒜ⒷⒸⒹ · 109 ⒜ⒷⒸⒹ · 110 ⒜ⒷⒸⒹ
111–120 · 121–130 · 131–140 · 141–150 · 151–160 · 161–170 · 171–180 · 181–190 · 191–200

READING SECTION

101 ⒜ⒷⒸⒹ · 102 ⒜ⒷⒸⒹ · 103 ⒜ⒷⒸⒹ · 104 ⒜ⒷⒸⒹ · 105 ⒜ⒷⒸⒹ · 106 ⒜ⒷⒸⒹ · 107 ⒜ⒷⒸⒹ · 108 ⒜ⒷⒸⒹ · 109 ⒜ⒷⒸⒹ · 110 ⒜ⒷⒸⒹ
111–120 · 121–130 · 131–140 · 141–150 · 151–160 · 161–170 · 171–180 · 181–190 · 191–200

答案紙

ACTUAL TEST 07

READING SECTION

ACTUAL TEST 08

READING SECTION

答案紙

ACTUAL TEST 09

READING SECTION

	A	B	C	D
101	Ⓐ	Ⓑ	Ⓒ	Ⓓ
102	Ⓐ	Ⓑ	Ⓒ	Ⓓ
103	Ⓐ	Ⓑ	Ⓒ	Ⓓ
104	Ⓐ	Ⓑ	Ⓒ	Ⓓ
105	Ⓐ	Ⓑ	Ⓒ	Ⓓ
106	Ⓐ	Ⓑ	Ⓒ	Ⓓ
107	Ⓐ	Ⓑ	Ⓒ	Ⓓ
108	Ⓐ	Ⓑ	Ⓒ	Ⓓ
109	Ⓐ	Ⓑ	Ⓒ	Ⓓ
110	Ⓐ	Ⓑ	Ⓒ	Ⓓ
111–120	Ⓐ	Ⓑ	Ⓒ	Ⓓ
121–130	Ⓐ	Ⓑ	Ⓒ	Ⓓ
131–140	Ⓐ	Ⓑ	Ⓒ	Ⓓ
141–150	Ⓐ	Ⓑ	Ⓒ	Ⓓ
151–160	Ⓐ	Ⓑ	Ⓒ	Ⓓ
161–170	Ⓐ	Ⓑ	Ⓒ	Ⓓ
171–180	Ⓐ	Ⓑ	Ⓒ	Ⓓ
181–190	Ⓐ	Ⓑ	Ⓒ	Ⓓ
191–200	Ⓐ	Ⓑ	Ⓒ	Ⓓ

ACTUAL TEST 10

READING SECTION

	A	B	C	D
101	Ⓐ	Ⓑ	Ⓒ	Ⓓ
102	Ⓐ	Ⓑ	Ⓒ	Ⓓ
103	Ⓐ	Ⓑ	Ⓒ	Ⓓ
104	Ⓐ	Ⓑ	Ⓒ	Ⓓ
105	Ⓐ	Ⓑ	Ⓒ	Ⓓ
106	Ⓐ	Ⓑ	Ⓒ	Ⓓ
107	Ⓐ	Ⓑ	Ⓒ	Ⓓ
108	Ⓐ	Ⓑ	Ⓒ	Ⓓ
109	Ⓐ	Ⓑ	Ⓒ	Ⓓ
110	Ⓐ	Ⓑ	Ⓒ	Ⓓ
111–120	Ⓐ	Ⓑ	Ⓒ	Ⓓ
121–130	Ⓐ	Ⓑ	Ⓒ	Ⓓ
131–140	Ⓐ	Ⓑ	Ⓒ	Ⓓ
141–150	Ⓐ	Ⓑ	Ⓒ	Ⓓ
151–160	Ⓐ	Ⓑ	Ⓒ	Ⓓ
161–170	Ⓐ	Ⓑ	Ⓒ	Ⓓ
171–180	Ⓐ	Ⓑ	Ⓒ	Ⓓ
181–190	Ⓐ	Ⓑ	Ⓒ	Ⓓ
191–200	Ⓐ	Ⓑ	Ⓒ	Ⓓ

新制 New TOEIC
閱讀超高分
最新多益改版黃金試題1000題

作　　者	Ki Taek Lee
譯　　者	林育珊
編　　輯	Gina Wang
審　　訂	Maddie Smith (Tests 1-3), Richard Luhrs (Tests 4-10)
校　　對	黃詩韻
內文排版	林書玉
封面設計	林書玉
製程管理	洪巧玲
發 行 人	黃朝萍
出 版 者	寂天文化事業股份有限公司
電　　話	+886-(0)2-2365-9739
傳　　真	+886-(0)2-2365-9835
網　　址	www.icosmos.com.tw
讀者服務	onlineservice@icosmos.com.tw
出版日期	2024 年 8 月 初版再刷　　（160125）